THE COMPLETE SHORT STORIES OF NATHANIEL HAWTHORNE

Powers

The Complete Short Stories of NATHANIEL HAWTHORNE

Doubleday & Company, Inc.
Garden City, New York

ISBN: 0-385-01560-7
Library of Congress Catalog Card Number 59-10561

Printed in the United States of America

CONTENTS

From MOSSES FROM AN OLD MANSE

From THE SNOW-IMAGE and OTHER TWICE-TOLD TALES

MISCELLANEOUS TALES

PREFACE

Between 1828, when Hawthorne's first published work appeared (FANSHAWE), and 1864, the year he died, Nathaniel Hawthorne produced just under a dozen novels, two juvenile volumes of adaptations of classical myths and biographies, a considerable amount of nonfiction collected variously as American, French and Italian, English Notebooks, and roughly one hundred tales and sketches. The tales and sketches were published over a period of ten or twelve years in such periodicals and annuals as *The Token*, the *New England Magazine*, the *Salem Gazette, The North American Review, Atlantic Monthly.* Sometimes they bore the author's real name, sometimes a pseudonym was attached, and at still other times the pieces appeared anonymously. Eventually Hawthorne began to gather his stories into volumes. The first of these collections, TWICE TOLD TALES, appeared in 1837 (and a revised edition, in 1851); MOSSES FROM AN OLD MANSE was published in 1846; and THE SNOW-IMAGE was brought out in 1851. It is from these sources that all but six of the selections in this current anthology were gleaned. These six tales—"The Ghost of Doctor Harris," "The Young Provincial," "The Haunted Quack," "The New England Village," "My Wife's Novel," and "The Bald Eagle"—were first brought together from their original sources in 1900, when they were included in the large paper, limited edition of THE COMPLETE WRITINGS OF NATHANIEL HAWTHORNE, published by Houghton Mifflin in twenty-two volumes. The editor of that edition identified "The Ghost of Doctor Harris" as having first been printed in the January 1900 issue of *The Nineteenth Century;* the other five had appeared anonymously in various issues of *The Token* in the early 1830s.

THE COMPLETE SHORT STORIES OF NATHANIEL HAWTHORNE contains seventy-two tales, the themes for which Hawthorne found among the traditions of New England. They are sometimes sorrowful, very often allegorical, seldom humorous, occasionally satirical, always fanciful and imaginative. This collection does not contain those shorter pieces which cannot be truly termed as short stories. Such familiar works as "A Rill from the Town Pump," "The Toll Gatherer's Day," "Main Street," "Sunday at Home," "Sights from a Steeple," "The Haunted Mind," and others have been omitted because they are sketches. This anthology also does not include any of the author's juvenile stories which were adaptations of classical myths and biographies, collected variously in volumes called A WONDER-BOOK, TANGLEWOOD TALES, and THE WHOLE HISTORY OF GRANDFATHER'S CHAIR.

Henry James spoke of the "haunted world of Hawthorne's imagination," and Anthony Trollope said, "In no American writer is there to be found the same predominance of weird imagination as in Hawthorne." Hawthorne was beguiled by the occult and the supernatural, and many of his stories have overtones of the mysterious. Perhaps even more, this New England author was concerned with Evil as a positive force in life. He wrote many allegories, all dark and brooding in mood, about the effects of sin upon the moral conscience.

Herman Melville "discovered" Hawthorne accidentally, while vacationing, when a young girl lent him her copy of MOSSES FROM AN OLD MANSE. He was struck by the fact that, "in spite of all the Indian summer sunlight on the hither side of Hawthorne's soul, the other side—like the dark half of the physical sphere—is shrouded in a blackness, ten times black." This blackness prevailed, too, in his stories about witchcraft, wherein he re-created the mystery, guilt, cruelty, and terror of the witch hunts. His ancestors had presided at the burnings of witches and, to him, the subject was not fiction.

Hawthorne's appearance on the nineteenth-century literary scene was something less than cosmic, and it was his contemporaries in the field of letters—rather than the reading public—who first appreciated the efforts of the shy, gentle man from Salem. In 1847 Edgar Allan Poe wrote: "The reputation of the author . . . has been confined, indeed, until very lately, to literary society; and I have not been wrong, perhaps, in citing him as the example, par excellence, in this country, of the privately admired and publicly-unappreciated man of genius. . . ." Henry James, Anthony Trollope, and Oliver Wendell Holmes echoed Poe's sentiments and lauded Hawthorne's accomplishments. Some of the opinions of these distinguished persons who knew and appreciated Hawthorne both as a man and as an author precede the tales in this collection. Their judgments have been upheld by modern critics, as well. Mark Van Doren, in his notable critical biography, NATHANIEL HAWTHORNE, comments that "at his highest . . . Hawthorne stands somehow in company with the Greek tragic poets."

D. J. K.

THE COMPLETE SHORT STORIES OF NATHANIEL HAWTHORNE

NATHANIEL HAWTHORNE

by Henry James

It is perhaps an advantage in writing of Nathaniel Hawthorne's work, that his life offers little opportunity to the biographer. The record of it makes so few exactions that in a critical account of him—even as brief as this—the work may easily take most of the place. He was one of those happy men of letters in whose course the great milestones are simply those of his ideas that found successful form. Born at Salem, Massachusetts, on July 4th, 1804, of established local Puritan—and in a conspicuous degree, sturdy seafaring—stock, he was educated at his birthplace and at Bowdoin College, Maine, where H. W. Longfellow was one of his fellow-students. Another was Franklin Pierce, who was to be elected President of the United States in 1852, and with whom Hawthorne formed relations that became an influence in his life. On leaving college in 1825 he returned to Salem to live, and in 1828 published in Boston a short romance called "Fanshaw," of which the scene, in spite of its being a "love story," is laid, but for a change of name, at Bowdoin, with professors and undergraduates for its male characters. The experiment was inevitably faint, but the author's beautiful touch had begun to feel its way. In 1837, after a dozen years spent in special solitude, as he later testified, at Salem, he collected as the first series of "Twice-Told Tales" various more or less unremunerated contributions to the magazines and annuals of the day. In 1845 appeared the second series, and in 1851 the two volumes were, with a preface peculiarly graceful and touching, reissued together; he is in general never more graceful than when prefatory. In 1851 and 1854 respectively came to light "The Snow Image" and "Mosses from an Old Manse," which form, with the previous double sheaf, his three main gatherings-in of the shorter fiction. I neglect, for brevity and as addressed to children "Grandfather's Chair" and "The Wonder Book" (1851), as well as "Tanglewood Tales" (1852). Of the other groups, some preceded, some followed, the appearance in 1850 of his second novel, "The Scarlet Letter."

These things—the experiments in the shorter fiction—had sounded, with their rare felicity, from the very first the note that was to be Hawthorne's distinguished mark,—that feeling for the latent romance of New England, which in summary form is the most final name to be given, I think, to his inspiration. This element, which is what at its best his genius most expresses, was far from obvious,—it had to be looked for; and Hawthorne found it, as he wandered and used, in the secret play of the Puritan faith: the secret, I say particularly, because the direct and ostensible, face to face with common tasks and small conditions (as I may call them without prejudice to their general grimness), arrived at forms of which the tender imagination could make little. It could make a great deal, on the other hand, of the spiritual contortions, the darkened outlook, of the ingrained sense of sin, of evil, and of responsibility. There had been other complications in the history of the community surrounding him,—savages from behind, soldiers from before, a cruel climate from every quarter and a pecuniary remittance from none. But the great complication was the pressing moral anxiety, the restless individual conscience. These things were developed at the cost of so many others, that there were almost no others left to help them to make a picture for the artist. The artist's imagination had to deck out the subject, to work it up, as we nowadays say; and Hawthorne's was,—on intensely chastened lines, indeed,—equal to the task. In that manner it came into exercise from the first, through the necessity of taking for granted, on the part of the society about him, a life of the spirit more complex than anything that met the mere eye of sense. It was a question of looking behind and beneath for the suggestive idea, the artistic motive; the effect of all of which was an invaluable training for the faculty that evokes and enhances. This ingenuity grew alert and irrepressible as it manoeuvred for the back view and turned up the under side of common aspects,—the laws secretly broken, the impulsive secretly felt, the hidden passions, the double lives, the dark corners, the closed rooms, the skeletons in the cupboard and at the feast. It made, in short, and cherished, for fancy's sake, a mystery and a glamour where there were otherwise none very ready to its hand; so that it ended by living in a world of things symbolic and allegoric, a presentation of objects casting, in every case, far behind them a shadow more curious and more amusing than the apparent figure. Any figure therefore easily became with him an emblem, any story a parable, any appearance a cover: things with which his concern is—gently, indulgently, skillfully, with the lightest hand in the world—to pivot them round and show the odd little stamp or sign that gives them their value for the collector.

The specimens he collected, as we may call them, are divisible into groups, but with the mark in common that they are all early products of the dry New England air. Some are myths and mysteries of old Massachusetts,—charming, ghostly passages of colonial history. Such are "The Gray Champion," and the four beautiful "Legends of the Province House." Others, like "Roger Malvin's Burial," "Rappaccini's Daughter," "Young Goodman Brown," are "moralities" without the moral, as it were; small cold apologues, frosty and exquisite, occasionally gathered from beyond the sea. Then there are the chapters of the fanciful all for fancy's sake, of the pure whimsical, and of observation merely amused and beguiled; pages, many of them, of friendly humorous reflections on what, in Salem or in Boston, a dreamer might meet in his walks. What Hawthorne encountered he instinctively embroidered, working it over with a fine, slow needle, and with flowers pale, rosy, or dusky, as the case might suggest. We have a handful of these in "The Great Carbuncle" and "The Great Stone Face," "The Seven Vagabonds," "The Threefold Destiny," "The Village Uncle," "The Toll Gatherer's Day," "A Rill from the Town Pump," and "Chippings with a Chisel." The inequalities in his work are not, to my sense, great; and in specifying, we take and leave with hesitation.

"The Scarlet Letter," in 1850, brought him immediate distinction, and has probably kept its place not only as the most original of his novels, but as the most distinguished piece of prose fiction that was to spring from American soil. He had received in 1839 an appointment to a small place in the Boston custom-house, where his labors were sordid and sterile, and he had given it up in permissible weariness. He had spent in 1841 near Roxbury, Massachusetts, a few months in the co-operative community of Brook Farm, a short-lived socialistic experiment. He had married in the following year and gone to live at the old Manse at Concord, where he remained till 1846, when, with a fresh fiscal engagement, he returned to his native town. It was in the intervals of his occupation at the Salem custom-house that "The Scarlet Letter" was written. The book has achieved the fortune of the small supreme group of novels: it has hung an ineffaceable image in the portrait gallery, the reserved inner cabinet, of literature. . . .

"The House of the Seven Gables," written during a residence of two years at Lenox, Massachusetts, was published in 1851. If there are probably no four books of any author among which, for a favorite, readers hesitate longer than between Hawthorne's four longest stories, there are at any rate many for whom this remains distinctly his largest and fullest production. Suffused as it is with a pleasant autumnal haze, it yet brushes more closely than its companions the surface of American life, comes a trifle nearer to being a novel of manners. . . .

Weary of Lenox, Hawthorne spent several months of 1852 at West Newton near Boston, where "The Blithedale Romance" was brought forth. He made the most, for the food of fancy, of what came under his hand,—happy in an appetite that could often find a feast in meagre materials. The third of his novels is an echo, delightfully poetized, of his residence at Brook Farm. "Transcendentalism" was in those days in New England much in the air; and the most comprehensive account of the partakers of this quaint experiment appears to have been held to be that they were Transcendentalists. More simply stated, they were young, candid radicals, reformers, philanthropists. The fact that it sprang—all irresponsibly indeed—from the observation of a known episode, gives "The Blithedale Romance" also a certain value as a picture of manners. . . . As we read it today, it has a soft, shy glamour, a touch of the poetry of far-off things. Nothing of the author's is a happier expression of what I have called his sense of the romance of New England.

In 1853 Franklin Pierce, then President, appointed him consul at Liverpool, which was the beginning of a residence of some seven years in England and in Italy, the period to which we owe "The Marble Faun" and "Our Old Home." The material for the latter of these was the first to be fathered, but the appearance of "The Marble Faun," begun in Rome in 1858 and finished during a second stay in England, preceded that of its companion. This is his only long drama on a foreign stage. Drawn from his own air, however, are much of its inspiration and its character. Hawthorne took with him to Italy, as he had done to England, more the old Puritan consciousness than he left behind. . . . The mystical, the mythical, are in "The Marble Faun" more than ever at hide-and-seek with the real. . . .

He returned to America in 1860, settled once more at Concord, and died at Plymouth, New Hampshire, in the arms of Franklin Pierce, in 1864. The Extracts, from his many note books, published by his wife and children after his death, the small "campaign" "Life of Franklin Pierce" (1852), two posthumous fragments, and those scraps and shreds of which his table drawers were still more exhaustively emptied, his literary catalogue—none of the longest—becomes complete.

The important item in this remainder is the close, ripe cluster, the series presented by himself, of his impressions of England. These admirable papers, with much of the same fascination, have something of the same uncomforted note with which he had surrendered himself to the charm of Italy: the mixture of sensibility and reluctance, of response and dissent, the strife between his sense of beauty and his sense of banishment. He came to the Old World late in life—though after dabbling for years, indeed, in the fancied phenomena of time, and with inevitable reserves, mistrusts, and antagonisms. The striking thing to my sense, however, is not what he missed but what he so ingeniously and vividly made out. If he had been, imaginatively, rather old in his youth, he was youthful in his age; and when all is said, we owe him, as a contribution to the immemorial process of lively repartee between the mother land and the daughter, the only pages of the business that can be said to belong to pure literature. He was capable of writing "The Marble Faun," and yet of declaring, in a letter from Rome, that he bitterly detested the place and should rejoice to bid it farewell for ever. Just so he was capable of drawing from English aspects a delight that they had yielded not even to Washington Irving, and yet of insisting, with a perversity that both smiled and frowned, that they rubbed him mainly all the wrong way. At home he had fingered the musty, but abroad he seemed to pine for freshness. In truth, for many persons his great, his most touching sign will have been his aloofness wherever he is. He is outside of everything, and an alien everywhere. He is an aesthetic solitary. His beautiful, light imagination is the wing that on the autumn evening just brushes the dusky window. It was a faculty that gave him much more a terrible sense of human abysses than a desire rashly to sound them and rise to the surface with his report. On the surface—the surface of the soul and the edge of the tragedy—he preferred to remain. He lingered, to weave his web, in the thin exterior air. This is a partial expression of his characteristic habit of dipping, of diving just for sport, into the moral world without being in the least a moralist. He had none of the heat nor of the dogmatism of that character; none of the impertinence, as we feel he would almost have held it, of any intermeddling. He never intermeddled; he was divertedly and discreetly contemplative, pausing oftenest wherever, amid prosaic aspects, there seemed most of an appeal to a sense for subtleties. But of all cynics he was the brightest and kindest, and the subtleties he spun are mere silken threads for string polished beads. His collection of moral mysteries is the cabinet of a dilettante.

TALE-WRITING—NATHANIEL HAWTHORNE

by Edgar A. Poe

In the preface to my sketches of New York Literati, while speaking of the broad distinction between the seeming public and real private opinion respecting our authors, I thus alluded to Nathaniel Hawthorne:—

> "For example, Mr. Hawthorne, the author of 'Twice-Told Tales,' is scarcely recognized by the press or by the public, and when noticed at all, is noticed merely to be damned by faint praise. Now, my own opinion of him is, that although his walk is limited and he is fairly to be charged with mannerism, treating all subjects in a similar tone of dreamy *innuendo*, yet in this walk he evinces extraordinary genius, having no rival either in America or elsewhere; and this opinion I have never heard gainsaid by any one literary person in the country. That this opinion, however, is a spoken and not a written one, is referable to the facts, first, that Mr. Hawthorne *is* a poor man, and, secondly, that he *is not* an ubiquitous quack."

The reputation of the author of "Twice-Told Tales" has been confined, indeed, until very lately, to literary society; and I have not been wrong, perhaps, in citing him as *the* example, *par excellence*, in this country, of the privately-admired and publicly-unappreciated man of genius. Within the last year or two, it is true, an occasional critic has been urged, by honest indignation, into very warm approval. . . . These criticisms, however, seemed to have little effect on the popular taste—at least, if we are to form any idea of the popular taste by reference to its expression in the newspapers, or by the sale of the author's book. It was never the fashion (until lately) to speak of him in any summary of our best authors. The daily critics would say, on such occasions, "Is there not Irving and Cooper, and Bryant and Paulding, and—Smith?" or, "Have we not Halleck and Dana, and Longfellow and—Thompson?" or, "Can we not point triumphantly to our own Sprague, Willis, Channing, Bancroft, Prescott and—Jenkins?" but these unanswerable queries were never wound up by the name of Hawthorne.

Beyond doubt, this inappreciation of him on the part of the public arose chiefly from the two causes to which I have referred—from the facts that he is neither a man of wealth nor a quack;—but these are insufficient to account for the whole effect. No small portion of it is attributable to the very marked idiosyncrasy of Mr. Hawthorne himself. In one sense, and in great measure, to be peculiar is to be original, and than the true originality there is no higher literary virtue. This true or commendable originality, however, implies not the uniform, but the continuous peculiarity—a peculiarity springing from ever-active vigor of fancy—better still if from ever-present force of imagination, giving its own hue, its own character to everything it touches, and, especially, *self impelled to touch everything.*

It is often said, inconsiderately, that very original writers always fail in popularity—that such and such persons are too original to be comprehended by the mass. "Too peculiar," should be the phrase, "too idiosyncratic." It is, in fact, the excitable, undisciplined and child-like popular mind which most keenly feels the original. The criticism of the conservatives, of the hackneys, of the cultivated old clergymen of the "North American Review," is precisely the criticism which condemns and alone condemns it. "It becometh not a divine," saith Lord Coke, "to be of a fiery and salamandrine spirit." Their conscience allowing them to move nothing themselves, these dignitaries have a holy horror of being moved. "Give us *quietude,*" they say. Opening their mouths with proper caution, they sigh forth the word "*Repose.*" And this is, indeed, the one thing they should be permitted to enjoy, if only upon the Christian principle of give and take.

The fact is, that if Mr. Hawthorne were really original, he could not fail of making himself felt by the public. But the fact is, he is *not* original in any sense. Those who speak of him as original, mean nothing more than that he differs in his manner or tone, and in his choice of subjects, from any author of their acquaintance—their acquaintance not extending to the German Tieck, whose manner, in *some* of his works, is absolutely identical with that *habitual* to Hawthorne. But it is clear that the element of the literary originality is novelty. The element of its appreciation by the reader is the reader's sense of the new. Whatever gives him a new and insomuch a pleasurable emotion, he considers original, and whoever frequently gives him such emotion, he considers an original writer. In a word, it is by the sum total of these emotions that he decides upon the writer's claim to originality. I may observe here, however, that there is clearly a point at which even novelty itself would cease to produce the legitimate originality, if we judge this originality, as we should, by the effect designed: this point is that at which *novelty becomes nothing novel;* and here the artist, *to preserve his originality,* will subside into the common-place. . . .

These points properly understood, it will be seen that the critic (unacquainted with Tieck) who reads a single tale or essay by Hawthorne, may be justified in thinking him original; but the tone, or manner, or choice of subject, which induces in this critic the sense of the new, will—if not in a second tale, at least in a third and all subsequent ones—not only fail of inducing it, but bring about an exactly antagonistic impression. In concluding a volume, and more especially in concluding all the volumes of the author, the critic will abandon his first design of calling him "original," and content himself with styling him "peculiar."

With the vague opinion that to be original is to be unpopular, I could, indeed, agree, were I to adopt an understanding of originality which, to my surprise, I have known adopted by many who have a right to be called critical. They have limited, in a love for mere words, the literary to the metaphysical originality. They regard as original in letters, only such combinations of thought, of incident, and so forth, as are, in fact, absolutely novel. It is clear, however, not only that it is the novelty of *effect* alone which is worth consideration, but that this effect is *best* wrought, for the end of all fictitious composition, pleasure, by shunning rather than by seeking the absolute novelty of combination. Originality, thus understood, tasks and startles the intellect, and so brings into undue action the faculties to which, in the lighter literature, we least appeal. And thus understood, it cannot fail to prove unpopular with the masses, who, seeking in this literature amusement, are positively offended by instruction. But the true originality—true in respect of its purposes—is that which, in bringing out the half-formed, the reluctant, or the unexpressed fancies of mankind, or in exciting the more delicate pulses of the heart's passion, or in giving birth to some universal sentiment or instinct in embryo, thus combines with the pleasurable effect of *apparent* novelty, a real egoistic delight. The reader, in the case first supposed, (that of the absolute novelty,) is excited, but embarrassed, disturbed, in some degree even pained at his own want of perception, at his own folly in not having himself hit upon the idea. In the second case, his pleasure is doubled. He is filled with an intrinsic and extrinsic delight. He feels and intensely enjoys the seeming novelty of the thought, enjoys it as really novel, as absolutely original with the writer—*and* himself. They two, he fancies, have, alone of all men, thought thus. They two have, together, created this thing. Henceforward there is a bond of sympathy between them, a sympathy which irradiates every subsequent page of the book.

There is a species of writing which, with some difficulty, may be admitted as a lower degree of what I have called the true original. In its perusal, we say to ourselves, not "how original this is!" nor "here is an idea which I and the author have alone entertained," but "here is a charmingly obvious fancy," or sometimes even, "here is a thought which I am not sure has ever occurred to myself, but which, of course, has occurred to all the rest of the world." This kind of composition (which still appertains to a high order) is usually designated as "the natural." It has little external resemblance, but strong internal affinity to the true original, if, indeed, as I have suggested, it is not of this latter an inferior degree. It is best exemplified, among English writers, in Addison, Irving and *Hawthorne*. The "ease" which is so often spoken of as its distinguishing feature, it has been the fashion to regard as ease in appearance alone, as a point of really difficult attainment. This idea, however, must be received with some reservation. The natural style is difficult only to those who should never intermeddle with it—to the unnatural. It is but the result of writing with the understanding, or with the instinct, that the *tone*, in composition, should be that which, at any given point or upon any given topic, would be the tone of the great mass of humanity. The author who, after the manner of the North Americans, is merely at *all* times *quiet*, is, of course, upon *most* occasions, merely silly or stupid, and has no more right to be thought "easy" or "natural" than has a cockney exquisite or the sleeping beauty in the waxworks.

The "peculiarity" or sameness, or monotone of Hawthorne, would, in its mere character of "peculiarity," and without reference to what *is* the peculiarity, suffice to deprive him of all chance of popular appreciation. But at his failure to be appreciated, we can, *of course*, no longer wonder, when we find him monotonous at decidedly the worst of all possible points—at that point which, having the least concern with Nature, is the farthest removed from the popular intellect, from the popular sentiment and from the popular taste. I allude to the strain of allegory which completely overwhelms the greater number of his subjects, and which in some measure interferes with the direct conduct of absolutely all.

In defence of allegory, (however, or for whatever object, employed,) there is scarcely one respectable word to be said. Its best appeals are made to the fancy—that is to say, to our sense of adaptation, not of matters proper, but of matters improper for the purpose, of the real with the unreal; having never more of intelligible connection than has something with nothing, never half so much of effective affinity as has the substance for the shadow. The deepest emotion aroused within us by the happiest allegory, *as* allegory, is a very, very imperfectly satisfied sense of the writer's ingenuity in overcoming a difficulty we should have preferred his not having attempted to overcome. The fallacy of the idea that allegory, in any of its moods, can be made to enforce a truth—that metaphor, for example, may illustrate as well as embellish an argument—could be promptly demonstrated: the converse of the supposed fact might be shown, indeed, with very little trouble—but these are topics foreign to my present purpose. One thing is clear, that if allegory ever establishes a fact, it is by dint of overturning a fiction. Where the suggested meaning runs through the obvious one in a *very* profound under-current, so as never to interfere with the upper one without our own volition, so as never to show itself unless *called* to the surface, there only, for the proper uses of fictitious narrative, is it available at all. Under the best circumstances, it must always interfere with that unity of effect which, to the artist, is worth all the allegory in the world. . . .

The obvious causes, however, which have prevented Mr. Hawthorne's *popularity*, do not suffice to condemn him in the eyes of the few who belong properly to books, and to whom books, perhaps, do not quite so properly belong. These few estimate an author, not as do the public, altogether by what he does, but in great measure—indeed, even in the greatest measure—by what he evinces a capability of doing. In this view, Hawthorne stands among literary people in America much in the same light as did Coleridge in England. The few, also, through a certain warping of the taste, which long pondering upon books as books merely never fails to induce, are not in condition to view the errors of a scholar as errors altogether. At any time these gentlemen are prone to think the public not right rather than an educated author wrong. But the simple truth is, that the writer who aims at impressing the people, is *always* wrong when he fails in forcing that people to receive the impression. How far Mr. Hawthorne has addressed the people at all, is, of course, not a question for me to decide. His books afford strong internal evidence of having been written to himself and his particular friends alone.

The tale proper affords the fairest field which can be afforded by the wide domains of mere prose, for the exercise of the highest genius. . . . History, philosophy, and other matters of that kind, we leave out of the question, of course. *Of course*, I say, and in spite of the graybeards. These graver topics, to the end of time, will be best illustrated by what a discriminating world, turning up its nose at the drab pamphlets, has agreed to understand as *talent*. The ordinary novel is objectionable, from its length, for reasons analogous to those which render length objectionable in the poem. As the novel cannot be read at one sitting, it cannot avail itself of the immense benefit of *totality*. Worldly interests, intervening during the pauses of perusal, modify, counteract and annul the impressions intended. But simple cessation in reading would, of itself, be sufficient to destroy the true unity. In the brief tale, however, the author is enabled to carry out his full design without interruption. During the hour of perusal, the soul of the reader is at the writer's control.

A skillful artist has constructed a tale. He has not fashioned his thoughts to accommodate his incidents, but having deliberately conceived a certain *single effect* to be wrought, he then invents such incidents, he then combines such events, and discusses them in such tone as may best serve him in establishing this preconceived effect. If his very first sentence tend not to the outbringing of this effect, then in his very first step has he committed a blunder. In the whole composition there should be no word written of which the tendency, direct or indirect, is not to the one pre-established design. And by such means, with such care and skill, a picture is at length painted which leaves in the mind of him who contemplates it with a kindred art, a sense of the fullest satisfaction. The idea of the tale, its thesis, has been presented unblemished, because undisturbed—an end absolutely demanded, yet, in the novel, altogether unattainable.

Of skillfully-constructed tales—I speak now without reference to other points, some of them more important than construction—there are very few American specimens. I am acquainted with no better one, upon the whole, than the "Murder Will Out" of Mr. Simms, and this has some glaring defects. The "Tales of a Traveler," by Irving, are graceful and impressive narratives—"The Young Italian" is especially good—but there is not one of the series which can be commended as a whole. . . . But in general skill of construction, the tales of Willis, I think, surpass those of any American writer—with the exception of Mr. Hawthorne.

I must defer to the better opportunity of a volume now in hand, a full discussion of his individual pieces, and hasten to conclude this paper with a summary of his merits and demerits.

He is peculiar and *not* original—unless in those detailed fancies and detached thoughts which his want of general originality will deprive of the appreciation due to them, in preventing them forever reaching the *public* eye. He is infinitely too fond of allegory, and can never hope for popularity so long as he persists in it. This he will not do, for allegory is at war with the whole tone of his nature, which disports itself never so well as when escaping from the mysticism of his Goodman Browns and White Old Maids into the hearty, genial, but still Indian-summer sunshine of his Wakefields and Little Annie's Rambles. Indeed, *his* spirit of "metaphor run-mad" is clearly imbibed from the phalanx and phalanstery atmosphere in which he has been so long struggling for breath. He has not half the material for the exclusiveness of authorship that he possesses for its universality. He has the purest style, the finest taste, the most available scholarship, the most delicate humor, the most touching pathos, the most radiant imagination, the most consummate ingenuity; and with these varied good qualities he has done *well* as a mystic. But is there any one of these qualities which should prevent his doing doubly as well in a career of honest, upright, sensible, prehensible and comprehensible things? Let him mend his pen, get a bottle of visible ink, come out from the Old Manse, cut Mr. Alcott, hang (if possible) the editor of "The Dial," and throw out of the window to the pigs all his odd numbers of "The North American Review."

From *Godey's Magazine and Lady's Book,* November 1847

THE GENIUS OF NATHANIEL HAWTHORNE

by Anthony Trollope

It is not sufficient for us to have a good thing and to enjoy it without knowing something of its nature, and inquiring how it has been produced, how far it is perfect, how far deficient, how it might have been improved, how it may have been marred. Would any one be contented to know that his watch told him the hour more or less correctly without understanding how it did so, and why correctly or why incorrectly? You shall have a horse that shall do all your work for you admirably out of doors, but bite and kick you if you go to him in the stable; or shall drag your buggy for you most obediently, but will never condescend to plow. How natural it is to look into the causes of the animal's proclivities! But when our intelligence is affected by something that comes to us from without, so as to make us aware that our inner self is being formed and reformed by what we receive,—as is the case with all that we read,—then the desire to search and ascertain of what kind is the instrument that is acting upon us becomes reasonably and naturally strong. It is not enough to have the book. We must know, if possible, how it was that the book became what it is, and why. How came it to pass that a man with no peculiar advantages of early education grew to be so many-sided as Shakespeare, and with every side so equal? How did he become so wise,—for you may glean from him such a book of proverbs that Solomon shall hardly furnish you with a better,—so pathetic, that not even Sophocles has equaled him? Could he have heard of the old Œdipus when he wrote his "Lear," and have understood it all?—so full of humor that not even Molière has excelled him; so happy in his pleasantries as to have rivaled Horace? And yet he was a poor player, who, as far as we can judge, never realized the extent of his own capacity. When one mind was so round, well-poised, and wholesome, why should another, also greatly gifted, be lop-sided, with all its very excellences tending toward malformation and disease,—as you shall see in a postman's legs or a blacksmith's arm, when all the strength collects itself in one part? How morbid were the natures of Byron and of Godwin and of Rousseau! How ill-natured was the genius of Swift; how impure and flashy that of Sterne; how preëminently, I might almost say predominantly, pure is that of Longfellow; how austere and unbending that of Milton! Then, again, there were others to whom the "totus teres atque rotundus" applies,—minds that were beautifully round, though the circles described were larger or smaller. Such were the minds of Homer and of Scott.

There never surely was a powerful, active, continually effective mind less round, more lop-sided, than that of NATHANIEL HAWTHORNE. If there were aught of dispraise in this, it would not be said by me,—by an Englishman of an American whom I knew, by an Englishman of letters of a brother on the other side of the water, much less by me, an English novelist, of an American novelist. The blacksmith, who is abnormally strong in his arm, gives the world the advantage of his strength. The poor bird, whose wretched life is sacrificed to the unnatural growth of that portion of him which the gourmands love, does produce the desired dainties in all their perfection. We could have hardly had "Childe Harold" except from a soured nature. The seraphic excellence of "Hiawatha" and "Evangeline" could have proceeded only from a mind which the world's roughness had neither toughened nor tainted. So from Hawthorne we could not have obtained that weird, mysterious, thrilling charm with which he has awed and delighted us had he not allowed his mind to revel in one direction, so as to lose its fair proportions.

I have been specially driven to think of this by the strong divergence between Hawthorne and myself. It has always been my object to draw my little pictures as like to life as possible, so that my readers should feel that they were dealing with people whom they might probably have known, but so to do it that the every-day good to be found among them should allure, and the every-day evil repel; and this I have attempted, believing that such ordinary good and ordinary evil would be more powerful in repelling or alluring than great and glowing incidents which, though they might interest, would not come home to the minds of readers. Hawthorne, on the other hand, has dealt with persons and incidents which were often but barely within the bounds of possibility,—which were sometimes altogether without those bounds, —and has determined that his readers should be carried out of their own little mundane ways, and brought into a world of imagination in which their intelligence might be raised, if only for a time, to something higher than the common needs of common life.

I will venture here to quote an extract from a letter written by Hawthorne to an American gentleman, a friend of his,—and of mine, though, if I remember rightly, I did not get it from him,—which he will recognize should he see this paper. As it is altogether about myself, perhaps I should do better to keep it to myself, but I will give it because it explains so accurately his own condition of mind in regard to novels; "It is odd enough that my own individual taste is for quite another class of novels than those which I myself am able to write. If I were to meet with such books as mine by another writer, I don't believe I should be able to get through them. Have you ever read the novels of Anthony Trollope? They precisely suit my taste; solid and substantial, written on strength of beef and through the inspiration of ale, and just as real as if some giant had hewn a great lump out of the earth, and put it under a glass case, with all its inhabitants going about their daily business, and not suspecting that they were made a show of." This is what he could read himself, but could not possibly have produced,—any more than I could have produced that "Marble Faun" which has been quite as much to my taste as was to his the fragment of common life which he has supposed me to put under a glass case in order that the frequenters at my little show might inspect at their ease all that was being done on that morsel of the earth's surface. How was it that his mind wandered away always into those fancies, not jocund as are usually those of the tellers of fairy tales, not high-flown as are the pictures generally drawn by the poets, with no fearful adventures though so sad, often by no means beautiful, without an attempt even at the picturesque, melancholy beyond compare, as though the writer had drawn all his experiences from untoward accidents? That some remnant of Puritan asceticism should be found in the writings of a novelist from Concord, in Massachusetts, would seem natural to an English reader,—though I doubt whether there be much of the flavor of the Mayflower left at present to pervade the literary parterres of Boston. But, had that been the Hawthorne flavor, readers both in England and in the States would have accepted it without surprise.

It is, however, altogether different, though ascetic enough. The predominating quality of Puritan life was hard, good sense,—a good sense which could value the realities of life while it rejected the frivolities,—a good sense to which buttered cakes, water-tight boots, and a pretty wife, or a kind husband could endear themselves. Hawthorne is severe, but his severity is never of a nature to form laws for life. His is a mixture of romance and austerity, quite as far removed from the realities of Puritanism as it is from the sentimentalism of poetry. He creates a melancholy which amounts almost to remorse in the minds of his readers. There falls upon them a conviction of some unutterable woe which is not altogether dispelled till other books and other incidents have had their effects. The woe is of course fictitious, and therefore endurable,—and therefore alluring. And woe itself has its charm. It is a fact that the really miserable will pity the comfortable insignificance of those who are not unhappy, and that they are apt even to boast of their own sufferings. There is a sublimity in mental and even in corporal torment which will sometimes make the position of Lucifer almost enviable. "All is not lost" with him! Prometheus chained, with the bird at his liver, had wherewithal to console himself in the magnificence of his thoughts. And so in the world of melancholy romance, of agony more realistic than melancholy, to which Hawthorne brings his readers, there is compensation to the reader in the feeling that, in having submitted himself to such sublime affliction, he has proved himself capable of sublimity. The bird that feeds upon your vitals would not have gorged himself with common flesh. You are beyond measure depressed by the weird tale that is told to you, but you become conscious of a certain grandness of nature in being susceptible of such suffering. When you hear what Hawthorne has done to others, you long to search his volumes. When he has operated upon you, you would not for worlds have foregone it. You have been ennobled by that familiarity with sorrow. You have been, as it were, sent through the fire and purged of so much of your dross. For a time, at least, you have been free from the mundane touch of that beef and ale with which novelists of a meaner school will certainly bring you in contact. No one will feel himself ennobled at once by having read one of my novels. But Hawthorne, when you have studied him, will be very precious to you. He will have plunged you into melancholy, he will have overshadowed you with black forebodings, he will almost have crushed you with imaginary sorrows; but he will have enabled you to feel yourself an inch taller during the process. Something of the sublimity of the transcendent, something of the mystery of the unfathomable, something of the brightness of the celestial, will have attached itself to you, and you will all but think that you too might live to be sublime, and revel in mingled light and mystery.

The creations of American literature generally are no doubt more given to the speculative,—less given to the realistic,—than are those of English literature. On our side of the water we deal more with beef and ale, and less with dreams. Even with the broad humor of Bret Harte, even with the broader humor of Artemus Ward and Mark Twain, there is generally present an undercurrent of melancholy, in which pathos and satire are intermingled. There was a touch of it even with the simple-going Cooper and the kindly Washington Irving. Melancholy and pathos, without the humor, are the springs on which all Longfellow's lines are set moving. But in no American writer is to be found the same predominance of weird imagination as in Hawthorne. There was something of it in M. G. Lewis—our Monk Lewis as he came to be called, from the name of a tale which he wrote; but with him, as with many others, we feel that they have been weird because they have desired to be so. They have struggled to achieve the tone with which their works are pervaded. With Hawthorne we are made to think that he could not have been anything else if he would. It is as though he could certainly have been nothing else in his own inner life. We know that such was not actually the case. Though a man singularly reticent,—what we generally call shy,—he could, when things went well with him, be argumentative, social, and cheery. I have seen him very happy over canvas-back ducks, and have heard him discuss, almost with violence, the superiority of American vegetables. Indeed, he once withered me with a scorn which was anything but mystic or melancholy because I expressed a patriotic preference for English peas. And yet his imagination was such that the creations of his brain could not have been other than such as I have described. Oliver Wendell Holmes has written a well-known story, weird and witch-like also, and has displayed much genius in the picture which he has given us of Elsie Venner. But the reader is at once aware that Holmes compelled himself to the construction of "Elsie Venner," and feels equally sure that Hawthorne wrote "The Marble Faun" because he could not help himself. . . .

"Mosses from an Old Manse" will be caviare to many. By this I intend no slight to the intelligence of the many readers who may not find themselves charmed by such narratives. In the true enjoyment of Hawthorne's work there is required a peculiar mood of mind. The reader should take a delight in looking round corners, and in seeing how places and things may be approached by other than the direct and obvious route. No writer impresses himself more strongly on the reader who will submit to him; but the reader must consent to put himself altogether under his author's guidance, and to travel by queer passages, the direction of which he will not perceive till, perhaps, he has got quite to the end of them. In "The Scarlet Letter," though there are many side paths, there is a direct road, so open that the obstinately straightforward traveler will find his way, though he will not, perhaps, see all that there is to be seen. In "The House of the Seven Gables" a kind of thoroughfare does at last make itself visible, though covered over with many tangles. In the volume of which I am now speaking there is no pathway at all. The reader must go where the writer may choose to take him, and must consent to change not only his ground, but the nature of his ground, every minute. This, as the name implies, is a collection of short stories,—and of course no thread or general plot is expected in such a compilation. But here the short narratives are altogether various in their style, no one of them giving any clew as to what may be expected to follow. They are, rather than tales, the jottings down of the author's own fancies, on matters which have subjected themselves to his brain, one after the other, in that promiscuous disorder in which his manner of thinking permitted him to indulge. He conceives a lovely woman, who has on her cheek a "birth-mark," so trifling as to be no flaw to her beauty. But her husband sees it, and, seeing it, can not rid himself of the remembrance of it. He is a man of science, concerned with the secrets of chemistry, and goes to work to concoct some ichor by which the mark may be eradicated. Just as success is being accomplished, the lady dies under the experiment. "You have aimed loftily," she says to her husband, at her last gasp; "you have done nobly. Do not repent." Whether the husband does repent we are not told; but the idea left is that, seeking something more than mortal perfection, he had thrown away the happiness which, as a mortal, he might have enjoyed. This is transcendental enough; but it is followed, a few pages on, by the record of Mrs. Bullfrog, who had got herself married to Mr. Bullfrog, as the natural possessor of all feminine loveliness, and then turns out to be a hideous virago, with false hair and false teeth, but who is at last accepted graciously by Bullfrog, because her money is real. The satire is intelligible, and is Hawthornean, but why Hawthorne should have brought himself to surround himself with objects so disagreeable the reader does not understand.

"The Select Party" is pleasant enough. It is held in a castle in the air, made magnificent with all architectural details, and there the Man of Fancy, who is its owner, entertains the Oldest Inhabitant, Nobody, M. Ondit, the Clerk of the Weather, Mother Carey, the Master Genius of his Age,—a young American, of course,—and sundry others, who among them have a good deal to say which is worth hearing. The student of Hawthorne will understand what quips and quirks will come from this mottled company.

Then there is an Italian, one Rappaccini, and his daughter, weird, ghostlike, and I must own very unintelligible. The young lady, however, has learned under the teaching of her father, who is part doctor, part gardener, and part conjurer, to exist on the essence of a flower which is fatal to everybody else. She becomes very detrimental to her lover, who has no such gifts, and the story ends as a tragedy. . . . "The Hall of Fantasy" is a mansion in which some unfortunates make their whole abode and business, and "contract habits which unfit them for all the real employments of life. Others,—but these are few,—possess the faculty, in their occasional visits, of discovering a purer truth than the world can impart." The reader can imagine to himself those who, under Hawthorne's guidance, would succeed and those who would fail by wandering into this hall. "The Procession of Life" is perhaps the strongest piece in the book,—the one most suggestive and most satisfactory. Hawthorne imagines that, by the blowing of some trumpet such as has never yet been heard, the inhabitants of the world shall be brought together under other circumstances than those which at present combine them. The poor now associate with the poor, the rich with the rich, the learned with the learned, the idle with the idle, the orthodox with the orthodox, and so on. By this new amalgamation the sick shall associate with the sick, the strong-bodied with the strong, the weak-bodied with the weak, the gifted with the gifted, the sorrowful with the sorrowful, the wicked with the wicked, and the good with the good. Here is a specimen of Hawthorne's manner in bringing the wicked together: "The hideous appeal has swept round the globe. Come all ye guilty ones, and rank yourselves in accordance with the brotherhood of crime. This, indeed, is an awful summons. I almost tremble to look at the strange partnerships that begin to be formed, reluctantly, but by the invincible necessity of like to like, in this part of the procession. A forger from the State prison seizes the arm of a distinguished financier. . . . Here comes a murderer with his clanking chain, and pairs himself,—horrible to tell!—with as pure and upright a man, in all observable respects, as ever partook of the consecrated bread and wine. . . . Why do that pair of flaunting girls, with the pert, affected laugh, and the sly leer at the bystander, intrude themselves into the same rank with yonder decorous matron and that somewhat prudish maiden?" The scope for irony and satire which Hawthorne could get from such a marshaling as this was unbounded.

There is a droll story, with a half-hidden meaning, called "Drowne's Wooden Image," in which Copley the painter is brought upon the scene, so that I am led to suppose that there was a Drowne who carved head-pieces for ships in Boston, and who, by some masterpiece in his trade and by the help of Hawthorne, has achieved a sort of immortality. Here the man, by dint of special energy on this special job,—he is supposed to be making a figure-head for a ship,—hews out of the wood a female Frankenstein, all alone, but lovely as was the other one hideous. The old idea, too, is conveyed that, as within every block of marble, so within every log of wood, there is a perfection of symmetry and beauty, to be reached by any one who may have the gift of properly stripping off the outlying matter.

"P.'s Correspondence" is the last I will mention. P. is a madman, who, in writing to his friend in Boston from his madhouse chamber, imagines himself to have met in London, Byron, Burns, Scott, and a score of other literary worthies, still alive as he supposes, but who by the stress of years have been changed in all their peculiarities, as men are changed when they live long. Byron becomes very religious, and professes excessive high-church tendencies, —as certain excellent and over-liberal friends of mine have in their old age become more timid and more conservative than they who were to the manner born. Hawthorne adds to this the joke that all his own American literary contemporaries,—men whom he knew to be alive, and with whom he probably was intimate,—are, alas! dead and gone. The madman weeps over Bryant, Whittier, and Longfellow, while he has been associating with Keats, Canning, and John Kemble.

Such is the nature of the Mosses from the old Manse each morsel of moss damp, tawny, and soft, as it ought to be, but each with enough of virus to give a sting to the tender hand that touches it. . . .

From *North American Review* September 1879

HAWTHORNE

by Oliver Wendell Holmes

. . . It was my fortune to be among the last of the friends who looked upon Hawthorne's living face. Late in the afternoon of the day before he left Boston on his last journey I called upon him at the hotel where he was staying. He had gone out but a moment before. Looking along the street, I saw a figure at some distance in advance which could only be his,—but how changed from his former port and figure! There was no mistaking the long iron-gray locks, the carriage of the head, and the general look of the natural outlines and movement; but he seemed to have shrunken in all his dimensions, and faltered along with an uncertain, feeble step, as if every movement were an effort. I joined him, and we walked together half an hour, during which time I learned so much of his state of mind and body as could be got at without worrying him with suggestive questions,—my object being to form an opinion of his condition, as I had been requested to do, and to give him some hints that might be useful to him on his journey.

His aspect, medically considered, was very unfavorable. There were persistent local symptoms, referred especially to the stomach,—"boring pain," distension, difficult digestion, with great wasting of flesh and strength. He was very gentle, very willing to answer questions, very docile to such counsel as I offered him, but evidently had no hope of recovering his health. He spoke as if his work were done, and he should write no more.

With all his obvious depression, there was no failing noticeable in his conversational powers. There was the same backwardness and hesitancy which in his best days it was hard for him to overcome, so that talking with him was almost like lovemaking, and his shy, beautiful soul had to be wooed from its bashful pudency like an unschooled maiden. The calm despondency with which he spoke about himself confirmed the unfavorable opinion suggested by his look and history. . . .

There was nothing in Mr. Hawthorne's aspect that gave warning of so sudden an end as that which startled us all. It seems probable that he died by the gentlest of all modes of release, fainting, without the trouble and confusion of coming back to life,—a way of ending liable to happen in any disease attended with much debility.

Mr. Hawthorne died in the town of Plymouth, New Hampshire, on the nineteenth of May. The moment, and even the hour, could not be told, for he had passed away without giving any sign of suffering, such as might call the attention of the friend near him. On Monday, the twenty-third of May, his body was given back to earth in the place where he had long lived, and which he had helped to make widely known,—the ancient town of Concord.

The day of his burial will always live in the memory of all who shared in its solemn, grateful duties. All the fair sights and sweet sounds of the opening season mingled their enchantments as if in homage to the dead master, who, as a lover of Nature and a student of life, had given such wealth of poetry to our New-England home, and invested the stern outlines of Puritan character with the colors of romance. It was the bridal day of the season, perfect in light as if heaven were looking on, perfect in air as if Nature herself were sighing for our loss. The orchards were all in fresh flower,—

> "One boundless blush, one white-empurpled shower
> Of mingled blossoms";—

the banks were literally blue with violets; the elms were putting out their tender leaves, just in that passing aspect which Raphael loved to pencil in the backgrounds of his holy pictures, not as yet printing deep shadows, but only mottling the sunshine at their feet. The birds were in full song; the pines were musical with the soft winds they sweetened. All was in faultless accord, and every heart was filled with the beauty that flooded the landscape.

The church where the funeral services were performed was luminous with the whitest blossoms of the luxuriant spring. A great throng of those who loved him, of those who honored his genius, of those who held him in kindly esteem as a neighbor and friend, filled the edifice. Most of those who were present wished to look once more at the features which they remembered with the lights and shadows of life's sunshine upon them. The cold moonbeam of death lay white on the noble forehead and still, placid features; but they never looked fuller of power than in this last aspect with which they met the eyes that were turned upon them.

In a patch of sunlight, flecked by the shade of tall, murmuring pines, at the summit of a gently swelling mound where the wild-flowers had climbed to find the light and the stirring of fresh breezes, the tired poet was laid beneath the green turf. Poet let us call him, though his chants were not modulated in the rhythm of verse. The element of poetry is air: we know the poet by his atmospheric effects, by the blue of his distances, by the softening of every hard outline he touches, by the silvery mist in which he veils deformity and clothes what is common so that it changes to awe-inspiring mystery, by the clouds of gold and purple which are the drapery of his dreams. And surely we have had but one prosewriter who could be compared with him in aërial perspective, if we may use the painter's term. If Irving is the Claude of our unrhymed poetry, Hawthorne is its Poussin.

The hand of the dead master shows itself in his every line. The shapes and scenes he pictures slide at once into our consciousness, as if they belonged there as much as our own homes and relatives. That limpid flow of expression, never laboring, never shallow, never hurried nor uneven nor turbid, but moving on with tranquil force, clear to the depths of its profoundest thought, shows itself with all its consummate perfections. Our literature could ill spare the rich ripe autumn of such a life as Hawthorne's, but he has left enough to keep his name in remembrance as long as the language in which he shaped his deep imaginations is spoken by human lips.

From *The Atlantic Monthly* July 1864

FROM

Twice-Told Tales

THE GRAY CHAMPION

There was once a time when New England groaned under the actual pressure of heavier wrongs than those threatened ones which brought on the Revolution. James II., the bigoted successor of Charles the Voluptuous, had annulled the charters of all the colonies, and sent a harsh and unprincipled soldier to take away our liberties and endanger our religion. The administration of Sir Edmund Andros lacked scarcely a single characteristic of tyranny: a Governor and Council, holding office from the King, and wholly independent of the country; laws made and taxes levied without concurrence of the people immediate or by their representatives; the rights of private citizens violated, and the titles of all landed property declared void; the voice of complaint stifled by restrictions on the press; and, finally, disaffection overawed by the first band of mercenary troops that ever marched on our free soil. For two years our ancestors were kept in sullen submission by that filial love which had invariably secured their allegiance to the mother country, whether its head chanced to be a Parliament, Protector, or Popish Monarch. Till these evil times, however, such allegiance had been merely nominal, and the colonists had ruled themselves, enjoying far more freedom than is even yet the privilege of the native subjects of Great Britain.

At length a rumor reached our shores that the Prince of Orange had ventured on an enterprise, the success of which would be the triumph of civil and religious rights and the salvation of New England. It was but a doubtful whisper; it might be false, or the attempt might fail; and, in either case, the man that stirred against King James would lose his head. Still the intelligence produced a marked effect. The people smiled mysteriously in the streets, and threw bold glances at their oppressors; while far and wide there was a subdued and silent agitation, as if the slightest signal would rouse the whole land from its sluggish despondency. Aware of their danger, the rulers resolved to avert it by an imposing display of strength, and perhaps to confirm their despotism by yet harsher measures. One afternoon in April, 1689, Sir Edmund Andros and his favorite councillors, being warm with wine, assembled the red-coats of the Governor's Guard, and made their appearance in the streets of Boston. The sun was near setting when the march commenced.

The roll of the drum at that unquiet crisis seemed to go through the streets, less as the martial music of the soldiers, than as a muster-call to the inhabitants themselves. A multitude, by various avenues, assembled in King Street, which was destined to be the scene, nearly a century afterwards, of another encounter between the troops of Britain, and a people struggling against her tyranny. Though more than sixty years had elapsed since the pilgrims came, this crowd of their descendants still showed the strong and sombre features of their character perhaps more strikingly in such a stern emergency than on happier occasions. There were the sober garb, the general severity of mien, the gloomy but undismayed expression, the scriptural forms of speech, and the confidence in Heaven's blessing on a righteous cause, which would have marked a band of the original Puritans, when threatened by some peril of the wilderness. Indeed, it was not yet time for the old spirit to be extinct; since there were men in the street that day who had worshipped there beneath the trees, before a house was reared to the God for whom they had become exiles. Old soldiers of the Parliament were here, too, smiling grimly at the thought that their aged arms might strike another blow against the house of Stuart. Here, also, were the veterans of King Philip's war, who had burned villages and slaughtered young and old, with pious fierceness, while the godly souls throughout the land were helping them with prayer. Several ministers were scattered among the crowd, which, unlike all other mobs, regarded them with such reverence, as if there were sanctity in their very garments. These holy men exerted their influence to quiet the people, but not to disperse them. Meantime, the purpose of the Governor, in disturbing the peace of the town at a period when the slightest commotion might throw the country into a ferment, was almost the universal subject of inquiry, and variously explained.

"Satan will strike his master-stroke presently," cried some, "because he knoweth that his time is short. All our godly pastors are to be dragged to prison! We shall see them at a Smithfield fire in King Street!"

Hereupon the people of each parish gathered closer round their minister, who looked calmly upwards and assumed a more apostolic dignity, as well befitted a candidate for the highest honor of his profession, the crown of martyrdom. It was actually fancied, at that period, that New England might have a John Rogers of her own to take the place of that worthy in the Primer.

"The Pope of Rome has given orders for a new St. Bartholomew!" cried others. "We are to be massacred, man and male child!"

Neither was this rumor wholly discredited, although the wiser class believed the Governor's object somewhat less atrocious. His predecessor under the old charter, Bradstreet, a venerable companion of the first settlers, was known to be in town. There were grounds for conjecturing, that Sir Edmund Andros intended at once to strike terror by a parade of military force, and to confound the opposite faction by possessing himself of their chief.

"Stand firm for the old charter Governor!" shouted the crowd, seizing upon the idea. "The good old Governor Bradstreet!"

While this cry was at the loudest, the people were surprised by the well-known figure of Governor Bradstreet himself, a patriarch of nearly ninety, who appeared on the elevated steps of a door, and, with characteristic mildness, besought them to submit to the constituted authorities.

"My children," concluded this venerable person, "do nothing rashly. Cry not aloud, but pray for the welfare of New England, and expect patiently what the Lord will do in this matter!"

The event was soon to be decided. All this time, the roll of the drum had been approaching through Cornhill, louder and deeper, till with reverberations from house to house, and the regular tramp of martial footsteps, it burst into the street. A double rank of soldiers made their appearance, occupying the whole breadth of the passage, with shouldered matchlocks, and matches burning, so as to present a row of fires in the dusk. Their steady march was like the progress of a machine, that would roll irresistibly over everything in its way. Next, moving slowly, with a confused clatter of hoofs on the pavement, rode a party of mounted gentlemen, the central figure being Sir Edmund Andros, elderly, but erect and soldier-like. Those around him were his favorite councillors, and the bitterest foes of New England. At his right hand rode Edward Randolph, our arch-enemy, that "blasted wretch," as Cotton Mather calls him, who achieved the downfall of our ancient government, and was followed with a sensible curse, through life and to his grave. On the other side was Bullivant, scattering jests and mockery as he rode along. Dudley came behind, with a downcast look, dreading, as well he might, to meet the indignant gaze of the people, who beheld him, their only countryman by birth, among the oppressors of his native land. The captain of a frigate in the harbor, and two or three civil officers under the Crown, were also there. But the figure which most attracted the public eye, and stirred up the deepest feeling, was the Episcopal clergyman of King's Chapel, riding haughtily among the magistrates in his priestly vestments, the fitting representative of prelacy and persecution, the union of church and state, and all those abominations which had driven the Puritans to the wilderness. Another guard of soldiers, in double rank, brought up the rear.

The whole scene was a picture of the condition of New England, and its moral, the deformity of any government that does not grow out of the nature of things and the character of the people. On one side the religious multitude, with their sad visages and dark attire, and on the other, the group of despotic rulers, with the high churchman in the midst, and here and there a crucifix at their bosoms, all magnificently clad, flushed with wine, proud of unjust authority, and scoffing at the universal groan. And the mercenary soldiers, waiting but the word to deluge the street with blood, showed the only means by which obedience could be secured.

"O Lord of Hosts," cried a voice among the crowd, "provide a Champion for thy people!"

This ejaculation was loudly uttered, and served as a herald's cry to introduce a remarkable personage. The crowd had rolled back, and were now huddled together nearly at the extremity of the street, while the soldiers had advanced no more than a third of its length. The intervening space was empty —a paved solitude, between lofty edifices, which threw almost a twilight shadow over it. Suddenly, there was seen the figure of an ancient man, who seemed to have emerged from among the people, and was walking by himself along the centre of the street, to confront the armed band. He wore the old Puritan dress, a dark cloak and a steeple-crowned hat, in the fashion of at least fifty years before, with a heavy sword upon his thigh, but a staff in his hand to assist the tremulous gait of age.

When at some distance from the multitude, the old man turned slowly round, displaying a face of antique majesty, rendered doubly venerable by the hoary beard that descended on his breast. He made a gesture at once of encouragement and warning, then turned again, and resumed his way.

"Who is this gray patriarch?" asked the young men of their sires.

"Who is this venerable brother?" asked the old men among themselves.

But none could make reply. The fathers of the people, those of fourscore years and upwards, were disturbed, deeming it strange that they should forget one of such evident authority, whom they must have known in their early days, the associate of Winthrop, and all the old councillors, giving laws, and making prayers, and leading them against the savage. The elderly men ought to have remembered him, too, with locks as gray in their youth, as their own were now. And the young! How could he have passed so utterly from their memories—that hoary sire, the relic of long-departed times, whose awful benediction had surely been bestowed on their uncovered heads, in childhood?

"Whence did he come? What is his purpose? Who can this old man be?" whispered the wondering crowd.

Meanwhile, the venerable stranger, staff in hand, was pursuing his solitary walk along the centre of the street. As he drew near the advancing soldiers, and as the roll of their drum came full upon his ear, the old man raised himself to a loftier mien, while the decrepitude of age seemed to fall from his shoulders, leaving him in gray but unbroken dignity. Now, he marched onward with a warrior's step, keeping time to the military music. Thus the aged form advanced on one side, and the whole parade of soldiers and magistrates on the other, till, when scarcely twenty yards remained between, the old man grasped his staff by the middle, and held it before him like a leader's truncheon.

"Stand!" cried he.

The eye, the face, and attitude of command; the solemn, yet warlike peal of that voice, fit either to rule a host in the battle-field or be raised to God in prayer, were irresistible. At the old man's word and outstretched arm, the roll of the drum was hushed at once, and the advancing line stood still. A tremulous enthusiasm seized upon the multitude. That stately form, combining the leader and the saint, so gray, so dimly seen, in such an ancient garb, could only belong to some old champion of the righteous cause, whom the oppressor's drum had summoned from his grave. They raised a shout of awe and exultation, and looked for the deliverance of New England.

The Governor, and the gentlemen of his party, perceiving themselves brought to an unexpected stand, rode hastily forward, as if they would have pressed their snorting and affrighted horses right against the hoary apparition. He, however, blenched not a step, but glancing his severe eye round the group, which half encompassed him, at last bent it sternly on Sir Edmund Andros. One would have thought that the dark old man was chief ruler there, and that the Governor and Council, with soldiers at their back, representing the whole power and authority of the Crown, had no alternative but obedience.

"What does this old fellow here?" cried Edward Randolph, fiercely. "On, Sir Edmund! Bid the soldiers forward, and give the dotard the same choice that you give all his countrymen—to stand aside or be trampled on!"

"Nay, nay, let us show respect to the good grandsire," said Bullivant, laughing. "See you not, he is some old round-headed dignitary, who hath lain asleep these thirty years, and knows nothing of the change of times? Doubtless, he thinks to put us down with a proclamation in Old Noll's name!"

"Are you mad, old man?" demanded Sir Edmund Andros, in loud and harsh tones. "How dare you stay the march of King James's Governor?"

"I have stayed the march of a King himself, ere now," replied the gray figure, with stern composure. "I am here, Sir Governor, because the cry of an oppressed people hath disturbed me in my secret place; and beseeching this favor earnestly of the Lord, it was vouchsafed me to appear once again on earth, in the good old cause of his saints. And what speak ye of James? There is no longer a Popish tyrant on the throne of England, and by to-morrow noon, his name shall be a byword in this very street, where ye would make it a word of terror. Back, thou that wast a Governor, back! With this night thy power is ended—to-morrow, the prison!—back, lest I foretell the scaffold!"

The people had been drawing nearer and nearer, and drinking in the words of their champion, who spoke in accents long disused, like one unaccustomed to converse, except with the dead of many years ago. But his voice stirred their souls. They confronted the soldiers, not wholly without arms, and ready to convert the very stones of the street into deadly weapons. Sir Edmund Andros looked at the old man; then he cast his hard and cruel eye over the multitude, and beheld them burning with that lurid wrath, so difficult to kindle or to quench; and again he fixed his gaze on the aged form, which stood obscurely in an open space, where neither friend nor foe had thrust himself. What were his thoughts, he uttered no word which might discover. But whether the oppressor were overawed by the Gray Champion's look, or perceived his peril in the threatening attitude of the people, it is certain that he gave back, and ordered his soldiers to commence a slow and guarded retreat. Before another sunset, the Governor, and all that rode so proudly with him, were prisoners, and long ere it was known that James had abdicated, King William was proclaimed throughout New England.

But where was the Gray Champion? Some reported that, when the troops had gone from King Street, and the people were thronging tumultuously in their rear, Bradstreet, the aged Governor, was seen to embrace a form more aged than his own. Others soberly affirmed, that while they marvelled at the venerable grandeur of his aspect, the old man had faded from their eyes, melting slowly into the hues of twilight, till, where he stood, there was an empty space. But all agreed that the hoary shape was gone. The men of that generation watched for his reappearance, in sunshine and in twilight, but never saw him more, nor knew when his funeral passed, nor where his gravestone was.

And who was the Gray Champion? Perhaps his name might be found in the records of that stern Court of Justice, which passed a sentence, too mighty for the age, but glorious in all after-times, for its humbling lesson to the monarch and its high example to the subject. I have heard, that whenever the descendants of the Puritans are to show the spirit of their sires, the old man appears again. When eighty years had passed, he walked once more in King Street. Five years later, in the twilight of an April morning, he stood on the green, beside the meeting-house, at Lexington, where now the obelisk of granite, with a slab of slate inlaid, commemorates the first fallen of the Revolution. And when our fathers were toiling at the breastwork on Bunker's Hill, all through that night the old warrior walked his rounds. Long, long may it be, ere he comes again! His hour is one of darkness, and adversity, and peril. But should domestic tyranny oppress us, or the invader's step pollute our soil, still may the Gray Champion come, for he is the type of New England's hereditary spirit; and his shadowy march, on the eve of danger, must ever be the pledge, that New England's sons will vindicate their ancestry.

THE WEDDING KNELL

There is a certain church in the city of New York which I have always regarded with peculiar interest, on account of a marriage there solemnized, under very singular circumstances, in my grandmother's girlhood. That venerable lady chanced to be a spectator of the scene, and ever after made it her favorite narrative. Whether the edifice now standing on the same site be the identical one to which she referred, I am not antiquarian enough to know; nor would it be worth while to correct myself, perhaps, of an agreeable error, by reading the date of its erection on the tablet over the door. It is a stately church, surrounded by an inclosure of the loveliest green, within which appear urns, pillars, obelisks, and other forms of monumental marble, the tributes of private affection, or more splendid memorials of historic dust. With such a place, though the tumult of the city rolls beneath its tower, one would be willing to connect some legendary interest.

The marriage might be considered as the result of an early engagement, though there had been two intermediate weddings on the lady's part, and forty years of celibacy on that of the gentleman. At sixty-five, Mr. Ellenwood was a shy, but not quite a secluded man; selfish, like all men who brood over their own hearts, yet manifesting on rare occasions a vein of generous sentiment; a scholar throughout life, though always an indolent one, because his studies had no definite object, either of public advantage or personal ambition; a gentleman, high bred and fastidiously delicate, yet sometimes requiring a considerable relaxation, in his behalf, of the common rules of society. In truth, there were so many anomalies in his character, and though shrinking with diseased sensibility from public notice, it had been his fatality so often to become the topic of the day, by some wild eccentricity of conduct, that people searched his lineage for an hereditary taint of insanity. But there was no need of this. His caprices had their origin in a mind that lacked the support of an engrossing purpose, and in feelings that preyed upon themselves for want of other food. If he were mad, it was the consequence, and not the cause, of an aimless and abortive life.

The widow was as complete a contrast to her third bridegroom, in everything but age, as can well be conceived. Compelled to relinquish her first engagement, she had been united to a man of twice her own years, to whom she became an exemplary wife, and by whose death she was left in possession of a splendid fortune. A southern gentleman, considerably younger than herself, succeeded to her hand, and carried her to Charleston, where, after many uncomfortable years, she found herself again a widow. It would have been singular, if any uncommon delicacy of feeling had survived through such a life as Mrs. Dabney's; it could not but be crushed and killed by her early disappointment, the cold duty of her first marriage, the dislocation of the heart's principles, consequent on a second union, and the unkindness of her southern husband, which had inevitably driven her to connect the idea of his death with that of her comfort. To be brief, she was that wisest, but unloveliest, variety of woman, a philosopher, bearing troubles of the heart with equanimity, dispensing with all that should have been her happiness, and making the best of what remained. Sage in most matters, the widow was perhaps the more amiable for the one frailty that made her ridiculous. Being childless, she could not remain beautiful by proxy, in the person of a daughter; she therefore refused to grow old and ugly, on any consideration; she struggled with Time, and held fast her roses in spite of him, till the venerable thief appeared to have relinquished the spoil, as not worth the trouble of acquiring it.

The approaching marriage of this woman of the world with such an unworldly man as Mr. Ellenwood was announced soon after Mrs. Dabney's return to her native city. Superficial observers, and deeper ones, seemed to concur in supposing that the lady must have borne no inactive part in arranging the affair; there were considerations of expediency which she would be far more likely to appreciate than Mr. Ellenwood; and there was just the specious phantom of sentiment and romance in this late union of two early lovers which sometimes makes a fool of a woman who has lost her true feelings among the accidents of life. All the wonder was, how the gentleman, with his lack of worldly wisdom and agonizing consciousness of ridicule, could have been induced to take a measure at once so prudent and so laughable. But while people talked the wedding-day arrived. The ceremony was to be solemnized according to the Episcopalian forms, and in open church, with a degree of publicity that attracted many spectators, who occupied the front seats of the galleries, and the pews near the altar and along the broad aisle. It had been arranged, or possibly it was the custom of the day, that the parties should proceed separately to church. By some accident the bridegroom was a little less punctual than the widow and her bridal attendants; with whose arrival, after this tedious, but necessary preface, the action of our tale may be said to commence.

The clumsy wheels of several old-fashioned coaches were heard, and the gentlemen and ladies composing the bridal party came through the church door with the sudden and gladsome effect of a burst of sunshine. The whole group, except the principal figure, was made up of youth and gayety. As they streamed up the broad aisle, while the pews and pillars seemed to brighten on either side, their steps were as buoyant as if they mistook the church for a ball-room, and were ready to dance hand in hand to the altar. So brilliant was the spectacle that few took notice of a singular phenomenon that had marked its entrance. At the moment when the bride's foot touched the threshold the bell swung heavily in the tower above her, and sent forth its deepest knell. The vibrations died away and returned with prolonged solemnity, as she entered the body of the church.

"Good heavens! what an omen," whispered a young lady to her lover.

"On my honor," replied the gentleman, "I believe the bell has the good taste to toll of its own accord. What has she to do with weddings? If you, dearest Julia, were approaching the altar the bell would ring out its merriest peal. It has only a funeral knell for her."

The bride and most of her company had been too much occupied with the bustle of entrance to hear the first boding stroke of the bell, or at least to reflect on the singularity of such a welcome to the altar. They therefore continued to advance with undiminished gayety. The gorgeous dresses of the time, the crimson velvet coats, the gold-laced hats, the hoop petticoats, the silk, satin, brocade, and embroidery, the buckles, canes, and swords, all displayed to the best advantage on persons suited to such finery, made the group appear more like a bright-colored picture than anything real. But by what perversity of taste had the artist represented his principal figure as so wrinkled and decayed, while yet he had decked her out in the brightest splendor of attire, as if the loveliest maiden had suddenly withered into age, and become a moral to the beautiful around her! On they went, however, and had glittered along about a third of the aisle, when another stroke of the bell seemed to fill the church with a visible gloom, dimming and obscuring the bright pageant, till it shone forth again as from a mist.

This time the party wavered, stopped, and huddled closer together, while a slight scream was heard from some of the ladies, and a confused whispering among the gentlemen. Thus tossing to and fro, they might have been fancifully compared to a splendid bunch of flowers, suddenly shaken by a puff of wind, which threatened to scatter the leaves of an old, brown, withered rose, on the same stalk with two dewy buds,—such being the emblem of the widow between her fair young bridemaids. But her heroism was admirable. She had started with an irrepressible shudder, as if the stroke of the bell had fallen directly on her heart; then, recovering herself, while her attendants were yet in dismay, she took the lead, and paced calmly up the aisle. The bell continued to swing, strike, and vibrate, with the same doleful regularity as when a corpse is on its way to the tomb.

"My young friends here have their nerves a little shaken," said the widow, with a smile, to the clergyman at the altar. "But so many weddings have been ushered in with the merriest peal of the bells, and yet turned out unhappily, that I shall hope for better fortune under such different auspices."

"Madam," answered the rector, in great perplexity, "this strange occurrence brings to my mind a marriage sermon of the famous Bishop Taylor, wherein he mingles so many thoughts of mortality and future woe, that, to speak somewhat after his own rich style, he seems to hang the bridal chamber in black, and cut the wedding garment out of a coffin pall. And it has been the custom of divers nations to infuse something of sadness into their marriage ceremonies, so to keep death in mind while contracting that engagement which is life's chiefest business. Thus we may draw a sad but profitable moral from this funeral knell."

But, though the clergyman might have given his moral even a keener point, he did not fail to dispatch an attendant to inquire into the mystery, and stop those sounds, so dismally appropriate to such a marriage. A brief space elapsed, during which the silence was broken only by whispers, and a few suppressed titterings, among the wedding party and the spectators, who, after the first shock, were disposed to draw an ill-natured merriment from the affair. The young have less charity for aged follies than the old for those of youth. The widow's glance was observed to wander, for an instant, towards a window of the church, as if searching for the time-worn marble that she had dedicated to her first husband; then her eyelids dropped over their faded orbs, and her thoughts were drawn irresistibly to another grave. Two buried men, with a voice at her ear, and a cry afar off, were calling her to lie down beside them. Perhaps, with momentary truth of feeling, she thought how much happier had been her fate, if, after years of bliss, the bell were now tolling for her funeral, and she were followed to the grave by the old affection of her earliest lover, long her husband. But why had she returned to him, when their cold hearts shrank from each other's embrace?

Still the death-bell tolled so mournfully, that the sunshine seemed to fade in the air. A whisper, communicated from those who stood nearest the windows, now spread through the church; a hearse, with a train of several coaches, was creeping along the street, conveying some dead man to the churchyard, while the bride awaited a living one at the altar. Immediately after, the footsteps of the bridegroom and his friends were heard at the door. The widow looked down the aisle, and clinched the arm of one of her bridemaids in her bony hand with such unconscious violence, that the fair girl trembled.

"You frighten me, my dear madam!" cried she. "For Heaven's sake, what is the matter?"

"Nothing, my dear, nothing," said the widow; then, whispering close to her ear, "There is a foolish fancy that I cannot get rid of. I am expecting my bridegroom to come into the church, with my first two husbands for groomsmen!"

"Look, look!" screamed the bridemaid. "What is here? The funeral!"

As she spoke, a dark procession paced into the church. First came an old man and woman, like chief mourners at a funeral, attired from head to foot in the deepest black, all but their pale features and hoary hair; he leaning on a staff, and supporting her decrepit form with his nerveless arm. Behind appeared another, and another pair, as aged, as black, and mournful as the first. As they drew near, the widow recognized in every face some trait of former friends, long forgotten, but now returning, as if from their old graves, to warn her to prepare a shroud; or, with purpose almost as unwelcome, to exhibit their wrinkles and infirmity, and claim her as their companion by the tokens of her own decay. Many a merry night had she danced with them, in youth. And now, in joyless age, she felt that some withered partner should request her hand, and all unite, in a dance of death, to the music of the funeral bell.

While these aged mourners were passing up the aisle, it was observed that, from pew to pew, the spectators shuddered with irrepressible awe, as some object, hitherto concealed by the intervening figures, came full in sight. Many turned away their faces; others kept a fixed and rigid stare; and a young girl giggled hysterically, and fainted with the laughter on her lips. When the spectral procession approached the altar, each couple separated, and slowly diverged, till, in the centre, appeared a form, that had been worthily ushered in with all this gloomy pomp, the death knell, and the funeral. It was the bridegroom in his shroud!

No garb but that of the grave could have befitted such a deathlike aspect; the eyes, indeed, had the wild gleam of a sepulchral lamp; all else was fixed in the stern calmness which old men wear in the coffin. The corpse stood motionless, but addressed the widow in accents that seemed to melt into the clang of the bell, which fell heavily on the air while he spoke.

"Come, my bride!" said those pale lips, "the hearse is ready. The sexton stands waiting for us at the door of the tomb. Let us be married; and then to our coffins!"

How shall the widow's horror be represented? It gave her the ghastliness of a dead man's bride. Her youthful friends stood apart, shuddering at the mourners, the shrouded bridegroom, and herself; the whole scene expressed, by the strongest imagery, the vain struggle of the gilded vanities of this world, when opposed to age, infirmity, sorrow, and death. The awestruck silence was first broken by the clergyman.

"Mr. Ellenwood," said he, soothingly, yet with somewhat of authority, "you are not well. Your mind has been agitated by the unusual circumstances in which you are placed. The ceremony must be deferred. As an old friend, let me entreat you to return home."

"Home! yes, but not without my bride," answered he, in the same hollow accents. "You deem this mockery; perhaps madness. Had I bedizened my aged and broken frame with scarlet and embroidery—had I forced my withered lips to smile at my dead heart—that might have been mockery, or madness. But now, let young and old declare, which of us has come hither without a wedding garment, the bridegroom or the bride!"

He stepped forward at a ghostly pace, and stood beside the widow, contrasting the awful simplicity of his shroud with the glare and glitter in which she had arrayed herself for this unhappy scene. None, that beheld them, could deny the terrible strength of the moral which his disordered intellect had contrived to draw.

"Cruel! cruel!" groaned the heart-stricken bride.

"Cruel!" repeated he; then, losing his deathlike composure in a wild bitterness: "Heaven judge which of us has been cruel to the other! In youth you deprived me of my happiness, my hopes, my aims; you took away all the substance of my life, and made it a dream without reality enough even to grieve at—with only a pervading gloom, through which I walked wearily, and cared not whither. But after forty years, when I have built my tomb, and would not give up the thought of resting there—no, not for such a life as we once pictured—you call me to the altar. At your summons I am here. But other husbands have enjoyed your youth, your beauty, your warmth of heart, and all that could be termed your life. What is there for me but your decay and death? And therefore I have bidden these funeral friends, and bespoken the sexton's deepest knell, and am come, in my shroud, to wed you, as with a burial service, that we may join our hands at the door of the sepulchre, and enter it together."

It was not frenzy; it was not merely the drunkenness of strong emotion, in a heart unused to it, that now wrought upon the bride. The stern lesson of the day had done its work; her worldliness was gone. She seized the bridegroom's hand.

"Yes!" cried she. "Let us wed, even at the door of the sepulchre! My life is gone in vanity and emptiness. But at its close there is one true feeling. It has made me what I was in youth; it makes me worthy of you. Time is no more for both of us. Let us wed for Eternity!"

With a long and deep regard, the bridegroom looked into her eyes, while a tear was gathering in his own. How strange that gush of human feeling from the frozen bosom of a corpse! He wiped away the tears even with his shroud.

"Beloved of my youth," said he, "I have been wild. The despair of my whole lifetime had returned at once, and maddened me. Forgive; and be forgiven. Yes; it is evening with us now; and we have realized none of our morning dreams of happiness. But let us join our hands before the altar, as lovers whom adverse circumstances have separated through life, yet who meet again as they are leaving it, and find their earthly affection changed into something holy as religion. And what is Time, to the married of Eternity?"

Amid the tears of many, and a swell of exalted sentiment, in those who felt aright, was solemnized the union of two immortal souls. The train of withered mourners, the hoary bridegroom in his shroud, the pale features of the aged bride, and the death-bell tolling through the whole, till its deep voice overpowered the marriage words, all marked the funeral of earthly hopes. But as the ceremony proceeded, the organ, as if stirred by the sympathies of this impressive scene, poured forth an anthem, first mingling with the dismal knell, then rising to a loftier strain, till the soul looked down upon its woe. And when the awful rite was finished, and with cold hand in cold hand, the Married of Eternity withdrew, the organ's peal of solemn triumph drowned the Wedding Knell.

THE MINISTER'S BLACK VEIL[1]

A PARABLE

The sexton stood in the porch of Milford meeting-house, pulling busily at the bell-rope. The old people of the village came stooping along the street. Children, with bright faces, tripped merrily beside their parents, or mimicked a graver gait, in the conscious dignity of their Sunday clothes. Spruce bachelors looked sidelong at the pretty maidens, and fancied that the Sabbath sunshine made them prettier than on week days. When the throng had mostly streamed into the porch, the sexton began to toll the bell, keeping his eye on the Reverend Mr. Hooper's door. The first glimpse of the clergyman's figure was the signal for the bell to cease its summons.

"But what has good Parson Hooper got upon his face?" cried the sexton in astonishment.

All within hearing immediately turned about, and beheld the semblance of Mr. Hooper, pacing slowly his meditative way towards the meeting-house. With one accord they started, expressing more wonder than if some strange minister were coming to dust the cushions of Mr. Hooper's pulpit.

"Are you sure it is our parson?" inquired Goodman Gray of the sexton.

"Of a certainty it is good Mr. Hooper," replied the sexton. "He was to have exchanged pulpits with Parson Shute, of Westbury; but Parson Shute sent to excuse himself yesterday, being to preach a funeral sermon."

[1]Another clergyman in New England, Mr. Joseph Moody, of York, Maine, who died about eighty years since, made himself remarkable by the same eccentricity that is here related of the Reverend Mr. Hooper. In his case, however, the symbol had a different import. In early life he had accidentally killed a beloved friend; and from that day till the hour of his own death, he hid his face from men.

The cause of so much amazement may appear sufficiently slight. Mr. Hooper, a gentlemanly person, of about thirty, though still a bachelor, was dressed with due clerical neatness, as if a careful wife had starched his band, and brushed the weekly dust from his Sunday's garb. There was but one thing remarkable in his appearance. Swathed about his forehead, and hanging down over his face, so low as to be shaken by his breath, Mr. Hooper had on a black veil. On a nearer view it seemed to consist of two folds of crape, which entirely concealed his features, except the mouth and chin, but probably did not intercept his sight, further than to give a darkened aspect to all living and inanimate things. With this gloomy shade before him, good Mr. Hooper walked onward, at a slow and quiet pace, stooping somewhat, and looking on the ground, as is customary with abstracted men, yet nodding kindly to those of his parishioners who still waited on the meeting-house steps. But so wonder-struck were they that his greeting hardly met with a return.

"I can't really feel as if good Mr. Hooper's face was behind that piece of crape," said the sexton.

"I don't like it," muttered an old woman, as she hobbled into the meeting-house. "He has changed himself into something awful, only by hiding his face."

"Our parson has gone mad!" cried Goodman Gray, following him across the threshold.

A rumor of some unaccountable phenomenon had preceded Mr. Hooper into the meeting-house, and set all the congregation astir. Few could refrain from twisting their heads towards the door; many stood upright, and turned directly about; while several little boys clambered upon the seats, and came down again with a terrible racket. There was a general bustle, a rustling of the women's gowns and shuffling of the men's feet, greatly at variance with that hushed repose which should attend the entrance of the minister. But Mr. Hooper appeared not to notice the perturbation of his people. He entered with an almost noiseless step, bent his head mildly to the pews on each side, and bowed as he passed his oldest parishioner, a white-haired great-grandsire, who occupied an arm-chair in the centre of the aisle. It was strange to observe how slowly this venerable man became conscious of something singular in the appearance of his pastor. He seemed not fully to partake of the prevailing wonder, till Mr. Hooper had ascended the stairs, and showed himself in the pulpit, face to face with his congregation, except for the black veil. That mysterious emblem was never once withdrawn. It shook with his measured breath, as he gave out the psalm; it threw its obscurity between him and the holy page, as he read the Scriptures; and while he prayed, the veil lay heavily on his uplifted countenance. Did he seek to hide it from the dread Being whom he was addressing?

Such was the effect of this simple piece of crape, that more than one woman of delicate nerves was forced to leave the meeting-house. Yet perhaps the pale-faced congregation was almost as fearful a sight to the minister, as his black veil to them.

Mr. Hooper had the reputation of a good preacher, but not an energetic one: he strove to win his people heavenward by mild, persuasive influences, rather than to drive them thither by the thunders of the Word. The sermon which he now delivered was marked by the same characteristics of style and manner as the general series of his pulpit oratory. But there was something, either in the sentiment of the discourse itself, or in the imagination of the auditors, which made it greatly the most powerful effort that they had ever heard from their pastor's lips. It was tinged, rather more darkly than usual, with the gentle gloom of Mr. Hooper's temperament. The subject had reference to secret sin, and those sad mysteries which we hide from our nearest and dearest, and would fain conceal from our own consciousness, even forgetting that the Omniscient can detect them. A subtle power was breathed into his words. Each member of the congregation, the most innocent girl, and the man of hardened breast, felt as if the preacher had crept upon them, behind his awful veil, and discovered their hoarded iniquity of deed or thought. Many spread their clasped hands on their bosoms. There was nothing terrible in what Mr. Hooper said, at least, no violence; and yet, with every tremor of his melancholy voice, the hearers quaked. An unsought pathos came hand in hand with awe. So sensible were the audience of some unwonted attribute in their minister, that they longed for a breath of wind to blow aside the veil, almost believing that a stranger's visage would be discovered, though the form, gesture, and voice were those of Mr. Hooper.

At the close of the services, the people hurried out with indecorous confusion, eager to communicate their pent-up amazement, and conscious of lighter spirits the moment they lost sight of the black veil. Some gathered in little circles, huddled closely together, with their mouths all whispering in the centre; some went homeward alone, wrapt in silent meditation; some talked loudly, and profaned the Sabbath day with ostentatious laughter. A few shook their sagacious heads, intimating that they could penetrate the mystery; while one or two affirmed that there was no mystery at all, but only that Mr. Hooper's eyes were so weakened by the midnight lamp, as to require a shade. After a brief interval, forth came good Mr. Hooper also, in the rear of his flock. Turning his veiled face from one group to another, he paid due reverence to the hoary heads, saluted the middle aged with kind dignity as their friend and spiritual guide, greeted the young with mingled authority and love, and laid his hands on the little children's heads to bless them. Such was always his custom on the Sabbath day. Strange and bewildered looks repaid him for his courtesy. None, as on former occasions, aspired to the honor of walking by their pastor's side. Old Squire Saunders, doubtless by an accidental lapse of memory, neglected to invite Mr. Hooper to his table, where the good clergyman had been wont to bless the food, almost every Sunday since his settlement. He returned, therefore, to the parsonage, and, at the moment of closing the door, was observed to look back upon the people, all of whom had their eyes fixed upon the minister. A sad smile gleamed faintly from beneath the black veil, and flickered about his mouth, glimmering as he disappeared.

"How strange," said a lady, "that a simple black veil, such as any woman might wear on her bonnet, should become such a terrible thing on Mr. Hooper's face!"

"Something must surely be amiss with Mr. Hooper's intellects," observed her husband, the physician of the village. "But the strangest part of the affair is the effect of this vagary, even on a sober-minded man like myself. The black veil, though it covers only our pastor's face, throws its influence over his whole person, and makes him ghostlike from head to foot. Do you not feel it so?"

"Truly do I," replied the lady; "and I would not be alone with him for the world. I wonder he is not afraid to be alone with himself!"

"Men sometimes are so," said her husband.

The afternoon service was attended with similar circumstances. At its conclusion, the bell tolled for the funeral of a young lady. The relatives and friends were assembled in the house, and the more distant acquaintances stood about the door, speaking of the good qualities of the deceased, when their talk was interrupted by the appearance of Mr. Hooper, still covered with his black veil. It was now an appropriate emblem. The clergyman stepped into the room where the corpse was laid, and bent over the coffin, to take a last farewell of his deceased parishioner. As he stooped, the veil hung straight down from his forehead, so that, if her eyelids had not been closed forever, the dead maiden might have seen his face. Could Mr. Hooper be fearful of her glance, that he so hastily caught back the black veil? A person who watched the interview between the dead and living, scrupled not to affirm, that, at the instant when the clergyman's features were disclosed, the corpse had slightly shuddered, rustling the shroud and muslin cap, though the countenance retained the composure of death. A superstitious old woman was the only witness of this prodigy. From the coffin Mr. Hooper passed into the chamber of the mourners, and thence to the head of the staircase, to make the funeral prayer. It was a tender and heart-dissolving prayer, full of sorrow, yet so imbued with celestial hopes, that the music of a heavenly harp, swept by the fingers of the dead, seemed faintly to be heard among the saddest accents of the minister. The people trembled, though they but darkly understood him when he prayed that they, and himself, and all of mortal race, might be ready, as he trusted this young maiden had been, for the dreadful hour that should snatch the veil from their faces. The bearers went heavily forth, and the mourners followed, saddening all the street, with the dead before them, and Mr. Hooper in his black veil behind.

"Why do you look back?" said one in the procession to his partner.

"I had a fancy," replied she, "that the minister and the maiden's spirit were walking hand in hand."

"And so had I, at the same moment," said the other.

That night, the handsomest couple in Milford village were to be joined in wedlock. Though reckoned a melancholy man, Mr. Hooper had a placid cheerfulness for such occasions, which often excited a sympathetic smile where livelier merriment would have been thrown away. There was no quality of his disposition which made him more beloved than this. The company at the wedding awaited his arrival with impatience, trusting that the strange awe, which had gathered over him throughout the day, would now be dispelled. But such was not the result. When Mr. Hooper came, the first thing that their eyes rested on was the same horrible black veil, which had added deeper gloom to the funeral, and could portend nothing but evil to the wedding. Such was its immediate effect on the guests that a cloud seemed to have rolled duskily from beneath the black crape, and dimmed the light of the candles. The bridal pair stood up before the minister. But the bride's cold fingers quivered in the tremulous hand of the bridegroom, and her deathlike paleness caused a whisper that the maiden who had been buried a few hours before was come from her grave to be married. If ever another wedding were so dismal, it was that famous one where they tolled the wedding knell. After performing the ceremony, Mr. Hooper raised a glass of wine to his lips, wishing happiness to the new-married couple in a strain of mild pleasantry that ought to have brightened the features of the guests, like a cheerful gleam from the hearth. At that instant, catching a glimpse of his figure in the looking-glass, the black veil involved his own spirit in the horror with which it overwhelmed all others. His frame shuddered, his lips grew white, he spilt the untasted wine upon the carpet, and rushed forth into the darkness. For the Earth, too, had on her Black Veil.

The next day, the whole village of Milford talked of little else than Parson Hooper's black veil. That, and the mystery concealed behind it, supplied a topic for discussion between acquaintances meeting in the street, and good women gossiping at their open windows. It was the first item of news that the tavernkeeper told to his guests. The children babbled of it on their way to school. One imitative little imp covered his face with an old black handkerchief, thereby so affrighting his playmates that the panic seized himself, and he well-nigh lost his wits by his own waggery.

It was remarkable that of all the busybodies and impertinent people in the parish, not one ventured to put the plain question to Mr. Hooper, wherefore he did this thing. Hitherto, whenever there appeared the slightest call for such interference, he had never lacked advisers, nor shown himself averse to be guided by their judgment. If he erred at all, it was by so painful a degree of self-distrust, that even the mildest censure would lead him to consider an indifferent action as a crime. Yet, though so well acquainted with this amiable weakness, no individual among his parishioners chose to make the black veil a subject of friendly remonstrance. There was a feeling of dread, neither plainly confessed nor carefully concealed, which caused each to shift the responsibility upon another, till at length it was found expedient to send a deputation of the church, in order to deal with Mr. Hooper about the mystery, before it should grow into a scandal. Never did an embassy so ill discharge its duties. The minister received them with friendly courtesy, but became silent, after they were seated, leaving to his visitors the whole burden of introducing their important business. The topic, it might be supposed, was obvious enough. There was the black veil swathed round Mr. Hooper's forehead, and concealing every feature above his placid mouth, on which, at times, they could perceive the glimmering of a melancholy smile. But that piece of crape, to their imagination, seemed to hang down before his heart, the symbol of a fearful secret between him and them. Were the veil but cast aside, they might speak freely of it, but not till then. Thus they sat a considerable time, speechless, confused, and shrinking uneasily from Mr. Hooper's eye, which they felt to be fixed upon them with an invisible glance. Finally, the deputies returned abashed to their constituents, pronouncing the matter too weighty to be handled, except by a council of the churches, if, indeed, it might not require a general synod.

But there was one person in the village unappalled by the awe with which the black veil had impressed all beside herself. When the deputies returned without an explanation, or even venturing to demand one, she, with the calm energy of her character, determined to chase away the strange cloud that appeared to be settling round Mr. Hooper, every moment more darkly than before. As his plighted wife, it should be her privilege to know what the black veil concealed. At the minister's first visit, therefore, she entered upon the subject with a direct simplicity, which made the task easier both for him and her. After he had seated himself, she fixed her eyes steadfastly upon the veil, but could discern nothing of the dreadful gloom that had so overawed the multitude: it was but a double fold of crape, hanging down from his forehead to his mouth, and slightly stirring with his breath.

"No," said she aloud, and smiling, "there is nothing terrible in this piece of crape, except that it hides a face which I am always glad to look upon. Come, good sir, let the sun shine from behind the cloud. First lay aside your black veil: then tell me why you put it on."

Mr. Hooper's smile glimmered faintly.

"There is an hour to come," said he, "when all of us shall cast aside our veils. Take it not amiss, beloved friend, if I wear this piece of crape till then."

"Your words are a mystery, too," returned the young lady. "Take away the veil from them, at least."

"Elizabeth, I will," said he, "so far as my vow may suffer me. Know, then, this veil is a type and a symbol, and I am bound to wear it ever, both in light and darkness, in solitude and before the gaze of multitudes, and as with strangers, so with my familiar friends. No mortal eye will see it withdrawn. This dismal shade must separate me from the world: even you, Elizabeth, can never come behind it!"

"What grievous affliction hath befallen you," she earnestly inquired, "that you should thus darken your eyes forever?"

"If it be a sign of mourning," replied Mr. Hooper, "I, perhaps, like most other mortals, have sorrows dark enough to be typified by a black veil."

"But what if the world will not believe that it is the type of an innocent sorrow?" urged Elizabeth. "Beloved and respected as you are, there may be whispers that you hide your face under the consciousness of secret sin. For the sake of your holy office, do away this scandal!"

The color rose into her cheeks as she intimated the nature of the rumors that were already abroad in the village. But Mr. Hooper's mildness did not forsake him. He even smiled again—that same sad smile, which always appeared like a faint glimmering of light, proceeding from the obscurity beneath the veil.

"If I hide my face for sorrow, there is cause enough," he merely replied; "and if I cover it for secret sin, what mortal might not do the same?"

And with this gentle, but unconquerable obstinacy did he resist all her entreaties. At length Elizabeth sat silent. For a few moments she appeared lost in thought, considering, probably, what new methods might be tried to withdraw her lover from so dark a fantasy, which, if it had no other meaning, was perhaps a symptom of mental disease. Though of a firmer character than his own, the tears rolled down her cheeks. But, in an instant, as it were, a new feeling took the place of sorrow: her eyes were fixed insensibly on the black veil, when, like a sudden twilight in the air, its terrors fell around her. She arose, and stood trembling before him.

"And do you feel it then, at last?" said he mournfully.

She made no reply, but covered her eyes with her hand, and turned to leave the room. He rushed forward and caught her arm.

"Have patience with me, Elizabeth!" cried he, passionately. "Do not desert me, though this veil must be between us here on earth. Be mine, and hereafter there shall be no veil over my face, no darkness between our souls! It is but a mortal veil—it is not for eternity! O! you know not how lonely I am, and how frightened, to be alone behind my black veil. Do not leave me in this miserable obscurity forever!"

"Lift the veil but once, and look me in the face," said she.

"Never! It cannot be!" replied Mr. Hooper.

"Then farewell!" said Elizabeth.

She withdrew her arm from his grasp, and slowly departed, pausing at the door, to give one long shuddering gaze, that seemed almost to penetrate the mystery of the black veil. But, even amid his grief, Mr. Hooper smiled to think that only a material emblem had separated him from happiness, though the horrors, which it shadowed forth, must be drawn darkly between the fondest of lovers.

From that time no attempts were made to remove Mr. Hooper's black veil, or, by a direct appeal, to discover the secret which it was supposed to hide. By persons who claimed a superiority to popular prejudice, it was reckoned merely an eccentric whim, such as often mingles with the sober actions of men otherwise rational, and tinges them all with its own semblance of insanity. But with the multitude, good Mr. Hooper was irreparably a bugbear. He could not walk the street with any peace of mind, so conscious was he that the gentle and timid would turn aside to avoid him, and that others would make it a point of hardihood to throw themselves in his way. The impertinence of the latter class compelled him to give up his customary walk at sunset to the burial ground; for when he leaned pensively over the gate, there would always be faces behind the gravestones, peeping at his black veil. A fable went the rounds that the stare of the dead people drove him thence. It grieved him, to the very depth of his kind heart, to observe how the children fled from his approach, breaking up their merriest sports, while his melancholy figure was yet afar off. Their instinctive dread caused him to feel more strongly than aught else, that a preternatural horror was interwoven with the threads of the black crape. In truth, his own antipathy to the veil was known to be so great, that he never willingly passed before a mirror, nor stooped to drink at a still fountain, lest, in its peaceful bosom, he should be affrighted by himself. This was what gave plausibility to the whispers, that Mr. Hooper's conscience tortured him for some great crime too horrible to be entirely concealed, or otherwise than so obscurely intimated. Thus, from beneath the black veil, there rolled a cloud into the sunshine, an ambiguity of sin or sorrow, which enveloped the poor minister, so that love or sympathy could never reach him. It was said that ghost and fiend consorted with him there. With self-shudderings and outward terrors, he walked continually in its shadow, groping darkly within his own soul, or gazing through a medium that saddened the whole world. Even the lawless wind, it was believed, respected his dreadful secret, and never blew aside the veil. But still good Mr. Hooper sadly smiled at the pale visages of the worldly throng as he passed by.

Among all its bad influences, the black veil had the one desirable effect, of making its wearer a very efficient clergyman. By the aid of his mysterious emblem—for there was no other apparent cause—he became a man of awful power over souls that were in agony for sin. His converts always regarded him with a dread peculiar to themselves, affirming, though but figuratively, that, before he brought them to celestial light, they had been with him behind the black veil. Its gloom, indeed, enabled him to sympathize with all dark affections. Dying sinners cried aloud for Mr. Hooper, and would not yield their breath till he appeared; though ever, as he stooped to whisper consolation, they shuddered at the veiled face so near their own. Such were the terrors of the black veil, even when Death had bared his visage! Strangers came long distances to attend service at his church, with the mere idle purpose of gazing at his figure, because it was forbidden them to behold his face. But many were made to quake ere they departed! Once, during Governor Belcher's administration, Mr. Hooper was appointed to preach the election sermon. Covered with his black veil, he stood before the chief magistrate, the council, and the representatives, and wrought so deep an impression, that the legislative measures of that year were characterized by all the gloom and piety of our earliest ancestral sway.

In this manner Mr. Hooper spent a long life, irreproachable in outward act, yet shrouded in dismal suspicions; kind and loving, though unloved, and dimly feared; a man apart from men, shunned in their health and joy, but ever summoned to their aid in mortal anguish. As years wore on, shedding their snows above his sable veil, he acquired a name throughout the New England churches, and they called him Father Hooper. Nearly all his parishioners, who were of mature age when he was settled, had been borne away by many a funeral: he had one congregation in the church, and a more crowded one in the churchyard; and having wrought so late into the evening, and done his work so well, it was now good Father Hooper's turn to rest.

Several persons were visible by the shaded candlelight, in the death chamber of the old clergyman. Natural connections he had none. But there was the decorously grave, though unmoved physician, seeking only to mitigate the last pangs of the patient whom he could not save. There were the deacons, and other eminently pious members of his church. There, also, was the Reverend Mr. Clark, of Westbury, a young and zealous divine, who had ridden in haste to pray by the bedside of the expiring minister. There was the nurse, no hired handmaiden of death, but one whose calm affection had endured thus long in secrecy, in solitude, amid the chill of age, and would not perish, even at the dying hour. Who, but Elizabeth! And there lay the hoary head of good Father Hooper upon the death pillow, with the black veil still swathed about his brow, and reaching down over his face, so that each more difficult gasp of his faint breath caused it to stir. All through life that piece of crape had hung between him and the world: it had separated him from cheerful brotherhood and woman's love, and kept him in the saddest of all prisons, his own heart; and still it lay upon his face, as if to deepen the gloom of his darksome chamber, and shade him from the sunshine of eternity.

For some time previous, his mind had been confused, wavering doubtfully between the past and the present, and hovering forward, as it were, at intervals, into the indistinctness of the world to come. There had been feverish turns, which tossed him from side to side, and wore away what little strength he had. But in his most convulsive struggles, and in the wildest vagaries of his intellect, when no other thought retained its sober influence, he still showed an awful solicitude lest the black veil should slip aside. Even if his bewildered soul could have forgotten, there was a faithful woman at his pillow, who, with averted eyes, would have covered that aged face, which she had last beheld in the comeliness of manhood. At length the death-stricken old man lay quietly in the torpor of mental and bodily exhaustion, with an imperceptible pulse, and breath that grew fainter and fainter, except when a long, deep, and irregular inspiration seemed to prelude the flight of his spirit.

The minister of Westbury approached the bedside.

"Venerable Father Hooper," said he, "the moment of your release is at hand. Are you ready for the lifting of the veil that shuts in time from eternity?"

Father Hooper at first replied merely by a feeble motion of his head; then, apprehensive, perhaps, that his meaning might be doubtful, he exerted himself to speak.

"Yea," said he, in faint accents, "my soul hath a patient weariness until that veil be lifted."

"And is it fitting," resumed the Reverend Mr. Clark, "that a man so given to prayer, of such a blameless example, holy in deed and thought, so far as mortal judgment may pronounce; is it fitting that a father in the church should leave a shadow on his memory, that may seem to blacken a life so pure? I pray you, my venerable brother, let not this thing be! Suffer us to be gladdened by your triumphant aspect as you go to your reward. Before the veil of eternity be lifted, let me cast aside this black veil from your face!"

And thus speaking, the Reverend Mr. Clark bent forward to reveal the mystery of so many years. But, exerting a sudden energy, that made all the beholders stand aghast, Father Hooper snatched both his hands from beneath the bedclothes, and pressed them strongly on the black veil, resolute to struggle, if the minister of Westbury would contend with a dying man.

"Never!" cried the veiled clergyman. "On earth, never!"

"Dark old man!" exclaimed the affrighted minister, "with what horrible crime upon your soul are you now passing to the judgment?"

Father Hooper's breath heaved; it rattled in his throat; but, with a mighty effort, grasping forward with his hands, he caught hold of life, and held it back till he should speak. He even raised himself in bed; and there he sat, shivering with the arms of death around him, while the black veil hung down, awful, at that last moment, in the gathered terrors of a lifetime. And yet the faint, sad smile, so often there, now seemed to glimmer from its obscurity, and linger on Father Hooper's lips.

"Why do you tremble at me alone?" cried he, turning his veiled face round the circle of pale spectators. "Tremble also at each other! Have men avoided me, and women shown no pity, and children screamed and fled, only for my black veil? What, but the mystery which it obscurely typifies, has made this piece of crape so awful? When the friend shows his inmost heart to his friend; the lover to his best beloved; when man does not vainly shrink from the eye of his Creator, loathsomely treasuring up the secret of his sin; then deem me a monster, for the symbol beneath which I have lived, and die! I look around me, and, lo! on every visage a Black Veil!"

While his auditors shrank from one another, in mutual affright, Father Hooper fell back upon his pillow, a veiled corpse, with a faint smile lingering on the lips. Still veiled, they laid him in his coffin, and a veiled corpse they bore him to the grave. The grass of many years has sprung up and withered on that grave, the burial stone is moss-grown, and good Mr. Hooper's face is dust; but awful is still the thought that it mouldered beneath the Black Veil!

THE MAYPOLE OF MERRY MOUNT

There is an admirable foundation for a philosophic romance in the curious history of the early settlement of Mount Wollaston, or Merry Mount. In the slight sketch here attempted, the facts, recorded on the grave pages of our New England annalists, have wrought themselves, almost spontaneously, into a sort of allegory. The masques, mummeries, and festive customs, described in the text, are in accordance with the manners of the age. Authority on these points may be found in Strutt's Book of English Sports and Pastimes.

Bright were the days at Merry Mount, when the Maypole was the banner staff of that gay colony! They who reared it, should their banner be triumphant, were to pour sunshine over New England's rugged hills, and scatter flower seeds throughout the soil. Jollity and gloom were contending for an empire. Midsummer eve had come, bringing deep verdure to the forest, and roses in her lap, of a more vivid hue than the tender buds of Spring. But May, or her mirthful spirit, dwelt all the year round at Merry Mount, sporting with the Summer months, and revelling with Autumn, and basking in the glow of Winter's fireside. Through a world of toil and care she flitted with a dreamlike smile, and came hither to find a home among the lightsome hearts of Merry Mount.

Never had the Maypole been so gayly decked as at sunset on midsummer eve. This venerated emblem was a pine-tree, which had preserved the slender grace of youth, while it equalled the loftiest height of the old wood monarchs. From its top streamed a silken banner, colored like the rainbow. Down nearly to the ground the pole was dressed with birchen boughs, and others of the liveliest green, and some with silvery leaves, fastened by ribbons that fluttered in fantastic knots of twenty different colors, but no sad ones. Garden flowers, and blossoms of the wilderness, laughed gladly forth amid the verdure, so fresh and dewy that they must have grown by magic on that happy pine-tree. Where this green and flowery splendor terminated, the shaft of the Maypole was stained with the seven brilliant hues of the banner at its top. On the lowest green bough hung an abundant wreath of roses, some that had been gathered in the sunniest spots of the forest, and others, of still richer blush, which the colonists had reared from English seed. O, people of the Golden Age, the chief of your husbandry was to raise flowers!

But what was the wild throng that stood hand in hand about the Maypole? It could not be that the fauns and nymphs, when driven from their classic groves and homes of ancient fable, had sought refuge, as all the persecuted did, in the fresh woods of the West. These were Gothic monsters, though perhaps of Grecian ancestry. On the shoulders of a comely youth uprose the head and branching antlers of a stag; a second, human in all other points, had the grim visage of a wolf; a third, still with the trunk and limbs of a mortal man, showed the beard and horns of a venerable he-goat. There was the likeness of a bear erect, brute in all but his hind legs, which were adorned with pink silk stockings. And here again, almost as wondrous, stood a real bear of the dark forest, lending each of his fore paws to the grasp of a human hand, and as ready for the dance as any in that circle. His inferior nature rose half way, to meet his companions as they stooped. Other faces wore the similitude of man or woman, but distorted or extravagant, with red noses pendulous before their mouths, which seemed of awful depth, and stretched from ear to ear in an eternal fit of laughter. Here might be seen the Salvage Man, well known in heraldry, hairy as a baboon, and girdled with green leaves. By his side, a noble figure, but still a counterfeit, appeared an Indian hunter, with feathery crest and wampum belt. Many of this strange company wore foolscaps, and had little bells appended to their garments, tinkling with a silvery sound, responsive to the inaudible music of their gleesome spirits. Some youths and maidens were of soberer garb, yet well maintained their places in the irregular throng by the expression of wild revelry upon their features. Such were the colonists of Merry Mount, as they stood in the broad smile of sunset round their venerated Maypole.

Had a wanderer, bewildered in the melancholy forest, heard their mirth, and stolen a half-affrighted glance, he might have fancied them the crew of Comus, some already transformed to brutes, some midway between man and beast, and the others rioting in the flow of tipsy jollity that foreran the change. But a band of Puritans, who watched the scene, invisible themselves, compared the masques to those devils and ruined souls with whom their superstition peopled the black wilderness.

Within the ring of monsters appeared the two airiest forms that had ever trodden on any more solid footing than a purple and golden cloud. One was a youth in glistening apparel, with a scarf of the rainbow pattern crosswise on his breast. His right hand held a gilded staff, the ensign of high dignity among the revellers, and his left grasped the slender fingers of a fair maiden, not less gayly decorated than himself. Bright roses glowed in contrast with the dark and glossy curls of each, and were scattered round their feet, or had sprung up spontaneously there. Behind this lightsome couple, so close to the Maypole that its boughs shaded his jovial face, stood the figure of an English priest, canonically dressed, yet decked with flowers, in heathen fashion, and wearing a chaplet of the native vine leaves. By the riot of his rolling eye, and the pagan decorations of his holy garb, he seemed the wildest monster there, and the very Comus of the crew.

"Votaries of the Maypole," cried the flower-decked priest, "merrily, all day long, have the woods echoed to your mirth. But be this your merriest hour, my hearts! Lo, here stand the Lord and Lady of the May, whom I, a clerk of Oxford, and high priest of Merry Mount, am presently to join in holy matrimony. Up with your nimble spirits, ye morris-dancers, green men, and glee maidens, bears and wolves, and horned gentlemen! Come; a chorus now, rich with the old mirth of Merry England, and the wilder glee of this fresh forest; and then a dance, to show the youthful pair what life is made of, and how airily they should go through it! All ye that love the Maypole, lend your voices to the nuptial song of the Lord and Lady of the May!"

This wedlock was more serious than most affairs of Merry Mount, where jest and delusion, trick and fantasy, kept up a continual carnival. The Lord and Lady of the May, though their titles must be laid down at sunset, were really and truly to be partners for the dance of life, beginning the measure that same bright eve. The wreath of roses, that hung from the lowest green bough of the Maypole, had been twined for them, and would be thrown over both their heads, in symbol of their flowery union. When the priest had spoken, therefore, a riotous uproar burst from the rout of monstrous figures.

"Begin you the stave, reverend Sir," cried they all; "and never did the woods ring to such a merry peal as we of the Maypole shall send up!"

Immediately a prelude of pipe, cithern, and viol, touched with practised minstrelsy, began to play from a neighboring thicket, in such a mirthful cadence that the boughs of the Maypole quivered to the sound. But the May Lord, he of the gilded staff, chancing to look into his Lady's eyes, was wonder struck at the almost pensive glance that met his own.

"Edith, sweet Lady of the May," whispered he reproachfully, "is yon wreath of roses a garland to hang above our graves, that you look so sad? O, Edith, this is our golden time! Tarnish it not by any pensive shadow of the mind; for it may be that nothing of futurity will be brighter than the mere remembrance of what is now passing."

"That was the very thought that saddened me! How came it in your mind too?" said Edith, in a still lower tone than he, for it was high treason to be sad at Merry Mount. "Therefore do I sigh amid this festive music. And besides, dear Edgar, I struggle as with a dream, and fancy that these shapes of our jovial friends are visionary, and their mirth unreal, and that we are no true Lord and Lady of the May. What is the mystery in my heart?"

Just then, as if a spell had loosened them, down came a little shower of withering rose leaves from the Maypole. Alas, for the young lovers! No sooner had their hearts glowed with real passion than they were sensible of something vague and unsubstantial in their former pleasures, and felt a dreary presentiment of inevitable change. From the moment that they truly loved, they had subjected themselves to earth's doom of care and sorrow, and troubled joy, and had no more a home at Merry Mount. That was Edith's mystery. Now leave we the priest to marry them, and the masquers to sport round the Maypole, till the last sunbeam be withdrawn from its summit, and the shadows of the forest mingle gloomily in the dance. Meanwhile, we may discover who these gay people were.

Two hundred years ago, and more, the old world and its inhabitants became mutually weary of each other. Men voyaged by thousands to the West: some to barter glass beads, and such like jewels, for the furs of the Indian hunter; some to conquer virgin empires; and one stern band to pray. But none of these motives had much weight with the colonists of Merry Mount. Their leaders were men who had sported so long with life, that when Thought and Wisdom came, even these unwelcome guests were led astray by the crowd of vanities which they should have put to flight. Erring Thought and perverted Wisdom were made to put on masques, and play the fool. The men of whom we speak, after losing the heart's fresh gayety, imagined a wild philosophy of pleasure, and came hither to act out their latest day-dream. They gathered followers from all that giddy tribe whose whole life is like the festal days of soberer men. In their train were minstrels, not unknown in London streets: wandering players, whose theatres had been the halls of noblemen; mummers, rope-dancers, and mounte-banks, who would long be missed at wakes, church ales, and fairs; in a word, mirth makers of every sort, such as abounded in that age, but now began to be discountenanced by the rapid growth of Puritanism. Light had their footsteps been on land, and as lightly they came across the sea. Many had been maddened by their previous troubles into a gay despair; others were as madly gay in the flush of youth, like the May Lord and his Lady; but whatever might be the quality of their mirth, old and young were gay at Merry Mount. The young deemed themselves happy. The elder spirits, if they knew that mirth was but the counterfeit of happiness, yet followed the false shadow wilfully, because at least her garments glittered brightest. Sworn triflers of a lifetime, they would not venture among the sober truths of life not even to be truly blest.

All the hereditary pastimes of Old England were transplanted hither. The King of Christmas was duly crowned, and the Lord of Misrule bore potent sway. On the Eve of St. John, they felled whole acres of the forest to make bonfires, and danced by the blaze all night, crowned with garlands, and throwing flowers into the flame. At harvest time, though their crop was of the smallest, they made an image with the sheaves of Indian corn, and wreathed it with autumnal garlands, and bore it home triumphantly. But what chiefly characterized the colonists of Merry Mount was their veneration for the Maypole. It has made their true history a poet's tale. Spring decked the hallowed emblem with young blossoms and fresh green boughs; Summer brought roses of the deepest blush, and the perfected foliage of the forest; Autumn enriched it with that red and yellow gorgeousness which converts each wildwood leaf into a painted flower; and Winter silvered it with sleet, and hung it round with icicles, till it flashed in the cold sunshine, itself a frozen sunbeam. Thus each alternate season did homage to the Maypole, and paid it a tribute of its own richest splendor. Its votaries danced round it, once, at least, in every month; sometimes they called it their religion, or their altar; but always, it was the banner staff of Merry Mount.

Unfortunately, there were men in the new world of a sterner faith than these Maypole worshippers. Not far from Merry Mount was a settlement of Puritans, most dismal wretches, who said their prayers before daylight, and then wrought in the forest or the cornfield till evening made it prayer time again. Their weapons were always at hand to shoot down the straggling savage. When they met in conclave, it was never to keep up the old English mirth, but to hear sermons three hours long, or to proclaim bounties on the heads of wolves and the scalps of Indians. Their festivals were fast days, and their chief pastime the singing of psalms. Woe to the youth or maiden who did but dream of a dance! The selectman nodded to the constable; and there sat the light-heeled reprobate in the stocks; or if he danced, it was round the whipping-post, which might be termed the Puritan Maypole.

A party of these grim Puritans, toiling through the difficult woods, each with a horseload of iron armor to burden his footsteps, would sometimes draw near the sunny precincts of Merry Mount. There were the silken colonists, sporting round their Maypole; perhaps teaching a bear to dance, or striving to communicate their mirth to the grave Indian; or masquerading in the skins of deer and wolves, which they had hunted for that especial purpose. Often, the whole colony were playing at blindman's bluff, magistrates and all, with their eyes bandaged, except a single scapegoat, whom the blinded sinners pursued by the tinkling of the bells at his garments. Once, it is said, they were seen following a flower-decked corpse, with merriment and festive music, to his grave. But did the dead man laugh? In the quietest times, they sang ballads and told tales, for the edification of their pious visitors; or perplexed them with juggling tricks; or grinned at them through horse collars; and when sport itself grew wearisome, they made game of their own stupidity, and began a yawning match. At the very least of these enormities, the men of iron shook their heads and frowned so darkly that the revellers looked up, imagining that a momentary cloud had over-cast the sunshine, which was to be perpetual there. On the other hand, the Puritans affirmed that, when a psalm was pealing from their place of worship, the echo which the forest sent them back seemed often like the chorus of a jolly catch, closing with a roar of laughter. Who but the fiend, and his bond slaves, the crew of Merry Mount, had thus disturbed them? In due time, a feud arose, stern and bitter on one side, and as serious on the other as anything could be among such light spirits as had sworn allegiance to the Maypole. The future complexion of New England was involved in this important quarrel. Should the grizzly saints establish their jurisdiction over the gay sinners, then would their spirits darken all the clime, and make it a land of clouded visages, of hard toil, of sermon and psalm forever. But should the banner staff of Merry Mount be fortunate, sunshine would break upon the hills, and flowers would beautify the forest, and late posterity do homage to the Maypole.

After these authentic passages from history, we return to the nuptials of the Lord and Lady of the May. Alas! we have delayed too long, and must darken our tale too suddenly. As we glance again at the Maypole, a solitary sunbeam is fading from the summit, and leaves only a faint, golden tinge blended with the hues of the rainbow banner. Even that dim light is now withdrawn, relinquishing the whole domain of Merry Mount to the evening gloom, which has rushed so instantaneously from the black surrounding woods. But some of these black shadows have rushed forth in human shape.

Yes, with the setting sun, the last day of mirth had passed from Merry Mount. The ring of gay masquers was disordered and broken; the stag lowered his antlers in dismay; the wolf grew weaker than a lamb; the bells of the morris-dancers tinkled with tremulous affright. The Puritans had played a characteristic part in the Maypole mummeries. Their darksome figures were intermixed with the wild shapes of their foes, and made the scene a picture of the moment, when waking thoughts start up amid the scattered fantasies of a dream. The leader of the hostile party stood in the centre of the circle, while the route of monsters cowered around him, like evil spirits in the presence of a dread magician. No fantastic foolery could look him in the face. So stern was the energy of his aspect, that the whole man, visage, frame, and soul, seemed wrought of iron, gifted with life and thought, yet all of one substance with his headpiece and breastplate. It was the Puritan of Puritans; it was Endicott himself!

"Stand off, priest of Baal!" said he, with a grim frown, and laying no reverent hand upon the surplice. "I know thee, Blackstone![1] Thou art the man who couldst not abide the rule even of thine own corrupted church, and hast come hither to preach iniquity, and to give example of it in thy life. But now shall it be seen that the Lord hath sanctified this wilderness for his peculiar people. Woe unto them that would defile it! And first, for this flower-decked abomination, the altar of thy worship!"

And with his keen sword Endicott assaulted the hallowed Maypole. Nor long did it resist his arm. It groaned with a dismal sound; it showered leaves and rosebuds upon the remorseless enthusiast; and finally, with all its green boughs and ribbons and flowers, symbolic of departed pleasures, down fell the banner staff of Merry Mount. As it sank, tradition says, the evening sky grew darker, and the woods threw forth a more sombre shadow.

"There," cried Endicott, looking triumphantly on his work, "there lies the only Maypole in New England! The thought is strong within me that, by its fall, is shadowed forth the fate of light and idle mirth makers, amongst us and our posterity. Amen, saith John Endicott."

"Amen!" echoed his followers.

But the votaries of the Maypole gave one groan for their idol. At the sound, the Puritan leader glanced at the crew of Comus, each a figure of broad mirth, yet, at this moment, strangely expressive of sorrow and dismay.

"Valiant captain," quoth Peter Palfrey, the Ancient of the band, "what order shall be taken with the prisoners?"

"I thought not to repent me of cutting down a Maypole," replied Endicott, "yet now I could find in my heart to plant it again, and give each of these bestial pagans one other dance round their idol. It would have served rarely for a whipping-post!"

"But there are pine-trees enow," suggested the lieutenant.

"True, good Ancient," said the leader. "Wherefore, bind the heathen crew, and bestow on them a small matter of stripes apiece, as earnest of our future justice. Set some of the rogues in the stocks to rest themselves, so soon as Providence shall bring us to one of our own well-ordered settlements, where such accommodations may be found. Further penalties, such as branding and cropping of ears, shall be thought of hereafter."

"How many stripes for the priest?" inquired Ancient Palfrey.

"None as yet," answered Endicott, bending his iron frown upon the culprit. "It must be for the Great and General Court to determine, whether stripes and long imprisonment, and other grievous penalty, may atone for his transgressions. Let him look to himself! For such as violate our civil order, it may be permitted us to show mercy. But woe to the wretch that troubleth our religion!"

"And this dancing bear," resumed the officer. "Must he share the stripes of his fellows?"

"Shoot him through the head!" said the energetic Puritan. "I suspect witchcraft in the beast."

"Here be a couple of shining ones," continued Peter Palfrey, pointing his

[1]Did Governor Endicott speak less positively, we should suspect a mistake here. The Rev. Mr. Blackstone, though an eccentric, is not known to have been an immoral man. We rather doubt his identity with the priest of Merry Mount.

weapon at the Lord and Lady of the May. "They seem to be of high station among these misdoers. Methinks their dignity will not be fitted with less than a double share of stripes."

Endicott rested on his sword, and closely surveyed the dress and aspect of the hapless pair. There they stood, pale, downcast, and apprehensive. Yet there was an air of mutual support, and of pure affection, seeking aid and giving it, that showed them to be man and wife, with the sanction of a priest upon their love. The youth, in the peril of the moment, had dropped his gilded staff, and thrown his arm about the Lady of the May, who leaned against his breast, too lightly to burden him, but with weight enough to express that their destinies were linked together, for good or evil. They looked first at each other, and then into the grim captain's face. There they stood, in the first hour of wedlock, while the idle pleasures, of which their companions were the emblems, had given place to the sternest cares of life, personified by the dark Puritans. But never had their youthful beauty seemed so pure and high as when its glow was chastened by adversity.

"Youth," said Endicott, "ye stand in an evil case thou and thy maiden wife. Make ready presently, for I am minded that ye shall both have a token to remember your wedding day!"

"Stern man," cried the May Lord, "how can I move thee? Were the means at hand, I would resist to the death. Being powerless, I entreat! Do with me as thou wilt, but let Edith go untouched!"

"Not so," replied the immitigable zealot. "We are not wont to show an idle courtesy to that sex, which requireth the stricter discipline. What sayest thou, maid? Shall thy silken bridegroom suffer thy share of the penalty, besides his own?"

"Be it death," said Edith, "and lay it all on me!"

Truly, as Endicott had said, the poor lovers stood in a woful case. Their foes were triumphant, their friends captive and abased, their home desolate, the benighted wilderness around them, and a rigorous destiny, in the shape of the Puritan leader, their only guide. Yet the deepening twilight could not altogether conceal that the iron man was softened; he smiled at the fair spectacle of early love; he almost sighed for the inevitable blight of early hopes.

"The troubles of life have come hastily on this young couple," observed Endicott. "We will see how they comport themselves under their present trials ere we burden them with greater. If, among the spoil, there be any garments of a more decent fashion, let them be put upon this May Lord and his Lady, instead of their glistening vanities. Look to it, some of you."

"And shall not the youth's hair be cut?" asked Peter Palfrey, looking with abhorrence at the lovelock and long glossy curls of the young man.

"Crop it forthwith, and that in the true pumpkin-shell fashion," answered the captain. "Then bring them along with us, but more gently than their fellows. There be qualities in the youth, which may make him valiant to fight, and sober to toil, and pious to pray; and in the maiden, that may fit her to become a mother in our Israel, bringing up babes in better nurture than her own hath been. Nor think ye, young ones, that they are the happiest, even in our lifetime of a moment, who misspend it in dancing round a Maypole!"

And Endicott, the severest Puritan of all who laid the rock foundation of New England, lifted the wreath of roses from the ruin of the Maypole, and threw it, with his own gauntleted hand, over the heads of the Lord and Lady of the May. It was a deed of prophecy. As the moral gloom of the world overpowers all systematic gayety, even so was their home of wild mirth made desolate amid the sad forest. They returned to it no more. But as their flowery garland was wreathed of the brightest roses that had grown there, so, in the tie that united them, were intertwined all the purest and best of their early joys. They went heavenward, supporting each other along the difficult path which it was their lot to tread, and never wasted one regretful thought on the vanities of Merry Mount.

THE GENTLE BOY

In the course of the year 1656, several of the people called Quakers, led, as they professed, by the inward movement of the spirit, made their appearance in New England. Their reputation, as holders of mystic and pernicious principles, having spread before them, the Puritans early endeavored to banish, and to prevent the further intrusion of the rising sect. But the measures by which it was intended to purge the land of heresy, though more than sufficiently vigorous, were entirely unsuccessful. The Quakers, esteeming persecution as a divine call to the post of danger, laid claim to a holy courage, unknown to the Puritans themselves, who had shunned the cross, by providing for the peaceable exercise of their religion in a distant wilderness. Though it was the singular fact, that every nation of the earth rejected the wandering enthusiasts who practised peace towards all man, the place of greatest uneasiness and peril, and therefore, in their eyes the most eligible, was the province of Massachusetts Bay.

The fines, imprisonments, and stripes, liberally distributed by our pious forefathers; the popular antipathy, so strong that it endured nearly a hundred years after actual persecution had ceased, were attractions as powerful for the Quakers, as peace, honor, and reward, would have been for the worldly minded. Every European vessel brought new cargoes of the sect, eager to testify against the oppression which they hoped to share; and when shipmasters were restrained by heavy fines from affording them passage, they made long and circuitous journeys through the Indian country, and appeared in the province as if conveyed by a supernatural power. Their enthusiasm, heightened almost to madness by the treatment which they received, produced actions contrary to the rules of decency, as well as of rational religion, and presented a singular contrast to the calm and staid deportment of their sectarian successors of the present day. The command of the spirit, inaudible except to the soul, and not to be controverted on grounds of human wisdom, was made a plea for most indecorous exhibitions, which, abstractedly considered, well deserved the moderate chastisement of the rod. These extravagances, and the persecution which was at once their cause and consequence, continued to increase, till, in the year 1659, the government of Massachusetts Bay indulged two members of the Quaker sect with the crown of martyrdom.

An indelible stain of blood is upon the hands of all who consented to this act, but a large share of the awful responsibility must rest upon the person then at the head of the government. He was a man of narrow mind and imperfect education, and his uncompromising bigotry was made hot and mischievous by violent and hasty passions; he exerted his influence indecorously and unjustifiably to compass the death of the enthusiasts; and his whole conduct, in respect to them, was marked by brutal cruelty. The Quakers, whose revengeful feelings were not less deep because they were inactive, remembered this man and his associates in after times. The historian of the sect affirms that, by the wrath of Heaven, a blight fell upon the land in the vicinity of the "bloody town" of Boston, so that no wheat would grow there; and he takes his stand, as it were, among the graves of the ancient persecutors, and triumphantly recounts the judgments that overtook them, in old age or at the parting hour. He tells us that they died suddenly and violently and in madness; but nothing can exceed the bitter mockery with which he records the loathsome disease, and "death by rottenness," of the fierce and cruel governor.

On the evening of the autumn day that had witnessed the martyrdom of two men of the Quaker persuasion, a Puritan settler was returning from the metropolis to the neighboring country town in which he resided. The air was cool, the sky clear, and the lingering twilight was made brighter by the rays of a young moon, which had now nearly reached the verge of the horizon. The traveller, a man of middle age, wrapped in a gray frieze cloak, quickened his pace when he had reached the outskirts of the town, for a gloomy extent of nearly four miles lay between him and his home. The low, straw-thatched houses were scattered at considerable intervals along the road, and the country having been settled but about thirty years, the tracts of original forest still bore no small proportion to the cultivated ground. The autumn wind wandered among the branches, whirling away the leaves from all except the pine-trees, and moaning as if it lamented the desolation of which it was the instrument. The road had penetrated the mass of woods that lay nearest to the town, and was just emerging into an open space, when the traveller's ears were saluted by a sound more mournful than even that of the wind. It was like the wailing of some one in distress, and it seemed to proceed from beneath a tall and lonely fir-tree, in the centre of a cleared but uninclosed and uncultivated field. The Puritan could not but remember that this was the very spot which had been made accursed a few hours before by the execution of the Quakers, whose bodies had been thrown together into one hasty grave, beneath the tree on which they suffered. He struggled, however, against the superstitious fears which belonged to the age, and compelled himself to pause and listen.

"The voice is most likely mortal, nor have I cause to tremble if it be otherwise," thought he, straining his eyes through the dim moonlight. "Methinks it is like the wailing of a child; some infant, it may be, which has strayed from its mother, and chanced upon this place of death. For the ease of mine own conscience I must search this matter out."

He therefore left the path, and walked somewhat fearfully across the field. Though now so desolate, its soil was pressed down and trampled by the thousand footsteps of those who had witnessed the spectacle of that day, all of whom had now retired, leaving the dead to their loneliness. The traveller at length reached the fir-tree, which from the middle upward was covered with living branches, although a scaffold had been erected beneath, and other preparations made for the work of death. Under this unhappy tree, which in after times was believed to drop poison with its dew, sat the one solitary mourner for innocent blood. It was a slender and light clad little boy, who leaned his face upon a hillock of fresh-turned and half-frozen earth, and wailed bitterly, yet in a suppressed tone, as if his grief might receive the punishment of crime. The Puritan, whose approach had been unperceived, laid his hand upon the child's shoulder, and addressed him compassionately.

"You have chosen a dreary lodging, my poor boy, and no wonder that you weep," said he. "But dry your eyes, and tell me where your mother dwells. I promise you, if the journey be not too far, I will leave you in her arms to-night."

The boy had hushed his wailing at once, and turned his face upward to the stranger. It was a pale, bright-eyed countenance, certainly not more than six years old, but sorrow, fear, and want had destroyed much of its infantile expression. The Puritan seeing the boy's frightened gaze, and feeling that he trembled under his hand, endeavored to reassure him.

"Nay, if I intended to do you harm, little lad, the readiest way were to leave you here. What! you do not fear to sit beneath the gallows on a new-made grave, and yet you tremble at a friend's touch. Take heart, child, and tell me what is your name and where is your home?"

"Friend," replied the little boy, in a sweet though faltering voice, "they call me Ilbrahim, and my home is here."

The pale, spiritual face, the eyes that seemed to mingle with the moonlight, the sweet, airy voice, and the outlandish name, almost made the Puritan believe that the boy was in truth a being which had sprung up out of the grave on which he sat. But perceiving that the apparition stood the test of a short mental prayer, and remembering that the arm which he had touched was lifelike, he adopted a more rational supposition. "The poor child is stricken in his intellect," thought he, "but verily his words are fearful in a place like this." He then spoke soothingly, intending to humor the boy's fantasy.

"Your home will scarce be comfortable, Ilbrahim, this cold autumn night, and I fear you are ill-provided with food. I am hastening to a warm supper and bed, and if you will go with me you shall share them!"

"I thank thee, friend, but though I be hungry, and shivering with cold, thou wilt not give me food nor lodging," replied the boy, in the quiet tone which despair had taught him, even so young. "My father was of the people whom all men hate. They have laid him under this heap of earth, and here is my home."

The Puritan, who had laid hold of little Ilbrahim's hand, relinquished it as if he were touching a loathsome reptile. But he possessed a compassionate heart, which not even religious prejudice could harden into stone.

"God forbid that I should leave this child to perish, though he comes of the accursed sect," said he to himself. "Do we not all spring from an evil root? Are we not all in darkness till the light doth shine upon us? He shall not perish, neither in body, nor, if prayer and instruction may avail for him, in soul." He then spoke aloud and kindly to Ilbrahim, who had again hid his face in the cold earth of the grave. "Was every door in the land shut against you, my child, that you have wandered to this unhallowed spot?"

"They drove me forth from the prison when they took my father thence," said the boy, "and I stood afar off watching the crowd of people, and when they were gone I came hither, and found only his grave. I knew that my father was sleeping here, and I said this shall be my home."

"No, child, no; not while I have a roof over my head, or a morsel to share with you!" exclaimed the Puritan, whose sympathies were now fully excited. "Rise up and come with me, and fear not any harm."

The boy wept afresh, and clung to the heap of earth as if the cold heart beneath it were warmer to him than any in a living breast. The traveller, however, continued to entreat him tenderly, and seeming to acquire some degree of confidence, he at length arose. But his slender limbs tottered with weakness, his little head grew dizzy, and he leaned against the tree of death for support.

"My poor boy, are you so feeble?" said the Puritan. "When did you taste food last?"

"I ate of bread and water with my father in the prison," replied Ilbrahim, "but they brought him none neither yesterday nor to-day, saying that he had eaten enough to bear him to his journey's end. Trouble not thyself for my hunger, kind friend, for I have lacked food many times ere now."

The traveller took the child in his arms and wrapped his cloak about him, while his heart stirred with shame and anger against the gratuitous cruelty of the instruments in this persecution. In the awakened warmth of his feelings he resolved that, at whatever risk, he would not forsake the poor little defenceless being whom Heaven had confided to his care. With this determination he left the accursed field, and resumed the homeward path from which the wailing of the boy had called him. The light and motionless burden scarcely impeded his progress, and he soon beheld the fire rays from the windows of the cottage which he, a native of a distant clime, had built in the western wilderness. It was surrounded by a considerable extent of cultivated ground, and the dwelling was situated in the nook of a wood-covered hill, whither it seemed to have crept for protection.

"Look up, child," said the Puritan to Ilbrahim, whose faint head had sunk upon his shoulder, "there is our home."

At the word "home," a thrill passed through the child's frame, but he continued silent. A few moments brought them to a cottage door, at which the owner knocked; for at that early period, when savages were wandering everywhere among the settlers, bolt and bar were indispensable to the security of a dwelling. The summons was answered by a bond-servant, a coarse-clad and dull-featured piece of humanity, who after ascertaining that his master was the applicant, undid the door, and held a flaring pine-knot torch to light him in. Farther back in the passage-way, the red blaze discovered a matronly woman, but no little crowd of children came bounding forth to greet their father's return. As the Puritan entered, he thrust aside his cloak, and displayed Ilbrahim's face to the female.

"Dorothy, here is a little outcast, whom Providence hath put into our hands," observed he. "Be kind to him, even as if he were of those dear ones who have departed from us."

"What pale and bright-eyed little boy is this, Tobias?" she inquired. "Is he one whom the wilderness folk have ravished from some Christian mother?"

"No, Dorothy, this poor child is no captive from the wilderness," he replied. "The heathen savage would have given him to eat of his scanty morsel, and to drink of his birchen cup; but Christian men, alas! had cast him out to die."

Then he told her how he had found him beneath the gallows, upon his father's grave; and how his heart had prompted him, like the speaking of an inward voice, to take the little outcast home, and be kind unto him. He acknowledged his resolution to feed and clothe him, as if he were his own child, and to afford him the instruction which should counteract the pernicious errors hitherto instilled into his infant mind. Dorothy was gifted with even a quicker tenderness than her husband, and she approved of all his doings and intentions.

"Have you a mother, dear child?" she inquired.

The tears burst forth from his full heart, as he attempted to reply; but Dorothy at length understood that he had a mother, who, like the rest of her sect, was a persecuted wanderer. She had been taken from the prison a short time before, carried into the uninhabited wilderness, and left to perish there by hunger or wild beasts. This was no uncommon method of disposing of the Quakers, and they were accustomed to boast that the inhabitants of the desert were more hospitable to them than civilized man.

"Fear not, little boy, you shall not need a mother, and a kind one," said Dorothy, when she had gathered this information. "Dry your tears, Ilbrahim, and be my child, as I will be your mother."

The good woman prepared the little bed, from which her own children had successively been borne to another resting-place. Before Ilbrahim would consent to occupy it, he knelt down, and as Dorothy listened to his simple and affecting prayer, she marvelled how the parents that had taught it to him could have been judged worthy of death. When the boy had fallen asleep, she bent over his pale and spiritual countenance, pressed a kiss upon his white brow, drew the bedclothes up about his neck, and went away with a pensive gladness in her heart.

Tobias Pearson was not among the earliest emigrants from the old country. He had remained in England during the first years of the civil war, in which he had borne some share as a cornet of dragoons, under Cromwell. But when the ambitious designs of his leader began to develop themselves, he quitted the army of the Parliament, and sought a refuge from the strife, which was no longer holy, among the people of his persuasion in the colony of Massachusetts. A more worldly consideration had perhaps an influence in drawing him thither; for New England offered advantages to men of unprosperous fortunes, as well as to dissatisfied religionists, and Pearson had hitherto found it difficult to provide for a wife and increasing family. To this supposed impurity of motive the more bigoted Puritans were inclined to impute the removal by death of all the children, for whose earthly good the father had been over-thoughtful. They had left their native country blooming like roses, and like roses they had perished in a foreign soil. Those expounders of the ways of Providence, who had thus judged their brother, and attributed his domestic sorrows to his sin, were not more charitable when they saw him and Dorothy endeavoring to fill up the void in their hearts by the adoption of an infant of the accursed sect. Nor did they fail to communicate their disapprobation to Tobias; but the latter, in reply, merely pointed at the little, quiet, lovely boy, whose appearance and deportment were indeed as powerful arguments as could possibly have been adduced in his own favor. Even his beauty, however, and his winning manners, sometimes produced an effect ultimately unfavorable; for the bigots, when the outer surfaces of their iron hearts had been softened and again grew hard, affirmed that no merely natural cause could have so worked upon them.

Their antipathy to the poor infant was also increased by the ill success of divers theological discussions, in which it was attempted to convince him of the errors of his sect. Ilbrahim, it is true, was not a skilful controversialist; but the feeling of his religion was strong as instinct in him, and he could neither be enticed nor driven from the faith which his father had died for. The odium of this stubbornness was shared in a great measure by the child's protectors, insomuch that Tobias and Dorothy very shortly began to experience a most bitter species of persecution, in the cold regards of many a friend whom they had valued. The common people manifested their opinions more openly. Pearson was a man of some consideration, being a representative to the General Court, and an approved lieutenant in the trainbands, yet within a week after his adoption of Ilbrahim he had been both hissed and hooted. Once, also, when walking through a solitary piece of woods, he heard a loud voice from some invisible speaker; and it cried, "What shall be done to the backslider? Lo! the scourge is knotted for him, even the whip of nine cords, and every cord three knots!" These insults irritated Pearson's temper for the moment; they entered also into his heart, and became imperceptible but powerful workers towards an end which his most secret thought had not yet whispered.

On the second Sabbath after Ilbrahim became a member of their family, Pearson and his wife deemed it proper that he should appear with them at public worship. They had anticipated some opposition to this measure from the boy, but he prepared himself in silence, and at the appointed hour was clad in the new mourning suit which Dorothy had wrought for him. As the parish was then, and during many subsequent years, unprovided with a bell, the signal for the commencement of religious exercises was the beat of a drum. At the first sound of that martial call to the place of holy and quiet thoughts, Tobias and Dorothy set forth, each holding a hand of little Ilbrahim, like two parents linked together by the infant of their love. On their path through the leafless woods they were overtaken by many persons of their acquaintance, all of whom avoided them, and passed by on the other side; but a severer trial awaited their constancy when they had descended the hill, and drew near the pine-built and undecorated house of prayer. Around the door, from which the drummer still sent forth his thundering summons, was drawn up a formidable phalanx, including several of the oldest members of the congregation, many of the middle aged, and nearly all the younger males. Pearson found it difficult to sustain their united and disapproving gaze, but Dorothy, whose mind was differently circumstanced, merely drew the boy closer to her, and faltered not in her approach. As they entered the door, they overheard the muttered sentiments of the assemblage, and when the reviling voices of the little children smote Ilbrahim's ear, he wept.

The interior aspect of the meeting-house was rude. The low ceiling, the unplastered walls, the naked wood work, and the undraperied pulpit, offered nothing to excite the devotion, which, without such external aids, often remains latent in the heart. The floor of the building was occupied by rows of long, cushionless benches, supplying the place of pews, and the broad aisle formed a sexual division, impassable except by children beneath a certain age.

Pearson and Dorothy separated at the door of the meeting-house, and Ilbrahim, being within the years of infancy, was retained under the care of the latter. The wrinkled beldams involved themselves in their rusty cloaks as he passed by; even the mild-featured maidens seemed to dread contamination; and many a stern old man arose, and turned his repulsive and unheavenly countenance upon the gentle boy, as if the sanctuary were polluted by his presence. He was a sweet infant of the skies that had strayed away from his home, and all the inhabitants of this miserable world closed up their impure hearts against him, drew back their earth-soiled garments from his touch, and said, "We are holier than thou."

Ilbrahim, seated by the side of his adopted mother, and retaining fast hold of her hand, assumed a grave and decorous demeanor, such as might befit a person of matured taste and understanding, who should find himself in a temple dedicated to some worship which he did not recognize but felt himself bound to respect. The exercises had not yet commenced, however, when the boy's attention was arrested by an event, apparently of trifling interest. A woman, having her face muffled in a hood, and a cloak drawn completely about her form, advanced slowly up the broad aisle and took a place upon the foremost bench. Ilbrahim's faint color varied, his nerves fluttered, he was unable to turn his eyes from the muffled female.

When the preliminary prayer and hymn were over, the minister arose, and having turned the hour-glass which stood by the great Bible, commenced his discourse. He was now well stricken in years, a man of pale, thin countenance, and his gray hairs were closely covered by a black velvet skullcap. In his younger days he had practically learned the meaning of persecution from Archbishop Laud, and he was not now disposed to forget the lesson against which he had murmured then. Introducing the often discussed subject of the Quakers, he gave a history of that sect, and a description of their tenets, in which error predominated, and prejudice distorted the aspect of what was true. He adverted to the recent measures in the province, and cautioned his hearers of weaker parts against calling in question the just severity which God-fearing magistrates had at length been compelled to exercise. He spoke of the danger of pity, in some cases a commendable and Christian virtue, but inapplicable to this pernicious sect. He observed that such was their devilish obstinacy in error, that even the little children, the sucking babes, were hardened and desperate heretics. He affirmed that no man, without Heaven's especial warrant, should attempt their conversion, lest while he lent his hand to draw them from the slough, he should himself be precipitated into its lowest depths.

The sands of the second hour were principally in the lower half of the glass when the sermon concluded. An approving murmur followed, and the clergyman, having given out a hymn, took his seat with much self-congratulation, and endeavored to read the effect of his eloquence in the visages of the people. But while voices from all parts of the house were tuning themselves to sing, a scene occurred, which, though not very unusual at that period in the province, happened to be without precedent in this parish.

The muffled female, who had hitherto sat motionless in the front rank of the audience, now arose, and with slow, stately, and unwavering step, ascended the pulpit stairs. The quiverings of incipient harmony were hushed, and the divine sat in speechless and almost terrified astonishment, while she undid the door, and stood up in the sacred desk from which his maledictions had just been thundered. She then divested herself of the cloak and hood, and appeared in a most singular array. A shapeless robe of sackcloth was girded about her waist with a knotted cord; her raven hair fell down upon her shoulders, and its blackness was defiled by pale streaks of ashes, which she had strown upon her head. Her eyebrows, dark and strongly defined, added to the deathly whiteness of a countenance, which, emaciated with want, and wild with enthusiasm and strange sorrows, retained no trace of earlier beauty. This figure stood gazing earnestly on the audience, and there was no sound, nor any movement, except a faint shuddering which every man observed in his neighbor, but was scarcely conscious of in himself. At length, when her fit of inspiration came, she spoke, for the first few moments, in a low voice, and not invariably distinct utterance. Her discourse gave evidence of an imagination hopelessly entangled with her reason; it was a vague and incomprehensible rhapsody, which, however, seemed to spread its own atmosphere round the hearer's soul, and to move his feelings by some influence unconnected with the words. As she proceeded, beautiful but shadowy images would sometimes be seen, like bright things moving in a turbid river; or a strong and singularly-shaped idea leaped forth, and seized at once on the understanding or the heart. But the course of her unearthly eloquence soon led her to the persecutions of her sect, and from thence the step was short to her own peculiar sorrows. She was naturally a woman of mighty passions, and hatred and revenge now wrapped themselves in the garb of piety; the character of her speech was changed, her images became distinct though wild, and her denunciations had an almost hellish bitterness.

"The Governor and his mighty men," she said, "have gathered together, taking counsel among themselves and saying, 'What shall we do unto this people—even unto the people that have come into this land to put our iniquity to the blush?' And lo! the devil entereth into the council chamber, like a lame man of low stature and gravely apparelled, with a dark and twisted countenance, and a bright, downcast eye. And he standeth up among the rulers; yea, he goeth to and fro, whispering to each; and every man lends his ear, for his word is 'Slay, slay!' But I say unto ye, Woe to them that slay! Woe to them that shed the blood of saints! Woe to them that have slain the husband, and cast forth the child, the tender infant, to wander homeless and hungry and cold, till he die; and have saved the mother alive, in the cruelty of their tender mercies! Woe to them in their lifetime! cursed are they in the delight and pleasure of their hearts! Woe to them in their death hour, whether it come swifty with blood and violence, or after long and lingering pain! Woe, in the dark house, in the rottenness of the grave, when the children's children shall revile the ashes of the fathers! Woe, woe, woe, at the judgment, when all the persecuted and all the slain in this bloody land, and the father, the mother, and the child, shall await them in a day that they cannot escape! Seed of the faith, seed of the faith, ye whose hearts are moving with a power that ye know not, arise, wash your hands of this innocent blood! Lift your voices, chosen ones; cry aloud, and call down a woe and a judgment with me!"

Having thus given vent to the flood of malignity which she mistook for inspiration, the speaker was silent. Her voice was succeeded by the hysteric shrieks of several women, but the feelings of the audience generally had not been drawn onward in the current with her own. They remained stupefied, stranded as it were, in the midst of a torrent, which deafened them by its roaring, but might not move them by its violence. The clergyman, who could not hitherto have ejected the usurper of his pulpit otherwise than by bodily force, now addressed her in the tone of just indignation and legitimate authority.

"Get you down, woman, from the holy place which you profane," he said. "Is it to the Lord's house that you come to pour forth the foulness of your heart and the inspiration of the devil? Get you down, and remember that the sentence of death is on you; yea, and shall be executed, were it but for this day's work!"

"I go, friend, I go, for the voice hath had its utterance," replied she, in a depressed and even mild tone. "I have done my mission unto thee and to thy people. Reward me with stripes, imprisonment, or death, as ye shall be permitted."

The weakness of exhausted passion caused her steps to totter as she descended the pulpit stairs. The people, in the mean while, were stirring to and fro on the floor of the house, whispering among themselves, and glancing towards the intruder. Many of them now recognized her as the woman who had assaulted the Governor with frightful language as he passed by the window of her prison; they knew, also, that she was adjudged to suffer death, and had been preserved only by an involuntary banishment into the wilderness. The new outrage, by which she had provoked her fate, seemed to render further lenity impossible; and a gentleman in military dress, with a stout man of inferior rank, drew towards the door of the meeting-house, and awaited her approach.

Scarcely did her feet press the floor, however, when an unexpected scene occurred. In that moment of her peril, when every eye frowned with death, a little timid boy pressed forth, and threw his arms round his mother.

"I am here, mother; it is I, and I will go with thee to prison," he exclaimed.

She gazed at him with a doubtful and almost frightened expression, for she knew that the boy had been cast out to perish, and she had not hoped to see his face again. She feared, perhaps, that it was but one of the happy visions with which her excited fancy had often deceived her, in the solitude of the desert or in prison. But when she felt his hand warm within her own, and heard his little eloquence of childish love, she began to know that she was yet a mother.

"Blessed art thou, my son," she sobbed. "My heart was withered; yea, dead with thee and with thy father; and now it leaps as in the first moment when I pressed thee to my bosom."

She knelt down and embraced him again and again, while the joy that could find no words expressed itself in broken accents, like the bubbles gushing up to vanish at the surface of a deep fountain. The sorrows of past years, and the darker peril that was nigh, cast not a shadow on the brightness of that fleeting moment. Soon, however, the spectators saw a change upon her face, as the consciousness of her sad estate returned, and grief supplied the fount of tears which joy had opened. By the words she uttered, it would seem that the indulgence of natural love had given her mind a momentary sense of its errors, and made her know how far she had strayed from duty in following the dictates of a wild fanaticism.

"In a doleful hour art thou returned to me, poor boy," she said, "for thy mother's path has gone darkening onward, till now the end is death. Son, son, I have borne thee in my arms when my limbs were tottering, and I have fed thee with the food that I was fainting for; yet I have ill performed a mother's part by thee in life, and now I leave thee no inheritance but woe and shame. Thou wilt go seeking through the world, and find all hearts closed against thee and their sweet affections turned to bitterness for my sake. My child, my child, how many a pang awaits thy gentle spirit, and I the cause of all!"

She hid her face on Ilbrahim's head, and her long, raven hair, discolored with the ashes of her mourning, fell down about him like a veil. A low and interrupted moan was the voice of her heart's anguish, and it did not fail to move the sympathies of many who mistook their involuntary virtue for a sin. Sobs were audible in the female section of the house, and every man who was a father drew his hand across his eyes. Tobias Pearson was agitated and uneasy, but a certain feeling like the consciousness of guilt oppressed him, so that he could not go forth and offer himself as the protector of the child. Dorothy, however, had watched her husband's eye. Her mind was free from the influence that had begun to work on his, and she drew near the Quaker woman, and addressed her in the hearing of all the congregation.

"Stranger, trust this boy to me, and I will be his mother," she said, taking Ilbrahim's hand. "Providence has signally marked out my husband to protect him, and he has fed at our table and lodged under our roof now many days, till our hearts have grown very strongly unto him. Leave the tender child with us, and be at ease concerning his welfare."

The Quaker rose from the ground, but drew the boy closer to her, while she gazed earnestly in Dorothy's face. Her mild but saddened features, and neat matronly attire, harmonized together, and were like a verse of fireside poetry. Her very aspect proved that she was blameless, so far as mortal could be so, in respect to God and man; while the enthusiast, in her robe of sackcloth and girdle of knotted cord, had as evidently violated the duties of the present life and the future, by fixing her attention wholly on the latter. The two females, as they held each a hand of Ilbrahim, formed a practical allegory; it was rational piety and unbridled fanaticism contending for the empire of a young heart.

"Thou art not of our people," said the Quaker, mournfully.

"No, we are not of your people," replied Dorothy, with mildness, "but we are Christians, looking upward to the same heaven with you. Doubt not that your boy shall meet you there, if there be a blessing on our tender and prayerful guidance of him. Thither, I trust, my own children have gone before me, for I also have been a mother; I am no longer so," she added, in a faltering tone, "and your son will have all my care."

"But will ye lead him in the path which his parents have trodden?" demanded the Quaker. "Can ye teach him the enlightened faith which his father has died for, and for which I, even I, am soon to become an unworthy martyr? The boy has been baptized in blood; will ye keep the mark fresh and ruddy upon his forehead?"

"I will not deceive you," answered Dorothy. "If your child become our child, we must breed him up in the instruction which Heaven has imparted to us; we must pray for him the prayers of our own faith; we must do towards him according to the dictates of our own consciences, and not of yours. Were we to act otherwise, we should abuse your trust, even in complying with your wishes."

The mother looked down upon her boy with a troubled countenance, and then turned her eyes upward to heaven. She seemed to pray internally, and the contention of her soul was evident.

"Friend," she said at length to Dorothy, "I doubt not that my son shall receive all earthly tenderness at thy hands. Nay, I will believe that even thy imperfect lights may guide him to a better world, for surely thou art on the path thither. But thou hast spoken of a husband. Doth he stand here among this multitude of people? Let him come forth, for I must know to whom I commit this most precious trust."

She turned her face upon the male auditors, and after a momentary delay, Tobias Pearson came forth from among them. The Quaker saw the dress which marked his military rank, and shook her head; but then she noted the hesitating air, the eyes that struggled with her own, and were vanquished; the color that went and came, and could find no resting-place. As she gazed, an unmirthful smile spread over her features, like sunshine that grows melancholy in some desolate spot. Her lips moved inaudibly, but at length she spake.

"I hear it, I hear it. The voice speaketh within me and saith, 'Leave thy child, Catharine, for his place is here, and go hence, for I have other work for thee. Break the bonds of natural affection, martyr thy love, and know that in all these things eternal wisdom hath its ends.' I go, friends; I go. Take ye my boy, my precious jewel. I go hence, trusting that all shall be well, and that even for his infant hands there is a labor in the vineyard."

She knelt down and whispered to Ilbrahim, who at first struggled and clung to his mother, with sobs and tears, but remained passive when she had kissed his cheek and arisen from the ground. Having held her hands over his head in mental prayer, she was ready to depart.

"Farewell, friends in mine extremity," she said to Pearson and his wife; "the good deed ye have done me is a treasure laid up in heaven, to be returned a thousand-fold hereafter. And farewell ye, mine enemies, to whom it is not permitted to harm so much as a hair of my head, nor to stay my footsteps even for a moment. The day is coming when ye shall call upon me to witness for ye to this one sin uncommitted, and I will rise up and answer."

She turned her steps towards the door, and the men who had stationed themselves to guard it, withdrew, and suffered her to pass. A general sentiment of pity overcame the virulence of religious hatred. Sanctified by her love and affliction, she went forth, and all the people gazed after her till she had journeyed up the hill, and was lost behind its brow. She went, the apostle of her own unquiet heart, to renew the wanderings of past years. For her voice had been already heard in many lands of Christendom; and she had pined in the cells of a Catholic Inquisition before she felt the lash and lay in the dungeons of the Puritans. Her mission had extended also to the followers of the Prophet, and from them she had received the courtesy and kindness which all the contending sects of our purer religion united to deny her. Her husband and herself had resided many months in Turkey, where even the Sultan's countenance was gracious to them; in that pagan land, too, was Ilbrahim's birthplace, and his oriental name was a mark of gratitude for the good deeds of an unbeliever.

When Pearson and his wife had thus acquired all the rights over Ilbrahim that could be delegated, their affection for him became like the memory of their native land, or their mild sorrow for the dead, a piece of the immovable furniture of their hearts. The boy, also, after a week or two of mental disquiet, began to gratify his protectors by many inadvertent proofs that he considered them as parents, and their house as home. Before the winter snows were melted, the persecuted infant, the little wanderer from a remote and heathen country, seemed native in the New England cottage, and inseparable from the warmth and security of its hearth. Under the influence of kind treatment, and in the consciousness that he was loved, Ilbrahim's demeanor lost a premature manliness, which had resulted from his earlier situation; he became more childlike, and his natural character displayed itself with freedom. It was in many respects a beautiful one, yet the disordered imaginations of both his father and mother had perhaps propagated a certain unhealthiness in the mind of the boy. In his general state, Ilbrahim would derive enjoyment from the most trifling events, and from every object about him; he seemed to discover rich treasures of happiness, by a faculty analogous to that of the witch hazel, which points to hidden gold where all is barren to the eye. His airy gayety, coming to him from a thousand sources, communicated itself to the family, and Ilbrahim was like a domesticated sunbeam, brightening moody countenances, and chasing away the gloom from the dark corners of the cottage.

On the other hand, as the susceptibility of pleasure is also that of pain, the exuberant cheerfulness of the boy's prevailing temper sometimes yielded to moments of deep depression. His sorrows could not always be followed up to their original source, but most frequently they appeared to flow, though Ilbrahim was young to be sad for such a cause, from wounded love. The flightiness of his mirth rendered him often guilty of offences against the decorum of a Puritan household, and on these occasions he did not invariably escape rebuke. But the slightest word of real bitterness, which he was infallible in distinguishing from pretended anger, seemed to sink into his heart and poison all his enjoyments, till he became sensible that he was entirely forgiven. Of the malice, which generally accompanies a superfluity of sensitiveness, Ilbrahim was altogether destitute: when trodden upon, he would not turn; when wounded, he could but die. His mind was wanting in the stamina for self-support; it was a plant that would twine beautifully round something stronger than itself, but if repulsed, or torn away, it had no choice but to wither on the ground. Dorothy's acuteness taught her that severity would crush the spirit of the child, and she nurtured him with the gentle care of one who handles a butterfly. Her husband manifested an equal affection, although it grew daily less productive of familiar caresses.

The feelings of the neighboring people, in regard to the Quaker infant and his protectors, had not undergone a favorable change, in spite of the momentary triumph which the desolate mother had obtained over their sympathies. The scorn and bitterness, of which he was the object, were very grievous to Ilbrahim, especially when any circumstance made him sensible that the children, his equals in age, partook of the enmity of their parents. His tender and social nature had already overflowed in attachments to everything about him, and still there was a residue of unappropriated love, which he yearned to bestow upon the little ones who were taught to hate him. As the warm days of spring came on, Ilbrahim was accustomed to remain for hours, silent and inactive, within hearing of the children's voices at their play; yet, with his usual delicacy of feeling, he avoided their notice, and would flee and hide himself from the smallest individual among them. Chance, however, at length seemed to open a medium of communication between his heart and theirs; it was by means of a boy about two years older than Ilbrahim, who was injured by a fall from a tree in the vicinity of Pearson's habitation. As the sufferer's own home was at some distance, Dorothy willingly received him under her roof, and became his tender and careful nurse.

Ilbrahim was the unconscious possessor of much skill in physiognomy, and it would have deterred him, in other circumstances, from attempting to make a friend of this boy. The countenance of the latter immediately impressed a beholder disagreeably, but it required some examination to discover that the cause was a very slight distortion of the mouth, and the irregular, broken line, and near approach of the eyebrows. Analogous, perhaps, to these trifling deformities, was an almost imperceptible twist of every joint, and the uneven prominence of the breast; forming a body, regular in its general outline, but faulty in almost all its details. The disposition of the boy was sullen and reserved, and the village schoolmaster stigmatized him as obtuse in intellect; although, at a later period of life, he evinced ambition and very peculiar talents. But whatever might be his personal or moral irregularities, Ilbrahim's heart seized upon, and clung to him, from the moment that he was brought wounded into the cottage; the child of persecution seemed to compare his own fate with that of the sufferer, and to feel that even different modes of misfortune had created a sort of relationship between them. Food, rest, and the fresh air, for which he languished, were neglected; he nestled continually by the bedside of the little stranger, and, with a fond jealousy, endeavored to be the medium of all the cares that were bestowed upon him. As the boy became convalescent, Ilbrahim contrived games suitable to his situation, or amused him by a faculty which he had perhaps breathed in with the air of his barbaric birthplace. It was that of reciting imaginary adventures, on the spur of the moment, and apparently in inexhaustible succession. His tales were of course monstrous, disjointed, and without aim; but they were curious on account of a vein of human tenderness which ran through them all, and was like a sweet, familiar face, encountered in the midst of wild and unearthly scenery. The auditor paid much attention to these romances, and sometimes interrupted them by brief remarks upon the incidents, displaying shrewdness above his years, mingled with a moral obliquity which grated very harshly against Ilbrahim's instinctive rectitude. Nothing, however, could arrest the progress of the latter's affection, and there were many proofs that it met with a response from the dark and stubborn nature on which it was lavished. The boy's parents at length removed him, to complete his cure under their own roof.

Ilbrahim did not visit his new friend after his departure; but he made anxious and continual inquiries respecting him, and informed himself of the day when he was to reappear among his playmates. On a pleasant summer afternoon, the children of the neighborhood had assembled in the little forest-crowned amphitheatre behind the meeting-house, and the recovering invalid was there, leaning on a staff. The glee of a score of untainted bosoms was heard in light and airy voices, which danced among the trees like sunshine become audible; the grown men of this weary world, as they journeyed by the spot, marvelled why life, beginning in such brightness, should proceed in gloom; and their hearts, or their imaginations, answered them and said, that the bliss of childhood gushes from its innocence. But it happened that an unexpected addition was made to the heavenly little band. It was Ilbrahim, who came towards the children with a look of sweet confidence on his fair and spiritual face, as if, having manifested his love to one of them, he had no longer to fear a repulse from their society. A hush came over their mirth the moment they beheld him, and they stood whispering to each other while he drew nigh; but, all at once, the devil of their fathers entered into the unbreeched fanatics, and sending up a fierce, shrill cry, they rushed upon the poor Quaker child. In an instant, he was the centre of a brood of baby-fiends, who lifted sticks against him, pelted him with stones, and displayed an instinct of destruction far more loathsome than the bloodthirstiness of manhood.

The invalid, in the meanwhile, stood apart from the tumult, crying out with a loud voice, "Fear not, Ilbrahim, come hither and take my hand;" and his unhappy friend endeavored to obey him. After watching the victim's struggling approach with a calm smile and unabashed eye, the foul-hearted little villain lifted his staff and struck Ilbrahim on the mouth, so forcibly that the blood issued in a stream. The poor child's arms had been raised to guard his head from the storm of blows; but now he dropped them at once. His persecutors beat him down, trampled upon him, dragged him by his long, fair locks, and Ilbrahim was on the point of becoming as veritable a martyr as ever entered bleeding into heaven. The uproar, however, attracted the notice of a few neighbors, who put themselves to the trouble of rescuing the little heretic, and of conveying him to Pearson's door.

Ilbrahim's bodily harm was severe, but long and careful nursing accomplished his recovery; the injury done to his sensitive spirit was more serious, though not so visible. Its signs were principally of a negative character, and to be discovered only by those who had previously known him. His gait was thenceforth slow, even, and unvaried by the sudden bursts of sprightlier motion, which had once corresponded to his overflowing gladness; his countenance was heavier, and its former play of expression, the dance of sunshine reflected from moving water, was destroyed by the cloud over his existence; his notice was attracted in a far less degree by passing events, and he appeared to find greater difficulty in comprehending what was new to him than at a happier period. A stranger, founding his judgment upon these circumstances, would have said that the dulness of the child's intellect widely contradicted the promise of his features; but the secret was in the direction of Ilbrahim's thoughts, which were brooding within him when they should naturally have been wandering abroad. An attempt of Dorothy to revive his former sportiveness was the single occasion on which his quiet demeanor yielded to a violent display of grief; he burst into passionate weeping, and ran and hid himself, for his heart had become so miserably sore that even the hand of kindness tortured it like fire. Sometimes, at night and probably in his dreams, he was heard to cry "Mother! Mother!" as if her place, which a stranger had supplied while Ilbrahim was happy, admitted of no substitute in his extreme affliction. Perhaps, among the many life-weary wretches then upon the earth, there was not one who combined innocence and misery like this poor, broken-hearted infant, so soon the victim of his own heavenly nature.

While this melancholy change had taken place in Ilbrahim, one of an earlier origin and of different character had come to its perfection in his adopted father. The incident with which this tale commences found Pearson in a state of religious dulness, yet mentally disquieted, and longing for a more fervid faith than he possessed. The first effect of his kindness to Ilbrahim was to produce a softened feeling, and incipient love for the child's whole sect; but joined to this, and resulting perhaps from self-suspicion, was a proud and ostentatious contempt of all their tenets and practical extravagances. In the course of much thought, however, for the subject struggled irresistibly into his mind, the foolishness of the doctrine began to be less evident, and the points which had particularly offended his reason assumed another aspect, or vanished entirely away. The work within him appeared to go on even while he slept, and that which had been a doubt, when he laid down to rest, would often hold the place of a truth, confirmed by some forgotten demonstration, when he recalled his thoughts in the morning. But while he was thus becoming assimilated to the enthusiasts, his contempt, in nowise decreasing towards them, grew very fierce against himself; he imagined, also, that every face of his acquaintance wore a sneer, and that every word addressed to him was a gibe. Such was his state of mind at the period of Ilbrahim's misfortune; and the emotions consequent upon that event completed the change, of which the child had been the original instrument.

In the mean time, neither the fierceness of the persecutors, nor the infatuation of their victims, had decreased. The dungeons were never empty; the streets of almost every village echoed daily with the lash; the life of a woman, whose mild and Christian spirit no cruelty could embitter, had been sacrificed; and more innocent blood was yet to pollute the hands that were so often raised in prayer. Early after the Restoration, the English Quakers represented to Charles II. that a "vein of blood was open in his dominions;" but though the displeasure of the voluptuous king was roused, his interference was not prompt. And now the tale must stride forward over many months, leaving Pearson to encounter ignominy and misfortune; his wife to a firm endurance of a thousand sorrows; poor Ilbrahim to pine and droop like a cankered rosebud; his mother to wander on a mistaken errand, neglectful of the holiest trust which can be committed to a woman.

A winter evening, a night of storm, had darkened over Pearson's habitation, and there were no cheerful faces to drive the gloom from his broad hearth. The fire, it is true, sent forth a glowing heat and a ruddy light, and large logs, dripping with half-melted snow, lay ready to be cast upon the embers. But the apartment was saddened in its aspect by the absence of much of the homely wealth which had once adorned it; for the exaction of repeated fines, and his own neglect of temporal affairs, had greatly impoverished the owner. And with the furniture of peace, the implements of war had likewise disappeared; the sword was broken, the helm and cuirass were cast away forever; the soldier had done with battles, and might not lift so much as his naked hand to guard his head. But the Holy Book remained, and the table on which it rested was drawn before the fire, while two of the persecuted sect sought comfort from its pages.

He who listened, while the other read, was the master of the house, now emaciated in form, and altered as to the expression and healthiness of his countenance; for his mind had dwelt too long among visionary thoughts, and his body had been worn by imprisonment and stripes. The hale and weather-beaten old man who sat beside him had sustained less injury from a far longer course of the same mode of life. In person he was tall and dignified, and, which alone would have made him hateful to the Puritans, his gray locks fell from beneath the broad-brimmed hat, and rested on his shoulders. As the old man read the sacred page the snow drifted against the windows, or eddied in at the crevices of the door, while a blast kept laughing in the chimney, and the blaze leaped fiercely up to seek it. And sometimes, when the wind struck the hill at a certain angle, and swept down by the cottage across the wintry plain, its voice was the most doleful that can be conceived; it came as if the Past were speaking, as if the Dead had contributed each a whisper, as if the Desolation of Ages were breathed in that one lamenting sound.

The Quaker at length closed the book, retaining however his hand between the pages which he had been reading, while he looked steadfastly at Pearson. The attitude and features of the latter might have indicated the endurance of bodily pain; he leaned his forehead on his hands, his teeth were firmly closed, and his frame was tremulous at intervals with a nervous agitation.

"Friend Tobias," inquired the old man, compassionately, "hast thou found no comfort in these many blessed passages of Scripture?"

"Thy voice has fallen on my ear like a sound afar off and indistinct," replied Pearson without lifting his eyes. "Yea, and when I have hearkened carefully the words seemed cold and lifeless, and intended for another and a lesser grief than mine. Remove the book," he added, in a tone of sullen bitterness. "I have no part in its consolations, and they do but fret my sorrow the more."

"Nay, feeble brother, be not as one who hath never known the light," said the elder Quaker earnestly, but with mildness. "Art thou he that wouldst be content to give all, and endure all, for conscience' sake; desiring even peculiar trials, that thy faith might be purified and thy heart weaned from worldly desires? And wilt thou sink beneath an affliction which happens alike to them that have their portion here below, and to them that lay up treasure in heaven? Faint not, for thy burden is yet light."

"It is heavy! It is heavier than I can bear!" exclaimed Pearson, with the impatience of a variable spirit. "From my youth upward I have been a man marked out for wrath; and year by year, yea, day after day, I have endured sorrows such as others know not in their lifetime. And now I speak not of the love that has been turned to hatred, the honor to ignominy, the ease and plentifulness of all things to danger, want, and nakedness. All this I could have borne, and counted myself blessed. But when my heart was desolate with many losses I fixed it upon the child of a stranger, and he became dearer to me than all my buried ones; and now he too must die as if my love were poison. Verily, I am an accursed man, and I will lay me down in the dust and lift up my head no more."

"Thou sinnest, brother, but it is not for me to rebuke thee; for I also have had my hours of darkness, wherein I have murmured against the cross," said the old Quaker. He continued, perhaps in the hope of distracting his companion's thoughts from his own sorrows. "Even of late was the light obscured within me, when the men of blood had banished me on pain of death, and the constables led me onward from village to village towards the wilderness. A strong and cruel hand was wielding the knotted cords; they sunk deep into the flesh, and thou mightst have tracked every reel and totter of my footsteps by the blood that followed. As we went on"—

"Have I not borne all this; and have I murmured?" interrupted Pearson impatiently.

"Nay, friend, but hear me," continued the other. "As we journeyed on, night darkened on our path, so that no man could see the rage of the persecutors or the constancy of my endurance, though Heaven forbid that I should glory therein. The lights began to glimmer in the cottage windows, and I could discern the inmates as they gathered in comfort and security, every man with his wife and children by their own evening hearth. At length we came to a tract of fertile land; in the dim light, the forest was not visible around it; and behold! there was a straw-thatched dwelling, which bore the very aspect of my home, far over the wild ocean, far in our own England. Then came bitter thoughts upon me; yea, remembrances that were like death to my soul. The happiness of my early days was painted to me; the disquiet of my manhood, the altered faith of my declining years. I remembered how I had been moved to go forth a wanderer when my daughter, the youngest, the dearest of my flock, lay on her dying bed, and"—

"Couldst thou obey the command at such a moment?" exclaimed Pearson, shuddering.

"Yea, yea," replied the old man hurriedly. "I was kneeling by her bedside when the voice spoke loud within me; but immediately I rose, and took my staff, and gat me gone. Oh! that it were permitted me to forget her woful look when I thus withdrew my arm, and left her journeying through the dark valley alone! for her soul was faint, and she had leaned upon my prayers. Now in that night of horror I was assailed by the thought that I had been an erring Christian and a cruel parent; yea, even my daughter, with her pale, dying features, seemed to stand by me and whisper, 'Father, you are deceived; go home and shelter your gray head.' O Thou, to whom I have looked in my farthest wanderings," continued the Quaker, raising his agitated eyes to heaven, "inflict not upon the bloodiest of our persecutors the unmitigated agony of my soul, when I believed that all I had done and suffered for Thee was at the instigation of a mocking fiend! But I yielded not; I knelt down and wrestled with the tempter, while the scourge bit more fiercely into the flesh. My prayer was heard, and I went on in peace and joy towards the wilderness."

The old man, though his fanaticism had generally all the calmness of reason, was deeply moved while reciting this tale; and his unwonted emotion seemed to rebuke and keep down that of his companion. They sat in silence, with their faces to the fire, imagining, perhaps, in its red embers new scenes of persecution yet to be encountered. The snow still drifted hard against the windows, and sometimes, as the blaze of the logs had gradually sunk, came down the spacious chimney and hissed upon the hearth. A cautious footstep might now and then be heard in a neighboring apartment, and the sound invariably drew the eyes of both Quakers to the door which led thither. When a fierce and riotous gust of wind had led his thoughts, by a natural association, to homeless travellers on such a night, Pearson resumed the conversation.

"I have well-nigh sunk under my own share of this trial," observed he, sighing heavily; "yet I would that it might be doubled to me, if so the child's mother could be spared. Her wounds have been deep and many, but this will be the sorest of all."

"Fear not for Catharine," replied the old Quaker, "for I know that valiant woman, and have seen how she can bear the cross. A mother's heart, indeed, is strong in her, and may seem to contend mightily with her faith; but soon she will stand up and give thanks that her son has been thus early an accepted sacrifice. The boy hath done his work, and she will feel that he is taken hence in kindness both to him and her. Blessed, blessed are they that with so little suffering can enter into peace!"

The fitful rush of the wind was now disturbed by a portentous sound; it was a quick and heavy knocking at the outer door. Pearson's wan countenance grew paler, for many a visit of persecution had taught him what to dread; the old man, on the other hand, stood up erect, and his glance was firm as that of the tried soldier who awaits his enemy.

"The men of blood have come to seek me," he observed with calmness. "They have heard how I was moved to return from banishment; and now am I to be led to prison, and thence to death. It is an end I have long looked for. I will open unto them, lest they say, 'Lo, he feareth!' "

"Nay, I will present myself before them," said Pearson, with recovered fortitude. "It may be that they seek me alone, and know not that thou abidest with me."

"Let us go boldly, both one and the other," rejoined his companion. "It is not fitting that thou or I should shrink."

They therefore proceeded through the entry to the door, which they opened, bidding the applicant "Come in, in God's name!" A furious blast of wind drove the storm into their faces, and extinguished the lamp; they had barely time to discern a figure, so white from head to foot with the drifted snow that it seemed like Winter's self, come in human shape, to seek refuge from its own desolation.

"Enter, friend, and do thy errand, be it what it may," said Pearson. "It must needs be pressing, since thou comest on such a bitter night."

"Peace be with this household," said the stranger, when they stood on the floor of the inner apartment.

Pearson started, the elder Quaker stirred the slumbering embers of the fire till they sent up a clear and lofty blaze; it was a female voice that had spoken; it was a female form that shone out, cold and wintry, in that comfortable light.

"Catharine, blessed woman!" exclaimed the old man, "art thou come to this darkened land again? art thou come to bear a valiant testimony as in former years? The scourge hath not prevailed against thee, and from the dungeon hast thou come forth triumphant; but strengthen, strengthen now thy heart, Catharine, for Heaven will prove thee yet this once, ere thou go to thy reward."

"Rejoice, friends!" she replied. "Thou who hast long been of our people, and thou whom a little child hath led to us, rejoice! Lo! I come, the messenger of glad tidings, for the day of persecution is overpast. The heart of the king, even Charles, hath been moved in gentleness towards us, and he hath sent forth his letters to stay the hands of the men of blood. A ship's company of our friends hath arrived at yonder town, and I also sailed joyfully among them."

As Catharine spoke, her eyes were roaming about the room, in search of him for whose sake security was dear to her. Pearson made a silent appeal to the old man, nor did the latter shrink from the painful task assigned him.

"Sister," he began, in a softened yet perfectly calm tone, "thou tellest us of His love, manifested in temporal good; and now must we speak to thee of that selfsame love, displayed in chastenings. Hitherto, Catharine, thou hast been as one journeying in a darksome and difficult path, and leading an infant by the hand; fain wouldst thou have looked heavenward continually, but still the cares of that little child have drawn thine eyes and thy affections to the earth. Sister! go on rejoicing, for his tottering footsteps shall impede thine own no more."

But the unhappy mother was not thus to be consoled; she shook like a leaf, she turned white as the very snow that hung drifted into her hair. The firm old man extended his hand and held her up, keeping his eye upon hers, as if to repress any outbreak of passion.

"I am a woman, I am but a woman; will He try me above my strength?" said Catharine very quickly, and almost in a whisper. "I have been wounded sore: I have suffered much; many things in the body; many in the mind; crucified in myself, and in them that were dearest to me. Surely," added she, with a long shudder, "He hath spared me in this one thing." She broke forth with sudden and irrepressible violence. "Tell me, man of cold heart, what has God done to me? Hath He cast me down, never to rise again? Hath He crushed my very heart in his hand? And thou, to whom I committed my child, how hast thou fulfilled thy trust? Give me back the boy, well, sound, alive, alive; or earth and Heaven shall avenge me!"

The agonized shriek of Catharine was answered by the faint, the very faint, voice of a child.

On this day it had become evident to Pearson, to his aged guest, and to Dorothy, that Ilbrahim's brief and troubled pilgrimage drew near its close. The two former would willingly have remained by him, to make use of the prayers and pious discourses which they deemed appropriate to the time, and which, if they be impotent as to the departing traveller's reception in the world whither it goes, may at least sustain him in bidding adieu to earth. But though Ilbrahim uttered no complaint, he was disturbed by the faces that looked upon him; so that Dorothy's entreaties, and their own conviction that the child's feet might tread heaven's pavement and not soil it, had induced the two Quakers to remove. Ilbrahim then closed his eyes and grew calm, and, except for now and then a kind and low word to his nurse, might have been thought to slumber. As nightfall came on, however, and the storm began to rise, something seemed to trouble the repose of the boy's mind, and to render his sense of hearing active and acute. If a passing wind lingered to shake the casement, he strove to turn his head towards it; if the door jarred to and fro upon its hinges, he looked long and anxiously thitherward; if the heavy voice of the old man, as he read the Scriptures, rose but a little higher, the child almost held his dying breath to listen; if a snow-drift swept by the cottage, with a sound like the trailing of a garment, Ilbrahim seemed to watch that some visitant should enter.

But, after a little time, he relinquished whatever secret hope had agitated him, and with one low, complaining whisper, turned his cheek upon the pillow. He then addressed Dorothy with his usual sweetness, and besought her to draw near him; she did so, and Ilbrahim took her hand in both of his, grasping it with a gentle pressure, as if to assure himself that he retained it. At intervals, and without disturbing the repose of his countenance, a very faint trembling passed over him from head to foot, as if a mild but somewhat cool wind had breathed upon him, and made him shiver. As the boy thus led her by the hand, in his quiet progress over the borders of eternity, Dorothy almost imagined that she could discern the near, though dim, delightfulness of the home he was about to reach; she would not have enticed the little wanderer back, though she bemoaned herself that she must leave him and return. But just when Ilbrahim's feet were pressing on the soil of Paradise he heard a voice behind him, and it recalled him a few, few paces of the weary path which he had travelled. As Dorothy looked upon his features, she perceived that their placid expression was again disturbed; her own thoughts had been so wrapped in him, that all sounds of the storm, and of human speech, were lost to her; but when Catharine's shriek pierced through the room, the boy strove to raise himself.

"Friend, she is come! Open unto her!" cried he.

In a moment his mother was kneeling by the bedside; she drew Ilbrahim to her bosom, and he nestled there, with no violence of joy, but contentedly, as if he were hushing himself to sleep. He looked into her face, and reading its agony, said, with feeble earnestness, "Mourn not, dearest mother. I am happy now." And with these words the gentle boy was dead.

The king's mandate to stay the New England persecutors was effectual in preventing further martyrdoms; but the colonial authorities, trusting in the remoteness of their situation, and perhaps in the supposed instability of the royal government, shortly renewed their severities in all other respects. Catharine's fanaticism had become wilder by the sundering of all human ties; and wherever a scourge was lifted there was she to receive the blow; and whenever a dungeon was unbarred thither she came, to cast herself upon the floor. But in process of time a more Christian spirit—a spirit of forbearance, though not of cordiality or approbation—began to pervade the land in regard to the persecuted sect. And then, when the rigid old Pilgrims eyed her rather in pity than in wrath; when the matrons fed her with the fragments of their children's food, and offered her a lodging on a hard and lowly bed; when no little crowd of schoolboys left their sports to cast stones after the roving enthusiast; then did Catharine return to Pearson's dwelling and made that her home.

As if Ilbrahim's sweetness yet lingered round his ashes; as if his gentle spirit came down from heaven to teach his parent a true religion, her fierce and vindictive nature was softened by the same griefs which had once irritated it. When the course of years had made the features of the unobtrusive mourner familiar in the settlement, she became a subject of not deep, but general, interest; a being on whom the otherwise superfluous sympathies of all might be bestowed. Every one spoke of her with that degree of pity which it is pleasant to experience; every one was ready to do her the little kindnesses which are not costly, yet manifest good will; and when at last she died, a long train of her once bitter persecutors followed her, with decent sadness and tears that were not painful, to her place by Ilbrahim's green and sunken grave.

MR. HIGGINBOTHAM'S CATASTROPHE

A young fellow, a tobacco pedlar by trade, was on his way from Morristown, where he had dealt largely with the Deacon of the Shaker settlement, to the village of Parker's Falls, on Salmon River. He had a neat little cart, painted green, with a box of cigars depicted on each side panel, and an Indian chief, holding a pipe and a golden tobacco stalk, on the rear. The pedlar drove a smart little mare, and was a young man of excellent character, keen at a bargain, but none the worse liked by the Yankees; who, as I have heard them say, would rather be shaved with a sharp razor than a dull one. Especially was he beloved by the pretty girls along the Connecticut, whose favor he used to court by presents of the best smoking tobacco in his stock; knowing well that the country lasses of New England are generally great performers on pipes. Moreover, as will be seen in the course of my story, the pedlar was inquisitive, and something of a tattler, always itching to hear the news and anxious to tell it again.

After an early breakfast at Morristown, the tobacco pedlar, whose name was Dominicus Pike, had travelled seven miles through a solitary piece of woods, without speaking a word to anybody but himself and his little gray mare. It being nearly seven o'clock, he was as eager to hold a morning gossip as a city shopkeeper to read the morning paper. An opportunity seemed at hand when, after lighting a cigar with a sun-glass, he looked up, and perceived a man coming over the brow of the hill, at the foot of which the pedlar had stopped his green cart. Dominicus watched him as he descended, and noticed that he carried a bundle over his shoulder on the end of a stick, and travelled with a weary, yet determined pace. He did not look as if he had started in the freshness of the morning, but had footed it all night, and meant to do the same all day.

"Good morning, mister," said Dominicus, when within speaking distance. "You go a pretty good jog. What's the latest news at Parker's Falls?"

The man pulled the broad brim of a gray hat over his eyes, and answered, rather suddenly, that he did not come from Parker's Falls, which, as being the limit of his own day's journey, the pedlar had naturally mentioned in his inquiry.

"Well then," rejoined Dominicus Pike, "let's have the latest news where you did come from. I'm not particular about Parker's Falls. Any place will answer."

Being thus importuned, the traveller—who was as ill looking a fellow as one would desire to meet in a solitary piece of woods—appeared to hesitate a little, as if he was either searching his memory for news, or weighing the expediency of telling it. At last, mounting on the step of the cart, he whispered in the ear of Dominicus, though he might have shouted aloud and no other mortal would have heard him.

"I do remember one little trifle of news," said he. "Old Mr. Higginbotham, of Kimballton, was murdered in his orchard, at eight o'clock last night, by an Irishman and a nigger. They strung him up to the branch of a St. Michael's pear-tree, where nobody would find him till the morning."

As soon as this horrible intelligence was communicated, the stranger betook himself to his journey again, with more speed than ever, not even turning his head when Dominicus invited him to smoke a Spanish cigar and relate all the particulars. The pedlar whistled to his mare and went up the hill, pondering on the doleful fate of Mr. Higginbotham whom he had known in the way of trade, having sold him many a bunch of long nines, and a great deal of pigtail, lady's twist, and fig tobacco. He was rather astonished at the rapidity with which the news had spread. Kimballton was nearly sixty miles distant in a straight line; the murder had been perpetrated only at eight o'clock the preceding night; yet Dominicus had heard of it at seven in the morning, when, in all probability, poor Mr. Higginbotham's own family had but just discovered his corpse, hanging on the St. Michael's pear-tree. The stranger on foot must have worn seven-league boots to travel at such a rate.

"Ill news flies fast, they say," thought Dominicus Pike; "but this beats railroads. The fellow ought to be hired to go express with the President's Message."

The difficulty was solved by supposing that the narrator had made a mistake of one day in the date of the occurrence; so that our friend did not hesitate to introduce the story at every tavern and country store along the road, expending a whole bunch of Spanish wrappers among at least twenty horrified audiences. He found himself invariably the first bearer of the intelligence, and was so pestered with questions that he could not avoid filling up the outline, till it became quite a respectable narrative. He met with one piece of corroborative evidence. Mr. Higginbotham was a trader; and a former clerk of his, to whom Dominicus related the facts, testified that the old gentleman was accustomed to return home through the orchard about nightfall, with the money and valuable papers of the store in his pocket. The clerk manifested but little grief at Mr. Higginbotham's catastrophe, hinting, what the pedlar had discovered in his own dealings with him, that he was a crusty old fellow, as close as a vice. His property would descend to a pretty niece who was now keeping school in Kimballton.

What with telling the news for the public good, and driving bargains for his own, Dominicus was so much delayed on the road that he chose to put up at a tavern, about five miles short of Parker's Falls. After supper, lighting one of his prime cigars, he seated himself in the bar-room, and went through the story of the murder, which had grown so fast that it took him half an hour to tell. There were as many as twenty people in the room, nineteen of whom received it all for gospel. But the twentieth was an elderly farmer, who had arrived on horseback a short time before, and was now seated in a corner smoking his pipe. When the story was concluded, he rose up very deliberately, brought his chair right in front of Dominicus, and stared him full in the face, puffing out the vilest tobacco smoke the pedlar had ever smelt.

"Will you make affidavit," demanded he, in the tone of a country justice taking an examination, "that old Squire Higginbotham of Kimballton was murdered in his orchard the night before last, and found hanging on his great pear-tree yesterday morning?"

"I tell the story as I heard it, mister," answered Dominicus, dropping his half-burnt cigar; "I don't say that I saw the thing done. So I can't take my oath that he was murdered exactly in that way."

"But I can take mine," said the farmer, "that if Squire Higginbotham was murdered night before last, I drank a glass of bitters with his ghost this morning. Being a neighbor of mine, he called me into his store, as I was riding by, and treated me, and then asked me to do a little business for him on the road. He didn't seem to know any more about his own murder than I did."

"Why, then, it can't be a fact!" exclaimed Dominicus Pike.

"I guess he'd have mentioned, if it was," said the old farmer; and he removed his chair back to the corner, leaving Dominicus quite down in the mouth.

Here was a sad resurrection of old Mr. Higginbotham! The pedlar had no heart to mingle in the conversation any more, but comforted himself with a glass of gin and water, and went to bed where, all night long, he dreamed of hanging on the St. Michael's pear-tree. To avoid the old farmer (whom he so detested that his suspension would have pleased him better than Mr. Higginbotham's), Dominicus rose in the gray of the morning, put the little mare into the green cart, and trotted swiftly away towards Parker's Falls. The fresh breeze, the dewy road, and the pleasant summer dawn, revived his spirits, and might have encouraged him to repeat the old story had there been anybody awake to hear it. But he met neither ox team, light wagon chaise, horseman, nor foot traveller, till, just as he crossed Salmon River, a man came trudging down to the bridge with a bundle over his shoulder, on the end of a stick.

"Good morning, mister," said the pedlar, reining in his mare. "If you come from Kimballton or that neighborhood, may be you can tell me the real fact about this affair of old Mr. Higginbotham. Was the old fellow actually murdered two or three nights ago, by an Irishman and a nigger?"

Dominicus had spoken in too great a hurry to observe, at first, that the stranger himself had a deep tinge of negro blood. On hearing this sudden question, the Ethiopian appeared to change his skin, its yellow hue becoming a ghastly white, while, shaking and stammering, he thus replied:—

"No! no! There was no colored man! It was an Irishman that hanged him last night, at eight o'clock. I came away at seven! His folks can't have looked for him in the orchard yet."

Scarcely had the yellow man spoken, when he interrupted himself, and though he seemed weary enough before, continued his journey at a pace which would have kept the pedlar's mare on a smart trot. Dominicus started after him in great perplexity. If the murder had not been committed till Tuesday night, who was the prophet that had foretold it, in all its circumstances, on Tuesday morning? If Mr. Higginbotham's corpse were not yet discovered by his own family, how came the mulatto, at above thirty miles' distance, to know that he was hanging in the orchard, especially as he had left Kimballton before the unfortunate man was hanged at all? These ambiguous circumstances, with the stranger's surprise and terror, made Dominicus think of raising a hue and cry after him, as an accomplice in the murder; since a murder, it seemed, had really been perpetrated.

"But let the poor devil go," thought the pedlar. "I don't want his black blood on my head; and hanging the nigger wouldn't unhang Mr. Higginbotham. Unhang the old gentleman! It's a sin, I know; but I should hate to have him come to life a second time, and give me the lie!"

With these meditations, Dominicus Pike drove into the street of Parker's Falls, which, as everybody knows, is as thriving a village as three cotton factories and a slitting mill can make it. The machinery was not in motion, and but a few of the shop doors unbarred, when he alighted in the stable yard of the tavern, and made it his first business to order the mare four quarts of oats. His second duty, of course, was to impart Mr. Higginbotham's catastrophe to the hostler. He deemed it advisable, however, not to be too positive as to the date of the direful fact, and also to be uncertain whether it were perpetrated by an Irishman and a mulatto, or by the son of Erin alone. Neither did he profess to relate it on his own authority, or that of any one person; but mentioned it as a report generally diffused.

The story ran through the town like fire among girdled trees, and became so much the universal talk that nobody could tell whence it had originated. Mr. Higginbotham was as well known at Parker's Falls as any citizen of the place, being part owner of the slitting mill, and a considerable stockholder in the cotton factories. The inhabitants felt their own prosperity interested in his fate. Such was the excitement, that the Parker's Falls Gazette anticipated its regular day of publication, and came out with half a form of blank paper and a column of double pica emphasized with capitals, and headed HORRID MURDER OF MR. HIGGINBOTHAM! Among other dreadful details, the printed account described the mark of the cord round the dead man's neck, and stated the number of thousand dollars of which he had been robbed; there was much pathos also about the affliction of his niece, who had gone from one fainting fit to another, ever since her uncle was found hanging on the St. Michael's pear-tree with his pockets inside out. The village poet likewise commemorated the young lady's grief in seventeen stanzas of a ballad. The selectmen held a meeting, and, in consideration of Mr. Higginbotham's claims on the town, determined to issue handbills, offering a reward of five hundred dollars for the apprehension of his murderers, and the recovery of the stolen property.

Meanwhile the whole population of Parker's Falls, consisting of shopkeepers, mistresses of boardinghouses, factory girls, millmen, and school boys rushed into the street and kept up such a terrible loquacity as more than compensated for the silence of the cotton machines, which refrained from their usual din out of respect to the deceased. Had Mr. Higginbotham cared about posthumous renown, his untimely ghost would have exulted in this tumult. Our friend Dominicus, in his vanity of heart, forgot his intended precautions, and mounting on the town pump, announced himself as the bearer of the authentic intelligence which had caused so wonderful a sensation. He immediately became the great man of the moment, and had just begun a new edition of the narrative, with a voice like a field preacher, when the mail stage drove into the village street. It had travelled all night, and must have shifted horses at Kimballton at three in the morning.

"Now we shall hear all the particulars," shouted the crowd.

The coach rumbled up to the piazza of the tavern, followed by a thousand people; for if any man had been minding his own business till then, he now left it at sixes and sevens, to hear the news. The pedlar, foremost in the race, discovered two passengers both of whom had been startled from a comfortable nap to find themselves in the centre of a mob. Every man assailing them with separate questions, all propounded at once, the couple were struck speechless, though one was a lawyer and the other a young lady.

"Mr. Higginbotham! Mr. Higginbotham! Tell us the particulars about old Mr. Higginbotham!" bawled the mob. "What is the coroner's verdict? Are the murderers apprehended? Is Mr. Higginbotham's niece come out of her fainting fits? Mr. Higginbotham! Mr. Higginbotham!!"

The coachman said not a word, except to swear awfully at the hostler for not bringing him a fresh team of horses. The lawyer inside had generally his wits about him even when asleep; the first thing he did, after learning the cause of the excitement, was to produce a large, red pocket-book. Meantime Dominicus Pike, being an extremely polite young man, and also suspecting that a female tongue would tell the story as glibly as a lawyer's, had handed the lady out of the coach. She was a fine, smart girl, now wide awake and bright as a button, and had such a sweet pretty mouth, that Dominicus would almost as lief have heard a love tale from it as a tale of murder.

"Gentlemen and ladies," said the lawyer to the shopkeepers, the millmen, and the factory girls, "I can assure you that some unaccountable mistake, or, more probably, a wilful falsehood, maliciously contrived to injure Mr. Higginbotham's credit, has excited this singular uproar. We passed through Kimballton at three o'clock this morning, and most certainly should have been informed of the murder had any been perpetrated. But I have proof nearly as strong as Mr. Higginbotham's own oral testimony, in the negative. Here is a note relating to a suit of his in the Connecticut courts, which was delivered me from that gentleman himself. I find it dated at ten o'clock last evening."

So saying, the lawyer exhibited the date and signature of the note, which irrefragably proved, either that this perverse Mr. Higginbotham was alive when he wrote it, or—as some deemed the more probable case, of two doubtful ones—that he was so absorbed in worldly business as to continue to transact it even after his death. But unexpected evidence was forthcoming. The young lady, after listening to the pedlar's explanation, merely seized a moment to smooth her gown and put her curls in order, and then appeared at the tavern door, making a modest signal to be heard.

"Good people," said she, "I am Mr. Higginbotham's niece."

A wondering murmur passed through the crowd on beholding her so rosy and bright; that same unhappy niece, whom they had supposed, on the authority of the Parker's Falls Gazette, to be lying at death's door in a fainting fit. But some shrewd fellows had doubted, all along, whether a young lady would be quite so desperate at the hanging of a rich old uncle.

"You see," continued Miss Higginbotham, with a smile, "that this strange story is quite unfounded as to myself; and I believe I may affirm it to be equally so in regard to my dear uncle Higginbotham. He has the kindness to give me a home in his house, though I contribute to my own support by teaching a school. I left Kimballton this morning to spend the vacation of commencement week with a friend, about five miles from Parker's Falls. My generous uncle, when he heard me on the stairs, called me to his bedside, and gave me two dollars and fifty cents to pay my stage fare, and another dollar for my extra expenses. He then laid his pocket-book under his pillow, shook hands with me, and advised me to take some biscuit in my bag, instead of breakfasting on the road. I feel confident, therefore, that I left my beloved relative alive, and trust that I shall find him so on my return."

The young lady courtesied at the close of her speech, which was so sensible and well worded, and delivered with such grace and propriety, that everybody thought her fit to be preceptress of the best academy in the State. But a stranger would have supposed that Mr. Higginbotham was an object of abhorrence at Parker's Falls, and that a thanksgiving had been proclaimed for his murder; so excessive was the wrath of the inhabitants on learning their mistake. The millmen resolved to bestow public honors on Dominicus Pike, only hesitating whether to tar and feather him, ride him on a rail, or refresh him with an ablution at the town pump, on the top of which he had declared himself the bearer of the news. The selectmen, by advice of the lawyer, spoke of prosecuting him for a misdemeanor, in circulating unfounded reports, to the great disturbance of the peace of the Commonwealth. Nothing saved Dominicus, either from mob law or a court of justice, but an eloquent appeal made by the young lady in his behalf. Addressing a few words of heartfelt gratitude to his benefactress, he mounted the green cart and rode out of town, under a discharge of artillery from the schoolboys, who found plenty of ammunition in the neighboring clay-pits and mud holes. As he turned his head to exchange a farewell glance with Mr. Higginbotham's niece, a ball, of the consistence of hasty pudding, hit him slap in the mouth, giving him a most grim aspect. His whole person was so bespattered with the like filthy missiles, that he had almost a mind to ride back, and supplicate for the threatened ablution at the town pump; for, though not meant in kindness, it would now have been a deed of charity.

However, the sun shone bright on poor Dominicus, and the mud, an emblem of all stains of undeserved opprobrium, was easily brushed off when dry. Being a funny rogue, his heart soon cheered up; nor could he refrain from a hearty laugh at the uproar which his story had excited. The handbills of the selectmen would cause the commitment of all the vagabonds in the State; the paragraph in the Parker's Falls Gazette would be reprinted from Maine to Florida, and perhaps form an item in the London newspapers; and many a miser would tremble for his money bags and life, on learning the catastrophe of Mr. Higginbotham. The pedlar meditated with much fervor on the charms of the young schoolmistress, and swore that Daniel Webster never spoke nor looked so like an angel as Miss Higginbotham, while defending him from the wrathful populace at Parker's Falls.

Dominicus was now on the Kimballton turnpike, having all along determined to visit that place, though business had drawn him out of the most direct road from Morristown. As he approached the scene of the supposed murder, he continued to revolve the circumstances in his mind, and was astonished at the aspect which the whole case assumed. Had nothing occurred to corroborate the story of the first traveller, it might now have been considered as a hoax; but the yellow man was evidently acquainted either with the report or the fact; and there was a mystery in his dismayed and guilty look on being abruptly questioned. When, to this singular combination of incidents, it was added that the rumor tallied exactly with Mr. Higginbotham's character and habits of life; and that he had an orchard, and a St. Michael's pear-tree, near which he always passed at nightfall: the circumstantial evidence appeared so strong that Dominicus doubted whether the autograph produced by the lawyer, or even the niece's direct testimony, ought to be equivalent. Making cautious inquiries along the road, the pedlar further learned that Mr. Higginbotham had in his service an Irishman of doubtful character, whom he had hired without a recommendation, on the score of economy.

"May I be hanged myself," exclaimed Dominicus Pike aloud, on reaching the top of a lonely hill, "if I'll believe old Higginbotham is unhanged till I see him with my own eyes, and hear it from his own mouth! And as he's a real shaver, I'll have the minister or some other responsible man for an indorser."

It was growing dusk when he reached the toll-house on Kimballton turnpike, about a quarter of a mile from the village of this name. His little mare was fast bringing him up with a man on horseback, who trotted through the gate a few rods in advance of him, nodded to the toll-gatherer, and kept on towards the village. Dominicus was acquainted with the tollman, and, while making change, the usual remarks on the weather passed between them.

"I suppose," said the pedlar, throwing back his whiplash, to bring it down like a feather on the mare's flank, "you have not seen anything of old Mr. Higginbotham within a day or two?"

"Yes," answered the toll-gatherer. "He passed the gate just before you drove up, and yonder he rides now, if you can see him through the dusk. He's been to Woodfield this afternoon, attending a sheriff's sale there. The old man generally shakes hands and has a little chat with me; but to-night, he nodded, —as if to say, 'Charge my toll,' and jogged on; for wherever he goes, he must always be at home by eight o'clock."

"So they tell me," said Dominicus.

"I never saw a man look so yellow and thin as the squire does," continued the toll-gatherer. "Says I to myself, to-night, he's more like a ghost or an old mummy than good flesh and blood."

The pedlar strained his eyes through the twilight, and could just discern the horseman now far ahead on the village road. He seemed to recognize the rear of Mr. Higginbotham; but through the evening shadows, and amid the dust from the horse's feet, the figure appeared dim and unsubstantial; as if the shape of the mysterious old man were faintly moulded of darkness and gray light. Dominicus shivered.

"Mr. Higginbotham has come back from the other world, by way of the Kimballton turnpike," thought he.

He shook the reins and rode forward, keeping about the same distance in the rear of the gray old shadow, till the latter was concealed by a bend of the road. On reaching this point, the pedlar no longer saw the man on horseback, but found himself at the head of the village street, not far from a number of stores and two taverns, clustered round the meeting-house steeple. On his left were a stone wall and a gate, the boundary of a wood-lot, beyond which lay an orchard, farther still, a mowing field, and last of all, a house. These were the premises of Mr. Higginbotham, whose dwelling stood beside the old highway, but had been left in the background by the Kimballton turnpike. Dominicus knew the place; and the little mare stopped short by instinct; for he was not conscious of tightening the reins.

"For the soul of me, I cannot get by this gate!" said he, trembling. "I never shall be my own man again, till I see whether Mr. Higginbotham is hanging on the St. Michael's pear-tree!"

He leaped from the cart, gave the rein a turn round the gate post, and ran along the green path of the wood-lot as if Old Nick were chasing behind. Just then the village clock tolled eight, and as each deep stroke fell, Dominicus gave a fresh bound and flew faster than before, till, dim in the solitary centre of the orchard, he saw the fated pear-tree. One great branch stretched from the old contorted trunk across the path, and threw the darkest shadow on that one spot. But something seemed to struggle beneath the branch!

The pedlar had never pretended to more courage than befits a man of peaceable occupation, nor could he account for his valor on this awful emergency. Certain it is, however, that he rushed forward, prostrated a sturdy Irishman with the butt end of his whip, and found—not indeed hanging on the St. Michael's pear-tree, but trembling beneath it, with a halter round his neck—the old, identical Mr. Higginbotham!

"Mr. Higginbotham," said Dominicus tremulously, "you're an honest man, and I'll take your word for it. Have you been hanged or not?"

If the riddle be not already guessed, a few words will explain the simple machinery by which this "coming event" was made to "cast its shadow before." Three men had plotted the robbery and murder of Mr. Higginbotham; two of them, successively, lost courage and fled, each delaying the crime one night by their disappearance; the third was in the act of perpetration, when a champion, blindly obeying the call of fate, like the heroes of old romance, appeared in the person of Dominicus Pike.

It only remains to say, that Mr. Higginbotham took the pedlar into high favor, sanctioned his addresses to the pretty schoolmistress, and settled his whole property on their children, allowing themselves the interest. In due time, the old gentleman capped the climax of his favors, by dying a Christian death, in bed, since which melancholy event Dominicus Pike has removed from Kimballton, and established a large tobacco manufactory in my native village.

WAKEFIELD

In some old magazine or newspaper I recollect a story, told as truth, of a man—let us call him Wakefield—who absented himself for a long time from his wife. The fact, thus abstractedly stated, is not very uncommon, nor—without a proper distinction of circumstances—to be condemned either as naughty or nonsensical. Howbeit, this, though far from the most aggravated, is perhaps the strangest, instance on record, of marital delinquency; and, moreover, as remarkable a freak as may be found in the whole list of human oddities. The wedded couple lived in London. The man, under pretence of going a journey, took lodgings in the next street to his own house, and there, unheard of by his wife or friends, and without the shadow of a reason for such self-banishment, dwelt upwards of twenty years. During that period, he beheld his home every day, and frequently the forlorn Mrs. Wakefield. And after so great a gap in his matrimonial felicity—when his death was reckoned certain, his estate settled, his name dismissed from memory, and his wife, long, long ago, resigned to her autumnal widowhood—he entered the door one evening, quietly, as from a day's absence, and became a loving spouse till death.

This outline is all that I remember. But the incident, though of the purest originality, unexampled, and probably never to be repeated, is one, I think, which appeals to the generous sympathies of mankind. We know, each for himself, that none of us would perpetrate such a folly, yet feel as if some other might. To my own contemplations, at least, it has often recurred, always exciting wonder, but with a sense that the story must be true, and a conception of its hero's character. Whenever any subject so forcibly affects the mind, time is well spent in thinking of it. If the reader choose, let him do his own meditation; or if he prefer to ramble with me through the twenty years of Wakefield's vagary, I bid him welcome; trusting that there will be a pervading spirit and a moral, even should we fail to find them, done up neatly, and condensed into the final sentence. Thought has always its efficacy, and every striking incident its moral.

What sort of a man was Wakefield? We are free to shape out our own idea, and call it by his name. He was now in the meridian of life; his matrimonial affections, never violent, were sobered into a calm, habitual sentiment; of all husbands, he was likely to be the most constant, because a certain sluggishness would keep his heart at rest, wherever it might be placed. He was intellectual, but not actively so; his mind occupied itself in long and lazy musings, that ended to no purpose, or had not vigor to attain it; his thoughts were seldom so energetic as to seize hold of words. Imagination, in the proper meaning of the term, made no part of Wakefield's gifts. With a cold but not depraved nor wandering heart, and a mind never feverish with riotous thoughts, nor perplexed with originality, who could have anticipated that our friend would entitle himself to a foremost place among the doers of eccentric deeds? Had his acquaintances been asked, who was the man in London the surest to perform nothing to-day which should be remembered on the morrow, they would have thought of Wakefield. Only the wife of his bosom might have hesitated. She, without having analyzed his character, was partly aware of a quiet selfishness, that had rusted into his inactive mind; of a peculiar sort of vanity, the most uneasy attribute about him; of a disposition to craft, which had seldom produced more positive effects than the keeping of petty secrets, hardly worth revealing; and, lastly, of what she called a little strangeness, sometimes, in the good man. This latter quality is indefinable, and perhaps nonexistent.

Let us now imagine Wakefield bidding adieu to his wife. It is the dusk of an October evening. His equipment is a drab great-coat, a hat covered with an oilcloth, top-boots, an umbrella in one hand and a small portmanteau in the other. He has informed Mrs. Wakefield that he is to take the night coach into the country. She would fain inquire the length of his journey, its object, and the probable time of his return; but, indulgent to his harmless love of mystery, interrogates him only by a look. He tells her not to expect him positively by the return coach, nor to be alarmed should he tarry three or four days; but, at all events, to look for him at supper on Friday evening. Wakefield himself, be it considered, has no suspicion of what is before him. He holds out his hand, she gives her own, and meets his parting kiss in the matter-of-course way of a ten years' matrimony; and forth goes the middle-aged Mr. Wakefield, almost resolved to perplex his good lady by a whole week's absence. After the door has closed behind him, she perceives it thrust partly open, and a vision of her husband's face, through the aperture, smiling on her, and gone in a moment. For the time, this little incident is dismissed without a thought. But, long afterwards, when she has been more years a widow than a wife, that smile recurs, and flickers across all her reminiscences of Wakefield's visage. In her many musings, she surrounds the original smile with a multitude of fantasies, which make it strange and awful: as, for instance, if she imagines him in a coffin, that parting look is frozen on his pale features; or, if she dreams of him in heaven, still his blessed spirit wears a quiet and crafty smile. Yet, for its sake, when all others have given him up for dead, she sometimes doubts whether she is a widow.

But our business is with the husband. We must hurry after him along the street, ere he lose his individuality, and melt into the great mass of London life. It would be vain searching for him there. Let us follow close at his heels, therefore, until, after several superfluous turns and doublings, we find him comfortably established by the fireside of a small apartment, previously bespoken. He is in the next street to his own, and at his journey's end. He can scarcely trust his good fortune, in having got thither unperceived—recollecting that, at one time, he was delayed by the throng, in the very focus of a lighted lantern; and, again, there were footsteps that seemed to tread behind his own, distinct from the multitudinous tramp around him; and, anon, he heard a voice shouting afar, and fancied that it called his name. Doubtless, a dozen busybodies had been watching him, and told his wife the whole affair. Poor Wakefield! Little knowest thou thine own insignificance in this great world! No mortal eye but mine has traced thee. Go quietly to thy bed, foolish man; and, on the morrow, if thou wilt be wise, get thee home to good Mrs. Wakefield, and tell her the truth. Remove not thyself, even for a little week, from thy place in her chaste bosom. Were she, for a single moment, to deem thee dead, or lost, or lastingly divided from her, thou wouldst be wofully conscious of a change in thy true wife forever after. It is perilous to make a chasm in human affections; not that they gape so long and wide—but so quickly close again!

Almost repenting of his frolic, or whatever it may be termed, Wakefield lies down betimes, and starting from his first nap, spreads forth his arms into the wide and solitary waste of the unaccustomed bed. "No,"—thinks he, gathering the bedclothes about him,—"I will not sleep alone another night."

In the morning he rises earlier than usual, and sets himself to consider what he really means to do. Such are his loose and rambling modes of thought that he has taken this very singular step with the consciousness of a purpose, indeed, but without being able to define it sufficiently for his own contemplation. The vagueness of the project, and the convulsive effort with which he plunges into the execution of it, are equally characteristic of a feeble-minded man. Wakefield sifts his ideas, however, as minutely as he may, and finds himself curious to know the progress of matters at home—how his exemplary wife will endure her widowhood of a week; and, briefly, how the little sphere of creatures and circumstances, in which he was a central object, will be affected by his removal. A morbid vanity, therefore, lies nearest the bottom of the affair. But, how is he to attain his ends? Not, certainly, by keeping close in this comfortable lodging, where, though he slept and awoke in the next street to his home, he is as effectually abroad as if the stage-coach had been whirling him away all night. Yet, should he reappear, the whole project is knocked in the head. His poor brains being hopelessly puzzled with this dilemma, he at length ventures out, partly resolving to cross the head of the street, and send one hasty glance towards his forsaken domicile. Habit—for he is a man of habits—takes him by the hand, and guides him, wholly unaware, to his own door, where, just at the critical moment, he is aroused by the scraping of his foot upon the step. Wakefield! whither are you going?

At that instant his fate was turning on the pivot. Little dreaming of the doom to which his first backward step devotes him, he hurries away, breathless with agitation hitherto unfelt, and hardly dares turn his head at the distant corner. Can it be that nobody caught sight of him? Will not the whole household—the decent Mrs. Wakefield, the smart maid servant, and the dirty little footboy—raise a hue and cry, through London streets, in pursuit of their fugitive lord and master? Wonderful escape! He gathers courage to pause and look homeward, but is perplexed with a sense of change about the familiar edifice, such as affects us all, when, after a separation of months or years, we again see some hill or lake, or work of art, with which we were friends of old. In ordinary cases, this indescribable impression is caused by the comparison and contrast between our imperfect reminiscences and the reality. In Wakefield, the magic of a single night has wrought a similar transformation, because, in that brief period, a great moral change has been effected. But this is a secret from himself. Before leaving the spot, he catches a far and momentary glimpse of his wife, passing athwart the front window, with her face turned towards the head of the street. The crafty nincompoop takes to his heels, scared with the idea that, among a thousand such atoms of mortality, her eye must have detected him. Right glad is his heart, though his brain be somewhat dizzy, when he finds himself by the coal fire of his lodgings.

So much for the commencement of this long whim-wham. After the initial conception, and the stirring up of the man's sluggish temperament to put it in practice, the whole matter evolves itself in a natural train. We may suppose him, as the result of deep deliberation, buying a new wig, of reddish hair, and selecting sundry garments, in a fashion unlike his customary suit of brown, from a Jew's old-clothes bag. It is accomplished. Wakefield is another man. The new system being now established, a retrograde movement to the old would be almost as difficult as the step that placed him in his unparalleled position. Furthermore, he is rendered obstinate by a sulkiness occasionally incident to his temper, and brought on at present by the inadequate sensation which he conceives to have been produced in the bosom of Mrs. Wakefield. He will not go back until she be frightened half to death. Well; twice or thrice has she passed before his sight, each time with a heavier step, a paler cheek, and more anxious brow; and in the third week of his non-appearance he detects a portent of evil entering the house, in the guise of an apothecary. Next day the knocker is muffled. Towards nightfall comes the chariot of a physician, and deposits its big-wigged and solemn burden at Wakefield's door, whence, after a quarter of an hour's visit, he emerges, perchance the herald of a funeral. Dear woman! Will she die? By this time, Wakefield is excited to something like energy of feeling, but still lingers away from his wife's bedside, pleading with his conscience that she must not be disturbed at such a juncture. If aught else restrains him, he does not know it. In the course of a few weeks she gradually recovers; the crisis is over; her heart is sad, perhaps, but quiet; and, let him return soon or late, it will never be feverish for him again. Such ideas glimmer through the mist of Wakefield's mind, and render him indistinctly conscious that an almost impassable gulf divides his hired apartment from his former home. "It is but in the next street!" he sometimes says. Fool! it is in another world. Hitherto, he has put off his return from one particular day to another; henceforward, he leaves the precise time undetermined. Not to-morrow—probably next week—pretty soon. Poor man! The dead have nearly as much chance of revisiting their earthly homes as the self-banished Wakefield.

Would that I had a folio to write, instead of an article of a dozen pages! Then might I exemplify how an influence beyond our control lays its strong hand on every deed which we do, and weaves its consequences into an iron tissue of necessity. Wakefield is spell-bound. We must leave him, for ten years or so, to haunt around his house, without once crossing the threshold, and to be faithful to his wife, with all the affection of which his heart is capable, while he is slowly fading out of hers. Long since, it must be remarked, he had lost the perception of singularity in his conduct.

Now for a scene! Amid the throng of a London street we distinguish a man, now waxing elderly, with few characteristics to attract careless observers, yet bearing, in his whole aspect, the handwriting of no common fate, for such as have the skill to read it. He is meagre; his low and narrow forehead is deeply wrinkled; his eyes, small and lustreless, sometimes wander apprehensively about him, but oftener seem to look inward. He bends his head, and moves with an indescribable obliquity of gait, as if unwilling to display his full front to the world. Watch him long enough to see what we have described, and you will allow that circumstances—which often produce remarkable men from nature's ordinary handiwork—have produced one such here. Next, leaving him to sidle along the footwalk, cast your eyes in the opposite direction, where a portly female, considerably in the wane of life, with a prayer-book in her hand, is proceeding to yonder church. She has the placid mien of settled widowhood. Her regrets have either died away, or have become so essential to her heart, that they would be poorly exchanged for joy. Just as the lean man and well-conditioned woman are passing, a slight obstruction occurs, and brings these two figures directly in contact. Their hands touch; the pressure of the crowd forces her bosom against his shoulder; they stand, face to face, staring into each other's eyes. After a ten years' separation, thus Wakefield meets his wife!

The throng eddies away, and carries them asunder. The sober widow, resuming her former pace, proceeds to church, but pauses in the portal, and throws a perplexed glance along the street. She passes in, however, opening her prayer-book as she goes. And the man! with so wild a face that busy and selfish London stands to gaze after him, he hurries to his lodgings, bolts the door, and throws himself upon the bed. The latent feelings of years break out; his feeble mind acquires a brief energy from their strength; all the miserable strangeness of his life is revealed to him at a glance: and he cries out, passionately, "Wakefield! Wakefield! You are mad!"

Perhaps he was so. The singularity of his situation must have so moulded him to himself, that, considered in regard to his fellow-creatures and the business of life, he could not be said to possess his right mind. He had contrived, or rather he had happened, to dissever himself from the world—to vanish—to give up his place and privileges with living men, without being admitted among the dead. The life of a hermit is nowise parallel to his. He was in the bustle of the city, as of old; but the crowd swept by and saw him not; he was, we may figuratively say, always beside his wife and at his hearth, yet must never feel the warmth of the one nor the affection of the other. It was Wakefield's unprecedented fate to retain his original share of human sympathies, and to be still involved in human interests, while he had lost his reciprocal influence on them. It would be a most curious speculation to trace out the effect of such circumstances on his heart and intellect, separately, and in unison. Yet, changed as he was, he would seldom be conscious of it, but deem himself the same man as ever; glimpses of the truth, indeed, would come, but only for the moment; and still he would keep saying, "I shall soon go back!"—nor reflect that he had been saying so for twenty years.

I conceive, also, that these twenty years would appear, in the retrospect, scarcely longer than the week to which Wakefield had at first limited his absence. He would look on the affair as no more than an interlude in the main business of his life. When, after a little while more, he should deem it time to reënter his parlor, his wife would clap her hands for joy, on beholding the middle-aged Mr. Wakefield. Alas, what a mistake! Would Time but await the close of our favorite follies, we should be young men, all of us, and till Doomsday.

One evening, in the twentieth year since he vanished, Wakefield is taking his customary walk towards the dwelling which he still calls his own. It is a gusty night of autumn, with frequent showers that patter down upon the pavement, and are gone before a man can put up his umbrella. Pausing near the house, Wakefield discerns, through the parlor windows of the second floor, the red glow and the glimmer and fitful flash of a comfortable fire. On the ceiling appears a grotesque shadow of good Mrs. Wakefield. The cap, the nose and chin, and the broad waist, form an admirable caricature, which dances, moreover, with the up-flickering and down-sinking blaze, almost too merrily for the shade of an elderly widow. At this instant a shower chances to fall, and is driven, by the unmannerly gust, full into Wakefield's face and bosom. He is quite penetrated with its autumnal chill. Shall he stand, wet and shivering here, when his own hearth has a good fire to warm him, and his own wife will run to fetch the gray coat and small-clothes, which, doubtless, she has kept carefully in the closet of their bed chamber? No! Wakefield is no such fool. He ascends the steps—heavily!—for twenty years have stiffened his legs since he came down—but he knows it not. Stay, Wakefield! Would you go to the sole home that is left you? Then step into your grave! The door opens. As he passes in, we have a parting glimpse of his visage, and recognize the crafty smile, which was the precursor of the little joke that he has ever since been playing off at his wife's expense. How unmercifully has he quizzed the poor woman! Well, a good night's rest to Wakefield!

This happy event—supposing it to be such—could only have occurred at an unpremeditated moment. We will not follow our friend across the threshold. He has left us much food for thought, a portion of which shall lend its wisdom to a moral, and be shaped into a figure. Amid the seeming confusion of our mysterious world, individuals are so nicely adjusted to a system, and systems to one another and to a whole, that, by stepping aside for a moment, a man exposes himself to a fearful risk of losing his place forever. Like Wakefield, he may become, as it were, the Outcast of the Universe.

THE GREAT CARBUNCLE[1]

A MYSTERY OF THE WHITE MOUNTAINS

At nightfall, once in the olden time, on the rugged side of one of the Crystal Hills, a party of adventurers were refreshing themselves, after a toilsome and fruitless quest for the Great Carbuncle. They had come thither, not as friends nor partners in the enterprise, but each, save one youthful pair, impelled by

[1]The Indian tradition, on which this somewhat extravagant tale is founded, is both too wild and too beautiful to be adequately wrought up in prose. Sullivan, in his History of Maine, written since the Revolution, remarks, that even then the existence of the Great Carbuncle was not entirely discredited.

his own selfish and solitary longing for this wondrous gem. Their feeling of brotherhood, however, was strong enough to induce them to contribute a mutual aid in building a rude hut of branches, and kindling a great fire of shattered pines, that had drifted down the headlong current of the Amonoosuck, on the lower bank of which they were to pass the night. There was but one of their number, perhaps, who had become so estranged from natural sympathies, by the absorbing spell of the pursuit, as to acknowledge no satisfaction at the sight of human faces, in the remote and solitary region whither they had ascended. A vast extent of wilderness lay between them and the nearest settlement, while scant a mile above their heads was that black verge where the hills throw off their shaggy mantle of forest trees, and either robe themselves in clouds or tower naked into the sky. The roar of the Amonoosuck would have been too awful for endurance if only a solitary man had listened, while the mountain stream talked with the wind.

The adventurers, therefore, exchanged hospitable greetings, and welcomed one another to the hut, where each man was the host, and all were the guests of the whole company. They spread their individual supplies of food on the flat surface of a rock, and partook of a general repast; at the close of which, a sentiment of good fellowship was perceptible among the party, though repressed by the idea, that the renewed search for the Great Carbuncle must make them strangers again in the morning. Seven men and one young woman, they warmed themselves together at the fire, which extended its bright wall along the whole front of their wigwam. As they observed the various and contrasted figures that made up the assemblage, each man looking like a caricature of himself, in the unsteady light that flickered over him, they came mutually to the conclusion, that an odder society had never met, in city or wilderness, on mountain or plain.

The eldest of the group, a tall, lean, weather-beaten man, some sixty years of age, was clad in the skins of wild animals, whose fashion of dress he did well to imitate, since the deer, the wolf, and the bear, had long been his most intimate companions. He was one of those ill-fated mortals, such as the Indians told of, whom, in their early youth, the Great Carbuncle smote with a peculiar madness, and became the passionate dream of their existence. All who visited that region knew him as the Seeker, and by no other name. As none could remember when he first took up the search, there went a fable in the valley of the Saco, that for his inordinate lust after the Great Carbuncle, he had been condemned to wander among the mountains till the end of time, still with the same feverish hopes at sunrise—the same despair at eve. Near this miserable Seeker sat a little elderly personage, wearing a high-crowned hat, shaped somewhat like a crucible. He was from beyond the sea, a Doctor Cacaphodel, who had wilted and dried himself into a mummy by continually stooping over charcoal furnaces, and inhaling unwholesome fumes during his researches in chemistry and alchemy. It was told of him, whether truly or not, that, at the commencement of his studies, he had drained his body of all its richest blood, and wasted it, with other inestimable ingredients, in an unsuccessful experiment—and had never been a well man since. Another of the adventurers was Master Ichabod Pigsnort, a weighty merchant and selectman of Boston, and an elder of the famous Mr. Norton's church. His enemies had a ridiculous story that Master Pigsnort was accustomed to spend a whole hour after prayer time, every morning and evening, in wallowing naked among an immense quantity of pine-tree shillings, which were the earliest silver coinage of Massachusetts. The fourth whom we shall notice had no name that his companions knew of, and was chiefly distinguished by a sneer that always contorted his thin visage, and by a prodigious pair of spectacles, which were supposed to deform and discolor the whole face of nature, to this gentleman's perception. The fifth adventurer likewise lacked a name, which was the greater pity, as he appeared to be a poet. He was a bright-eyed man, but wofully pined away, which was no more than natural, if, as some people affirmed, his ordinary diet was fog, morning mist, and a slice of the densest cloud within his reach, sauced with moonshine, whenever he could get it. Certain it is, that the poetry which flowed from him had a smack of all these dainties. The sixth of the party was a young man of haughty mien, and sat somewhat apart from the rest, wearing his plumed hat loftily among his elders, while the fire glittered on the rich embroidery of his dress, and gleamed intensely on the jewelled pommel of his sword. This was the Lord de Vere, who, when at home, was said to spend much of his time in the burial vault of his dead progenitors, rummaging their mouldy coffins in search of all the earthly pride and vainglory that was hidden among bones and dust; so that, besides his own share, he had the collected haughtiness of his whole line of ancestry.

Lastly, there was a handsome youth in rustic garb, and by his side a blooming little person, in whom a delicate shade of maiden reserve was just melting into the rich glow of a young wife's affection. Her name was Hannah, and her husband's Matthew; two homely names, yet well enough adapted to the simple pair, who seemed strangely out of place among the whimsical fraternity whose wits had been set agog by the Great Carbuncle.

Beneath the shelter of one hut, in the bright blaze of the same fire, sat this varied group of adventurers, all so intent upon a single object, that, of whatever else they began to speak, their closing words were sure to be illuminated with the Great Carbuncle. Several related the circumstances that brought them thither. One had listened to a traveller's tale of this marvellous stone in his own distant country, and had immediately been seized with such a thirst for beholding it as could only be quenched in its intensest lustre. Another, so long ago as when the famous Captain Smith visited these coasts, had seen it blazing far at sea, and had felt no rest in all the intervening years till now that he took up the search. A third, being encamped on a hunting expedition full forty miles south of the White Mountains, awoke at midnight, and beheld the Great Carbuncle gleaming like a meteor, so that the shadows of the trees fell backward from it. They spoke of the innumerable attempts which had been made to reach the spot, and of the singular fatality which had hitherto withheld success from all adventurers, though it might seem so easy to follow to its source a light that overpowered the moon, and almost matched the sun. It was observable that each smiled scornfully at the madness of every other in anticipating better fortune than the past, yet nourished a scarcely hidden conviction that he would himself be the favored one. As if to allay their too sanguine hopes, they recurred to the Indian traditions that a spirit kept watch about the gem, and bewildered those who sought it either by removing it from peak to peak of the higher hills, or by calling up a mist from the enchanted lake over which it hung. But these tales were deemed unworthy of credit, all professing to believe that the search had been baffled by want of sagacity or perseverance in the adventurers, or such other causes as might naturally obstruct the passage to any given point among the intricacies of forest, valley, and mountain.

In a pause of the conversation the wearer of the prodigious spectacles looked round upon the party, making each individual, in turn, the object of the sneer which invariably dwelt upon his countenance.

"So, fellow-pilgrims," said he, "here we are, seven wise men, and one fair damsel—who, doubtless, is as wise as any graybeard of the company: here we are, I say, all bound on the same goodly enterprise. Methinks, now, it were not amiss that each of us declare what he proposes to do with the Great Carbuncle, provided he have the good hap to clutch it. What says our friend in the bear skin? How mean you, good sir, to enjoy the prize which you have been seeking, the Lord knows how long, among the Crystal Hills?"

"How enjoy it!" exclaimed the aged Seeker, bitterly. "I hope for no enjoyment from it; that folly has passed long ago! I keep up the search for this accursed stone because the vain ambition of my youth has become a fate upon me in old age. The pursuit alone is my strength,—the energy of my soul,—the warmth of my blood,—and the pith and marrow of my bones! Were I to turn my back upon it I should fall down dead on the hither side of the Notch, which is the gateway of this mountain region. Yet not to have my wasted lifetime back again would I give up my hopes of the Great Carbuncle! Having found it, I shall bear it to a certain cavern that I wot of, and there, grasping it in my arms, lie down and die, and keep it buried with me forever."

"O wretch, regardless of the interests of science!" cried Doctor Cacaphodel, with philosophic indignation. "Thou art not worthy to behold, even from afar off, the lustre of this most precious gem that ever was concocted in the laboratory of Nature. Mine is the sole purpose for which a wise man may desire the possession of the Great Carbuncle. Immediately on obtaining it—for I have a presentiment, good people, that the prize is reserved to crown my scientific reputation—I shall return to Europe, and employ my remaining years in reducing it to its first elements. A portion of the stone will I grind to impalpable powder; other parts shall be dissolved in acids, or whatever solvents will act upon so admirable a composition; and the remainder I design to melt in the crucible, or set on fire with the blow-pipe. By these various methods I shall gain an accurate analysis, and finally bestow the result of my labors upon the world in a folio volume."

"Excellent!" quoth the man with the spectacles. "Nor need you hesitate, learned sir, on account of the necessary destruction of the gem; since the perusal of your folio may teach every mother's son of us to concoct a Great Carbuncle of his own."

"But, verily," said Master Ichabod Pigsnort, "for mine own part I object to the making of these counterfeits, as being calculated to reduce the marketable value of the true gem. I tell ye frankly, sirs, I have an interest in keeping up the price. Here have I quitted my regular traffic, leaving my warehouse in the care of my clerks, and putting my credit to great hazard, and, furthermore, have put myself in peril of death or captivity by the accursed heathen savages—and all this without daring to ask the prayers of the congregation, because the quest for the Great Carbuncle is deemed little better than a traffic with the Evil One. Now think ye that I would have done this grievous wrong to my soul, body, reputation, and estate, without a reasonable chance of profit?"

"Not I, pious Master Pigsnort," said the man with the spectacles. "I never laid such a great folly to thy charge."

"Truly, I hope not," said the merchant. "Now, as touching this Great Carbuncle, I am free to own that I have never had a glimpse of it; but be it only the hundredth part so bright as people tell, it will surely outvalue the Great Mogul's best diamond, which he holds at an incalculable sum. Wherefore, I am minded to put the Great Carbuncle on shipboard, and voyage with it to England, France, Spain, Italy, or into Heathendom, if Providence should send me thither, and, in a word, dispose of the gem to the best bidder among the potentates of the earth, that he may place it among his crown jewels. If any of ye have a wiser plan, let him expound it."

"That have I, thou sordid man!" exclaimed the poet. "Dost thou desire nothing brighter than gold that thou wouldst transmute all this ethereal lustre into such dross as thou wallowest in already? For myself, hiding the jewel under my cloak, I shall hie me back to my attic chamber, in one of the darksome alleys of London. There, night and day, will I gaze upon it; my soul shall drink its radiance; it shall be diffused throughout my intellectual powers, and gleam brightly in every line of poesy that I indite. Thus, long ages after I am gone, the splendor of the Great Carbuncle will blaze around my name!"

"Well said, Master Poet!" cried he of the spectacles. "Hide it under thy cloak, sayest thou? Why, it will gleam through the holes, and make thee look like a jack-o'-lantern!"

"To think!" ejaculated the Lord de Vere, rather to himself than his companions, the best of whom he held utterly unworthy of his intercourse—"to think that a fellow in a tattered cloak should talk of conveying the Great Carbuncle to a garret in Grub Street! Have not I resolved within myself that the whole earth contains no fitter ornament for the great hall of my ancestral castle? There shall it flame for ages, making a noonday of midnight, glittering on the suits of armor, the banners, and escutcheons, that hang around the wall, and keeping bright the memory of heroes. Wherefore have all other adventurers sought the prize in vain but that I might win it, and make it a symbol of the glories of our lofty line? And never, on the diadem of the White Mountains, did the Great Carbuncle hold a place half so honored as is reserved for it in the hall of the De Veres!"

"It is a noble thought," said the Cynic, with an obsequious sneer. "Yet, might I presume to say so, the gem would make a rare sepulchral lamp, and would display the glories of your lordship's progenitors more truly in the ancestral vault than in the castle hall."

"Nay, forsooth," observed Matthew, the young rustic, who sat hand in hand with his bride, "the gentleman has bethought himself of a profitable use for this bright stone. Hannah here and I are seeking it for a like purpose."

"How, fellow!" exclaimed his lordship, in surprise. "What castle hall hast thou to hang it in?"

"No castle," replied Matthew, "but as neat a cottage as any within sight of the Crystal Hills. Ye must know, friends, that Hannah and I, being wedded the last week, have taken up the search of the Great Carbuncle, because we shall need its light in the long winter evenings; and it will be such a pretty thing to show the neighbors when they visit us. It will shine through the house so that we may pick up a pin in any corner, and will set all the windows aglowing as if there were a great fire of pine knots in the chimney. And then how pleasant, when we awake in the night, to be able to see one another's faces!"

There was a general smile among the adventurers at the simplicity of the young couple's project in regard to this wondrous and invaluable stone, with which the greatest monarch on earth might have been proud to adorn his palace. Especially the man with spectacles, who had sneered at all the company in turn, now twisted his visage into such an expression of ill-natured mirth, that Matthew asked him, rather peevishly, what he himself meant to do with the Great Carbuncle.

"The Great Carbuncle!" answered the Cynic, with ineffable scorn. "Why, you blockhead, there is no such thing in *rerum natura*. I have come three thousand miles, and am resolved to set my foot on every peak of these mountains, and poke my head into every chasm, for the sole purpose of demonstrating to the satisfaction of any man one whit less an ass than thyself that the Great Carbuncle is all a humbug!"

Vain and foolish were the motives that had brought most of the adventurers to the Crystal Hills; but none so vain, so foolish, and so impious too, as that of the scoffer with the prodigious spectacles. He was one of those wretched and evil men whose yearnings are downward to the darkness, instead of heavenward, and who, could they but extinguish the lights which God hath kindled for us, would count the midnight gloom their chiefest glory. As the Cynic spoke, several of the party were startled by a gleam of red splendor, that showed the huge shapes of the surrounding mountains and the rock-bestrewn bed of the turbulent river with an illumination unlike that of their fire on the trunks and black boughs of the forest trees. They listened for the roll of thunder, but heard nothing, and were glad that the tempest came not near them. The stars, those dial points of heaven, now warned the adventurers to close their eyes on the blazing logs, and open them, in dreams, to the glow of the Great Carbuncle.

The young married couple had taken their lodgings in the farthest corner of the wigwam, and were separated from the rest of the party by a curtain of curiously-woven twigs, such as might have hung, in deep festoons, around the bridal-bower of Eve. The modest little wife had wrought this piece of tapestry while the other guests were talking. She and her husband fell asleep with hands tenderly clasped, and awoke from visions of unearthly radiance to meet the more blessed light of one another's eyes. They awoke at the same instant, and with one happy smile beaming over their two faces, which grew brighter with their consciousness of the reality of life and love. But no sooner did she recollect where they were, than the bride peeped through the interstices of the leafy curtain, and saw that the outer room of the hut was deserted.

"Up, dear Matthew!" cried she, in haste. "The strange folk are all gone! Up, this very minute, or we shall lose the Great Carbuncle!"

In truth, so little did these poor young people deserve the mighty prize which had lured them thither, that they had slept peacefully all night, and till the summits of the hills were glittering with sunshine; while the other adventurers had tossed their limbs in feverish wakefulness, or dreamed of climbing precipices, and set off to realize their dreams with the earliest peep of dawn. But Matthew and Hannah, after their calm rest, were as light as two young deer, and merely stopped to say their prayers and wash themselves in a cold pool of the Amonoosuck, and then to taste a morsel of food, ere they turned their faces to the mountain-side. It was a sweet emblem of conjugal affection, as they toiled up the difficult ascent, gathering strength from the mutual aid which they afforded. After several little accidents, such as a torn robe, a lost shoe, and the entanglement of Hannah's hair in a bough, they reached the upper verge of the forest, and were now to pursue a more adventurous course. The innumerable trunks and heavy foliage of the trees had hitherto shut in their thoughts, which now shrank affrighted from the region of wind and cloud and naked rocks and desolate sunshine, that rose immeasurably above them. They gazed back at the obscure wilderness which they had traversed, and longed to be buried again in its depths rather than trust themselves to so vast and visible a solitude.

"Shall we go on?" said Matthew, throwing his arm round Hannah's waist, both to protect her and to comfort his heart by drawing her close to it.

But the little bride, simple as she was, had a woman's love of jewels, and could not forego the hope of possessing the very brightest in the world, in spite of the perils with which it must be won.

"Let us climb a little higher," whispered she, yet tremulously, as she turned her face upward to the lonely sky.

"Come, then," said Matthew, mustering his manly courage and drawing her along with him, for she became timid again the moment that he grew bold.

And upward, accordingly, went the pilgrims of the Great Carbuncle, now treading upon the tops and thickly-interwoven branches of dwarf pines, which, by the growth of centuries, though mossy with age, had barely reached three feet in altitude. Next, they came to masses and fragments of naked rock heaped confusedly together, like a cairn reared by giants in memory of a giant chief. In this bleak realm of upper air nothing breathed, nothing grew; there was no life but what was concentrated in their two hearts, they had climbed so high that Nature herself seemed no longer to keep them company. She lingered beneath them, within the verge of the forest trees, and sent a farewell glance after her children as they strayed where her own green footprints had never been. But soon they were to be hidden from her eye. Densely and dark the mists began to gather below, casting black spots of shadow on the vast landscape, and sailing heavily to one centre, as if the loftiest mountain peak had summoned a council of its kindred clouds. Finally, the vapors welded themselves, as it were, into a mass, presenting the appearance of a pavement over which the wanderers might have trodden, but where they would vainly have sought an avenue to the blessed earth which they had lost. And the lovers yearned to behold that green earth again, more intensely, alas! than, beneath a clouded sky, they had ever desired a glimpse of heaven. They even felt it a relief to their desolation when the mists, creeping gradually up the mountain, concealed its lonely peak, and thus annihilated, at least for them, the whole region of visible space. But they drew closer together, with a fond and melancholy gaze, dreading lest the universal cloud should snatch them from each other's sight.

Still, perhaps, they would have been resolute to climb as far and as high, between earth and heaven, as they could find foothold, if Hannah's strength had not begun to fail, and with that, her courage also. Her breath grew short. She refused to burden her husband with her weight, but often tottered against his side, and recovered herself each time by a feebler effort. At last, she sank down on one of the rocky steps of the acclivity.

"We are lost, dear Matthew," said she, mournfully. "We shall never find our way to the earth again. And oh how happy we might have been in our cottage!"

"Dear heart!—we will yet be happy there," answered Matthew. "Look! In this direction, the sunshine penetrates the dismal mist. By its aid, I can direct our course to the passage of the Notch. Let us go back, love, and dream no more of the Great Carbuncle!"

"The sun cannot be yonder," said Hannah, with despondence. "By this time it must be noon. If there could ever be any sunshine here, it would come from above our heads."

"But look!" repeated Matthew, in a somewhat altered tone. "It is brightening every moment. If not sunshine, what can it be?"

Nor could the young bride any longer deny that a radiance was breaking through the mist, and changing its dim hue to a dusky red, which continually grew more vivid, as if brilliant particles were interfused with the gloom. Now, also, the cloud began to roll away from the mountain, while, as it heavily withdrew, one object after another started out of its impenetrable obscurity into sight, with precisely the effect of a new creation, before the indistinctness of the old chaos had been completely swallowed up. As the process went on, they saw the gleaming of water close at their feet, and found themselves on the very border of a mountain lake, deep, bright, clear, and calmly beautiful, spreading from brim to brim of a basin that had been scooped out of the solid rock. A ray of glory flashed across its surface. The pilgrims looked whence it should proceed, but closed their eyes with a thrill of awful admiration, to exclude the fervid splendor that glowed from the brow of a cliff impending over the enchanted lake. For the simple pair had reached that lake of mystery, and found the long-sought shrine of the Great Carbuncle!

They threw their arms around each other, and trembled at their own success; for, as the legends of this wondrous gem rushed thick upon their memory, they felt themselves marked out by fate—and the consciousness was fearful. Often, from childhood upward, they had seen it shining like a distant star. And now that star was throwing its intensest lustre on their hearts. They seemed changed to one another's eyes, in the red brilliancy that flamed upon their cheeks, while it lent the same fire to the lake, the rocks, and sky, and to the mists which had rolled back before its power. But, with their next glance, they beheld an object that drew their attention even from the mighty stone. At the base of the cliff, directly beneath the Great Carbuncle, appeared the figure of a man, with his arms extended in the act of climbing, and his face turned upward, as if to drink the full gush of splendor. But he stirred not, no more than if changed to marble.

"It is the Seeker," whispered Hannah, convulsively grasping her husband's arm. "Matthew, he is dead."

"The joy of success has killed him," replied Matthew, trembling violently. "Or, perhaps, the very light of the Great Carbuncle was death!"

"The Great Carbuncle," cried a peevish voice behind them. "The Great Humbug! If you have found it, prithee point it out to me."

They turned their heads, and there was the Cynic, with his prodigious spectacles set carefully on his nose, staring now at the lake, now at the rocks, now at the distant masses of vapor, now right at the Great Carbuncle itself, yet seemingly as unconscious of its light as if all the scattered clouds were condensed about his person. Though its radiance actually threw the shadow of the unbeliever at his own feet, as he turned his back upon the glorious jewel, he would not be convinced that there was the least glimmer there.

"Where is your Great Humbug?" he repeated. "I challenge you to make me see it!"

"There," said Matthew, incensed at such perverse blindness, and turning the Cynic round towards the illuminated cliff. "Take off those abominable spectacles, and you cannot help seeing it!"

Now these colored spectacles probably darkened the Cynic's sight, in at least as great a degree as the smoked glasses through which people gaze at an eclipse. With resolute bravado, however, he snatched them from his nose, and fixed a bold stare full upon the ruddy blaze of the Great Carbuncle. But scarcely had he encountered it, when, with a deep, shuddering groan, he dropped his head, and pressed both hands across his miserable eyes. Thenceforth there was, in very truth, no light of the Great Carbuncle, nor any other light on earth, nor light of heaven itself, for the poor Cynic. So long accustomed to view all objects through a medium that deprived them of every glimpse of brightness, a single flash of so glorious a phenomenon, striking upon his naked vision, had blinded him forever.

"Matthew," said Hannah, clinging to him, "let us go hence!"

Matthew saw that she was faint, and kneeling down, supported her in his arms, while he threw some of the thrillingly cold water of the enchanted lake upon her face and bosom. It revived her, but could not renovate her courage.

"Yes, dearest!" cried Matthew, pressing her tremulous form to his breast, —"we will go hence, and return to our humble cottage. The blessed sunshine and the quiet moonlight shall come through our window. We will kindle the cheerful glow of our hearth, at eventide, and be happy in its light. But never again will we desire more light than all the world may share with us."

"No," said his bride, "for how could we live by day, or sleep by night, in this awful blaze of the Great Carbuncle!"

Out of the hollow of their hands, they drank each a draught from the lake, which presented them its waters uncontaminated by an earthly lip. Then, lending their guidance to the blinded Cynic, who uttered not a word, and even stifled his groans in his own most wretched heart, they began to descend the mountain. Yet, as they left the shore, till then untrodden, of the spirit's lake, they threw a farewell glance towards the cliff, and beheld the vapors gathering in dense volumes, through which the gem burned duskily.

As touching the other pilgrims of the Great Carbuncle, the legend goes on to tell, that the worshipful Master Ichabod Pigsnort soon gave up the quest as a desperate speculation, and wisely resolved to betake himself again to his warehouse, near the town dock, in Boston. But, as he passed through the

Notch of the mountains, a war party of Indians captured our unlucky merchant, and carried him to Montreal, there holding him in bondage, till, by the payment of a heavy ransom, he had wofully subtracted from his hoard of pine-tree shillings. By his long absence, moreover, his affairs had become so disordered that, for the rest of his life, instead of wallowing in silver, he had seldom a sixpence worth of copper. Doctor Cacaphodel, the alchemist, returned to his laboratory with a prodigious fragment of granite, which he ground to powder, dissolved in acids, melted in the crucible, and burned with the blow-pipe, and published the result of his experiments in one of the heaviest folios of the day. And, for all these purposes, the gem itself could not have answered better than the granite. The poet, by a somewhat similar mistake, made prize of a great piece of ice, which he found in a sunless chasm of the mountains, and swore that it corresponded, in all points, with his idea of the Great Carbuncle. The critics say, that, if his poetry lacked the splendor of the gem, it retained all the coldness of the ice. The Lord de Vere went back to his ancestral hall, where he contented himself with a wax-lighted chandelier, and filled, in due course of time, another coffin in the ancestral vault. As the funeral torches gleamed within that dark receptacle, there was no need of the Great Carbuncle to show the vanity of earthly pomp.

The Cynic, having cast aside his spectacles, wandered about the world, a miserable object, and was punished with an agonizing desire of light, for the wilful blindness of his former life. The whole night long, he would lift his splendor-blasted orbs to the moon and stars; he turned his face eastward, at sunrise, as duly as a Persian idolater; he made a pilgrimage to Rome, to witness the magnificent illumination of St. Peter's Church; and finally perished in the great fire of London, into the midst of which he had thrust himself, with the desperate idea of catching one feeble ray from the blaze that was kindling earth and heaven.

Matthew and his bride spent many peaceful years, and were fond of telling the legend of the Great Carbuncle. The tale, however, towards the close of their lengthened lives, did not meet with the full credence that had been accorded to it by those who remembered the ancient lustre of the gem. For it is affirmed that, from the hour when two mortals had shown themselves so simply wise as to reject a jewel which would have dimmed all earthly things, its splendor waned. When other pilgrims reached the cliff, they found only an opaque stone, with particles of mica glittering on its surface. There is also a tradition that, as the youthful pair departed, the gem was loosened from the forehead of the cliff, and fell into the enchanted lake, and that, at noontide, the Seeker's form may still be seen to bend over its quenchless gleam.

Some few believe that this inestimable stone is blazing as of old, and say that they have caught its radiance, like a flash of summer lightning, far down the valley of the Saco. And be it owned that, many a mile from the Crystal Hills, I saw a wondrous light around their summits, and was lured, by the faith of poesy, to be the latest pilgrim of the GREAT CARBUNCLE.

THE PROPHETIC PICTURES[1]

"But this painter!" cried Walter Ludlow, with animation. "He not only excels in his peculiar art, but possesses vast acquirements in all other learning and science. He talks Hebrew with Dr. Mather, and gives lectures in anatomy to Dr. Boylston. In a word, he will meet the best instructed man among us on his own ground. Moreover, he is a polished gentleman—a citizen of the world—yes, a true cosmopolite; for he will speak like a native of each clime and country of the globe except our own forests, whither he is now going. Nor is all this what I most admire in him."

"Indeed!" said Elinor, who had listened with a woman's interest to the description of such a man. "Yet this is admirable enough."

"Surely it is," replied her lover, "but far less so than his natural gift of adapting himself to every variety of character, insomuch that all men—and all women too, Elinor—shall find a mirror of themselves in this wonderful painter. But the greatest wonder is yet to be told."

"Nay, if he have more wonderful attributes than these," said Elinor, laughing, "Boston is a perilous abode for the poor gentleman. Are you telling me of a painter or a wizard?"

"In truth," answered he, "that question might be asked much more seriously than you suppose. They say that he paints not merely a man's features, but his mind and heart. He catches the secret sentiments and passions, and throws them upon the canvas, like sunshine—or perhaps, in the portraits of dark-souled men, like a gleam of infernal fire. It is an awful gift," added Walter, lowering his voice from its tone of enthusiasm. "I shall be almost afraid to sit to him."

"Walter, are you in earnest?" exclaimed Elinor.

"For Heaven's sake, dearest Elinor, do not let him paint the look which you now wear," said her lover, smiling, though rather perplexed. "There: it is passing away now, but when you spoke you seemed frightened to death, and very sad besides. What were you thinking of?"

"Nothing, nothing," answered Elinor hastily. "You paint my face with your own fantasies. Well, come for me to-morrow, and we will visit this wonderful artist."

But when the young man had departed, it cannot be denied that a remarkable expression was again visible on the fair and youthful face of his mistress. It was a sad and anxious look, little in accordance with what should have been the feelings of a maiden on the eve of wedlock. Yet Walter Ludlow was the chosen of her heart.

"A look!" said Elinor to herself. "No wonder that it startled him, if it expressed what I sometimes feel. I know, by my own experience, how frightful

[1]This story was suggested by an anecdote of Stuart, related in Dunlap's *History of the Arts of Design*,—a most entertaining book to the general reader, and a deeply interesting one, we should think, to the artist.

a look may be. But it was all fancy. I thought nothing of it at the time—I have seen nothing of it since—I did but dream it."

And she busied herself about the embroidery of a ruff, in which she meant that her portrait should be taken.

The painter, of whom they had been speaking, was not one of those native artists who, at a later period than this, borrowed their colors from the Indians, and manufactured their pencils of the furs of wild beasts. Perhaps, if he could have revoked his life and prearranged his destiny, he might have chosen to belong to that school without a master, in the hope of being at least original, since there were no works of art to imitate nor rules to follow. But he had been born and educated in Europe. People said that he had studied the grandeur or beauty of conception, and every touch of the master hand, in all the most famous pictures, in cabinets and galleries, and on the walls of churches, till there was nothing more for his powerful mind to learn. Art could add nothing to its lessons, but Nature might. He had therefore visited a world whither none of his professional brethren had preceded him, to feast his eyes on visible images that were noble and picturesque, yet had never been transferred to canvas. America was too poor to afford other temptations to an artist of eminence, though many of the colonial gentry, on the painter's arrival, had expressed a wish to transmit their lineaments to posterity by means of his skill. Whenever such proposals were made, he fixed his piercing eyes on the applicant, and seemed to look him through and through. If he beheld only a sleek and comfortable visage, though there were a gold-laced coat to adorn the picture and golden guineas to pay for it, he civilly rejected the task and the reward. But if the face were the index of any thing uncommon, in thought, sentiment, or experience; or if he met a beggar in the street, with a white beard and a furrowed brow; or if sometimes a child happened to look up and smile, he would exhaust all the art on them that he denied to wealth.

Pictorial skill being so rare in the colonies, the painter became an object of general curiosity. If few or none could appreciate the technical merit of his productions, yet there were points, in regard to which the opinion of the crowd was as valuable as the refined judgment of the amateur. He watched the effect that each picture produced on such untutored beholders, and derived profit from their remarks, while they would as soon have thought of instructing Nature herself as him who seemed to rival her. Their admiration, it must be owned, was tinctured with the prejudices of the age and country. Some deemed it an offence against the Mosaic law, and even a presumptuous mockery of the Creator, to bring into existence such lively images of his creatures. Others, frightened at the art which could raise phantoms at will, and keep the form of the dead among the living, were inclined to consider the painter as a magician, or perhaps the famous Black Man, of old witch times, plotting mischief in a new guise. These foolish fancies were more than half believed among the mob. Even in superior circles his character was invested with a vague awe, partly rising like smoke wreaths from the popular superstitions, but chiefly caused by the varied knowledge and talents which he made subservient to his profession.

Being on the eve of marriage, Walter Ludlow and Elinor were eager to obtain their portraits, as the first of what, they doubtless hoped, would be a long series of family pictures. The day after the conversation above recorded they visited the painter's rooms. A servant ushered them into an apartment, where, though the artist himself was not visible, there were personages whom they could hardly forbear greeting with reverence. They knew, indeed, that the whole assembly were but pictures, yet felt it impossible to separate the idea of life and intellect from such striking counterfeits. Several of the portraits were known to them, either as distinguished characters of the day or their private acquaintances. There was Governor Burnett, looking as if he had just received an undutiful communication from the House of Representatives, and were inditing a most sharp response. Mr. Cooke hung beside the ruler whom he opposed, sturdy, and somewhat puritanical, as befitted a popular leader. The ancient lady of Sir William Phipps eyed them from the wall, in ruff and farthingale,—an imperious old dame, not unsuspected of witchcraft. John Winslow, then a very young man, wore the expression of warlike enterprise, which long afterwards made him a distinguished general. Their personal friends were recognized at a glance. In most of the pictures, the whole mind and character were brought out on the countenance, and concentrated into a single look, so that, to speak paradoxically, the originals hardly resembled themselves so strikingly as the portraits did.

Among these modern worthies there were two old bearded Saints, who had almost vanished into the darkening canvas. There was also a pale, but unfaded Madonna, who had perhaps been worshipped in Rome, and now regarded the lovers with such a mild and holy look that they longed to worship too.

"How singular a thought," observed Walter Ludlow, "that this beautiful face has been beautiful for above two hundred years! Oh, if all beauty would endure so well! Do you not envy her, Elinor?"

"If earth were heaven, I might," she replied. "But where all things fade, how miserable to be the one that could not fade!"

"This dark old St. Peter has a fierce and ugly scowl, saint though he be," continued Walter. "He troubles me. But the Virgin looks kindly at us."

"Yes; but very sorrowfully, methinks," said Elinor.

The easel stood beneath these three old pictures, sustaining one that had been recently commenced. After a little inspection, they began to recognize the features of their own minister, the Rev. Dr. Colman, growing into shape and life, as it were, out of a cloud.

"Kind old man!" exclaimed Elinor. "He gazes at me as if he were about to utter a word of paternal advice."

"And at me," said Walter, "as if he were about to shake his head and rebuke me for some suspected iniquity. But so does the original. I shall never feel quite comfortable under his eye till we stand before him to be married."

They now heard a footstep on the floor, and turning, beheld the painter, who had been some moments in the room, and had listened to a few of their remarks. He was a middle-aged man, with a countenance well worthy of his own pencil. Indeed, by the picturesque, though careless arrangement of his rich dress, and, perhaps, because his soul dwelt always among painted shapes, he looked somewhat like a portrait himself. His visitors were sensible of a kindred between the artist and his works, and felt as if one of the pictures had stepped from the canvas to salute them.

Walter Ludlow, who was slightly known to the painter, explained the object of their visit. While he spoke, a sunbeam was falling athwart his figure and Elinor's, with so happy an effect that they also seemed living pictures of youth and beauty, gladdened by bright fortune. The artist was evidently struck.

"My easel is occupied for several ensuing days, and my stay in Boston must be brief," said he, thoughtfully; then, after an observant glance, he added: "but your wishes shall be gratified, though I disappoint the Chief Justice and Madam Oliver. I must not lose this opportunity, for the sake of painting a few ells of broadcloth and brocade."

The painter expressed a desire to introduce both their portraits into one picture, and represent them engaged in some appropriate action. This plan would have delighted the lovers, but was necessarily rejected, because so large a space of canvas would have been unfit for the room which it was intended to decorate. Two half-length portraits were therefore fixed upon. After they had taken leave, Walter Ludlow asked Elinor, with a smile, whether she knew what an influence over their fates the painter was about to acquire.

"The old women of Boston affirm," continued he, "that after he has once got possession of a person's face and figure, he may paint him in any act or situation whatever—and the picture will be prophetic. Do you believe it?"

"Not quite," said Elinor, smiling. "Yet if he has such magic, there is something so gentle in his manner that I am sure he will use it well."

It was the painter's choice to proceed with both the portraits at the same time, assigning as a reason, in the mystical language which he sometimes used, that the faces threw light upon each other. Accordingly he gave now a touch to Walter, and now to Elinor, and the features of one and the other began to start forth so vividly that it appeared as if his triumphant art would actually disengage them from the canvas. Amid the rich light and deep shade, they beheld their phantom selves. But, though the likeness promised to be perfect, they were not quite satisfied with the expression; it seemed more vague than in most of the painter's works. He, however, was satisfied with the prospect of success, and being much interested in the lovers, employed his leisure moments, unknown to them, in making a crayon sketch of their two figures. During their sittings, he engaged them in conversation, and kindled up their faces with characteristic traits, which, though continually varying, it was his purpose to combine and fix. At length he announced that at their next visit both the portraits would be ready for delivery.

"If my pencil will but be true to my conception, in the few last touches which I meditate," observed he, "these two pictures will be my very best performances. Seldom, indeed, has an artist such subjects."

While speaking, he still bent his penetrative eye upon them, nor withdrew it till they had reached the bottom of the stairs.

Nothing, in the whole circle of human vanities, takes stronger hold of the imagination than this affair of having a portrait painted. Yet why should it be so? The looking-glass, the polished globes of the andirons, the mirror-like water, and all other reflecting surfaces, continually present us with portraits, or rather ghosts, of ourselves, which we glance at, and straightway forget them. But we forget them only because they vanish. It is the idea of duration—of earthly immortality—that gives such a mysterious interest to our own portraits. Walter and Elinor were not insensible to this feeling, and hastened to the painter's room, punctually at the appointed hour, to meet those pictured shapes which were to be their representatives with posterity. The sunshine flashed after them into the apartment, but left it somewhat gloomy as they closed the door.

Their eyes were immediately attracted to their portraits, which rested against the farthest wall of the room. At the first glance, through the dim light and the distance, seeing themselves in precisely their natural attitudes, and with all the air that they recognized so well, they uttered a simultaneous exclamation of delight.

"There we stand," cried Walter, enthusiastically, "fixed in sunshine forever! No dark passions can gather on our faces!"

"No," said Elinor, more calmly; "no dreary change can sadden us."

This was said while they were approaching, and had yet gained only an imperfect view of the pictures. The painter, after saluting them, busied himself at a table in completing a crayon sketch, leaving his visitors to form their own judgment as to his perfected labors. At intervals, he sent a glance from beneath his deep eyebrows, watching their countenances in profile, with his pencil suspended over the sketch. They had now stood some moments, each in front of the other's picture, contemplating it with entranced attention, but without uttering a word. At length, Walter stepped forward—then back—viewing Elinor's portrait in various lights, and finally spoke.

"Is there not a change?" said he, in a doubtful and meditative tone. "Yes; the perception of it grows more vivid the longer I look. It is certainly the same picture that I saw yesterday; the dress—the features—all are the same; and yet something is altered."

"Is then the picture less like than it was yesterday?" inquired the painter, now drawing near, with irrepressible interest.

"The features are perfect, Elinor," answered Walter, "and, at the first glance, the expression seemed also hers. But, I could fancy that the portrait has changed countenance, while I have been looking at it. The eyes are fixed on mine with a strangely sad and anxious expression. Nay, it is grief and terror! Is this like Elinor?"

"Compare the living face with the pictured one," said the painter.

Walter glanced sidelong at his mistress, and started. Motionless and absorbed—fascinated, as it were—in contemplation of Walter's portrait, Elinor's face had assumed precisely the expression of which he had just been complaining. Had she practised for whole hours before a mirror, she could not have caught the look so successfully. Had the picture itself been a mirror, it could not have thrown back her present aspect with stronger and more melancholy truth. She appeared quite unconscious of the dialogue between the artist and her lover.

"Elinor," exclaimed Walter, in amazement, "what change has come over you?"

She did not hear him, nor desist from her fixed gaze, till he seized her hand, and thus attracted her notice; then, with a sudden tremor, she looked from the picture to the face of the original.

"Do you see no change in your portrait?" asked she.

"In mine?—None!" replied Walter, examining it. "But let me see! Yes; there is a slight change—an improvement, I think, in the picture, though none in the likeness. It has a livelier expression than yesterday, as if some bright thought were flashing from the eyes, and about to be uttered from the lips. Now that I have caught the look, it becomes very decided."

While he was intent on these observations, Elinor turned to the painter. She regarded him with grief and awe, and felt that he repaid her with sympathy and commiseration, though wherefore, she could but vaguely guess.

"That look!" whispered she, and shuddered. "How came it there?"

"Madam," said the painter, sadly, taking her hand, and leading her apart, "in both these pictures, I have painted what I saw. The artist—the true artist—must look beneath the exterior. It is his gift—his proudest, but often a melancholy one—to see the inmost soul, and, by a power indefinable even to himself, to make it glow or darken upon the canvas, in glances that express the thought and sentiment of years. Would that I might convince myself of error in the present instance!"

They had now approached the table, on which were heads in chalk, hands almost as expressive as ordinary faces, ivied church towers, thatched cottages, old thunder-stricken trees, Oriental and antique costume, and all such picturesque vagaries of an artist's idle moments. Turning them over, with seeming carelessness, a crayon sketch of two figures was disclosed.

"If I have failed," continued he—"if your heart does not see itself reflected in your own portrait—if you have no secret cause to trust my delineation of the other—it is not yet too late to alter them. I might change the action of these figures too. But would it influence the event?"

He directed her notice to the sketch. A thrill ran through Elinor's frame; a shriek was upon her lips; but she stifled it, with the self-command that becomes habitual to all who hide thoughts of fear and anguish within their bosoms. Turning from the table, she perceived that Walter had advanced near enough to have seen the sketch, though she could not determine whether it had caught his eye.

"We will not have the pictures altered," said she, hastily. "If mine is sad, I shall but look the gayer for the contrast."

"Be it so," answered the painter, bowing. "May your griefs be such fanciful ones that only your picture may mourn for them! For your joys—may they be true and deep, and paint themselves upon this lovely face till it quite belie my art!"

After the marriage of Walter and Elinor, the pictures formed the two most splendid ornaments of their abode. They hung side by side, separated by a narrow panel, appearing to eye each other constantly, yet always returning the gaze of the spectator. Travelled gentlemen, who professed a knowledge of such subjects, reckoned these among the most admirable specimens of modern portraiture; while common observers compared them with the originals, feature by feature, and were rapturous in praise of the likeness. But it was on a third class—neither travelled connoisseurs nor common observers, but people of natural sensibility—that the pictures wrought their strongest effect. Such persons might gaze carelessly at first, but, becoming interested, would return day after day, and study these painted faces like the pages of a mystic volume. Walter Ludlow's portrait attracted their earliest notice. In the absence of himself and his bride, they sometimes disputed as to the expression which the painter had intended to throw upon the features; all agreeing that there was a look of earnest import, though no two explained it alike. There was less diversity of opinion in regard to Elinor's picture. They differed, indeed, in their attempts to estimate the nature and depth of the gloom that dwelt upon her face, but agreed that it was gloom, and alien from the natural temperament of their youthful friend. A certain fanciful person announced, as the result of much scrutiny, that both these pictures were parts of one design, and that the melancholy strength of feeling, in Elinor's countenance, bore reference to the more vivid emotion, or, as he termed it, the wild passion, in that of Walter. Though unskilled in the art, he even began a sketch, in which the action of the two figures was to correspond with their mutual expression.

It was whispered among friends that, day by day, Elinor's face was assuming a deeper shade of pensiveness, which threatened soon to render her too true a counterpart of her melancholy picture. Walter, on the other hand, instead of acquiring the vivid look which the painter had given him on the canvas, became reserved and downcast, with no outward flashes of emotion, however it might be smouldering within. In course of time, Elinor hung a gorgeous curtain of purple silk, wrought with flowers and fringed with heavy golden tassels, before the pictures, under pretence that the dust would tarnish their hues, or the light dim them. It was enough. Her visitors felt, that the massive folds of the silk must never be withdrawn, nor the portraits mentioned in her presence.

Time wore on; and the painter came again. He had been far enough to the north to see the silver cascade of the Crystal Hills, and to look over the vast round of cloud and forest from the summit of New England's loftiest mountain. But he did not profane that scene by the mockery of his art. He had also lain in a canoe on the bosom of Lake George, making his soul the mirror of its loveliness and grandeur, till not a picture in the Vatican was more vivid than his recollection. He had gone with the Indian hunters to Niagara, and there, again, had flung his hopeless pencil down the precipice, feeling that he could as soon paint the roar, as aught else that goes to make up the wondrous cataract. In truth, it was seldom his impulse to copy natural scenery, except as a framework for the delineations of the human form and face, instinct with thought, passion, or suffering. With store of such his adventurous ramble had enriched him: the stern dignity of Indian chiefs; the dusky loveliness of Indian girls; the domestic life of wigwams; the stealthy march; the battle beneath gloomy pine-trees; the frontier fortress with its garrison; the anomaly of the old French partisan, bred in courts, but grown gray in shaggy deserts; such were the scenes and portraits that he had sketched. The glow of perilous moments; flashes of wild feeling; struggles of fierce power,—love, hate, grief, frenzy; in a word, all the worn-out heart of the old earth had been revealed to him under a new form. His portfolio was filled with graphic illustrations of the volume of his memory, which genius would transmute into its own substance, and imbue with immortality. He felt that the deep wisdom in his art, which he had sought so far, was found.

But amid stern or lovely nature, in the perils of the forest or its overwhelming peacefulness, still there had been two phantoms, the companions of his way. Like all other men around whom an engrossing purpose wreathes itself, he was insulated from the mass of human kind. He had no aim—no pleasure—no sympathies—but what were ultimately connected with his art.

Though gentle in manner and upright in intent and action, he did not possess kindly feelings; his heart was cold; no living creature could be brought near enough to keep him warm. For these two beings, however, he had felt, in its greatest intensity, the sort of interest which always allied him to the subjects of his pencil. He had pried into their souls with his keenest insight, and pictured the result upon their features with his utmost skill, so as barely to fall short of that standard which no genius ever reached, his own severe conception. He had caught from the duskiness of the future—at least, so he fancied—a fearful secret, and had obscurely revealed it on the portraits. So much of himself—of his imagination and all other powers—had been lavished on the study of Walter and Elinor, that he almost regarded them as creations of his own, like the thousands with which he had peopled the realms of Picture. Therefore did they flit through the twilight of the woods, hover on the mist of waterfalls, look forth from the mirror of the lake, nor melt away in the noontide sun. They haunted his pictorial fancy, not as mockeries of life, nor pale goblins of the dead, but in the guise of portraits, each with the unalterable expression which his magic had evoked from the caverns of the soul. He could not recross the Atlantic till he had again beheld the originals of those airy pictures.

"O glorious Art!" thus mused the enthusiastic painter as he trod the street, "thou art the image of the Creator's own. The innumerable forms, that wander in nothingness, start into being at thy beck. The dead live again. Thou recallest them to their old scenes, and givest their gray shadows the lustre of a better life, at once earthly and immortal. Thou snatchest back the fleeting moments of History. With thee there is no Past, for, at thy touch, all that is great becomes forever present; and illustrious men live through long ages, in the visible performance of the very deeds which made them what they are. O potent Art! as thou bringest the faintly revealed Past to stand in that narrow strip of sunlight, which we call Now, canst thou summon the shrouded Future to meet her there? Have I not achieved it? Am I not thy Prophet?"

Thus, with a proud, yet melancholy fervor, did he almost cry aloud, as he passed through the toilsome street, among people that knew not of his reveries, nor could understand nor care for them. It is not good for man to cherish a solitary ambition. Unless there be those around him by whose example he may regulate himself, his thoughts, desires, and hopes will become extravagant, and he the semblance, perhaps the reality, of a madman. Reading other bosoms with an acuteness almost preternatural, the painter failed to see the disorder of his own.

"And this should be the house," said he, looking up and down the front, before he knocked. "Heaven help my brains! That picture! Methinks it will never vanish. Whether I look at the windows or the door, there it is framed within them, painted strongly, and glowing in the richest tints—the faces of the portraits—the figures and action of the sketch!"

He knocked.

"The Portraits! Are they within?" inquired he of the domestic; then recollecting himself—"your master and mistress! Are they at home?"

"They are, sir," said the servant, adding, as he noticed that picturesque aspect of which the painter could never divest himself, "and the Portraits too!"

The guest was admitted into a parlor, communicating by a central door with an interior room of the same size. As the first apartment was empty, he passed to the entrance of the second, within which his eyes were greeted by those living personages, as well as their pictured representatives, who had long been the objects of so singular an interest. He involuntarily paused on the threshold.

They had not perceived his approach. Walter and Elinor were standing before the portraits, whence the former had just flung back the rich and voluminous folds of the silken curtain, holding its golden tassel with one hand, while the other grasped that of his bride. The pictures, concealed for months, gleamed forth again in undiminished splendor, appearing to throw a sombre light across the room, rather than to be disclosed by a borrowed radiance. That of Elinor had been almost prophetic. A pensiveness, and next a gentle sorrow, had successively dwelt upon her countenance, deepening, with the lapse of time, into a quiet anguish. A mixture of affright would now have made it the very expression of the portrait. Walter's face was moody and dull, or animated only by fitful flashes, which left a heavier darkness for their momentary illumination. He looked from Elinor to her portrait, and thence to his own, in the contemplation of which he finally stood absorbed.

The painter seemed to hear the step of Destiny approaching behind him, on its progress towards its victims. A strange thought darted into his mind. Was not his own the form in which that destiny had embodied itself, and he a chief agent of the coming evil which he had foreshadowed?

Still, Walter remained silent before the picture, communing with it as with his own heart, and abandoning himself to the spell of evil influence that the painter had cast upon the features. Gradually his eyes kindled; while as Elinor watched the increasing wildness of his face, her own assumed a look of terror; and when at last he turned upon her, the resemblance of both to their portraits was complete.

"Our fate is upon us!" howled Walter. "Die!"

Drawing a knife, he sustained her, as she was sinking to the ground, and aimed it at her bosom. In the action, and in the look and attitude of each, the painter beheld the figures of his sketch. The picture, with all its tremendous coloring, was finished.

"Hold, madman!" cried he, sternly.

He had advanced from the door, and interposed himself between the wretched beings, with the same sense of power to regulate their destiny as to alter a scene upon the canvas. He stood like a magician, controlling the phantoms which he had evoked.

"What!" muttered Walter Ludlow, as he relapsed from fierce excitement into silent gloom. "Does Fate impede its own decree?"

"Wretched lady!" said the painter, "did I not warn you?"

"You did," replied Elinor, calmly, as her terror gave place to the quiet grief which it had disturbed. "But—I loved him!"

Is there not a deep moral in the tale? Could the result of one, or all our deeds, be shadowed forth and set before us, some would call it Fate, and hurry onward, others be swept along by their passionate desires, and none be turned aside by the PROPHETIC PICTURES.

DAVID SWAN

A FANTASY

We can be but partially acquainted even with the events which actually influence our course through life, and our final destiny. There are innumerable other events—if such they may be called—which come close upon us, yet pass away without actual results, or even betraying their near approach, by the reflection of any light or shadow across our minds. Could we know all the vicissitudes of our fortunes, life would be too full of hope and fear, exultation or disappointment, to afford us a single hour of true serenity. This idea may be illustrated by a page from the secret history of David Swan.

We have nothing to do with David until we find him, at the age of twenty, on the high road from his native place to the city of Boston, where his uncle, a small dealer in the grocery line, was to take him behind the counter. Be it enough to say that he was a native of New Hampshire, born of respectable parents, and had received an ordinary school education, with a classic finish by a year at Gilmanton Academy. After journeying on foot from sunrise till nearly noon of a summer's day, his weariness and the increasing heat determined him to sit down in the first convenient shade, and await the coming up of the stage-coach. As if planted on purpose for him, there soon appeared a little tuft of maples, with a delightful recess in the midst, and such a fresh bubbling spring that it seemed never to have sparkled for any wayfarer but David Swan. Virgin or not, he kissed it with his thirsty lips, and then flung himself along the brink, pillowing his head upon some shirts and a pair of pantaloons, tied up in a striped cotton handkerchief. The sunbeams could not reach him; the dust did not yet rise from the road after the heavy rain of yesterday; and his grassy lair suited the young man better than a bed of down. The spring murmured drowsily beside him; the branches waved dreamily across the blue sky overhead; and a deep sleep, perchance hiding dreams within its depths, fell upon David Swan. But we are to relate events which he did not dream of.

While he lay sound asleep in the shade, other people were wide awake, and passed to and fro, afoot, on horseback, and in all sorts of vehicles, along the sunny road by his bedchamber. Some looked neither to the right hand nor the left, and knew not that he was there; some merely glanced that way, without admitting the slumberer among their busy thoughts; some laughed to see how soundly he slept; and several, whose hearts were brimming full of scorn, ejected their venomous superfluity on David Swan. A middle-aged widow, when nobody else was near, thrust her head a little way into the recess, and vowed that the young fellow looked charming in his sleep. A temperance lecturer saw him, and wrought poor David into the texture of his evening's discourse, as an awful instance of dead drunkenness by the roadside. But censure, praise, merriment, scorn, and indifference were all one, or rather all nothing, to David Swan.

He had slept only a few moments when a brown carriage, drawn by a handsome pair of horses, bowled easily along, and was brought to a stand-still nearly in front of David's resting-place. A linchpin had fallen out, and permitted one of the wheels to slide off. The damage was slight, and occasioned merely a momentary alarm to an elderly merchant and his wife, who were returning to Boston in the carriage. While the coachman and a servant were replacing the wheel, the lady and gentleman sheltered themselves beneath the maple-trees, and there espied the bubbling fountain, and David Swan asleep beside it. Impressed with the awe which the humblest sleeper usually sheds around him, the merchant trod as lightly as the gout would allow; and his spouse took good heed not to rustle her silk gown, lest David should start up all of a sudden.

"How soundly he sleeps!" whispered the old gentleman. "From what a depth he draws that easy breath! Such sleep as that, brought on without an opiate, would be worth more to me than half my income; for it would suppose health and an untroubled mind."

"And youth, besides," said the lady. "Healthy and quiet age does not sleep thus. Our slumber is no more like his than our wakefulness."

The longer they looked the more did this elderly couple feel interested in the unknown youth, to whom the wayside and the maple shade were as a secret chamber, with the rich gloom of damask curtains brooding over him. Perceiving that a stray sunbeam glimmered down upon his face, the lady contrived to twist a branch aside, so as to intercept it. And having done this little act of kindness, she began to feel like a mother to him.

"Providence seems to have laid him here," whispered she to her husband, "and to have brought us hither to find him, after our disappointment in our cousin's son. Methinks I can see a likeness to our departed Henry. Shall we waken him?"

"To what purpose?" said the merchant, hesitating. "We know nothing of the youth's character."

"That open countenance!" replied his wife, in the same hushed voice, yet earnestly. "This innocent sleep!"

While these whispers were passing, the sleeper's heart did not throb, nor his breath become agitated, nor his features betray the least token of interest. Yet Fortune was bending over him, just ready to let fall a burden of gold. The old merchant had lost his only son, and had no heir to his wealth except a distant relative, with whose conduct he was dissatisfied. In such cases, people sometimes do stranger things than to act the magician, and awaken a young man to splendor who fell asleep in poverty.

"Shall we not waken him?" repeated the lady, persuasively.

"The coach is ready, sir," said the servant, behind.

The old couple started, reddened, and hurried away, mutually wondering that they should ever have dreamed of doing anything so very ridiculous. The merchant threw himself back in the carriage, and occupied his mind with the plan of a magnificent asylum for unfortunate men of business. Meanwhile, David Swan enjoyed his nap.

The carriage could not have gone above a mile or two, when a pretty young girl came along, with a tripping pace, which showed precisely how her little heart was dancing in her bosom. Perhaps it was this merry kind of motion that caused—is there any harm in saying it?—her garter to slip its knot. Conscious that the silken girth—if silk it were—was relaxing its hold, she turned aside into the shelter of the maple-trees, and there found a young man asleep by the spring! Blushing as red as any rose that she should have intruded into a gentleman's bedchamber, and for such a purpose, too, she was about to make her escape on tiptoe. But there was peril near the sleeper. A monster of a bee had been wandering overhead—buzz, buzz, buzz—now among the leaves, now flashing through the strips of sunshine, and now lost in the dark shade, till finally he appeared to be settling on the eyelid of David Swan. The sting of a bee is sometimes deadly. As free hearted as she was innocent, the girl attacked the intruder with her handkerchief, brushed him soundly, and drove him from beneath the maple shade. How sweet a picture! This good deed accomplished, with quickened breath, and a deeper blush, she stole a glance at the youthful stranger for whom she had been battling with a dragon in the air.

"He is handsome!" thought she, and blushed redder yet.

How could it be that no dream of bliss grew so strong within him, that, shattered by its very strength, it should part asunder, and allow him to perceive the girl among its phantoms? Why, at least, did no smile of welcome brighten upon his face? She was come, the maid whose soul, according to the old and beautiful idea, had been severed from his own, and whom, in all his vague but passionate desires, he yearned to meet. Her, only, could he love with a perfect love; him, only, could she receive into the depths of her heart; and now her image was faintly blushing in the fountain, by his side; should it pass away, its happy lustre would never gleam upon his life again.

"How sound he sleeps!" murmured the girl.

She departed, but did not trip along the road so lightly as when she came.

Now, this girl's father was a thriving country merchant in the neighborhood, and happened, at that identical time, to be looking out for just such a young man as David Swan. Had David formed a wayside acquaintance with the daughter, he would have become the father's clerk, and all else in natural succession. So here, again, had good fortune—the best of fortunes—stolen so near that her garments brushed against him; and he knew nothing of the matter.

The girl was hardly out of sight when two men turned aside beneath the maple shade. Both had dark faces, set off by cloth caps, which were drawn down aslant over their brows. Their dresses were shabby, yet had a certain smartness. These were a couple of rascals who got their living by whatever the devil sent them, and now, in the interim of other business, had staked the joint profits of their next piece of villany on a game of cards, which was to have been decided here under the trees. But, finding David asleep by the spring, one of the rogues whispered to his fellow,—

"Hist!—Do you see that bundle under his head?"

The other villain nodded, winked, and leered.

"I'll bet you a horn of brandy," said the first, "that the chap has either a pocket-book, or a snug little hoard of small change, stowed away amongst his shirts. And if not there, we shall find it in his pantaloons pocket."

"But how if he wakes?" said the other.

His companion thrust aside his waistcoat, pointed to the handle of a dirk, and nodded.

"So be it!" muttered the second villain.

They approached the unconscious David, and, while one pointed the dagger towards his heart, the other began to search the bundle beneath his head. Their two faces, grim, wrinkled, and ghastly with guilt and fear, bent over their victim, looking horrible enough to be mistaken for fiends, should he suddenly awake. Nay, had the villains glanced aside into the spring, even they would hardly have known themselves as reflected there. But David Swan had never worn a more tranquil aspect, even when asleep on his mother's breast.

"I must take away the bundle," whispered one.

"If he stirs, I'll strike," muttered the other.

But, at this moment, a dog, scenting along the ground, came in beneath the maple-trees, and gazed alternately at each of these wicked men, and then at the quiet sleeper. He then lapped out of the fountain.

"Pshaw!" said one villain. "We can do nothing now. The dog's master must be close behind."

"Let's take a drink and be off," said the other.

The man with the dagger thrust back the weapon into his bosom, and drew forth a pocket pistol, but not of that kind which kills by a single discharge. It was a flask of liquor, with a block-tin tumbler screwed upon the mouth. Each drank a comfortable dram, and left the spot, with so many jests, and such laughter at their unaccomplished wickedness, that they might be said to have gone on their way rejoicing. In a few hours they had forgotten the whole affair, nor once imagined that the recording angel had written down the crime of murder against their souls, in letters as durable as eternity. As for David Swan, he still slept quietly, neither conscious of the shadow of death when it hung over him, nor of the glow of renewed life when that shadow was withdrawn.

He slept, but no longer so quietly as at first. An hour's repose had snatched, from his elastic frame, the weariness with which many hours of toil had burdened it. Now he stirred—now, moved his lips, without a sound—now, talked, in an inward tone, to the noonday spectres of his dream. But a noise of wheels came rattling louder and louder along the road, until it dashed through the dispersing mist of David's slumber—and there was the stage-coach. He started up with all his ideas about him.

"Halloo, driver!—Take a passenger?" shouted he.

"Room on top!" answered the driver.

Up mounted David, and bowled away merrily towards Boston, without so much as a parting glance at that fountain of dreamlike vicissitude. He knew not that a phantom of Wealth had thrown a golden hue upon its waters—nor that one of Love had sighed softly to their murmur—nor that one of Death had threatened to crimson them with his blood—all, in the brief hour since he lay down to sleep. Sleeping or waking, we hear not the airy footsteps of the strange things that almost happen. Does it not argue a superintending Providence that, while viewless and unexpected events thrust themselves continually athwart our path, there should still be regularity enough in mortal life to render foresight even partially available?

THE HOLLOW OF THE THREE HILLS

In those strange old times, when fantastic dreams and madmen's reveries were realized among the actual circumstances of life, two persons met together at an appointed hour and place. One was a lady, graceful in form and fair of feature, though pale and troubled, and smitten with an untimely blight in what should have been the fullest bloom of her years; the other was an ancient and meanly-dressed woman, of ill-favored aspect, and so withered, shrunken, and decrepit, that even the space since she began to decay must have exceeded the ordinary term of human existence. In the spot where they encountered, no mortal could observe them. Three little hills stood near each other, and down in the midst of them sunk a hollow basin, almost mathematically circular, two or three hundred feet in breadth, and of such depth that a stately cedar might but just be visible above the sides. Dwarf pines were numerous upon the hills, and partly fringed the outer verge of the intermediate hollow, within which there was nothing but the brown grass of October, and here and there a tree trunk that had fallen long ago, and lay mouldering with no green successor from its roots. One of these masses of decaying wood, formerly a majestic oak, rested close beside a pool of green and sluggish water at the bottom of the basin. Such scenes as this (so gray tradition tells) were once the resort of the Power of Evil and his plighted subjects; and here, at midnight or on the dim verge of evening, they were said to stand round the mantling pool, disturbing its putrid waters in the performance of an impious baptismal rite. The chill beauty of an autumnal sunset was now gilding the three hill-tops, whence a paler tint stole down their sides into the hollow.

"Here is our pleasant meeting come to pass," said the aged crone, "according as thou hast desired. Say quickly what thou wouldst have of me, for there is but a short hour that we may tarry here."

As the old withered woman spoke, a smile glimmered on her countenance, like lamplight on the wall of a sepulchre. The lady trembled, and cast her eyes upward to the verge of the basin, as if meditating to return with her purpose unaccomplished. But it was not so ordained.

"I am a stranger in this land, as you know," said she at length. "Whence I come it matters not; but I have left those behind me with whom my fate was intimately bound, and from whom I am cut off forever. There is a weight in my bosom that I cannot away with, and I have come hither to inquire of their welfare."

"And who is there by this green pool that can bring thee news from the ends of the earth?" cried the old woman, peering into the lady's face. "Not from my lips mayst thou hear these tidings; yet, be thou bold, and the daylight shall not pass away from yonder hill-top before thy wish be granted."

"I will do your bidding though I die," replied the lady desperately.

The old woman seated herself on the trunk of the fallen tree, threw aside the hood that shrouded her gray locks, and beckoned her companion to draw near.

"Kneel down," she said, "and lay your forehead on my knees."

She hesitated a moment, but the anxiety that had long been kindling burned fiercely up within her. As she knelt down, the border of her garment was dipped into the pool; she laid her forehead on the old woman's knees, and the latter drew a cloak about the lady's face, so that she was in darkness. Then she heard the muttered words of prayer, in the midst of which she started, and would have arisen.

"Let me flee,—let me flee and hide myself, that they may not look upon me!" she cried. But, with returning recollection, she hushed herself, and was still as death.

For it seemed as if other voices—familiar in infancy, and unforgotten through many wanderings, and in all the vicissitudes of her heart and fortune—were mingling with the accents of the prayer. At first the words were faint and indistinct, not rendered so by distance, but rather resembling the dim pages of a book which we strive to read by an imperfect and gradually brightening light. In such a manner, as the prayer proceeded, did those voices strengthen upon the ear; till at length the petition ended, and the conversation of an aged man, and of a woman broken and decayed like himself, became distinctly audible to the lady as she knelt. But those strangers appeared not to stand in the hollow depth between the three hills. Their voices were encompassed and reëchoed by the walls of a chamber, the windows of which were rattling in the breeze; the regular vibration of a clock, the crackling of a fire, and the tinkling of the embers as they fell among the ashes, rendered the scene almost as vivid as if painted to the eye. By a melancholy hearth sat these two old people, the man calmly despondent, the woman querulous and tearful, and their words were all of sorrow. They spoke of a daughter, a wanderer they knew not where, bearing dishonor along with her, and leaving shame and affliction to bring their gray heads to the grave. They alluded also to other and more recent woe, but in the midst of their talk their voices seemed to melt into the sound of the wind sweeping mournfully among the autumn leaves; and when the lady lifted her eyes, there was she kneeling in the hollow between three hills.

"A weary and lonesome time yonder old couple have of it," remarked the old woman, smiling in the lady's face.

"And did you also hear them?" exclaimed she, a sense of intolerable humiliation triumphing over her agony and fear.

"Yea; and we have yet more to hear," replied the old woman. "Wherefore, cover thy face quickly."

Again the withered hag poured forth the monotonous words of a prayer that was not meant to be acceptable in heaven; and soon, in the pauses of her breath, strange murmurings began to thicken, gradually increasing so as to drown and overpower the charm by which they grew. Shrieks pierced through the obscurity of sound, and were succeeded by the singing of sweet female voices, which, in their turn, gave way to a wild roar of laughter, broken suddenly by groanings and sobs, forming altogether a ghastly confusion of terror and mourning and mirth. Chains were rattling, fierce and stern voices uttered threats, and the scourge resounded at their command. All these noises deepened and became substantial to the listener's ear, till she could distinguish every soft and dreamy accent of the love songs that died causelessly into funeral hymns. She shuddered at the unprovoked wrath which blazed up like the spontaneous kindling of flame, and she grew faint at the fearful merriment raging miserably around her. In the midst of this wild scene, where unbound passions jostled each other in a drunken career, there was one solemn voice of a man, and a manly and melodious voice it might once have been. He went to and fro continually, and his feet sounded upon the floor. In each member of that frenzied company, whose own burning thoughts had become their exclusive world, he sought an auditor for the story of his individual wrong, and interpreted their laughter and tears as his reward of scorn or pity. He spoke of woman's perfidy, of a wife who had broken her holiest vows, of a home and heart made desolate. Even as he went on, the shout, the laugh, the shriek, the sob, rose up in unison, till they changed into the hollow, fitful, and uneven sound of the wind, as it fought among the pine-trees on those three lonely hills. The lady looked up, and there was the withered woman smiling in her face.

"Couldst thou have thought there were such merry times in a mad-house?" inquired the latter.

"True, true," said the lady to herself; "there is mirth within its walls, but misery, misery without."

"Wouldst thou hear more?" demanded the old woman.

"There is one other voice I would fain listen to again," replied the lady, faintly.

"Then, lay down thy head speedily upon my knees, that thou mayst get thee hence before the hour be past."

The golden skirts of day were yet lingering upon the hills, but deep shades obscured the hollow and the pool, as if sombre night were rising thence to overspread the world. Again that evil woman began to weave her spell. Long did it proceed unanswered, till the knolling of a bell stole in among the intervals of her words, like a clang that had travelled far over valley and rising ground, and was just ready to die in the air. The lady shook upon her companion's knees as she heard that boding sound. Stronger it grew and sadder, and deepened into the tone of a death bell, knolling dolefully from some ivy-mantled tower, and bearing tidings of mortality and woe to the cottage, to the hall, and to the solitary wayfarer, that all might weep for the doom appointed in turn to them. Then came a measured tread, passing slowly, slowly on, as of mourners with a coffin, their garments trailing on the ground, so that the ear could measure the length of their melancholy array. Before them went the priest, reading the burial service, while the leaves of his book were rustling in the breeze. And though no voice but his was heard to speak aloud, still there were revilings and anathemas, whispered but distinct, from women and from men, breathed against the daughter who had wrung the aged hearts of her parents,—the wife who had betrayed the trusting fondness of her husband,—the mother who had sinned against natural affection, and left her child to die. The sweeping sound of the funeral train faded away like a thin vapor, and the wind, that just before had seemed to shake the coffin pall, moaned sadly round the verge of the Hollow between three Hills. But when the old woman stirred the kneeling lady, she lifted not her head.

"Here has been a sweet hour's sport!" said the withered crone, chuckling to herself.

THE VISION OF THE FOUNTAIN

At fifteen I became a resident in a country village, more than a hundred miles from home. The morning after my arrival—a September morning, but warm and bright as any in July—I rambled into a wood of oaks, with a few walnut-trees intermixed, forming the closest shade above my head. The ground was rocky, uneven, overgrown with bushes and clumps of young saplings, and traversed only by cattle paths. The track which I chanced to follow led me to a crystal spring, with a border of grass as freshly green as on May morning, and overshadowed by the limb of a great oak. One solitary sunbeam found its way down, and played like a goldfish in the water.

From my childhood I have loved to gaze into a spring. The water filled a circular basin, small but deep, and set round with stones, some of which were covered with slimy moss, the others naked, and of variegated hue, reddish, white, and brown. The bottom was covered with coarse sand, which sparkled in the lonely sunbeam, and seemed to illuminate the spring with an unborrowed light. In one spot the gush of the water violently agitated the sand, but without obscuring the fountain, or breaking the glassiness of its surface. It appeared as if some living creature were about to emerge—the Naiad of the spring, perhaps—in the shape of a beautiful young woman, with a gown of filmy water moss, a belt of rainbow drops, and a cold, pure, passionless countenance. How would the beholder shiver, pleasantly yet fearfully, to see her sitting on one of the stones, paddling her white feet in the ripples, and throwing up water to sparkle in the sun! Wherever she laid her hands on grass and flowers, they would immediately be moist as with morning dew. Then would she set about her labors, like a careful housewife, to clear the fountain of withered leaves, and bits of slimy wood, and old acorns from the oaks above, and grains of corn left by cattle in drinking, till the bright sand, in the bright water, was like a treasury of diamonds. But, should the intruder approach too near, he would find only the drops of a summer shower glistening about the spot where he had seen her.

Reclining on the border of grass, where the dewy goddess should have been, I bent forward, and a pair of eyes met mine within the watery mirror. They were the reflection of my own. I looked again, and lo! another face, deeper in the fountain than my own image, more distinct in all the features, yet faint as thought. The vision had the aspect of a fair young girl, with locks of paly gold. A mirthful expression laughed in the eyes and dimpled over the whole shadowy countenance, till it seemed just what a fountain would be, if, while dancing merrily into the sunshine, it should assume the shape of woman. Through the dim rosiness of the cheeks I could see the brown leaves, the slimy twigs, the acorns, and the sparkling sand. The solitary sunbeam was diffused among the golden hair, which melted into its faint brightness, and became a glory round that head so beautiful!

My description can give no idea how suddenly the fountain was thus tenanted, and how soon it was left desolate. I breathed, and there was the face!

I held my breath, and it was gone! Had it passed away, or faded into nothing? I doubted whether it had ever been.

My sweet readers, what a dreamy and delicious hour did I spend, where that vision found and left me! For a long time I sat perfectly still, waiting till it should reappear, and fearful that the slightest motion, or even the flutter of my breath, might frighten it away. Thus have I often started from a pleasant dream, and then kept quiet in hopes to while it back. Deep were my musings, as to the race and attributes of that ethereal being. Had I created her? Was she the daughter of my fancy, akin to those strange shapes which peep under the lids of children's eyes? And did her beauty gladden me, for that one moment, and then die? Or was she a water nymph within the fountain, or fairy, or woodland goddess, peeping over my shoulder, or the ghost of some forsaken maid who had drowned herself for love? Or, in good truth, had a lovely girl, with a warm heart and lips that would bear pressure, stolen softly behind me, and thrown her image into the spring?

I watched and waited, but no vision came again. I departed, but with a spell upon me which drew me back, that same afternoon, to the haunted spring. There was the water gushing, the sand sparkling, and the sunbeam glimmering. There the vision was not, but only a great frog, the hermit of that solitude, who immediately withdrew his speckled snout and made himself invisible, all except a pair of long legs, beneath a stone. Methought he had a devilish look! I could have slain him as an enchanter who kept the mysterious beauty imprisoned in the fountain.

Sad and heavy, I was returning to the village. Between me and the church spire rose a little hill, and on its summit a group of trees, insulated from all the rest of the wood, with their own share of radiance hovering on them from the west, and their own solitary shadow falling to the east. The afternoon being far declined, the sunshine was almost pensive, and the shade almost cheerful; glory and gloom were mingled in the placid light; as if the spirits of the Day and Evening had met in friendship under those trees, and found themselves akin. I was admiring the picture, when the shape of a young girl emerged from behind the clump of oaks. My heart knew her; it was the Vision; but so distant and ethereal did she seem, so unmixed with earth, so imbued with the pensive glory of the spot where she was standing, that my spirit sunk within me, sadder than before. How could I ever reach her?

While I gazed, a sudden shower came pattering down upon the leaves. In a moment the air was full of brightness, each raindrop catching a portion of sunlight as it fell, and the whole gentle shower appearing like a mist, just substantial enough to bear the burden of radiance. A rainbow, vivid as Niagara's, was painted in the air. Its southern limb came down before the group of trees, and enveloped the fair Vision, as if the hues of heaven were the only garment for her beauty. When the rainbow vanished, she, who had seemed a part of it, was no longer there. Was her existence absorbed in nature's loveliest phenomenon, and did her pure frame dissolve away in the varied light? Yet, I would not despair of her return; for, robed in the rainbow, she was the emblem of Hope.

Thus did the vision leave me; and many a doleful day succeeded to the parting moment. By the spring, and in the wood, and on the hill, and through the village; at dewy sunrise, burning noon, and at that magic hour of sunset when she had vanished from my sight, I sought her, but in vain. Weeks came and went, months rolled away, and she appeared not in them. I imparted my mystery to none, but wandered to and fro, or sat in solitude, like one that had caught a glimpse of heaven, and could take no more joy on earth. I withdrew into an inner world, where my thoughts lived and breathed, and the Vision in the midst of them. Without intending it, I became at once the author and hero of a romance, conjuring up rivals, imagining events, the actions of others and my own, and experiencing every change of passion, till jealousy and despair had their end in bliss. Oh, had I the burning fancy of my early youth, with manhood's colder gift, the power of expression, your hearts, sweet ladies, should flutter at my tale!

In the middle of January I was summoned home. The day before my departure, visiting the spots which had been hallowed by the Vision, I found that the spring had a frozen bosom, and nothing but the snow and a glare of winter sunshine on the hill of the rainbow. "Let me hope," thought I, "or my heart will be as icy as the fountain, and the whole world as desolate as this snowy hill." Most of the day was spent in preparing for the journey, which was to commence at four o'clock the next morning. About an hour after supper, when all was in readiness, I descended from my chamber to the sitting-room, to take leave of the old clergyman and his family with whom I had been an inmate. A gust of wind blew out my lamp as I passed through the entry.

According to their invariable custom, so pleasant a one when the fire blazes cheerfully, the family were sitting in the parlor, with no other light than what came from the hearth. As the good clergyman's scanty stipend compelled him to use all sorts of economy, the foundation of his fires was always a large heap of tan, or ground bark, which would smoulder away, from morning till night, with a dull warmth and no flame. This evening the heap of tan was newly put on, and surmounted with three sticks of red oak, full of moisture, and a few pieces of dry pine, that had not yet kindled. There was no light, except the little that came sullenly from two half-burned brands, without even glimmering on the andirons. But I knew the position of the old minister's arm-chair, and also where his wife sat, with her knitting-work, and how to avoid his two daughters, one a stout country lass, and the other a consumptive girl. Groping through the gloom, I found my own place next to that of the son, a learned collegian, who had come home to keep school in the village during the winter vacation. I noticed that there was less room than usual, to-night, between the collegian's chair and mine.

As people are always taciturn in the dark, not a word was said for some time after my entrance. Nothing broke the stillness but the regular click of the matron's knitting-needles. At times, the fire threw out a brief and dusky gleam, which twinkled on the old man's glasses, and hovered doubtfully round our circle, but was far too faint to portray the individuals who composed it. Were we not like ghosts? Dreamy as the scene was, might it not be a type of the mode in which departed people, who had known and loved each other here, would hold communion in eternity? We were aware of each other's presence, not by sight, nor sound, nor touch, but by an inward consciousness. Would it not be so among the dead?

The silence was interrupted by the consumptive daughter, addressing a remark to some one in the circle whom she called Rachel. Her tremulous and decayed accents were answered by a single word, but in a voice that made me start, and bend towards the spot whence it had proceeded. Had I ever heard that sweet, low tone? If not, why did it rouse up so many old recollections, or mockeries of such, the shadows of things familiar, yet unknown, and fill my mind with confused images of her features who had spoken, though buried in the gloom of the parlor? Whom had my heart recognized, that it throbbed so? I listened to catch her gentle breathing, and strove, by the intensity of my gaze, to picture forth a shape where none was visible.

Suddenly the dry pine caught; the fire blazed up with a ruddy glow; and where the darkness had been, there was she—the Vision of the Fountain! A spirit of radiance only, she had vanished with the rainbow, and appeared again in the firelight, perhaps to flicker with the blaze, and be gone. Yet, her cheek was rosy and life-like, and her features, in the bright warmth of the room, were even sweeter and tenderer than my recollection of them. She knew me! The mirthful expression that had laughed in her eyes and dimpled over her countenance, when I beheld her faint beauty in the fountain, was laughing and dimpling there now. One moment our glance mingled—the next, down rolled the heap of tan upon the kindled wood—and darkness snatched away the Daughter of the Light, and gave her back to me no more!

Fair ladies, there is nothing more to tell. Must the simple mystery be revealed, then, that Rachel was the daughter of the village squire, and had left home for a boarding-school, the morning after I arrived and returned the day before my departure? If I transformed her to an angel, it is what every youthful lover does for his mistress. Therein consists the essence of my story. But slight the change, sweet maids, to make angels of yourselves!

FANCY'S SHOW BOX

A MORALITY

What is Guilt? A stain upon the soul. And it is a point of vast interest whether the soul may contract such stains, in all their depth and flagrancy, from deeds which may have been plotted and resolved upon, but which, physically, have never had existence. Must the fleshly hand and visible frame of man set its seal to the evil designs of the soul, in order to give them their entire validity against the sinner? Or, while none but crimes perpetrated are cognizable before an earthly tribunal, will guilty thoughts—of which guilty deeds are no more than shadows—will these draw down the full weight of a condemning sentence, in the supreme court of eternity? In the solitude of a midnight chamber or in a desert, afar from men or in a church, while the body is kneeling, the soul may pollute itself even with those crimes which we are accustomed to deem altogether carnal. If this be true, it is a fearful truth.

Let us illustrate the subject by an imaginary example. A venerable gentleman, one Mr. Smith, who had long been regarded as a pattern of moral excellence, was warming his aged blood with a glass or two of generous wine. His children being gone forth about their worldly business, and his grandchildren at school, he sat alone, in a deep, luxurious arm-chair, with his feet beneath a richly-carved mahogany table. Some old people have a dread of solitude, and when better company may not be had, rejoice even to hear the quiet breathing of a babe, asleep upon the carpet. But Mr. Smith, whose silver hair was the bright symbol of a life unstained, except by such spots as are inseparable from human nature, had no need of a babe to protect him by its purity, nor of a grown person to stand between him and his own soul. Nevertheless, either Manhood must converse with Age, or Womanhood must soothe him with gentle cares, or Infancy must sport around his chair, or his thoughts will stray into the misty region of the past, and the old man be chill and sad. Wine will not always cheer him. Such might have been the case with Mr. Smith, when, through the brilliant medium of his glass of old Madeira, he beheld three figures entering the room. These were Fancy, who had assumed the garb and aspect of an itinerant showman, with a box of pictures on her back; and Memory, in the likeness of a clerk, with a pen behind her ear, an inkhorn at her buttonhole, and a huge manuscript volume beneath her arm; and lastly, behind the other two, a person shrouded in a dusky mantle, which concealed both face and form. But Mr. Smith had a shrewd idea that it was Conscience.

How kind of Fancy, Memory, and Conscience to visit the old gentleman, just as he was beginning to imagine that the wine had neither so bright a sparkle nor so excellent a flavor as when himself and the liquor were less aged! Through the dim length of the apartment, where crimson curtains muffled the glare of sunshine and created a rich obscurity, the three guests drew near the silver-haired old man. Memory, with a finger between the leaves of her huge volume, placed herself at his right hand. Conscience, with her face still hidden in the dusky mantle, took her station on the left, so as to be next his heart; while Fancy set down her picture box upon the table, with the magnifying glass convenient to his eye. We can sketch merely the outlines of two or three out of the many pictures which, at the pulling of a string, successively peopled the box with the semblances of living scenes.

One was a moonlight picture: in the background, a lowly dwelling; and in front, partly shadowed by a tree, yet besprinkled with flakes of radiance, two youthful figures, male and female. The young man stood with folded arms, a haughty smile upon his lip, and a gleam of triumph in his eye, as he glanced downward at the kneeling girl. She was almost prostrate at his feet, evidently sinking under a weight of shame and anguish, which hardly allowed her to lift her clasped hands in supplication. Her eyes she could not lift. But neither her agony, nor the lovely features on which it was depicted, nor the slender grace of the form which it convulsed, appeared to soften the obduracy of the young man. He was the personification of triumphant scorn. Now, strange to say, as old Mr. Smith peeped through the magnifying glass, which made the objects start out from the canvas with magical deception, he began to recognize the farm-house, the tree, and both the figures of the picture. The young man, in times long past, had often met his gaze within the looking-glass; the girl was the very image of his first love—his cottage love—his Martha Burroughs!

Mr. Smith was scandalized. "O vile and slanderous picture!" he exclaims. "When have I triumphed over ruined innocence? Was not Martha wedded, in her teens, to David Tomkins, who won her girlish love, and long enjoyed her affection as a wife? And ever since his death she has lived a reputable widow!" Meantime, Memory was turning over the leaves of her volume, rustling them to and fro with uncertain fingers, until, among the earlier pages, she found one which had reference to this picture. She reads it, close to the old gentleman's ear; it is a record merely of sinful thought, which never was embodied in an act; but while Memory is reading, Conscience unveils her face, and strikes a dagger to the heart of Mr. Smith. Though not a death-blow, the torture was extreme.

The exhibition proceeded. One after another, Fancy displayed her pictures, all of which appeared to have been painted by some malicious artist on purpose to vex Mr. Smith. Not a shadow of proof could have been adduced, in any earthly court, that he was guilty of the slightest of those sins which were thus made to stare him in the face. In one scene there was a table set out, with several bottles, and glasses half filled with wine, which threw back the dull ray of an expiring lamp. There had been mirth and revelry, until the hands of the clock stood just at midnight, when murder stepped between the boon companions. A young man had fallen on the floor, and lay stone dead, with a ghastly wound crushed into his temple, while over him, with a delirium of mingled rage and horror in his countenance, stood the youthful likeness of Mr. Smith. The murdered youth wore the features of Edward Spencer! "What does this rascal of a painter mean?" cries Mr. Smith, provoked beyond all patience. "Edward Spencer was my earliest and dearest friend, true to me as I to him, through more than half a century. Neither I, nor any other, ever murdered him. Was he not alive within five years, and did he not, in token of our long friendship, bequeath me his gold-headed cane and a mourning ring?" Again had Memory been turning over her volume, and fixed at length upon so confused a page that she surely must have scribbled it when she was tipsy. The purport was, however, that while Mr. Smith and Edward Spencer were heating their young blood with wine, a quarrel had flashed up between them, and Mr. Smith, in deadly wrath, had flung a bottle at Spencer's head. True, it missed its aim, and merely smashed a looking-glass; and the next morning, when the incident was imperfectly remembered, they had shaken hands with a hearty laugh. Yet, again, while Memory was reading, Conscience unveiled her face, struck a dagger to the heart of Mr. Smith, and quelled his remonstrance with her iron frown. The pain was quite excruciating.

Some of the pictures had been painted with so doubtful a touch, and in colors so faint and pale, that the subjects could barely be conjectured. A dull, semi-transparent mist had been thrown over the surface of the canvas, into which the figures seemed to vanish, while the eye sought most earnestly to fix them. But in every scene, however dubiously portrayed, Mr. Smith was invariably haunted by his own lineaments, at various ages, as in a dusty mirror. After poring several minutes over one of these blurred and almost indistinguishable pictures, he began to see that the painter had intended to represent him, now in the decline of life, as stripping the clothes from the backs of three half-starved children. "Really, this puzzles me!" quoth Mr. Smith, with the irony of conscious rectitude. "Asking pardon of the painter, I pronounce him a fool, as well as a scandalous knave. A man of my standing in the world to be robbing little children of their clothes! Ridiculous!" But while he spoke, Memory had searched her fatal volume, and found a page, which, with her sad, calm voice, she poured into his ear. It was not altogether inapplicable to the misty scene. It told how Mr. Smith had been grievously tempted by many devilish sophistries, on the ground of a legal quibble, to commence a lawsuit against three orphan children, joint heirs to a considerable estate. Fortunately, before he was quite decided, his claims had turned out nearly as devoid of law as justice. As Memory ceased to read, Conscience again thrust aside her mantle, and would have struck her victim with the envenomed dagger, only that he struggled and clasped his hands before his heart. Even then, however, he sustained an ugly gash.

Why should we follow Fancy through the whole series of those awful pictures? Painted by an artist of wondrous power, and terrible acquaintance with the secret soul, they embodied the ghosts of all the never perpetrated sins that had glided through the lifetime of Mr. Smith. And could such beings of cloudy fantasy, so near akin to nothingness, give valid evidence against him at the day of judgment? Be that the case or not, there is reason to believe that one truly penitential tear would have washed away each hateful picture, and left the canvas white as snow. But Mr. Smith, at a prick of Conscience too keen to be endured, bellowed aloud, with impatient agony, and suddenly discovered that his three guests were gone. There he sat alone, a silver-haired and highly-venerated old man, in the rich gloom of the crimson-curtained room, with no box of pictures on the table, but only a decanter of most excellent Madeira. Yet his heart still seemed to fester with the venom of the dagger.

Nevertheless, the unfortunate old gentleman might have argued the matter with Conscience, and alleged many reasons wherefore she should not smite him so pitilessly. Were we to take up his cause, it should be somewhat in the following fashion: A scheme of guilt, till it be put in execution, greatly resembles a train of incidents in a projected tale. The latter, in order to produce a sense of reality in the reader's mind, must be conceived with such proportionate strength by the author as to seem, in the glow of fancy, more like truth, past, present, or to come, than purely fiction. The prospective sinner, on the other hand, weaves his plot of crime, but seldom or never feels a perfect certainty that it will be executed. There is a dreaminess diffused about his thoughts, in a dream, as it were, he strikes the death-blow into his victim's heart, and starts to find an indelible blood-stain on his hand. Thus a novel writer or a dramatist, in creating a villain of romance and fitting him with evil deeds, and the villain of actual life, in projecting crimes that will be perpetrated, may almost meet each other half-way between reality and fancy. It is not until the crime is accomplished that guilt clinches its gripe upon the guilty heart, and claims it for its own. Then, and not before, sin is actually felt and acknowledged, and, if unaccompanied by repentance, grows a thousand-fold more virulent by its self-consciousness. Be it considered, also, that men often over-estimate their capacity for evil. At a distance, while its attendant circumstances do not press upon their notice, and its results are dimly seen, they can bear to contemplate it. They may take the steps which lead to crime, impelled by the same sort of mental action as in working out a mathematical problem, yet be powerless with compunction at the final moment. They knew not what deed it was that they deemed themselves resolved to do. In truth, there is no such thing in man's nature as a settled and full resolve, either for good or evil, except at the very moment of execution. Let us hope, therefore, that all the dreadful consequences of sin will not be incurred, unless the act have set its seal upon the thought.

Yet, with the slight fancy work which we have framed, some sad and awful truths are interwoven. Man must not disclaim his brotherhood, even with the guiltiest, since, though his hand be clean, his heart has surely been polluted by the flitting phantoms of iniquity. He must feel that, when he shall knock at the gate of heaven, no semblance of an unspotted life can entitle him to entrance there. Penitence must kneel, and Mercy come from the footstool of the throne, or that golden gate will never open!

DR. HEIDEGGER'S EXPERIMENT

That very singular man, old Dr. Heidegger, once invited four venerable friends to meet him in his study. There were three white-bearded gentlemen, Mr. Medbourne, Colonel Killigrew, and Mr. Gascoigne, and a withered gentlewoman, whose name was the Widow Wycherly. They were all melancholy old creatures, who had been unfortunate in life, and whose greatest misfortune it was that they were not long ago in their graves. Mr. Medbourne, in the vigor of his age, had been a prosperous merchant, but had lost his all by a frantic speculation, and was now little better than a mendicant. Colonel Killigrew had wasted his best years, and his health and substance, in the pursuit of sinful pleasures, which had given birth to a brood of pains, such as the gout, and divers other torments of soul and body. Mr. Gascoigne was a ruined politician, a man of evil fame, or at least had been so till time had buried him from the knowledge of the present generation, and made him obscure instead of infamous. As for the Widow Wycherly, tradition tells us that she was a great beauty in her day; but, for a long while past, she had lived in deep seclusion, on account of certain scandalous stories which had prejudiced the gentry of the town against her. It is a circumstance worth mentioning that each of these three old gentlemen, Mr. Medbourne, Colonel Killigrew, and Mr. Gascoigne, were early lovers of the Widow Wycherly, and had once been on the point of cutting each other's throats for her sake. And, before proceeding further, I will merely hint that Dr. Heidegger and all his four guests were sometimes thought to be a little beside themselves,—as is not unfrequently the case with old people, when worried either by present troubles or woful recollections.

"My dear old friends," said Dr. Heidegger, motioning them to be seated, "I am desirous of your assistance in one of those little experiments with which I amuse myself here in my study."

If all stories were true, Dr. Heidegger's study must have been a very curious place. It was a dim, old-fashioned chamber, festooned with cobwebs, and besprinkled with antique dust. Around the walls stood several oaken bookcases, the lower shelves of which were filled with rows of gigantic folios and black-letter quartos, and the upper with little parchment-covered duodecimos. Over the central bookcase was a bronze bust of Hippocrates, with which, according to some authorities, Dr. Heidegger was accustomed to hold consultations in all difficult cases of his practice. In the obscurest corner of the room stood a tall and narrow oaken closet, with its door ajar, within which doubtfully appeared a skeleton. Between two of the bookcases hung a looking-glass, presenting its high and dusty plate within a tarnished gilt frame. Among many wonderful stories related of this mirror, it was fabled that the spirits of all the doctor's deceased patients dwelt within its verge, and would stare him in the face whenever he looked thitherward. The opposite side of the chamber was ornamented with the full-length portrait of a young lady, arrayed in the faded magnificence of silk, satin, and brocade, and with a visage as faded as her dress. Above half a century ago, Dr. Heidegger had been on the point of marriage with this young lady; but, being affected with some slight disorder, she had swallowed one of her lover's prescriptions, and died on the bridal evening. The greatest curiosity of the study remains to be mentioned; it was a ponderous folio volume, bound in black leather, with massive silver clasps. There were no letters on the back, and nobody could tell the title of the book. But it was well known to be a book of magic; and once, when a chambermaid had lifted it, merely to brush away the dust, the skeleton had rattled in its closet, the picture of the young lady had stepped one foot upon the floor, and several ghastly faces had peeped forth from the mirror; while the brazen head of Hippocrates frowned, and said,—"Forbear!"

Such was Dr. Heidegger's study. On the summer afternoon of our tale a small round table, as black as ebony, stood in the centre of the room, sustaining a cut-glass vase of beautiful form and elaborate workmanship. The sunshine came through the window, between the heavy festoons of two faded damask curtains, and fell directly across this vase; so that a mild splendor was reflected from it on the ashen visages of the five old people who sat around. Four champagne glasses were also on the table.

"My dear old friends," repeated Dr. Heidegger, "may I reckon on your aid in performing an exceedingly curious experiment?"

Now Dr. Heidegger was a very strange old gentleman, whose eccentricity had become the nucleus for a thousand fantastic stories. Some of these fables, to my shame be it spoken, might possibly be traced back to my own veracious self; and if any passages of the present tale should startle the reader's faith, I must be content to bear the stigma of a fiction monger.

When the doctor's four guests heard him talk of his proposed experiment, they anticipated nothing more wonderful than the murder of a mouse in an air pump, or the examination of a cobweb by the microscope, or some similar nonsense, with which he was constantly in the habit of pestering his intimates. But without waiting for a reply, Dr. Heidegger hobbled across the chamber, and returned with the same ponderous folio, bound in black leather, which common report affirmed to be a book of magic. Undoing the silver clasps, he opened the volume, and took from among its black-letter pages a rose, or what was once a rose, though now the green leaves and crimson petals had assumed one brownish hue, and the ancient flower seemed ready to crumble to dust in the doctor's hands.

"This rose," said Dr. Heidegger, with a sigh, "this same withered and crumbling flower, blossomed five and fifty years ago. It was given me by Sylvia Ward, whose portrait hangs yonder; and I meant to wear it in my bosom at our wedding. Five and fifty years it has been treasured between the leaves of this old volume. Now, would you deem it possible that this rose of half a century could ever bloom again?"

"Nonsense!" said the Widow Wycherly, with a peevish toss of her head. "You might as well ask whether an old woman's wrinkled face could ever bloom again."

"See!" answered Dr. Heidegger.

He uncovered the vase, and threw the faded rose into the water which it contained. At first, it lay lightly on the surface of the fluid, appearing to imbibe none of its moisture. Soon, however, a singular change began to be visible. The crushed and dried petals stirred, and assumed a deepening tinge of crimson, as if the flower were reviving from a deathlike slumber; the slender stalk and twigs of foliage became green; and there was the rose of half a century, looking as fresh as when Sylvia Ward had first given it to her lover. It was scarcely full blown; for some of its delicate red leaves curled modestly around its moist bosom, within which two or three dewdrops were sparkling.

"That is certainly a very pretty deception," said the doctor's friends; carelessly, however, for they had witnessed greater miracles at a conjurer's show; "pray how was it effected?"

"Did you never hear of the 'Fountain of Youth?'" asked Dr. Heidegger, "which Ponce De Leon, the Spanish adventurer, went in search of two or three centuries ago?"

"But did Ponce De Leon ever find it?" said the Widow Wycherly.

"No," answered Dr. Heidegger, "for he never sought it in the right place. The famous Fountain of Youth, if I am rightly informed, is situated in the southern part of the Floridian peninsula, not far from Lake Macaco. Its source is overshadowed by several gigantic magnolias, which, though numberless centuries old, have been kept as fresh as violets by the virtues of this wonderful water. An acquaintance of mine, knowing my curiosity in such matters, has sent me what you see in the vase."

"Ahem!" said Colonel Killigrew, who believed not a word of the doctor's story; "and what may be the effect of this fluid on the human frame?"

"You shall judge for yourself, my dear colonel," replied Dr. Heidegger; "and all of you, my respected friends, are welcome to so much of this admirable fluid as may restore to you the bloom of youth. For my own part, having had much trouble in growing old, I am in no hurry to grow young again. With your permission, therefore, I will merely watch the progress of the experiment."

While he spoke, Dr. Heidegger had been filling the four champagne glasses with the water of the Fountain of Youth. It was apparently impregnated with an effervescent gas, for little bubbles were continually ascending from the depths of the glasses, and bursting in silvery spray at the surface. As the liquor diffused a pleasant perfume, the old people doubted not that it possessed cordial and comfortable properties; and though utter sceptics as to its rejuvenescent power, they were inclined to swallow it at once. But Dr. Heidegger besought them to stay a moment.

"Before you drink, my respectable old friends," said he, "it would be well that, with the experience of a lifetime to direct you, you should draw up a few general rules for your guidance, in passing a second time through the perils of youth. Think what a sin and shame it would be, if, with your peculiar advantages, you should not become patterns of virtue and wisdom to all the young people of the age!"

The doctor's four venerable friends made him no answer, except by a feeble and tremulous laugh; so very ridiculous was the idea that, knowing how closely repentance treads behind the steps of error, they should ever go astray again.

"Drink, then," said the doctor, bowing: "I rejoice that I have so well selected the subjects of my experiment."

With palsied hands, they raised the glasses to their lips. The liquor, if it really possessed such virtues as Dr. Heidegger imputed to it, could not have been bestowed on four human beings who needed it more wofully. They looked as if they had never known what youth or pleasure was, but had been the offspring of Nature's dotage, and always the gray, decrepit, sapless, miserable creatures, who now sat stooping round the doctor's table, without life enough in their souls or bodies to be animated even by the prospect of growing young again. They drank off the water, and replaced their glasses on the table.

Assuredly there was an almost immediate improvement in the aspect of the party, not unlike what might have been produced by a glass of generous wine, together with a sudden glow of cheerful sunshine brightening over all their visages at once. There was a healthful suffusion on their cheeks, instead of the ashen hue that had made them look so corpse-like. They gazed at one another, and fancied that some magic power had really begun to smooth away the deep and sad inscriptions which Father Time had been so long engraving on their brows. The Widow Wycherly adjusted her cap, for she felt almost like a woman again.

"Give us more of this wondrous water!" cried they, eagerly. "We are younger—but we are still too old! Quick—give us more!"

"Patience, patience!" quoth Dr. Heidegger, who sat watching the experiment with philosophic coolness. "You have been a long time growing old. Surely, you might be content to grow young in half an hour! But the water is at your service."

Again he filled their glasses with the liquor of youth, enough of which still remained in the vase to turn half the old people in the city to the age of their own grandchildren. While the bubbles were yet sparkling on the brim, the doctor's four guests snatched their glasses from the table, and swallowed the contents at a single gulp. Was it delusion? even while the draught was passing down their throats, it seemed to have wrought a change on their whole systems. Their eyes grew clear and bright; a dark shade deepened among their silvery locks, they sat around the table, three gentlemen of middle age, and a woman, hardly beyond her buxom prime.

"My dear widow, you are charming!" cried Colonel Killigrew, whose eyes had been fixed upon her face, while the shadows of age were flitting from it like darkness from the crimson daybreak.

The fair widow knew, of old, that Colonel Killigrew's compliments were not always measured by sober truth; so she started up and ran to the mirror, still dreading that the ugly visage of an old woman would meet her gaze. Meanwhile, the three gentlemen behaved in such a manner as proved that the water of the Fountain of Youth possessed some intoxicating qualities; unless, indeed, their exhilaration of spirits were merely a lightsome dizziness caused by the sudden removal of the weight of years. Mr. Gascoigne's mind seemed to run on political topics, but whether relating to the past, present, or future, could not easily be determined, since the same ideas and phrases have been in vogue these fifty years. Now he rattled forth full-throated sentences about patriotism, national glory, and the people's right; now he muttered some perilous stuff or other, in a sly and doubtful whisper, so cautiously that even his own conscience could scarcely catch the secret; and now, again, he spoke in measured accents, and a deeply deferential tone, as if a royal ear were listening to his well-turned periods. Colonel Killigrew all this time had been trolling forth a jolly bottle song, and ringing his glass in symphony with the chorus, while his eyes wandered toward the buxom figure of the Widow Wycherly. On the other side of the table, Mr. Medbourne was involved in a calculation of dollars and cents, with which was strangely intermingled a project for supplying the East Indies with ice, by harnessing a team of whales to the polar icebergs.

As for the Widow Wycherly, she stood before the mirror courtesying and simpering to her own image, and greeting it as the friend whom she loved better than all the world beside. She thrust her face close to the glass, to see whether some long-remembered wrinkle or crow's foot had indeed vanished. She examined whether the snow had so entirely melted from her hair that the venerable cap could be safely thrown aside. At last, turning briskly away, she came with a sort of dancing step to the table.

"My dear old doctor," cried she, "pray favor me with another glass!"

"Certainly, my dear madam, certainly!" replied the complaisant doctor; "see! I have already filled the glasses."

There, in fact, stood the four glasses, brimful of this wonderful water, the delicate spray of which, as it effervesced from the surface, resembled the tremulous glitter of diamonds. It was now so nearly sunset that the chamber had grown duskier than ever; but a mild and moonlike splendor gleamed from within the vase, and rested alike on the four guests and on the doctor's venerable figure. He sat in a highbacked, elaborately-carved, oaken arm-chair, with a gray dignity of aspect that might have well befitted that very Father Time, whose power had never been disputed, save by this fortunate company. Even while quaffing the third draught of the Fountain of Youth, they were almost awed by the expression of his mysterious visage.

But, the next moment, the exhilarating gush of young life shot through their veins. They were now in the happy prime of youth. Age, with its miserable train of cares and sorrows and diseases, was remembered only as the trouble of a dream, from which they had joyously awoke. The fresh gloss of the soul, so early lost, and without which the world's successive scenes had been but a gallery of faded pictures, again threw its enchantment over all their prospects. They felt like new-created beings in a new-created universe.

"We are young! We are young!" they cried exultingly.

Youth, like the extremity of age, had effaced the strongly-marked characteristics of middle life, and mutually assimilated them all. They were a group of merry youngsters, almost maddened with the exuberant frolicsomeness of their years. The most singular effect of their gayety was an impulse to mock the infirmity and decrepitude of which they had so lately been the victims. They laughed loudly at their old-fashioned attire, the wide-skirted coats and flapped waistcoats of the young men, and the ancient cap and gown of the blooming girl. One limped across the floor like a gouty grandfather; one set a pair of spectacles astride of his nose, and pretended to pore over the black-letter pages of the book of magic; a third seated himself in an arm-chair, and strove to imitate the venerable dignity of Dr. Heidegger. Then all shouted mirthfully, and leaped about the room. The Widow Wycherly—if so fresh a damsel could be called a widow—tripped up to the doctor's chair, with a mischievous merriment in her rosy face.

"Doctor, you dear old soul," cried she, "get up and dance with me!" And then the four young people laughed louder than ever, to think what a queer figure the poor old doctor would cut.

"Pray excuse me," answered the doctor quietly. "I am old and rheumatic, and my dancing days were over long ago. But either of these gay young gentlemen will be glad of so pretty a partner."

"Dance with me, Clara!" cried Colonel Killigrew.

"No, no, I will be her partner!" shouted Mr. Gascoigne.

"She promised me her hand, fifty years ago!" exclaimed Mr. Medbourne.

They all gathered round her. One caught both her hands in his passionate grasp—another threw his arm about her waist—the third buried his hand among the glossy curls that clustered beneath the widow's cap. Blushing, panting, struggling, chiding, laughing, her warm breath fanning each of their faces by turns, she strove to disengage herself, yet still remained in their triple embrace. Never was there a livelier picture of youthful rivalship, with bewitching beauty for the prize. Yet, by a strange deception, owing to the duskiness of the chamber, and the antique dresses which they still wore, the tall mirror is said to have reflected the figures of the three old, gray, withered grandsires, ridiculously contending for the skinny ugliness of a shrivelled grandam.

But they were young: their burning passions proved them so. Inflamed to madness by the coquetry of the girl-widow, who neither granted nor quite withheld her favors, the three rivals began to interchange threatening glances. Still keeping hold of the fair prize, they grappled fiercely at one another's throats. As they struggled to and fro, the table was overturned, and the vase dashed into a thousand fragments. The precious Water of Youth flowed in a bright stream across the floor, moistening the wings of a butterfly, which, grown old in the decline of summer, had alighted there to die. The insect fluttered lightly through the chamber, and settled on the snowy head of Dr. Heidegger.

"Come, come, gentlemen!—come, Madam Wycherly," exclaimed the doctor, "I really must protest against this riot."

They stood still and shivered; for it seemed as if gray Time were calling them back from their sunny youth, far down into the chill and darksome vale of years. They looked at old Dr. Heidegger, who sat in his carved arm-chair, holding the rose of half a century, which he had rescued from among the fragments of the shattered vase. At the motion of his hand, the four rioters resumed their seats; the more readily, because their violent exertions had wearied them, youthful though they were.

"My poor Sylvia's rose!" ejaculated Dr. Heidegger, holding it in the light of the sunset clouds; "it appears to be fading again."

And so it was. Even while the party were looking at it, the flower continued to shrivel up, till it became as dry and fragile as when the doctor had first thrown it into the vase. He shook off the few drops of moisture which clung to its petals.

"I love it as well thus as in its dewy freshness," observed he, pressing the withered rose to his withered lips. While he spoke, the butterfly fluttered down from the doctor's snowy head, and fell upon the floor.

His guests shivered again. A strange chillness, whether of the body or spirit they could not tell, was creeping gradually over them all. They gazed at one another, and fancied that each fleeting moment snatched away a charm, and left a deepening furrow where none had been before. Was it an illusion? Had the changes of a lifetime been crowded into so brief a space, and were they now four aged people, sitting with their old friend, Dr. Heidegger?

"Are we grown old again, so soon?" cried they, dolefully.

In truth they had. The Water of Youth possessed merely a virtue more transient than that of wine. The delirium which it created had effervesced away. Yes! they were old again. With a shuddering impulse, that showed her a woman still, the widow clasped her skinny hands before her face, and wished that the coffin lid were over it, since it could be no longer beautiful.

"Yes, friends, ye are old again," said Dr. Heidegger, "and lo! the Water of Youth is all lavished on the ground. Well—I bemoan it not; for if the fountain gushed at my very doorstep, I would not stoop to bathe my lips in it—no, though its delirium were for years instead of moments. Such is the lesson ye have taught me!"

But the doctor's four friends had taught no such lesson to themselves. They resolved forthwith to make a pilgrimage to Florida, and quaff at morning, noon, and night, from the Fountain of Youth.

NOTE.—In an English review, not long since, I have been accused of plagiarizing the idea of this story from a chapter in one of the novels of Alexandre Dumas. There has undoubtedly been a plagiarism on one side or the other; but as my story was written a good deal more than twenty years ago, and as the novel is of considerably more recent date, I take pleasure in thinking that M. Dumas has done me the honor to appropriate one of the fanciful conceptions of my earlier days. He is heartily welcome to it; nor is it the only instance, by many, in which the great French romancer has exercised the privilege of commanding genius by confiscating the intellectual property of less famous people to his own use and behoof.

September, 1860.

LEGENDS OF THE PROVINCE HOUSE

I. HOWE'S MASQUERADE

One afternoon, last summer, while walking along Washington Street, my eye was attracted by a signboard protruding over a narrow archway, nearly opposite the Old South Church. The sign represented the front of a stately edifice, which was designated as the "Old Province House, kept by Thomas Waite." I was glad to be thus reminded of a purpose, long entertained, of visiting and rambling over the mansion of the old royal governors of Massachusetts; and entering the arched passage, which penetrated through the middle of a brick row of shops, a few steps transported me from the busy heart of modern Boston into a small and secluded court-yard. One side of this space was occupied by the square front of the Province House, three stories high, and surmounted by a cupola, on the top of which a gilded Indian was discernible, with his bow bent and his arrow on the string, as if aiming at the weathercock on the spire of the Old South. The figure has kept this attitude for seventy years or more, ever since good Deacon Drowne, a cunning carver of wood, first stationed him on his long sentinel's watch over the city.

The Province House is constructed of brick, which seems recently to have been overlaid with a coat of light-colored paint. A flight of red freestone steps, fenced in by a balustrade of curiously wrought iron, ascends from the court-yard to the spacious porch, over which is a balcony, with an iron balustrade of similar pattern and workmanship to that beneath. These letters and figures—16 P. S. 79—are wrought into the iron work of the balcony, and probably express the date of the edifice, with the initials of its founder's name. A wide door with double leaves admitted me into the hall or entry, on the right of which is the entrance to the bar-room.

It was in this apartment, I presume, that the ancient governors held their levees, with vice-regal pomp, surrounded by the military men, the councillors, the judges, and other officers of the crown, while all the loyalty of the province thronged to do them honor. But the room, in its present condition, cannot boast even of faded magnificence. The panelled wainscot is covered with dingy paint, and acquires a duskier hue from the deep shadow into which the Province House is thrown by the brick block that shuts it in from Washington Street. A ray of sunshine never visits this apartment any more than the glare of the festal torches, which have been extinguished from the era of the Revolution. The most venerable and ornamental object is a chimney-piece set round with Dutch tiles of blue-figured China, representing scenes from Scripture; and, for aught I know, the lady of Pownall or Bernard may have sat beside this fire-place, and told her children the story of each blue tile. A bar in modern style, well replenished with decanters, bottles, cigar boxes, and net-work bags of lemons, and provided with a beer pump and a soda fount, extends along one side of the room. At my entrance, an elderly person was smacking his lips with a zest which satisfied me that the cellars of the Province House still hold good liquor, though doubtless of other vintages than were quaffed by the old governors. After sipping a glass of port sangaree, prepared by the skilful hands of Mr. Thomas Waite, I besought that worthy successor and representative of so many historic personages to conduct me over their time honored mansion.

He readily complied; but, to confess the truth, I was forced to draw strenuously upon my imagination, in order to find aught that was interesting in a house which, without its historic associations, would have seemed merely such a tavern as is usually favored by the custom of decent city boarders, and old-fashioned country gentlemen. The chambers, which were probably spacious in former times, are now cut up by partitions, and subdivided into little nooks, each affording scanty room for the narrow bed and chair and dressing-table of a single lodger. The great staircase, however, may be termed, without much hyperbole, a feature of grandeur and magnificencc. It winds through the midst of the house by flights of broad steps, each flight terminating in a square landing-place, whence the ascent is continued towards the cupola. A carved balustrade, freshly painted in the lower stories, but growing dingier as we ascend, borders the staircase with its quaintly twisted and intertwined pillars, from top to bottom. Up these stairs the military boots, or perchance the gouty shoes, of many a governor have trodden, as the wearers mounted to the cupola, which afforded them so wide a view over their metropolis and the surrounding country. The cupola is an octagon, with several windows, and a door opening upon the roof. From this station, as I pleased myself with imagining, Gage may have beheld his disastrous victory on Bunker Hill (unless one of the tri-mountains intervened), and Howe have marked the approaches of Washington's besieging army; although the buildings since erected in the vicinity have shut out almost every object, save the steeple of the Old South, which seems almost within arm's length. Descending from the cupola, I paused in the garret to observe the ponderous white-oak framework, so much more massive than the frames of modern houses, and thereby resembling an antique skeleton. The brick walls, the materials of which were imported from Holland, and the timbers of the mansion, are still as sound as ever; but the floors and other interior parts being greatly decayed, it is contemplated to gut the whole, and build a new house within the ancient frame and brick work. Among other inconveniences of the present edifice, mine host mentioned that any jar or motion was apt to shake down the dust of ages out of the ceiling of one chamber upon the floor of that beneath it.

We stepped forth from the great front window into the balcony, where, in old times, it was doubtless the custom of the king's representative to show himself to a loyal populace, requiting their huzzas and tossed-up hats with stately bendings of his dignified person. In those days the front of the Province House looked upon the street; and the whole site now occupied by the brick range of stores, as well as the present courtyard, was laid out in grass plats, overshadowed by trees and bordered by a wrought-iron fence. Now, the old aristocratic edifice hides its time-worn visage behind an upstart modern building; at one of the back windows I observed some pretty tailoresses, sewing and chatting and laughing, with now and then a careless glance towards the balcony. Descending thence, we again entered the bar-room, where the elderly gentleman above mentioned, the smack of whose lips had spoken so favorably for Mr. Waite's good liquor, was still lounging in his chair. He seemed to be, if not a lodger, at least a familiar visitor of the house, who might be supposed to have his regular score at the bar, his summer seat at the open window, and his prescriptive corner at the winter's fireside. Being of a sociable aspect, I ventured to address him with a remark calculated to draw forth his historical reminiscences, if any such were in his mind; and it gratified me to discover, that, between memory and tradition, the old gentleman was really possessed of some very pleasant gossip about the Province House. The portion of his talk which chiefly interested me was the outline of the following legend. He professed to have received it at one or two removes from an eye-witness; but this derivation, together with the lapse of time, must have afforded opportunities for many variations of the narrative; so that despairing of literal and absolute truth, I have not scrupled to make such further changes as seemed conducive to the reader's profit and delight.

At one of the entertainments given at the Province House, during the latter part of the siege of Boston, there passed a scene which has never yet been satisfactorily explained. The officers of the British army, and the loyal gentry of the province, most of whom were collected within the beleaguered town, had been invited to a masked ball; for it was the policy of Sir William Howe to hide the distress and danger of the period, and the desperate aspect of the siege, under an ostentation of festivity. The spectacle of this evening, if the oldest members of the provincial court circle might be believed, was the most gay and gorgeous affair that had occurred in the annals of the government. The brilliantly-lighted apartments were thronged with figures that seemed to have stepped from the dark canvas of historic portraits, or to have flitted forth from the magic pages of romance, or at least to have flown hither from one of the London theatres, without a change of garments. Steeled knights of the Conquest, bearded statesmen of Queen Elizabeth, and high-ruffled ladies of her court, were mingled with characters of comedy, such as a party-colored Merry Andrew, jingling his cap and bells; a Falstaff, almost as provocative of laughter as his prototype; and a Don Quixote, with a bean pole for a lance, and a pot lid for a shield.

But the broadest merriment was excited by a group of figures ridiculously dressed in old regimentals, which seemed to have been purchased at a military rag fair, or pilfered from some receptacle of the castoff clothes of both the French and British armies. Portions of their attire had probably been worn at the siege of Louisburg, and the coats of most recent cut might have been rent and tattered by sword, ball, or bayonet, as long ago as Wolfe's victory. One of these worthies—a tall, lank figure, brandishing a rusty sword of immense longitude—purported to be no less a personage than General George Washington; and the other principal officers of the American army, such as Gates, Lee, Putnam, Schuyler, Ward and Heath, were represented by similar scarecrows. An interview in the mock heroic style, between the rebel warriors and the British commander-in-chief, was received with immense applause, which came loudest of all from the loyalists of the colony. There was one of the guests, however, who stood apart, eyeing these antics sternly and scornfully, at once with a frown and a bitter smile.

It was an old man, formerly of high station and great repute in the province, and who had been a very famous soldier in his day. Some surprise had been expressed that a person of Colonel Joliffe's known whig principles, though now too old to take an active part in the contest, should have remained in Boston during the siege, and especially that he should consent to show himself in the mansion of Sir William Howe. But thither he had come, with a fair granddaughter under his arm; and there, amid all the mirth and buffoonery, stood this stern old figure, the best sustained character in the masquerade, because so well representing the antique spirit of his native land. The other guests affirmed that Colonel Joliffe's black puritanical scowl threw a shadow round about him; although in spite of his sombre influence their gayety continued to blaze higher, like—(an ominous comparison)—the flickering brilliancy of a lamp which has but a little while to burn. Eleven strokes, full half an hour ago, had pealed from the clock of the Old South, when a rumor was circulated among the company that some new spectacle or pageant was about to be exhibited, which should put a fitting close to the splendid festivities of the night.

"What new jest has your Excellency in hand?" asked the Rev. Mather Byles, whose Presbyterian scruples had not kept him from the entertainment. "Trust me, sir, I have already laughed more than beseems my cloth at your Homeric confabulation with yonder ragamuffin General of the rebels. One other such fit of merriment, and I must throw off my clerical wig and band."

"Not so, good Doctor Byles," answered Sir William Howe; "if mirth were a crime, you had never gained your doctorate in divinity. As to this new foolery, I know no more about it than yourself; perhaps not so much. Honestly now, Doctor, have you not stirred up the sober brains of some of your countrymen to enact a scene in our masquerade?"

"Perhaps," slyly remarked the granddaughter of Colonel Joliffe, whose high spirit had been stung by many taunts against New England,—"perhaps we are to have a mask of allegorical figures. Victory, with trophies from Lexington and Bunker Hill—Plenty, with her overflowing horn, to typify the present abundance in this good town—and Glory, with a wreath for his Excellency's brow."

Sir William Howe smiled at words which he would have answered with one of his darkest frowns had they been uttered by lips that wore a beard. He was spared the necessity of a retort, by a singular interruption. A sound of music was heard without the house, as if proceeding from a full band of military instruments stationed in the street, playing not such a festal strain as was suited to the occasion, but a slow funeral march. The drums appeared to be muffled, and the trumpets poured forth a wailing breath, which at once hushed the merriment of the auditors, filling all with wonder, and some with apprehension. The idea occurred to many that either the funeral procession of some great personage had halted in front of the Province House, or that a corpse, in a velvet-covered and gorgeously-decorated coffin, was about to be borne from the portal. After listening a moment, Sir William Howe called, in a stern voice, to the leader of the musicians, who had hitherto enlivened the entertainment with gay and lightsome melodies. The man was drum-major to one of the British regiments.

"Dighton," demanded the general, "what means this foolery? Bid your band silence that dead march—or, by my word, they shall have sufficient cause for their lugubrious strains! Silence it, sirrah!"

"Please your honor," answered the drum-major, whose rubicund visage had lost all its color, "the fault is none of mine. I and my band are all here together, and I question whether there be a man of us that could play that march without book. I never heard it but once before, and that was at the funeral of his late Majesty, King George the Second."

"Well, well!" said Sir William Howe, recovering his composure—"it is the prelude to some masquerading antic. Let it pass."

A figure now presented itself, but among the many fantastic masks that were dispersed through the apartments none could tell precisely from whence it came. It was a man in an old-fashioned dress of black serge, and having the aspect of a steward or principal domestic in the household of a nobleman or great English landholder. This figure advanced to the outer door of the mansion, and throwing both its leaves wide open, withdrew a little to one side and looked back towards the grand staircase as if expecting some person to descend. At the same time the music in the street sounded a loud and doleful summons. The eyes of Sir William Howe and his guests being directed to the staircase, there appeared, on the uppermost landing-place that was discernible from the bottom, several personages descending towards the door. The foremost was a man of stern visage, wearing a steeple-crowned hat and a skull-cap beneath it; a dark cloak, and huge wrinkled boots that came half-way up his legs. Under his arm was a rolled-up banner, which seemed to be the banner of England, but strangely rent and torn; he had a sword in his right hand, and grasped a Bible in his left. The next figure was of milder aspect, yet full of dignity, wearing a broad ruff, over which descended a beard, a gown of wrought velvet, and a doublet and hose of black satin. He carried a roll of manuscript in his hand. Close behind these two came a young man of very striking countenance and demeanor, with deep thought and contemplation on his brow, and perhaps a flash of enthusiasm in his eye. His garb, like that of his predecessors, was of an antique fashion, and there was a stain of blood upon his ruff. In the same group with these were three or four others, all men of dignity and evident command, and bearing themselves like personages who were accustomed to the gaze of the multitude. It was the idea of the beholders that these figures went to join the mysterious funeral that had halted in front of the Province House; yet that supposition seemed to be contradicted by the air of triumph with which they waved their hands, as they crossed the threshold and vanished through the portal.

"In the devil's name what is this?" muttered Sir William Howe to a gentleman beside him; "a procession of the regicide judges of King Charles the martyr?"

"These," said Colonel Joliffe, breaking silence almost for the first time that evening,—"these, if I interpret them aright, are the Puritan governors—the rulers of the old original Democracy of Massachusetts. Endicott, with the banner from which he had torn the symbol of subjection, and Winthrop, and Sir Henry Vane, and Dudley, Haynes, Bellingham, and Leverett."

"Why had that young man a stain of blood upon his ruff?" asked Miss Joliffe.

"Because, in after years," answered her grandfather, "he laid down the wisest head in England upon the block for the principles of liberty."

"Will not your Excellency order out the guard?" whispered Lord Percy, who, with other British officers, had now assembled round the General. "There may be a plot under this mummery."

"Tush! we have nothing to fear," carelessly replied Sir William Howe. "There can be no worse treason in the matter than a jest, and that somewhat of the dullest. Even were it a sharp and bitter one, our best policy would be to laugh it off. See—here come more of these gentry."

Another group of characters had now partly descended the staircase. The first was a venerable and white-bearded patriarch, who cautiously felt his way downward with a staff. Treading hastily behind him, and stretching forth his gauntleted hand as if to grasp the old man's shoulder, came a tall, soldier-like figure, equipped with a plumed cap of steel, a bright breastplate, and a long sword, which rattled against the stairs. Next was seen a stout man, dressed in rich and courtly attire, but not of courtly demeanor; his gait had the swinging motion of a seaman's walk; and chancing to stumble on the staircase, he suddenly grew wrathful, and was heard to mutter an oath. He was followed by a noble-looking personage in a curled wig, such as are represented in the portraits of Queen Anne's time and earlier; and the breast of his coat was decorated with an embroidered star. While advancing to the door, he bowed to the right hand and to the left, in a very gracious and insinuating style; but as he crossed the threshold, unlike the early Puritan governors, he seemed to wring his hands with sorrow.

"Prithee, play the part of a chorus, good Doctor Byles," said Sir William Howe. "What worthies are these?"

"If it please your Excellency they lived somewhat before my day," answered the doctor; "but doubtless our friend, the Colonel, has been hand and glove with them."

"Their living faces I never looked upon," said Colonel Joliffe, gravely; "although I have spoken face to face with many rulers of this land, and shall greet yet another with an old man's blessing ere I die. But we talk of these figures. I take the venerable patriarch to be Bradstreet, the last of the Puritans, who was governor at ninety, or thereabouts. The next is Sir Edmund Andros, a tyrant, as any New England school-boy will tell you; and therefore the people cast him down from his high seat into a dungeon. Then comes Sir William Phipps, shepherd, cooper, sea-captain, and governor—may many of his countrymen rise as high from as low an origin! Lastly, you saw the gracious Earl of Bellamont, who ruled us under King William."

"But what is the meaning of it all?" asked Lord Percy.

"Now, were I a rebel," said Miss Joliffe, half aloud, "I might fancy that the ghosts of these ancient governors had been summoned to form the funeral procession of royal authority in New England."

Several other figures were now seen at the turn of the staircase. The one in advance had a thoughtful, anxious, and somewhat crafty expression of face, and in spite of his loftiness of manner, which was evidently the result both of an ambitious spirit and of long continuance in high stations, he seemed not incapable of cringing to a greater than himself. A few steps behind came an officer in a scarlet and embroidered uniform, cut in a fashion old enough to have been worn by the Duke of Marlborough. His nose had a rubicund tinge, which, together with the twinkle of his eye, might have marked him as a lover of the wine cup and good fellowship; notwithstanding which tokens he appeared ill at ease, and often glanced around him as if apprehensive of some secret mischief. Next came a portly gentleman, wearing a coat of shaggy cloth, lined with silken velvet; he had sense, shrewdness, and humor in his face, and a folio volume under his arm; but his aspect was that of a man vexed and tormented beyond all patience, and harassed almost to death. He went hastily down, and was followed by a dignified person, dressed in a purple velvet suit, with very rich embroidery; his demeanor would have possessed much stateliness, only that a grievous fit of the gout compelled him to hobble from stair to stair, with contortions of face and body. When Dr. Byles beheld this figure on the staircase, he shivered as with an ague, but continued to watch him steadfastly, until the gouty gentleman had reached the threshold, made a gesture of anguish and despair, and vanished into the outer gloom, whither the funeral music summoned him.

"Governor Belcher!—my old patron!—in his very shape and dress!" gasped Doctor Byles. "This is an awful mockery!"

"A tedious foolery, rather," said Sir William Howe, with an air of indifference. "But who were the three that preceded him?"

"Governor Dudley, a cunning politician—yet his craft once brought him to a prison," replied Colonel Joliffe. "Governor Shute, formerly a Colonel under Marlborough, and whom the people frightened out of the province; and learned Governor Burnet, whom the legislature tormented into a mortal fever."

"Methinks they were miserable men, these royal governors of Massachusetts," observed Miss Joliffe. "Heavens, how dim the light grows!"

It was certainly a fact that the large lamp which illuminated the staircase now burned dim and duskily: so that several figures, which passed hastily down the stairs and went forth from the porch, appeared rather like shadows than persons of fleshly substance. Sir William Howe and his guests stood at the doors of the contiguous apartments, watching the progress of this singular pageant, with various emotions of anger, contempt, or half-acknowledged fear, but still with an anxious curiosity. The shapes which now seemed hastening to join the mysterious procession were recognized rather by striking peculiarities of dress, or broad characteristics of manner, than by any perceptible resemblance of features to their prototypes. Their faces, indeed, were invariably kept in deep shadow. But Doctor Byles, and other gentlemen who had long been familiar with the successive rulers of the province, were heard to whisper the names of Shirley, of Pownall, of Sir Francis Bernard, and of the well-remembered Hutchinson; thereby confessing that the actors, whoever they might be, in this spectral march of governors, had succeeded in putting on some distant portraiture of the real personages. As they vanished from the door, still did these shadows toss their arms into the gloom of night, with a dread expression of woe. Following the mimic representative of Hutchinson came a military figure, holding before his face the cocked hat which he had taken from his powdered head; but his epaulettes and other insignia of rank were those of a general officer, and something in his mien reminded the beholders of one who had recently been master of the Province House, and chief of all the land.

"The shape of Gage, as true as in a looking-glass," exclaimed Lord Percy, turning pale.

"No, surely," cried Miss Joliffe, laughing hysterically; "it could not be Gage, or Sir William would have greeted his old comrade in arms! Perhaps he will not suffer the next to pass unchallenged."

"Of that be assured, young lady," answered Sir William Howe, fixing his eyes, with a very marked expression, upon the immovable visage of her grandfather. "I have long enough delayed to pay the ceremonies of a host to these departing guests. The next that takes his leave shall receive due courtesy."

A wild and dreary burst of music came through the open door. It seemed as if the procession, which had been gradually filling up its ranks, were now about to move, and that this loud peal of the wailing trumpets, and roll of the muffled drums, were a call to some loiterer to make haste. Many eyes, by an irresistible impulse, were turned upon Sir William Howe, as if it were he whom the dreary music summoned to the funeral of departed power.

"See!—here comes the last!" whispered Miss Joliffe, pointing her tremulous finger to the staircase.

A figure had come into view as if descending the stairs; although so dusky was the region whence it emerged, some of the spectators fancied that they had seen this human shape suddenly moulding itself amid the gloom. Downward the figure came, with a stately and martial tread, and reaching the lowest stair was observed to be a tall man, booted and wrapped in a military cloak, which was drawn up around the face so as to meet the flapped brim of a laced hat. The features, therefore, were completely hidden. But the British officers deemed that they had seen that military cloak before, and even recognized the frayed embroidery on the collar, as well as the gilded scabbard of a sword which protruded from the folds of the cloak, and glittered in a vivid gleam of light. Apart from these trifling particulars, there were characteristics of gait and bearing which impelled the wondering guests to glance from the shrouded figure to Sir William Howe, as if to satisfy themselves that their host had not suddenly vanished from the midst of them.

With a dark flush of wrath upon his brow they saw the General draw his sword and advance to meet the figure in the cloak before the latter had stepped one pace upon the floor.

"Villain, unmuffle yourself!" cried he. "You pass no farther!"

The figure, without blenching a hair's breadth from the sword which was pointed at his breast, made a solemn pause and lowered the cape of the cloak from about his face, yet not sufficiently for the spectators to catch a glimpse of it. But Sir William Howe had evidently seen enough. The sternness of his countenance gave place to a look of wild amazement, if not horror, while he recoiled several steps from the figure, and let fall his sword upon the floor. The martial shape again drew the cloak about his features and passed on; but reaching the threshold, with his back towards the spectators, he was seen to stamp his foot and shake his clinched hands in the air. It was afterwards affirmed that Sir William Howe had repeated that selfsame gesture of rage and sorrow, when, for the last time, and as the last royal governor, he passed through the portal of the Province House.

"Hark!—the procession moves," said Miss Joliffe.

The music was dying away along the street, and its dismal strains were mingled with the knell of midnight from the steeple of the Old South, and with the roar of artillery, which announced that the beleaguering army of Washington had intrenched itself upon a nearer height than before. As the deep boom of the cannon smote upon his ear, Colonel Joliffe raised himself to the full height of his aged form, and smiled sternly on the British General.

"Would your Excellency inquire further into the mystery of the pageant?" said he.

"Take care of your gray head!" cried Sir William Howe, fiercely, though with a quivering lip. "It has stood too long on a traitor's shoulders!"

"You must make haste to chop it off, then," calmly replied the Colonel; "for a few hours longer, and not all the power of Sir William Howe, nor of his master, shall cause one of these gray hairs to fall. The empire of Britain in this ancient province is at its last gasp to-night;—almost while I speak it is a dead corpse;—and methinks the shadows of the old governors are fit mourners at its funeral!"

With these words Colonel Joliffe threw on his cloak, and drawing his granddaughter's arm within his own, retired from the last festival that a British ruler ever held in the old province of Massachusetts Bay. It was supposed that the Colonel and the young lady possessed some secret intelligence in regard to the mysterious pageant of that night. However this might be, such knowledge has never become general. The actors in the scene have vanished into deeper obscurity than even that wild Indian band who scattered the cargoes of the tea ships on the waves, and gained a place in history, yet left no names. But superstition, among other legends of this mansion, repeats the wondrous tale, that on the anniversary night of Britain's discomfiture the ghosts of the ancient governors of Massachusetts still glide through the portal of the Province House. And, last of all, comes a figure shrouded in a military cloak, tossing his clinched hands into the air, and stamping his iron-shod boots upon the broad freestone steps, with a semblance of feverish despair, but without the sound of a foot-tramp.

When the truth-telling accents of the elderly gentleman were hushed, I drew a long breath and looked round the room, striving, with the best energy of my imagination, to throw a tinge of romance and historic grandeur over the realities of the scene. But my nostrils snuffed up a scent of cigar smoke, clouds of which the narrator had emitted by way of visible emblem, I suppose, of the nebulous obscurity of his tale. Moreover, my gorgeous fantasies were wofully disturbed by the rattling of the spoon in a tumbler of whiskey punch, which Mr. Thomas Waite was mingling for a customer. Nor did it add to the picturesque appearance of the panelled walls that the slate of the Brookline stage was suspended against them, instead of the armorial escutcheon of some far-descended governor. A stage-driver sat at one of the windows, reading a penny paper of the day—the Boston Times—and presenting a figure which could nowise be brought into any picture of "Times in Boston" seventy or a hundred years ago. On the window seat lay a bundle, neatly done up in brown paper, the direction of which I had the idle curiosity to read. "Miss SUSAN HUGGINS, at the PROVINCE HOUSE." A pretty chambermaid, no doubt. In truth, it is desperately hard work, when we attempt to throw the spell of hoar antiquity over localities with which the living world, and the day that is passing over us, have aught to do. Yet, as I glanced at the stately staircase down which the procession of the old governors had descended, and as I emerged through the venerable portal whence their figures had preceded me, it gladdened me to be conscious of a thrill of awe. Then, diving through the narrow archway, a few strides transported me into the densest throng of Washington Street.

II. EDWARD RANDOLPH'S PORTRAIT

The old legendary guest of the Province House abode in my remembrance from midsummer till January. One idle evening last winter, confident that he would be found in the snuggest corner of the bar-room, I resolved to pay him another visit, hoping to deserve well of my country by snatching from oblivion some else unheard-of fact of history. The night was chill and raw, and rendered boisterous by almost a gale of wind, which whistled along Washington Street, causing the gas-lights to flare and flicker within the lamps. As I hurried onward, my fancy was busy with a comparison between the present aspect of the street and that which it probably wore when the British governors inhabited the mansion whither I was now going. Brick edifices in those times were few, till a succession of destructive fires had swept, and swept again, the wooden dwellings and warehouses from the most populous quarters of the town. The buildings stood insulated and independent, not, as now, merging their separate existences into connected ranges, with a front of tiresome identity,—but each possessing features of its own, as if the owner's individual taste had shaped it,—and the whole presenting a picturesque irregularity, the absence of which is hardly compensated by any beauties of our modern architecture. Such a scene, dimly vanishing from the eye by the ray of here and there a tallow candle, glimmering through the small panes of scattered windows, would form a sombre contrast to the street as I beheld it, with the gas-lights blazing from corner to corner, flaming within the shops, and throwing a noonday brightness through the huge plates of glass.

But the black, lowering sky, as I turned my eyes upward, wore, doubtless, the same visage as when it frowned upon the ante-revolutionary New Englanders. The wintry blast had the same shriek that was familiar to their ears. The Old South Church, too, still pointed its antique spire into the darkness, and was lost between earth and heaven; and as I passed, its clock, which had warned so many generations how transitory was their lifetime, spoke heavily and slow the same unregarded moral to myself. "Only seven o'clock," thought I. "My old friend's legends will scarcely kill the hours 'twixt this and bedtime."

Passing through the narrow arch, I crossed the court-yard, the confined precincts of which were made visible by a lantern over the portal of the Province House. On entering the bar-room, I found, as I expected, the old tradition monger seated by a special good fire of anthracite, compelling clouds of smoke from a corpulent cigar. He recognized me with evident pleasure; for my rare properties as a patient listener invariably make me a favorite with elderly gentlemen and ladies of narrative propensities. Drawing a chair to the fire, I desired mine host to favor us with a glass apiece of whiskey punch, which was speedily prepared, steaming hot, with a slice of lemon at the bottom, a dark-red stratum of port wine upon the surface, and a sprinkling of nutmeg strewn over all. As we touched our glasses together, my legendary friend made himself known to me as Mr. Bela Tiffany; and I rejoiced at the oddity of the name, because it gave his image and character a sort of individuality in my conception. The old gentleman's draught acted as a solvent upon his memory, so that it overflowed with tales, traditions, anecdotes of famous dead people, and traits of ancient manners, some of which were childish as a nurse's lullaby, while others might have been worth the notice of the grave historian. Nothing impressed me more than a story of a black mysterious picture, which used to hang in one of the chambers of the Province House, directly above the room where we were now sitting. The following is as correct a version of the fact as the reader would be likely to obtain from any other source, although, assuredly, it has a tinge of romance approaching to the marvellous.

In one of the apartments of the Province House there was long preserved an ancient picture, the frame of which was as black as ebony, and the canvas itself so dark with age, damp, and smoke, that not a touch of the painter's art could be discerned. Time had thrown an impenetrable veil over it, and left to tradition and fable and conjecture to say what had once been there portrayed. During the rule of many successive governors, it had hung, by prescriptive and undisputed right, over the mantel-piece of the same chamber; and it still kept its place when Lieutenant-Governor Hutchinson assumed the administration of the province, on the departure of Sir Francis Bernard.

The Lieutenant-Governor sat, one afternoon, resting his head against the carved back of his stately arm-chair, and gazing up thoughtfully at the void blackness of the picture. It was scarcely a time for such inactive musing, when affairs of the deepest moment required the ruler's decision; for, within that very hour Hutchinson had received intelligence of the arrival of a British fleet, bringing three regiments from Halifax to overawe the insubordination of the people. These troops awaited his permission to occupy the fortress of Castle William, and the town itself. Yet, instead of affixing his signature to an official order, there sat the Lieutenant-Governor, so carefully scrutinizing the black waste of canvas that his demeanor attracted the notice of two young persons who attended him. One, wearing a military dress of buff, was his kinsman, Francis Lincoln, the Provincial Captain of Castle William; the other, who sat on a low stool beside his chair, was Alice Vane, his favorite niece.

She was clad entirely in white, a pale, ethereal creature, who, though a native of New England, had been educated abroad, and seemed not merely a stranger from another clime, but almost a being from another world. For several years, until left an orphan, she had dwelt with her father in sunny Italy, and there had acquired a taste and enthusiasm for sculpture and painting which she found few opportunities of gratifying in the undecorated dwellings of the colonial gentry. It was said that the early productions of her own pencil exhibited no inferior genius, though, perhaps, the rude atmosphere of New England had cramped her hand, and dimmed the glowing colors of her fancy. But observing her uncle's steadfast gaze, which appeared to search through the mist of years to discover the subject of the picture, her curiosity was excited.

"Is it known, my dear uncle," inquired she, "what this old picture once represented? Possibly, could it be made visible, it might prove a masterpiece of some great artist—else, why has it so long held such a conspicuous place?"

As her uncle, contrary to his usual custom (for he was as attentive to all the humors and caprices of Alice as if she had been his own best-beloved child), did not immediately reply, the young Captain of Castle William took that office upon himself.

"This dark old square of canvas, my fair cousin," said he, "has been an heirloom in the Province House from time immemorial. As to the painter, I can tell you nothing; but, if half the stories told of it be true, not one of the great Italian masters has ever produced so marvellous a piece of work as that before you."

Captain Lincoln proceeded to relate some of the strange fables and fantasies which, as it was impossible to refute them by ocular demonstration, had grown to be articles of popular belief, in reference to this old picture. One of the wildest, and at the same time the best accredited, accounts, stated it to be an original and authentic portrait of the Evil One, taken at a witch meeting near Salem; and that its strong and terrible resemblance had been confirmed by several of the confessing wizards and witches, at their trial, in open court. It was likewise affirmed that a familiar spirit or demon abode behind the blackness of the picture, and had shown himself, at seasons of public calamity, to more than one of the royal governors. Shirley, for instance, had beheld this ominous apparition, on the eve of General Abercrombie's shameful and bloody defeat under the walls of Ticonderoga. Many of the servants of the Province House had caught glimpses of a visage frowning down upon them, at morning or evening twilight,—or in the depths of night, while raking up the fire that glimmered on the hearth beneath; although, if any were bold enough to hold a torch before the picture, it would appear as black and undistinguishable as ever. The oldest inhabitant of Boston recollected that his father, in whose days the portrait had not wholly faded out of sight, had once looked upon it, but would never suffer himself to be questioned as to the face which was there represented. In connection with such stories, it was remarkable that over the top of the frame there were some ragged remnants of black silk, indicating that a veil had formerly hung down before the picture, until the duskiness of time had so effectually concealed it. But, after all, it was the most singular part of the affair that so many of the pompous governors of Massachusetts had allowed the obliterated picture to remain in the state chamber of the Province House.

"Some of these fables are really awful," observed Alice Vane, who had occasionally shuddered, as well as smiled, while her cousin spoke. "It would be almost worth while to wipe away the black surface of the canvas, since the original picture can hardly be so formidable as those which fancy paints instead of it."

"But would it be possible," inquired her cousin, "to restore this dark picture to its pristine hues?"

"Such arts are known in Italy," said Alice.

The Lieutenant-Governor had roused himself from his abstracted mood, and listened with a smile to the conversation of his young relatives. Yet his voice had something peculiar in its tones when he under-took the explanation of the mystery.

"I am sorry, Alice, to destroy your faith in the legends of which you are so fond," remarked he; "but my antiquarian researches have long since made me acquainted with the subject of this picture—if picture it can be called—which is no more visible, nor ever will be, than the face of the long buried man whom it once represented. It was the portrait of Edward Randolph, the founder of this house, a person famous in the history of New England."

"Of that Edward Randolph," exclaimed Captain Lincoln, "who obtained the repeal of the first provincial charter, under which our forefathers had enjoyed almost democratic privileges! He that was styled the arch-enemy of New England, and whose memory is still held in detestation as the destroyer of our liberties!"

"It was the same Randolph," answered Hutchinson, moving uneasily in his chair. "It was his lot to taste the bitterness of popular odium."

"Our annals tell us," continued the Captain of Castle William, "that the curse of the people followed this Randolph where he went, and wrought evil in all the subsequent events of his life, and that its effect was seen likewise in the manner of his death. They say, too, that the inward misery of that curse worked itself outward, and was visible on the wretched man's countenance, making it too horrible to be looked upon. If so, and if this picture truly represented his aspect, it was in mercy that the cloud of blackness has gathered over it."

"These traditions are folly to one who has proved, as I have, how little of historic truth lies at the bottom," said the Lieutenant-Governor. "As regards the life and character of Edward Randolph, too implicit credence has been given to Dr. Cotton Mather, who—I must say it, though some of his blood runs in my veins—has filled our early history with old women's tales, as fanciful and extravagant as those of Greece or Rome."

"And yet," whispered Alice Vane, "may not such fables have a moral? And, methinks, if the visage of this portrait be so dreadful, it is not without a cause that it has hung so long in a chamber of the Province House. When the rulers feel themselves irresponsible, it were well that they should be reminded of the awful weight of a people's curse."

The Lieutenant-Governor started, and gazed for a moment at his niece, as if her girlish fantasies had struck upon some feeling in his own breast, which all his policy or principles could not entirely subdue. He knew, indeed, that Alice, in spite of her foreign education, retained the native sympathies of a New England girl.

"Peace, silly child," cried he, at last, more harshly than he had ever before addressed the gentle Alice. "The rebuke of a king is more to be dreaded than the clamor of a wild, misguided multitude. Captain Lincoln, it is decided. The fortress of Castle William must be occupied by the royal troops. The two remaining regiments shall be billeted in the town, or encamped upon the

Common. It is time, after years of tumult, and almost rebellion, that his majesty's government should have a wall of strength about it."

"Trust, sir—trust yet awhile to the loyalty of the people," said Captain Lincoln; "nor teach them that they can ever be on other terms with British soldiers than those of brotherhood, as when they fought side by side through the French War. Do not convert the streets of your native town into a camp. Think twice before you give up old Castle William, the key of the province, into other keeping than that of true-born New Englanders."

"Young man, it is decided," repeated Hutchinson, rising from his chair. "A British officer will be in attendance this evening, to receive the necessary instructions for the disposal of the troops. Your presence also will be required. Till then, farewell."

With these words the Lieutenant-Governor hastily left the room, while Alice and her cousin more slowly followed, whispering together, and once pausing to glance back at the mysterious picture. The Captain of Castle William fancied that the girl's air and mien were such as might have belonged to one of those spirits of fable—fairies, or creatures of a more antique mythology—who sometimes mingled their agency with mortal affairs, half in caprice, yet with a sensibility to human weal or woe. As he held the door for her to pass, Alice beckoned to the picture and smiled.

"Come forth, dark and evil Shape!" cried she. "It is thine hour!"

In the evening, Lieutenant-Governor Hutchinson sat in the same chamber where the foregoing scene had occurred, surrounded by several persons whose various interests had summoned them together. There were the Selectmen of Boston, plain, patriarchal fathers of the people, excellent representatives of the old puritanical founders, whose sombre strength had stamped so deep an impress upon the New England character. Contrasting with these were one or two members of Council, richly dressed in the white wigs, the embroidered waistcoats and other magnificence of the time, and making a somewhat ostentatious display of courtier-like ceremonial. In attendance, likewise, was a major of the British army, awaiting the Lieutenant-Governor's orders for the landing of the troops, which still remained on board the transports. The Captain of Castle William stood beside Hutchinson's chair with folded arms, glancing rather haughtily at the British officer, by whom he was soon to be superseded in his command. On a table, in the centre of the chamber, stood a branched silver candlestick, throwing down the glow of half a dozen wax-lights upon a paper apparently ready for the Lieutenant-Governor's signature.

Partly shrouded in the voluminous folds of one of the window curtains, which fell from the ceiling to the floor, was seen the white drapery of a lady's robe. It may appear strange that Alice Vane should have been there at such a time; but there was something so childlike, so wayward, in her singular character, so apart from ordinary rules, that her presence did not surprise the few who noticed it. Meantime, the chairman of the Selectmen was addressing to the Lieutenant-Governor a long and solemn protest against the reception of the British troops into the town.

"And if your Honor," concluded this excellent but somewhat prosy old gentleman, "shall see fit to persist in bringing these mercenary sworders and musketeers into our quiet streets, not on our heads be the responsibility. Think, sir, while there is yet time, that if one drop of blood be shed, that blood shall be an eternal stain upon your Honor's memory. You, sir, have written with an able pen the deeds of our forefathers. The more to be desired is it, therefore, that yourself should deserve honorable mention, as a true patriot and upright ruler, when your own doings shall be written down in history."

"I am not insensible, my good sir, to the natural desire to stand well in the annals of my country," replied Hutchinson, controlling his impatience into courtesy, "nor know I any better method of attaining that end than by withstanding the merely temporary spirit of mischief, which, with your pardon, seems to have infected elder men than myself. Would you have me wait till the mob shall sack the Province House, as they did my private mansion? Trust me, sir, the time may come when you will be glad to flee for protection to the king's banner, the raising of which is now so distasteful to you."

"Yes," said the British major, who was impatiently expecting the Lieutenant-Governor's orders. "The demagogues of this Province have raised the devil and cannot lay him again. We will exorcise him, in God's name and the king's."

"If you meddle with the devil, take care of his claws!" answered the Captain of Castle William, stirred by the taunt against his countrymen.

"Craving your pardon, young sir," said the venerable Selectman, "let not an evil spirit enter into your words. We will strive against the oppressor with prayer and fasting, as our forefathers would have done. Like them, moreover, we will submit to whatever lot a wise Providence may send us,—always, after our own best exertions to amend it."

"And there peep forth the devil's claws!" muttered Hutchinson, who well understood the nature of Puritan submission. "This matter shall be expedited forthwith. When there shall be a sentinel at every corner, and a court of guard before the town house, a loyal gentleman may venture to walk abroad. What to me is the outcry of a mob, in this remote province of the realm? The king is my master, and England is my country! Upheld by their armed strength, I set my foot upon the rabble, and defy them!"

He snatched a pen, and was about to affix his signature to the paper that lay on the table, when the Captain of Castle William placed his hand upon his shoulder. The freedom of the action, so contrary to the ceremonious respect which was then considered due to rank and dignity, awakened general surprise, and in none more than in the Lieutenant-Governor himself. Looking angrily up, he perceived that his young relative was pointing his finger to the opposite wall. Hutchinson's eye followed the signal; and he saw, what had hitherto been unobserved, that a black silk curtain was suspended before the mysterious picture, so as completely to conceal it. His thoughts immediately recurred to the scene of the preceding afternoon; and, in his surprise, confused by indistinct emotions, yet sensible that his niece must have had an agency in this phenomenon, he called loudly upon her.

"Alice!—come hither, Alice!"

No sooner had he spoken than Alice Vane glided from her station, and pressing one hand across her eyes, with the other snatched away the sable curtain that concealed the portrait. An exclamation of surprise burst from every beholder; but the Lieutenant-Governor's voice had a tone of horror.

"By Heaven!" said he, in a low, inward murmur, speaking rather to himself than to those around him, "if the spirit of Edward Randolph were to appear among us from the place of torment, he could not wear more of the terrors of hell upon his face!"

"For some wise end," said the aged Selectman, solemnly, "hath Providence scattered away the mist of years that had so long hid this dreadful effigy. Until this hour no living man hath seen what we behold!"

Within the antique frame, which so recently had inclosed a sable waste of canvas, now appeared a visible picture, still dark, indeed, in its hues and shadings, but thrown forward in strong relief. It was a half-length figure of a gentleman in a rich but very old-fashioned dress of embroidered velvet, with a broad ruff and a beard, and wearing a hat, the brim of which overshadowed his forehead. Beneath this cloud the eyes had a peculiar glare, which was almost lifelike. The whole portrait started so distinctly out of the background, that it had the effect of a person looking down from the wall at the astonished and awe-stricken spectators. The expression of the face, if any words can convey an idea of it, was that of a wretch detected in some hideous guilt, and exposed to the bitter hatred and laughter and withering scorn of a vast surrounding multitude. There was the struggle of defiance, beaten down and overwhelmed by the crushing weight of ignominy. The torture of the soul had come forth upon the countenance. It seemed as if the picture, while hidden behind the cloud of immemorial years, had been all the time acquiring an intenser depth and darkness of expression, till now it gloomed forth again, and threw its evil omen over the present hour. Such, if the wild legend may be credited, was the portrait of Edward Randolph, as he appeared when a people's curse had wrought its influence upon his nature.

" 'Twould drive me mad—that awful face!" said Hutchinson, who seemed fascinated by the contemplation of it.

"Be warned, then!" whispered Alice. "He trampled on a people's right. Behold his punishment—and avoid a crime like his!"

The Lieutenant-Governor actually trembled for an instant; but, exerting his energy—which was not, however, his most characteristic feature—he strove to shake off the spell of Randolph's countenance.

"Girl!" cried he, laughing bitterly as he turned to Alice, "have you brought hither your painter's art—your Italian spirit of intrigue—your tricks of stage effect —and think to influence the councils of rulers and the affairs of nations by such shallow contrivances? See here!"

"Stay yet a while," said the Selectman, as Hutchinson again snatched the pen; "for if ever mortal man received a warning from a tormented soul, your Honor is that man!"

"Away!" answered Hutchinson fiercely. "Though yonder senseless picture cried 'Forbear!'—it should not move me!"

Casting a scowl of defiance at the pictured face (which seemed at that moment to intensify the horror of its miserable and wicked look), he scrawled on the paper, in characters that betokened it a deed of desperation, the name of Thomas Hutchinson. Then, it is said, he shuddered, as if that signature had granted away his salvation.

"It is done," said he; and placed his hand upon his brow.

"May Heaven forgive the deed," said the soft, sad accents of Alice Vane, like the voice of a good spirit flitting away.

When morning came there was a stifled whisper through the household, and spreading thence about the town, that the dark, mysterious picture had started from the wall, and spoken face to face with Lieutenant-Governor Hutchinson. If such a miracle had been wrought, however, no traces of it remained behind, for within the antique frame nothing could be discerned save the impenetrable cloud, which had covered the canvas since the memory of man. If the figure had, indeed, stepped forth, it had fled back, spirit-like, at the daydawn, and hidden itself behind a century's obscurity. The truth probably was, that Alice Vane's secret for restoring the hues of the picture had merely effected a temporary renovation. But those who, in that brief interval, had beheld the awful visage of Edward Randolph, desired no second glance, and ever afterwards trembled at the recollection of the scene, as if an evil spirit had appeared visibly among them. And as for Hutchinson, when, far over the ocean, his dying hour drew on, he gasped for breath, and complained that he was choking with the blood of the Boston Massacre; and Francis Lincoln, the former Captain of Castle William, who was standing at his bedside, perceived a likeness in his frenzied look to that of Edward Randolph. Did his broken spirit feel, at that dread hour, the tremendous burden of a People's curse?

At the conclusion of this miraculous legend, I inquired of mine host whether the picture still remained in the chamber over our heads; but Mr. Tiffany informed me that it had long since been removed, and was supposed to be hidden in some out-of-the-way corner of the New England Museum. Perchance some curious antiquary may light upon it there, and, with the assistance of Mr. Howorth, the picture cleaner, may supply a not unnecessary proof of the authenticity of the facts here set down. During the progress of the story a storm had been gathering abroad, and raging and rattling so loudly in the upper regions of the Province House, that it seemed as if all the old governors and great men were running riot above stairs while Mr. Bela Tiffany babbled of them below. In the course of generations, when many people have lived and died in an ancient house, the whistling of the wind through its crannies, and the creaking of its beams and rafters, become strangely like the tones of the human voice, or thundering laughter, or heavy footsteps treading the deserted chambers. It is as if the echoes of half a century were revived. Such were the ghostly sounds that roared and murmured in our ears when I took leave of the circle round the fireside of the Province House, and plunging down the door steps, fought my way homeward against a drifting snow-storm.

III. LADY ELEANORE'S MANTLE

Mine excellent friend, the landlord of the Province House, was pleased, the other evening, to invite Mr. Tiffany and myself to an oyster supper. This slight mark of respect and gratitude, as he handsomely observed, was far less than the ingenious tale-teller, and I, the humble note-taker of his narratives, had fairly earned, by the public notice which our joint lucubrations had attracted to his establishment. Many a cigar had been smoked within his premises—many a glass of wine, or more potent aqua vitæ, had been quaffed—many a dinner had been eaten by curious strangers, who, save for the fortunate conjunction of Mr. Tiffany and me, would never have ventured through that darksome avenue which gives access to the historic precincts of the Province House. In short, if any credit be due to the courteous assurances of Mr. Thomas Waite, we had brought his forgotten mansion almost as effectually into public view as if we had thrown down the vulgar range of shoe shops and dry goods stores, which hides its aristocratic front from Washington Street. It may be unadvisable, however, to speak too loudly of the increased custom of the house, lest Mr. Waite should find it difficult to renew the lease on so favorable terms as heretofore.

Being thus welcomed as benefactors, neither Mr. Tiffany nor myself felt any scruple in doing full justice to the good things that were set before us. If the feast were less magnificent than those same panelled walls had witnessed in a by-gone century,—if mine host presided with somewhat less of state than might have befitted a successor of the royal Governors,—if the guests made a less imposing show than the bewigged and powdered and embroided dignitaries, who erst banqueted at the gubernatorial table, and now sleep, within their armorial tombs on Copp's Hill, or round King's Chapel,—yet never, I may boldly say, did a more comfortable little party assemble in the Province House, from Queen Anne's days to the Revolution. The occasion was rendered more interesting by the presence of a venerable personage, whose own actual reminiscences went back to the epoch of Gage and Howe, and even supplied him with a doubtful anecdote or two of Hutchinson. He was one of that small, and now all but extinguished, class, whose attachment to royalty, and to the colonial institutions and customs that were connected with it, had never yielded to the democratic heresies of after times. The young queen of Britain has not a more loyal subject in her realm—perhaps not one who would kneel before her throne with such reverential love—as this old grandsire, whose head has whitened beneath the mild sway of the Republic, which still, in his mellower moments, he terms a usurpation. Yet prejudices so obstinate have not made him an ungentle or impracticable companion. If the truth must be told, the life of the aged loyalist has been of such a scrambling and unsettled character,—he has had so little choice of friends and been so often destitute of any,—that I doubt whether he would refuse a cup of kindness with either Oliver Cromwell or John Hancock,—to say nothing of any democrat now upon the stage. In another paper of this series I may perhaps give the reader a closer glimpse of his portrait.

Our host, in due season, uncorked a bottle of Madeira, of such exquisite perfume and admirable flavor that he surely must have discovered it in an ancient bin, down deep beneath the deepest cellar, where some jolly old butler stored away the Governor's choicest wine, and forgot to reveal the secret on his death-bed. Peace to his red-nosed ghost, and a libation to his memory! This precious liquor was imbibed by Mr. Tiffany with peculiar zest; and after sipping the third glass, it was his pleasure to give us one of the oddest legends which he had yet raked from the storehouse where he keeps such matters. With some suitable adornments from my own fancy, it ran pretty much as follows.

Not long after Colonel Shute had assumed the government of Massachusetts Bay, now nearly a hundred and twenty years ago, a young lady of rank and fortune arrived from England, to claim his protection as her guardian. He was her distant relative, but the nearest who had survived the gradual extinction of her family; so that no more eligible shelter could be found for the rich and high-born Lady Eleanore Rochcliffe than within the Province House of a transatlantic colony. The consort of Governor Shute, moreover, had been as a mother to her childhood, and was now anxious to receive her, in the hope that a beautiful young woman would be exposed to infinitely less peril from the primitive society of New England than amid the artifices and corruptions of a court. If either the Governor or his lady had especially consulted their own comfort, they would probably have sought to devolve the responsibility on other hands; since, with some noble and splendid traits of character, Lady Eleanore was remarkable for a harsh, unyielding pride, a haughty consciousness of her hereditary and personal advantages, which made her almost incapable of control. Judging from many traditionary anecdotes, this peculiar temper was hardly less than a monomania; or, if the acts which it inspired were those of a sane person, it seemed due from Providence that pride so sinful should be followed by as severe a retribution. That tinge of the marvellous, which is thrown over so many of these half-forgotten legends, has probably imparted an additional wildness to the strange story of Lady Eleanore Rochcliffe.

The ship in which she came passenger had arrived at Newport, whence Lady Eleanore was conveyed to Boston in the Governor's coach, attended by a small escort of gentlemen on horseback. The ponderous equipage, with its four black horses, attracted much notice as it rumbled through Cornhill, surrounded by the prancing steeds of half a dozen cavaliers, with swords dangling to their stirrups and pistols at their holsters. Through the large glass windows of the coach, as it rolled along, the people could discern the figure of Lady Eleanore, strangely combining an almost queenly stateliness with the grace and beauty of a maiden in her teens. A singular tale had gone abroad among the ladies of the province, that their fair rival was indebted for much of the irresistible charm of her appearance to a certain article of dress—an embroidered mantle—which had been wrought by the most skilful artist in London, and possessed even magical properties of adornment. On the present occasion, however, she owed nothing to the witchery of dress, being clad in a riding habit of velvet, which would have appeared stiff and ungraceful on any other form.

The coachman reined in his four black steeds, and the whole cavalcade came to a pause in front of the contorted iron balustrade that fenced the Province House from the public street. It was an awkward coincidence that the bell of the Old South was just then tolling for a funeral; so that, instead of a gladsome peal with which it was customary to announce the arrival of distinguished strangers, Lady Eleanore Rochcliffe was ushered by a doleful clang, as if calamity had come embodied in her beautiful person.

"A very great disrespect!" exclaimed Captain Langford, an English officer, who had recently brought dispatches to Governor Shute. "The funeral should have been deferred, lest Lady Eleanore's spirits be affected by such a dismal welcome."

"With your pardon, sir," replied Doctor Clarke, a physician, and a famous champion of the popular party, "whatever the heralds may pretend, a dead beggar must have precedence of a living queen. King Death confers high privileges."

These remarks were interchanged while the speakers waited a passage through the crowd, which had gathered on each side of the gateway, leaving an open avenue to the portal of the Province House. A black slave in livery now leaped from behind the coach, and threw open the door; while at the same moment Governor Shute descended the flight of steps from his mansion, to assist Lady Eleanore in alighting. But the Governor's stately approach was anticipated in a manner that excited general astonishment. A pale young man, with his black hair all in disorder, rushed from the throng, and prostrated himself beside the coach, thus offering his person as a footstool for Lady Eleanore Rochcliffe to tread upon. She held back an instant, yet with an expression as if doubting whether the young man were worthy to bear the weight of her footstep, rather than dissatisfied to receive such awful reverence from a fellow-mortal.

"Up, sir," said the Governor, sternly, at the same time lifting his cane over the intruder. "What means the Bedlamite by this freak?"

"Nay," answered Lady Eleanore playfully, but with more scorn than pity in her tone, "your Excellency shall not strike him. When men seek only to be trampled upon, it were a pity to deny them a favor so easily granted—and so well deserved!"

Then, though as lightly as a sunbeam on a cloud, she placed her foot upon the cowering form, and extended her hand to meet that of the Governor. There was a brief interval, during which Lady Eleanore retained this attitude; and never, surely, was there an apter emblem of aristocracy and hereditary pride trampling on human sympathies and the kindred of nature, than these two figures presented at that moment. Yet the spectators were so smitten with her beauty, and so essential did pride seem to the existence of such a creature, that they gave a simultaneous acclamation of applause.

"Who is this insolent young fellow?" inquired Captain Langford, who still remained beside Doctor Clarke. "If he be in his senses, his impertinence demands the bastinado. If mad, Lady Eleanore should be secured from further inconvenience, by his confinement."

"His name is Jervase Helwyse," answered the Doctor; " a youth of no birth or fortune, or other advantages, save the mind and soul that nature gave him; and being secretary to our colonial agent in London, it was his misfortune to meet this Lady Eleanore Rochcliffe. He loved her—and her scorn has driven him mad."

"He was mad so to aspire," observed the English officer.

"It may be so," said Doctor Clarke, frowning as he spoke. "But I tell you, sir, I could well-nigh doubt the justice of the Heaven above us if no signal humiliation overtake this lady, who now treads so haughtily into yonder mansion. She seeks to place herself above the sympathies of our common nature, which envelops all human souls. See, if that nature do not assert its claim over her in some mode that shall bring her level with the lowest!"

"Never!" cried Captain Langford indignantly—"neither in life, nor when they lay her with her ancestors."

Not many days afterwards the Governor gave a ball in honor of Lady Eleanore Rochcliffe. The principal gentry of the colony received invitations, which were distributed to their residences, far and near, by messengers on horseback, bearing missives sealed with all the formality of official dispatches. In obedience to the summons, there was a general gathering of rank, wealth, and beauty; and the wide door of the Province House had seldom given admittance to more numerous and honorable guests than on the evening of Lady Eleanore's ball. Without much extravagance of eulogy, the spectacle might even be termed splendid; for, according to the fashion of the times, the ladies shone in rich silks and satins, outspread over wide-projecting hoops; and the gentlemen glittered in gold embroidery, laid unsparingly upon the purple, or scarlet, or sky-blue velvet, which was the material of their coats and waistcoats. The latter article of dress was of great importance, since it enveloped the wearer's body nearly to the knees, and was perhaps bedizened with the amount of his whole year's income, in golden flowers and foliage. The altered taste of the present day—a taste symbolic of a deep change in the whole system of society—would look upon almost any of those gorgeous figures as ridiculous; although that evening the guests sought their reflections in the pier-glasses, and rejoiced to catch their own glitter amid the glittering crowd. What a pity that one of the stately mirrors has not preserved a picture of the scene, which, by the very traits that were so transitory, might have taught us much that would be worth knowing and remembering!

Would, at least, that either painter or mirror could convey to us some faint idea of a garment, already noticed in this legend,—the Lady Eleanore's embroidered mantle,—which the gossips whispered was invested with magic properties, so as to lend a new and untried grace to her figure each time that she put it on! Idle fancy as it is, this mysterious mantle has thrown an awe around my image of her, partly from its fabled virtues, and partly because it was the handiwork of a dying woman, and, perchance, owed the fantastic grace of its conception to the delirium of approaching death.

After the ceremonial greetings had been paid, Lady Eleanore Rochcliffe stood apart from the mob of guests, insulating herself within a small and distinguished circle, to whom she accorded a more cordial favor than to the general throng. The waxen torches threw their radiance vividly over the scene, bringing out its brilliant points in strong relief; but she gazed carelessly, and with now and then an expression of weariness or scorn, tempered with such feminine grace that her auditors scarcely perceived the moral deformity of which it was the utterance. She beheld the spectacle not with vulgar ridicule, as disdaining to be pleased with the provincial mockery of a court festival, but with the deeper scorn of one whose spirit held itself too high to participate in the enjoyment of other human souls. Whether or no the recollections of those who saw her that evening were influenced by the strange events with which she was subsequently connected, so it was that her figure ever after recurred to them as marked by something wild and unnatural,—although, at the time, the general whisper was of her exceeding beauty, and of the indescribable charm which her mantle threw around her. Some close observers, indeed, detected a feverish flush and alternate paleness of countenance, with a corresponding flow and revulsion of spirits, and once or twice a painful and helpless betrayal of lassitude, as if she were on the point of sinking to the ground. Then, with a nervous shudder, she seemed to arouse her energies and threw some bright and playful yet half-wicked sarcasm into the conversation. There was so strange a characteristic in her manners and sentiments that it astonished every right-minded listener; till looking in her face, a lurking and incomprehensible glance and smile perplexed them with doubts both as to her seriousness and sanity. Gradually, Lady Eleanore Rochcliffe's circle grew smaller, till only four gentlemen remained in it. These were Captain Langford, the English officer before mentioned; a Virginian planter, who had come to Massachusetts on some political errand; a young Episcopal clergyman, the grandson of a British earl; and, lastly, the private secretary of Governor Shute, whose obsequiousness had won a sort of tolerance from Lady Eleanore.

At different periods of the evening the liveried servants of the Province House passed among the guests, bearing huge trays of refreshments and French and Spanish wines. Lady Eleanore Rochcliffe, who refused to wet her beautiful lips even with a bubble of Champagne, had sunk back into a large damask chair, apparently overwearied either with the excitement of the scene or its tedium, and while, for an instant, she was unconscious of voices, laughter and music, a young man stole forward, and knelt down at her feet. He bore a salver in his hand, on which was a chased silver goblet, filled to the brim with wine, which he offered as reverentially as to a crowned queen, or rather with the awful devotion of a priest doing sacrifice to his idol. Conscious that some one touched her robe, Lady Eleanore started, and unclosed her eyes upon the pale, wild features and dishevelled hair of Jervase Helwyse.

"Why do you haunt me thus?" said she, in a languid tone, but with a kindlier feeling than she ordinarily permitted herself to express. "They tell me that I have done you harm."

"Heaven knows if that be so," replied the young man solemnly. "But, Lady Eleanore, in requital of that harm, if such there be, and for your own earthly and heavenly welfare, I pray you to take one sip of this holy wine, and then to pass the goblet round among the guests. And this shall be a symbol that you have not sought to withdraw yourself from the chain of human sympathies—which whoso would shake off must keep company with fallen angels."

"Where has this mad fellow stolen that sacramental vessel?" exclaimed the Episcopal clergyman.

This question drew the notice of the guests to the silver cup, which was recognized as appertaining to the communion plate of the Old South Church; and, for aught that could be known, it was brimming over with the consecrated wine.

"Perhaps it is poisoned," half whispered the Governor's secretary.

"Pour it down the villain's throat!" cried the Virginian fiercely.

"Turn him out of the house!" cried Captain Langford, seizing Jervase Helwyse so roughly by the shoulder that the sacramental cup was overturned, and its contents sprinkled upon Lady Eleanore's mantle. "Whether knave, fool, or Bedlamite, it is intolerable that the fellow should go at large."

"Pray, gentlemen, do my poor admirer no harm," said Lady Eleanore, with a faint and weary smile. "Take him out of my sight, if such be your pleasure; for I can find in my heart to do nothing but laugh at him; whereas, in all decency and conscience, it would become me to weep for the mischief I have wrought!"

But while the by-standers were attempting to lead away the unfortunate young man, he broke from them, and with a wild, impassioned earnestness, offered a new and equally strange petition to Lady Eleanore. It was no other than that she should throw off the mantle, which, while he pressed the silver cup of wine upon her, she had drawn more closely around her form, so as almost to shroud herself within it.

"Cast it from you!" exclaimed Jervase Helwyse, clasping his hands in an agony of entreaty. "It may not yet be too late! Give the accursed garment to the flames!"

But Lady Eleanore, with a laugh of scorn, drew the rich folds of the embroidered mantle over her head, in such a fashion as to give a completely new aspect to her beautiful face, which—half hidden, half revealed—seemed to belong to some being of mysterious character and purposes.

"Farewell, Jervase Helwyse!" said she. "Keep my image in your remembrance, as you behold it now."

"Alas, lady!" he replied, in a tone no longer wild, but sad as a funeral bell. "We must meet shortly, when your face may wear another aspect—and that shall be the image that must abide within me."

He made no more resistance to the violent efforts of the gentlemen and servants, who almost dragged him out of the apartment, and dismissed him roughly from the iron gate of the Province House. Captain Langford, who had been very active in this affair, was returning to the presence of Lady Eleanore Rochcliffe, when he encountered the physician, Doctor Clarke, with whom he had held some casual talk on the day of her arrival. The doctor stood apart, separated from Lady Eleanore by the width of the room, but eying her with such keen sagacity that Captain Langford involuntarily gave him credit for the discovery of some deep secret.

"You appear to be smitten, after all, with the charms of this queenly maiden," said he, hoping thus to draw forth the physician's hidden knowledge.

"God forbid!" answered Doctor Clarke, with a grave smile; "and if you be wise you will put up the same prayer for yourself. Woe to those who shall be smitten by this beautiful Lady Eleanore! But yonder stands the Governor—and I have a word or two for his private ear. Good night!"

He accordingly advanced to Governor Shute, and addressed him in so low a tone that none of the by-standers could catch a word of what he said, although the sudden change of his Excellency's hitherto cheerful visage betokened that the communication could be of no agreeable import. A very few moments afterwards it was announced to the guests that an unforeseen circumstance rendered it necessary to put a premature close to the festival.

The ball at the Province House supplied a topic of conversation for the colonial metropolis for some days after its occurrence, and might still longer have been the general theme, only that a subject of all-engrossing interest thrust it, for a time, from the public recollection. This was the appearance of a dreadful epidemic, which, in that age and long before and afterwards, was wont to slay its hundreds and thousands on both sides of the Atlantic. On the occasion of which we speak, it was distinguished by a peculiar virulence, insomuch that it has left its traces—its pit-marks, to use an appropriate figure—on the history of the country, the affairs of which were thrown into confusion by its ravages. At first, unlike its ordinary course, the disease seemed to confine itself to the higher circles of society, selecting its victims from among the proud, the well-born, and the wealthy, entering unabashed into stately chambers, and lying down with the slumberers in silken beds. Some of the most distinguished guests of the Province House—even those whom the haughty Lady Eleanore Rochcliffe had deemed not unworthy of her favor—were stricken by this fatal scourge. It was noticed, with an ungenerous bitterness of feeling, that the four gentlemen—the Virginian, the British officer, the young clergyman, and the Governor's secretary—who had been her most devoted attendants on the evening of the ball, were the foremost on whom the plague stroke fell. But the disease, pursuing its onward progress, soon ceased to be exclusively a prerogative of aristocracy. Its red brand was no longer conferred like a noble's star, or an order of knight-hood. It threaded its way through the narrow and crooked streets, and entered the low, mean, darksome dwellings, and laid its hand of death upon the artisans and laboring classes of the town. It compelled rich and poor to feel themselves brethren then; and stalking to and fro across the Three Hills, with a fierceness which made it almost a new pestilence, there was that mighty conqueror—that scourge and horror of our forefathers—the Small-Pox!

We cannot estimate the affright which this plague inspired of yore, by contemplating it as the fangless monster of the present day. We must remember, rather, with what awe we watched the gigantic footsteps of the Asiatic cholera, striding from shore to shore of the Atlantic, and marching like destiny upon cities far remote which flight had already half depopulated. There is no other fear so horrible and unhumanizing as that which makes man dread to breathe heaven's vital air lest it be poison, or to grasp the hand of a brother or friend lest the gripe of the pestilence should clutch him. Such was the dismay that now followed in the track of the disease, or ran before it throughout the town. Graves were hastily dug, and the pestilential relics as hastily covered, because the dead were enemies of the living, and strove to draw them headlong, as it were, into their own dismal pit. The public councils were suspended, as if mortal wisdom might relinquish its devices, now that an unearthly usurper had found his way into the ruler's mansion. Had an enemy's fleet been hovering on the coast, or his armies trampling on our soil, the people would probably have committed their defence to that same direful conqueror who had wrought their own calamity, and would permit no interference with his sway. This conqueror had a symbol of his triumphs. It was a blood-red flag, that fluttered in the tainted air, over the door of every dwelling into which the Small-Pox had entered.

Such a banner was long since waving over the portal of the Province House; for thence, as was proved by tracking its footsteps back, had all this dreadful mischief issued. It had been traced back to a lady's luxurious chamber—to the proudest of the proud—to her that was so delicate, and hardly owned herself of earthly mould—to the haughty one, who took her stand above human sympathies—to Lady Eleanore! There remained no room for doubt that the contagion had lurked in that gorgeous mantle, which threw so strange a grace around her at the festival. Its fantastic splendor had been conceived in the delirious brain of a woman on her death-bed, and was the last toil of her stiffening fingers, which had interwoven fate and misery with its golden threads. This dark tale, whispered at first, was now bruited far and wide. The people raved against the Lady Eleanore, and cried out that her pride and scorn had evoked a fiend, and that, between them both, this monstrous evil had been born. At times, their rage and despair took the semblance of grinning mirth; and whenever the red flag of the pestilence was hoisted over another and yet another door, they clapped their hands and shouted through the streets, in bitter mockery: "Behold a new triumph for the Lady Eleanore!"

One day, in the midst of these dismal times, a wild figure approached the portal of the Province House, and folding his arms, stood contemplating the scarlet banner which a passing breeze shook fitfully, as if to fling abroad the contagion that it typified. At length, climbing one of the pillars by means of the iron balustrade, he took down the flag and entered the mansion, waving it above his head. At the foot of the staircase he met the Governor, booted and spurred, with his cloak drawn around him, evidently on the point of setting forth upon a journey.

"Wretched lunatic, what do you seek here?" exclaimed Shute, extending his cane to guard himself from contact. "There is nothing here but Death. Back—or you will meet him!"

"Death will not touch me, the banner-bearer of the pestilence!" cried Jervase Helwyse, shaking the red flag aloft. "Death, and the Pestilence, who wears the aspect of the Lady Eleanore, will walk through the streets to-night, and I must march before them with this banner!"

"Why do I waste words on the fellow?" muttered the Governor, drawing his cloak across his mouth. "What matters his miserable life, when none of us are sure of twelve hours' breath? On, fool, to your own destruction!"

He made way for Jervase Helwyse, who immediately ascended the staircase, but, on the first landing place, was arrested by the firm grasp of a hand upon his shoulder. Looking fiercely up, with a madman's impulse to struggle with and rend asunder his opponent, he found himself powerless beneath a calm, stern eye, which possessed the mysterious property of quelling frenzy at its height. The person whom he had now encountered was the physician, Doctor Clarke, the duties of whose sad profession had led him to the Province House, where he was an infrequent guest in more prosperous times.

"Young man, what is your purpose?" demanded he.

"I seek the Lady Eleanore," answered Jervase Helwyse, submissively.

"All have fled from her," said the physician. "Why do you seek her now? I tell you, youth, her nurse fell death-stricken on the threshold of that fatal chamber. Know ye not, that never came such a curse to our shores as this lovely Lady Eleanore?—that her breath has filled the air with poison?—that she has shaken pestilence and death upon the land, from the folds of her accursed mantle?"

"Let me look upon her!" rejoined the mad youth, more wildly. "Let me behold her, in her awful beauty, clad in the regal garments of the pestilence! She and Death sit on a throne together. Let me kneel down before them!"

"Poor youth!" said Doctor Clarke; and, moved by a deep sense of human weakness, a smile of caustic humor curled his lip even then. "Wilt thou still worship the destroyer and surround her image with fantasies the more magnificent, the more evil she has wrought? Thus man doth ever to his tyrants. Approach, then! Madness, as I have noted, has that good efficacy, that it will guard you from contagion—and perchance its own cure may be found in yonder chamber."

Ascending another flight of stairs, he threw open a door and signed to Jervase Helwyse that he should enter. The poor lunatic, it seems probable, had cherished a delusion that his haughty mistress sat in state, unharmed herself by the pestilential influence, which, as by enchantment, she scattered round about her. He dreamed, no doubt, that her beauty was not dimmed, but brightened into superhuman splendor. With such anticipations, he stole reverentially to the door at which the physician stood, but paused upon the threshold, gazing fearfully into the gloom of the darkened chamber.

"Where is the Lady Eleanore?" whispered he.

"Call her," replied the physician.

"Lady Eleanore!—Princess!—Queen of Death!" cried Jervase Helwyse, advancing three steps into the chamber. "She is not here! There, on yonder table, I behold the sparkle of a diamond which once she wore upon her bosom. There"—and he shuddered—"there hangs her mantle, on which a dead woman embroidered a spell of dreadful potency. But where is the Lady Eleanore?"

Something stirred within the silken curtains of a canopied bed; and a low moan was uttered, which, listening intently, Jervase Helwyse began to distinguish as a woman's voice, complaining dolefully of thirst. He fancied, even, that he recognized its tones.

"My throat!—my throat is scorched," murmured the voice. "A drop of water!"

"What thing art thou?" said the brain-stricken youth, drawing near the bed and tearing asunder its curtains. "Whose voice hast thou stolen for thy murmurs and miserable petitions, as if Lady Eleanore could be conscious of mortal infirmity? Fie! Heap of diseased mortality, why lurkest thou in my lady's chamber?"

"O Jervase Helwyse," said the voice—and as it spoke the figure contorted itself, struggling to hide its blasted face—"look not now on the woman you once loved! The curse of Heaven hath stricken me, because I would not call man my brother, nor woman sister. I wrapped myself in PRIDE as in a MANTLE, and scorned the sympathies of nature; and therefore has nature made this wretched body the medium of a dreadful sympathy. You are avenged—they are all avenged—Nature is avenged—for I am Eleanore Rochcliffe!"

The malice of his mental disease, the bitterness lurking at the bottom of his heart, mad as he was, for a blighted and ruined life, and love that had been paid with cruel scorn, awoke within the breast of Jervase Helwyse. He shook his finger at the wretched girl, and the chamber echoed, the curtains of the bed were shaken, with his outburst of insane merriment.

"Another triumph for the Lady Eleanore!" he cried. "All have been her victims! Who so worthy to be the final victim as herself?"

Impelled by some new fantasy of his crazed intellect, he snatched the fatal mantle and rushed from the chamber and the house. That night a procession passed, by torchlight, through the streets, bearing in the midst the figure of a woman, enveloped with a richly embroidered mantle; while in advance stalked Jervase Helwyse, waving the red flag of the pestilence. Arriving opposite the

Province House, the mob burned the effigy, and a strong wind came and swept away the ashes. It was said that, from that very hour, the pestilence abated, as if its sway had some mysterious connection, from the first plague stroke to the last, with Lady Eleanore's Mantle. A remarkable uncertainty broods over that unhappy lady's fate. There is a belief, however, that in a certain chamber of this mansion a female form may sometimes be duskily discerned, shrinking into the darkest corner and muffling her face within an embroidered mantle. Supposing the legend true, can this be other than the once proud Lady Eleanore?

Mine host and the old loyalist and I bestowed no little warmth of applause upon this narrative, in which we had all been deeply interested; for the reader can scarcely conceive how unspeakably the effect of such a tale is heightened when, as in the present case, we may repose perfect confidence in the veracity of him who tells it. For my own part, knowing how scrupulous is Mr. Tiffany to settle the foundation of his facts, I could not have believed him one whit the more faithfully had he professed himself an eye-witness of the doings and sufferings of poor Lady Eleanore. Some sceptics, it is true, might demand documentary evidence, or even require him to produce the embroidered mantle, forgetting that—Heaven be praised—it was consumed to ashes. But now the old loyalist, whose blood was warmed by the good cheer, began to talk, in his turn, about the traditions of the Province House, and hinted that he, if it were agreeable, might add a few reminiscences to our legendary stock. Mr. Tiffany having no cause to dread a rival, immediately besought him to favor us with a specimen; my own entreaties, of course, were urged to the same effect; and our venerable guest, well pleased to find willing auditors, awaited only the return of Mr. Thomas Waite, who had been summoned forth to provide accommodations for several new arrivals. Perchance the public—but be this as its own caprice and ours shall settle the matter—may read the result in another Tale of the Province House.

IV. OLD ESTHER DUDLEY

Our host having resumed the chair, he, as well as Mr. Tiffany and myself, expressed much eagerness to be made acquainted with the story to which the loyalist had alluded. That venerable man first of all saw fit to moisten his throat with another glass of wine, and then, turning his face towards our coal fire, looked steadfastly for a few moments into the depths of its cheerful glow. Finally, he poured forth a great fluency of speech. The generous liquid that he had imbibed, while it warmed his age-chilled blood, likewise took off the chill from his heart and mind, and gave him an energy to think and feel, which we could hardly have expected to find beneath the snows of four-score winters. His feelings, indeed, appeared to me more excitable than those of a younger man; or at least, the same degree of feeling manifested itself by more visible effects than if his judgment and will had possessed the potency of meridian life. At the pathetic passages of his narrative he readily melted into tears. When a breath of indignation swept across his spirit the blood flushed his withered visage even to the roots of his white hair; and he shook his clinched fist at the trio of peaceful auditors, seeming to fancy enemies in those who felt very kindly towards the desolate old soul. But ever and anon, sometimes in the midst of his most earnest talk, this ancient person's intellect would wander vaguely, losing its hold of the matter in hand, and groping for it amid misty shadows. Then would he cackle forth a feeble laugh, and express a doubt whether his wits—for by that phrase it pleased our ancient friend to signify his mental powers—were not getting a little the worse for wear.

Under these disadvantages, the old loyalist's story required more revision to render it fit for the public eye than those of the series which have preceded it; nor should it be concealed that the sentiment and tone of the affair may have undergone some slight, or perchance more than slight, metamorphosis, in its transmission to the reader through the medium of a thorough-going democrat. The tale itself is a mere sketch, with no involution of plot, nor any great interest of events, yet possessing, if I have rehearsed it aright, that pensive influence over the mind which the shadow of the old Province House flings upon the loiterer in its court-yard.

The hour had come—the hour of defeat and humiliation—when Sir William Howe was to pass over the threshold of the Province House, and embark, with no such triumphal ceremonies as he once promised himself, on board the British fleet. He bade his servants and military attendants go before him, and lingered a moment in the loneliness of the mansion, to quell the fierce emotions that struggled in his bosom as with a death throb. Preferable, then, would he have deemed his fate, had a warrior's death left him a claim to the narrow territory of a grave within the soil which the King had given him to defend. With an ominous perception that, as his departing footsteps echoed adown the staircase, the sway of Britain was passing forever from New England, he smote his clinched hand on his brow, and cursed the destiny that had flung the shame of a dismembered empire upon him.

"Would to God," cried he, hardly repressing his tears of rage, "that the rebels were even now at the doorstep! A blood-stain upon the floor should then bear testimony that the last British ruler was faithful to his trust."

The tremulous voice of a woman replied to his exclamation.

"Heaven's cause and the King's are one," it said. "Go forth, Sir William Howe, and trust in Heaven to bring back a Royal Governor in triumph."

Subduing, at once, the passion to which he had yielded only in the faith that it was unwitnessed, Sir William Howe became conscious that an aged woman, leaning on a gold-headed staff, was standing betwixt him and the door. It was old Esther Dudley, who had dwelt almost immemorial years in this mansion, until her presence seemed as inseparable from it as the recollections of its history. She was the daughter of an ancient and once eminent family, which had fallen into poverty and decay, and left its last descendant no resource save the bounty of the King, nor any shelter except within the walls of the Province House. An office in the household, with merely nominal duties, had been assigned to her as a pretext for the payment of a small pension, the greater part of which she expended in adorning herself with an antique magnificence of attire. The claims of Esther Dudley's gentle blood were acknowledged by all the successive Governors; and they treated her with the punctilious courtesy which it was her foible to demand, not always with success, from a neglectful world. The only actual share which she assumed in the business of the mansion was to glide through its passages and public chambers, late at night, to see that the servants had dropped no fire from their flaring torches, nor left embers crackling and blazing on the hearths. Perhaps it was this invariable custom of walking her rounds in the hush of midnight that caused the superstition of the times to invest the old woman with attributes of awe and mystery; fabling that she had entered the portal of the Province House, none knew whence, in the train of the first Royal Governor, and that it was her fate to dwell there till the last should have departed. But Sir William Howe, if he ever heard this legend, had forgotten it.

"Mistress Dudley, why are you loitering here?" asked he, with some severity of tone. "It is my pleasure to be the last in this mansion of the King."

"Not so, if it please your Excellency," answered the time-stricken woman. "This roof has sheltered me long. I will not pass from it until they bear me to the tomb of my forefathers. What other shelter is there for old Esther Dudley, save the Province House or the grave?"

"Now Heaven forgive me!" said Sir William Howe to himself. "I was about to leave this wretched old creature to starve or beg. Take this, good Mistress Dudley," he added, putting a purse into her hands. "King George's head on these golden guineas is sterling yet, and will continue so, I warrant you, even should the rebels crown John Hancock their king. That purse will buy a better shelter than the Province House can now afford."

"While the burden of life remains upon me, I will have no other shelter than this roof," persisted Esther Dudley, striking her staff upon the floor with a gesture that expressed immovable resolve. "And when your Excellency returns in triumph, I will totter into the porch to welcome you."

"My poor old friend!" answered the British General,—and all his manly and martial pride could no longer restrain a gush of bitter tears. "This is an evil hour for you and me. The Province which the King intrusted to my charge is lost. I go hence in misfortune—perchance in disgrace—to return no more. And you, whose present being is incorporated with the past—who have seen Governor after Governor, in stately pageantry, ascend these steps—whose whole life has been an observance of majestic ceremonies, and a worship of the King—how will you endure the change? Come with us! Bid farewell to a land that has shaken off its allegiance, and live still under a royal government, at Halifax."

"Never, never!" said the pertinacious old dame. "Here will I abide; and King George shall still have one true subject in his disloyal Province."

"Beshrew the old fool!" muttered Sir William Howe, growing impatient of her obstinacy, and ashamed of the emotion into which he had been betrayed. "She is the very moral of old-fashioned prejudice, and could exist nowhere but in this musty edifice. Well, then, Mistress Dudley, since you will needs tarry, I give the Province House in charge to you. Take this key, and keep it safe until myself, or some other Royal Governor, shall demand it of you."

Smiling bitterly at himself and her, he took the heavy key of the Province House, and delivering it into the old lady's hands, drew his cloak around him for departure. As the General glanced back at Esther Dudley's antique figure, he deemed her well fitted for such a charge, as being so perfect a representative of the decayed past—of an age gone by, with its manners, opinions, faith and feelings, all fallen into oblivion or scorn—of what had once been a reality, but was now merely a vision of faded magnificence. Then Sir William Howe strode forth, smiting his clinched hands together, in the fierce anguish of his spirit; and old Esther Dudley was left to keep watch in the lonely Province House, dwelling there with memory; and if Hope ever seemed to flit around her, still was it Memory in disguise.

The total change of affairs that ensued on the departure of the British troops did not drive the venerable lady from her stronghold. There was not, for many years afterwards, a Governor of Massachusetts; and the magistrates, who had charge of such matters, saw no objection to Esther Dudley's residence in the Province House, especially as they must otherwise have paid a hireling for taking care of the premises, which with her was a labor of love. And so they left her the undisturbed mistress of the old historic edifice. Many and strange were the fables which the gossips whispered about her, in all the chimney corners of the town. Among the time-worn articles of furniture that had been left in the mansion there was a tall, antique mirror, which was well worthy of a tale by itself, and perhaps may hereafter be the theme of one. The gold of its heavily-wrought frame was tarnished, and its surface so blurred, that the old woman's figure, whenever she paused before it, looked indistinct and ghost-like. But it was the general belief that Esther could cause the Governors of the overthrown dynasty, with the beautiful ladies who had once adorned their festivals, the Indian chiefs who had come up to the Province House to hold council or swear allegiance, the grim Provincial warriors, the severe clergymen—in short, all the pageantry of gone days—all the figures that ever swept across the broad plate of glass in former times—she could cause the whole to reappear, and people the inner world of the mirror with shadows of old life. Such legends as these, together with the singularity of her isolated existence, her age, and the infirmity that each added winter flung upon her, made Mistress Dudley the object both of fear and pity; and it was partly the result of either sentiment that, amid all the angry license of the times, neither wrong nor insult ever fell upon her unprotected head. Indeed, there was so much haughtiness in her demeanor towards intruders, among whom she reckoned all persons acting under the new authorities, that it was really an affair of no small nerve to look her in the face. And to do the people justice, stern republicans as they had now become, they were well content that the old gentlewoman, in her hoop petticoat and faded embroidery, should still haunt the palace of ruined pride and overthrown power, the symbol of a departed system, embodying a history in her person. So Esther Dudley dwelt year after year in the Province House, still reverencing all that others had flung aside, still faithful to her King, who, so long as the venerable dame yet held her post, might be said to retain one true subject in New England, and one spot of the empire that had been wrested from him.

And did she dwell there in utter loneliness? Rumor said, not so. Whenever her chill and withered heart desired warmth, she was wont to summon a black slave of Governor Shirley's from the blurred mirror, and send him in search of guests who had long ago been familiar in those deserted chambers. Forth went the sable messenger, with the starlight or the moonshine gleaming through him, and did his errand in the burial ground, knocking at the iron doors of tombs, or upon the marble slabs that covered them, and whispering to those within: "My mistress, old Esther Dudley, bids you to the Province House at midnight." And punctually as the clock of the Old South told twelve came the shadows of the Olivers, the Hutchinsons, the Dudleys, all the grandees of a by-gone generation, gliding beneath the portal into the well-known mansion, where Esther mingled with them as if she likewise were a shade. Without vouching for the truth of such traditions, it is certain that Mistress Dudley sometimes assembled a few of the stanch, though crestfallen, old tories, who had lingered in the rebel town during those days of wrath and tribulation. Out of a cobwebbed bottle, containing liquor that a royal Governor might have smacked his lips over, they quaffed healths to the King, and babbled treason to the Republic, feeling as if the protecting shadow of the throne were still flung around them. But, draining the last drops of their liquor, they stole timorously homeward, and answered not again if the rude mob reviled them in the street.

Yet Esther Dudley's most frequent and favored guests were the children of the town. Towards them she was never stern. A kindly and loving nature, hindered elsewhere from its free course by a thousand rocky prejudices, lavished itself upon these little ones. By bribes of gingerbread of her own making, stamped with a royal crown, she tempted their sunny sportiveness beneath the gloomy portal of the Province House, and would often beguile them to spend a whole playday there, sitting in a circle round the verge of her hoop petticoat, greedily attentive to her stories of a dead world. And when these little boys and girls stole forth again from the dark, mysterious mansion, they went bewildered, full of old feelings that graver people had long ago forgotten, rubbing their eyes at the world around them as if they had gone astray into ancient times, and become children of the past. At home, when their parents asked where they had loitered such a weary while, and with whom they had been at play, the children would talk of all the departed worthies of the Province, as far back as Governor Belcher and the haughty dame of Sir William Phipps. It would seem as though they had been sitting on the knees of these famous personages, whom the grave had hidden for half a century, and had toyed with the embroidery of their rich waistcoats, or roguishly pulled the long curls of their flowing wigs. "But Governor Belcher has been dead this many a year," would the mother say to her little boy. "And did you really see him at the Province House?" "Oh yes, dear mother! yes!" the half-dreaming child would answer. "But when old Esther had done speaking about him he faded away out of his chair." Thus, without affrighting her little guests, she led them by the hand into the chambers of her own desolate heart, and made childhood's fancy discern the ghosts that haunted there.

Living so continually in her own circle of ideas, and never regulating her mind by a proper reference to present things, Esther Dudley appears to have grown partially crazed. It was found that she had no right sense of the progress and true state of the Revolutionary War, but held a constant faith that the armies of Britain were victorious on every field, and destined to be ultimately triumphant. Whenever the town rejoiced for a battle won by Washington, or Gates, or Morgan, or Greene, the news, in passing through the door of the Province House, as through the ivory gate of dreams, became metamorphosed into a strange tale of the prowess of Howe, Clinton, or Cornwallis. Sooner or later it was her invincible belief the colonies would be prostrate at the footstool of the King. Sometimes she seemed to take for granted that such was already the case. On one occasion, she startled the towns-people by a brilliant illumination of the Province House, with candles at every pane of glass, and a transparency of the King's initials and a crown of light in the great balcony window. The figure of the aged woman in the most gorgeous of her mildewed velvets and brocades was seen passing from casement to casement, until she paused before the balcony, and flourished a huge key above her head. Her wrinkled visage actually gleamed with triumph, as if the soul within her were a festal lamp.

"What means this blaze of light? What does old Esther's joy portend?" whispered a spectator. "It is frightful to see her gliding about the chambers, and rejoicing there without a soul to bear her company."

"It is as if she were making merry in a tomb," said another.

"Pshaw! It is no such mystery," observed an old man, after some brief exercise of memory. "Mistress Dudley is keeping jubilee for the King of England's birthday."

Then the people laughed aloud, and would have thrown mud against the blazing transparency of the King's crown and initials, only that they pitied the poor old dame, who was so dismally triumphant amid the wreck and ruin of the system to which she appertained.

Oftentimes it was her custom to climb the weary staircase that wound upward to the cupola, and thence strain her dimmed eyesight seaward and countryward, watching for a British fleet, or for the march of a grand procession, with the King's banner floating over it. The passengers in the street below would discern her anxious visage, and send up a shout, "When the golden Indian on the Province House shall shoot his arrow, and when the cock on the Old South spire shall crow, then look for a Royal Governor again!"—for this had grown a byword through the town. And at last, after long, long years, old Esther Dudley knew, or perchance she only dreamed, that a Royal Governor was on the eve of returning to the Province House, to receive the heavy key which Sir William Howe had committed to her charge. Now it was the fact that intelligence bearing some faint analogy to Esther's version of it was current among the townspeople. She set the mansion in the best order that her means allowed, and, arraying herself in silks and tarnished gold, stood long before the blurred mirror to admire her own magnificence. As she gazed, the gray and withered lady moved her ashen lips, murmuring half aloud, talking to shapes that she saw within the mirror, to shadows of her own fantasies, to the household friends of memory, and bidding them rejoice with her and come forth to meet the Governor. And while absorbed in this communion, Mistress Dudley heard the tramp of many footsteps in the street, and, looking out at the window, beheld what she construed as the Royal Governor's arrival.

"O happy day! O blessed, blessed hour!" she exclaimed. "Let me but bid him welcome within the portal, and my task in the Province House, and on earth, is done!"

Then with tottering feet, which age and tremulous joy caused to tread amiss, she hurried down the grand staircase, her silks sweeping and rustling as she went, so that the sound was as if a train of spectral courtiers were thronging from the dim mirror. And Esther Dudley fancied that as soon as the wide door should be flung open, all the pomp and splendor of by-gone times would pace majestically into the Province House, and the gilded tapestry of the past would be brightened by the sunshine of the present. She turned the key—withdrew it from the lock—unclosed the door—and stepped across the threshold. Advancing up the court-yard appeared a person of most dignified mien, with tokens, as Esther interpreted them, of gentle blood, high rank, and long-accustomed authority, even in his walk and every gesture. He was richly dressed, but wore a gouty shoe, which, however, did not lessen the stateliness of his gait. Around and behind him were people in plain civic dresses, and two or three war-worn veterans, evidently officers of rank, arrayed in a uniform of blue and buff. But Esther Dudley, firm in the belief that had fastened its roots about her heart, beheld only the principal personage, and never doubted that this was the long-looked-for Governor, to whom she was to surrender up her charge. As he approached, she involuntarily sank down on her knees and tremblingly held forth the heavy key.

"Receive my trust! take it quickly!" cried she; "for methinks Death is striving to snatch away my triumph. But he comes too late. Thank Heaven for this blessed hour! God save King George!"

"That, Madam, is a strange prayer to be offered up at such a moment," replied the unknown guest of the Province House, and courteously removing his hat, he offered his arm to raise the aged woman. "Yet, in reverence for your gray hairs and long-kept faith, Heaven forbid that any here should say you nay. Over the realms which still acknowledge his sceptre, God save King George!"

Esther Dudley started to her feet, and hastily clutching back the key, gazed with fearful earnestness at the stranger; and dimly and doubtfully, as if suddenly awakened from a dream, her bewildered eyes half recognized his face. Years ago she had known him among the gentry of the province. But the ban of the King had fallen upon him! How, then, came the doomed victim here? Proscribed, excluded from mercy, the monarch's most dreaded and hated foe, this New England merchant had stood triumphantly against a kingdom's strength; and his foot now trod upon humbled Royalty, as he ascended the steps of the Province House, the people's chosen Governor of Massachusetts.

"Wretch, wretch that I am!" muttered the old woman, with such a heart-broken expression that the tears gushed from the stranger's eyes. "Have I bidden a traitor welcome? Come, Death! come quickly!"

"Alas, venerable lady!" said Governor Hancock, lending her his support with all the reverence that a courtier would have shown to a queen. "Your life has been prolonged until the world has changed around you. You have treasured up all that time has rendered worthless—the principles, feelings, manners, modes of being and acting, which another generation has flung aside—and you are a symbol of the past. And I, and these around me—we represent a new race of men—living no longer in the past, scarcely in the present—but projecting our lives forward into the future. Ceasing to model ourselves on ancestral superstitions, it is our faith and principle to press onward, onward! Yet," continued he, turning to his attendants, "let us reverence, for the last time, the stately and gorgeous prejudices of the tottering Past!"

While the Republican Governor spoke, he had continued to support the helpless form of Esther Dudley; her weight grew heavier against his arm; but at last, with a sudden effort to free herself, the ancient woman sank down beside one of the pillars of the portal. The key of the Province House fell from her grasp, and clanked against the stone.

"I have been faithful unto death," murmured she. "God save the King!"

"She hath done her office!" said Hancock solemnly. "We will follow her reverently to the tomb of her ancestors; and then, my fellow-citizens, onward—onward! We are no longer children of the Past!"

As the old loyalist concluded his narrative, the enthusiasm which had been fitfully flashing within his sunken eyes, and quivering across his wrinkled visage, faded away, as if all the lingering fire of his soul were extinguished. Just then, too, a lamp upon the mantel-piece threw out a dying gleam, which vanished as speedily as it shot upward, compelling our eyes to grope for one another's features by the dim glow of the hearth. With such a lingering fire, methought, with such a dying gleam, had the glory of the ancient system vanished from the Province House, when the spirit of old Esther Dudley took its flight. And now, again, the clock of the Old South threw its voice of ages on the breeze, knolling the hourly knell of the Past, crying out far and wide through the multitudinous city, and filling our ears, as we sat in the dusky chamber, with its reverberating depth of tone. In that same mansion—in that very chamber—what a volume of history had been told off into hours, by the same voice that was now trembling in the air. Many a Governor had heard those midnight accents, and longed to exchange his stately cares for slumber. And as for mine host and Mr. Bela Tiffany and the old loyalist and me, we had babbled about dreams of the past, until we almost fancied that the clock was still striking in a bygone century. Neither of us would have wondered, had a hoop-petticoated phantom of Esther Dudley tottered into the chamber, walking her rounds in the hush of midnight, as of yore, and motioned us to quench the fading embers of the fire, and leave the historic precincts to herself and her kindred shades. But as no such vision was vouchsafed, I retired unbidden, and would advise Mr. Tiffany to lay hold of another auditor, being resolved not to show my face in the Province House for a good while hence—if ever.

THE VILLAGE UNCLE

AN IMAGINARY RETROSPECT.

Come! another log upon the hearth. True, our little parlor is comfortable, especially here, where the old man sits in his old arm-chair; but on Thanksgiving night the blaze should dance higher up the chimney, and send a shower of sparks into the outer darkness. Toss on an armful of those dry oak chips, the last relics of the Mermaid's knee timbers, the bones of your namesake, Susan. Higher yet, and clearer be the blaze, till our cottage windows glow the ruddiest in the village, and the light of our household mirth flash far across the bay to Nahant. And now, come, Susan, come, my children, draw your chairs round me, all of you. There is a dimness over your figures! You sit quivering indistinctly with each motion of the blaze, which eddies about you like a flood, so that you all have the look of visions, or people that dwell only in the firelight, and will vanish from existence as completely as your own shadows when the flame shall sink among the embers. Hark! let me listen for the swell of the surf; it should be audible a mile inland on a night like this. Yes; there I catch the sound, but only an uncertain murmur, as if a good way down over the beach; though, by the almanac, it is high tide at eight o'clock, and the billows must now be dashing within thirty yards of our door. Ah! the old man's ears are failing him; and so is his eyesight, and perhaps his mind; else you would not all be so shadowy in the blaze of his Thanksgiving fire.

How strangely the past is peeping over the shoulders of the present! To judge by my recollections, it is but a few moments since I sat in another room; yonder model of a vessel was not there, nor the old chest of drawers, nor Susan's profile and mine, in that gilt frame; nothing, in short, except this same fire, which glimmered on books, papers, and a picture, and half discovered my solitary figure in a looking-glass. But it was paler than my rugged old self, and younger, too, by almost half a century. Speak to me, Susan; speak, my beloved ones; for the scene is glimmering on my sight again, and as it brightens you fade away. Oh, I should be loath to lose my treasure of past happiness, and become once more what I was then; a hermit in the depths of my own mind; sometimes yawning over drowsy volumes, and anon a scribbler of wearier trash than what I read; a man who had wandered out of the real world and got into its shadow, where his troubles, joys, and vicissitudes were of such slight stuff that he hardly knew whether he lived, or only dreamed of living. Thank Heaven, I am an old man now, and have done with all such vanities.

Still this dimness of mine eyes! Come nearer, Susan, and stand before the fullest blaze of the hearth. Now I behold you illuminated from head to foot, in your clean cap and decent gown, with the dear lock of gray hair across your forehead, and a quiet smile about your mouth, while the eyes alone are concealed by the red gleam of the fire upon your spectacles. There, you made me tremble again. When the flame quivered, my sweet Susan, you quivered with it, and grew indistinct, as if melting into the warm light, that my last glimpse of you might be as visionary as the first was, full many a year since. Do you remember it? You stood on the little bridge over the brook that runs across King's Beach into the sea. It was twilight; the waves rolling in, the wind sweeping by, the crimson clouds fading in the west, and the silver moon brightening above the hill; and on the bridge were you, fluttering in the breeze like a sea-bird that might skim away at your pleasure. You seemed a daughter of the viewless wind, a creature of the ocean foam and the crimson light, whose merry life was spent in dancing on the crests of the billows, that threw up their spray to support your footsteps. As I drew nearer I fancied you akin to the race of mermaids, and thought how pleasant it would be to dwell with you among the quiet coves, in the shadow of the cliffs, and to roam along secluded beaches of the purest sand; and when our northern shores grew bleak, to haunt the islands, green and lonely, far amid summer seas. And yet it gladdened me, after all this nonsense, to find you nothing but a pretty young girl, sadly perplexed with the rude behavior of the wind about your petticoats.

Thus I did with Susan as with most other things in my earlier days, dipping her image into my mind and coloring it of a thousand fantastic hues, before I could see her as she really was. Now, Susan, for a sober picture of our village! It was a small collection of dwellings that seemed to have been cast up by the sea, with the rockweed and marine plants that it vomits after a storm, or to have come ashore among the pipe staves and other lumber which had been washed from the deck of an eastern schooner. There was just space for the narrow and sandy street, between the beach in front and a precipitous hill that lifted its rocky forehead in the rear, among a waste of juniper bushes and the wild growth of a broken pasture. The village was picturesque in the variety of its edifices, though all were rude. Here stood a little old hovel, built perhaps of driftwood; there a row of boat-houses; and beyond them a two-story dwelling, of dark and weather-beaten aspect, the whole intermixed with one or two snug cottages, painted white, a sufficiency of pigsties, and a shoemaker's shop. Two grocery stores stood opposite each other, in the centre of the village. These were the places of resort, at their idle hours, of a hardy throng of fishermen, in red baize shirts, oil-cloth trousers, and boots of brown leather covering the whole leg; true seven-league boots, but fitter to wade the ocean than walk the earth. The wearers seemed amphibious, as if they did but creep out of salt water to sun themselves; nor would it have been wonderful to see their lower limbs covered with clusters of little shell-fish, such as cling to rocks and old ship timber over which the tide ebbs and flows. When their fleet of boats was weather-bound, the butchers raised their price, and the spit was busier than the frying-pan: for this was a place of fish, and known as such, to all the country round about; the very air was fishy, being perfumed with dead sculpins, hardheads, and dogfish strewn plentifully on the beach. You see, children, the village is but little changed since your mother and I were young.

How like a dream it was, when I bent over a pool of water one pleasant morning, and saw that the ocean had dashed its spray over me and made me a fisherman! There were the tarpaulin, the baize shirt, the oil-cloth trousers and seven-league boots, and there my own features, but so reddened with sunburn and sea-breezes, that methought I had another face, and on the other shoulders too. The sea-gulls and the loons and I had now all one trade; we skimmed the crested waves and sought our prey beneath them, the man with as keen enjoyment as the birds. Always, when the east grew purple, I launched my dory, my little flat-bottomed skiff, and rowed cross-handed to Point Ledge, the Middle Ledge, or, perhaps beyond Egg Rock; often, too, did I anchor off Dread Ledge, a spot of peril to ships unpiloted; and sometimes spread an adventurous sail and tracked across the bay to South Shore, casting my lines in sight of Scituate. Ere nightfall, I hauled my skiff high and dry on the beach, laden with red rock cod, or the white-bellied ones of deep water; haddock, bearing the black marks of Saint Peter's fingers near the gills; the long-bearded hake, whose liver holds oil enough for a midnight lamp; and now and then a mighty halibut, with a back broad as my boat. In the autumn, I tolled and caught those lovely fish, the mackerel. When the wind was high, —when the whale-boats, anchored off the Point, nodded their slender masts at each other, and the dories pitched and tossed in the surf,—when Nahant Beach was thundering three miles off, and the spray broke a hundred feet in air round the distant base of Egg Rock,—when the brimful and boisterous sea threatened to tumble over the street of our village,—then I made a holiday on shore.

Many such a day did I sit snugly in Mr. Bartlett's store, attentive to the yarns of Uncle Parker; uncle to the whole village by right of seniority, but of southern blood, with no kindred in New England. His figure is before me now, enthroned upon a mackerel barrel: a lean old man, of great height, but bent with years, and twisted into an uncouth shape by seven broken limbs; furrowed also, and weather-worn, as if every gale, for the better part of a century, had caught him somewhere on the sea. He looked like a harbinger of tempest; a shipmate of the Flying Dutchman. After innumerable voyages aboard men-of-war and merchant-men, fishing schooners and chebacco boats, the old salt had become master of a handcart, which he daily trundled about the vicinity, and sometimes blew his fish-horn through the streets of Salem. One of Uncle Parker's eyes had been blown out with gunpowder, and the other did but glimmer in its socket. Turning it upward as he spoke, it was his delight to tell of cruises against the French, and battles with his own shipmates, when he and an antagonist used to be seated astride of a sailor's chest, each fastened down by a spike nail through his trousers, and there to fight it out. Sometimes he expatiated on the delicious flavor of the hagden, a greasy and goose-like fowl, which the sailors catch with hook and line on the Grand Banks. He dwelt with rapture on an interminable winter at the Isle of Sables, where he had gladdened himself, amid polar snows, with the rum and sugar saved from the wreck of a West India schooner. And wrathfully did he shake his fist, as he related how a party of Cape Cod men had robbed him and his companions of their lawful spoil, and sailed away with every keg of old Jamaica, leaving him not a drop to drown his sorrow. Villains they were, and of that wicked brotherhood who are said to tie lanterns to horses' tails, to mislead the mariner along the dangerous shores of the Cape.

Even now, I seem to see the group of fishermen, with that old salt in the midst. One fellow sits on the counter, a second bestrides an oil barrel, a third lolls at his length on a parcel of new cod lines, and another has planted the tarry seat of his trousers on a heap of salt, which will shortly be sprinkled over a lot of fish. They are a likely set of men. Some have voyaged to the East Indies or the Pacific, and most of them have sailed in Marblehead schooners to Newfoundland; a few have been no farther than the Middle Banks, and one or two have always fished along the shore; but, as Uncle Parker used to say, they have all been christened in salt water, and know more than men ever learn in the bushes. A curious figure, by way of contrast, is a fish dealer from far-up country, listening with eyes wide open to narratives that might startle Sinbad the Sailor. Be it well with you, my brethren! Ye are all gone, some to your graves ashore, and others to the depths of ocean; but my faith is strong that ye are happy; for whenever I behold your forms, whether in dream or vision, each departed friend is puffing his long nine, and a mug of the right black strap goes round from lip to lip.

But where was the mermaid in those delightful times? At a certain window near the centre of the village appeared a pretty display of gingerbread men and horses, picture-books and ballads, small fish-hooks, pins, needles, sugar-plums, and brass thimbles, articles on which the young fishermen used to expend their money from pure gallantry. What a picture was Susan behind the counter! A slender maiden, though the child of rugged parents, she had the slimmest of all waists, brown hair curling on her neck, and a complexion rather pale, except when the sea-breeze flushed it. A few freckles became beauty-spots beneath her eyelids. How was it, Susan, that you talked and acted so carelessly, yet always for the best, doing whatever was right in your own eyes, and never once doing wrong in mine, nor shocked a taste that had been morbidly sensitive till now? And whence had you that happiest gift of brightening every topic with an unsought gayety, quiet but irresistible, so that even gloomy spirits felt your sunshine, and did not shrink from it? Nature wrought the charm. She made you a frank, simple, kind-hearted, sensible, and mirthful girl. Obeying nature, you did free things without indelicacy, displayed a maiden's thoughts to every eye, and proved yourself as innocent as naked Eve.

It was beautiful to observe how her simple and happy nature mingled itself with mine. She kindled a domestic fire within my heart, and took up her dwelling there, even in that chill and lonesome cavern, hung round with glittering icicles of fancy. She gave me warmth of feeling, while the influence of my mind made her contemplative. I taught her to love the moonlight hour, when the expanse of the encircled bay was smooth as a great mirror and slept in a transparent shadow; while beyond Nahant the wind rippled the dim ocean into a dreamy brightness, which grew faint afar off without becoming gloomier. I held her hand and pointed to the long surf wave, as it rolled calmly on the beach, in an unbroken line of silver; we were silent together till its deep and peaceful murmur had swept by us. When the Sabbath sun shone down into the recesses of the cliffs, I led the mermaid thither, and told her that those huge, gray, shattered rocks, and her native sea, that raged forever like a storm against them, and her own slender beauty in so stern a scene, were all combined into a strain of poetry. But on the Sabbath eve, when her mother had gone early to bed, and her gentle sister had smiled and left us, as we sat alone by the quiet hearth, with household things around, it was her turn to make me feel that here was a deeper poetry, and that this was the dearest hour of all. Thus went on our wooing till I had shot wild fowl enough to feather our bridal bed, and the Daughter of the Sea was mine.

I built a cottage for Susan and myself, and made a gateway in the form of a Gothic arch, by setting up a whale's jaw-bones. We bought a heifer with her first calf, and had a little garden on the hill-side, to supply us with potatoes and green sauce for our fish. Our parlor, small and neat, was ornamented with our two profiles in one gilt frame, and with shells and pretty pebbles on the mantel-piece, selected from the sea's treasury of such things, on Nahant Beach. On the desk, beneath the looking-glass, lay the Bible, which I had begun to read aloud at the book of Genesis, and the singing-book that Susan used for her evening psalm. Except the almanac, we had no other literature. All that I heard of books was when an Indian history, or tale of shipwreck, was sold by a pedlar or wandering subscription man, to some one in the village, and read through its owner's nose to a slumberous auditory. Like my brother fishermen, I grew into the belief that all human erudition was collected in our pedagogue, whose green spectacles and solemn phiz, as he passed to his little school-house amid a waste of sand, might have gained him a diploma from any college in New England. In truth I dreaded him. When our children were old enough to claim his care, you remember, Susan, how I frowned, though you were pleased, at this learned man's encomiums on their proficiency. I feared to trust them even with the alphabet; it was the key to a fatal treasure.

But I loved to lead them by their little hands along the beach, and point to nature in the vast and the minute, the sky, the sea, the green earth, the pebbles, and the shells. Then did I discourse of the mighty works and co-extensive goodness of the Deity, with the simple wisdom of a man whose mind had profited by lonely days upon the deep, and his heart by the strong and pure affections of his evening home. Sometimes my voice lost itself in a tremulous depth; for I felt His eye upon me as I spoke. Once, while my wife and all of us were gazing at ourselves, in the mirror left by the tide in a hollow of the sand, I pointed to the pictured heaven below, and bade her observe how religion was strewn everywhere in our path; since even a casual pool of water recalled the idea of that home whither we were travelling, to rest forever with our children. Suddenly, your image, Susan, and all the little faces made up of yours and mine, seemed to fade away and vanish around me, leaving a pale visage like my own of former days within the frame of a large looking-glass. Strange illusion!

My life glided on, the past appearing to mingle with the present and absorb the future, till the whole lies before me at a glance. My manhood has long been waning with a stanch decay; my earlier contemporaries, after lives of unbroken health, are all at rest, without having known the weariness of later age; and now, with a wrinkled forehead and thin white hair as badges of my dignity, I have become the patriarch, the Uncle of the village. I love that name; it widens the circle of my sympathies; it joins all the youthful to my household in the kindred of affection.

Like Uncle Parker, whose rheumatic bones were dashed against Egg Rock, full forty years ago, I am a spinner of long yarns. Seated on the gunwale of a dory, or on the sunny side of a boat-house, where the warmth is grateful to my limbs, or by my own hearth, when a friend or two are there, I overflow with talk, and yet am never tedious. With a broken voice I give utterance to much wisdom. Such, Heaven be praised! is the vigor of my faculties, that many a forgotten usage, and traditions ancient in my youth, and early adventures of myself or others, hitherto effaced by things more recent, acquire new distinctness in my memory. I remember the happy days when the haddock were more numerous on all the fishing grounds than sculpins in the surf; when the deep-water cod swam close in shore, and the dogfish, with his poisonous horn, had not learned to take the hook. I can number every equinoctial storm in which the sea has overwhelmed the street, flooded the cellars of the village, and hissed upon our kitchen hearth. I give the history of the great whale that was landed on Whale Beach, and whose jaws, being now my gateway, will last for ages after my coffin shall have passed beneath them. Thence it is an easy digression to the halibut, scarcely smaller than the whale, which ran out six cod lines, and hauled my dory to the mouth of Boston Harbor, before I could touch him with the gaff.

If melancholy accidents be the theme of conversation, I tell how a friend of mine was taken out of his boat by an enormous shark; and the sad, true tale of a young man on the eve of marriage, who had been nine days missing, when his drowned body floated into the very pathway, on Marblehead Neck, that had often led him to the dwelling of his bride,—as if the dripping corpse would have come where the mourner was. With such awful fidelity did that lover return to fulfil his vows! Another favorite story is of a crazy maiden who conversed with angels and had the gift of prophecy, and whom all the village loved and pitied, though she went from door to door accusing us of sin, exhorting to repentance, and foretelling our destruction by flood or earthquake. If the young men boast their knowledge of the ledges and sunken rocks, I speak of pilots who knew the wind by its scent and the wave by its taste, and could have steered blindfold to any port between Boston and Mount Desert, guided only by the rote of the shore,—the peculiar sound of the surf on each island, beach, and line of rocks, along the coast. Thus do I talk, and all my auditors grow wise while they deem it pastime.

I recollect no happier portion of my life than this, my calm old age. It is like the sunny and sheltered slope of a valley, where, late in the autumn, the grass is greener than in August, and intermixed with golden dandelions that have not been seen till now, since the first warmth of the year. But with me the verdure and the flowers are not frost-bitten in the midst of winter. A playfulness has revisited my mind; a sympathy with the young and gay; an unpainful interest in the business of others; a light and wandering curiosity; arising, perhaps, from the sense that my toil on earth is ended, and the brief hour till bedtime may be spent in play. Still I have fancied that there is a depth of feeling and reflection under this superficial levity peculiar to one who has lived long and is soon to die.

Show me anything that would make an infant smile, and you shall behold a gleam of mirth over the hoary ruin of my visage. I can spend a pleasant hour in the sun, watching the sports of the village children on the edge of the surf: now they chase the retreating wave far down over the wet sand; now it steals softly up to kiss their naked feet; now it comes onward with threatening front, and roars after the laughing crew, as they scamper beyond its reach. Why should not an old man be merry too, when the great sea is at play with those little children? I delight, also, to follow in the wake of a pleasure party of young men and girls, strolling along the beach after an early supper at the Point. Here, with handkerchiefs at nose, they bend over a heap of eel-grass, entangled in which is a dead skate, so oddly accoutred with two legs and a long tail that they mistake him for a drowned animal. A few steps farther the ladies scream, and the gentlemen make ready to protect them against a young shark of the dogfish kind, rolling with a lifelike motion in the tide that has thrown him up. Next, they are smit with wonder at the black shells of a wagon load of live lobsters, packed in rock-weed for the country market. And when they reach the fleet of dories, just hauled ashore after the day's fishing, how do I laugh in my sleeve, and sometimes roar outright, at the simplicity of these young folks and the sly humor of the fishermen! In winter, when our village is thrown into a bustle by the arrival of perhaps a score of country dealers, bargaining for frozen fish, to be transported hundreds of miles, and eaten fresh in Vermont or Canada, I am a pleased but idle spectator in the throng. For I launch my boat no more.

When the shore was solitary I have found a pleasure that seemed even to exalt my mind, in observing the sports or contentions of two gulls, as they wheeled and hovered about each other, with hoarse screams, one moment flapping on the foam of the wave, and then soaring aloft, till their white bosoms melted into the upper sunshine. In the calm of the summer sunset I drag my aged limbs, with a little ostentation of activity, because I am so old, up to the rocky brow of the hill. There I see the white sails of many a vessel, outward bound or homeward from afar, and the black trail of a vapor behind the eastern steamboat; there, too, is the sun going down, but not in gloom, and there the illimitable ocean mingling with the sky, to remind me of Eternity.

But sweetest of all is the hour of cheerful musing and pleasant talk, that comes between the dusk and the lighted candle, by my glowing fireside. And never, even on the first Thanksgiving night, when Susan and I sat alone with our hopes, nor the second, when a stranger had been sent to gladden us, and be the visible image of our affection, did I feel such joy as now. All that belong to me are here; Death has taken none, nor Disease kept them away, nor Strife divided them from their parents or each other; with neither poverty nor riches to disturb them, nor the misery of desires beyond their lot, they have kept New England's festival round the patriarch's board. For I am a patriarch! Here I sit among my descendants, in my old arm-chair and immemorial corner, while the firelight throws an appropriate glory round my venerable frame. Susan! My children! Something whispers me that this happiest hour must be the final one, and that nothing remains but to bless you all, and depart with a treasure of recollected joys to heaven. Will you meet me there? Alas! your figures grow indistinct, fading into pictures on the air, and now to fainter outlines, while the fire is glimmering on the walls of a familiar room, and shows the book that I flung down, the sheet that I left half written, some fifty years ago. I lift my eyes to the looking-glass and perceive myself alone, unless those be the mermaid's features retiring into the depths of the mirror with a tender and melancholy smile.

Ah! one feels a chillness, not bodily, but about the heart, and, moveover, a foolish dread of looking behind him, after these pastimes. I can imagine precisely how a magician would sit down in gloom and terror, after dismissing the shadows that had personated dead or distant people, and stripping his cavern of the unreal splendor which had changed it to a palace. And now for a moral to my reverie. Shall it be that, since fancy can create so bright a dream of happiness, it were better to dream on from youth to age, than to awake and strive doubtfully for something real. Oh, the slight tissue of a dream can no more preserve us from the stern reality of misfortune than a robe of cobweb could repel the wintry blast. Be this the moral then. In chaste and warm affections, humble wishes, and honest toil for some useful end, there is health for the mind, and quiet for the heart, the prospect of a happy life, and the fairest hope of heaven.

THE AMBITIOUS GUEST

One September night a family had gathered round their hearth, and piled it high with the driftwood of mountain streams, the dry cones of the pine, and the splintered ruins of great trees that had come crashing down the precipice. Up the chimney roared the fire, and brightened the room with its broad blaze. The faces of the father and mother had a sober gladness; the children laughed; the eldest daughter was the image of Happiness at seventeen; and the aged grandmother, who sat knitting in the warmest place, was the image of Happiness grown old. They had found the "herb, heart's-ease," in the bleakest spot of all New England. This family were situated in the Notch of the White Hills, where the wind was sharp throughout the year, and pitilessly cold in the winter,—giving their cottage all its fresh inclemency before it descended on the valley of the Saco. They dwelt in a cold spot and a dangerous one; for a mountain towered above their heads, so steep, that the stones would often rumble down its sides and startle them at midnight.

The daughter had just uttered some simple jest that filled them all with mirth, when the wind came through the Notch and seemed to pause before their cottage—rattling the door, with a sound of wailing and lamentation, before it passed into the valley. For a moment it saddened them, though there was nothing unusual in the tones. But the family were glad again when they perceived that the latch was lifted by some traveller, whose footsteps had been unheard amid the dreary blast which heralded his approach, and wailed as he was entering, and went moaning away from the door.

Though they dwelt in such a solitude, these people held daily converse with the world. The romantic pass of the Notch is a great artery, through which the life-blood of internal commerce is continually throbbing between Maine, on one side, and the Green Mountains and the shores of the St. Lawrence, on the other. The stage-coach always drew up before the door of the cottage. The wayfarer, with no companion but his staff, paused here to exchange a word, that the sense of loneliness might not utterly overcome him ere he could pass through the cleft of the mountain, or reach the first house in the valley. And here the teamster, on his way to Portland market, would put up for the night; and, if a bachelor, might sit an hour beyond the usual bedtime, and steal a kiss from the mountain maid at parting. It was one of those primitive taverns where the traveller pays only for food and lodging, but meets with a homely kindness beyond all price. When the footsteps were heard, therefore, between the outer door and the inner one, the whole family rose up, grandmother, children, and all, as if about to welcome some one who belonged to them, and whose fate was linked with theirs.

The door was opened by a young man. His face at first wore the melancholy expression, almost despondency, of one who travels a wild and bleak road, at nightfall and alone, but soon brightened up when he saw the kindly warmth of his reception. He felt his heart spring forward to meet them all, from the old woman, who wiped a chair with her apron, to the little child that held out its arms to him. One glance and smile placed the stranger on a footing of innocent familiarity with the eldest daughter.

"Ah, this fire is the right thing!" cried he; "especially when there is such a pleasant circle round it. I am quite benumbed; for the Notch is just like the pipe of a great pair of bellows; it has blown a terrible blast in my face all the way from Bartlett."

"Then you are going towards Vermont?" said the master of the house, as he helped to take a light knap-sack off the young man's shoulders.

"Yes; to Burlington, and far enough beyond," replied he. "I meant to have been at Ethan Crawford's to-night; but a pedestrian lingers along such a road as this. It is no matter; for, when I saw this good fire, and all your cheerful faces, I felt as if you had kindled it on purpose for me, and were waiting my arrival. So I shall sit down among you, and make myself at home."

The frank-hearted stranger had just drawn his chair to the fire when something like a heavy footstep was heard without, rushing down the steep side of the mountain, as with long and rapid strides, and taking such a leap in passing the cottage as to strike the opposite precipice. The family held their breath, because they knew the sound, and their guest held his by instinct.

"The old mountain has thrown a stone at us, for fear we should forget him," said the landlord, recovering himself. "He sometimes nods his head and threatens to come down; but we are old neighbors, and agree together pretty well upon the whole. Besides we have a sure place of refuge hard by if he should be coming in good earnest."

Let us now suppose the stranger to have finished his supper of bear's meat; and, by his natural felicity of manner, to have placed himself on a footing of kindness with the whole family, so that they talked as freely together as if he belonged to their mountain brood. He was of a proud, yet gentle spirit—haughty and reserved among the rich and great; but ever ready to stoop his head to the lowly cottage door, and be like a brother or a son at the poor man's fireside. In the household of the Notch he found warmth and simplicity of feeling, the pervading intelligence of New England, and a poetry of native growth, which they had gathered when they little thought of it from the mountain peaks and chasms, and at the very threshold of their romantic and dangerous abode. He had travelled far and alone; his whole life, indeed, had been a solitary path; for, with the lofty caution of his nature, he had kept himself apart from those who might otherwise have been his companions. The family, too, though so kind and hospitable, had that consciousness of unity among themselves, and separation from the world at large, which, in every domestic circle, should still keep a holy place where no stranger may intrude. But this evening a prophetic sympathy impelled the refined and educated youth to pour out his heart before the simple mountaineers, and constrained them to answer him with the same free confidence. And thus it should have been. Is not the kindred of a common fate a closer tie than that of birth?

The secret of the young man's character was a high and abstracted ambition. He could have borne to live an undistinguished life, but not to be forgotten in the grave. Yearning desire had been transformed to hope; and hope, long cherished, had become like certainty, that, obscurely as he journeyed now, a glory was to beam on all his pathway,—though not, perhaps, while he was treading it. But when posterity should gaze back into the gloom of what was now the present, they would trace the brightness of his footsteps, brightening as meaner glories faded, and confess that a gifted one had passed from his cradle to his tomb with none to recognize him.

"As yet," cried the stranger—his cheek glowing and his eye flashing with enthusiasm—"as yet, I have done nothing. Were I to vanish from the earth to-morrow, none would know so much of me as you: that a nameless youth came up at nightfall from the valley of the Saco, and opened his heart to you in the evening, and passed through the Notch by sunrise, and was seen no more. Not a soul would ask, 'Who was he? Whither did the wanderer go?' But I cannot die till I have achieved my destiny. Then, let Death come! I shall have built my monument!"

There was a continual flow of natural emotion, gushing forth amid abstracted reverie, which enabled the family to understand this young man's sentiments, though so foreign from their own. With quick sensibility of the ludicrous, he blushed at the ardor into which he had been betrayed.

"You laugh at me," said he, taking the eldest daughter's hand, and laughing himself. "You think my ambition as nonsensical as if I were to freeze myself to death on the top of Mount Washington, only that people might spy at me from the country round about. And, truly, that would be a noble pedestal for a man's statue!"

"It is better to sit here by this fire," answered the girl, blushing, "and be comfortable and contented, though nobody thinks about us."

"I suppose," said her father, after a fit of musing, "there is something natural in what the young man says; and if my mind had been turned that way, I might have felt just the same. It is strange, wife, how his talk has set my head running on things that are pretty certain never to come to pass."

"Perhaps they may," observed the wife. "Is the man thinking what he will do when he is a widower?"

"No, no!" cried he, repelling the idea with reproachful kindness. "When I think of your death, Esther, I think of mine, too. But I was wishing we had a good farm in Bartlett, or Bethlehem, or Littleton, or some other township round the White Mountains; but not where they could tumble on our heads. I should want to stand well with my neighbors and be called Squire, and sent to General Court for a term or two; for a plain, honest man may do as much good there as a lawyer. And when I should be grown quite an old man, and you an old woman, so as not to be long apart, I might die happy enough in my bed, and leave you all crying around me. A slate gravestone would suit me as well as a marble one—with just my name and age, and a verse of a hymn, and something to let people know that I lived an honest man and died a Christian."

"There now!" exclaimed the stranger; "it is our nature to desire a monument, be it slate or marble, or a pillar of granite, or a glorious memory in the universal heart of man."

"We're in a strange way, to-night," said the wife, with tears in her eyes. "They say it's a sign of something, when folks' minds go a wandering so. Hark to the children!"

They listened accordingly. The younger children had been put to bed in another room, but with an open door between, so that they could be heard talking busily among themselves. One and all seemed to have caught the infection from the fireside circle, and were outvying each other in wild wishes, and childish projects of what they would do when they came to be men and women. At length a little boy, instead of addressing his brothers and sisters, called out to his mother.

"I'll tell you what I wish, mother," cried he. "I want you and father and grandma'm, and all of us, and the stranger too, to start right away, and go and take a drink out of the basin of the Flume!"

Nobody could help laughing at the child's notion of leaving a warm bed, and dragging them from a cheerful fire, to visit the basin of the Flume,—a brook, which tumbles over the precipice, deep within the Notch. The boy had hardly spoken when a wagon rattled along the road, and stopped a moment before the door. It appeared to contain two or three men, who were cheering their hearts with the rough chorus of a song, which resounded, in broken notes, between the cliffs, while the singers hesitated whether to continue their journey or put up here for the night.

"Father," said the girl, "they are calling you by name."

But the good man doubted whether they had really called him, and was unwilling to show himself too solicitous of gain by inviting people to patronize his house. He therefore did not hurry to the door; and the lash being soon applied, the travellers plunged into the Notch, still singing and laughing, though their music and mirth came back drearily from the heart of the mountain.

"There, mother!" cried the boy, again. "They'd have given us a ride to the Flume."

Again they laughed at the child's pertinacious fancy for a night ramble. But it happened that a light cloud passed over the daughter's spirit; she looked gravely into the fire, and drew a breath that was almost a sigh. It forced its way, in spite of a little struggle to repress it. Then starting and blushing, she looked quickly round the circle, as if they had caught a glimpse into her bosom. The stranger asked what she had been thinking of.

"Nothing," answered she, with a downcast smile. "Only I felt lonesome just then."

"Oh, I have always had a gift of feeling what is in other people's hearts," said he, half seriously. "Shall I tell the secrets of yours? For I know what to think when a young girl shivers by a warm hearth, and complains of lonesomeness at her mother's side. Shall I put these feelings into words?"

"They would not be a girl's feelings any longer if they could be put into words," replied the mountain nymph, laughing, but avoiding his eye.

All this was said apart. Perhaps a germ of love was springing in their hearts, so pure that it might blossom in Paradise, since it could not be matured on earth; for women worship such gentle dignity as his; and the proud, contemplative, yet kindly soul is oftenest captivated by simplicity like hers. But while they spoke softly, and he was watching the happy sadness, the lightsome shadows, the shy yearnings of a maiden's nature, the wind through the Notch took a deeper and drearier sound. It seemed, as the fanciful stranger said, like the choral strain of the spirits of the blast, who in old Indian times had their dwelling among these mountains, and made their heights and recesses a sacred region. There was a wail along the road, as if a funeral were passing. To chase away the gloom, the family threw pine branches on their fire, till the dry leaves crackled and the flame arose, discovering once again a scene of peace and humble happiness. The light hovered about them fondly, and caressed them all. There were the little faces of the children, peeping from their bed apart, and here the father's frame of strength, the mother's subdued and careful mien, the high-browed youth, the budding girl, and the good old grandam, still knitting in the warmest place. The aged woman looked up from her task, and, with fingers ever busy, was the next to speak.

"Old folks have their notions," said she, "as well as young ones. You've been wishing and planning; and letting your heads run on one thing and another, till you've set my mind a wandering too. Now what should an old woman wish for, when she can go but a step or two before she comes to her grave? Children, it will haunt me night and day till I tell you."

"What is it, mother?" cried the husband and wife at once.

Then the old woman, with an air of mystery which drew the circle closer round the fire, informed them that she had provided her grave-clothes some years before,—a nice linen shroud, a cap with a muslin ruff, and everything of a finer sort than she had worn since her wedding day. But this evening an old superstition had strangely recurred to her. It used to be said, in her younger days, that if anything were amiss with a corpse, if only the ruff were not smooth, or the cap did not set right, the corpse in the coffin and beneath the clods would strive to put up its cold hands and arrange it. The bare thought made her nervous.

"Don't talk so, grandmother!" said the girl, shuddering.

"Now,"—continued the old woman, with singular earnestness, yet smiling strangely at her own folly,—"I want one of you, my children—when your mother is dressed and in the coffin—I want one of you to hold a looking-glass over my face. Who knows but I may take a glimpse at myself, and see whether all's right?"

"Old and young, we dream of graves and monuments," murmured the stranger youth. "I wonder how mariners feel when the ship is sinking, and they, unknown and undistinguished, are to be buried together in the ocean—that wide and nameless sepulchre?"

For a moment, the old woman's ghastly conception so engrossed the minds of her hearers that a sound abroad in the night, rising like the roar of a blast, had grown broad, deep, and terrible, before the fated group were conscious of it. The house and all within it trembled; the foundations of the earth seemed to be shaken, as if this awful sound were the peal of the last trump. Young and old exchanged one wild glance, and remained an instant, pale, affrighted, without utterance, or power to move. Then the same shriek burst simultaneously from all their lips.

"The Slide! The Slide!"

The simplest words must intimate, but not portray, the unutterable horror of the catastrophe. The victims rushed from their cottage, and sought refuge in what they deemed a safer spot—where, in contemplation of such an emergency, a sort of barrier had been reared. Alas! they had quitted their security, and fled right into the pathway of destruction. Down came the whole side of the mountain, in a cataract of ruin. Just before it reached the house, the stream broke into two branches—shivered not a window there, but overwhelmed the whole vicinity, blocked up the road, and annihilated everything in its dreadful course. Long ere the thunder of the great Slide had ceased to roar among the mountains, the mortal agony had been endured, and the victims were at peace. Their bodies were never found.

The next morning, the light smoke was seen stealing from the cottage chimney up the mountain side. Within, the fire was yet smouldering on the hearth, and the chairs in a circle round it, as if the inhabitants had but gone forth to view the devastation of the Slide, and would shortly return, to thank Heaven for their miraculous escape. All had left separate tokens, by which those who had known the family were made to shed a tear for each. Who has not heard their name? The story has been told far and wide, and will forever be a legend of these mountains. Poets have sung their fate.

There were circumstances which led some to suppose that a stranger had been received into the cottage on this awful night, and had shared the catastrophe of all its inmates. Others denied that there were sufficient grounds for such a conjecture. Woe for the high-souled youth, with his dream of Earthly Immortality! His name and person utterly unknown; his history, his way of life, his plans, a mystery never to be solved, his death and his existence equally a doubt! Whose was the agony of that death moment?

THE SISTER YEARS

Last night, between eleven and twelve o'clock, when the Old Year was leaving her final footprints on the borders of Time's empire, she found herself in possession of a few spare moments, and sat down—of all places in the world—on the steps of our new City Hall. The wintry moonlight showed that she looked weary of body and sad of heart, like many another wayfarer of earth. Her garments, having been exposed to much foul weather and rough usage, were in very ill condition; and as the hurry of her journey had never before allowed her to take an instant's rest, her shoes were so worn as to be scarcely worth the mending. But, after trudging only a little distance farther, this poor Old Year was destined to enjoy a long, long sleep. I forgot to mention that, when she seated herself on the steps, she deposited by her side a very capacious bandbox, in which, as is the custom among travellers of her sex, she carried a great deal of valuable property. Besides this luggage, there was a folio book under her arm, very much resembling the annual volume of a newspaper. Placing this volume across her knees, and resting her elbows upon it, with her forehead in her hands, the weary, bedraggled, world-worn Old Year heaved a heavy sigh, and appeared to be taking no very pleasant retrospect of her past existence.

While she thus awaited the midnight knell that was to summon her to the innumerable sisterhood of departed Years, there came a young maiden treading lightsomely on tiptoe along the street, from the direction of the Railroad Depot. She was evidently a stranger, and perhaps had come to town by the evening train of cars. There was a smiling cheerfulness in this fair maiden's face, which bespoke her fully confident of a kind reception from the multitude of people with whom she was soon to form acquaintance. Her dress was rather too airy for the season, and was bedizened with fluttering ribbons and other vanities, which were likely soon to be rent away by the fierce storms or to fade in the hot sunshine, amid which she was to pursue her changeful course. But still she was a wonderfully pleasant looking figure, and had so much promise and such an indescribable hopefulness in her aspect, that hardly anybody could meet her without anticipating some very desirable thing—the consummation of some long-sought good—from her kind offices. A few dismal characters there may be, here and there about the world, who have so often been trifled with by young maidens as promising as she, that they have now ceased to pin any faith upon the skirts of the New Year. But, for my own part, I have great faith in her; and should I live to see fifty more such, still, from each of these successive sisters, I shall reckon upon receiving something that will be worth living for.

The New Year—for this young maiden was no less a personage—carried all her goods and chattels in a basket of no great size or weight, which hung upon her arm. She greeted the disconsolate Old Year with great affection, and sat down beside her on the steps of the City Hall, waiting for the signal to begin her rambles through the world. The two were own sisters, being both granddaughters of Time; and though one looked so much older than the other, it was rather owing to hardships and trouble than to age, since there was but a twelvemonth's difference between them.

"Well, my dear sister," said the New Year, after the first salutations, "you look almost tired to death. What have you been about during your sojourn in this part of Infinite Space?"

"Oh, I have it all recorded here in my Book of Chronicles," answered the Old Year, in a heavy tone. "There is nothing that would amuse you; and you will soon get sufficient knowledge of such matters from your own personal experience. It is but tiresome reading."

Nevertheless, she turned over the leaves of the folio, and glanced at them by the light of the moon, feeling an irresistible spell of interest in her own biography, although its incidents were remembered without pleasure. The volume, though she termed it her Book of Chronicles, seemed to be neither more nor less than the "Salem Gazette" for 1838; in the accuracy of which journal this sagacious Old Year had so much confidence that she deemed it needless to record her history with her own pen.

"What have you been doing in the political way?" asked the New Year.

"Why, my course here in the United States," said the Old Year,—"though perhaps I ought to blush at the confession,—my political course, I must acknowledge, has been rather vacillatory, sometimes inclining towards the Whigs—then causing the Administration party to shout for triumph—and now again uplifting what seemed the almost prostrate banner of the Opposition; so that historians will hardly know what to make of me in this respect. But the Loco Focos"—

"I do not like these party nicknames," interrupted her sister, who seemed remarkably touchy about some points. "Perhaps we shall part in better humor if we avoid any political discussion."

"With all my heart," replied the Old Year, who had already been tormented half to death with squabbles of this kind. "I care not if the names of Whig or Tory, with their interminable brawls about Banks and the Sub-Treasury, Abolition, Texas, the Florida War, and a million of other topics—which you will learn soon enough for your own comfort—I care not, I say, if no whisper of these matters ever reaches my ears again. Yet they have occupied so large a share of my attention that I scarcely know what else to tell you. There has indeed been a curious sort of war on the Canada border, where blood has streamed in the names of Liberty and Patriotism; but it must remain for some future, perhaps far distant Year, to tell whether or no those holy names have been rightfully invoked. Nothing so much depresses me, in my view of mortal affairs, as to see high energies wasted, and human life and happiness thrown away, for ends that appear oftentimes unwise, and still oftener remain unaccomplished. But the wisest people and the best keep a steadfast faith that the progress of Mankind is onward and upward, and that the toil and anguish of the path serve to wear away the imperfections of the Immortal Pilgrim, and will be felt no more when they have done their office."

"Perhaps," cried the hopeful New Year,—"perhaps I shall see that happy day!"

"I doubt whether it be so close at hand," answered the Old Year, gravely smiling. "You will soon grow weary of looking for that blessed consummation, and will turn for amusement (as has frequently been my own practice) to the affairs of some sober little city, like this of Salem. Here we sit on the steps of the new City Hall, which has been completed under my administration; and it would make you laugh to see how the game of politics, of which the Capitol at Washington is the great chess-board, is here played in miniature. Burning Ambition finds its fuel here; here Patriotism speaks boldly in the people's behalf, and virtuous Economy demands retrenchment in the emoluments of a lamplighter; here the Aldermen range their senatorial dignity around the Mayor's chair of state, and the Common Council feel that they have liberty in charge. In short, human weakness and strength, passion and policy, Man's tendencies, his aims and modes of pursuing them, his individual character and his character in the mass, may be studied almost as well here as on the theatre of nations: and with this great advantage, that, be the lesson ever so disastrous, its Liliputian scope still makes the beholder smile."

"Have you done much for the improvement of the City?" asked the New Year. "Judging from what little I have seen, it appears to be ancient and time-worn."

"I have opened the Railroad," said the elder Year, "and half a dozen times a day you will hear the bell (which once summoned the Monks of a Spanish Convent to their devotions) announcing the arrival or departure of the cars. Old Salem now wears a much livelier expression than when I first beheld her. Strangers rumble down from Boston by hundreds at a time. New faces throng in Essex Street. Railroad hacks and omnibuses rattle over the pavements. There is a perceptible increase of oyster shops, and other establishments for the accommodation of a transitory diurnal multitude. But a more important change awaits the venerable town. An immense accumulation of musty prejudices will be carried off by the free circulation of society. A peculiarity of character, of which the inhabitants themselves are hardly sensible, will be rubbed down and worn away by the attrition of foreign substances. Much of the result will be good; there will likewise be a few things not so good. Whether for better or worse, there will be a probable diminution of the moral influence of wealth, and the sway of an aristocratic class, which, from an era far beyond my memory, has held firmer dominion here than in any other New England town."

The Old Year having talked away nearly all of her little remaining breath, now closed her Book of Chronicles, and was about to take her departure. But her sister detained her a while longer, by inquiring the contents of the huge bandbox which she was so painfully lugging along with her.

"These are merely a few trifles," replied the Old Year, "which I have picked up in my rambles, and am going to deposit in the receptacle of things past and forgotten. We sisterhood of Years never carry anything really valuable out of the world with us. Here are patterns of most of the fashions which I brought into vogue, and which have already lived out their allotted term. You will supply their place with others equally ephemeral. Here, put up in little China pots, like rouge, is a considerable lot of beautiful women's bloom, which the disconsolate fair ones owe me a bitter grudge for stealing. I have likewise a quantity of men's dark hair, instead of which, I have left gray locks, or none at all. The tears of widows and other afflicted mortals, who have received comfort during the last twelve months, are preserved in some dozens of essence bottles, well corked and sealed. I have several bundles of love-letters, eloquently breathing an eternity of burning passion, which grew cold and perished almost before the ink was dry. Moreover, here is an assortment of many thousand broken promises, and other broken ware, all very light and packed into little space. The heaviest articles in my possession are a large parcel of disappointed hopes, which a little while ago were buoyant enough to have inflated Mr. Lauriat's balloon."

"I have a fine lot of hopes here in my basket," remarked the New Year. "They are a sweet-smelling flower—a species of rose."

"They soon lose their perfume," replied the sombre Old Year. "What else have you brought to insure a welcome from the discontented race of mortals?"

"Why, to say the truth, little or nothing else," said her sister, with a smile, —"save a few new Annuals and Almanacs, and some New Year's gifts for the children. But I heartily wish well to poor mortals, and mean to do all I can for their improvement and happiness."

"It is a good resolution," rejoined the Old Year; "and, by the way, I have a plentiful assortment of good resolutions, which have now grown so stale and musty that I am ashamed to carry them any farther. Only for fear that the City authorities would send Constable Mansfield with a warrant after me, I should toss them into the street at once. Many other matters go to make up the contents of my bandbox, but the whole lot would not fetch a single bid, even at an auction of worn-out furniture; and as they are worth nothing either to you or anybody else, I need not trouble you with a longer catalogue."

"And must I also pick up such worthless luggage in my travels?" asked the New Year.

"Most certainly—and well, if you have no heavier load to bear," replied the other. "And now, my dear sister, I must bid you farewell, earnestly advising and exhorting you to expect no gratitude nor good-will from this peevish, unreasonable, inconsiderate, ill-intending, and worse-behaving world. However warmly its inhabitants may seem to welcome you, yet, do what you may, and lavish on them what means of happiness you please, they will still be complaining, still craving what it is not in your power to give, still looking forward to some other Year for the accomplishment of projects which ought never to have been formed, and which, if successful, would only provide new occasions of discontent. If these ridiculous people ever see anything tolerable in you, it will be after you are gone forever."

"But I," cried the fresh-hearted New Year, "I shall try to leave men wiser than I find them. I will offer them freely whatever good gifts Providence permits me to distribute, and will tell them to be thankful for what they have, and humbly hopeful for more; and surely, if they are not absolute fools, they will condescend to be happy, and will allow me to be a happy Year. For my happiness must depend on them."

"Alas for you, then, my poor sister!" said the Old Year, sighing, as she uplifted her burden. "We, grandchildren of Time, are born to trouble. Happiness, they say, dwells in the mansions of Eternity; but we can only lead mortals thither, step by step, with reluctant murmurings, and ourselves must perish on the threshold. But hark! my task is done."

The clock in the tall steeple of Dr. Emerson's church struck twelve; there was a response from Dr. Flint's, in the opposite quarter of the city; and while the strokes were yet dropping into the air, the Old Year either flitted or faded away,—and not the wisdom and might of Angels, to say nothing of the remorseful yearnings of the millions who had used her ill, could have prevailed with that departed Year to return one step. But she, in the company of Time and all her kindred, must hereafter hold a reckoning with Mankind. So shall it be, likewise, with the maidenly New Year, who, as the clock ceased to strike, arose from the steps of the City Hall, and set out rather timorously on her earthly course.

"A happy New Year!" cried a watchman, eying her figure very questionably, but without the least suspicion that he was addressing the New Year in person.

"Thank you kindly!" said the New Year; and she gave the watchman one of the roses of hope from her basket. "May this flower keep a sweet smell, long after I have bidden you good-by."

Then she stepped on more briskly through the silent streets; and such as were awake at the moment heard her footfall, and said,—"The New Year is come!" Wherever there was a knot of midnight roisterers they quaffed her health. She sighed, however, to perceive that the air was tainted—as the atmosphere of this world must continually be—with the dying breaths of mortals who had lingered just long enough for her to bury them. But there were millions left alive to rejoice at her coming; and so she pursued her way with confidence, strewing emblematic flowers on the doorstep of almost every dwelling, which some persons will gather up and wear in their bosoms, and others will trample under foot. The Carrier Boy can only say further that, early this morning, she filled his basket with New Year's Addresses, assuring him that the whole City, with our new Mayor, and the Aldermen and Common Council at its head, would make a general rush to secure copies. Kind Patrons, will not you redeem the pledge of the NEW YEAR?

THE SEVEN VAGABONDS

Rambling on foot in the spring of my life and the summer of the year, I came one afternoon to a point which gave me the choice of three directions. Straight before me the main road extended its dusty length to Boston; on the left a branch went towards the sea, and would have lengthened my journey a trifle of twenty or thirty miles; while, by the right-hand path I might have gone over hills and lakes to Canada, visiting in my way the celebrated town of Stamford. On a level spot of grass, at the foot of the guide-post, appeared an object which, though locomotive on a different principle, reminded me of Gulliver's portable mansion among the Brobdignags. It was a huge covered wagon, or, more properly, a small house on wheels, with a door on one side and a window shaded by green blinds on the other. Two horses, munching provender out of the baskets which muzzled them, were fastened near the vehicle: a delectable sound of music proceeded from the interior; and I immediately conjectured that this was some itinerant show halting at the confluence of the roads to intercept such idle travellers as myself. A shower had long been climbing up the western sky, and now hung so blackly over my onward path that it was a point of wisdom to seek shelter here.

"Halloo! Who stands guard here? Is the door-keeper asleep?" cried I, approaching a ladder of two or three steps which was let down from the wagon.

The music ceased at my summons, and there appeared at the door, not the sort of figure that I had mentally assigned to the wandering showman, but a most respectable old personage, whom I was sorry to have addressed in so free a style. He wore a snuff-colored coat and smallclothes, with white top-boots, and exhibited the mild dignity of aspect and manner which may often be noticed in aged schoolmasters, and sometimes in deacons, selectmen, or other potentates of that kind. A small piece of silver was my passport within his premises, where I found only one other person, hereafter to be described.

"This is a dull day for business," said the old gentleman, as he ushered me in; "but I merely tarry here to refresh the cattle, being bound for the camp-meeting at Stamford."

Perhaps the movable scene of this narrative is still peregrinating New England, and may enable the reader to test the accuracy of my description. The spectacle—for I will not use the unworthy term of puppet show—consisted of a multitude of little people assembled on a miniature stage. Among them were artisans of every kind, in the attitudes of their toil, and a group of fair ladies and gay gentlemen standing ready for the dance; a company of foot-soldiers formed a line across the stage, looking stern, grim, and terrible enough, to make it a pleasant consideration that they were but three inches high; and conspicuous above the whole was seen a Merry Andrew, in the pointed cap and motley coat of his profession. All the inhabitants of this mimic world were motionless, like the figures in a picture, or like that people who one moment were alive in the midst of their business and delights, and the next were transformed to statues, preserving an eternal semblance of labor that was ended, and pleasure that could be felt no more. Anon, however, the old gentleman turned the handle of a barrel organ, the first note of which produced a most enlivening effect upon the figures, and awoke them all to their proper occupations and amusements. By the self-same impulse the tailor plied his needle, the blacksmith's hammer descended upon the anvil, and the dancers whirled away on feathery tiptoes; the company of soldiers broke into platoons, retreated from the stage, and were succeeded by a troop of horse, who came prancing onward with such a sound of trumpets and trampling of hoofs as might have startled Don Quixote himself; while an old toper, of inveterate ill habits, uplifted his black bottle and took off a hearty swig. Meantime the Merry Andrew began to caper and turn somersets, shaking his sides, nodding his head, and winking his eyes in as life-like a manner as if he were ridiculing the nonsense of all human affairs, and making fun of the whole multitude beneath him. At length the old magician (for I compared the showman to Prospero entertaining his guests with a mask of shadows) paused that I might give utterance to my wonder.

"What an admirable piece of work is this!" exclaimed I, lifting up my hands in astonishment.

Indeed I liked the spectacle, and was tickled with the old man's gravity as he presided at it, for I had none of that foolish wisdom which reproves every occupation that is not useful in this world of vanities. If there be a faculty which I possess more perfectly than most men, it is that of throwing myself mentally into situations foreign to my own, and detecting, with a cheerful eye, the desirable circumstances of each. I could have envied the life of this gray-headed showman, spent as it had been in a course of safe and pleasurable adventure, in driving his huge vehicle sometimes through the sands of Cape Cod, and sometimes over the rough forest roads of the north and east, and halting now on the green before a village meeting-house, and now in a paved square of the metropolis. How often must his heart have been gladdened by the delight of children as they viewed these animated figures! or his pride indulged by haranguing learnedly to grown men on the mechanical powers which produced such wonderful effects, or his gallantry brought into play (for this is an attribute which such grave men do not lack) by the visits of pretty maidens! And then with how fresh a feeling must he return, at intervals, to his own peculiar home!

"I would I were assured of as happy a life as his," thought I.

Though the showman's wagon might have accommodated fifteen or twenty spectators, it now contained only himself and me, and a third person at whom I threw a glance on entering. He was a neat and thin young man of two or three and twenty; his drab hat, and green frock coat with velvet collar, were smart, though no longer new; while a pair of green spectacles that seemed needless to his brisk little eyes gave him something of a scholar-like and literary air. After allowing me a sufficient time to inspect the puppets, he advanced with a bow, and drew my attention to some books in a corner of the wagon. These he forthwith began to extol with an amazing volubility of well-sounding words, and an ingenuity of praise that won him my heart, as being myself one of the most merciful of critics. Indeed his stock required some considerable powers of commendation in the salesman; there were several ancient friends of mine, the novels of those happy days when my affections wavered between the Scottish Chiefs and Thomas Thumb; besides a few of later date, whose merits had not been acknowledged by the public. I was glad to find that dear little venerable volume, the New England Primer, looking as antique as ever, though in its thousandth new edition; a bundle of superannuated gilt picture-books made such a child of me, that partly for the glittering covers, and partly for the fairy tales within, I bought the whole; and an assortment of ballads and popular theatrical songs drew largely on my purse. To balance these expenditures, I meddled neither with sermons, nor science, nor morality, though volumes of each were there; nor with a Life of Franklin in the coarsest of paper, but so showily bound that it was emblematical of the Doctor himself, in the court-dress which he refused to wear at Paris; nor with Webster's Spelling-Book, nor some of Byron's minor poems, nor half a dozen little Testaments at twenty-five cents each.

Thus far the collection might have been swept from some great bookstore, or picked up at an evening auction room; but there was one small blue-covered pamphlet, which the pedlar handed me with so peculiar an air, that I purchased it immediately at his own price; and then, for the first time, the thought struck me, that I had spoken face to face with the veritable author of a printed book. The literary man now evinced a great kindness for me, and I ventured to inquire which way he was travelling.

"Oh," said he, "I keep company with this old gentleman here, and we are moving now towards the camp-meeting at Stamford."

He then explained to me that for the present season he had rented a corner of the wagon as a bookstore, which, as he wittily observed, was a true Circulating Library, since there were few parts of the country where it had not gone its rounds. I approved of the plan exceedingly, and began to sum up within my mind the many uncommon felicities in the life of a book pedlar, especially when his character resembled that of the individual before me. At a high rate was to be reckoned the daily and hourly enjoyment of such interviews as the present, in which he seized upon the admiration of a passing stranger, and made him aware that a man of literary taste, and even of literary achievement, was travelling the country in a showman's wagon. A more valuable, yet not infrequent, triumph, might be won in his conversations with some elderly clergyman, long vegetating in a rocky, woody, watery back settlement of New England, who, as he recruited his library from the pedlar's stock of sermons, would exhort him to seek a college education and become the first scholar in his class. Sweeter and prouder yet would be his sensations when, talking poetry while he sold spelling-books, he should charm the mind, and haply touch the heart, of a fair country schoolmistress, herself an unhonored poetess, a wearer of blue stockings which none but himself took pains to look at. But the scene of his completest glory would be when the wagon had halted for the night, and his stock of books was transferred to some crowded bar-room. Then would he recommend to the multifarious company, whether traveller from the city, or teamster from the hills, or neighboring squire, or the landlord himself, or his loutish hostler, works suited to each particular taste and capacity; proving, all the while, by acute criticism and profound remark, that the lore in his books was even exceeded by that in his brain.

Thus happily would he traverse the land; sometimes a herald before the march of Mind; sometimes walking arm in arm with awful Literature; and reaping everywhere a harvest of real and sensible popularity, which the secluded bookworms, by whose toil he lived, could never hope for.

"If ever I meddle with literature," thought I, fixing myself in adamantine resolution, "it shall be as a travelling bookseller."

Though it was still mid afternoon, the air had now grown dark about us, and a few drops of rain came down upon the roof of our vehicle, pattering like the feet of birds that had flown thither to rest. A sound of pleasant voices made us listen, and there soon appeared half-way up the ladder the pretty person of a young damsel, whose rosy face was so cheerful that even amid the gloomy light it seemed as if the sunbeams were peeping under her bonnet. We next saw the dark and handsome features of a young man, who, with easier gallantry than might have been expected in the heart of Yankee land, was assisting her into the wagon. It became immediately evident to us, when the two strangers stood within the door, that they were of a profession kindred to those of my companions; and I was delighted with the more than hospitable, the even paternal, kindness of the old showman's manner, as he welcomed them; while the man of literature hastened to lead the merry-eyed girl to a seat on the long bench.

"You are housed but just in time, my young friends," said the master of the wagon. "The sky would have been down upon you within five minutes."

The young man's reply marked him as a foreigner, not by any variation from the idiom and accent of good English, but because he spoke with more caution and accuracy than if perfectly familiar with the language.

"We knew that a shower was hanging over us," said he, "and consulted whether it were best to enter the house on the top of yonder hill, but seeing your wagon in the road"—

"We agreed to come hither," interrupted the girl, with a smile, "because we should be more at home in a wandering house like this."

I meanwhile, with many a wild and undetermined fantasy, was narrowly inspecting these two doves that had flown into our ark. The young man, tall, agile, and athletic, wore a mass of black shining curls clustering round a dark and vivacious countenance, which, if it had not greater expression, was at least more active, and attracted readier notice, than the quiet faces of our countrymen. At his first appearance he had been laden with a neat mahogany box, of about two feet square, but very light in proportion to its size, which he had immediately unstrapped from his shoulders and deposited on the floor of the wagon.

The girl had nearly as fair a complexion as our own beauties, and a brighter one than most of them; the lightness of her figure, which seemed calculated to traverse the whole world without weariness, suited well with the glowing cheerfulness of her face; and her gay attire, combining the rainbow hues of crimson, green, and a deep orange, was as proper to her lightsome aspect as if she had been born in it. This gay stranger was appropriately burdened with that mirth-inspiring instrument, the fiddle, which her companion took from her hands, and shortly began the process of tuning. Neither of us—the previous company of the wagon—needed to inquire their trade; for this could be no mystery to frequenters of brigade musters, ordinations, cattle-shows, commencements, and other festal meetings in our sober land; and there is a dear friend of mine who will smile when this page recalls to his memory a chivalrous deed performed by us, in rescuing the showbox of such a couple from a mob of great double-fisted countrymen.

"Come," said I to the damsel of gay attire, "shall we visit all the wonders of the world together?"

She understood the metaphor at once; though indeed it would not much have troubled me if she had assented to the literal meaning of my words. The mahogany box was placed in a proper position, and I peeped in through its small round magnifying window, while the girl sat by my side, and gave short descriptive sketches, as one after another the pictures were unfolded to my view. We visited together, at least our imaginations did, full many a famous city, in the streets of which I had long yearned to tread; once, I remember, we were in the harbor of Barcelona, gazing townwards; next, she bore me through the air to Sicily, and bade me look up at blazing Ætna; then we took wing to Venice, and sat in a gondola beneath the arch of the Rialto; and anon she sat me down among the thronged spectators at the coronation of Napoleon. But there was one scene, its locality she could not tell, which charmed my attention longer than all those gorgeous palaces and churches, because the fancy haunted me that I myself, the preceding summer, had beheld just such a humble meeting-house, in just such a pine-surrounded nook, among our own green mountains. All these pictures were tolerably executed, though far inferior to the girl's touches of description; nor was it easy to comprehend how, in so few sentences, and these, as I supposed, in a language foreign to her, she contrived to present an airy copy of each varied scene. When we had travelled through the vast extent of the mahogany box I looked into my guide's face.

"Where are you going, my pretty maid?" inquired I, in the words of an old song.

"Ah," said the gay damsel, "you might as well ask where the summer wind is going. We are wanderers here, and there, and everywhere. Wherever there is mirth, our merry hearts are drawn to it. To-day, indeed, the people have told us of a great frolic and festival in these parts; so perhaps we may be needed at what you call the camp-meeting at Stamford."

Then in my happy youth, and while her pleasant voice yet sounded in my ears, I sighed; for none but myself, I thought, should have been her companion in a life which seemed to realize my own wild fancies, cherished all through visionary boyhood to that hour. To these two strangers the world was in its golden age, not that indeed it was less dark and sad than ever, but because its weariness and sorrow had no community with their ethereal nature. Wherever they might appear in their pilgrimage of bliss, Youth would echo back their gladness, care-stricken Maturity would rest a moment from its toil, and Age, tottering among the graves, would smile in withered joy for their sakes. The lonely cot, the narrow and gloomy street, the sombre shade, would catch a passing gleam like that now shining on ourselves, as these bright spirits wandered by. Blessed pair, whose happy home was throughout all the earth! I looked at my shoulders, and thought them broad enough to sustain those pictured towns and mountains; mine, too, was an elastic foot, as tireless as the wing of the bird of paradise; mine was then an untroubled heart, that would have gone singing on its delightful way.

"O maiden!" said I aloud, "why did you not come hither alone?"

While the merry girl and myself were busy with the showbox, the unceasing rain had driven another wayfarer into the wagon. He seemed pretty nearly of the old showman's age, but much smaller, leaner, and more withered than he, and less respectably clad in a patched suit of gray; withal, he had a thin, shrewd countenance, and a pair of diminutive gray eyes, which peeped rather too keenly out of their puckered sockets. This old fellow had been joking with the showman, in a manner which intimated previous acquaintance; but perceiving that the damsel and I had terminated our affairs, he drew forth a folded document, and presented it to me. As I had anticipated, it proved to be a circular, written in a very fair and legible hand, and signed by several distinguished gentlemen whom I had never heard of, stating that the bearer had encountered every variety of misfortune, and recommending him to the notice of all charitable people. Previous disbursements had left me no more than a five-dollar bill, out of which, however, I offered to make the beggar a donation, provided he would give me change for it. The object of my beneficence looked keenly in my face, and discerned that I had none of that abominable spirit, characteristic though it be, of a full-blooded Yankee, which takes pleasure in detecting every little harmless piece of knavery.

"Why, perhaps," said the ragged old mendicant, "if the bank is in good standing, I can't say but I may have enough about me to change your bill."

"It is a bill of the Suffolk Bank," said I, "and better than the specie."

As the beggar had nothing to object, he now produced a small buff-leather bag, tied up carefully with a shoestring. When this was opened, there appeared a very comfortable treasure of silver coins, of all sorts and sizes; and I even fancied that I saw, gleaming among them, the golden plumage of that rare bird in our currency, the American Eagle. In this precious heap was my bank-note deposited, the rate of exchange being considerably against me. His wants being thus relieved, the destitute man pulled out of his pocket an old pack of greasy cards, which had probably contributed to fill the buff-leather bag in more ways than one.

"Come," said he, "I spy a rare fortune in your face, and for twenty-five cents more, I'll tell you what it is."

I never refuse to take a glimpse into futurity; so, after shuffling the cards, and when the fair damsel had cut them, I dealt a portion to the prophetic beggar. Like others of his profession, before predicting the shadowy events that were moving on to meet me, he gave proof of his preternatural science by describing scenes through which I had already passed. Here let me have credit for a sober fact. When the old man had read a page in his book of fate, he bent his keen gray eyes on mine, and proceeded to relate, in all its minute particulars, what was then the most singular event of my life. It was one which I had no purpose to disclose till the general unfolding of all secrets; nor would it be a much stranger instance of inscrutable knowledge, or fortune conjecture, if the beggar were to meet me in the street to-day, and repeat, word for word, the page which I have here written. The fortune-teller, after predicting a destiny which Time seems loath to make good, put up his cards, secreted his treasure bag, and began to converse with the other occupants of the wagon.

"Well, old friend," said the showman, "you have not yet told us which way your face is turned this afternoon."

"I am taking a trip northward, this warm weather," replied the conjurer, "across the Connecticut first, and then up through Vermont, and may be into Canada before the fall. But I must stop and see the breaking up of the camp-meeting at Stamford."

I began to think that all the vagrants in New England were converging to the camp-meeting, and had made this wagon their rendezvous by the way. The showman now proposed that, when the shower was over, they should pursue the road to Stamford together, it being sometimes the policy of these people to form a sort of league and confederacy.

"And the young lady too," observed the gallant bibliopolist, bowing to her profoundly, "and this foreign gentleman, as I understand, are on a jaunt of pleasure to the same spot. It would add incalculably to my own enjoyment, and I presume to that of my colleague and his friend, if they could be prevailed upon to join our party."

This arrangement met with approbation on all hands, nor were any of those concerned more sensible of its advantages than myself, who had no title to be included in it. Having already satisfied myself as to the several modes in which the four others attained felicity, I next set my mind at work to discover what enjoyments were peculiar to the old "Straggler," as the people of the country would have termed the wandering mendicant and prophet. As he pretended to familiarity with the Devil, so I fancied that he was fitted to pursue and take delight in his way of life, by possessing some of the mental and moral characteristics, the lighter and more comic ones, of the Devil in popular stories. Among them might be reckoned a love of deception for its own sake, a shrewd eye and keen relish for human weakness and ridiculous infirmity, and the talent of petty fraud. Thus to this old man there would be pleasure even in the consciousness so insupportable to some minds, that his whole life was a cheat upon the world, and that, so far as he was concerned with the public, his little cunning had the upper hand of its united wisdom. Every day would furnish him with a succession of minute and pungent triumphs: as when, for instance, his importunity wrung a pittance out of the heart of a miser; or when my silly good nature transferred a part of my slender purse to his plump leather bag; or when some ostentatious gentleman should throw a coin to the ragged beggar who was richer than himself; or when, though he would not always be so decidedly diabolical, his pretended wants should make him a sharer in the scanty living of real indigence. And then what an inexhaustible field of enjoyment, both as enabling him to discern so much folly and achieve such quantities of minor mischief, was opened to his sneering spirit by his pretensions to prophetic knowledge.

All this was a sort of happiness which I could conceive of, though I had little sympathy with it. Perhaps, had I been then inclined to admit it, I might have found that the roving life was more proper to him than to either of his companions; for Satan, to whom I had compared the poor man, has delighted, ever since the time of Job, in "wandering up and down upon the earth;" and indeed a crafty disposition which operates not in deep-laid plans, but in disconnected tricks, could not have an adequate scope, unless naturally impelled to a continual change of scene and society. My reflections were here interrupted.

"Another visitor!" exclaimed the old showman.

The door of the wagon had been closed against the tempest, which was roaring and blustering with prodigious fury and commotion, and beating violently against our shelter, as if it claimed all those homeless people for its lawful prey, while we, caring little for the displeasure of the elements, sat comfortably talking. There was now an attempt to open the door, succeeded by a voice uttering some strange, unintelligible gibberish, which my companions mistook for Greek, and I suspected to be thieves' Latin. However, the showman stepped forward, and gave admittance to a figure which made me imagine, either that our wagon had rolled back two hundred years into past ages, or that the forest and its old inhabitants had sprung up around us by enchantment.

It was a red Indian, armed with his bow and arrow. His dress was a sort of cap, adorned with a single feather of some wild bird, and a frock of blue cotton girded tight about him; on his breast, like orders of knighthood, hung a crescent and a circle, and other ornaments of silver; while a small crucifix betokened that our Father the Pope had interposed between the Indian and the Great Spirit, whom he had worshipped in his simplicity. This son of the wilderness and pilgrim of the storm took his place silently in the midst of us. When the first surprise was over, I rightly conjectured him to be one of the Penobscot tribe, parties of which I had often seen, in their summer excursions down our Eastern rivers. There they paddle their birch canoes among the coasting schooners, and build their wigwam beside some roaring mill-dam, and drive a little trade in basket work where their fathers hunted deer. Our new visitor was probably wandering through the country towards Boston, subsisting on the careless charity of the people, while he turned his archery to profitable account by shooting at cents, which were to be the prize of his successful aim.

The Indian had not long been seated ere our merry damsel sought to draw him into conversation. She, indeed, seemed all made up of sunshine in the month of May; for there was nothing so dark and dismal that her pleasant mind could not cast a glow over it; and the wild man, like a fir-tree in his native forest, soon began to brighten into a sort of sombre cheerfulness. At length, she inquired whether his journey had any particular end or purpose.

"I go shoot at the camp-meeting at Stamford," replied the Indian.

"And here are five more," said the girl, "all aiming at the camp-meeting too. You shall be one of us, for we travel with light hearts; and as for me, I sing merry songs, and tell merry tales, and am full of merry thoughts, and I dance merrily along the road, so that there is never any sadness among them that keep me company. But, oh, you would find it very dull indeed to go all the way to Stamford alone!"

My ideas of the aboriginal character led me to fear that the Indian would prefer his own solitary musings to the gay society thus offered him; on the contrary, the girl's proposal met with immediate acceptance, and seemed to animate him with a misty expectation of enjoyment. I now gave myself up to a course of thought which, whether it flowed naturally from this combination of events, or was drawn forth by a wayward fancy, caused my mind to thrill as if I were listening to deep music. I saw mankind, in this weary old age of the world, either enduring a sluggish existence amid the smoke and dust of cities, or, if they breathed a purer air, still lying down at night with no hope but to wear out to-morrow, and all the to-morrows which make up life, among the same dull scenes and in the same wretched toil that had darkened the sunshine of to-day. But there were some, full of the primeval instinct, who preserved the freshness of youth to their latest years by the continual excitement of new objects, new pursuits, and new associates; and cared little, though their birthplace might have been here in New England, if the grave should close over them in Central Asia. Fate was summoning a parliament of these free spirits; unconscious of the impulse which directed them to a common centre, they had come hither from far and near, and last of all appeared the representative of those mighty vagrants who had chased the deer during thousands of years, and were chasing it now in the Spirit Land. Wandering down through the waste of ages, the woods had vanished around his path; his arm had lost somewhat of its strength, his foot of its fleetness, his mien of its wild regality, his heart and mind of their savage virtue and uncultured force; but here, untamable to the routine of artificial life, roving now along the dusty road as of old over the forest leaves, here was the Indian still.

"Well," said the old showman, in the midst of my meditations, "here is an honest company of us—one, two, three, four, five, six—all going to the camp-meeting at Stamford. Now, hoping no offence, I should like to know where this young gentleman may be going?"

I started. How came I among these wanderers? The free mind, that preferred its own folly to another's wisdom; the open spirit, that found companions everywhere; above all, the restless impulse, that had so often made me wretched in the midst of enjoyments; these were my claims to be of their society.

"My friends!" cried I, stepping into the centre of the wagon, "I am going with you to the camp-meeting at Stamford."

"But in what capacity?" asked the old showman, after a moment's silence. "All of us here can get our bread in some creditable way. Every honest man should have his livelihood. You, sir, as I take it, are a mere strolling gentleman."

I proceeded to inform the company that, when Nature gave me a propensity to their way of life, she had not left me altogether destitute of qualifications for it; though I could not deny that my talent was less respectable, and might be less profitable, than the meanest of theirs. My design, in short, was to imitate the story-tellers of whom Oriental travellers have told us, and become an itinerant novelist, reciting my own extemporaneous fictions to such audiences as I could collect.

"Either this," said I, "is my vocation, or I have been born in vain."

The fortune-teller, with a sly wink to the company, proposed to take me as an apprentice to one or other of his professions, either of which, undoubtedly, would have given full scope to whatever inventive talent I might possess. The bibliopolist spoke a few words in opposition to my plan, influenced partly, I suspect, by the jealousy of authorship, and partly by an apprehension that the *viva voce* practice would become general among novelists, to the infinite detriment of the book trade. Dreading a rejection, I solicited the interest of the merry damsel.

"Mirth," cried I, most aptly appropriating the words of L'Allegro, "to thee I sue! Mirth, admit me of thy crew!"

"Let us indulge the poor youth," said Mirth, with a kindness which made me love her dearly, though I was no such coxcomb as to misinterpret her motives. "I have espied much promise in him. True, a shadow sometimes flits across his brow, but the sunshine is sure to follow in a moment. He is never guilty of a sad thought, but a merry one is twin born with it. We will take him with us; and you shall see that he will set us all a-laughing before we reach the camp-meeting at Stamford."

Her voice silenced the scruples of the rest, and gained me admittance into the league; according to the terms of which, without a community of goods or profits, we were to lend each other all the aid, and avert all the harm, that might be in our power. This affair settled, a marvellous jollity entered into the whole tribe of us, manifesting itself characteristically in each individual. The old showman, sitting down to his barrel organ, stirred up the souls of the pygmy people with one of the quickest tunes in the music book; tailors, blacksmiths, gentlemen and ladies, all seemed to share in the spirit of the occasion; and the Merry Andrew played his part more facetiously than ever, nodding and winking particularly at me. The young foreigner flourished his fiddle bow with a master's hand, and gave an inspiring echo to the showman's melody. The bookish man and the merry damsel started up simultaneously to dance; the former enacting the double shuffle in a style which everybody must have witnessed ere Election week was blotted out of time; while the girl, setting her arms akimbo with both hands at her slim waist, displayed such light rapidity of foot, and harmony of varying attitude and motion, that I could not conceive how she ever was to stop; imagining, at the moment, that Nature had made her, as the old showman had made his puppets, for no earthly purpose but to dance jigs. The Indian bellowed forth a succession of most hideous outcries, somewhat affrighting us till we interpreted them as the war-song, with which, in imitation of his ancestors, he was prefacing the assault on Stamford. The conjurer, meanwhile, sat demurely in a corner, extracting a sly enjoyment from the whole scene, and, like the facetious Merry Andrew, directing his queer glance particularly at me.

As for myself, with great exhilaration of fancy, I began to arrange and color the incidents of a tale, wherewith I proposed to amuse an audience that very evening; for I saw that my associates were a little ashamed of me, and that no time was to be lost in obtaining a public acknowledgment of my abilities.

"Come, fellow-laborers," at last said the old showman, whom we had elected President; "the shower is over, and we must be doing our duty by these poor souls at Stamford."

"We'll come among them in procession with music and dancing," cried the merry damsel.

Accordingly—for it must be understood that our pilgrimage was to be performed on foot—we sallied joyously out of the wagon, each of us, even the old gentleman in his white top-boots, giving a great skip as we came down the ladder. Above our heads there was such a glory of sunshine and splendor of clouds, and such brightness of verdure below, that, as I modestly remarked at the time, Nature seemed to have washed her face, and put on the best of her jewelry and a fresh green gown, in honor of our confederation. Casting our eyes northward, we beheld a horseman approaching leisurely, and splashing through the little puddles on the Stamford road. Onward he came, sticking up in his saddle with rigid perpendicularity, a tall, thin figure in rusty black, whom the showman and the conjurer shortly recognized to be, what his aspect sufficiently indicated, a travelling preacher of great fame among the Methodists. What puzzled us was the fact that his face appeared turned from, instead of to, the camp-meeting at Stamford. However, as this new votary of the wandering life drew near the little green space where the guide-post and our wagon were situated, my six fellow-vagabonds and myself rushed forward and surrounded him, crying out with united voices,—

"What news, what news from the camp-meeting at Stamford?"

The missionary looked down in surprise at as singular a knot of people as could have been selected from all his heterogeneous auditors. Indeed, considering that we might all be classified under the general head of Vagabond, there was great diversity of character among the grave old showman, the sly, prophetic beggar, the fiddling foreigner and his merry damsel, the smart bibliopolist, the sombre Indian, and myself, the itinerant novelist, a slender youth of eighteen. I even fancied that a smile was endeavoring to disturb the iron gravity of the preacher's mouth.

"Good people," answered he, "the camp-meeting is broke up."

So saying, the Methodist minister switched his steed and rode westward. Our union being thus nullified by the removal of its object, we were sundered at once to the four winds of heaven. The fortune-teller giving a nod to all, and a peculiar wink to me, departed on his northern tour, chuckling within himself as he took the Stamford road. The old showman and his literary coadjutor were already tackling their horses to the wagon, with a design to peregrinate southwest along the sea-coast. The foreigner and the merry damsel took their laughing leave, and pursued the eastern road, which I had that day trodden; as they passed away, the young man played a lively strain and the girl's happy spirit broke into a dance: and thus, dissolving, as it were, into sunbeams and gay music, that pleasant pair departed from my view. Finally, with a pensive shadow thrown across my mind, yet envious of the light philosophy of my late companions, I joined myself to the Penobscot Indian and set forth towards the distant city.

THE WHITE OLD MAID

The moonbeams came through two deep and narrow windows, and showed a spacious chamber richly furnished in an antique fashion. From one lattice the shadow of the diamond panes was thrown upon the floor; the ghostly light, through the other, slept upon a bed, falling between the heavy silken curtains, and illuminating the face of a young man. But, how quietly the slumberer lay! how pale his features! and how like a shroud the sheet was wound about his frame! Yes; it was a corpse, in its burial clothes.

Suddenly, the fixed features seemed to move with dark emotion. Strange fantasy! It was but the shadow of the fringed curtain waving betwixt the dead face and the moonlight, as the door of the chamber opened and a girl stole softly to the bedside. Was there delusion in the moonbeams, or did her gesture and her eye betray a gleam of triumph, as she bent over the pale corpse—pale as itself—and pressed her living lips to the cold ones of the dead? As she drew back from that long kiss, her features writhed as if a proud heart were fighting with its anguish. Again it seemed that the features of the corpse had moved responsive to her own. Still an illusion! The silken curtain had waved, a second time, betwixt the dead face and the moonlight, as another fair young girl unclosed the door, and glided, ghost-like, to the bedside. There the two maidens stood, both beautiful, with the pale beauty of the dead between them. But she who had first entered was proud and stately, and the other a soft and fragile thing.

"Away!" cried the lofty one. "Thou hadst him living! The dead is mine!"

"Thine!" returned the other, shuddering. "Well hast thou spoken! The dead is thine!"

The proud girl started, and stared into her face with a ghastly look. But a wild and mournful expression passed across the features of the gentle one; and weak and helpless, she sank down on the bed, her head pillowed beside that of the corpse, and her hair mingling with his dark locks. A creature of hope and joy, the first draught of sorrow had bewildered her.

"Edith!" cried her rival.

Edith groaned, as with a sudden compression of the heart; and removing her cheek from the dead youth's pillow, she stood upright, fearfully encountering the eyes of the lofty girl.

"Wilt thou betray me?" said the latter, calmly.

"Till the dead bid me speak, I will be silent," answered Edith. "Leave us alone together! Go, and live many years, and then return, and tell me of thy life. He, too, will be here! Then, if thou tellest of sufferings more than death, we will both forgive thee."

"And what shall be the token?" asked the proud girl, as if her heart acknowledged a meaning in these wild words.

"This lock of hair," said Edith, lifting one of the dark, clustering curls that lay heavily on the dead man's brow.

The two maidens joined their hands over the bosom of the corpse, and appointed a day and hour, far, far in time to come, for their next meeting in that chamber. The statelier girl gave one deep look at the motionless countenance, and departed—yet turned again and trembled ere she closed the door, almost believing that her dead lover frowned upon her. And Edith, too! Was not her white form fading into the moonlight? Scorning her own weakness she went forth, and perceived that a negro slave was waiting in the passage with a wax-light, which he held between her face and his own, and regarded her, as she thought, with an ugly expression of merriment. Lifting his torch on high, the slave lighted her down the staircase, and undid the portal of the mansion. The young clergyman of the town had just ascended the steps, and bowing to the lady, passed in without a word.

Years, many years, rolled on; the world seemed new again, so much older was it grown since the night when those pale girls had clasped their hands across the bosom of the corpse. In the interval, a lonely woman had passed from youth to extreme age, and was known by all the town as the "Old Maid in the Winding Sheet." A taint of insanity had affected her whole life, but so quiet, sad, and gentle, so utterly free from violence, that she was suffered to pursue her harmless fantasies, unmolested by the world, with whose business or pleasures she had nought to do. She dwelt alone, and never came into the daylight, except to follow funerals. Whenever a corpse was borne along the street in sunshine, rain, or snow; whether a pompous train of the rich and proud thronged after it, or few and humble were the mourners, behind them came the lonely woman in a long white garment which the people called her shroud. She took no place among the kindred or the friends, but stood at the door to hear the funeral prayer, and walked in the rear of the procession, as one whose earthly charge it was to haunt the house of mourning, and be the shadow of affliction, and see that the dead were duly buried. So long had this been her custom that the inhabitants of the town deemed her a part of every funeral, as much as the coffin pall, or the very corpse itself, and augured ill of the sinner's destiny unless the "Old Maid in the Winding Sheet" came gliding, like a ghost, behind. Once, it is said, she affrighted a bridal party with her pale presence, appearing suddenly in the illuminated hall, just as the priest was uniting a false maid to a wealthy man, before her lover had been dead a year. Evil was the omen to that marriage! Sometimes she stole forth by moonlight and visited the graves of venerable Integrity, and wedded Love, and virgin Innocence, and every spot where the ashes of a kind and faithful heart were mouldering. Over the hillocks of those favored dead would she stretch out her arms, with a gesture, as if she were scattering seeds; and many believed that she brought them from the garden of Paradise; for the graves which she had visited were green beneath the snow, and covered with sweet flowers from April to November. Her blessing was better than a holy verse upon the tombstone. Thus wore away her long, sad, peaceful, and fantastic life, till few were so old as she, and the people of later generations wondered how the dead had ever been buried, or mourners had endured their grief, without the "Old Maid in the Winding Sheet."

Still years went on, and still she followed funerals, and was not yet summoned to her own festival of death. One afternoon the great street of the town was all alive with business and bustle, though the sun now gilded only the upper half of the church spire, having left the housetops and loftiest trees in shadow. The scene was cheerful and animated, in spite of the sombre shade between the high brick buildings. Here were pompous merchants, in white wigs and laced velvet; the bronzed faces of sea-captains; the foreign garb and air of Spanish creoles; and the disdainful port of natives of Old England; all contrasted with the rough aspect of one or two back settlers, negotiating sales of timber from forests where axe had never sounded. Sometimes a lady passed, swelling roundly forth in an embroidered petticoat, balancing her steps in high-heeled shoes, and courtesying with lofty grace to the punctilious obeisances of the gentlemen. The life of the town seemed to have its very centre not far from an old mansion that stood somewhat back from the pavement, surrounded by neglected grass, with a strange air of loneliness, rather deepened than dispelled by the throng so near it. Its site would have been suitably occupied by a magnificent Exchange or a brick block, lettered all over with various signs; or the large house itself might have made a noble tavern, with the "King's Arms" swinging before it, and guests in every chamber, instead of the present solitude. But owing to some dispute about the right of inheritance, the mansion had been long without a tenant, decaying from year to year, and throwing the stately gloom of its shadow over the busiest part of the town. Such was the scene, and such the time, when a figure unlike any that have been described was observed at a distance down the street.

"I espy a strange sail, yonder," remarked a Liverpool captain; "that woman in the long white garment!"

The sailor seemed much struck by the object, as were several others who, at the same moment, caught a glimpse of the figure that had attracted his notice. Almost immediately the various topics of conversation gave place to speculations, in an undertone, on this unwonted occurrence.

"Can there be a funeral so late this afternoon?" inquired some.

They looked for the signs of death at every door—the sexton, the hearse, the assemblage of black-clad relatives—all that makes up the woful pomp of funerals. They raised their eyes, also, to the sun-gilt spire of the church, and wondered that no clang proceeded from its bell, which had always tolled till now when this figure appeared in the light of day. But none had heard that a corpse was to be borne to its home that afternoon, nor was there any token of a funeral, except the apparition of the "Old Maid in the Winding Sheet."

"What may this portend?" asked each man of his neighbor.

All smiled as they put the question, yet with a certain trouble in their eyes, as if pestilence or some other wide calamity were prognosticated by the untimely intrusion among the living of one whose presence had always been associated with death and woe. What a comet is to the earth was that sad woman to the town. Still she moved on, while the hum of surprise was hushed at her approach, and the proud and the humble stood aside, that her white garment might not wave against them. It was a long, loose robe, of spotless purity. Its wearer appeared very old, pale, emaciated, and feeble, yet glided onward without the unsteady pace of extreme age. At one point of her course a little rosy boy burst forth from a door, and ran, with open arms, towards the ghostly woman, seeming to expect a kiss from her bloodless lips. She made a slight pause, fixing her eye upon him with an expression of no earthly sweetness, so that the child shivered and stood awe-struck, rather than affrighted, while the Old Maid passed on. Perhaps her garment might have been polluted even by an infant's touch; perhaps her kiss would have been death to the sweet boy within a year.

"She is but a shadow," whispered the superstitious. "The child put forth his arms and could not grasp her robe!"

The wonder was increased when the Old Maid passed beneath the porch of the deserted mansion, ascended the moss-covered steps, lifted the iron knocker, and gave three raps. The people could only conjecture that some old remembrance, troubling her bewildered brain, had impelled the poor woman hither to visit the friends of her youth; all gone from their home long since and forever, unless their ghosts still haunted it—fit company for the "Old Maid in the Winding Sheet." An elderly man approached the steps, and, reverently uncovering his gray locks, essayed to explain the matter.

"None, Madam," said he, "have dwelt in this house these fifteen years agone—no, not since the death of old Colonel Fenwicke, whose funeral you may remember to have followed. His heirs, being ill agreed among themselves, have let the mansion-house go to ruin."

The Old Maid looked slowly round with a slight gesture of one hand, and a finger of the other upon her lip, appearing more shadow-like than ever in the obscurity of the porch. But again she lifted the hammer, and gave, this time, a single rap. Could it be that a footstep was now heard coming down the staircase of the old mansion, which all conceived to have been so long untenanted? Slowly, feebly, yet heavily, like the pace of an aged and infirm person, the step approached, more distinct on every downward stair, till it reached the portal. The bar fell on the inside; the door was opened. One upward glance towards the church spire, whence the sunshine had just faded, was the last that the people saw of the "Old Maid in the Winding Sheet."

"Who undid the door?" asked many.

This question, owing to the depth of shadow beneath the porch, no one could satisfactorily answer. Two or three aged men, while protesting against an inference which might be drawn, affirmed that the person within was a negro, and bore a singular resemblance to old Cæsar, formerly a slave in the house, but freed by death some thirty years before.

"Her summons has waked up a servant of the old family," said one, half seriously.

"Let us wait here," replied another. "More guests will knock at the door, anon. But the gate of the graveyard should be thrown open!"

Twilight had overspread the town before the crowd began to separate, or the comments on this incident were exhausted. One after another was wending his way homeward, when a coach—no common spectacle in those days—drove slowly into the street. It was an old-fashioned equipage, hanging close to the ground, with arms on the panels, a footman behind, and a grave, corpulent coachman seated high in front—the whole giving an idea of solemn state and dignity. There was something awful in the heavy rumbling of the wheels. The coach rolled down the street, till, coming to the gateway of the deserted mansion, it drew up, and the footman sprang to the ground.

"Whose grand coach is this?" asked a very inquisitive body.

The footman made no reply, but ascended the steps of the old house, gave three raps with the iron hammer, and returned to open the coach door. An old man, possessed of the heraldic lore so common in that day, examined the shield of arms on the panel.

"Azure, a lion's head erased, between three flower-de-luces," said he; then whispered the name of the family to whom these bearings belonged. The last inheritor of his honors was recently dead, after a long residence amid the splendor of the British court, where his birth and wealth had given him no mean station. "He left no child," continued the herald, "and these arms, being in a lozenge, betoken that the coach appertains to his widow."

Further disclosures, perhaps, might have been made, had not the speaker suddenly been struck dumb by the stern eye of an ancient lady who thrust forth her head from the coach, preparing to descend. As she emerged, the people saw that her dress was magnificent, and her figure dignified, in spite of age and infirmity—a stately ruin but with a look, at once, of pride and wretchedness. Her strong and rigid features had an awe about them, unlike that of the white Old Maid, but as of something evil. She passed up the steps, leaning on a gold-headed cane; the door swung open as she ascended—and the light of a torch glittered on the embroidery of her dress, and gleamed on the pillars of the porch. After a momentary pause—a glance backwards—and then a desperate effort—she went in. The decipherer of the coat of arms had ventured up the lowest step, and shrinking back immediately, pale and tremulous, affirmed that the torch was held by the very image of old Cæsar.

"But such a hideous grin," added he, "was never seen on the face of mortal man, black or white! It will haunt me till my dying day."

Meantime, the coach had wheeled round, with a prodigious clatter on the pavement, and rumbled up the street, disappearing in the twilight, while the ear still tracked its course. Scarcely was it gone, when the people began to question whether the coach and attendants, the ancient lady, the spectre of old Cæsar, and the Old Maid herself, were not all a strangely combined delusion, with some dark purport in its mystery. The whole town was astir, so that, instead of dispersing, the crowd continually increased, and stood gazing up at the windows of the mansion, now silvered by the brightening moon. The elders, glad to indulge the narrative propensity of age, told of the long-faded splendor of the family, the entertainments they had given, and the guests, the greatest of the land, and even titled and noble ones from abroad, who had passed beneath that portal. These graphic reminiscences seemed to call up the ghosts of those to whom they referred. So strong was the impression on some of the more imaginative hearers, that two or three were seized with trembling fits, at one and the same moment, protesting that they had distinctly heard three other raps of the iron knocker.

"Impossible!" exclaimed others. "See! The moon shines beneath the porch, and shows every part of it, except in the narrow shade of that pillar. There is no one there!"

"Did not the door open?" whispered one of these fanciful persons.

"Didst thou see it, too?" said his companion, in a startled tone.

But the general sentiment was opposed to the idea that a third visitant had made application at the door of the deserted house. A few, however, adhered to this new marvel, and even declared that a red gleam like that of a torch had shone through the great front window, as if the negro were lighting a guest up the staircase. This, too, was pronounced a mere fantasy. But at once the whole multitude started, and each man beheld his own terror painted in the faces of all the rest.

"What an awful thing is this!" cried they.

A shriek too fearfully distinct for doubt had been heard within the mansion, breaking forth suddenly, and succeeded by a deep stillness, as if a heart had burst in giving it utterance. The people knew not whether to fly from the very sight of the house, or to rush trembling in, and search out the strange mystery. Amid their confusion and affright, they are somewhat reassured by the appearance of their clergyman, a venerable patriarch, and equally a saint, who had taught them and their fathers the way to heaven for more than the space of an ordinary lifetime. He was a reverend figure, with long, white hair upon his shoulders, a white beard upon his breast, and a back so bent over his staff that he seemed to be looking downward continually, as if to choose a proper grave for his weary frame. It was some time before the good old man, being deaf and of impaired intellect, could be made to comprehend such portions of the affair as were comprehensible at all. But, when possessed of the facts, his energies assumed unexpected vigor.

"Verily," said the old gentleman, "it will be fitting that I enter the mansion-house of the worthy Colonel Fenwicke, lest any harm should have befallen that true Christian woman whom ye call the 'Old Maid in the Winding Sheet.'"

Behold, then, the venerable clergyman ascending the steps of the mansion, with a torch-bearer behind him. It was the elderly man who had spoken to the Old Maid, and the same who had afterwards explained the shield of arms and recognized the features of the negro. Like their predecessors, they gave three raps with the iron hammer.

"Old Cæsar cometh not," observed the priest. "Well I wot he no longer doth service in this mansion."

"Assuredly, then, it was something worse, in old Cæsar's likeness!" said the other adventurer.

"Be it as God wills," answered the clergyman. "See! my strength, though it be much decayed, hath sufficed to open this heavy door. Let us enter and pass up the staircase."

Here occurred a singular exemplification of the dreamy state of a very old man's mind. As they ascended the wide flight of stairs, the aged clergyman appeared to move with caution, occasionally standing aside, and oftener bending his head, as it were in salutation, thus practising all the gestures of one who makes his way through a throng. Reaching the head of the staircase, he looked around with sad and solemn benignity, laid aside his staff, bared his hoary locks, and was evidently on the point of commencing a prayer.

"Reverend Sir," said his attendant, who conceived this a very suitable prelude to their further search, "would it not be well that the people join with us in prayer?"

"Welladay!" cried the old clergyman, staring strangely around him. "Art thou here with me, and none other? Verily, past times were present to me, and I deemed that I was to make a funeral prayer, as many a time heretofore, from the head of this staircase. Of a truth, I saw the shades of many that are gone. Yea, I have prayed at their burials, one after another, and the 'Old Maid in the Winding Sheet' hath seen them to their graves!"

Being now more thoroughly awake to their present purpose, he took his staff and struck forcibly on the floor, till there came an echo from each deserted chamber, but no menial to answer their summons. They therefore walked along the passage, and again paused, opposite to the great front window through which was seen the crowd, in the shadow and partial moonlight of the street beneath. On their right hand was the open door of a chamber, and a closed one on their left. The clergyman pointed his cane to the carved oak panel of the latter.

"Within that chamber," observed he, "a whole life-time since, did I sit by the death-bed of a goodly young man, who, being now at the last gasp"—

Apparently there was some powerful excitement in the ideas which had now flashed across his mind. He snatched the torch from his companion's hand,

and threw open the door with such sudden violence that the flame was extinguished, leaving them no other light than the moonbeams, which fell through two windows into the spacious chamber. It was sufficient to discover all that could be known. In a high-backed oaken arm-chair, upright, with her hands clasped across her breast, and her head thrown back, sat the "Old Maid in the Winding Sheet." The stately dame had fallen on her knees, with her forehead on the holy knees of the Old Maid, one hand upon the floor and the other pressed convulsively against her heart. It clutched a lock of hair, once sable, now discolored with a greenish mould. As the priest and layman advanced into the chamber, the Old Maid's features assumed such a semblance of shifting expression that they trusted to hear the whole mystery explained by a single word. But it was only the shadow of a tattered curtain waving betwixt the dead face and the moonlight.

"Both dead!" said the venerable man. "Then who shall divulge the secret? Methinks it glimmers to and fro in my mind, like the light and shadow across the Old Maid's face. And now 't is gone!"

PETER GOLDTHWAITE'S TREASURE

"And so, Peter, you won't even consider of the business?" said Mr. John Brown, buttoning his surtout over the snug rotundity of his person, and drawing on his gloves. "You positively refuse to let me have this crazy old house, and the land under and adjoining, at the price named?"

"Neither at that, nor treble the sum," responded the gaunt, grizzled, and threadbare Peter Goldthwaite. "The fact is, Mr. Brown, you must find another site for your brick block, and be content to leave my estate with the present owner. Next summer, I intend to put a splendid new mansion over the cellar of the old house."

"Pho, Peter!" cried Mr. Brown, as he opened the kitchen door; "content yourself with building castles in the air, where house-lots are cheaper than on earth, to say nothing of the cost of bricks and mortar. Such foundations are solid enough for your edifices, while this underneath us is just the thing for mine; and so we may both be suited. What say you again?"

"Precisely what I said before, Mr. Brown," answered Peter Goldthwaite. "And as for castles in the air, mine may not be as magnificent as that sort of architecture, but perhaps as substantial, Mr. Brown, as the very respectable brick block with dry goods stores, tailors' shops, and banking rooms on the lower floor, and lawyers' offices in the second story, which you are so anxious to substitute."

"And the cost, Peter, eh?" said Mr. Brown, as he withdrew, in something of a pet. "That, I suppose, will be provided for, off-hand, by drawing a check on Bubble Bank!"

John Brown and Peter Goldthwaite had been jointly known to the commercial world between twenty and thirty years before, under the firm of Goldthwaite & Brown; which copartnership, however, was speedily dissolved by the natural incongruity of its constituent parts. Since that event, John Brown, with exactly the qualities of a thousand other John Browns, and by just such plodding methods as they used, had prospered wonderfully, and become one of the wealthiest John Browns on earth. Peter Goldthwaite, on the contrary, after innumerable schemes, which ought to have collected all the coin and paper currency of the country into his coffers, was as needy a gentleman as ever wore a patch upon his elbow. The contrast between him and his former partner may be briefly marked; for Brown never reckoned upon luck, yet always had it; while Peter made luck the main condition of his projects, and always missed it. While the means held out, his speculations had been magnificent, but were chiefly confined, of late years, to such small business as adventures in the lottery. Once he had gone on a gold-gathering expedition somewhere to the South, and ingeniously contrived to empty his pockets more thoroughly than ever; while others, doubtless, were filling theirs with native bullion by the handful. More recently he had expended a legacy of a thousand or two of dollars in purchasing Mexican scrip, and thereby became the proprietor of a province; which, however, so far as Peter could find out, was situated where he might have had an empire for the same money,—in the clouds. From a search after this valuable real estate Peter returned so gaunt and threadbare that, on reaching New England, the scarecrows in the cornfields beckoned to him, as he passed by. "They did but flutter in the wind," quoth Peter Goldthwaite. No, Peter, they beckoned, for the scarecrows knew their brother!

At the period of our story his whole visible income would not have paid the tax of the old mansion in which we find him. It was one of those rusty, moss-grown, many-peaked wooden houses, which are scattered about the streets of our elder towns, with a beetle-browed second story projecting over the foundation, as if it frowned at the novelty around it. This old paternal edifice, needy as he was, and though, being centrally situated on the principal street of the town, it would have brought him a handsome sum, the sagacious Peter had his own reasons for never parting with, either by auction or private sale. There seemed, indeed, to be a fatality that connected him with his birthplace; for, often as he had stood on the verge of ruin, and standing there even now, he had not yet taken the step beyond it which would have compelled him to surrender the house to his creditors. So here he dwelt with bad luck till good should come.

Here then in his kitchen, the only room where a spark of fire took off the chill of a November evening, poor Peter Goldthwaite had just been visited by his rich old partner. At the close of their interview, Peter, with rather a mortified look, glanced downwards at his dress, parts of which appeared as ancient as the days of Goldthwaite & Brown. His upper garment was a mixed surtout, wofully faded, and patched with newer stuff on each elbow; beneath this he wore a threadbare black coat, some of the silk buttons of which had been replaced with others of a different pattern; and lastly, though he lacked not a pair of gray pantaloons, they were very shabby ones, and had been partially turned brown by the frequent toasting of Peter's shins before a scanty fire. Peter's person was in keeping with his goodly apparel. Gray-headed, hollow-eyed, pale-cheeked, and lean-bodied, he was the perfect picture of a man who had fed on windy schemes and empty hopes, till he could neither live on such unwholesome trash, nor stomach more substantial food.

But, withal, this Peter Goldthwaite, crack-brained simpleton as, perhaps, he was, might have cut a very brilliant figure in the world, had he employed his imagination in the airy business of poetry, instead of making it a demon of mischief in mercantile pursuits. After all, he was no bad fellow, but as harmless as a child, and as honest and honorable, and as much of the gentleman which nature meant him for, as an irregular life and depressed circumstances will permit any man to be.

As Peter stood on the uneven bricks of his hearth, looking round at the disconsolate old kitchen, his eyes began to kindle with the illumination of an enthusiasm that never long deserted him. He raised his hand, clinched it, and smote it energetically against the smoky panel over the fireplace.

"The time is come!" said he. "With such a treasure at command, it were folly to be a poor man any longer. To-morrow morning I will begin with the garret, nor desist till I have torn the house down!"

Deep in the chimney-corner, like a witch in a dark cavern, sat a little old woman, mending one of the two pairs of stockings wherewith Peter Goldthwaite kept his toes from being frostbitten. As the feet were ragged past all darning, she had cut pieces out of a cast-off flannel petticoat, to make new soles. Tabitha Porter was an old maid, upwards of sixty years of age, fifty-five of which she had sat in that same chimney-corner, such being the length of time since Peter's grandfather had taken her from the almshouse. She had no friend but Peter, nor Peter any friend but Tabitha; so long as Peter might have a shelter for his own head, Tabitha would know where to shelter hers; or, being homeless elsewhere, she would take her master by the hand and bring him to her native home, the almshouse. Should it ever be necessary, she loved him well enough to feed him with her last morsel, and clothe him with her under petticoat. But Tabitha was a queer old woman, and, though never infected with Peter's flightiness, had become so accustomed to his freaks and follies that she viewed them all as matters of course. Hearing him threaten to tear the house down, she looked quietly up from her work.

"Best leave the kitchen till the last, Mr. Peter," said she.

"The sooner we have it all down the better," said Peter Goldthwaite. "I am tired to death of living in this cold, dark, windy, smoky, creaking, groaning, dismal old house. I shall feel like a younger man when we get into my splendid brick mansion, as, please Heaven, we shall by this time next autumn. You shall have a room on the sunny side, old Tabby, finished and furnished as best may suit your own notions."

"I should like it pretty much such a room as this kitchen," answered Tabitha. "It will never be like home to me till the chimney-corner gets as black with smoke as this; and that won't be these hundred years. How much do you mean to lay out on the house, Mr. Peter?"

"What is that to the purpose?" exclaimed Peter, loftily. "Did not my great-granduncle, Peter Goldthwaite, who died seventy years ago, and whose namesake I am, leave treasure enough to build twenty such?"

"I can't say but he did, Mr. Peter," said Tabitha, threading her needle.

Tabitha well understood that Peter had reference to an immense hoard of the precious metals, which was said to exist somewhere in the cellar or walls, or under the floors, or in some concealed closet, or other out-of-the-way nook of the house. This wealth, according to tradition, had been accumulated by a former

Peter Goldthwaite, whose character seems to have borne a remarkable similitude to that of the Peter of our story. Like him he was a wild projector, seeking to heap up gold by the bushel and the cartload, instead of scraping it together, coin by coin. Like Peter the second, too, his projects had almost invariably failed, and, but for the magnificent success of the final one, would have left him with hardly a coat and pair of breeches to his gaunt and grizzled person. Reports were various as to the nature of his fortunate speculation: one intimating that the ancient Peter had made the gold by alchemy; another, that he had conjured it out of people's pockets by the black art; and a third, still more unaccountable, that the devil had given him free access to the old provincial treasury. It was affirmed, however, that some secret impediment had debarred him from the enjoyment of his riches, and that he had a motive for concealing them from his heir, or at any rate had died without disclosing the place of deposit. The present Peter's father had faith enough in the story to cause the cellar to be dug over. Peter himself chose to consider the legend as an indisputable truth, and, amid his many troubles, had this one consolation that, should all other resources fail, he might build up his fortunes by tearing his house down. Yet, unless he felt a lurking distrust of the golden tale, it is difficult to account for his permitting the paternal roof to stand so long, since he had never yet seen the moment when his predecessor's treasure would not have found plenty of room in his own strong box. But now was the crisis. Should he delay the search a little longer, the house would pass from the lineal heir, and with it the vast heap of gold, to remain in its burial-place, till the ruin of the aged walls should discover it to strangers of a future generation.

"Yes!" cried Peter Goldthwaite, again, "to-morrow I will set about it."

The deeper he looked at the matter the more certain of success grew Peter. His spirits were naturally so elastic that even now, in the blasted autumn of his age, he could often compete with the spring-time gayety of other people. Enlivened by his brightening prospects, he began to caper about the kitchen like a hobgoblin, with the queerest antics of his lean limbs, and gesticulations of his starved features. Nay, in the exuberance of his feelings, he seized both of Tabitha's hands, and danced the old lady across the floor, till the oddity of her rheumatic motions set him into a roar of laughter, which was echoed back from the rooms and chambers, as if Peter Goldthwaite were laughing in every one. Finally he bounded upward, almost out of sight, into the smoke that clouded the roof of the kitchen, and, alighting safely on the floor again, endeavored to resume his customary gravity.

"To-morrow, at sunrise," he repeated, taking his lamp to retire to bed, "I'll see whether this treasure be hid in the wall of the garret."

"And as we're out of wood, Mr. Peter," said Tabitha, puffing and panting with her late gymnastics, "as fast as you tear the house down, I'll make a fire with the pieces."

Gorgeous that night were the dreams of Peter Goldthwaite! At one time he was turning a ponderous key in an iron door not unlike the door of a sepulchre, but which, being opened, disclosed a vault heaped up with gold coin, as plentifully as golden corn in a granary. There were chased goblets, also, and tureens, salvers, dinner dishes, and dish covers of gold, or silver gilt, besides chains and other jewels, incalculably rich, though tarnished with the damps of the vault; for, of all the wealth that was irrevocably lost to man, whether buried in the earth or sunken in the sea, Peter Goldthwaite had found it in this one treasure-place. Anon, he had returned to the old house as poor as ever, and was received at the door by the gaunt and grizzled figure of a man whom he might have mistaken for himself, only that his garments were of a much elder fashion. But the house, without losing its former aspect, had been changed into a palace of the precious metals. The floors, walls, and ceiling were of burnished silver; the doors, the window frames, the cornices, the balustrades, and the steps of the staircase, of pure gold; and silver, with gold bottoms, were the chairs, and gold, standing on silver legs, the high chests of drawers, and silver the bedsteads, with blankets of woven gold, and sheets of silver tissue. The house had evidently been transmuted by a single touch; for it retained all the marks that Peter remembered, but in gold or silver instead of wood; and the initials of his name, which, when a boy, he had cut in the wooden door-post, remained as deep in the pillar of gold. A happy man would have been Peter Goldthwaite except for a certain ocular deception, which, whenever he glanced backwards, caused the house to darken from its glittering magnificence into the sordid gloom of yesterday.

Up, betimes, rose Peter, seized an axe, hammer, and saw, which he had placed by his bedside, and hied him to the garret. It was but scantily lighted up, as yet, by the frosty fragments of a sunbeam, which began to glimmer through the almost opaque bull's-eyes of the window. A moralizer might find abundant themes for his speculative and impracticable wisdom in a garret. There is the limbo of departed fashions, aged trifles of a day, and whatever was valuable only to one generation of men, and which passed to the garret when that generation passed to the grave, not for safe keeping, but to be out of the way. Peter saw piles of yellow and musty account-books, in parchment covers, wherein creditors, long dead and buried, had written the names of dead and buried debtors in ink now so faded that their moss-grown tombstones were more legible. He found old moth-eaten garments all in rags and tatters, or Peter would have put them on. Here was a naked and rusty sword, not a sword of service, but a gentleman's small French rapier, which had never left its scabbard till it lost it. Here were canes of twenty different sorts, but no gold-headed ones, and shoe-buckles of various pattern and material, but not silver nor set with precious stones. Here was a large box full of shoes, with high heels and peaked toes. Here, on a shelf, were a multitude of phials, half-filled with old apothecaries' stuff, which, when the other half had done its business on Peter's ancestors, had been brought hither from the death chamber. Here—not to give a longer inventory of articles that will never be put up at auction—was the fragment of a full-length looking-glass, which, by the dust and dimness of its surface, made the picture of these old things look older than the reality. When Peter, not knowing that there was a mirror there, caught the faint traces of his own figure, he partly imagined that the former Peter Goldthwaite had come back, either to assist or impede his search for the hidden wealth. And at that moment a strange notion glimmered through his brain that he was the identical Peter who had concealed the gold, and ought to know whereabout it lay. This, however, he had unaccountably forgotten.

"Well, Mr. Peter!" cried Tabitha, on the garret stairs. "Have you torn the house down enough to heat the teakettle?"

"Not yet, old Tabby," answered Peter; "but that's soon done—as you shall see."

With the word in his mouth, he uplifted the axe, and laid about him so vigorously that the dust flew, the boards crashed, and, in a twinkling, the old woman had an apron full of broken rubbish.

"We shall get our winter's wood cheap," quoth Tabitha.

The good work being thus commenced, Peter beat down all before him, smiting and hewing at the joists and timbers, unclinching spike-nails, ripping and tearing away boards, with a tremendous racket, from morning till night. He took care, however, to leave the outside shell of the house untouched, so that the neighbors might not suspect what was going on.

Never, in any of his vagaries, though each had made him happy while it lasted, had Peter been happier than now. Perhaps, after all, there was something in Peter Goldthwaite's turn of mind, which brought him an inward recompense for all the external evil that it caused. If he were poor, ill-clad, even hungry, and exposed, as it were, to be utterly annihilated by a precipice of impending ruin, yet only his body remained in these miserable circumstances, while his aspiring soul enjoyed the sunshine of a bright futurity. It was his nature to be always young, and the tendency of his mode of life to keep him so. Gray hairs were nothing, no, nor wrinkles, nor infirmity; he might look old, indeed, and be somewhat disagreeably connected with a gaunt old figure, much the worse for wear; but the true, the essential Peter was a young man of high hopes, just entering on the world. At the kindling of each new fire, his burnt-out youth rose afresh from the old embers and ashes. It rose exulting now. Having lived thus long—not too long, but just to the right age—a susceptible bachelor, with warm and tender dreams, he resolved, so soon as the hidden gold should flash to light, to go a-wooing, and win the love of the fairest maid in town. What heart could resist him? Happy Peter Goldthwaite!

Every evening—as Peter had long absented himself from his former lounging-places, at insurance offices, news-rooms, and bookstores, and as the honor of his company was seldom requested in private circles—he and Tabitha used to sit down sociably by the kitchen hearth. This was always heaped plentifully with the rubbish of his day's labor. As the foundation of the fire, there would be a goodly-sized backlog of red oak, which, after being sheltered from rain or damp above a century, still hissed with the heat, and distilled streams of water from each end, as if the tree had been cut down within a week or two. Next these were large sticks, sound, black, and heavy, which had lost the principle of decay, and were indestructible except by fire, wherein they glowed like red-hot bars of iron. On this solid basis, Tabitha would rear a lighter structure, composed of the splinters of door panels, ornamented mouldings, and such quick combustibles, which caught like straw, and threw a brilliant blaze high up the spacious flue, making its sooty sides visible almost to the chimney-top. Meantime, the gleam of the old kitchen would be chased out of the cob-webbed corners, and away from the dusky cross-beams overhead, and driven nobody could tell whither, while Peter smiled like a gladsome man, and Tabitha seemed a picture of comfortable age. All this, of course, was but an emblem of the bright fortune which the destruction of the house would shed upon its occupants.

While the dry pine was flaming and crackling, like an irregular discharge of fairy musketry, Peter sat looking and listening, in a pleasant state of excitement. But, when the brief blaze and uproar were succeeded by the dark-red glow, the substantial heat, and the deep singing sound, which were to last throughout the evening, his humor became talkative. One night, the hundredth time, he teased Tabitha to tell him something new about his great-granduncle.

"You have been sitting in that chimney-corner fifty-five years, old Tabby, and must have heard many a tradition about him," said Peter. "Did not you tell me that, when you first came to the house, there was an old woman sitting where you sit now, who had been housekeeper to the famous Peter Goldthwaite?"

"So there was, Mr. Peter," answered Tabitha, "and she was near about a hundred years old. She used to say that she and old Peter Goldthwaite had often spent a sociable evening by the kitchen fire—pretty much as you and I are doing now, Mr. Peter."

"The old fellow must have resembled me in more points than one," said Peter, complacently, "or he never would have grown so rich. But, methinks, he might have invested the money better than he did—no interest!—nothing but good security!—and the house to be torn down to come at it! What made him hide it so snug, Tabby?"

"Because he could not spend it," said Tabitha; "for as often as he went to unlock the chest, the Old Scratch came behind and caught his arm. The money, they say, was paid Peter out of his purse; and he wanted Peter to give him a deed of this house and land, which Peter swore he would not do."

"Just as I swore to John Brown, my old partner," remarked Peter. "But this is all nonsense, Tabby! I don't believe the story."

"Well, it may not be just the truth," said Tabitha; "for some folks say that Peter did make over the house to the Old Scratch, and that's the reason it has always been so unlucky to them that lived in it. And as soon as Peter had given him the deed, the chest flew open, and Peter caught up a handful of the gold. But, lo and behold!—there was nothing in his fist but a parcel of old rags."

"Hold your tongue, you silly old Tabby!" cried Peter in great wrath. "They were as good golden guineas as ever bore the effigies of the king of England. It seems as if I could recollect the whole circumstance, and how I, or old Peter, or whoever it was, thrust in my hand, or his hand, and drew it out all of a blaze with gold. Old rags, indeed!"

But it was not an old woman's legend that would discourage Peter Goldthwaite. All night long he slept among pleasant dreams, and awoke at daylight with a joyous throb of the heart, which few are fortunate enough to feel beyond their boyhood. Day after day he labored hard without wasting a moment, except at meal times, when Tabitha summoned him to the pork and cabbage, or such other sustenance as she had picked up, or Providence had sent them. Being a truly pious man, Peter never failed to ask a blessing; if the food were none of the best, then so much the more earnestly, as it was more needed;—nor to return thanks, if the dinner had been scanty, yet for the good appetite, which was better than a sick stomach at a feast. Then did he hurry back to his toil, and, in a moment, was lost to sight in a cloud of dust from the old walls, though sufficiently perceptible to the ear by the clatter which he raised in the midst of it. How enviable is the consciousness of being usefully employed! Nothing troubled Peter; or nothing but those phantoms of the mind which seem like vague recollections, yet have also the aspect of presentiments. He often paused, with his axe uplifted in the air, and said to himself,—"Peter Goldthwaite, did you never strike this blow before?"—or, "Peter, what need of tearing the whole house down? Think a little while, and you will remember where the gold is hidden." Days and weeks passed on, however, without any remarkable discovery. Sometimes, indeed, a lean, gray rat peeped forth at the lean, gray man, wondering what devil had got into the old house, which had always been so peaceable till now. And, occasionally, Peter sympathized with the sorrows of a female mouse, who had brought five or six pretty, little, soft and delicate young ones into the world just in time to see them crushed by its ruin. But, as yet, no treasure!

By this time, Peter, being as determined as Fate and as diligent as Time, had made an end with the uppermost regions, and got down to the second story, where he was busy in one of the front chambers. It had formerly been the state bed-chamber, and was honored by tradition as the sleeping apartment of Governor Dudley, and many other eminent guests. The furniture was gone. There were remnants of faded and tattered paper-hangings, but larger spaces of bare wall ornamented with charcoal sketches, chiefly of people's heads in profile. These being specimens of Peter's youthful genius, it went more to his heart to obliterate them than if they had been pictures on a church wall by Michael Angelo. One sketch, however, and that the best one, affected him differently. It represented a ragged man, partly supporting himself on a spade, and bending his lean body over a hole in the earth, with one hand extended to grasp something that he had found. But close behind him, with a fiendish laugh on his features, appeared a figure with horns, a tufted tail, and a cloven hoof.

"Avaunt, Satan!" cried Peter. "The man shall have his gold!"

Uplifting his axe, he hit the horned gentleman such a blow on the head as not only demolished him, but the treasure-seeker also, and caused the whole scene to vanish like magic. Moreover, his axe broke quite through the plaster and laths, and discovered a cavity.

"Mercy on us, Mr. Peter, are you quarreling with the Old Scratch?" said Tabitha, who was seeking some fuel to put under the pot.

Without answering the old woman, Peter broke down a further space of the wall, and laid open a small closet or cupboard, on one side of the fireplace, about breast high from the ground. It contained nothing but a brass lamp, covered with verdigris, and a dusty piece of parchment. While Peter inspected the latter, Tabitha seized the lamp, and began to rub it with her apron.

"There is no use in rubbing it, Tabitha," said Peter. "It is not Aladdin's lamp, though I take it to be a token of as much luck. Look here, Tabby!"

Tabitha took the parchment and held it close to her nose, which was saddled with a pair of iron-bound spectacles. But no sooner had she began to puzzle over it than she burst into a chuckling laugh, holding both her hands against her sides.

"You can't make a fool of the old woman!" cried she. "This is your own handwriting, Mr. Peter! the same as in the letter you sent me from Mexico."

"There is certainly a considerable resemblance," said Peter, again examining the parchment. "But you know yourself, Tabby, that this closet must have been plastered up before you came to the house, or I came into the world. No, this is old Peter Goldthwaite's writing; these columns of pounds, shillings, and pence are his figures, denoting the amount of the treasure; and this at the bottom is, doubtless, a reference to the place of concealment. But the ink has either faded or peeled off, so that it is absolutely illegible. What a pity!"

"Well, this lamp is as good as new. That's some comfort," said Tabitha.

"A lamp!" thought Peter. "That indicates light on my researches."

For the present, Peter felt more inclined to ponder on this discovery than to resume his labors. After Tabitha had gone down stairs, he stood poring over the parchment, at one of the front windows, which was so obscured with dust that the sun could barely throw an uncertain shadow of the casement across the floor. Peter forced it open, and looked out upon the great street of the town, while the sun looked in at his old house. The air, though mild, and even warm, thrilled Peter as with a dash of water.

It was the first day of the January thaw. The snow lay deep upon the house-tops, but was rapidly dissolving into millions of water-drops, which sparkled downwards through the sunshine, with the noise of a summer shower beneath the eaves. Along the street, the trodden snow was as hard and solid as a pavement of white marble, and had not yet grown moist in the spring-like temperature. But when Peter thrust forth his head, he saw that the inhabitants, if not the town, were already thawed out by this warm day, after two or three weeks of winter weather. It gladdened him—a gladness with a sigh breathing through it—to see the stream of ladies, gliding along the slippery sidewalks, with their red cheeks set off by quilted hoods, boas, and sable capes, like roses amidst a new kind of foliage. The sleigh-bells jingled to and fro continually: sometimes announcing the arrival of a sleigh from Vermont, laden with the frozen bodies of porkers, or sheep, and perhaps a deer or two; sometimes of a regular market-man, with chickens, geese, and turkeys, comprising the whole colony of a barn yard; and sometimes of a farmer and his dame, who had come to town partly for the ride, partly to go a-shopping, and partly for the sale of some eggs and butter. This couple rode in an old-fashioned square sleigh, which had served them twenty winters, and stood twenty summers in the sun beside their door. Now, a gentleman and lady skimmed the snow in an elegant car, shaped somewhat like a cockle-shell. Now, a stage-sleigh, with its cloth curtains thrust aside to admit the sun, dashed rapidly down the street, whirling in and out among the vehicles that obstructed its passage. Now came, round a corner, the similitude of Noah's ark on runners, being an immense open sleigh with seats for fifty people, and drawn by a dozen horses. This spacious receptacle was populous with merry maids and merry bachelors, merry girls and boys, and merry old folks, all alive with fun, and grinning to the full width of their mouths. They kept up a buzz of babbling voices and low laughter, and sometimes burst into a deep, joyous shout, which the spectators answered with three cheers, while a gang of roguish boys let drive their snowballs right among the pleasure party. The sleigh passed on, and, when concealed by a bend of the street, was still audible by a distant cry of merriment.

Never had Peter beheld a livelier scene than was constituted by all these accessories: the bright sun, the flashing water-drops, the gleaming snow, the cheerful multitude, the variety of rapid vehicles, and the jingle jangle of merry bells which made the heart dance to their music. Nothing dismal was to be seen, except that peaked piece of antiquity, Peter Goldthwaite's house, which might well look sad externally, since such a terrible consumption was preying on its insides. And Peter's gaunt figure, half visible in the projecting second story, was worthy of his house.

"Peter! How goes it, friend Peter?" cried a voice across the street, as Peter was drawing in his head. "Look out here, Peter!"

Peter looked, and saw his old partner, Mr. John Brown, on the opposite sidewalk, portly and comfortable, with his furred cloak thrown open, disclosing a handsome surtout beneath. His voice had directed the attention of the whole town to Peter Goldthwaite's window, and to the dusty scarecrow which appeared at it.

"I say, Peter," cried Mr. Brown again, "what the devil are you about there, that I hear such a racket whenever I pass by? You are repairing the old house, I suppose,—making a new one of it,—eh?"

"Too late for that, I am afraid, Mr. Brown," replied Peter. "If I make it new, it will be new inside and out, from the cellar upwards."

"Had not you better let me take the job?" said Mr. Brown, significantly.

"Not yet!" answered Peter, hastily shutting the window; for, ever since he had been in search of the treasure, he hated to have people stare at him.

As he drew back, ashamed of his outward poverty, yet proud of the secret wealth within his grasp, a haughty smile shone out on Peter's visage, with precisely the effect of the dim sunbeams in the squalid chamber. He endeavored to assume such a mien as his ancestor had probably worn, when he gloried in the building of a strong house for a home to many generations of his posterity. But the chamber was very dark to his snow-dazzled eyes, and very dismal too, in contrast with the living scene that he had just looked upon. His brief glimpse into the street had given him a forcible impression of the manner in which the world kept itself cheerful and prosperous, by social pleasures and an intercourse of business, while he, in seclusion, was pursuing an object that might possibly be a phantasm, by a method which most people would call madness. It is one great advantage of a gregarious mode of life that each person rectifies his mind by other minds, and squares his conduct to that of his neighbors, so as seldom to be lost in eccentricity. Peter Goldthwaite had exposed himself to this influence by merely looking out of the window. For a while, he doubted whether there were any hidden chest of gold, and, in that case, whether he was so exceedingly wise to tear the house down, only to be convinced of its non-existence.

But this was momentary. Peter, the Destroyer, resumed the task which fate had assigned him, nor faltered again till it was accomplished. In the course of his search, he met with many things that are usually found in the ruins of an old house, and also with some that are not. What seemed most to the purpose was a rusty key, which had been thrust into a chink of the wall, with a wooden label appended to the handle, bearing the initials, P.G. Another singular discovery was that of a bottle of wine, walled up in an old oven. A tradition ran in the family, that Peter's grandfather, a jovial officer in the old French War, had set aside many dozens of the precious liquor for the benefit of topers then unborn. Peter needed no cordial to sustain his hopes, and therefore kept the wine to gladden his success. Many halfpence did he pick up, that had been lost through the cracks of the floor, and some few Spanish coins, and the half of a broken sixpence, which had doubtless been a love token. There was likewise a silver coronation medal of George the Third. But old Peter Goldthwaite's strong box fled from one dark corner to another, or otherwise eluded the second Peter's clutches, till, should he seek much farther, he must burrow into the earth.

We will not follow him in his triumphant progress, step by step. Suffice it that Peter worked like a steam-engine, and finished, in that one winter, the job which all the former inhabitants of the house, with time and the elements to aid them, had only half done in a century. Except the kitchen, every room and chamber was now gutted. The house was nothing but a shell,—the apparition of a house,—as unreal as the painted edifices of a theatre. It was like the perfect rind of a great cheese, in which a mouse had dwelt and nibbled till it was a cheese no more. And Peter was the mouse.

What Peter had torn down, Tabitha had burned up; for she wisely considered that, without a house, they should need no wood to warm it; and therefore economy was nonsense. Thus the whole house might be said to have dissolved in smoke, and flown up among the clouds, through the great black flue of the kitchen chimney. It was an admirable parallel to the feat of the man who jumped down his own throat.

On the night between the last day of winter and the first of spring, every chink and cranny had been ransacked, except within the precincts of the kitchen. This fated evening was an ugly one. A snow-storm had set in some hours before, and was still driven and tossed about the atmosphere by a real hurricane, which fought against the house as if the prince of the air, in person, were putting the final stroke to Peter's labors. The framework being so much weakened, and the inward props removed, it would have been no marvel if, in some stronger wrestle of the blast, the rotten walls of the edifice, and all the peaked roofs, had come crushing down upon the owner's head. He, however, was careless of the peril, but as wild and restless as the night itself, or as the flame that quivered up the chimney at each roar of the tempestuous wind.

"The wine, Tabitha!" he cried. "My grandfather's rich old wine! We will drink it now!"

Tabitha arose from her smoke-blackened bench in the chimney-corner, and placed the bottle before Peter, close beside the old brass lamp, which had likewise been the prize of his researches. Peter held it before his eyes, and, looking through the liquid medium, beheld the kitchen illuminated with a golden glory, which also enveloped Tabitha and gilded her silver hair, and converted her mean garments into robes of queenly splendor. It reminded him of his golden dream.

"Mr. Peter," remarked Tabitha, "must the wine be drunk before the money is found?"

"The money *is* found!" exclaimed Peter, with a sort of fierceness. "The chest is within my reach. I will not sleep, till I have turned this key in the rusty lock. But, first of all, let us drink!"

There being no corkscrew in the house, he smote the neck of the bottle with old Peter Goldthwaite's rusty key, and decapitated the sealed cork at a single blow. He then filled two little china teacups, which Tabitha had brought from the cupboard. So clear and brilliant was this aged wine that it shone within the cups, and rendered the sprig of scarlet flowers, at the bottom of each, more distinctly visible than when there had been no wine there. Its rich and delicate perfume wasted itself round the kitchen.

"Drink, Tabitha!" cried Peter. "Blessings on the honest old fellow who set aside this good liquor for you and me! And here's to Peter Goldthwaite's memory!"

"And good cause have we to remember him," quoth Tabitha, as she drank.

How many years, and through what changes of fortune and various calamity, had that bottle hoarded up its effervescent joy, to be quaffed at last by two such boon companions! A portion of the happiness of the former age had been kept for them, and was now set free, in a crowd of rejoicing visions, to sport amid the storm and desolation of the present time. Until they have finished the bottle, we must turn our eyes elsewhere.

It so chanced that, on this stormy night, Mr. John Brown found himself ill at ease in his wire-cushioned arm-chair, by the glowing grate of anthracite which heated his handsome parlor. He was naturally a good sort of a man, and kind and pitiful whenever the misfortunes of others happened to reach his heart through the padded vest of his own prosperity. This evening he had thought much about his old partner, Peter Goldthwaite, his strange vagaries, and continual ill luck, the poverty of his dwelling, at Mr. Brown's last visit, and Peter's crazed and haggard aspect when he had talked with him at the window.

"Poor fellow!" thought Mr. John Brown. "Poor, crackbrained Peter Goldthwaite! For old acquaintance' sake, I ought to have taken care that he was comfortable this rough winter."

These feelings grew so powerful that, in spite of the inclement weather, he resolved to visit Peter Goldthwaite immediately. The strength of the impulse was really singular. Every shriek of the blast seemed a summons, or would have seemed so, had Mr. Brown been accustomed to hear the echoes of his own fancy in the wind. Much amazed at such active benevolence, he huddled himself in his cloak, muffled his throat and ears in comforters and handkerchiefs, and, thus fortified, bade defiance to the tempest. But the powers of the air had rather the best of the battle. Mr. Brown was just weathering the corner, by Peter Goldthwaite's house, when the hurricane caught him off his feet, tossed him face downward into a snow bank, and proceeded to bury his protuberant part beneath fresh drifts. There seemed little hope of his reappearance earlier than the next thaw. At the same moment his hat snatched away, and whirled aloft into some far distant region, whence no tidings have as yet returned.

Nevertheless Mr. Brown contrived to burrow a passage through the snowdrift, and, with his bare head bent against the storm, floundered onward to Peter's door. There was such a creaking and groaning and rattling, and such an ominous shaking throughout the crazy edifice, that the loudest rap would have been inaudible to those within. He therefore entered, without ceremony, and groped his way to the kitchen.

His intrusion, even there, was unnoticed. Peter and Tabitha stood with their backs to the door, stooping over a large chest, which, apparently, they had just dragged from a cavity, or concealed closet, on the left side of the chimney. By the lamp in the old woman's hand, Mr. Brown saw that the chest was barred and clamped with iron, strengthened with iron plates and studded with iron nails, so as to be a fit receptacle in which the wealth of one century might be hoarded up for the wants of another. Peter Goldthwaite was inserting a key into the lock.

"O Tabitha!" cried he, with tremulous rapture, "how shall I endure the effulgence? The gold!—the bright, bright gold! Methinks I can remember my last glance at it, just as the iron-plated lid fell down. And ever since, being seventy years, it has been blazing in secret, and gathering its splendor against this glorious moment! It will flash upon us like the noonday sun!"

"Then shade your eyes, Mr. Peter!" said Tabitha, with somewhat less patience than usual. "But, for mercy's sake, do turn the key!"

And, with a strong effort of both hands, Peter did force the rusty key through the intricacies of the rusty lock. Mr. Brown, in the meantime, had drawn near, and thrust his eager visage between those of the other two, at the instant that Peter threw up the lid. No sudden blaze illuminated the kitchen.

"What's here?" exclaimed Tabitha, adjusting her spectacles, and holding the lamp over the open chest. "Old Peter Goldthwaite's hoard of old rags."

"Pretty much so, Tabby," said Mr. Brown, lifting a handful of the treasure.

Oh, what a ghost of dead and buried wealth had Peter Goldthwaite raised, to scare himself out of his scanty wits withal! Here was the semblance of an incalculable sum, enough to purchase the whole town, and build every street anew, but which, vast as it was, no sane man would have given a solid sixpence for. What then, in sober earnest, were the delusive treasures of the chest? Why, here were old provincial bills of credit, and treasury notes, and bills of land, banks, and all other bubbles of the sort, from the first issue, above a century and a half ago, down nearly to the Revolution. Bills of a thousand pounds were intermixed with parchment pennies, and worth no more than they.

"And this, then, is old Peter Goldthwaite's treasure!" said John Brown. "Your namesake, Peter, was something like yourself; and, when the provincial currency had depreciated fifty or seventy-five percent, he bought it up in expectation of a rise. I have heard my grandfather say that old Peter gave his father a mortgage of this very house and land, to raise cash for his silly project. But the currency kept sinking, till nobody would take it as a gift; and there was old Peter Goldthwaite, like Peter the second, with thousands in his strong box and hardly a coat to his back. He went mad upon the strength of it. But, never mind, Peter! It is just the sort of capital for building castles in the air."

"The house will be down about our ears!" cried Tabitha, as the wind shook it with increasing violence.

"Let it fall!" said Peter, folding his arms, as he seated himself upon the chest.

"No, no, my old friend Peter," said John Brown. "I have house room for you and Tabby, and a safe vault for the chest of treasure. To-morrow we will try to come to an agreement about the sale of this old house. Real estate is well up, and I could afford you a pretty handsome price."

"And I," observed Peter Goldthwaite, with reviving spirits, "have a plan for laying out the cash to great advantage."

"Why, as to that," muttered John Brown to himself, "we must apply to the next court for a guardian to take care of the solid cash; and if Peter insists upon speculating, he may do it, to his heart's content, with old Peter Goldthwaite's Treasure."

THE SHAKER BRIDAL

One day, in the sick chamber of Father Ephraim, who had been forty years the presiding elder over the Shaker settlement at Goshen, there was an assemblage of several of the chief men of the sect. Individuals had come from the rich establishment at Lebanon, from Canterbury, Harvard, and Alfred, and from all the other localities where this strange people have fertilized the rugged hills of New England by their systematic industry. An elder was likewise there, who had made a pilgrimage of a thousand miles from a village of the faithful in Kentucky, to visit his spiritual kindred, the children of the sainted mother Ann. He had partaken of the homely abundance of their tables, had quaffed the far-famed Shaker cider, and had joined in the sacred dance, every step of which is believed to alienate the enthusiast from earth, and bear him onward to heavenly purity and bliss. His brethren of the north had now courteously invited him to be present on an occasion, when the concurrence of every eminent member of their community was peculiarly desirable.

The venerable Father Ephraim sat in his easy chair, not only hoary headed and infirm with age, but worn down by a lingering disease, which, it was evident, would very soon transfer his patriarchal staff to other hands. At his footstool stood a man and woman, both clad in the Shaker garb.

"My brethren," said Father Ephraim to the surrounding elders, feebly exerting himself to utter these few words, "here are the son and daughter to whom I would commit the trust of which Providence is about to lighten my weary shoulders. Read their faces, I pray you, and say whether the inward movement of the spirit hath guided my choice aright."

Accordingly, each elder looked at the two candidates with a most scrutinizing gaze. The man, whose name was Adam Colburn, had a face sunburnt with labor in the fields, yet intelligent, thoughtful, and traced with cares enough for a whole lifetime, though he had barely reached middle age. There was something severe in his aspect, and a rigidity throughout his person, characteristics that caused him generally to be taken for a school-master; which vocation, in fact, he had formerly exercised for several years. The woman, Martha Pierson, was somewhat above thirty, thin and pale, as a Shaker sister almost invariably is, and not entirely free from that corpse-like appearance which the garb of the sisterhood is so well calculated to impart.

"This pair are still in the summer of their years," observed the elder from Harvard, a shrewd old man. "I would like better to see the hoar-frost of autumn on their heads. Methinks, also, they will be exposed to peculiar temptations, on account of the carnal desires which have heretofore subsisted between them."

"Nay, brother," said the elder from Canterbury, "the hoar-frost and the black-frost hath done its work on Brother Adam and Sister Martha, even as we sometimes discern its traces in our cornfields, while they are yet green. And why should we question the wisdom of our venerable Father's purpose although this pair, in their early youth, have loved one another as the world's people love? Are there not many brethren and sisters among us, who have lived long together in wedlock, yet, adopting our faith, find their hearts purified from all but spiritual affection?"

Whether or no the early loves of Adam and Martha had rendered it inexpedient that they should now preside together over a Shaker village, it was certainly most singular that such should be the final result of many warm and tender hopes. Children of neighboring families, their affection was older even than their school-days; it seemed an innate principle, interfused among all their sentiments and feelings, and not so much a distinct remembrance, as connected with their whole volume of remembrances. But, just as they reached a proper age for their union, misfortunes had fallen heavily on both, and made it necessary that they should resort to personal labor for a bare subsistence. Even under these circumstances, Martha Pierson would probably have consented to unite her fate with Adam Colburn's, and, secure of the bliss of mutual love, would patiently have awaited the less important gifts of fortune. But Adam, being of a calm and cautious character, was loath to relinquish the advantages which a single man possesses for raising himself in the world. Year after year, therefore, their marriage had been deferred. Adam Colburn had followed many vocations, had travelled far, and seen much of the world and of life. Martha had earned her bread sometimes as a seamstress, sometimes as help to a farmer's wife, sometimes as school-mistress of the village children, sometimes as a nurse or watcher of the sick, thus acquiring a varied experience, the ultimate use of which she little anticipated. But nothing had gone prosperously with either of the lovers; at no subsequent moment would matrimony have been so prudent a measure as when they had first parted, in the opening bloom of life, to seek a better fortune. Still they had held fast their mutual faith. Martha might have been the wife of a man who sat among the senators of his native state, and Adam could have won the hand, as he had unintentionally won the heart, of a rich and comely widow. But neither of them desired good fortune save to share it with the other.

At length that calm despair which occurs only in a strong and somewhat stubborn character, and yields to no second spring of hope, settled down on the spirit of Adam Colburn. He sought an interview with Martha, and proposed that they should join the Society of Shakers. The converts of this sect are oftener driven within its hospitable gates by worldly misfortune than drawn thither by fanaticism, and are received without inquisition as to their motives. Martha, faithful still, had placed her hand in that of her lover, and accompanied him to the Shaker village. Here the natural capacity of each, cultivated and strengthened by the difficulties of their previous lives, had soon gained them an important rank in the Society, whose members are generally below the ordinary standard of intelligence. Their faith and feelings had, in some degree, become assimilated to those of their fellow-worshippers. Adam Colburn gradually acquired reputation, not only in the management of the temporal affairs of the Society, but as a clear and efficient preacher of their doctrines. Martha was not less distinguished in the duties proper to her sex. Finally, when the infirmities of Father Ephraim had admonished him to seek a successor in his patriarchal office, he thought of Adam and Martha, and proposed to renew, in their persons, the primitive form of Shaker government, as established by Mother Ann. They were to be the Father and Mother of the village. The simple ceremony, which would constitute them such, was now to be performed.

"Son Adam, and daughter Martha," said the venerable Father Ephraim, fixing his aged eyes piercingly upon them, "if ye can conscientiously undertake this charge, speak, that the brethren may not doubt of your fitness."

"Father," replied Adam, speaking with the calmness of his character, "I came to your village a disappointed man, weary of the world, worn out with continual trouble, seeking only a security against evil fortune, as I had no hope of good. Even my wishes of worldly success were almost dead within me. I came hither as a man might come to a tomb, willing to lie down in its gloom and coldness, for the sake of its peace and quiet. There was but one earthly affection in my breast, and it had grown calmer since my youth; so that I was satisfied to bring Martha to be my sister, in our new abode. We are brother and sister; nor would I have it otherwise. And in this peaceful village I have found all that I hoped for,—all that I desire. I will strive, with my best strength, for the spiritual and temporal good of our community. My conscience is not doubtful in this matter. I am ready to receive the trust."

"Thou hast spoken well, son Adam," said the Father. "God will bless thee in the office which I am about to resign."

"But our sister!" observed the elder from Harvard, "hath she not likewise a gift to declare her sentiments?"

Martha started, and moved her lips, as if she would have made a formal reply to this appeal. But, had she attempted it, perhaps the old recollections, the long-repressed feelings of childhood, youth, and womanhood, might have gushed from her heart, in words that it would have been profanation to utter there.

"Adam has spoken," said she hurriedly; "his sentiments are likewise mine."

But while speaking these few words, Martha grew so pale that she looked fitter to be laid in her coffin than to stand in the presence of Father Ephraim and the elders; she shuddered, also, as if there were something awful or horrible in her situation and destiny. It required, indeed, a more than feminine strength of nerve, to sustain the fixed observance of men so exalted and famous throughout the sect as these were. They had overcome their natural sympathy with human frailties and affections. One, when he joined the Society, had brought with him his wife and children, but never, from that hour, had spoken a fond word to the former, or taken his best-loved child upon his knee. Another, whose family refused to follow him, had been enabled—such was his gift of holy fortitude—to leave them to the mercy of the world. The youngest of the elders, a man of about fifty, had been bred from infancy in a Shaker village, and was said never to have clasped a woman's hand in his own, and to have no conception of a closer tie than the cold fraternal one of the sect. Old Father Ephraim was the most awful character of all. In his youth he had been a dissolute libertine, but was converted by Mother Ann herself, and had partaken of the wild fanaticism of the early Shakers. Tradition whispered, at the firesides of the village, that Mother Ann had been compelled to sear his heart of flesh with a red-hot iron before it could be purified from earthly passions.

However that might be, poor Martha had a woman's heart, and a tender one, and it quailed within her, as she looked round at those strange old men, and from them to the calm features of Adam Colburn. But perceiving that the elders eyed her doubtfully, she gasped for breath, and again spoke.

"With what strength is left me by my many troubles," said she, "I am ready to undertake this charge, and to do my best in it."

"My children, join your hands," said Father Ephraim.

They did so. The elders stood up around, and the Father feebly raised himself to a more erect position, but continued sitting in his great chair.

"I have bidden you to join your hands," said he, "not in earthly affection, for ye have cast off its chains forever; but as brother and sister in spiritual love, and helpers of one another in your allotted task. Teach unto others the faith which ye have received. Open wide your gates,—I deliver you the keys thereof,—open them wide to all who will give up the iniquities of the world, and come hither to lead lives of purity and peace. Receive the weary ones, who have known the vanity of earth,—receive the little children, that they may never learn that miserable lesson. And a blessing be upon your labors; so that the time may hasten on, when the mission of Mother Ann shall have wrought its full effect,—when children shall no more be born and die, and the last survivor of mortal race, some old and weary man like me, shall see the sun go down, nevermore to rise on a world of sin and sorrow!"

The aged Father sank back exhausted, and the surrounding elders deemed, with good reason, that the hour was come when the new heads of the village must enter on their patriarchal duties. In their attention to Father Ephraim, their eyes were turned from Martha Pierson, who grew paler and paler, unnoticed even by Adam Colburn. He, indeed, had withdrawn his hand from hers, and folded his arms with a sense of satisfied ambition. But paler and paler grew Martha by his side, till, like a corpse in its burial clothes, she sank down at the feet of her early lover; for, after many trials firmly borne, her heart could endure the weight of its desolate agony no longer.

ENDICOTT AND THE RED CROSS

At noon of an autumnal day, more than two centuries ago, the English colors were displayed by the standard-bearer of the Salem trainband, which had mustered for martial exercise under the orders of John Endicott. It was a period when the religious exiles were accustomed often to buckle on their armor, and practise the handling of their weapons of war. Since the first settlement of New England, its prospects had never been so dismal. The dissensions between Charles the First and his subjects were then, and for several years afterwards, confined to the floor of Parliament. The measures of the King and ministry were rendered more tyrannically violent by an opposition, which had not yet acquired sufficient confidence in its own strength to resist royal injustice with the sword. The bigoted and haughty primate, Laud, Archbishop of Canterbury, controlled the religious affairs of the realm, and was consequently invested with powers which might have wrought the utter ruin of the two Puritan colonies, Plymouth and Massachusetts. There is evidence on record that our forefathers perceived their danger, but were resolved that their infant country should not fall without a struggle, even beneath the giant strength of the King's right arm.

Such was the aspect of the times when the folds of the English banner, with the Red Cross in its field, were flung out over a company of Puritans. Their leader, the famous Endicott, was a man of stern and resolute countenance, the effect of which was heightened by a grizzled beard that swept the upper portion of his breastplate. This piece of armor was so highly polished that the whole surrounding scene had its image in the glittering steel. The central object in the mirrored picture was an edifice of humble architecture with neither steeple nor bell to proclaim it—what nevertheless it was—the house of prayer. A token of the perils of the wilderness was seen in the grim head of a wolf, which had just been slain within the precincts of the town, and according to the regular mode of claiming the bounty, was nailed on the porch of the meeting-house. The blood was still plashing on the doorstep. There happened to be visible, at the same noontide hour, so many other characteristics of the times and manners of the Puritans, that we must endeavor to represent them in a sketch, though far less vividly than they were reflected in the polished breastplate of John Endicott.

In close vicinity to the sacred edifice appeared that important engine of Puritanic authority, the whipping-post—with the soil around it well trodden by the feet of evil doers, who had there been disciplined. At one corner of the meeting-house was the pillory, and at the other the stocks; and, by a singular good fortune for our sketch, the head of an Episcopalian and suspected Catholic was grotesquely incased in the former machine; while a fellow-criminal, who had boisterously quaffed a health to the king, was confined by the legs in the latter. Side by side, on the meeting-house steps, stood a male and a female figure. The man was a tall, lean, haggard personification of fanaticism, bearing on his breast this label,—A WANTON GOSPELLER—which betokened that he had dared to give interpretations of Holy Writ unsanctioned by the infallible judgment of the civil and religious rulers. His aspect showed no lack of zeal to maintain his heterodoxies, even at the stake. The woman wore a cleft stick on her tongue, in appropriate retribution for having wagged that unruly member against the elders of the church; and her countenance and gestures gave much cause to apprehend that, the moment the stick should be removed, a repetition of the offence would demand new ingenuity in chastising it.

The above-mentioned individuals had been sentenced to undergo their various modes of ignominy, for the space of one hour at noonday. But among the crowd were several whose punishment would be life-long; some, whose ears had been cropped, like those of puppy dogs; others, whose cheeks had been branded with the initials of their misdemeanors; one, with his nostrils slit and seared; and another, with a halter about his neck, which he was forbidden ever to take off, or to conceal beneath his garments. Methinks he must have been grievously tempted to affix the other end of the rope to some convenient beam or bough. There was likewise a young woman, with no mean share of beauty, whose doom it was to wear the letter A on the breast of her gown, in the eyes of all the world and her own children. And even her own children knew what that initial signified. Sporting with her infamy, the lost and desperate creature had embroidered the fatal token in scarlet cloth, with golden thread and the nicest art of needlework; so that the capital A might have been thought to mean Admirable, or anything rather than Adulteress.

Let not the reader argue, from any of these evidences of iniquity, that the times of the Puritans were more vicious than our own, when, as we pass along the very street of this sketch, we discern no badge of infamy on man or woman. It was the policy of our ancestors to search out even the most secret sins, and expose them to shame, without fear or favor, in the broadest light of the noonday sun. Were such the custom now, perchance we might find materials for a no less piquant sketch than the above.

Except the malefactors whom we have described, and the diseased or infirm persons, the whole male population of the town, between sixteen years and sixty, were seen in the ranks of the trainband. A few stately savages, in all the pomp and dignity of the primeval Indian, stood gazing at the spectacle. Their flint-headed arrows were but childish weapons compared with the matchlocks of the Puritans, and would have rattled harmlessly against the steel caps and hammered iron breastplates which inclosed each soldier in an individual fortress. The valiant John Endicott glanced with an eye of pride at his sturdy followers, and prepared to renew the martial toils of the day.

"Come, my stout hearts!" quoth he, drawing his sword. "Let us show these poor heathen that we can handle our weapons like men of might. Well for them, if they put us not to prove it in earnest!"

The iron-breasted company straightened their line, and each man drew the heavy butt of his matchlock close to his left foot, thus awaiting the orders of the captain. But, as Endicott glanced right and left along the front, he discovered a personage at some little distance with whom it behooved him to hold a parley. It was an elderly gentleman, wearing a black cloak and band, and a high-crowned hat, beneath which was a velvet skull-cap, the whole being the garb of a Puritan minister. This reverend person bore a staff which seemed to have been recently cut in the forest, and his shoes were bemired as if he had been travelling on foot through the swamps of the wilderness. His aspect was perfectly that of a pilgrim, heightened also by an apostolic dignity. Just as Endicott perceived him he laid aside his staff, and stooped to drink at a bubbling fountain which gushed into the sunshine about a score of yards from the corner of the meeting-house. But, ere the good man drank, he turned his face heavenward in thankfulness, and then, holding back his gray beard with one hand, he scooped up his simple draught in the hollow of the other.

"What, ho! good Mr. Williams," shouted Endicott. "You are welcome back again to our town of peace. How does our worthy Governor Winthrop? And what news from Boston?"

"The Governor hath his health, worshipful Sir," answered Roger Williams, now resuming his staff, and drawing near. "And for the news, here is a letter, which, knowing I was to travel hitherward to-day, his Excellency committed to my charge. Belike it contains tidings of much import; for a ship arrived yesterday from England."

Mr. Williams, the minister of Salem and of course known to all the spectators, had now reached the spot where Endicott was standing under the banner of his company, and put the Governor's epistle into his hand. The broad seal was impressed with Winthrop's coat of arms. Endicott hastily unclosed the letter and began to read, while, as his eye passed down the page, a wrathful change came over his manly countenance. The blood glowed through it, till it seemed to be kindling with an internal heat; nor was it unnatural to suppose that his breastplate would likewise become red-hot with the angry fire of the bosom which it covered. Arriving at the conclusion, he shook the letter fiercely in his hand, so that it rustled as loud as the flag above his head.

"Black tidings these, Mr. Williams," said he; "blacker never came to New England. Doubtless you know their purport?"

"Yea, truly," replied Roger Williams; "for the Governor consulted, respecting this matter, with my brethren in the ministry at Boston; and my opinion was likewise asked. And his Excellency entreats you by me, that the news be not suddenly noised abroad, lest the people be stirred up unto some outbreak, and thereby give the King and the Archbishop a handle against us."

"The Governor is a wise man—a wise man, and a meek and moderate," said Endicott, setting his teeth grimly. "Nevertheless, I must do according to my own best judgment. There is neither man, woman, nor child in New England, but has a concern as dear as life in these tidings; and if John Endicott's voice be loud enough, man, woman, and child shall hear them. Soldiers, wheel into a hollow square! Ho, good people! Here are news for one and all of you."

The soldiers closed in around their captain; and he and Roger Williams stood together under the banner of the Red Cross; while the women and the aged men pressed forward, and the mothers held up their children to look Endicott in the face. A few taps of the drum gave signal for silence and attention.

"Fellow-soldiers,—fellow-exiles," began Endicott, speaking under strong excitement, yet powerfully restraining it, "wherefore did ye leave your native country? Wherefore, I say, have we left the green and fertile fields, the cottages, or, perchance, the old gray halls, where we were born and bred, the churchyards where our forefathers lie buried? Wherefore have we come hither to set up our own tombstones in a wilderness? A howling wilderness it is! The wolf and the bear meet us within halloo of our dwellings. The savage lieth in wait for us in the dismal shadow of the woods. The stubborn roots of the trees break our ploughshares, when we would till the earth. Our children cry for bread, and we must dig in the sands of the sea-shore to satisfy them. Wherefore, I say again, have we sought this country of a rugged soil and wintry sky? Was it not for the enjoyment of our civil rights? Was it not for liberty to worship God according to our conscience?"

"Call you this liberty of conscience?" interrupted a voice on the steps of the meeting-house.

It was the Wanton Gospeller. A sad and quiet smile flitted across the mild visage of Roger Williams. But Endicott, in the excitement of the moment, shook his sword wrathfully at the culprit—an ominous gesture from a man like him.

"What hast thou to do with conscience, thou knave?" cried he. "I said liberty to worship God, not license to profane and ridicule him. Break not in upon my speech, or I will lay thee neck and heels till this time to-morrow! Hearken to me, friends, nor heed that accursed rhapsodist. As I was saying, we have sacrificed all things, and have come to a land whereof the old world hath scarcely heard, that we might make a new world unto ourselves, and painfully seek a path from hence to heaven. But what think ye now? This son of a Scotch tyrant—this grandson of a Papistical and adulterous Scotch woman, whose death proved that a golden crown doth not always save an anointed head from the block"—

"Nay, brother, nay," interposed Mr. Williams; "thy words are not meet for a secret chamber, far less for a public street."

"Hold thy peace, Roger Williams!" answered Endicott, imperiously. "My spirit is wiser than thine for the business now in hand. I tell ye, fellow-exiles, that Charles of England, and Laud, our bitterest persecutor, arch-priest of Canterbury, are resolute to pursue us even hither. They are taking counsel, saith this letter, to send over a governor-general, in whose breast shall be deposited all the law and equity of the land. They are minded, also, to establish the idolatrous forms of English Episcopacy; so that, when Laud shall kiss the Pope's toe, as cardinal of Rome, he may deliver New England, bound hand and foot, into the power of his master!"

A deep groan from the auditors,—a sound of wrath, as well as fear and sorrow,—responded to this intelligence.

"Look ye to it, brethren," resumed Endicott, with increasing energy. "If this king and this arch-prelate have their will, we shall briefly behold a cross on the spire of this tabernacle which we have builded, and a high altar within its walls, with wax tapers burning round it at noonday. We shall hear the sacring bell, and the voices of the Romish priests saying the mass. But think ye, Christian men, that these abominations may be suffered without a sword drawn? without a shot fired? without blood spilt, yea, on the very stairs of the pulpit? No,—be ye strong of hand and stout of heart! Here we stand on our own soil, which we have bought with our goods, which we have won with our swords, which we have cleared with our axes, which we have tilled with the sweat of our brows, which we have sanctified with our prayers to the God that brought us hither! Who shall enslave us here? What have we to do with this mitred prelate,—with this crowned king? What have we to do with England?"

Endicott gazed round at the excited countenances of the people, now full of his own spirit, and then turned suddenly to the standard-bearer, who stood close behind him.

"Officer, lower your banner!" said he.

The officer obeyed; and, brandishing his sword, Endicott thrust it through the cloth, and, with his left hand, rent the Red Cross completely out of the banner. He then waved the tattered ensign above his head.

"Sacrilegious wretch!" cried the high-churchman in the pillory, unable longer to restrain himself, "thou hast rejected the symbol of our holy religion!"

"Treason, treason!" roared the royalist in the stocks. "He hath defaced the King's banner!"

"Before God and man, I will avouch the deed," answered Endicott. "Beat a flourish, drummer!—shout, soldiers and people!—in honor of the ensign of New England. Neither Pope nor Tyrant hath part in it now!"

With a cry of triumph, the people gave their sanction to one of the boldest exploits which our history records. And forever honored be the name of Endicott! We look back through the mist of ages, and recognize in the rending of the Red Cross from New England's banner the first omen of that deliverance which our fathers consummated after the bones of the stern Puritan had lain more than a century in the dust.

THE LILY'S QUEST

AN APOLOGUE

Two lovers, once upon a time, had planned a little summer-house, in the form of an antique temple, which it was their purpose to consecrate to all manner of refined and innocent enjoyments. There they would hold pleasant intercourse with one another and the circle of their familiar friends; there they would give festivals of delicious fruit; there they would hear lightsome music, intermingled with the strains of pathos which make joy more sweet; there they would read poetry and fiction, and permit their own minds to flit away in day-dreams and romance; there, in short—for why should we shape out the vague sunshine of their hopes?—there all pure delights were to cluster like roses among the pillars of the edifice, and blossom ever new and spontaneously. So, one breezy and cloudless afternoon, Adam Forrester and Lilias Fay set out upon a ramble over the wide estate which they were to possess together, seeking a proper site for their Temple of Happiness. They were themselves a fair and happy spectacle, fit priest and priestess for such a shrine; although, making poetry of the pretty name of Lilias, Adam Forrester was wont to call her LILY, because her form was as fragile, and her cheek almost as pale.

As they passed hand in hand down the avenue of drooping elms that led from the portal of Lilias Fay's paternal mansion, they seemed to glance like winged creatures through the strips of sunshine, and to scatter brightness where the deep shadows fell. But setting forth at the same time with this youthful pair, there was a dismal figure, wrapped in a black velvet cloak that might have been made of a coffin pall, and with a sombre hat such as mourners wear drooping its broad brim over his heavy brows. Glancing behind them, the lovers well knew who it was that followed, but wished from their hearts that he had been elsewhere, as being a companion so strangely unsuited to their joyous errand. It was a near relative of Lilias Fay, an old man by the name of Walter Gascoigne, who had long labored under the burden of a melancholy spirit, which was sometimes maddened into absolute insanity, and always had a tinge of it. What a contrast between the young pilgrims of bliss and their unbidden associate! They looked as if moulded of heaven's sunshine, and he of earth's gloomiest shade; they flitted along like Hope and Joy roaming hand in hand through life; while his darksome figure stalked behind, a type of all the woful influences which life could fling upon them. But the three had not gone far when they reached a spot that pleased the gentle Lily, and she paused.

"What sweeter place shall we find than this?" said she. "Why should we seek farther for the site of our Temple?"

It was indeed a delightful spot of earth, though undistinguished by any very prominent beauties, being merely a nook in the shelter of a hill, with the prospect of a distant lake in one direction, and of a church spire in another. There were vistas and pathways leading onward and onward into the green woodlands, and vanishing away in the glimmering shade. The Temple, if erected here, would look towards the west: so that the lovers could shape all sorts of magnificent dreams out of the purple, violet, and gold of the sunset sky; and few of their anticipated pleasures were dearer than this sport of fantasy.

"Yes," said Adam Forrester, "we might seek all day and find no lovelier spot. We will build our Temple here."

But their sad old companion, who had taken his stand on the very site which they proposed to cover with a marble floor, shook his head and frowned; and the young man and the Lily deemed it almost enough to blight the spot, and desecrate it for their airy Temple, that his dismal figure had thrown its shadow there. He pointed to some scattered stones, the remnants of a former structure, and to flowers such as young girls delight to nurse in their gardens, but which had now relapsed into the wild simplicity of nature.

"Not here!" cried old Walter Gascoigne. "Here, long ago, other mortals built their Temple of Happiness. Seek another site for yours!"

"What!" exclaimed Lilias Fay. "Have any ever planned such a Temple save ourselves?"

"Poor child!" said her gloomy kinsman. "In one shape or other, every mortal has dreamed your dream."

Then he told the lovers how, not, indeed, an antique Temple, but a dwelling, had once stood there, and that a dark-clad guest had dwelt among its inmates, sitting forever at the fireside, and poisoning all their household mirth. Under this type, Adam Forrester and Lilias saw that the old man spake of Sorrow. He told of nothing that might not be recorded in the history of almost every household; and yet his hearers felt as if no sunshine ought to fall upon a spot where human grief had left so deep a stain; or, at least, that no joyous Temple should be built there.

"This is very sad," said the Lily, sighing.

"Well, there are lovelier spots than this," said Adam Forrester, soothingly, —"spots which sorrow has not blighted."

So they hastened away, and the melancholy Gascoigne followed them, looking as if he had gathered up all the gloom of the deserted spot, and was bearing it as a burden of inestimable treasure. But still they rambled on, and soon found themselves in a rocky dell through the midst of which ran a streamlet with ripple and foam, and a continual voice of inarticulate joy. It was a wild retreat, walled on either side with gray precipices, which would have frowned somewhat too sternly, had not a profusion of green shrubbery rooted itself into their crevices, and wreathed gladsome foliage around their solemn brows. But the chief joy of the dell was in the little stream, which seemed like the presence of a blissful child, with nothing earthly to do save to babble merrily and disport itself, and make every living soul its playfellow, and throw the sunny gleams of its spirit upon all.

"Here, here is the spot!" cried the two lovers with one voice as they reached a level space on the brink of a small cascade. "This glen was made on purpose for our Temple!"

"And the glad song of the brook will be always in our ears," said Lilias Fay.

"And its long melody shall sing the bliss of our lifetime," said Adam Forrester.

"Ye must build no Temple here!" murmured their dismal companion.

And there again was the old lunatic, standing just on the spot where they meant to rear their lightsome dome, and looking like the embodied symbol of some great woe, that, in forgotten days, had happened there. And, alas! there had been woe, nor that alone. A young man, more than a hundred years before, had lured hither a girl that loved him, and on this spot had murdered her, and washed his bloody hands in the stream which sung so merrily. And ever since the victim's death shrieks were often heard to echo between the cliffs.

"And see!" cried old Gascoigne, "is the stream yet pure from the stain of the murderer's hands?"

"Methinks it has a tinge of blood," faintly answered the Lily; and being as slight as the gossamer, she trembled and clung to her lover's arm, whispering, "Let us flee from this dreadful vale!"

"Come, then," said Adam Forrester, as cheerily as he could, "we shall soon find a happier spot."

They set forth again, young Pilgrims on that quest which millions—which every child of Earth—has tried in turn. And were the Lily and her lover to be more fortunate than all those millions? For a long time it seemed not so. The dismal shape of the old lunatic still glided behind them; and for every spot that looked lovely in their eyes, he had some legend of human wrong or suffering, so miserably sad that his auditors could never afterwards connect the idea of joy with the place where it had happened. Here, a heart-broken woman, kneeling to her child, had been spurned from his feet; here, a desolate old creature had prayed to the evil one, and had received a fiendish malignity of soul in answer to her prayer; here, a new-born infant, sweet blossom of life, had been found dead, with the impress of its mother's fingers round its throat; and here, under a shattered oak, two lovers had been stricken by lightning, and fell blackened corpses in each other's arms. The dreary Gascoigne had a gift to know whatever evil and lamentable thing had stained the bosom of Mother Earth; and when his funereal voice had told the tale, it appeared like a prophecy of future woe as well as a tradition of the past. And now, by their sad demeanor, you would have fancied that the pilgrim lovers were seeking, not a temple of earthly joy, but a tomb for themselves and their posterity.

"Where in this world," exclaimed Adam Forrester, despondingly, "shall we build our Temple of Happiness?"

"Where in this world, indeed!" repeated Lilias Fay; and being faint and weary, the more so by the heaviness of her heart, the Lily drooped her head and sat down on the summit of a knoll, repeating, "Where in this world shall we build our Temple?"

"Ah! have you already asked yourselves that question?" said their companion, his shaded features growing even gloomier with the smile that dwelt on them; "yet there is a place, even in this world, where ye may build it."

While the old man spoke, Adam Forrester and Lilias had carelessly thrown their eyes around, and perceived that the spot where they had chanced to pause possessed a quiet charm, which was well enough adapted to their present mood of mind. It was a small rise of ground, with a certain regularity of shape, that had perhaps been bestowed by art; and a group of trees, which almost surrounded it, threw their pensive shadows across and far beyond, although some softened glory of the sunshine found its way there. The ancestral mansion, wherein the lovers would dwell together, appeared on one side, and the ivied church, where they were to worship, on another. Happening to cast their eyes on the ground they smiled, yet with a sense of wonder, to see that a pale lily was growing at their feet.

"We will build our Temple here," said they, simultaneously, and with an indescribable conviction that they had at last found the very spot.

Yet, while they uttered this exclamation, the young man and the Lily turned an apprehensive glance at their dreary associate, deeming it hardly possible that some tale of earthly affliction should not make those precincts loathsome, as in every former case. The old man stood just behind them, so as to form the chief figure in the group, with his sable cloak muffling the lower part of his visage, and his sombre hat over-shadowing his brows. But he gave no word of dissent from their purpose; and an inscrutable smile was accepted by the lovers as a token that here had been no footprint of guilt or sorrow to desecrate the site of their Temple of Happiness.

In a little time longer, while summer was still in its prime, the fairy structure of the Temple arose on the summit of the knoll, amid the solemn shadows of the trees, yet often gladdened with bright sunshine. It was built of white marble, with slender and graceful pillars supporting a vaulted dome; and beneath the centre of this dome, upon a pedestal, was a slab of dark-veined marble, on which books and music might be strewn. But there was a fantasy among the people of the neighborhood that the edifice was planned after an ancient mausoleum and was intended for a tomb, and that the central slab of dark-veined marble was to be inscribed with the names of buried ones. They doubted, too, whether the form of Lilias Fay could appertain to a creature of this earth, being so very delicate, and growing every day more fragile, so that she looked as if the summer breeze should snatch her up and waft her heavenward. But still she watched the daily growth of the Temple; and so did old Walter Gascoigne, who now made that spot his continual haunt, leaning whole hours together on his staff, and giving as deep attention to the work as though it had been indeed a tomb. In due time it was finished, and a day appointed for a simple rite of dedication.

On the preceding evening, after Adam Forrester had taken leave of his mistress, he looked back towards the portal of her dwelling, and felt a strange thrill of fear; for he imagined that, as the setting sunbeams faded from her figure, she was exhaling away, and that something of her ethereal substance was withdrawn with each lessening gleam of light. With his farewell glance a shadow had fallen over the portal and Lilias was invisible. His foreboding spirit deemed it an omen at the time, and so it proved; for the sweet earthly form, by which the Lily had been manifested to the world, was found lifeless the next morning in the Temple, with her head resting on her arms, which were folded upon the slab of dark-veined marble. The chill winds of the earth had long since breathed a blight into this beautiful flower, so that a loving hand had now transplanted it, to blossom brightly in the garden of Paradise.

But alas, for the Temple of Happiness! In his unutterable grief, Adam Forrester had no purpose more at heart than to convert this Temple of many delightful hopes into a tomb, and bury his dead mistress there. And lo! a wonder! Digging a grave beneath the Temple's marble floor, the sexton found no virgin earth, such as was meet to receive the maiden's dust, but an ancient sepulchre, in which were treasured up the bones of generations that had died long ago. Among those forgotten ancestors was the Lily to be laid. And when the funeral procession brought Lilias thither in her coffin, they beheld old Walter Gascoigne standing beneath the dome of the Temple, with his cloak of pall and face of darkest gloom; and wherever that figure might take its stand the spot would seem a sepulchre. He watched the mourners as they lowered the coffin down.

"And so," said he to Adam Forrester, with the strange smile in which his insanity was wont to gleam forth, "you have found no better foundation for your happiness than on a grave!"

But as the Shadow of Affliction spoke, a vision of Hope and Joy had its birth in Adam's mind, even from the old man's taunting words; for then he knew what was betokened by the parable in which the Lily and himself had acted; and the mystery of Life and Death was opened to him.

"Joy! joy!" he cried, throwing his arms towards heaven, "on a grave be the site of our Temple; and now our happiness is for Eternity!"

With those words, a ray of sunshine broke through the dismal sky, and glimmered down into the sepulchre; while, at the same moment, the shape of old Walter Gascoigne stalked drearily away, because his gloom, symbolic of all earthly sorrow, might no longer abide there, now that the darkest riddle of humanity was read.

EDWARD FANE'S ROSEBUD

There is hardly a more difficult exercise of fancy than, while gazing at a figure of melancholy age, to recreate its youth, and, without entirely obliterating the identity of form and features, to restore those graces which time has snatched away. Some old people, especially women, so age-worn and woful are they, seem never to have been young and gay. It is easier to conceive that such gloomy phantoms were sent into the world as withered and decrepit as we behold them now, with sympathies only for pain and grief, to watch at death-beds and weep at funerals. Even the sable garments of their widowhood appear essential to their existence; all their attributes combine to render them darksome shadows, creeping strangely amid the sunshine of human life. Yet it is no unprofitable task to take one of these doleful creatures, and set fancy resolutely at work to brighten the dim eye, and darken the silvery locks, and paint the ashen cheek with rose color, and repair the shrunken and crazy form, till a dewy maiden shall be seen in the old matron's elbow-chair. The miracle being wrought, then let the years roll back again, each sadder than the last, and the whole weight of age and sorrow settle down upon the youthful figure. Wrinkles and furrows, the handwriting of Time, may thus be deciphered, and found to contain deep lessons of thought and feeling. Such profit might be derived by a skilful observer from my much-respected friend, the Widow Toothaker, a nurse of great repute, who has breathed the atmosphere of sick-chambers and dying breaths these forty years.

See! she sits cowering over her lonesome hearth, with her gown and upper petticoat drawn upward, gathering thriftly into her person the whole warmth of the fire, which, now at nightfall, begins to dissipate the autumnal chill of her chamber. The blaze quivers capriciously in front, alternately glimmering into the deepest chasms of her wrinkled visage, and then permitting a ghostly dimness to mar the outlines of her venerable figure. And Nurse Toothaker holds a teaspoon in her right hand, with which to stir up the contents of a tumbler in her left, whence steams a vapory fragrance, abhorred of temperance societies. Now she sips—now stirs—now sips again. Her sad old heart has need to be revived by the rich infusion of Geneva, which is mixed half and half with hot water, in the tumbler. All day long she has been sitting by a death-pillow, and quitted it for her home only when the spirit of her patient left the clay and went homeward too. But now are her melancholy meditations cheered, and her torpid blood warmed, and her shoulders lightened of at least twenty ponderous years, by a draught from the true Fountain of Youth in a case bottle. It is strange that men should deem that fount a fable, when its liquor fills more bottles than the congress water! Sip it again, good nurse, and see whether a second draught will not take off another score of years, and perhaps ten more, and show us, in your high-backed chair, the blooming damsel who plighted troths with Edward Fane. Get you gone, Age and Widowhood! Come back, unwedded Youth! But, alas! the charm will not work. In spite of fancy's most potent spell, I can see only an old dame cowering over the fire, a picture of decay and desolation, while the November blast roars at her in the chimney, and fitful showers rush suddenly against the window.

Yet there was a time when Rose Grafton—such was the pretty maiden name of Nurse Toothaker—possessed beauty that would have gladdened this dim and dismal chamber as with sunshine. It won for her the heart of Edward Fane, who has since made so great a figure in the world and is now a grand old gentleman, with powdered hair, and as gouty as a lord. These early lovers thought to have walked hand in hand through life. They had wept together for Edward's little sister Mary, whom Rose tended in her sickness, partly because she was the sweetest child that ever lived or died, but more for love of him. She was but three years old. Being such an infant, Death could not embody his terrors in her little corpse; nor did Rose fear to touch the dead child's brow, though chill, as she curled the silken hair around it, nor to take her tiny hand and clasp a flower within its fingers. Afterward, when she looked through the pane of glass in the coffin lid, and beheld Mary's face, it seemed not so much like death, or life, as like a waxwork, wrought into the perfect image of a child asleep, and dreaming of its mother's smile. Rose thought her too fair a thing to be hidden in the grave, and wondered that an angel did not snatch up little Mary's coffin, and bear the slumbering babe to heaven, and bid her wake immortal. But when the sods were laid on little Mary, the heart of Rose was troubled. She shuddered at the fantasy, that, in grasping the child's cold fingers, her virgin hand had exchanged a first greeting with mortality, and could never lose the earthly taint. How many a greeting since! But as yet, she was a fair young girl, with the dew-drops of fresh feeling in her bosom; and instead of Rose, which seemed to mature a name for her half-opened beauty, her lover called her Rosebud.

The rosebud was destined never to bloom for Edward Fane. His mother was a rich and haughty dame with all the aristocratic prejudices of colonial times. She scorned Rose Grafton's humble parentage, and caused her son to break his faith, though, had she let him choose, he would have prized his Rosebud above the richest diamond. The lovers parted, and have seldom met again. Both may have visited the same mansions, but not at the same time; for one was bidden to the festal hall, and the other to the sick-chamber; he was the guest of Pleasure and Prosperity, and she of Anguish. Rose, after their separation, was long secluded within the dwelling of Mr. Toothaker, whom she married with the revengeful hope of breaking her false lover's heart. She went to her bridegroom's arms with bitterer tears, they say, than young girls ought to shed at the threshold of the bridal chamber. Yet, though her husband's head was getting gray, and his heart had been chilled with an autumnal frost, Rose soon began to love him, and wondered at her own conjugal affection. He was all she had to love; there were no children.

In a year or two, poor Mr. Toothaker was visited with a wearisome infirmity, which settled in his joints, and made him weaker than a child. He crept forth about his business, and came home at dinner time and eventide, not with the manly tread that gladdens a wife's heart, but slowly, feebly, jotting down each dull footstep with a melancholy dub of his staff. We must pardon his pretty wife, if she sometimes blushed to own him. Her visitors, when they heard him coming, looked for the appearance of some old, old man; but he dragged his nerveless limbs into the parlor—and there was Mr. Toothaker! The disease increasing, he never went into the sunshine, save with a staff in his right hand and his left on his wife's shoulder, bearing heavily downward, like a dead man's hand. Thus, a slender woman, still looking maiden-like, she supported his tall, broad-chested frame along the pathway of their little garden, and plucked the roses for her gray-haired husband, and spoke soothingly, as to an infant. His mind was palsied with his body; its utmost energy was peevishness. In a few months more, she helped him up the staircase, with a pause at every step, and a longer one upon the landing-place, and a heavy glance behind, as he crossed the threshold of his chamber. He knew, poor man, that the precincts of those four walls would thenceforth be his world—his world, his home, his tomb—at once a dwelling and a burial-place, till he were borne to a darker and a narrower one. But Rose was with him in the tomb. He leaned upon her in his daily passage from the bed to the chair by the fireside, and back again from the weary chair to the joyless bed—his bed and hers—their marriage-bed; till even this short journey ceased, and his head lay all day upon the pillow, and hers all night beside it. How long poor Mr. Toothaker was kept in misery! Death seemed to draw near the door, and often to lift the latch, and sometimes to thrust his ugly skull into the chamber, nodding to Rose, and pointing at her husband, but still delayed to enter. "This bedridden wretch cannot escape me!" quoth Death. "I will go forth and run a race with the swift, and fight a battle with the strong, and come back for Toothaker at my leisure!" Oh, when the deliverer came so near, in the dull anguish of her worn-out sympathies, did she never long to cry, "Death, come in!"

But, no! We have no right to ascribe such a wish to our friend Rose. She never failed in a wife's duty to her poor sick husband. She murmured not, though a glimpse of the sunny sky was as strange to her as him, nor answered peevishly, though his complaining accents roused her from her sweetest dream, only to share his wretchedness. He knew her faith, yet nourished a cankered jealousy; and when the slow disease had chilled all his heart, save one lukewarm spot, which Death's frozen fingers were searching for, his last words were: "What would my Rose have done for her first love, if she has been so true and kind to a sick old man like me!" And then his poor soul crept away, and left the body lifeless, though hardly more so than for years before, and Rose a widow, though in truth it was the wedding-night that widowed her. She felt glad, it must be owned, when Mr. Toothaker was buried, because his corpse had retained such a likeness to the man half alive, that she hearkened for the sad murmur of his voice, bidding her shift his pillow. But all through the next winter, though the grave had held him many a month, she fancied him calling from that cold bed, "Rose! Rose! come put a blanket on my feet!"

So now the Rosebud was the Widow Toothaker. Her troubles had come early, and, tedious as they seemed, had passed before all her bloom was fled. She was still fair enough to captivate a bachelor, or, with a widow's cheerful gravity, she might have won a widower, stealing into his heart in the very guise of his dead wife. But the Widow Toothaker had no such projects. By her watchings and continual cares her heart had become knit to her first husband with a constancy which changed its very nature, and made her love him for his infirmities, and infirmity for his sake. When the palsied old man was gone, even her early lover could not have supplied his place. She had dwelt in a sick-chamber, and been the companion of a half-dead wretch, till she could scarcely breathe in a free air, and felt ill at ease with the healthy and the happy. She missed the fragrance of the doctor's stuff. She walked the chamber with a noiseless footfall. If visitors came in she spoke in soft and soothing accents, and was startled and shocked by their loud voices. Often, in the lonesome evening, she looked timorously from the fireside to the bed, with almost a hope of recognizing a ghastly face upon the pillow. Then went her thoughts sadly to her husband's grave. If one impatient throb had wronged him in his lifetime,—if she had secretly repined because her buoyant youth was imprisoned with his torpid age,—if ever, while slumbering beside him, a treacherous dream had admitted another into her heart,—yet the sick man had been preparing a revenge which the dead now claimed. On his painful pillow he had cast a spell around her; his groans and misery had proved more captivating charms than gayety and youthful grace; in his semblance Disease itself had won the Rosebud for a bride; nor could his death dissolve the nuptials. By that indissoluble bond she had gained a home in every sick-chamber, and nowhere else: there were her brethren and sisters; thither her husband summoned her with that voice which had seemed to issue from the grave of Toothaker. At length she recognized her destiny.

We have beheld her as the maid, the wife, the widow; now we see her in a separate and insulated character; she was, in all her attributes, Nurse Toothaker. And Nurse Toothaker alone, with her own shrivelled lips, could make known her experience in that capacity. What a history might she record of the great sicknesses in which she has gone hand in hand with the exterminating angel! She remembers when the small-pox hoisted a red banner on almost every house along the street. She has witnessed when the typhus fever swept off a whole household, young and old, all but a lonely mother, who vainly shrieked to follow her last loved one. Where would be Death's triumph, if none lived to weep? She can speak of strange maladies that have broken out, as if spontaneously, but were found to have been imported from foreign lands, with rich silks and other merchandise, the costliest portion of the cargo. And once, she recollects, the people died of what was considered a new pestilence, till the doctors traced it to the ancient grave of a young girl, who thus caused many deaths a hundred years after her own burial. Strange, that such black mischief should lurk in a maiden's grave! She loves to tell how strong men fight with fiery fevers, utterly refusing to give up their breath; and how consumptive virgins fade out of the world, scarcely reluctant, as if their lovers were wooing them to a far country. Tell us, thou fearful woman! tell us the death secrets! Fain would I search out the meaning of words, faintly gasped with intermingled sobs and broken sentences, half audibly spoken between earth and the judgment seat!

An awful woman! She is the patron saint of young physicians, and the bosom friend of old ones. In the mansions where she enters, the inmates provide themselves black garments; the coffin maker follows her; and the bell tolls as she comes away from the threshold. Death himself has met her at so many a bedside, that he puts forth his bony hand to greet Nurse Toothaker. She is an awful woman! And, oh! is it conceivable, that this handmaid of human infirmity and affliction—so darkly stained, so thoroughly imbued with all that is saddest in the doom of mortals—can ever again be bright and gladsome, even though bathed in the sunshine of eternity? By her long communion with woe has she not forfeited her inheritance of immortal joy? Does any germ of bliss survive within her?

Hark!—an eager knocking at Nurse Toothaker's door. She starts from her drowsy reverie, sets aside the empty tumbler and teaspoon, and lights a lamp at the dim embers of the fire. Rap, rap, rap! again; and she hurries adown the staircase, wondering which of her friends can be at death's door now, since there is such an earnest messenger at Nurse Toothaker's. Again the peal resounds, just as her hand is on the lock. "Be quick, Nurse Toothaker!" cries a man on the doorsteps; "old General Fane is taken with the gout in his stomach, and has sent for you to watch by his death-bed. Make haste, for there is no time to lose!" "Fane! Edward Fane! And has he sent for me at last? I am ready! I will get on my cloak and begone. So," adds the sable-gowned, ashen-visaged, funereal old figure, "Edward Fane remembers his Rosebud!"

Our question is answered. There is a germ of bliss within her. Her long-hoarded constancy—her memory of the bliss that was—remaining amid the gloom of her after life like a sweet-smelling flower in a coffin, is a symbol that all may be renewed. In some happier clime the Rosebud may revive again with all the dewdrops in its bosom.

THE THREEFOLD DESTINY

A FAIRY LEGEND

I have sometimes produced a singular and not unpleasing effect, so far as my own mind was concerned, by imagining a train of incidents in which the spirit and mechanism of the fairy legend should be combined with the characters and manners of familiar life. In the little tale which follows, a subdued tinge of the wild and wonderful is thrown over a sketch of New England personages and scenery, yet, it is hoped, without entirely obliterating the sober hues of nature. Rather than a story of events claiming to be real, it may be considered as an allegory, such as the writers of the last century would have expressed in the shape of an Eastern tale, but to which I have endeavored to give a more life-like warmth than could be infused into those fanciful productions.

In the twilight of a summer eve, a tall, dark figure, over which long and remote travel had thrown an outlandish aspect, was entering a village, not in "Fairy Londe," but within our own familiar boundaries. The staff on which this traveller leaned had been his companion from the spot where it grew, in the jungles of Hindostan; the hat that overshadowed his sombre brow had shielded him from the suns of Spain: but his cheek had been blackened by the red-hot wind of an Arabian desert, and had felt the frozen breath of an Arctic region. Long sojourning amid wild and dangerous men, he still wore beneath his vest the ataghan which he had once struck into the throat of a Turkish robber. In every foreign clime he had lost something of his New England characteristics; and, perhaps, from every people he had unconsciously borrowed a new peculiarity; so that when the world-wanderer again trod the street of his native village it is no wonder that he passed unrecognized, though exciting the gaze and curiosity of all. Yet, as his arm casually touched that of a young woman who was wending her way to an evening lecture she started, and almost uttered a cry.

"Ralph Cranfield!" was the name that she half articulated.

"Can that be my old playmate, Faith Egerton?" thought the traveller, looking round at her figure, but without pausing.

Ralph Cranfield, from his youth upward, had felt himself marked out for a high destiny. He had imbibed the idea—we say not whether it were revealed to him by witchcraft, or in a dream of prophecy, or that his brooding fancy had palmed its own dictates upon him as the oracles of a Sibyl!—but he had imbibed the idea, and held it firmest among his articles of faith, that three marvellous events of his life were to be confirmed to him by three signs.

The first of these three fatalities, and perhaps the one on which his youthful imagination had dwelt most fondly, was the discovery of the maid who alone, of all the maids on earth, could make him happy by her love. He was to roam around the world till he should meet a beautiful woman wearing on her bosom a jewel in the shape of a heart; whether of pearl, or ruby, or emerald, or carbuncle, or a changeful opal, or perhaps a priceless diamond, Ralph Cranfield little cared, so long as it were a heart of one peculiar shape. On encountering this lovely stranger, he was bound to address her thus: "Maiden, I have brought you a heavy heart. May I rest its weight on you?" And if she were his fated bride—if their kindred souls were destined to form a union here below, which all eternity should only bind more closely—she would reply, with her finger on the heart-shaped jewel,—"This token, which I have worn so long, is the assurance that you may!"

And, secondly, Ralph Cranfield had a firm belief that there was a mighty treasure hidden somewhere in the earth, of which the burial-place would be revealed to none but him. When his feet should press upon the mysterious spot, there would be a hand before him pointing downward—whether carved of marble, or hewn in gigantic dimensions on the side of a rocky precipice, or perchance a hand of flame in empty air, he could not tell; but, at least, he would discern a hand, the forefinger pointing downward, and beneath it the Latin word EFFODE—Dig! and digging thereabouts, the gold in coin or ingots, the precious stones, or of whatever else the treasure might consist, would be certain to reward his toil.

The third and last of the miraculous events in the life of this high-destined man was to be the attainment of extensive influence and sway over his fellow-creatures. Whether he were to be a king and founder of an hereditary throne, or the victorious leader of a people contending for their freedom, or the apostle of a purified and regenerated faith, was left for futurity to show. As messengers of the sign by which Ralph Cranfield might recognize the summons, three venerable men were to claim audience of him. The chief among them, a dignified and majestic person, arrayed, it may be supposed, in the flowing garments of an ancient sage, would be the bearer of a wand or prophet's rod. With this wand, or rod, or staff, the venerable sage would trace a certain figure in the air, and then proceed to make known his heaven-instructed message: which, if obeyed, must lead to glorious results.

With this proud fate before him, in the flush of his imaginative youth, Ralph Cranfield had set forth to seek the maid, the treasure, and the venerable sage with his gift of extended empire. And had he found them? Alas! it was not with the aspect of a triumphant man, who had achieved a nobler destiny than all his fellows, but rather with the gloom of one struggling against peculiar and continual adversity, that he now passed homeward to his mother's cottage. He had come back, but only for a time, to lay aside the pilgrim's staff, trusting that his weary manhood would regain somewhat of the elasticity of youth, in the spot where his threefold fate had been foreshown him. There had been few changes in the village; for it was not one of those thriving places where a year's prosperity makes more than the havoc of a century's decay; but like a gray hair in a young man's head, an antiquated little town, full of old maids, and aged elms, and moss-grown dwellings. Few seemed to be the changes here. The drooping elms, indeed, had a more majestic spread; the weather-blackened houses were adorned with a denser thatch of verdant moss; and doubtless there were a few more gravestones in the burial ground, inscribed with names that had once been familiar in the village street. Yet, summing up all the mischief that ten years had wrought, it seemed scarcely more than if Ralph Cranfield had gone forth that very morning, and dreamed a day-dream till the twilight, and then turned back again. But his heart grew cold because the village did not remember him as he remembered the village.

"Here is the change!" sighed he, striking his hand upon his breast. "Who is this man of thought and care, weary with world-wandering and heavy with disappointed hopes? The youth returns not, who went forth so joyously!"

And now Ralph Cranfield was at his mother's gate, in front of the small house where the old lady, with slender but sufficient means, had kept herself comfortable during her son's long absence. Admitting himself within the enclosure, he leaned against a great, old tree, trifling with his own impatience, as people often do in those intervals when years are summed into a moment. He took a minute survey of the dwelling—its windows brightened with the sky gleam, its doorway, with the half of a millstone for a step, and the faintly-traced path waving thence to the gate. He made friends again with his childhood's friend, the old tree against which he leaned; and glancing his eye adown its trunk, beheld something that excited a melancholy smile. It was a half obliterated inscription—the Latin word EFFODE—which he remembered to have carved in the bark of the tree, with a whole day's toil, when he had first begun to muse about his exalted destiny. It might be accounted a rather singular coincidence, that the bark just above the inscription, had put forth an excrescence, shaped not unlike a hand, with the forefinger pointing obliquely at the word of fate. Such, at least, was its appearance in the dusky light.

"Now a credulous man," said Ralph Cranfield carelessly to himself, "might suppose that the treasure which I have sought round the world lies buried, after all, at the very door of my mother's dwelling. That would be a jest indeed!"

More he thought not about the matter; for now the door was opened, and an elderly woman appeared on the threshold, peering into the dusk to discover who it might be that had intruded on her premises, and was standing in the shadow of her tree. It was Ralph Cranfield's mother. Pass we over their greeting, and leave the one to her joy and the other to his rest,—if quiet rest be found.

But when morning broke, he arose with a troubled brow; for his sleep and his wakefulness had alike been full of dreams. All the fervor was rekindled with which he had burned of yore to unravel the threefold mystery of his fate. The crowd of his early visions seemed to have awaited him beneath his mother's roof, and thronged riotously around to welcome his return. In the well-remembered chamber, on the pillow where his infancy had slumbered, he had passed a wilder night than ever in an Arab tent, or when he had reposed his head in the ghastly shades of a haunted forest. A shadowy maid had stolen to his bedside, and laid her finger on the scintillating heart; a hand of flame had glowed amid the darkness, pointing downward to a mystery within the earth; a hoary sage had waved his prophetic wand, and beckoned the dreamer onward to a chair of state. The same phantoms, though fainter in the daylight, still flitted about the cottage, and mingled among the crowd of familiar faces that were drawn thither by the news of Ralph Cranfield's return, to bid him welcome for his mother's sake. There they found him, a tall, dark, stately man of foreign aspect, courteous in demeanor and mild of speech, yet with an abstracted eye, which seemed often to snatch a glance at the invisible.

Meantime the widow Cranfield went bustling about the house, full of joy that she again had somebody to love, and be careful of, and for whom she might vex and tease herself with the petty troubles of daily life. It was nearly noon when she looked forth from the door, and descried three personages of note coming along the street, through the hot sunshine and the masses of elm-tree shade. At length they reached her gate and undid the latch.

"See, Ralph!" exclaimed she, with maternal pride, "here is Squire Hawkwood and the two other selectmen, coming on purpose to see you! Now do tell them a good long story about what you have seen in foreign parts."

The foremost of the three visitors, Squire Hawkwood, was a very pompous, but excellent old gentleman, the head and prime mover in all the affairs of the village, and universally acknowledged to be one of the sagest men on earth. He wore, according to a fashion even then becoming antiquated, a three-cornered hat, and carried a silver-headed cane, the use of which seemed to be rather for flourishing in the air than for assisting the progress of his legs. His two companions were elderly and respectable yeomen, who, retaining an ante-revolutionary reverence for rank and hereditary wealth, kept a little in the Squire's rear. As they approached along the pathway, Ralph Cranfield sat in an oaken elbow chair, half unconsciously gazing at the three visitors, and enveloping their homely figures in the misty romance that pervaded his mental world.

"Here," thought he, smiling at the conceit, "here come three elderly personages, and the first of the three is a venerable sage with a staff. What if this embassy should bring me the message of my fate!"

While Squire Hawkwood and his colleagues entered, Ralph rose from his seat and advanced a few steps to receive them, and his stately figure and dark countenance, as he bent courteously towards his guests, had a natural dignity, contrasting well with the bustling importance of the Squire. The old gentleman, according to invariable custom, gave an elaborate preliminary flourish with his cane in the air, then removed his three-cornered hat in order to wipe his brow, and finally proceeded to make known his errand.

"My colleagues and myself," began the Squire, "are burdened with momentous duties, being jointly selectmen of this village. Our minds, for the space of three days past, have been laboriously bent on the selection of a suitable person to fill a most important office, and take upon himself a charge and rule which, wisely considered, may be ranked no lower than those of kings and potentates. And whereas you, our native townsman, are of good natural intellect, and well cultivated by foreign travel, and that certain vagaries and fantasies of your youth are doubtless long ago corrected; taking all these matters, I say, into due consideration, we are of opinion that Providence hath sent you hither, at this juncture, for our very purpose."

During this harangue, Cranfield gazed fixedly at the speaker, as if he beheld something mysterious and unearthly in his pompous little figure, and as if the Squire had worn the flowing robes of an ancient sage, instead of a square-skirted coat, flapped waistcoat, velvet breeches and silk stockings. Nor was his wonder without sufficient cause; for the flourish of the Squire's staff, marvellous to relate, had described precisely the signal in the air which was to ratify the message of the prophetic Sage whom Cranfield had sought around the world.

"And what," inquired Ralph Cranfield, with a tremor in his voice, "what may this office be, which is to equal me with kings and potentates?"

"No less than instructor of our village school," answered Squire Hawkwood; "the office being now vacant by the death of the venerable Master Whitaker, after a fifty years' incumbency."

"I will consider of your proposal," replied Ralph Cranfield, hurriedly, "and will make known my decision within three days."

After a few more words the village dignitary and his companions took their leave. But to Cranfield's fancy their images were still present, and became more and more invested with the dim awfulness of figures which had first appeared to him in a dream, and afterwards had shown themselves in his waking moments, assuming homely aspects among familiar things. His mind dwelt upon the features of the Squire, till they grew confused with those of the visionary Sage, and one appeared but the shadow of the other. The same visage, he now thought, had looked forth upon him from the Pyramid of Cheops; the same form had beckoned to him among the colonnades of the Alhambra; the same figure had mistily revealed itself through the ascending steam of the Great Geyser. At every effort of his memory he recognized some trait of the dreamy Messenger of Destiny in this pompous, bustling, self-important, little great man of the village. Amid such musings Ralph Cranfield sat all day in the cottage, scarcely hearing and vaguely answering his mother's thousand questions about his travels and adventures. At sunset he roused himself to take a stroll, and, passing the aged elm-tree, his eye was again caught by the semblance of a hand pointing downward at the half-obliterated inscription.

As Cranfield walked down the street of the village, the level sunbeams threw his shadow far before him; and he fancied that as his shadow walked among distant objects, so had there been a presentiment stalking in advance of him throughout his life. And when he drew near each object, over which his tall shadow had preceded him, still it proved to be one of the familiar recollections of his infancy and youth. Every crook in the pathway was remembered. Even the more transitory characteristics of the scene were the same as in by-gone days. A company of cows were grazing on the grassy roadside, and refreshed him with their fragrant breath. "It is sweeter," thought he, "than the perfume which was wafted to our ship from the Spice Islands." The round little figure of a child rolled from a doorway, and lay laughing almost beneath Cranfield's feet. The dark and stately man stooped down and, lifting the infant, restored him to his mother's arms. "The children," said he to himself —and sighed and smiled—"the children are to be my charge!" And while a flow of natural feeling gushed like a well-spring in his heart, he came to a dwelling which he could nowise forbear to enter. A sweet voice, which seemed to come from a deep and tender soul, was warbling a plaintive little air within.

He bent his head and passed through the lowly door. As his foot sounded upon the threshold, a young woman advanced from the dusky interior of the house, at first hastily, and then with a more uncertain step, till they met face to face. There was a singular contrast in their two figures: he dark and picturesque—one who had battled with the world, whom all suns had shone upon, and whom all winds had blown on a varied course; she neat, comely, and quiet—quiet even in her agitation, as if all her emotions had been subdued to the peaceful tenor of her life. Yet their faces, all unlike as they were, had an expression that seemed not so alien, a glow of kindred feeling flashing upward anew from half-extinguished embers.

"You are welcome home!" said Faith Egerton.

But Cranfield did not immediately answer; for his eye had been caught by an ornament in the shape of a Heart which Faith wore as a brooch upon her bosom. The material was the ordinary white quartz; and he recollected having himself shaped it out of one of those Indian arrowheads which are so often found in the ancient haunts of the red men. It was precisely on the pattern of that worn by the visionary Maid. When Cranfield departed on his shadowy search he had bestowed this brooch, in a gold setting, as a parting gift to Faith Egerton.

"So, Faith, you have kept the Heart!" said he at length.

"Yes," said she, blushing deeply; then more gayly, "and what else have you brought me from beyond the sea?"

"Faith!" replied Ralph Cranfield, uttering the fated words by an uncontrollable impulse, "I have brought you nothing but a heavy heart! May I rest its weight on you?"

"This token which I have worn so long," said Faith, laying her tremulous finger on the Heart, "is the assurance that you may!"

"Faith! Faith!" cried Cranfield, clasping her in his arms, "you have interpreted my wild and weary dream!"

Yes, the wild dream was awake at last. To find the mysterious treasure, he was to till the earth around his mother's dwelling, and reap its products! Instead of warlike command, or regal or religious sway, he was to rule over the village children! And now the visionary Maid had faded from his fancy, and in her place he saw the playmate of his childhood! Would all who cherish such wild wishes but look around them, they would oftenest find their sphere of duty, of prosperity, and happiness, within those precincts and in that station where Providence itself has cast their lot. Happy they who read the riddle without a weary world search, or a lifetime spent in vain!

FROM

Mosses From an Old Manse

THE BIRTHMARK

In the latter part of the last century there lived a man of science, an eminent proficient in every branch of natural philosophy, who not long before our story opens had made experience of a spiritual affinity more attractive than any chemical one. He had left his laboratory to the care of an assistant, cleared his fine countenance from the furnace smoke, washed the stain of acids from his fingers, and persuaded a beautiful woman to become his wife. In those days when the comparatively recent discovery of electricity and other kindred mysteries of Nature seemed to open paths into the region of miracle, it was not unusual for the love of science to rival the love of woman in its depth and absorbing energy. The higher intellect, the imagination, the spirit, and even the heart might all find their congenial aliment in pursuits which, as some of their ardent votaries believed, would ascend from one step of powerful intelligence to another, until the philosopher should lay his hand on the secret of creative force and perhaps make new worlds for himself. We know not whether Aylmer possessed this degree of faith in man's ultimate control over Nature. He had devoted himself, however, too unreservedly to scientific studies ever to be weaned from them by any second passion. His love for his young wife might prove the stronger of the two; but it could only be by intertwining itself with his love of science, and uniting the strength of the latter to his own.

Such a union accordingly took place, and was attended with truly remarkable consequences and a deeply impressive moral. One day, very soon after their marriage, Aylmer sat gazing at his wife with a trouble in his countenance that grew stronger until he spoke.

"Georgiana," said he, "has it never occurred to you that the mark upon your cheek might be removed?"

"No, indeed," said she, smiling; but perceiving the seriousness of his manner, she blushed deeply. "To tell you the truth it has been so often called a charm that I was simple enough to imagine it might be so."

"Ah, upon another face perhaps it might," replied her husband; "but never on yours. No, dearest Georgiana, you came so nearly perfect from the hand of Nature that this slightest possible defect, which we hesitate whether to term a defect or a beauty, shocks me, as being the visible mark of earthly imperfection."

"Shocks you, my husband!" cried Georgiana, deeply hurt; at first reddening with momentary anger, but then bursting into tears. "Then why did you take me from my mother's side? You cannot love what shocks you!"

To explain this conversation it must be mentioned that in the centre of Georgiana's left cheek there was a singular mark, deeply interwoven, as it were, with the texture and substance of her face. In the usual state of her complexion—a healthy though delicate bloom—the mark wore a tint of deeper crimson, which imperfectly defined its shape amid the surrounding rosiness. When she blushed it gradually became more indistinct, and finally vanished amid the triumphant rush of blood that bathed the whole cheek with its brilliant glow. But if any shifting motion caused her to turn pale there was the mark again, a crimson stain upon the snow, in what Aylmer sometimes deemed an almost fearful distinctness. Its shape bore not a little similarity to the human hand, though of the smallest pygmy size. Georgiana's lovers were wont to say that some fairy at her birth hour had laid her tiny hand upon the infant's cheek, and left this impress there in token of the magic endowments that were to give her such sway over all hearts. Many a desperate swain would have risked life for the privilege of pressing his lips to the mysterious hand. It must not be concealed, however, that the impression wrought by this fairy sign manual varied exceedingly, according to the difference of temperament in the beholders. Some fastidious persons—but they were exclusively of her own sex—affirmed that the bloody hand, as they chose to call it, quite destroyed the effect of Georgiana's beauty, and rendered her countenance even hideous. But it would be as reasonable to say that one of those small blue stains which sometimes occur in the purest statuary marble would convert the Eve of Powers to a monster. Masculine observers, if the birthmark did not heighten their admiration, contented themselves with wishing it away, that the world might possess one living specimen of ideal loveliness without the semblance of a flaw. After his marriage,—for he thought little or nothing of the matter before,—Aylmer discovered that this was the case with himself.

Had she been less beautiful,—if Envy's self could have found aught else to sneer at,—he might have felt his affection heightened by the prettiness of this mimic hand, now vaguely portrayed, now lost, now stealing forth again and glimmering to and fro with every pulse of emotion that throbbed within her heart; but seeing her otherwise so perfect, he found this one defect grow more and more intolerable with every moment of their united lives. It was the fatal flaw of humanity which Nature, in one shape or another, stamps ineffaceably on all her productions, either to imply that they are temporary and finite, or that their perfection must be wrought by toil and pain. The crimson hand expressed the ineludible gripe in which mortality clutches the highest and purest of earthly mould, degrading them into kindred with the lowest, and even with the very brutes, like whom their visible frames return to dust. In this manner, selecting it as the symbol of his wife's liability to sin, sorrow, decay, and death, Aylmer's sombre imagination was not long in rendering the birthmark a frightful object, causing him more trouble and horror than ever Georgiana's beauty, whether of soul or sense, had given him delight.

At all the seasons which should have been their happiest, he invariably and without intending it, nay, in spite of a purpose to the contrary, reverted to this one disastrous topic. Trifling as it at first appeared, it so connected itself with innumerable trains of thought and modes of feeling that it became the central point of all. With the morning twilight Aylmer opened his eyes upon his wife's face and recognized the symbol of imperfection; and when they sat together at the evening hearth his eyes wandered stealthily to her cheek, and beheld, flickering with the blaze of the wood fire, the spectral hand that wrote mortality where he would fain have worshipped. Georgiana soon learned to shudder at his gaze. It needed but a glance with the peculiar expression that his face often wore to change the roses of her cheek into a death-like paleness, amid which the crimson hand was brought strongly out, like a bas-relief of ruby on the whitest marble.

Late one night when the lights were growing dim, so as hardly to betray the stain on the poor wife's cheek, she herself, for the first time, voluntarily took up the subject.

"Do you remember, my dear Aylmer," said she, with a feeble attempt at a smile, "have you any recollection of a dream last night about this odious hand?"

"None! none whatever!" replied Aylmer, starting; but then he added, in a dry, cold tone, affected for the sake of concealing the real depth of his emotion, "I might well dream of it; for before I fell asleep it had taken a pretty firm hold of my fancy."

"And you did dream of it?" continued Georgiana, hastily; for she dreaded lest a gush of tears should interrupt what she had to say. "A terrible dream! I wonder that you can forget it. Is it possible to forget this one expression?—'It is in her heart now; we must have it out!' Reflect, my husband; for by all means I would have you recall that dream."

The mind is in a sad state when Sleep, the all-involving, cannot confine her spectres within the dim region of her sway, but suffers them to break forth, affrighting this actual life with secrets that perchance belong to a deeper one. Aylmer now remembered his dream. He had fancied himself with his servant Aminadab, attempting an operation for the removal of the birthmark; but the deeper went the knife, the deeper sank the hand, until at length its tiny grasp appeared to have caught hold of Georgiana's heart; whence, however, her husband was inexorably resolved to cut or wrench it away.

When the dream had shaped itself perfectly in his memory, Aylmer sat in his wife's presence with a guilty feeling. Truth often finds its way to the mind close muffled in robes of sleep, and then speaks with uncompromising directness of matters in regard to which we practise an unconscious self-deception during our waking moments. Until now he had not been aware of the tyrannizing influence acquired by one idea over his mind, and of the lengths which he might find in his heart to go for the sake of giving himself peace.

"Aylmer," resumed Georgiana, solemnly, "I know not what may be the cost to both of us to rid me of this fatal birthmark. Perhaps its removal may cause cureless deformity; or it may be the stain goes as deep as life itself. Again: do we know that there is a possibility, on any terms, of unclasping the firm gripe of this little hand which was laid upon me before I came into the world?"

"Dearest Georgiana, I have spent much thought upon the subject," hastily interrupted Aylmer. "I am convinced of the perfect practicability of its removal."

"If there be the remotest possibility of it," continued Georgiana, "let the attempt be made at whatever risk. Danger is nothing to me; for life, while this hateful mark makes me the object of your horror and disgust,—life is a burden which I would fling down with joy. Either remove this dreadful hand, or take my wretched life! You have deep science. All the world bears witness of it. You have achieved great wonders. Cannot you remove this little, little mark, which I cover with the tips of two small fingers? Is this beyond your power, for the sake of your own peace, and to save your poor wife from madness?"

"Noblest, dearest, tenderest wife," cried Aylmer, rapturously, "doubt not my power. I have already given this matter the deepest thought—thought which might almost have enlightened me to create a being less perfect than yourself. Georgiana, you have led me deeper than ever into the heart of science. I feel myself fully competent to render this dear cheek as faultless as its fellow; and then, most beloved, what will be my triumph when I shall have corrected what Nature left imperfect in her fairest work! Even Pygmalion, when his sculptured woman assumed life, felt not greater ecstasy than mine will be."

"It is resolved, then," said Georgiana, faintly smiling. "And, Aylmer, spare me not, though you should find the birthmark take refuge in my heart at last."

Her husband tenderly kissed her cheek—her right cheek—not that which bore the impress of the crimson hand.

The next day Aylmer apprised his wife of a plan that he had formed whereby he might have opportunity for the intense thought and constant watchfulness which the proposed operation would require; while Georgiana, likewise, would enjoy the perfect repose essential to its success. They were to seclude themselves in the extensive apartments occupied by Aylmer as a laboratory, and where, during his toilsome youth, he had made discoveries in the elemental powers of Nature that had roused the admiration of all the learned societies in Europe. Seated calmly in this laboratory, the pale philosopher had investigated the secrets of the highest cloud region and of the profoundest mines; he had satisfied himself of the causes that kindled and kept alive the fires of the volcano; and had explained the mystery of fountains, and how it is that they gush forth, some so bright and pure, and others with such rich medicinal virtues, from the dark bosom of the earth. Here, too, at an earlier period, he had studied the wonders of the human frame, and attempted to fathom the very process by which Nature assimilates all her precious influences from earth and air, and from the spiritual world, to create and foster man, her masterpiece. The latter pursuit, however, Aylmer had long laid aside in unwilling recognition of the truth—against which all seekers sooner or later stumble—that our great creative Mother, while she amuses us with apparently working in the broadest sunshine, is yet severely careful to keep her own secrets, and, in spite of her pretended openness, shows us nothing but results. She permits us, indeed, to mar, but seldom to mend, and, like a jealous patentee, on no account to make. Now, however, Aylmer resumed these half-forgotten investigations; not, of course, with such hopes or wishes as first suggested them; but because they involved much physiological truth and lay in the path of his proposed scheme for the treatment of Georgiana.

As he led her over the threshold of the laboratory, Georgiana was cold and tremulous. Aylmer looked cheerfully into her face, with intent to reassure her, but was so startled with the intense glow of the birthmark upon the whiteness of her cheek that he could not restrain a strong convulsive shudder. His wife fainted.

"Aminadab! Aminadab!" shouted Aylmer, stamping violently on the floor.

Forthwith there issued from an inner apartment a man of low stature, but bulky frame, with shaggy hair hanging about his visage, which was grimed with the vapors of the furnace. This personage had been Aylmer's underworker during his whole scientific career, and was admirably fitted for that office by his great mechanical readiness, and the skill with which, while incapable of comprehending a single principle, he executed all the details of his master's experiments. With his vast strength, his shaggy hair, his smoky aspect, and the indescribable earthiness that incrusted him, he seemed to represent man's physical nature; while Aylmer's slender figure, and pale, intellectual face, were no less apt a type of the spiritual element.

"Throw open the door of the boudoir, Aminadab," said Aylmer, "and burn a pastil."

"Yes, master," answered Aminadab, looking intently at the lifeless form of Georgiana; and then he muttered to himself, "If she were my wife, I'd never part with that birthmark."

When Georgiana recovered consciousness she found herself breathing an atmosphere of penetrating fragrance, the gentle potency of which had recalled her from her deathlike faintness. The scene around her looked like enchantment. Aylmer had converted those smoky, dingy, sombre rooms, where he had spent his brightest years in recondite pursuits, into a series of beautiful apartments not unfit to be the secluded abode of a lovely woman. The walls were hung with gorgeous curtains, which imparted the combination of grandeur and grace that no other species of adornment can achieve; and as they fell from the ceiling to the floor, their rich and ponderous folds, concealing all angles and straight lines, appeared to shut in the scene from infinite space. For aught Georgiana knew, it might be a pavilion among the clouds. And Aylmer, excluding the sunshine, which would have interfered with his chemical processes, had supplied its place with perfumed lamps, emitting flames of various hue, but all uniting in a soft, impurpled radiance. He now knelt by his wife's side, watching her earnestly, but without alarm; for he was confident in his science, and felt that he could draw a magic circle round her within which no evil might intrude.

"Where am I? Ah, I remember," said Georgiana, faintly; and she placed her hand over her cheek to hide the terrible mark from her husband's eyes.

"Fear not, dearest!" exclaimed he. "Do not shrink from me! Believe me, Georgiana, I even rejoice in this single imperfection, since it will be such a rapture to remove it."

"Oh, spare me!" sadly replied his wife. "Pray do not look at it again. I never can forget that convulsive shudder."

In order to soothe Georgiana, and, as it were, to release her mind from the burden of actual things, Aylmer now put in practice some of the light and playful secrets which science had taught him among its profounder lore. Airy figures, absolutely bodiless ideas, and forms of unsubstantial beauty came and danced before her, imprinting their momentary footsteps on beams of light. Though she had some indistinct idea of the method of these optical phenomena, still the illusion was almost perfect enough to warrant the belief that her husband possessed sway over the spiritual world. Then again, when she felt a wish to look forth from her seclusion, immediately, as if her thoughts were answered, the procession of external existence flitted across a screen. The scenery and the figures of actual life were perfectly represented, but with that bewitching, yet indescribable difference which always makes a picture, an image, or a shadow so much more attractive than the original. When wearied of this, Aylmer bade her cast her eyes upon a vessel containing a quantity of earth. She did so, with little interest at first; but was soon startled to perceive the germ of a plant shooting upward from the soil. Then came the slender stalk; the leaves gradually unfolded themselves; and amid them was a perfect and lovely flower.

"It is magical!" cried Georgiana. "I dare not touch it."

"Nay, pluck it," answered Aylmer,—"pluck it, and inhale its brief perfume while you may. The flower will wither in a few moments and leave nothing save its brown seed vessels; but thence may be perpetuated a race as ephemeral as itself."

But Georgiana had no sooner touched the flower than the whole plant suffered a blight, its leaves turning coal-black as if by the agency of fire.

"There was too powerful a stimulus," said Aylmer, thoughtfully.

To make up for this abortive experiment, he proposed to take her portrait by a scientific process of his own invention. It was to be effected by rays of light striking upon a polished plate of metal. Georgiana assented; but, on looking at the result, was affrighted to find the features of the portrait blurred and indefinable; while the minute figure of a hand appeared where the cheek should have been. Aylmer snatched the metallic plate and threw it into a jar of corrosive acid.

Soon, however, he forgot these mortifying failures. In the intervals of study and chemical experiment he came to her flushed and exhausted, but seemed invigorated by her presence, and spoke in glowing language of the resources of his art. He gave a history of the long dynasty of the alchemists, who spent so many ages in quest of the universal solvent by which the golden principle might be elicited from all things vile and base. Aylmer appeared to believe that, by the plainest scientific logic, it was altogether within the limits of possibility to discover this long-sought medium; "but," he added, "a philosopher who should go deep enough to acquire the power would attain too lofty a wisdom to stoop to the exercise of it." Not less singular were his opinions in regard to the elixir vitæ. He more than intimated that it was at his option to concoct a liquid that should prolong life for years, perhaps interminably; but that it would produce a discord in Nature which all the world, and chiefly the quaffer of the immortal nostrum, would find cause to curse.

"Aylmer, are you in earnest?" asked Georgiana, looking at him with amazement and fear. "It is terrible to possess such power, or even to dream of possessing it."

"Oh, do not tremble, my love," said her husband. "I would not wrong either you or myself by working such inharmonious effects upon our lives; but I would have you consider how trifling, in comparison, is the skill requisite to remove this little hand."

At the mention of the birthmark, Georgiana, as usual, shrank as if a redhot iron had touched her cheek.

Again Aylmer applied himself to his labors. She could hear his voice in the distant furnace room giving directions to Aminadab, whose harsh, uncouth, misshapen tones were audible in response, more like the grunt or growl of a brute than human speech. After hours of absence, Aylmer reappeared and proposed that she should now examine his cabinet of chemical products and natural treasures of the earth. Among the former he showed her a small vial, in which, he remarked, was contained a gentle yet most powerful fragrance, capable of impregnating all the breezes that blow across a kingdom. They were of inestimable value, the contents of that little vial; and, as he said so, he threw some of the perfume into the air and filled the room with piercing and invigorating delight.

"And what is this?" asked Georgiana, pointing to a small crystal globe containing a gold-colored liquid. "It is so beautiful to the eye that I could imagine it the elixir of life."

"In one sense it is," replied Aylmer; "or, rather, the elixir of immortality. It is the most precious poison that ever was concocted in this world. By its aid I could apportion the lifetime of any mortal at whom you might point your finger. The strength of the dose would determine whether he were to linger out years, or drop dead in the midst of a breath. No king on his guarded throne could keep his life if I, in my private station, should deem that the welfare of millions justified me in depriving him of it."

"Why do you keep such a terrific drug?" inquired Georgiana in horror.

"Do not mistrust me, dearest," said her husband, smiling; "its virtuous potency is yet greater than its harmful one. But see! here is a powerful cosmetic. With a few drops of this in a vase of water, freckles may be washed away as easily as the hands are cleansed. A stronger infusion would take the blood out of the cheek, and leave the rosiest beauty a pale ghost."

"Is it with this lotion that you intend to bathe my cheek?" asked Georgiana, anxiously.

"Oh, no," hastily replied her husband; "this is merely superficial. Your case demands a remedy that shall go deeper."

In his interviews with Georgiana, Aylmer generally made minute inquiries as to her sensations and whether the confinement of the rooms and the temperature of the atmosphere agreed with her. These questions had such a particular drift that Georgiana began to conjecture that she was already subjected to certain physical influences, either breathed in with the fragrant air or taken with her food. She fancied likewise, but it might be altogether fancy, that there was a stirring up of her system—a strange, indefinite sensation creeping through her veins, and tingling, half painfully, half pleasurably, at her heart. Still, whenever she dared to look into the mirror, there she beheld herself pale as a white rose and with the crimson birthmark stamped upon her cheek. Not even Aylmer now hated it so much as she.

To dispel the tedium of the hours which husband found it necessary to devote to the processes of combination and analysis, Georgiana turned over the volumes of his scientific library. In many dark old tomes she met with chapters full of romance and poetry. They were the works of the philosophers of the middle ages, such as Albertus Magnus, Cornelius Agrippa, Paracelsus, and the famous friar who created the prophetic Brazen Head. All these antique naturalists stood in advance of their centuries, yet were imbued with some of their credulity, and therefore were believed, and perhaps imagined themselves to have acquired from the investigation of Nature a power above Nature, and from physics a sway over the spiritual world. Hardly less curious and imaginative were the early volumes of the Transactions of the Royal Society, in which the members, knowing little of the limits of natural possibility, were continually recording wonders or proposing methods whereby wonders might be wrought.

But to Georgiana the most engrossing volume was a large folio from her husband's own hand, in which he had recorded every experiment of his scientific career, its original aim, the methods adopted for its development, and its final success or failure, with the circumstances to which either event was attributable. The book, in truth, was both the history and emblem of his ardent, ambitious, imaginative, yet practical and laborious life. He handled physical details as if there were nothing beyond them; yet spiritualized them all, and redeemed himself from materialism by his strong and eager aspiration towards the infinite. In his grasp the veriest clod of earth assumed a soul. Georgiana, as she read, reverenced Aylmer and loved him more profoundly than ever, but with a less entire dependence on his judgment than heretofore. Much as he had accomplished, she could not but observe that his most splendid successes were almost invariably failures, if compared with the ideal at which he aimed. His brightest diamonds were the merest pebbles, and felt to be so by himself, in comparison with the inestimable gems which lay hidden beyond his reach. The volume, rich with achievements that had won renown for its author, was yet as melancholy a record as ever mortal hand had penned. It was the sad confession and continual exemplification of the shortcomings of the composite man, the spirit burdened with clay and working in matter, and of the despair that assails the higher nature at finding itself so miserably thwarted by the earthly part. Perhaps every man of genius in whatever sphere might recognize the image of his own experience in Aylmer's journal.

So deeply did these reflections affect Georgiana that she laid her face upon the open volume and burst into tears. In this situation she was found by her husband.

"It is dangerous to read in a sorcerer's books," said he with a smile, though his countenance was uneasy and displeased. "Georgiana, there are pages in that volume which I can scarcely glance over and keep my senses. Take heed lest it prove as detrimental to you."

"It has made me worship you more than ever," said she.

"Ah, wait for this one success," rejoined he, "then worship me if you will. I shall deem myself hardly unworthy of it. But come, I have sought you for the luxury of your voice. Sing to me, dearest."

So she poured out the liquid music of her voice to quench the thirst of his spirit. He then took his leave with a boyish exuberance of gayety, assuring her that her seclusion would endure but a little longer, and that the result was already certain. Scarcely had he departed when Georgiana felt irresistibly impelled to follow him. She had forgotten to inform Aylmer of a symptom which for two or three hours past had begun to excite her attention. It was a sensation in the fatal birthmark, not painful, but which induced a restlessness throughout her system. Hastening after her husband, she intruded for the first time into the laboratory.

The first thing that struck her eye was the furnace, that hot and feverish worker, with the intense glow of its fire, which by the quantities of soot clustered above it seemed to have been burning for ages. There was a distilling apparatus in full operation. Around the room were retorts, tubes, cylinders, crucibles, and other apparatus of chemical research. An electrical machine stood ready for immediate use. The atmosphere felt oppressively close, and was tainted with gaseous odors which had been tormented forth by the processes of science. The severe and homely simplicity of the apartment, with its naked walls and brick pavement, looked strange, accustomed as Georgiana had become to the fantastic elegance of her boudoir. But what chiefly, indeed almost solely, drew her attention, was the aspect of Aylmer himself.

He was pale as death, anxious and absorbed, and hung over the furnace as if it depended upon his utmost watchfulness whether the liquid which it was distilling should be the draught of immortal happiness or misery. How different from the sanguine and joyous mien that he had assumed for Georgiana's encouragement!

"Carefully now, Aminadab; carefully, thou human machine; carefully, thou man of clay!" muttered Aylmer, more to himself than his assistant. "Now, if there be a thought too much or too little, it is all over."

"Ho! ho!" mumbled Aminadab. "Look, master! look!"

Aylmer raised his eyes hastily, and at first reddened, then grew paler than ever, on beholding Georgiana. He rushed towards her and seized her arm with a gripe that left the print of his fingers upon it.

"Why do you come hither? Have you no trust in your husband?" cried he, impetuously. "Would you throw the blight of that fatal birthmark over my labors? It is not well done. Go, prying woman, go!"

"Nay, Aylmer," said Georgiana with the firmness of which she possessed no stinted endowment, "it is not you that have a right to complain. You mistrust your wife; you have concealed the anxiety with which you watch the development of this experiment. Think not so unworthily of me, my husband. Tell me all the risk we run, and fear not that I shall shrink; for my share in it is far less than your own."

"No, no, Georgiana!" said Aylmer, impatiently; "it must not be."

"I submit," replied she calmly. "And, Aylmer, I shall quaff whatever draught you bring me; but it will be on the same principle that would induce me to take a dose of poison if offered by your hand."

"My noble wife," said Aylmer, deeply moved, "I knew not the height and depth of your nature until now. Nothing shall be concealed. Know, then, that this crimson hand, superficial as it seems, has clutched its grasp into your being with a strength of which I had no previous conception. I have already administered agents powerful enough to do aught except to change your entire physical system. Only one thing remains to be tried. If that fail us we are ruined."

"Why did you hesitate to tell me this?" asked she.

"Because, Georgiana," said Aylmer, in a low voice, "there is danger."

"Danger? There is but one danger—that this horrible stigma shall be left upon my cheek!" cried Georgiana. "Remove it, remove it, whatever be the cost, or we shall both go mad!"

"Heaven knows your words are too true," said Aylmer, sadly. "And now, dearest, return to your boudoir. In a little while all will be tested."

He conducted her back and took leave of her with a solemn tenderness which spoke far more than his words how much was now at stake. After his departure Georgiana became rapt in musings. She considered the character of

Aylmer, and did it completer justice than at any previous moment. Her heart exulted, while it trembled, at his honorable love—so pure and lofty that it would accept nothing less than perfection nor miserably make itself contented with an earthlier nature than he had dreamed of. She felt how much more precious was such a sentiment than that meaner kind which would have borne with the imperfection for her sake, and have been guilty of treason to holy love by degrading its perfect idea to the level of the actual; and with her whole spirit she prayed that, for a single moment, she might satisfy his highest and deepest conception. Longer than one moment she well knew it could not be; for his spirit was ever on the march, ever ascending, and each instant required something that was beyond the scope of the instant before.

The sound of her husband's footsteps aroused her. He bore a crystal goblet containing a liquor colorless as water, but bright enough to be the draught of immortality. Aylmer was pale; but it seemed rather the consequence of a highly-wrought state of mind and tension of spirit than of fear or doubt.

"The concoction of the draught has been perfect," said he, in answer to Georgiana's look. "Unless all my science have deceived me, it cannot fail."

"Save on your account, my dearest Aylmer," observed his wife, "I might wish to put off this birthmark of mortality by relinquishing mortality itself in preference to any other mode. Life is but a sad possession to those who have attained precisely the degree of moral advancement at which I stand. Were I weaker and blinder it might be happiness. Were I stronger, it might be endured hopefully. But, being what I find myself, methinks I am of all mortals the most fit to die."

"You are fit for heaven without tasting death!" replied her husband. "But why do we speak of dying? The draught cannot fail. Behold its effect upon this plant."

On the window seat there stood a geranium diseased with yellow blotches, which had overspread all its leaves. Aylmer poured a small quantity of the liquid upon the soil in which it grew. In a little time, when the roots of the plant had taken up the moisture, the unsightly blotches began to be extinguished in a living verdure.

"There needed no proof," said Georgiana, quietly. "Give me the goblet. I joyfully stake all upon your word."

"Drink, then, thou lofty creature!" exclaimed Aylmer, with fervid admiration. "There is no taint of imperfection on thy spirit. Thy sensible frame, too, shall soon be all perfect."

She quaffed the liquid and returned the goblet to his hand.

"It is grateful," said she with a placid smile. "Methinks it is like water from a heavenly fountain; for it contains I know not what of unobtrusive fragrance and deliciousness. It allays a feverish thirst that had parched me for many days. Now, dearest, let me sleep. My earthly senses are closing over my spirit like the leaves around the heart of a rose at sunset."

She spoke the last words with a gentle reluctance, as if it required almost more energy than she could command to pronounce the faint and lingering syllables. Scarcely had they loitered through her lips ere she was lost in slumber. Aylmer sat by her side, watching her aspect with the emotions proper to a man the whole value of whose existence was involved in the process now to be tested. Mingled with this mood, however, was the philosophic investigation characteristic of the man of science. Not the minutest symptom escaped him. A heightened flush of the cheek, a slight irregularity of breath, a quiver of the eyelid, a hardly perceptible tremor through the frame,—such were the details which, as the moments passed, he wrote down in his folio volume. Intense thought had set its stamp upon every previous page of that volume, but the thoughts of years were all concentrated upon the last.

While thus employed, he failed not to gaze often at the fatal hand, and not without a shudder. Yet once, by a strange and unaccountable impulse, he pressed it with his lips. His spirit recoiled, however, in the very act; and Georgiana, out of the midst of her deep sleep, moved uneasily and murmured as if in remonstrance. Again Aylmer resumed his watch. Nor was it without avail. The crimson hand, which at first had been strongly visible upon the marble paleness of Georgiana's cheek, now grew more faintly outlined. She remained not less pale than ever; but the birthmark, with every breath that came and went, lost somewhat of its former distinctness. Its presence had been awful; its departure was more awful still. Watch the stain of the rainbow fading out of the sky, and you will know how that mysterious symbol passed away.

"By Heaven! it is well-nigh gone!" said Aylmer to himself, in almost irrepressible ecstasy. "I can scarcely trace it now. Success! success! And now it is like the faintest rose color. The lightest flush of blood across her cheek would overcome it. But she is so pale!"

He drew aside the window curtain and suffered the light of natural day to fall into the room and rest upon her cheek. At the same time he heard a gross, hoarse chuckle, which he had long known as his servant Aminadab's expression of delight.

"Ah, clod! ah, earthly mass!" cried Aylmer, laughing in a sort of frenzy, "you have served me well! Matter and spirit—earth and heaven—have both done their part in this! Laugh, thing of the senses! You have earned the right to laugh."

These exclamations broke Georgiana's sleep. She slowly unclosed her eyes and gazed into the mirror which her husband had arranged for that purpose. A faint smile flitted over her lips when she recognized how barely perceptible was now that crimson hand which had once blazed forth with such disastrous brilliancy as to scare away all their happiness. But then her eyes sought Aylmer's face with a trouble and anxiety that he could by no means account for.

"My poor Aylmer!" murmured she.

"Poor? Nay, richest, happiest, most favored!" exclaimed he. "My peerless bride, it is successful! You are perfect!"

"My poor Aylmer," she repeated, with a more than human tenderness, "you have aimed loftily; you have done nobly. Do not repent that with so high and pure a feeling, you have rejected the best the earth could offer. Aylmer, dearest Aylmer, I am dying!"

Alas! it was too true! The fatal hand had grappled with the mystery of life, and was the bond by which an angelic spirit kept itself in union with a mortal frame. As the last crimson tint of the birthmark—that sole token of human imperfection—faded from her cheek, the parting breath of the now perfect woman passed into the atmosphere, and her soul, lingering a moment near her husband, took its heavenward flight. Then a hoarse, chuckling laugh was heard again! Thus ever does the gross fatality of earth exult in its invariable triumph over the immortal essence which, in this dim sphere of half development, demands the completeness of a higher state. Yet, had Aylmer reached a profounder wisdom, he need not thus have flung away the happiness which would have woven his mortal life of the selfsame texture with the celestial. The momentary circumstance was too strong for him; he failed to look beyond the shadowy scope of time, and, living once for all in eternity, to find the perfect future in the present.

A SELECT PARTY

A Man of Fancy made an entertainment at one of his castles in the air, and invited a select number of distinguished personages to favor him with their presence. The mansion, though less splendid than many that have been situated in the same region, was nevertheless of a magnificence such as is seldom witnessed by those acquainted only with terrestrial architecture. Its strong foundations and massive walls were quarried out of a ledge of heavy and sombre clouds which had hung brooding over the earth, apparently as dense and ponderous as its own granite, throughout a whole autumnal day. Perceiving that the general effect was gloomy,—so that the airy castle looked like a feudal fortress, or a monastery of the Middle Ages, or a state-prison of our own times, rather than the home of pleasure and repose which he intended it to be,—the owner, regardless of expense, resolved to gild the exterior from top to bottom. Fortunately, there was just then a flood of evening sunshine in the air. This being gathered up and poured abundantly upon the roof and walls, imbued them with a kind of solemn cheerfulness; while the cupolas and pinnacles were made to glitter with the purest gold, and all the hundred windows gleamed with a glad light, as if the edifice itself were rejoicing in its heart. And now, if the people of the lower world chanced to be looking upward out of the turmoil of their petty perplexities, they probably mistook the castle in the air for a heap of sunset clouds to which the magic of light and shade had imparted the aspect of a fantastically constructed mansion. To such beholders it was unreal, because they lacked the imaginative faith. Had they been worthy to pass within its portal, they would have recognized the truth, that the dominions which the spirit conquers for itself, among unrealities become a thousand times more real than the earth whereon they stamp their feet, saying, "This is solid and substantial; this may be called a fact."

At the appointed hour, the host stood in his great saloon to receive the company. It was a vast and noble room, the vaulted ceiling of which was supported by double rows of gigantic pillars that had been hewn entire out of masses of variegated clouds. So brilliantly were they polished, and so exquisitely wrought by the sculptor's skill, as to resemble the finest specimens of emerald, porphyry, opal, and chrysolite, thus producing a delicate richness of effect which their immense size rendered not incompatible with grandeur. To each of these pillars a meteor was suspended. Thousands of these ethereal lustres are continually wandering about the firmament, burning out to waste, yet capable of imparting a useful radiance to any person who has the art of converting them to domestic purposes. As managed in the saloon, they are far more economical than ordinary lamplight. Such, however, was the intensity of their blaze that it had been found expedient to cover each meteor with a globe of evening mist, thereby muffling the too potent glow and soothing it into a mild and comfortable splendor. It was like the brilliancy of a powerful yet chastened imagination—a light which seemed to hide whatever was unworthy to be noticed and give effect to every beautiful and noble attribute. The guests, therefore, as they advanced up the centre of the saloon appeared to better advantage than ever before in their lives.

The first that entered, with old-fashioned punctuality, was a venerable figure in the costume of by-gone days, with his white hair flowing down over his shoulders and a reverend beard upon his breast. He leaned upon a staff, the tremulous stroke of which, as he set it carefully upon the floor, reëchoed through the saloon at every footstep. Recognizing at once this celebrated personage, whom it had cost him a vast deal of trouble and research to discover, the host advanced nearly three fourths of the distance down between the pillars to meet and welcome him.

"Venerable sir," said the Man of Fancy, bending to the floor, "the honor of this visit would never be forgotten were my term of existence to be as happily prolonged as your own."

The old gentleman received the compliment with gracious condescension. He then thrust up his spectacles over his forehead and appeared to take a critical survey of the saloon.

"Never within my recollection," observed he, "have I entered a more spacious and noble hall. But are you sure that it is built of solid materials and that the structure will be permanent?"

"Oh, never fear, my venerable friend," replied the host. "In reference to a lifetime like your own, it is true, my castle may well be called a temporary edifice. But it will endure long enough to answer all the purposes for which it was erected."

But we forget that the reader has not yet been made acquainted with the guest. It was no other than that universally accredited character so constantly referred to in all seasons of intense cold or heat; he that remembers the hot Sunday and the cold Friday; the witness of a past age, whose negative reminiscences find their way into every newspaper, yet whose antiquated and dusky abode is so overshadowed by accumulated years and crowded back by modern edifices that none but the Man of Fancy could have discovered it; it was, in short, that twin brother of Time, and great-grandsire of mankind, and hand-and-glove associate of all forgotten men and things—the Oldest Inhabitant. The host would willingly have drawn him into conversation, but succeeded only in eliciting a few remarks as to the oppressive atmosphere of this present summer evening compared with one which the guest had experienced about fourscore years ago. The old gentleman, in fact, was a good deal overcome by his journey among the clouds, which, to a frame so earth-incrusted by long continuance in a lower region, was unavoidably more fatiguing than to younger spirits. He was therefore conducted to an easy-chair, well cushioned and stuffed with vaporous softness, and left to take a little repose.

The Man of Fancy now discerned another guest, who stood so quietly in the shadow of one of the pillars that he might easily have been overlooked.

"My dear sir," exclaimed the host, grasping him warmly by the hand, "allow me to greet you as the hero of the evening. Pray do not take it as an empty compliment; for if there were not another guest in my castle, it would be entirely pervaded with your presence."

"I thank you," answered the unpretending stranger; "but, though you happened to overlook me, I have not just arrived. I came very early; and, with your permission, shall remain after the rest of the company have retired."

And who does the reader imagine was this unobtrusive guest? It was the famous performer of acknowledged impossibilities—a character of superhuman capacity and virtue, and, if his enemies are to be credited, of no less remarkable weaknesses and defects. With a generosity with which he alone sets us an example, we will glance merely at his nobler attributes. He it is, then, who prefers the interests of others to his own, and a humble station to an exalted one. Careless of fashion, custom, the opinions of men, and the influence of the press, he assimilates his life to the standard of ideal rectitude, and thus proves himself the one independent citizen of our free country. In point of ability, many people declare him to be the only mathematician capable of squaring the circle; the only mechanic acquainted with the principle of perpetual motion; the only scientific philosopher who can compel water to run up hill; the only writer of the age whose genius is equal to the production of an epic poem; and finally, so various are his accomplishments, the only professor of gymnastics who has succeeded in jumping down his own throat. With all these talents, however, he is so far from being considered a member of good society that it is the severest censure of any fashionable assemblage to affirm that this remarkable individual was present. Public orators, lecturers and theatrical performers particularly eschew his company. For especial reasons we are not at liberty to disclose his name, and shall mention only one other trait,—a most singular phenomenon in natural philosophy,—that, when he happens to cast his eyes upon a looking-glass, he beholds Nobody reflected there!

Several other guests now made their appearance; and among them, chattering with immense volubility, a brisk little gentleman of universal vogue in private society, and not unknown in the public journals under the title of Monsieur On-Dit. The name would seem to indicate a Frenchman; but, whatever be his country, he is thoroughly versed in all the languages of the day, and can express himself quite as much to the purpose in English as in any other tongue. No sooner were the ceremonies of salutation over than this talkative little person put his mouth to the host's ear and whispered three secrets of state, an important piece of commercial intelligence, and a rich item of fashionable scandal. He then assured the Man of Fancy that he would not fail to circulate in the society of the lower world a minute description of this magnificent castle in the air and of the festivities at which he had the honor to be a guest. So saying, Monsieur On-Dit made his bow and hurried from one to another of the company, with all of whom he seemed to be acquainted and to possess some topic of interest or amusement for every individual. Coming at last to the Oldest Inhabitant, who was slumbering comfortably in the easy-chair, he applied his mouth to that venerable ear.

"What do you say?" cried the old gentleman, starting from his nap and putting up his hand to serve the purpose of an ear trumpet.

Monsieur On-Dit bent forward again and repeated his communication.

"Never within my memory," exclaimed the Oldest Inhabitant, lifting his hands in astonishment, "has so remarkable an incident been heard of."

Now came in the Clerk of the Weather, who had been invited out of deference to his official station, although the host was well aware that his conversation was likely to contribute but little to the general enjoyment. He soon, indeed, got into a corner with his acquaintance of long ago, the Oldest Inhabitant, and began to compare notes with him in reference to the great storms, gales of wind, and other atmospherical facts that had occurred during a century past. It rejoiced the Man of Fancy that his venerable and much-respected guest had met with so congenial an associate. Entreating them both to make themselves perfectly at home, he now turned to receive the Wandering Jew. This personage, however, had latterly grown so common by mingling in all sorts of society and appearing at the beck of every entertainer, that he could hardly be deemed a proper guest in a very exclusive circle. Besides, being covered with dust from his continual wanderings along the highways of the world, he really looked out of place in a dress party; so that the host felt relieved of an incommodity when the restless individual in question, after a brief stay, took his departure on a ramble towards Oregon.

The portal was now thronged by a crowd of shadowy people with whom the Man of Fancy had been acquainted in his visionary youth. He had invited them hither for the sake of observing how they would compare, whether advantageously or otherwise, with the real characters to whom this maturer life had introduced him. They were beings of crude imagination, such as glide before a young man's eye and pretend to be actual inhabitants of the earth; the wise and witty with whom he would hereafter hold intercourse; the generous and heroic friends whose devotion would be requited with his own; the beautiful dream woman who would become the helpmate of his human toils and sorrows, and at once the source and partaker of his happiness. Alas! it is not good for the fullgrown man to look too closely at these old acquaintances, but rather to reverence them at a distance through the medium of years that have gathered duskily between. There was something laughably untrue in their pompous stride and exaggerated sentiment; they were neither human nor tolerable likenesses of humanity, but fantastic maskers, rendering heroism and nature alike ridiculous by the grave absurdity of their pretensions to such attributes; and as for the peerless dream lady, behold! there advanced up the saloon, with a movement like a jointed doll, a sort of wax figure of an angel, a creature as cold as moonshine, an artifice in petticoats, with an intellect of pretty phrases and only the semblance of a heart, yet in all these particulars the true type of a young man's imaginary mistress. Hardly could the host's punctilious courtesy restrain a smile as he paid his respects to this unreality, and met the sentimental glance with which the Dream sought to remind him of their former love passages.

"No, no, fair lady," murmured he betwixt sighing and smiling, "my taste is changed; I have learned to love what Nature makes better than my own creations in the guise of womanhood."

"Ah, false one," shrieked the dream lady, pretending to faint, but dissolving into thin air, out of which came the deplorable murmur of her voice, "your inconstancy has annihilated me."

"So be it," said the cruel Man of Fancy to himself; "and a good riddance too."

Together with these shadows, and from the same region, there came an uninvited multitude of shapes which at any time during his life had tormented the Man of Fancy in his moods of morbid melancholy or had haunted him in the delirium of fever. The walls of his castle in the air were not dense enough to keep them out, nor would the strongest of earthly architecture have availed to their exclusion. Here were those forms of dim terror which had beset him at the entrance of life, waging warfare with his hopes; here were strange uglinesses of earlier date, such as haunt children in the night-time. He was particularly startled by the vision of a deformed old black woman whom he imagined as lurking in the garret of his native home, and who, when he was an infant, had once come to his bedside and grinned at him in the crisis of a scarlet fever. This same black shadow, with others almost as hideous, now glided among the pillars of the magnificent saloon, grinning recognition, until the man shuddered anew at the forgotten terrors of his childhood. It amused him, however, to observe the black woman, with the mischievous caprice peculiar to such beings, steal up to the chair of the Oldest Inhabitant and peep into his half-dreamy mind.

"Never within my memory," muttered that venerable personage, aghast, "did I see such a face."

Almost immediately after the unrealities just described, arrived a number of guests whom incredulous readers may be inclined to rank equally among creatures of imagination. The most noteworthy were an incorruptible Patriot; a Scholar without pedantry; a Priest without worldly ambition; and a Beautiful Woman without pride or coquetry; a Married Pair whose life had never been disturbed by incongruity of feeling; a Reformer untrammelled by his theory; and a Poet who felt no jealousy towards other votaries of the lyre. In truth, however, the host was not one of the cynics who consider these patterns of excellence, without the fatal flaw, such rarities in the world; and he had invited them to his select party chiefly out of humble deference to the judgment of society, which pronounces them almost impossible to be met with.

"In my younger days," observed the Oldest Inhabitant, "such characters might be seen at the corner of every street."

Be that as it might, these specimens of perfection proved to be not half so entertaining companions as people with the ordinary allowance of faults.

But now appeared a stranger, whom the host had no sooner recognized than, with an abundance of courtesy unlavished on any other, he hastened down the whole length of the saloon in order to pay him emphatic honor. Yet he was a young man in poor attire, with no insignia of rank or acknowledged eminence, nor anything to distinguish him among the crowd except a high, white forehead, beneath which a pair of deepest eyes were glowing with warm light. It was such a light as never illuminates the earth save when a great heart burns as the household fire of a grand intellect. And who was he?—who but the Master Genius for whom our country is looking anxiously into the mist of Time, as destined to fulfil the great mission of creating an American literature, hewing it, as it were, out of the unwrought granite of our intellectual quarries? From him, whether moulded in the form of an epic poem or assuming a guise altogether new as the spirit itself may determine, we are to receive our first great original work, which shall do all that remains to be achieved for our glory among the nations. How this child of a mighty destiny had been discovered by the Man of Fancy it is of little consequence to mention. Suffice it that he dwells as yet unhonored among men, unrecognized by those who have known him from his cradle; the noble countenance which should be distinguished by a halo diffused around it passes daily amid the throng of people toiling and troubling themselves about the trifles of a moment, and none pay reverence to the worker of immortality. Nor does it matter much to him, in his triumph over all the ages, though a generation or two of his own times shall do themselves the wrong to disregard him.

By this time Monsieur On-Dit had caught up the stranger's name and destiny, and was busily whispering the intelligence among the other guests.

"Pshaw!" said one. "There can never be an American genius."

"Pish!" cried another. "We have already as good poets as any in the world. For my part I desire to see no better."

And the Oldest Inhabitant, when it was proposed to introduce him to the Master Genius, begged to be excused, observing that a man who had been honored with the acquaintance of Dwight, and Freneau, and Joel Barlow, might be allowed a little austerity of taste.

The saloon was now fast filling up by the arrival of other remarkable characters, among whom were noticed Davy Jones, the distinguished nautical personage, and a rude, carelessly-dressed, harum-scarum sort of elderly fellow, known by the nickname of Old Harry. The latter, however, after being shown to a dressing-room, reappeared with his gray hair nicely combed, his clothes brushed, a clean dicky on his neck, and altogether so changed in aspect as to merit the more respectful appellation of Venerable Henry. Joel Doe and Richard Roe came arm in arm, accompanied by a Man of Straw, a fictitious indorser, and several persons who had no existence except as voters in closely-contested elections. The celebrated Seatsfield, who now entered, was at first supposed to belong to the same brotherhood, until he made it apparent that he was a real man of flesh and blood and had his earthly domicile in Germany. Among the latest comers, as might reasonably be expected, arrived a guest from the far future.

"Do you know him? do you know him?" whispered Monsieur On-Dit, who seemed to be acquainted with everybody. "He is the representative of Posterity,—the man of an age to come."

"And how came he here?" asked a figure who was evidently the prototype of the fashion plate in a magazine, and might be taken to represent the vanities of the passing moment. "The fellow infringes upon our rights by coming before his time."

"But you forget where we are," answered the Man of Fancy, who overheard the remark. "The lower earth, it is true, will be forbidden ground to him for many long years hence; but a castle in the air is a sort of no man's land, where Posterity may make acquaintance with us on equal terms."

No sooner was his identity known than a throng of guests gathered about Posterity, all expressing the most generous interest in his welfare, and many boasting of the sacrifices which they had made, or were willing to make, in his behalf. Some, with as much secrecy as possible, desired his judgment upon certain copies of verses or great manuscript rolls of prose; others accosted him with the familiarity of old friends, taking it for granted that he was perfectly cognizant of their names and characters. At length, finding himself thus beset, Posterity was put quite beside his patience.

"Gentlemen, my good friends," cried he, breaking loose from a misty poet who strove to hold him by the button, "I pray you to attend to your own business, and leave me to take care of mine! I expect to owe you nothing, unless it be certain national debts, and other encumbrances and impediments, physical and moral, which I shall find it troublesome enough to remove from my path. As to your verses, pray read them to your contemporaries. Your names are as strange to me as your faces; and even were it otherwise,—let me whisper you a secret,—the cold, icy memory which one generation may retain of another is but a poor recompense to barter life for. Yet, if your heart is set on being known to me, the surest, the only method is to live truly and wisely for your own age, whereby, if the native force be in you, you may likewise live for posterity."

"It is nonsense," murmured the Oldest Inhabitant, who, as a man of the past, felt jealous that all notice should be withdrawn from himself to be lavished on the future, "sheer nonsense to waste so much thought on what only is to be."

To divert the minds of his guests, who were considerably abashed by this little incident, the Man of Fancy led them through several apartments of the castle, receiving their compliments upon the taste and varied magnificence that were displayed in each. One of these rooms was filled with moonlight, which did not enter through the window, but was the aggregate of all the moonshine that is scattered around the earth on a summer night while no eyes are awake to enjoy its beauty. Airy spirits had gathered it up, wherever they found it gleaming on the broad bosom of a lake, or silvering the meanders of a stream, or glimmering among the wind-stirred boughs of a wood, and had garnered it in this one spacious hall. Along the walls, illuminated by the mild intensity of the moonshine, stood a multitude of ideal statues, the original conceptions of the great works of ancient or modern art, which the sculptors did but imperfectly succeed in putting into marble; for it is not to be supposed that the pure idea of an immortal creation ceases to exist; it is only necessary to know where they are deposited in order to obtain possession of them. In the alcoves of another vast apartment was arranged a splendid library, the volumes of which were inestimable, because they consisted not of actual performances, but of the works which the authors only planned, without ever finding the happy season to achieve them. To take familiar instances, here were the untold tales of Chaucer's Canterbury Pilgrims; the unwritten cantos of the Fairy Queen; the conclusion of Coleridge's Christabel; and the whole of Dryden's projected epic on the subject of King Arthur. The shelves were crowded; for it would not be too much to affirm that every author has imagined and shaped out in his thought more and far better works than those which actually proceeded from his pen. And here, likewise, were the unrealized conceptions of youthful poets who died of the very strength of their own genius before the world had caught one inspired murmur from their lips.

When the peculiarities of the library and statue gallery were explained to the Oldest Inhabitant, he appeared infinitely perplexed, and exclaimed, with more energy than usual, that he had never heard of such a thing within his memory, and, moreover, did not at all understand how it could be.

"But my brain, I think," said the good old gentleman, "is getting not so clear as it used to be. You young folks, I suppose, can see your way through these strange matters. For my part, I give it up."

"And so do I," muttered the Old Harry. "It is enough to puzzle the—Ahem!"

Making as little reply as possible to these observations, the Man of Fancy preceded the company to another noble saloon, the pillars of which were solid golden sunbeams taken out of the sky in the first hour in the morning. Thus, as they retained all their living lustre, the room was filled with the most cheerful radiance imaginable, yet not too dazzling to be borne with comfort and delight. The windows were beautifully adorned with curtains made of the many-colored clouds of sunrise, all imbued with virgin light, and hanging in magnificent festoons from the ceiling to the floor. Moreover, there were fragments of rainbows scattered through the room; so that the guests, astonished at one another, reciprocally saw their heads made glorious by the seven primary hues; or, if they chose,—as who would not?—they could grasp a rainbow in the air and convert it to their own apparel and adornment. But the morning light and scattered rainbows were only a type and symbol of the real wonders of the apartment. By an influence akin to magic, yet perfectly natural, whatever means and opportunities of joy are neglected in the lower world had been carefully gathered up and deposited in the saloon of morning sunshine. As may well be conceived, therefore, there was material enough to supply, not merely a joyous evening, but also a happy lifetime, to more than as many people as that spacious apartment could contain. The company seemed to renew their youth; while that pattern and proverbial standard of innocence, the Child Unborn, frolicked to and fro among them, communicating his own unwrinkled gayety to all who had the good fortune to witness his gambols.

"My honored friends," said the Man of Fancy, after they had enjoyed themselves a while, "I am now to request your presence in the banqueting hall, where a slight collation is awaiting you."

"Ah, well said!" ejaculated a cadaverous figure, who had been invited for no other reason than that he was pretty constantly in the habit of dining with Duke Humphrey. "I was beginning to wonder whether a castle in the air were provided with a kitchen."

It was curious, in truth, to see how instantaneously the guests were diverted from the high moral enjoyments which they had been tasting with so much apparent zest by a suggestion of the more solid as well as liquid delights of the festive board. They thronged eagerly in the rear of the host, who now ushered them into a lofty and extensive hall, from end to end of which was arranged a table, glittering all over with innumerable dishes and drinking vessels of gold. It is an uncertain point whether these rich articles of plate were made for the occasion out of molten sunbeams, or recovered from the wrecks of Spanish galleons that had lain for ages at the bottom of the sea. The upper end of the table was overshadowed by a canopy, beneath which was placed a chair of elaborate magnificence, which the host himself declined to occupy, and besought his guests to assign it to the worthiest among them. As a suitable homage to his incalculable antiquity and eminent distinction, the post of honor was at first tendered to the Oldest Inhabitant. He, however, eschewed it, and requested the favor of a bowl of gruel at a side table, where he could refresh himself with a quiet nap. There was some little hesitation as to the next candidate, until Posterity took the Master Genius of our country by the hand and led him to the chair of state beneath the princely canopy. When once they beheld him in his true place, the company acknowledged the justice of the selection by a long thunder roll of vehement applause.

Then was served up a banquet, combining, if not all the delicacies of the season, yet all the rarities which careful purveyors had met with in the flesh, fish, and vegetable markets of the land of Nowhere. The bill of fare being unfortunately lost, we can only mention a phœnix, roasted in its own flames, cold potted birds of paradise, ice-creams from the Milky Way, and whip syllabubs and flummery from the Paradise of Fools, whereof there was a very great consumption. As for drinkables, the temperance people contented themselves with water as usual; but it was the water of the Fountain of Youth; the ladies sipped Nepenthe; the lovelorn, the careworn, and the sorrow-stricken were supplied with brimming goblets of Lethe; and it was shrewdly conjectured that a certain golden vase, from which only the more distinguished guests were invited to partake, contained nectar that had been mellowing ever since the days of classical mythology. The cloth being removed, the company, as usual, grew eloquent over their liquor, and delivered themselves of a succession of brilliant speeches,—the task of reporting which we resign to the more adequate ability of Counsellor Gill, whose indispensable coöperation the Man of Fancy had taken the precaution to secure.

When the festivity of the banquet was at its most ethereal point, the Clerk of the Weather was observed to steal from the table and thrust his head between the purple and golden curtains of one of the windows.

"My fellow-guests," he remarked aloud, after carefully noting the signs of the night, "I advise such of you as live at a distance to be going as soon as possible; for a thunder storm is certainly at hand."

"Mercy on me!" cried Mother Carey, who had left her brood of chickens and come hither in gossamer drapery, with pink silk stockings. "How shall I ever get home?"

All now was confusion and hasty departure, with but little superfluous leave-taking. The Oldest Inhabitant, however, true to the rule of those long-past days in which his courtesy had been studied, paused on the threshold of the meteor-lighted hall to express his vast satisfaction at the entertainment.

"Never, within my memory," observed the gracious old gentleman, "has it been my good fortune to spend a pleasanter evening or in more select society."

The wind here took his breath away, whirled his three-cornered hat into infinite space, and drowned what further compliments it had been his purpose to bestow. Many of the company had bespoken will-o'-the-wisps to convoy them home; and the host, in his general beneficence, had engaged the Man in the

Moon, with an immense horn lantern, to be the guide of such desolate spinsters as could do no better for themselves. But a blast of the rising tempest blew out all their lights in the twinkling of an eye. How, in the darkness that ensued, the guests contrived to get back to earth, or whether the greater part of them contrived to get back at all, or are still wandering among clouds, mists, and puffs of tempestuous wind, bruised by the beams and rafters of the overthrown castle in the air, and deluded by all sorts of unrealities, are points that concern themselves much more than the writer or the public. People should think of these matters before they thrust themselves on a pleasure party into the realm of Nowhere.

YOUNG GOODMAN BROWN

Young Goodman Brown came forth at sunset into the street at Salem village; but put his head back, after crossing the threshold, to exchange a parting kiss with his young wife. And Faith, as the wife was aptly named, thrust her own pretty head into the street, letting the wind play with the pink ribbons of her cap while she called to Goodman Brown.

"Dearest heart," whispered she, softly and rather sadly, when her lips were close to his ear, "prithee put off your journey until sunrise and sleep in your own bed to-night. A lone woman is troubled with such dreams and such thoughts that she's afeard of herself sometimes. Pray tarry with me this night, dear husband, of all nights in the year." (Halloween)

"My love and my Faith," replied young Goodman Brown, "of all nights in the year, this one night must I tarry away from thee. My journey, as thou callest it, forth and back again, must needs be done 'twixt now and sunrise. What, my sweet, pretty wife, dost thou doubt me already, and we but three months married?"

"Then God bless you!" said Faith, with the pink ribbons; "and may you find all well when you come back."

"Amen!" cried Goodman Brown. "Say thy prayers, dear Faith, and go to bed at dusk, and no harm will come to thee."

So they parted; and the young man pursued his way until, being about to turn the corner by the meeting-house, he looked back and saw the head of Faith still peeping after him with a melancholy air, in spite of her pink ribbons.

"Poor little Faith!" thought he, for his heart smote him. "What a wretch am I to leave her on such an errand! She talks of dreams, too. Methought as she spoke there was trouble in her face, as if a dream had warned her what work is to be done to-night. But no, no; 't would kill her to think it. Well, she's a blessed angel on earth; and after this one night I'll cling to her skirts and follow her to heaven."

With this excellent resolve for the future, Goodman Brown felt himself justified in making more haste on his present evil purpose. He had taken a dreary road, darkened by all the gloomiest trees of the forest, which barely stood aside to let the narrow path creep through, and closed immediately behind. It was all as lonely as could be; and there is this peculiarity in such a solitude, that the traveller knows not who may be concealed by the innumerable trunks and the thick boughs overhead; so that with lonely footsteps he may yet be passing through an unseen multitude.

"There may be a devilish Indian behind every tree," said Goodman Brown to himself; and he glanced fearfully behind him as he added, "What if the devil himself should be at my very elbow!"

His head being turned back, he passed a crook of the road, and, looking forward again, beheld the figure of a man, in grave and decent attire, seated at the foot of an old tree. He arose at Goodman Brown's approach and walked onward side by side with him.

"You are late, Goodman Brown," said he. "The clock of the Old South was striking as I came through Boston, and that is full fifteen minutes agone."

"Faith kept mc back a while," replied the young man, with a tremor in his voice, caused by the sudden appearance of his companion, though not wholly unexpected.

It was now deep dusk in the forest, and deepest in that part of it where these two were journeying. As nearly as could be discerned, the second traveller was about fifty years old, apparently in the same rank of life as Goodman Brown, and bearing a considerable resemblance to him, though perhaps more in expression than features. Still they might have been taken for father and son. And yet, though the elder person was as simply clad as the younger, and as simple in manner too, he had an indescribable air of one who knew the world, and who would not have felt abashed at the governor's dinner table or in King William's court, were it possible that his affairs should call him thither. But the only thing about him that could be fixed upon as remarkable was his staff, which bore the likeness of a great black snake, so curiously wrought that it might almost be seen to twist and wriggle itself like a living serpent. This, of course, must have been an ocular deception, assisted by the uncertain light.

"Come, Goodman Brown," cried his fellow-traveller, "this is a dull pace for the beginning of a journey. Take my staff, if you are so soon weary."

"Friend," said the other, exchanging his slow pace for a full stop, "having kept covenant by meeting thee here, it is my purpose now to return whence I came. I have scruples touching the matter thou wot'st of."

"Sayest thou so?" replied he of the serpent, smiling apart. "Let us walk on, nevertheless, reasoning as we go; and if I convince thee not thou shalt turn back. We are but a little way in the forest yet."

"Too far! too far!" exclaimed the goodman, unconsciously resuming his walk. "My father never went into the woods on such an errand, nor his father before him. We have been a race of honest men and good Christians since the days of the martyrs; and shall I be the first of the name of Brown that ever took this path and kept"—

"Such company, thou wouldst say," observed the elder person, interpreting his pause. "Well said, Goodman Brown! I have been as well acquainted with your family as with ever a one among the Puritans; and that's no trifle to say. I helped your grandfather, the constable, when he lashed the Quaker woman so smartly through the streets of Salem; and it was I that brought your father a pitch-pine knot, kindled at my own hearth, to set fire to an Indian village, in King Philip's war. They were my good friends, both; and many a pleasant walk have we had along this path, and returned merrily after midnight. I would fain be friends with you for their sake."

"If it be as thou sayest," replied Goodman Brown, "I marvel they never spoke of these matters; or, verily, I marvel not, seeing that the least rumor of the sort would have driven them from New England. We are a people of prayer, and good works to boot, and abide no such wickedness."

"Wickedness or not," said the traveller with the twisted staff, "I have a very general acquaintance here in New England. The deacons of many a church have drunk the communion wine with me; the selectmen of divers towns make me their chairman; and a majority of the Great and General Court are firm supporters of my interest. The governor and I, too— But these are state secrets."

"Can this be so?" cried Goodman Brown, with a stare of amazement at his undisturbed companion. "Howbeit, I have nothing to do with the governor and council; they have their own ways, and are no rule for a simple husbandman like me. But, were I to go on with thee, how should I meet the eye of that good old man, our minister, at Salem village? Oh, his voice would make me tremble both Sabbath day and lecture day."

Thus far the elder traveller had listened with due gravity; but now burst into a fit of irrepressible mirth, shaking himself so violently that his snake-like staff actually seemed to wriggle in sympathy.

"Ha! ha! ha!" shouted he again and again; then composing himself, "Well, go on, Goodman Brown, go on; but, prithee, don't kill me with laughing."

"Well, then, to end the matter at once," said Goodman Brown, considerably nettled, "there is my wife, Faith. It would break her dear little heart; and I'd rather break my own."

"Nay, if that be the case," answered the other, "e'en go thy ways, Goodman Brown. I would not for twenty old women like the one hobbling before us that Faith should come to any harm."

As he spoke he pointed his staff at a female figure on the path, in whom Goodman Brown recognized a very pious and exemplary dame, who had taught him his catechism in youth, and was still his moral and spiritual adviser, jointly with the minister and Deacon Gookin.

"A marvel, truly, that Goody Cloyse should be so far in the wilderness at nightfall," said he. "But with your leave, friend, I shall take a cut through the woods until we have left this Christian woman behind. Being a stranger to you, she might ask whom I was consorting with and whither I was going."

"Be it so," said his fellow-traveller. "Betake you to the woods, and let me keep the path."

Accordingly the young man turned aside, but took care to watch his companion, who advanced softly along the road until he had come within a staff's length of the old dame. She, meanwhile, was making the best of her way, with singular speed for so aged a woman, and mumbling some indistinct words—a prayer, doubtless—as she went. The traveller put forth his staff and touched her withered neck with what seemed the serpent's tail.

"The devil!" screamed the pious old lady.

"Then Goody Cloyse knows her old friend?" observed the traveller, confronting her and leaning on his writhing stick.

"Ah, forsooth, and is it your worship indeed?" cried the good dame. "Yea, truly is it, and in the very image of my old gossip, Goodman Brown, the grandfather of the silly fellow that now is. But—would your worship believe it? —my broomstick hath strangely disappeared, stolen, as I suspect, by that unhanged witch, Goody Cory, and that, too, when I was all anointed with the juice of smallage, and cinquefoil, and wolf's bane"—

"Mingled with fine wheat and the fat of a new-born babe," said the shape of old Goodman Brown.

"Ah, your worship knows the recipe," cried the old lady, cackling aloud. "So, as I was saying, being all ready for the meeting, and no horse to ride on, I made up my mind to foot it; for they tell me there is a nice young man to be taken into communion to-night. But now your good worship will lend me your arm, and we shall be there in a twinkling."

"That can hardly be," answered her friend. "I may not spare you my arm, Goody Cloyse; but here is my staff, if you will."

So saying, he threw it down at her feet, where, perhaps, it assumed life, being one of the rods which its owner had formerly lent to the Egyptian magi. Of this fact, however, Goodman Brown could not take cognizance. He had cast up his eyes in astonishment, and, looking down again, beheld neither Goody Cloyse nor the serpentine staff, but his fellow-traveller alone, who waited for him as calmly as if nothing had happened.

"That old woman taught me my catechism," said the young man; and there was a world of meaning in this simple comment.

They continued to walk onward, while the elder traveller exhorted his companion to make good speed and persevere in the path, discoursing so aptly that his arguments seemed rather to spring up in the bosom of his auditor than to be suggested by himself. As they went, he plucked a branch of maple to serve for a walking stick, and began to strip it of the twigs and little boughs, which were wet with evening dew. The moment his fingers touched them they became strangely withered and dried up as with a week's sunshine. Thus the pair proceeded, at a good free pace, until suddenly, in a gloomy hollow of the road, Goodman Brown sat himself down on the stump of a tree and refused to go any farther.

"Friend," said he, stubbornly, "my mind is made up. Not another step will I budge on this errand. What if a wretched old woman do choose to go to the devil when I thought she was going to heaven: is that any reason why I should quit my dear Faith and go after her?"

"You will think better of this by and by," said his acquaintance, composedly. "Sit here and rest yourself a while; and when you feel like moving again, there is my staff to help you along."

Without more words, he threw his companion the maple stick, and was as speedily out of sight as if he had vanished into the deepening gloom. The young man sat a few moments by the roadside, applauding himself greatly, and thinking with how clear a conscience he should meet the minister in his morning walk, nor shrink from the eye of good old Deacon Gookin. And what calm sleep would be his that very night, which was to have been spent so wickedly, but so purely and sweetly now, in the arms of Faith! Amidst these pleasant and praiseworthy meditations, Goodman Brown heard the tramp of horses along the road, and deemed it advisable to conceal himself within the verge of the forest, conscious of the guilty purpose that had brought him thither, though now so happily turned from it.

On came the hoof tramps and the voices of the riders, two grave old voices, conversing soberly as they drew near. These mingled sounds appeared to pass along the road, within a few yards of the young man's hiding-place; but, owing doubtless to the depth of the gloom at that particular spot, neither the travellers nor their steeds were visible. Though their figures brushed the small boughs by the wayside, it could not be seen that they intercepted, even for a moment, the faint gleam from the strip of bright sky athwart which they must have passed. Goodman Brown alternately crouched and stood on tiptoe, pulling aside the branches and thrusting forth his head as far as he durst without discerning so much as a shadow. It vexed him the more, because he could have sworn, were such a thing possible, that he recognized the voices of the minister and Deacon Gookin, jogging along quietly, as they were wont to do, when bound to some ordination or ecclesiastical council. While yet within hearing, one of the riders stopped to pluck a switch.

"Of the two, reverend sir," said the voice like the deacon's, "I had rather miss an ordination dinner than tonight's meeting. They tell me that some of our community are to be here from Falmouth and beyond, and others from Connecticut and Rhode Island, besides several of the Indian powwows, who, after their fashion, know almost as much deviltry as the best of us. Moreover, there is a goodly young woman to be taken into communion."

"Mighty well, Deacon Gookin!" replied the solemn old tones of the minister. "Spur up, or we shall be late. Nothing can be done, you know, until I get on the ground."

The hoofs clattered again; and the voices, talking so strangely in the empty air, passed on through the forest, where no church had ever been gathered or solitary Christian prayed. Whither, then, could these holy men be journeying so deep into the heathen wilderness? Young Goodman Brown caught hold of a tree for support, being ready to sink down on the ground, faint and overburdened with the heavy sickness of his heart. He looked up to the sky, doubting whether there really was a heaven above him. Yet there was the blue arch, and the stars brightening in it.

"With heaven above and Faith below, I will yet stand firm against the devil!" cried Goodman Brown.

While he still gazed upward into the deep arch of the firmament and had lifted his hands to pray, a cloud, though no wind was stirring, hurried across the zenith and hid the brightening stars. The blue sky was still visible, except directly overhead, where this black mass of cloud was sweeping swiftly northward. Aloft in the air, as if from the depths of the cloud, came a confused and doubtful sound of voices. Once the listener fancied that he could distinguish the accents of towns-people of his own, men and women, both pious and ungodly, many of whom he had met at the communion table, and had seen others rioting at the tavern. The next moment, so indistinct were the sounds, he doubted whether he had heard aught but the murmur of the old forest, whispering without a wind. Then came a stronger swell of those familiar tones, heard daily in the sunshine at Salem village, but never until now from a cloud of night. There was one voice, of a young woman, uttering lamentations, yet with an uncertain sorrow, and entreating for some favor, which, perhaps, it would grieve her to obtain; and all the unseen multitude, both saints and sinners, seemed to encourage her onward.

"Faith!" shouted Goodman Brown, in a voice of agony and desperation; and the echoes of the forest mocked him, crying, "Faith! Faith!" as if bewildered wretches were seeking her all through the wilderness.

The cry of grief, rage, and terror was yet piercing the night, when the unhappy husband held his breath for a response. There was a scream, drowned immediately in a louder murmur of voices, fading into far-off laughter, as the dark cloud swept away, leaving the clear and silent sky above Goodman Brown. But something fluttered lightly down through the air and caught on the branch of a tree. The young man seized it, and beheld a pink ribbon.

"My Faith is gone!" cried he, after one stupefied moment. "There is no good on earth; and sin is but a name. Come, devil; for to thee is this world given."

And, maddened with despair, so that he laughed loud and long, did Goodman Brown grasp his staff and set forth again, at such a rate that he seemed to fly along the forest path rather than to walk or run. The road grew wilder and drearier and more faintly traced, and vanished at length, leaving him in the heart of the dark wilderness, still rushing onward with the instinct that guides mortal man to evil. The whole forest was peopled with frightful sounds—the creaking of the trees, the howling of wild beasts, and the yell of Indians; while sometimes the wind tolled like a distant church bell, and sometimes gave a broad roar around the traveller, as if all Nature were laughing him to scorn. But he was himself the chief horror of the scene, and shrank not from its other horrors.

"Ha! ha! ha!" roared Goodman Brown when the wind laughed at him. "Let us hear which will laugh loudest. Think not to frighten me with your deviltry. Come witch, come wizard, come Indian powwow, come devil himself, and here comes Goodman Brown. You may as well fear him as he fear you."

In truth, all through the haunted forest there could be nothing more frightful than the figure of Goodman Brown. On he flew among the black pines, brandishing his staff with frenzied gestures, now giving vent to an inspiration of horrid blasphemy, and now shouting forth such laughter as set all the echoes of the forest laughing like demons around him. The fiend in his own shape is less hideous than when he rages in the breast of man. Thus sped the demoniac on his course, until, quivering among the trees, he saw a red light before him, as when the felled trunks and branches of a clearing have been set on fire, and throw up their lurid blaze against the sky, at the hour of midnight. He paused, in a lull of the tempest that had driven him onward, and heard the swell of what seemed a hymn, rolling solemnly from a distance with the weight of many voices. He knew the tune; it was a familiar one in the choir of the village meeting-house. The verse died heavily away, and was lengthened by a chorus, not of human voices, but of all the sounds of the benighted wilderness pealing in awful harmony together. Goodman Brown cried out, and his cry was lost to his own ear by its unison with the cry of the desert.

In the interval of silence he stole forward until the light glared full upon his eyes. At one extremity of an open space, hemmed in by the dark wall of the forest, arose a rock, bearing some rude, natural resemblance either to an altar or a pulpit, and surrounded by four blazing pines, their tops aflame, their stems untouched, like candles at an evening meeting. The mass of foliage that had overgrown the summit of the rock was all on fire, blazing high into the night and fitfully illuminating the whole field. Each pendent twig and leafy festoon was in a blaze. As the red light arose and fell, a numerous congregation alternately shone forth, then disappeared in shadow, and again grew, as it were, out of the darkness, peopling the heart of the solitary woods at once.

"A grave and dark-clad company," quoth Goodman Brown.

In truth they were such. Among them, quivering to and fro between gloom and splendor, appeared faces that would be seen next day at the council board of the province, and others which, Sabbath after Sabbath, looked devoutly heavenward, and benignantly over the crowded pews, from the holiest pulpits in the land. Some affirm that the lady of the governor was there. At least there were high dames well known to her, and wives of honored husbands, and widows, a great multitude, and ancient maidens, all of excellent repute, and fair young girls, who trembled lest their mothers should espy them. Either the sudden gleams of light flashing over the obscure field bedazzled Goodman Brown, or he recognized a score of the church members of Salem village famous for their especial sanctity. Good old Deacon Gookin had arrived, and waited at the skirts of that venerable saint, his revered pastor. But, irreverently consorting with these grave, reputable, and pious people, these elders of the church, these chaste dames and dewy virgins, there were men of dissolute lives and women of spotted fame, wretches given over to all mean and filthy vice, and suspected even of horrid crimes. It was strange to see that the good shrank not from the wicked, nor were the sinners abashed by the saints. Scattered also among their pale-faced enemies were the Indian priests, or powwows, who had often scared their native forest with more hideous incantations than any known to English witchcraft.

"But where is Faith?" thought Goodman Brown; and, as hope came into his heart, he trembled.

Another verse of the hymn arose, a slow and mournful strain, such as the pious love, but joined to words which expressed all that our nature can conceive of sin, and darkly hinted at far more. Unfathomable to mere mortals is the lore of fiends. Verse after verse was sung; and still the chorus of the desert swelled between like the deepest tone of a mighty organ; and with the final peal of that dreadful anthem there came a sound, as if the roaring wind, the rushing streams, the howling beasts, and every other voice of the unconcerted wilderness were mingling and according with the voice of guilty man in homage to the prince of all. The four blazing pines threw up a loftier flame, and obscurely discovered shapes and visages of horror on the smoke wreaths above the impious assembly. At the same moment the fire on the rock shot redly forth and formed a glowing arch above its base, where now appeared a figure. With reverence be it spoken, the figure bore no slight similitude, both in garb and manner, to some grave divine of the New England churches.

"Bring forth the converts!" cried a voice that echoed through the field and rolled into the forest.

At the word, Goodman Brown stepped forth from the shadow of the trees and approached the congregation, with whom he felt a loathful brotherhood by the sympathy of all that was wicked in his heart. He could have well-nigh sworn that the shape of his own dead father beckoned him to advance, looking downward from a smoke wreath, while a woman, with dim features of despair, threw out her hand to warn him back. Was it his mother? But he had no power to retreat one step, nor to resist, even in thought, when the minister and good old Deacon Gookin seized his arms and led him to the blazing rock. Thither came also the slender form of a veiled female, led between Goody Cloyse, that pious teacher of the catechism, and Martha Carrier, who had received the devil's promise to be queen of hell. A rampant hag was she. And there stood the proselytes beneath the canopy of fire.

"Welcome, my children," said the dark figure, "to the communion of your race. Ye have found thus young your nature and your destiny. My children, look behind you!"

They turned; and flashing forth, as it were, in a sheet of flame, the fiend worshippers were seen; the smile of welcome gleamed darkly on every visage.

"There," resumed the sable form, "are all whom ye have reverenced from youth. Ye deemed them holier than yourselves, and shrank from your own sin, contrasting it with their lives of righteousness and prayerful aspirations heavenward. Yet here are they all in my worshipping assembly. This night it shall be granted you to know their secret deeds: how hoary-bearded elders of the church have whispered wanton words to the young maids of their households; how many a woman, eager for widows' weeds, has given her husband a drink at bedtime and let him sleep his last sleep in her bosom; how beardless youths have made haste to inherit their fathers' wealth; and how fair damsels —blush not, sweet ones—have dug little graves in the garden, and bidden me, the sole guest, to an infant's funeral. By the sympathy of your human hearts for sin ye shall scent out all the places—whether in church, bed-chamber, street, field, or forest—where crime has been committed, and shall exult to behold the whole earth one stain of guilt, one mighty blood spot. Far more than this. It shall be yours to penetrate, in every bosom, the deep mystery of sin, the fountain of all wicked arts, and which inexhaustibly supplies more evil impulses than human power—than my power at its utmost—can make manifest in deeds. And now, my children, look upon each other."

They did so; and, by the blaze of the hell-kindled torches, the wretched man beheld his Faith, and the wife her husband, trembling before that unhallowed altar.

"Lo, there ye stand, my children," said the figure, in a deep and solemn tone, almost sad with its despairing awfulness, as if his once angelic nature could yet mourn for our miserable race. "Depending upon one another's hearts, ye had still hoped that virtue were not all a dream. Now are ye undeceived. Evil is the nature of mankind. Evil must be your only happiness. Welcome again, my children, to the communion of your race."

"Welcome," repeated the fiend worshippers, in one cry of despair and triumph.

And there they stood, the only pair, as it seemed, who were yet hesitating on the verge of wickedness in this dark world. A basin was hollowed, naturally, in the rock. Did it contain water, reddened by the lurid light? or was it blood? or, perchance, a liquid flame? Herein did the shape of evil dip his hand and prepare to lay the mark of baptism upon their foreheads, that they might be partakers of the mystery of sin, more conscious of the secret guilt of others, both in deed and thought, than they could now be of their own. The husband cast one look at his pale wife, and Faith at him. What polluted wretches would the next glance show them to each other, shuddering alike at what they disclosed and what they saw!

"Faith! Faith!" cried the husband, "look up to heaven, and resist the wicked one."

Whether Faith obeyed he knew not. Hardly had he spoken when he found himself amid calm night and solitude, listening to a roar of the wind which died heavily away through the forest. He staggered against the rock, and felt it chill and damp; while a hanging twig, that had been all on fire, besprinkled his cheek with the coldest dew.

The next morning young Goodman Brown came slowly into the street of Salem village, staring around him like a bewildered man. The good old minister was taking a walk along the graveyard to get an appetite for breakfast and meditate his sermon, and bestowed a blessing, as he passed, on Goodman Brown. He shrank from the venerable saint as if to avoid an anathema. Old Deacon Gookin was at domestic worship, and the holy words of his prayer were heard through the open window. "What God doth the wizard pray to?" quoth Goodman Brown. Goody Cloyse, that excellent old Christian, stood in the early sunshine at her own lattice, catechizing a little girl who had brought her a pint of morning's milk. Goodman Brown snatched away the child as from the grasp of the fiend himself. Turning the corner by the meeting-house, he spied the head of Faith, with the pink ribbons, gazing anxiously forth, and bursting into such joy at sight of him that she skipped along the street and almost kissed her husband before the whole village. But Goodman Brown looked sternly and sadly into her face, and passed on without a greeting.

Had Goodman Brown fallen asleep in the forest and only dreamed a wild dream of a witch-meeting?

Be it so if you will; but, alas! it was a dream of evil omen for young Goodman Brown. A stern, a sad, a darkly meditative, a distrustful, if not a desperate man did he become from the night of that fearful dream. On the Sabbath day, when the congregation were singing a holy psalm, he could not listen because an anthem of sin rushed loudly upon his ear and drowned all the blessed strain. When the minister spoke from the pulpit with power and fervid eloquence, and, with his hand on the open Bible, of the sacred truths of our religion, and of saint-like lives and triumphant deaths, and of future bliss or misery unutterable, then did Goodman Brown turn pale, dreading lest the roof should thunder down upon the gray blasphemer and his hearers. Often, awaking suddenly at midnight, he shrank from the bosom of Faith; and at morning or eventide, when the family knelt down at prayer, he scowled and muttered to himself, and gazed sternly at his wife, and turned away. And when he had lived long, and was borne to his grave a hoary corpse, followed by Faith, an aged woman, and children and grandchildren, a goodly procession, besides neighbors not a few, they carved no hopeful verse upon his tombstone, for his dying hour was gloom.

RAPPACCINI'S DAUGHTER

(FROM THE WRITINGS OF AUBÉPINE)

We do not remember to have seen any translated specimens of the productions of M. de l'Aubépine—a fact the less to be wondered at, as his very name is unknown to many of his own countrymen as well as to the student of foreign literature. As a writer, he seems to occupy an unfortunate position between the Transcendentalists (who, under one name or another, have their share in all the current literature of the world) and the great body of pen-and-ink men who address the intellect and sympathies of the multitude. If not too refined, at all events too remote, too shadowy, and unsubstantial in his modes of development to suit the taste of the latter class, and yet too popular to satisfy the spiritual or metaphysical requisitions of the former, he must necessarily find himself without an audience, except here and there an individual or possibly an isolated clique. His writings, to do them justice, are not altogether destitute of fancy and originality; they might have won him greater reputation but for an inveterate love of allegory, which is apt to invest his plots and characters with the aspect of scenery and people in the clouds, and to steal away the human warmth out of his conceptions. His fictions are sometimes historical, sometimes of the present day, and sometimes, so far as can be discovered, have little or no reference either to time or space. In any case, he generally contents himself with a very slight embroidery of outward manners,—the faintest possible counterfeit of real life,—and endeavors to create an interest by some less obvious peculiarity of the subject. Occasionally a breath of Nature, a raindrop of pathos and tenderness, or a gleam of humor, will find its way into the midst of his fantastic imagery, and make us feel as if, after all, we were yet within the limits of our native earth. We will only add to this very cursory notice that M. de l'Aubépine's productions, if the reader chance to take them in precisely the proper point of view, may amuse a leisure hour as well as those of a brighter man; if otherwise, they can hardly fail to look excessively like nonsense.

Our author is voluminous; he continues to write and publish with as much praiseworthy and indefatigable prolixity as if his efforts were crowned with the brilliant success that so justly attends those of Eugene Sue. His first appearance was by a collection of stories in a long series of volumes entitled "Contes deux fois racontées." The titles of some of his more recent works (we quote from memory) are as follows: "Le Voyage Céleste à Chemin de Fer," 3 tom., 1838; "Le nouveau Père Adam et la nouvelle Mère Eve," 2 tom., 1839; "Roderic; ou le Serpent à l'estomac," 2 tom., 1840; "Le Culte du Feu," a folio volume of ponderous research into the religion and ritual of the old Persian Ghebers, published in 1841; "La Soirée du Chateau en Espagne," 1 tom., 8vo, 1842; and "L'Artiste du Beau; ou le Papillon Mécanique," 5 tom., 4to, 1843. Our somewhat wearisome perusal of this startling catologue of volumes has left behind it a certain personal affection and sympathy, though by no means admiration, for M. de l'Aubépine; and we would fain do the little in our power towards introducing him favorably to the American public. The ensuing tale is a translation of his "Beatrice; ou la Belle Empoisonneuse," recently published in "La Revue Anti-Aristocratique." This journal, edited by the Comte de Bearhaven, has for some years past led the defence of liberal principles and popular rights with a faithfulness and ability worthy of all praise.

A young man, named Giovanni Guasconti, came, very long ago, from the more southern region of Italy, to pursue his studies at the University of Padua. Giovanni, who had but a scanty supply of gold ducats in his pocket, took lodgings in a high and gloomy chamber of an old edifice which looked not unworthy to have been the palace of a Paduan noble, and which, in fact, exhibited over its entrance the armorial bearings of a family long since extinct. The young stranger, who was not unstudied in the great poem of his country, recollected that one of the ancestors of this family, and perhaps an occupant of this very mansion, had been pictured by Dante as a partaker of the immortal agonies of his Inferno. These reminiscences and associations, together with the tendency to heartbreak natural to a young man for the first time out of his native sphere, caused Giovanni to sigh heavily as he looked around the desolate and ill-furnished apartment.

"Holy Virgin, signor!" cried old Dame Lisabetta, who, won by the youth's remarkable beauty of person, was kindly endeavoring to give the chamber a habitable air, "what a sigh was that to come out of a young man's heart! Do you find this old mansion gloomy? For the love of Heaven, then, put your head out of the window, and you will see as bright sunshine as you have left in Naples."

Guasconti mechanically did as the old woman advised, but could not quite agree with her that the Paduan sunshine was as cheerful as that of southern Italy. Such as it was, however, it fell upon a garden beneath the window and expended its fostering influences on a variety of plants, which seemed to have been cultivated with exceeding care.

"Does this garden belong to the house?" asked Giovanni.

"Heaven forbid, signor, unless it were fruitful of better pot herbs than any that grow there now," answered old Lisabetta. "No; that garden is cultivated by the own hands of Signor Giacomo Rappaccini, the famous doctor, who, I warrant him, has been heard of as far as Naples. It is said that he distils these plants into medicines that are as potent as a charm. Oftentimes you may see the signor doctor at work, and perchance the signora, his daughter, too, gathering the strange flowers that grow in the garden."

The old woman had now done what she could for the aspect of the chamber; and, commending the young man to the protection of the saints, took her departure.

Giovanni still found no better occupation than to look down into the garden beneath his window. From its appearance, he judged it to be one of those botanic gardens which were of earlier date in Padua than elsewhere in Italy or in the world. Or, not improbably, it might once have been the pleasure-place of an opulent family; for there was the ruin of a marble fountain in the centre, sculptured with rare art, but so wofully shattered that it was impossible to trace the original design from the chaos of remaining fragments. The water, however, continued to gush and sparkle into the sunbeams as cheerfully as ever. A little gurgling sound ascended to the young man's window, and made him feel as if the fountain were an immortal spirit that sung its song unceasingly and without heeding the vicissitudes around it, while one century imbodied it in marble and another scattered the perishable garniture on the soil. All about the pool into which the water subsided grew various plants, that seemed to require a plentiful supply of moisture for the nourishment of gigantic leaves, and, in some instances, flowers gorgeously magnificent. There was one shrub in particular, set in a marble vase in the midst of the pool, that bore a profusion of purple blossoms, each of which had the lustre and richness of a gem; and the whole together made a show so resplendent that it seemed enough to illuminate the garden, even had there been no sunshine. Every portion of the soil was peopled with plants and herbs, which, if less beautiful, still bore tokens of assiduous care, as if all had their individual virtues, known to the scientific mind that fostered them. Some were placed in urns, rich with old carving, and others in common garden pots; some crept serpent-like along the ground or climbed on high, using whatever means of ascent was offered them. One plant had wreathed itself round a statue of Vertumnus, which was thus quite veiled and shrouded in a drapery of hanging foliage, so happily arranged that it might have served a sculptor for a study.

While Giovanni stood at the window he heard a rustling behind a screen of leaves, and became aware that a person was at work in the garden. His figure soon emerged into view, and showed itself to be that of no common laborer, but a tall, emaciated, sallow, and sickly-looking man, dressed in a scholar's garb of black. He was beyond the middle term of life, with gray hair, a thin, gray beard, and a face singularly marked with intellect and cultivation, but which could never, even in his more youthful days, have expressed much warmth of heart.

Nothing could exceed the intentness with which this scientific gardener examined every shrub which grew in his path: it seemed as if he was looking into their inmost nature, making observations in regard to their creative essence, and discovering why one leaf grew in this shape and another in that, and wherefore such and such flowers differed among themselves in hue and perfume. Nevertheless, in spite of this deep intelligence on his part, there was no approach to intimacy between himself and these vegetable existences. On the contrary, he avoided their actual touch or the direct inhaling of their odors with a caution that impressed Giovanni most disagreeably; for the man's demeanor was that of one walking among malignant influences, such as savage beasts, or deadly snakes, or evil spirits, which, should he allow them one moment of license, would wreak upon him some terrible fatality. It was strangely frightful to the young man's imagination to see this air of insecurity in a person cultivating a garden, that most simple and innocent of human toils, and which had been alike the joy and labor of the unfallen parents of the race. Was this garden, then, the Eden of the present world? And this man, with such a perception of harm in what his own hands caused to grow,—was he the Adam?

The distrustful gardener, while plucking away the dead leaves or pruning the too luxuriant growth of the shrubs, defended his hands with a pair of thick gloves. Nor were these his only armor. When, in his walk through the garden, he came to the magnificent plant that hung its purple gems beside the marble fountain, he placed a kind of mask over his mouth and nostrils, as if all this beauty did but conceal a deadlier malice; but, finding his task still too dangerous, he drew back, removed the mask, and called loudly, but in the infirm voice of a person affected with inward disease,—

"Beatrice! Beatrice!"

"Here am I, my father. What would you?" cried a rich and youthful voice from the window of the opposite house—a voice as rich as a tropical sunset, and which made Giovanni, though he knew not why, think of deep hues of purple or crimson and of perfumes heavily delectable. "Are you in the garden?"

"Yes, Beatrice," answered the gardener, "and I need your help."

Soon there emerged from under a sculptured portal the figure of a young girl, arrayed with as much richness of taste as the most splendid of the flowers, beautiful as the day, and with a bloom so deep and vivid that one shade more would have been too much. She looked redundant with life, health, and energy; all of which attributes were bound down and compressed, as it were, and girdled tensely, in their luxuriance, by her virgin zone. Yet Giovanni's fancy must have grown morbid while he looked down into the garden; for the impression which the fair stranger made upon him was as if here were another flower, the human sister of those vegetable ones, as beautiful as they, more beautiful than the richest of them, but still to be touched only with a glove, nor to be approached without a mask. As Beatrice came down the garden path, it was observable that she handled and inhaled the odor of several of the plants which her father had most sedulously avoided.

"Here, Beatrice," said the latter, "see how many needful offices require to be done to our chief treasure. Yet, shattered as I am, my life might pay the penalty of approaching it so closely as circumstances demand. Henceforth, I fear, this plant must be consigned to your sole charge."

"And gladly will I undertake it," cried again the rich tones of the young lady, as she bent towards the magnificent plant and opened her arms as if to embrace it. "Yes, my sister, my splendor, it shall be Beatrice's task to nurse and serve thee; and thou shalt reward her with thy kisses and perfumed breath, which to her is as the breath of life."

Then, with all the tenderness in her manner that was so strikingly expressed in her words, she busied herself with such attentions as the plant seemed to require; and Giovanni, at his lofty window, rubbed his eyes and almost doubted whether it were a girl tending her favorite flower, or one sister performing the duties of affection to another. The scene soon terminated. Whether Dr. Rappaccini had finished his labors in the garden, or that his watchful eye had caught the stranger's face, he now took his daughter's arm and retired. Night was already closing in; oppressive exhalations seemed to proceed from the plants and steal upward past the open window; and Giovanni, closing the lattice, went to his couch and dreamed of a rich flower and beautiful girl. Flower and maiden were different, and yet the same, and fraught with some strange peril in either shape.

But there is an influence in the light of morning that tends to rectify whatever errors of fancy, or even of judgment, we may have incurred during the sun's decline, or among the shadows of the night, or in the less wholesome glow of moonshine. Giovanni's first movement, on starting from sleep, was to throw open the window and gaze down into the garden which his dreams had made so fertile of mysteries. He was surprised and a little ashamed to find how real and matter-of-fact an affair it proved to be, in the first rays of the sun which gilded the dew-drops that hung upon leaf and blossom, and, while giving a brighter beauty to each rare flower, brought everything within the limits of ordinary experience. The young man rejoiced that, in the heart of the barren city, he had the privilege of overlooking this spot of lovely and luxuriant vegetation. It would serve, he said to himself, as a symbolic language to keep him in communion with Nature. Neither the sickly and thoughtworn Dr. Giacomo Rappaccini, it is true, nor his brilliant daughter, were now visible; so that Giovanni could not determine how much of the singularity which he attributed to both was due to their own qualities and how much to his wonder-working fancy; but he was inclined to take a most rational view of the whole matter.

In the course of the day he paid his respects to Signor Pietro Baglioni, professor of medicine in the university, a physician of eminent repute, to whom Giovanni had brought a letter of introduction. The professor was an elderly personage, apparently of genial nature, and habits that might almost be called jovial. He kept the young man to dinner, and made himself very agreeable by the freedom and liveliness of his conversation, especially when warmed by a flask or two of Tuscan wine. Giovanni, conceiving that men of science, inhabitants of the same city, must needs be on familiar terms with one another, took an opportunity to mention the name of Dr. Rappaccini. But the professor did not respond with so much cordiality as he had anticipated.

"Ill would it become a teacher of the divine art of medicine," said Professor Pietro Baglioni, in answer to a question of Giovanni, "to withhold due and well-considered praise of a physician so eminently skilled as Rappaccini; but, on the other hand, I should answer it but scantily to my conscience were I to permit a worthy youth like yourself, Signor Giovanni, the son of an ancient friend, to imbibe erroneous ideas respecting a man who might hereafter chance to hold your life and death in his hands. The truth is, our worshipful Dr. Rappaccini has as much science as any member of the faculty—with perhaps one single exception—in Padua, or all Italy; but there are certain grave objections to his professional character."

"And what are they?" asked the young man.

"Has my friend Giovanni any disease of body or heart, that he is so inquisitive about physicians?" said the professor, with a smile. "But as for Rappaccini, it is said of him—and I, who know the man well, can answer for its truth—that he cares infinitely more for science than for mankind. His patients are interesting to him only as subjects for some new experiment. He would sacrifice human life, his own among the rest, or whatever else was dearest to him, for the sake of adding so much as a grain of mustard seed to the great heap of his accumulated knowledge."

"Methinks he is an awful man indeed," remarked Guasconti, mentally recalling the cold and purely intellectual aspect of Rappaccini. "And yet, worshipful professor, is it not a noble spirit? Are there many men capable of so spiritual a love of science?"

"God forbid," answered the professor, somewhat testily; "at least, unless they take sounder views of the healing art than those adopted by Rappaccini. It is his theory that all medicinal virtues are comprised within those substances which we term vegetable poisons. These he cultivates with his own hands, and is said even to have produced new varieties of poison, more horribly deleterious than Nature, without the assistance of this learned person, would ever have plagued the world withal. That the signor doctor does less mischief than might be expected with such dangerous substances is undeniable. Now and then, it must be owned, he has effected, or seemed to effect, a marvellous cure; but, to tell you my private mind, Signor Giovanni, he should receive little credit for such instances of success,—they being probably the work of chance,—but should be held strictly accountable for his failures, which may justly be considered his own work."

The youth might have taken Baglioni's opinions with many grains of allowance had he known that there was a professional warfare of long continuance between him and Dr. Rappaccini, in which the latter was generally thought to have gained the advantage. If the reader be inclined to judge for himself, we refer him to certain black-letter tracts on both sides, preserved in the medical department of the University of Padua.

"I know not, most learned professor," returned Giovanni, after musing on what had been said of Rappaccini's exclusive zeal for science,—"I know not how dearly this physician may love his art; but surely there is one object more dear to him. He has a daughter."

"Aha!" cried the professor, with a laugh. "So now our friend Giovanni's secret is out. You have heard of this daughter, whom all the young men in Padua are wild about, though not half a dozen have ever had the good hap to see her face. I know little of the Signora Beatrice save that Rappaccini is said to have instructed her deeply in his science, and that, young and beautiful as fame reports her, she is already qualified to fill a professor's chair. Perchance her father destines her for mine! Other absurd rumors there be, not worth talking about or listening to. So now, Signor Giovanni, drink off your glass of lachryma."

Guasconti returned to his lodgings somewhat heated with the wine he had quaffed, and which caused his brain to swim with strange fantasies in reference to Dr. Rappaccini and the beautiful Beatrice. On his way, happening to pass by a florist's, he bought a fresh bouquet of flowers.

Ascending to his chamber, he seated himself near the window, but within the shadow thrown by the depth of the wall, so that he could look down into the garden with little risk of being discovered. All beneath his eye was a solitude. The strange plants were basking in the sunshine, and now and then nodding gently to one another, as if in acknowledgment of sympathy and kindred. In the midst, by the shattered fountain, grew the magnificent shrub, with its purple gems clustering all over it; they glowed in the air, and gleamed back again out of the depths of the pool, which thus seemed to overflow with colored radiance from the rich reflection that was steeped in it. At first, as we have said, the garden was a solitude. Soon, however,—as Giovanni had half hoped, half feared, would be the case,—a figure appeared beneath the antique sculptured portal, and came down between the rows of plants, inhaling their various perfumes as if she were one of those beings of old classic fable that lived upon sweet odors. On again beholding Beatrice, the young man was even startled to perceive how much her beauty exceeded his recollection of it; so brilliant, so vivid, was its character, that she glowed amid the sunlight, and, as Giovanni whispered to himself, positively illuminated the more shadowy intervals of the garden path. Her face being now more revealed than on the former occasion, he was struck by its expression of simplicity and sweetness,—qualities that had not entered into his idea of her character, and which made him ask anew what manner of mortal she might be. Nor did he fail again to observe, or imagine, an analogy between the beautiful girl and the gorgeous shrub that hung its gemlike flowers over the fountain,—a resemblance which Beatrice seemed to have indulged a fantastic humor in heightening, both by the arrangement of her dress and the selection of its hues.

Approaching the shrub, she threw open her arms, as with a passionate ardor, and drew its branches into an intimate embrace—so intimate that her features were hidden in its leafy bosom and her glistening ringlets all intermingled with the flowers.

"Give me thy breath, my sister," exclaimed Beatrice; "for I am faint with common air. And give me this flower of thine, which I separate with gentlest fingers from the stem and place it close beside my heart."

With these words the beautiful daughter of Rappaccini plucked one of the richest blossoms of the shrub, and was about to fasten it in her bosom. But now, unless Giovanni's draughts of wine had bewildered his senses, a singular incident occurred. A small orange-colored reptile, of the lizard or chameleon species, chanced to be creeping along the path, just at the feet of Beatrice. It appeared to Giovanni,—but, at the distance from which he gazed, he could scarcely have seen anything so minute,—it appeared to him, however, that a drop or two of moisture from the broken stem of the flower descended upon the lizard's head. For an instant the reptile contorted itself violently, and then lay motionless in the sunshine. Beatrice observed this remarkable phenomenon, and crossed herself, sadly, but without surprise; nor did she therefore hesitate to arrange the fatal flower in her bosom. There it blushed, and almost glimmered with the dazzling effect of a precious stone, adding to her dress and aspect the one appropriate charm which nothing else in the world could have supplied. But Giovanni, out of the shadow of his window, bent forward and shrank back, and murmured and trembled.

"Am I awake? Have I my senses?" said he to himself. "What is this being? Beautiful shall I call her, or inexpressibly terrible?"

Beatrice now strayed carelessly through the garden, approaching closer beneath Giovanni's window, so that he was compelled to thrust his head quite out of its concealment in order to gratify the intense and painful curiosity which she excited. At this moment there came a beautiful insect over the garden wall; it had, perhaps, wandered through the city, and found no flowers or verdure among those antique haunts of men until the heavy perfumes of Dr. Rappaccini's shrubs had lured it from afar. Without alighting on the flowers, this winged brightness seemed to be attracted by Beatrice, and lingered in the air and fluttered about her head. Now, here it could not be but that Giovanni Guasconti's eyes deceived him. Be that as it might, he fancied that, while Beatrice was gazing at the insect with childish delight, it grew faint and fell at her feet; its bright wings shivered; it was dead—from no cause that he could discern, unless it were the atmosphere of her breath. Again Beatrice crossed herself and sighed heavily as she bent over the dead insect.

An impulsive movement of Giovanni drew her eyes to the window. There she beheld the beautiful head of the young man—rather a Grecian than an Italian head, with fair, regular features, and a glistening of gold among his ringlets—gazing down upon her like a being that hovered in mid air. Scarcely knowing what he did, Giovanni threw down the bouquet which he had hitherto held in his hand.

"Signora," said he, "there are pure and healthful flowers. Wear them for the sake of Giovanni Guasconti."

"Thanks, signor," replied Beatrice, with her rich voice, that came forth as it were like a gush of music, and with a mirthful expression half childish and half woman-like. "I accept your gift, and would fain recompense it with this precious purple flower; but if I toss it into the air it will not reach you. So Signor Guasconti must even content himself with my thanks."

She lifted the bouquet from the ground, and then, as if inwardly ashamed at having stepped aside from her maidenly reserve to respond to a stranger's greeting, passed swiftly homeward through the garden. But few as the moments were, it seemed to Giovanni, when she was on the point of vanishing beneath the sculptured portal, that his beautiful bouquet was already beginning to wither in her grasp. It was an idle thought; there could be no possibility of distinguishing a faded flower from a fresh one at so great a distance.

For many days after this incident the young man avoided the window that looked into Dr. Rappaccini's garden, as if something ugly and monstrous would have blasted his eyesight had he been betrayed into a glance. He felt conscious of having put himself, to a certain extent, within the influence of an unintelligible power by the communication which he had opened with Beatrice. The wisest course would have been, if his heart were in any real danger, to quit his lodgings and Padua itself at once; the next wiser, to have accustomed himself, as far as possible, to the familiar and daylight view of Beatrice—thus bringing her rigidly and systematically within the limits of ordinary experience. Least of all, while avoiding her sight, ought Giovanni to have remained so near this extraordinary being that the proximity and possibility even of intercourse should give a kind of substance and reality to the wild vagaries which his imagination ran riot continually in producing. Guasconti had not a deep heart—or, at all events, its depths were not sounded now; but he had a quick fancy, and an ardent southern temperament, which rose every instant to a higher fever pitch. Whether or no Beatrice possessed those terrible attributes, that fatal breath, the affinity with those so beautiful and deadly flowers which were indicated by what Giovanni had witnessed, she had at least instilled a fierce and subtle poison into his system. It was not love, although her rich beauty was a madness to him; nor horror, even while he fancied her spirit to be imbued with the same baneful essence that seemed to pervade her physical frame; but a wild offspring of both love and horror that had each parent in it, and burned like one and shivered like the other. Giovanni knew not what to dread; still less did he know what to hope; yet hope and dread kept a continual warfare in his breast, alternately vanquishing one another and starting up afresh to renew the contest. Blessed are all simple emotions, be they dark or bright! It is the lurid intermixture of the two that produces the illuminating blaze of the infernal regions.

Sometimes he endeavored to assuage the fever of his spirit by a rapid walk through the streets of Padua or beyond its gates: his footsteps kept time with the throbbings of his brain, so that the walk was apt to accelerate itself to a race. One day he found himself arrested; his arm was seized by a portly personage, who had turned back on recognizing the young man and expended much breath in overtaking him.

"Signor Giovanni! Stay, my young friend!" cried he. "Have you forgotten me? That might well be the case if I were as much altered as yourself."

It was Baglioni, whom Giovanni had avoided ever since their first meeting, from a doubt that the professor's sagacity would look too deeply into his secrets. Endeavoring to recover himself, he stared forth wildly from his inner world into the outer one and spoke like a man in a dream.

"Yes; I am Giovanni Guasconti. You are Professor Pietro Baglioni. Now let me pass!"

"Not yet, not yet, Signor Giovanni Guasconti," said the professor, smiling, but at the same time scrutinizing the youth with an earnest glance. "What! did I grow up side by side with your father? and shall his son pass me like a stranger in these old streets of Padua? Stand still, Signor Giovanni; for we must have a word or two before we part."

"Speedily, then, most worshipful professor, speedily," said Giovanni, with feverish impatience. "Does not your worship see that I am in haste?"

Now, while he was speaking there came a man in black along the street, stooping and moving feebly like a person in inferior health. His face was all overspread with a most sickly and sallow hue, but yet so pervaded with an expression of piercing and active intellect that an observer might easily have overlooked the merely physical attributes and have seen only this wonderful energy. As he passed, this person exchanged a cold and distant salutation with Baglioni, but fixed his eyes upon Giovanni with an intentness that seemed to bring out whatever was within him worthy of notice. Nevertheless, there was a peculiar quietness in the look, as if taking merely a speculative, not a human, interest in the young man.

"It is Dr. Rappaccini!" whispered the professor when the stranger had passed. "Has he ever seen your face before?"

"Not that I know," answered Giovanni, starting at the name.

"He *has* seen you! he must have seen you!" said Baglioni, hastily. "For some purpose or other, this man of science is making a study of you. I know that look of his! It is the same that coldly illuminates his face as he bends over a bird, a mouse, or a butterfly, which, in pursuance of some experiment, he has killed by the perfume of a flower; a look as deep as Nature itself, but without Nature's warmth of love. Signor Giovanni, I will stake my life upon it, you are the subject of one of Rappaccini's experiments!"

"Will you make a fool of me?" cried Giovanni, passionately. "*That,* signor professor, were an untoward experiment."

"Patience! patience!" replied the imperturbable professor. "I tell thee, my poor Giovanni, that Rappaccini has a scientific interest in thee. Thou hast fallen into fearful hands! And the Signora Beatrice,—what part does she act in this mystery?"

But Guasconti, finding Baglioni's pertinacity intolerable, here broke away, and was gone before the professor could again seize his arm. He looked after the young man intently and shook his head.

"This must not be," said Baglioni to himself. "The youth is the son of my old friend, and shall not come to any harm from which the arcana of medical science can preserve him. Besides, it is too insufferable an impertinence in Rappaccini, thus to snatch the lad out of my own hands, as I may say, and make use of him for his infernal experiments. This daughter of his! It shall be looked to. Perchance, most learned Rappaccini, I may foil you where you little dream of it!"

Meanwhile Giovanni had pursued a circuitous route, and at length found himself at the door of his lodgings. As he crossed the threshold he was met by old Lisabetta, who smirked and smiled, and was evidently desirous to attract his attention; vainly, however, as the ebullition of his feelings had momentarily subsided into a cold and dull vacuity. He turned his eyes full upon the withered face that was puckering itself into a smile, but seemed to behold it not. The old dame, therefore, laid her grasp upon his cloak.

"Signor! signor!" whispered she, still with a smile over the whole breadth of her visage, so that it looked not unlike a grotesque carving in wood, darkened by centuries. "Listen, signor! There is a private entrance into the garden!"

"What do you say?" exclaimed Giovanni, turning quickly about, as if an inanimate thing should start into feverish life. "A private entrance into Dr. Rappaccini's garden?"

"Hush! hush! not so loud!" whispered Lisabetta, putting her hand over his mouth. "Yes; into the worshipful doctor's garden, where you may see all his fine shrubbery. Many a young man in Padua would give gold to be admitted among those flowers."

Giovanni put a piece of gold into her hand.

"Show me the way," said he.

A surmise, probably excited by his conversation with Baglioni, crossed his mind, that this interposition of old Lisabetta might perchance be connected with the intrigue, whatever were its nature, in which the professor seemed to suppose that Dr. Rappaccini was involving him. But such a suspicion, though it disturbed Giovanni, was inadequate to restrain him. The instant that he was aware of the possibility of approaching Beatrice, it seemed an absolute necessity of his existence to do so. It mattered not whether she were angel or demon; he was irrevocably within her sphere, and must obey the law that whirled him onward, in ever-lessening circles, towards a result which he did not attempt to foreshadow; and yet, strange to say, there came across him a sudden doubt whether this intense interest on his part were not delusory; whether it were really of so deep and positive a nature as to justify him in now thrusting himself into an incalculable position; whether it were not merely the fantasy of a young man's brain, only slightly or not at all connected with his heart.

He paused, hesitated, turned half about, but again went on. His withered guide led him along several obscure passages, and finally undid a door, through which, as it was opened, there came the sight and sound of rustling leaves, with the broken sunshine glimmering among them. Giovanni stepped forth, and, forcing himself through the entanglement of a shrub that wreathed its tendrils over the hidden entrance, stood beneath his own window in the open area of Dr. Rappaccini's garden.

How often is it the case that, when impossibilities have come to pass and dreams have condensed their misty substance into tangible realities, we find ourselves calm, and even coldly self-possessed, amid circumstances which it would have been a delirium of joy or agony to anticipate! Fate delights to thwart us thus. Passion will choose his own time to rush upon the scene, and lingers sluggishly behind when an appropriate adjustment of events would seem to summon his appearance. So was it now with Giovanni. Day after day his pulses had throbbed with feverish blood at the improbable idea of an interview with Beatrice, and of standing with her, face to face, in this very garden, basking in the Oriental sunshine of her beauty, and snatching from her full gaze the mystery which he deemed the riddle of his own existence. But now there was a singular and untimely equanimity within his breast. He threw a glance around the garden to discover if Beatrice or her father were present, and, perceiving that he was alone, began a critical observation of the plants.

The aspect of one and all of them dissatisfied him; their gorgeousness seemed fierce, passionate, and even unnatural. There was hardly an individual shrub which a wanderer, straying by himself through a forest, would not have been startled to find growing wild, as if an unearthly face had glared at him out of the thicket. Several also would have shocked a delicate instinct by an appearance of artificialness indicating that there had been such commixture, and, as it were, adultery, of various vegetable species, that the production was no longer of God's making, but the monstrous offspring of man's depraved fancy, glowing with only an evil mockery of beauty. They were probably the result of experiment, which in one or two cases had succeeded in mingling plants individually lovely into a compound possessing the questionable and ominous character that distinguished the whole growth of the garden. In fine, Giovanni recognized but two or three plants in the collection, and those of a kind that he well knew to be poisonous. While busy with these contemplations he heard the rustling of a silken garment, and, turning, beheld Beatrice emerging from beneath the sculptured portal.

Giovanni had not considered with himself what should be his deportment; whether he should apologize for his intrusion into the garden, or assume that he was there with the privity at least, if not by the desire, of Dr. Rappaccini or his daughter; but Beatrice's manner placed him at his ease, though leaving him still in doubt by what agency he had gained admittance. She came lightly along the path and met him near the broken fountain. There was surprise in her face, but brightened by a simple and kind expression of pleasure.

"You are a connoisseur in flowers, signor," said Beatrice, with a smile, alluding to the bouquet which he had flung her from the window. "It is no marvel, therefore, if the sight of my father's rare collection has tempted you to take a nearer view. If he were here, he could tell you many strange and interesting facts as to the nature and habits of these shrubs; for he has spent a lifetime in such studies, and this garden is his world."

"And yourself, lady," observed Giovanni, "if fame says true,—you likewise are deeply skilled in the virtues indicated by these rich blossoms and these spicy perfumes. Would you deign to be my instructress, I should prove an apter scholar than if taught by Signor Rappaccini himself."

"Are there such idle rumors?" asked Beatrice, with the music of a pleasant laugh. "Do people say that I am skilled in my father's science of plants? What a jest is there! No; though I have grown up among these flowers, I know no more of them than their hues and perfume; and sometimes methinks I would fain rid myself of even that small knowledge. There are many flowers here, and those not the least brilliant, that shock and offend me when they meet my eye. But pray, signor, do not believe these stories about my science. Believe nothing of me save what you see with your own eyes."

"And must I believe all that I have seen with my own eyes?" asked Giovanni, pointedly, while the recollection of former scenes made him shrink. "No, signora; you demand too little of me. Bid me believe nothing save what comes from your own lips."

It would appear that Beatrice understood him. There came a deep flush to her cheek; but she looked full into Giovanni's eyes, and responded to his gaze of uneasy suspicion with a queenlike haughtiness.

"I do so bid you, signor," she replied. "Forget whatever you may have fancied in regard to me. If true to the outward senses, still it may be false in its essence; but the words of Beatrice Rappaccini's lips are true from the depths of the heart outward. Those you may believe."

A fervor glowed in her whole aspect and beamed upon Giovanni's consciousness like the light of truth itself; but while she spoke there was a fragrance in the atmosphere around her, rich and delightful, though evanescent, yet which the young man, from an indefinable reluctance, scarcely dared to draw into his lungs. It might be the odor of the flowers. Could it be Beatrice's breath which thus embalmed her words with a strange richness, as if by steeping them in her heart? A faintness passed like a shadow over Giovanni and flitted away; he seemed to gaze through the beautiful girl's eyes into her transparent soul, and felt no more doubt or fear.

The tinge of passion that had colored Beatrice's manner vanished; she became gay, and appeared to derive a pure delight from her communion with the youth not unlike what the maiden of a lonely island might have felt conversing with a voyager from the civilized world. Evidently her experience of life had been confined within the limits of that garden. She talked now about matters as simple as the daylight or summer clouds, and now asked questions in reference to the city, or Giovanni's distant home, his friends, his mother, and his sisters—questions indicating such seclusion, and such lack of familiarity with modes and forms, that Giovanni responded as if to an infant. Her spirit gushed out before him like a fresh rill that was just catching its first glimpse of the sunlight and wondering at the reflections of earth and sky which were flung into its bosom. There came thoughts, too, from a deep source, and fantasies of a gemlike brilliancy, as if diamonds and rubies sparkled upward among the bubbles of the fountain. Ever and anon there gleamed across the young man's mind a sense of wonder that he should be walking side by side with the being who had so wrought upon his imagination, whom he had idealized in such hues of terror, in whom he had positively witnessed such manifestations of dreadful attributes,—that he should be conversing with Beatrice like a brother, and should find her so human and so maidenlike. But such reflections were only momentary; the effect of her character was too real not to make itself familiar at once.

In this free intercourse they had strayed through the garden, and now, after many turns among its avenues, were come to the shattered fountain, beside which grew the magnificent shrub, with its treasury of glowing blossoms. A fragrance was diffused from it which Giovanni recognized as identical with that which he had attributed to Beatrice's breath, but incomparably more powerful. As her eyes fell upon it, Giovanni beheld her press her hand to her bosom as if her heart were throbbing suddenly and painfully.

"For the first time in my life," murmured she, addressing the shrub, "I had forgotten thee."

"I remember, signora," said Giovanni, "that you once promised to reward me with one of these living gems for the bouquet which I had the happy boldness to fling to your feet. Permit me now to pluck it as a memorial of this interview."

He made a step towards the shrub with extended hand; but Beatrice darted forward, uttering a shriek that went through his heart like a dagger. She caught his hand and drew it back with the whole force of her slender figure. Giovanni felt her touch thrilling through his fibres.

"Touch it not!" exclaimed she, in a voice of agony. "Not for thy life! It is fatal!"

Then, hiding her face, she fled from him and vanished beneath the sculptured portal. As Giovanni followed her with his eyes, he beheld the emaciated figure and pale intelligence of Dr. Rappaccini, who had been watching the scene, he knew not how long, within the shadow of the entrance.

No sooner was Guasconti alone in his chamber than the image of Beatrice came back to his passionate musings, invested with all the witchery that had been gathering around it ever since his first glimpse of her, and now likewise imbued with a tender warmth of girlish womanhood. She was human; her nature was endowed with all gentle and feminine qualities; she was worthiest to be worshipped; she was capable, surely, on her part, of the height and heroism of love. Those tokens which he had hitherto considered as proofs of a frightful peculiarity in her physical and moral system were now either forgotten, or, by the subtle sophistry of passion transmitted into a golden crown of enchantment, rendering Beatrice the more admirable by so much as she was the more unique. Whatever had looked ugly was now beautiful; or, if incapable of such a change, it stole away and hid itself among those shapeless half ideas which throng the dim region beyond the daylight of our perfect consciousness. Thus did he spend the night, nor fell asleep until the dawn had begun to awake the slumbering flowers in Dr. Rappaccini's garden, whither Giovanni's dreams doubtless led him. Up rose the sun in his due season, and, flinging his beams upon the young man's eyelids, awoke him to a sense of pain. When thoroughly aroused, he became sensible of a burning and tingling agony in his hand—in his right hand—the very hand which Beatrice had grasped in her own when he was on the point of plucking one of the gem-like flowers. On the back of that hand there was now a purple print like that of four small fingers, and the likeness of a slender thumb upon his wrist.

Oh, how stubbornly does love,—or even that cunning semblance of love which flourishes in the imagination, but strikes no depth of root into the heart,—how stubbornly does it hold its faith until the moment comes when it is doomed to vanish into thin mist! Giovanni wrapped a handkerchief about his hand and wondered what evil thing had stung him, and soon forgot his pain in a reverie of Beatrice.

After the first interview, a second was in the inevitable course of what we call fate. A third; a fourth; and a meeting with Beatrice in the garden was no longer an incident in Giovanni's daily life, but the whole space in which he might be said to live; for the anticipation and memory of that ecstatic hour made up the remainder. Nor was it otherwise with the daughter of Rappaccini. She watched for the youth's appearance, and flew to his side with confidence as unreserved as if they had been playmates from early infancy—as if they were such playmates still. If, by any unwonted chance, he failed to come at the appointed moment, she stood beneath the window and sent up the rich sweetness of her tones to float around him in his chamber and echo and reverberate throughout his heart: "Giovanni! Giovanni! Why tarriest thou? Come down!" And down he hastened into that Eden of poisonous flowers.

But, with all this intimate familiarity, there was still a reserve in Beatrice's demeanor, so rigidly and invariably sustained that the idea of infringing it scarcely occurred to his imagination. By all appreciable signs, they loved; they had looked love with eyes that conveyed the holy secret from the depths of one soul into the depths of the other, as if it were too sacred to be whispered by the way; they had even spoken love in those gushes of passion when their spirits darted forth in articulated breath like tongues of long-hidden flame; and yet there had been no seal of lips, no clasp of hands, nor any slightest caress such as love claims and hallows. He had never touched one of the gleaming ringlets of her hair; her garment—so marked was the physical barrier between them—had never been waved against him by a breeze. On the few occasions when Giovanni had seemed tempted to overstep the limit, Beatrice grew so sad, so stern, and withal wore such a look of desolate separation, shuddering at itself, that not a spoken word was requisite to repel him. At such times he was startled at the horrible suspicions that rose, monster-like, out of the caverns of his heart and stared him in the face; his love grew thin and faint as the morning mist, his doubts alone had substance. But, when Beatrice's face brightened again after the momentary shadow, she was transformed at once from the mysterious, questionable being whom he had watched with so much awe and horror; she was now the beautiful and unsophisticated girl whom he felt that his spirit knew with a certainty beyond all other knowledge.

A considerable time had now passed since Giovanni's last meeting with Baglioni. One morning, however, he was disagreeably surprised by a visit from the professor, whom he had scarcely thought of for whole weeks, and would willingly have forgotten still longer. Given up as he had long been to a pervading excitement, he could tolerate no companions except upon condition of their perfect sympathy with his present state of feeling. Such sympathy was not to be expected from Professor Baglioni.

The visitor chatted carelessly for a few moments about the gossip of the city and the university, and then took up another topic.

"I have been reading an old classic author lately," said he, "and met with a story that strangely interested me. Possibly you may remember it. It is of an Indian prince, who sent a beautiful woman as a present to Alexander the Great. She was as lovely as the dawn and gorgeous as the sunset; but what especially distinguished her was a certain rich perfume in her breath—richer than a garden of Persian roses. Alexander, as was natural to a youthful conqueror, fell in love at first sight with this magnificent stranger; but a certain sage physician, happening to be present, discovered a terrible secret in regard to her."

"And what was that?" asked Giovanni, turning his eyes downward to avoid those of the professor.

"That this lovely woman," continued Baglioni, with emphasis, "had been nourished with poisons from her birth upward, until her whole nature was so imbued with them that she herself had become the deadliest poison in existence. Poison was her element of life. With that rich perfume of her breath she blasted the very air. Her love would have been poison—her embrace death. Is not this a marvellous tale?"

"A childish fable," answered Giovanni, nervously starting from his chair. "I marvel how your worship finds time to read such nonsense among your graver studies."

"By the by," said the professor, looking uneasily about him, "what singular fragrance is this in your apartment? Is it the perfume of your gloves? It is faint, but delicious; and yet, after all, by no means agreeable. Were I to breathe it long, methinks it would make me ill. It is like the breath of a flower; but I see no flowers in the chamber."

"Nor are there any," replied Giovanni, who had turned pale as the professor spoke; "nor, I think, is there any fragrance except in your worship's imagination. Odors, being a sort of element combined of the sensual and the spiritual, are apt to deceive us in this manner. The recollection of a perfume, the bare idea of it, may easily be mistaken for a present reality."

"Aye; but my sober imagination does not often play such tricks," said Baglioni; "and, were I to fancy any kind of odor, it would be that of some vile apothecary drug, wherewith my fingers are likely enough to be imbued. Our worshipful friend Rappaccini, as I have heard, tinctures his medicaments with odors richer than those of Araby. Doubtless, likewise, the fair and learned Signora Beatrice would minister to her patients with draughts as sweet as a maiden's breath; but woe to him that sips them!"

Giovanni's face evinced many contending emotions. The tone in which the professor alluded to the pure and lovely daughter of Rappaccini was a torture to his soul; and yet the intimation of a view of her character, opposite to his own, gave instantaneous distinctness to a thousand dim suspicions, which now grinned at him like so many demons. But he strove hard to quell them and to respond to Baglioni with a true lover's perfect faith.

"Signor professor," said he, "you were my father's friend; perchance, too, it is your purpose to act a friendly part towards his son. I would fain feel nothing towards you save respect and deference; but I pray you to observe, signor, that there is one subject on which we must not speak. You know not the Signora Beatrice. You cannot, therefore, estimate the wrong—the blasphemy, I may even say—that is offered to her character by a light or injurious word."

"Giovanni! my poor Giovanni!" answered the professor, with a calm expression of pity, "I know this wretched girl far better than yourself. You shall hear the truth in respect to the poisoner Rappaccini and his poisonous daughter; yes, poisonous as she is beautiful. Listen; for, even should you do violence to my gray hairs, it shall not silence me. That old fable of the Indian woman has become a truth by the deep and deadly science of Rappaccini and in the person of the lovely Beatrice."

Giovanni groaned and hid his face.

"Her father," continued Baglioni, "was not restrained by natural affection from offering up his child in this horrible manner as the victim of his insane zeal for science; for, let us do him justice, he is as true a man of science as ever distilled his own heart in an alembic. What, then, will be your fate? Beyond a doubt you are selected as the material of some new experiment. Perhaps the result is to be death; perhaps a fate more awful still. Rappaccini, with what he calls the interest of science before his eyes, will hesitate at nothing."

"It is a dream," muttered Giovanni to himself; "surely it is a dream."

"But," resumed the professor, "be of good cheer, son of my friend. It is not yet too late for the rescue. Possibly we may even succeed in bringing back this miserable child within the limits of ordinary nature, from which her father's madness has estranged her. Behold this little silver vase! It was wrought by the hands of the renowned Benvenuto Cellini, and is well worthy to be a love gift to the fairest dame in Italy. But its contents are invaluable. One little sip of this antidote would have rendered the most virulent poisons of the Borgias innocuous. Doubt not that it will be as efficacious against those of Rappaccini. Bestow the vase, and the precious liquid within it, on your Beatrice, and hopefully await the result."

Baglioni laid a small, exquisitely wrought silver vial on the table and withdrew, leaving what he had said to produce its effect upon the young man's mind.

"We will thwart Rappaccini yet," thought he, chuckling to himself, as he descended the stairs; "but, let us confess the truth of him, he is a wonderful man—a wonderful man indeed; a vile empiric, however, in his practice, and therefore not to be tolerated by those who respect the good old rules of the medical profession."

Throughout Giovanni's whole acquaintance with Beatrice, he had occasionally, as we have said, been haunted by dark surmises as to her character; yet so thoroughly had she made herself felt by him as a simple, natural, most affectionate, and guileless creature, that the image now held up by Professor Baglioni looked as strange and incredible as if it were not in accordance with his own original conception. True, there were ugly recollections connected with his first glimpses of the beautiful girl; he could not quite forget the bouquet that withered in her grasp, and the insect that perished amid the sunny air, by no ostensible agency save the fragrance of her breath. These incidents, however, dissolving in the pure light of her character, had no longer the efficacy of facts, but were acknowledged as mistaken fantasies, by whatever testimony of the senses they might appear to be substantiated. There is something truer and more real than what we can see with the eyes and touch with the finger. On such better evidence had Giovanni founded his confidence in Beatrice, though rather by the necessary force of her high attributes than by any deep and generous faith on his part. But now his spirit was incapable of sustaining itself at the height to which the early enthusiasm of passion had exalted it; he fell down, grovelling among earthly doubts, and defiled therewith the pure whiteness of Beatrice's image. Not that he gave her up; he did but distrust. He resolved to institute some decisive test that should satisfy him, once for all, whether there were those dreadful peculiarities in her physical nature which could not be supposed to exist without some corresponding monstrosity of soul. His eyes, gazing down afar, might have deceived him as to the lizard, the insect, and the flowers; but if he could witness, at the distance of a few paces, the sudden blight of one fresh and healthful flower in Beatrice's hand, there would be room for no further question. With this idea he hastened to the florist's and purchased a bouquet that was still gemmed with the morning dew-drops.

It was now the customary hour of his daily interview with Beatrice. Before descending into the garden, Giovanni failed not to look at his figure in the mirror,—a vanity to be expected in a beautiful young man, yet, as displaying itself at that troubled and feverish moment, the token of a certain shallowness of feeling and insincerity of character. He did gaze, however, and said to himself that his features had never before possessed so rich a grace, nor his eyes such vivacity, nor his cheeks so warm a hue of superabundant life.

"At least," thought he, "her poison has not yet insinuated itself into my system. I am no flower to perish in her grasp."

With that thought he turned his eyes on the bouquet, which he had never once laid aside from his hand. A thrill of indefinable horror shot through his frame on perceiving that those dewy flowers were already beginning to droop; they wore the aspect of things that had been fresh and lovely yesterday. Giovanni grew white as marble, and stood motionless before the mirror, staring at his own reflection there as at the likeness of something frightful. He remembered Baglioni's remark about the fragrance that seemed to pervade the chamber. It must have been the poison in his breath! Then he shuddered—shuddered at himself. Recovering from his stupor, he began to watch with curious eye a spider that was busily at work hanging its web from the antique cornice of the apartment, crossing and recrossing the artful system of interwoven lines—as vigorous and active a spider as ever dangled from an old ceiling. Giovanni bent towards the insect, and emitted a deep, long breath. The spider suddenly ceased its toil; the web vibrated with a tremor originating in the body of the small artisan. Again Giovanni sent forth a breath, deeper, longer, and imbued with a venomous feeling out of his heart: he knew not whether he were wicked, or only desperate. The spider made a convulsive gripe with his limbs and hung dead across the window.

"Accursed! accursed!" muttered Giovanni, addressing himself. "Hast thou grown so poisonous that this deadly insect perishes by thy breath?"

At that moment a rich, sweet voice came floating up from the garden.

"Giovanni! Giovanni! It is past the hour! Why tarriest thou? Come down!"

"Yes," muttered Giovanni again. "She is the only being whom my breath may not slay! Would that it might!"

He rushed down, and in an instant was standing before the bright and loving eyes of Beatrice. A moment ago his wrath and despair had been so fierce that he could have desired nothing so much as to wither her by a glance; but with her actual presence there came influences which had too real an existence to be at once shaken off: recollections of the delicate and benign power of her feminine nature, which had so often enveloped him in a religious calm; recollections of many a holy and passionate outgush of her heart, when the pure fountain had been unsealed from its depths and made visible in its transparency to his mental eye; recollections which, had Giovanni known how to estimate them, would have assured him that all this ugly mystery was but an earthly illusion, and that, whatever mist of evil might seem to have gathered over her, the real Beatrice was a heavenly angel. Incapable as he was of such high faith, still her presence had not utterly lost its magic. Giovanni's rage was quelled into an aspect of sullen insensibility. Beatrice, with a quick spiritual sense, immediately felt that there was a gulf of blackness between them which neither he nor she could pass. They walked on together, sad and silent, and came thus to the marble fountain and to its pool of water on the ground, in the midst of which grew the shrub that bore gem-like blossoms. Giovanni was affrighted at the eager enjoyment—the appetite, as it were—with which he found himself inhaling the fragrance of the flowers.

"Beatrice," asked he, abruptly, "whence came this shrub?"

"My father created it," answered she, with simplicity.

"Created it! created it!" repeated Giovanni. "What mean you, Beatrice?"

"He is a man fearfully acquainted with the secrets of Nature," replied Beatrice; "and, at the hour when I first drew breath, this plant sprang from the soil, the offspring of his science, of his intellect, while I was but his earthly child. Approach it not!" continued she, observing with terror that Giovanni was drawing nearer to the shrub. "It has qualities that you little dream of. But I, dearest Giovanni,—I grew up and blossomed with the plant and was nourished with its breath. It was my sister, and I loved it with a human affection; for, alas!—hast thou not suspected it?—there was an awful doom."

Here Giovanni frowned so darkly upon her that Beatrice paused and trembled. But her faith in his tenderness reassured her, and made her blush that she had doubted for an instant.

"There was an awful doom," she continued, "the effect of my father's fatal love of science, which estranged me from all society of my kind. Until Heaven sent thee, dearest Giovanni, oh, how lonely was thy poor Beatrice!"

"Was it a hard doom?" asked Giovanni, fixing his eyes upon her.

"Only of late have I known how hard it was," answered she, tenderly. "Oh, yes; but my heart was torpid, and therefore quiet."

Giovanni's rage broke forth from his sullen gloom like a lightning flash out of a dark cloud.

"Accursed one!" cried he, with venomous scorn and anger. "And, finding thy solitude wearisome, thou hast severed me likewise from all the warmth of life and enticed me into thy region of unspeakable horror!"

"Giovanni!" exclaimed Beatrice, turning her large bright eyes upon his face. The force of his words had not found its way into her mind; she was merely thunderstruck.

"Yes, poisonous thing!" repeated Giovanni, beside himself with passion. "Thou hast done it! Thou hast blasted me! Thou hast filled my veins with poison! Thou hast made me as hateful, as ugly, as loathsome and deadly a creature as thyself—a world's wonder of hideous monstrosity! Now, if our breath be happily as fatal to ourselves as to all others, let us join our lips in one kiss of unutterable hatred, and so die!"

"What has befallen me?" murmured Beatrice, with a low moan out of her heart. "Holy Virgin, pity me, a poor heart-broken child!"

"Thou,—dost thou pray?" cried Giovanni, still with the same fiendish scorn. "Thy very prayers, as they come from thy lips, taint the atmosphere with death. Yes, yes; let us pray! Let us to church and dip our fingers in the holy water at the portal! They that come after us will perish as by a pestilence! Let us sign crosses in the air! It will be scattering curses abroad in the likeness of holy symbols!"

"Giovanni," said Beatrice, calmly, for her grief was beyond passion, "why dost thou join thyself with me thus in those terrible words? I, it is true, am the horrible thing thou namest me. But thou,—what hast thou to do, save with one other shudder at my hideous misery to go forth out of the garden and mingle with thy race, and forget that there ever crawled on earth such a monster as poor Beatrice?"

"Dost thou pretend ignorance?" asked Giovanni, scowling upon her. "Behold! this power have I gained from the pure daughter of Rappaccini."

There was a swarm of summer insects flitting through the air in search of the food promised by the flower odors of the fatal garden. They circled round Giovanni's head, and were evidently attracted towards him by the same influence which had drawn them for an instant within the sphere of several of the shrubs. He sent forth a breath among them, and smiled bitterly at Beatrice as at least a score of the insects fell dead upon the ground.

"I see it! I see it!" shrieked Beatrice. "It is my father's fatal science! No, no, Giovanni; it was not I! Never! never! I dreamed only to love thee and be with thee a little time, and so to let thee pass away, leaving but thine image in mine heart; for, Giovanni, believe it, though my body be nourished with poison, my spirit is God's creature, and craves love as its daily food. But my father,—he has united us in this fearful sympathy. Yes; spurn me, tread upon me, kill me! Oh, what is death after such words as thine? But it was not I. Not for a world of bliss would I have done it."

Giovanni's passion had exhausted itself in its outburst from his lips. There now came across him a sense, mournful, and not without tenderness, of the intimate and peculiar relationship between Beatrice and himself. They stood, as it were, in an utter solitude, which would be made none the less solitary by the densest throng of human life. Ought not, then, the desert of humanity around them to press this insulated pair closer together? If they should be cruel to one another, who was there to be kind to them? Besides, thought Giovanni, might there not still be a hope of his returning within the limits of ordinary nature, and leading Beatrice, the redeemed Beatrice, by the hand? O, weak, and selfish, and unworthy spirit, that could dream of an earthly union and earthly happiness as possible, after such deep love had been so bitterly wronged as was Beatrice's love by Giovanni's blighting words! No, no; there could be no such hope. She must pass heavily, with that broken heart, across the borders of Time—she must bathe her hurts in some fount of paradise, and forget her grief in the light of immortality, and *there* be well.

But Giovanni did not know it.

"Dear Beatrice," said he, approaching her, while she shrank away as always at his approach, but now with a different impulse, "dearest Beatrice, our fate is not yet so desperate. Behold! there is a medicine, potent, as a wise physician has assured me, and almost divine in its efficacy. It is composed of ingredients the most opposite to those by which thy awful father has brought this calamity upon thee and me. It is distilled of blessed herbs. Shall we not quaff it together, and thus be purified from evil?"

"Give it me!" said Beatrice, extending her hand to receive the little silver vial which Giovanni took from his bosom. She added, with a peculiar emphasis, "I will drink; but do thou await the result."

She put Baglioni's antidote to her lips; and, at the same moment, the figure of Rappaccini emerged from the portal and came slowly towards the marble fountain. As he drew near, the pale man of science seemed to gaze with a triumphant expression at the beautiful youth and maiden, as might an artist who should spend his life in achieving a picture or a group of statuary and finally be satisfied with his success. He paused; his bent form grew erect with conscious power; he spread out his hands over them in the attitude of a father imploring a blessing upon his children; but those were the same hands that had thrown poison into the stream of their lives. Giovanni trembled. Beatrice shuddered nervously, and pressed her hand upon her heart.

"My daughter," said Rappaccini, "thou art no longer lonely in the world. Pluck one of those precious gems from thy sister shrub and bid thy bridegroom wear it in his bosom. It will not harm him now. My science and the sympathy between thee and him have so wrought within his system that he now stands apart from common men, as thou dost, daughter of my pride and triumph, from ordinary women. Pass on, then, through the world, most dear to one another and dreadful to all besides!"

"My father," said Beatrice, feebly,—and still as she spoke she kept her hand upon her heart,—"wherefore didst thou inflict this miserable doom upon thy child?"

"Miserable!" exclaimed Rappaccini. "What mean you, foolish girl? Dost thou deem it misery to be endowed with marvellous gifts against which no power nor strength could avail an enemy—misery, to be able to quell the mightiest with a breath—misery, to be as terrible as thou art beautiful? Wouldst thou, then, have preferred the condition of a weak woman, exposed to all evil and capable of none?"

"I would fain have been loved, not feared," murmured Beatrice, sinking down upon the ground. "But now it matters not. I am going, father, where the evil which thou hast striven to mingle with my being will pass away like a dream—like the fragrance of these poisonous flowers, which will no longer taint my breath among the flowers of Eden. Farewell, Giovanni! Thy words of hatred are like lead within my heart; but they, too, will fall away as I ascend. Oh, was there not, from the first, more poison in thy nature than in mine?"

To Beatrice,—so radically had her earthly part been wrought upon by Rappaccini's skill,—as poison had been life, so the powerful antidote was death; and thus the poor victim of man's ingenuity and of thwarted nature, and of the fatality that attends all such efforts of perverted wisdom, perished there, at the feet of her father and Giovanni. Just at that moment Professor Pietro Baglioni looked forth from the window, and called loudly, in a tone of triumph mixed with horror, to the thunderstricken man of science,—

"Rappaccini! Rappaccini! and is *this* the upshot of your experiment!"

MRS. BULLFROG

It makes me melancholy to see how like fools some very sensible people act in the matter of choosing wives. They perplex their judgments by a most undue attention to little niceties of personal appearance, habits, disposition, and other trifles which concern nobody but the lady herself. An unhappy gentleman, resolving to wed nothing short of perfection, keeps his heart and hand till both get so old and withered that no tolerable woman will accept them. Now this is the very height of absurdity. A kind Providence has so skilfully adapted sex to sex and the mass of individuals to each other, that, with certain obvious exceptions, any male and female may be moderately happy in the married state. The true rule is to ascertain that the match is fundamentally a good one, and then to take it for granted that all minor objections, should there be such, will vanish, if you let them alone. Only put yourself beyond hazard as to the real basis of matrimonial bliss, and it is scarcely to be imagined what miracles, in the way of recognizing smaller incongruities, connubial love will effect.

For my own part I freely confess that, in my bachelorship, I was precisely such an over-curious simpleton as I now advise the reader not to be. My early habits had gifted me with a feminine sensibility and too exquisite refinement. I was the accomplished graduate of a dry goods store, where, by dint of ministering to the whims of fine ladies, and suiting silken hose to delicate limbs, and handling satins, ribbons, chintzes, calicoes, tapes, gauze, and cambric needles, I grew up a very ladylike sort of a gentleman. It is not assuming too much to affirm that the ladies themselves were hardly so ladylike as Thomas Bullfrog. So painfully acute was my sense of female imperfection, and such varied excellence did I require in the woman whom I could love, that there was an awful risk of my getting no wife at all, or of being driven to perpetrate matrimony with my own image in the looking-glass. Besides the fundamental principle already hinted at, I demanded the fresh bloom of youth, pearly teeth, glossy ringlets, and the whole list of lovely items, with the utmost delicacy of habits and sentiments, a silken texture of mind, and, above all, a virgin heart. In a word, if a young angel just from paradise, yet dressed in earthly fashion, had come and offered me her hand, it is by no means certain that I should have taken it. There was every chance of my becoming a most miserable old bachelor, when, by the best luck in the world, I made a journey into another state, and was smitten by, and smote again, and wooed, won, and married, the present Mrs. Bullfrog, all in the space of a fortnight. Owing to these extempore measures, I not only gave my bride credit for certain perfections which have not as yet come to light, but also overlooked a few trifling defects, which, however, glimmered on my perception long before the close of the honeymoon. Yet, as there was no mistake about the fundamental principle aforesaid, I soon learned, as will be seen, to estimate Mrs. Bullfrog's deficiencies and superfluities at exactly their proper value.

The same morning that Mrs. Bullfrog and I came together as a unit, we took two seats in the stage-coach and began our journey towards my place of business. There being no other passengers, we were as much alone and as free to give vent to our raptures as if I had hired a hack for the matrimonial jaunt. My bride looked charmingly in a green silk calash and riding habit of pelisse cloth; and whenever her red lips parted with a smile, each tooth appeared like an inestimable pearl. Such was my passionate warmth that—we had rattled out of the village, gentle reader, and were lonely as Adam and Eve in paradise—I plead guilty to no less freedom than a kiss. The gentle eye of Mrs. Bullfrog scarcely rebuked me for the profanation. Emboldened by her indulgence, I threw back the calash from her polished brow, and suffered my fingers, white and delicate as her own, to stray among those dark and glossy curls which realized my daydreams of rich hair.

"My love," said Mrs. Bullfrog, tenderly, "you will disarrange my curls."

"Oh, no, my sweet Laura!" replied I, still playing with the glossy ringlets. "Even your fair hand could not manage a curl more delicately than mine. I propose myself the pleasure of doing up your hair in papers every evening at the same time with my own."

"Mr. Bullfrog," repeated she, "you must not disarrange my curls."

This was spoken in a more decided tone than I had happened to hear, until then, from my gentlest of all gentle brides. At the same time she put up her hand and took mine prisoner; but merely drew it away from the forbidden ringlet, and then immediately released it. Now, I am a fidgety little man, and always love to have something in my fingers; so that, being debarred from my wife's curls, I looked about me for any other plaything. On the front seat of the coach there was one of those small baskets in which travelling ladies who are too delicate to appear at a public table generally carry a supply of gingerbread, biscuits and cheese, cold ham, and other light refreshments, merely to sustain nature to the journey's end. Such airy diet will sometimes keep them in pretty good flesh for a week together. Laying hold of this same little basket, I thrust my hand under the newspaper with which it was carefully covered.

"What's this, my dear?" cried I; for the black neck of a bottle had popped out of the basket.

"A bottle of Kalydor, Mr. Bullfrog," said my wife, coolly taking the basket from my hands and replacing it on the front seat.

There was no possibility of doubting my wife's word; but I never knew genuine Kalydor, such as I use for my own complexion, to smell so much like cherry brandy. I was about to express my fears that the lotion would injure her skin, when an accident occurred which threatened more than a skin-deep injury. Our Jehu had carelessly driven over a heap of gravel and fairly capsized the coach, with the wheels in the air and our heels where our heads should have been. What became of my wits I cannot imagine; they have always had a perverse trick of deserting me just when they were most needed; but so it chanced, that in the confusion of our overthrow I quite forgot that there was a Mrs. Bullfrog in the world. Like many men's wives, the good lady served her husband as a stepping-stone. I had scrambled out of the coach and was instinctively settling my cravat, when somebody brushed roughly by me, and I heard a smart thwack upon the coachman's ear.

"Take that, you villain!" cried a strange, hoarse voice. "You have ruined me, you blackguard! I shall never be the woman I have been!"

And then came a second thwack, aimed at the driver's other ear; but which missed it, and hit him on the nose, causing a terrible effusion of blood. Now, who or what fearful apparition was inflicting this punishment on the poor fellow remained an impenetrable mystery to me. The blows were given by a person of grisly aspect, with a head almost bald, and sunken cheeks, apparently of the feminine gender, though hardly to be classed in the gentler sex. There being no teeth to modulate the voice, it had a mumbled fierceness, not passionate, but stern, which absolutely made me quiver like calf's-foot jelly. Who could the phantom be? The most awful circumstance of the affair is yet to be told: for this ogre, or whatever it was, had a riding habit like Mrs. Bullfrog's, and also a green silk calash dangling down her back by the strings. In my terror and turmoil of mind I could imagine nothing less than that the Old Nick, at the moment of our overturn, had annihilated my wife and jumped into her petticoats. This idea seemed the more probable, since I could nowhere perceive Mrs. Bullfrog alive, nor, though I looked very sharply about the coach, could I detect any traces of that beloved woman's dead body. There would have been a comfort in giving her Christian burial.

"Come, sir, bestir yourself! Help this rascal to set up the coach," said the hobgoblin to me; then, with a terrific screech to three countrymen at a distance, "Here, you fellows, ain't you ashamed to stand off when a poor woman is in distress?"

The countrymen, instead of fleeing for their lives, came running at full speed, and laid hold of the topsy-turvy coach. I, also, though a small-sized man, went to work like a son of Anak. The coachman, too, with the blood still streaming from his nose, tugged and toiled most manfully, dreading, doubtless, that the next blow might break his head. And yet, bemauled as the poor fellow had been, he seemed to glance at me with an eye of pity, as if my case were more deplorable than his. But I cherished a hope that all would turn out a dream, and seized the opportunity, as we raised the coach, to jam two of my fingers under the wheel, trusting that the pain would awaken me.

"Why, here we are, all to rights again!" exclaimed a sweet voice behind. "Thank you for your assistance, gentlemen. My dear Mr. Bullfrog, how you perspire! Do let me wipe your face. Don't take this little accident too much to heart, good driver. We ought to be thankful that none of our necks are broken."

"We might have spared one neck out of the three," muttered the driver, rubbing his ear and pulling his nose, to ascertain whether he had been cuffed or not. "Why, the woman's a witch!"

I fear that the reader will not believe, yet it is positively a fact, that there stood Mrs. Bullfrog, with her glossy ringlets curling on her brow, and two rows of orient pearls gleaming between her parted lips, which wore a most angelic smile. She had regained her riding habit and calash from the grisly phantom, and was, in all respects, the lovely woman who had been sitting by my side at the instant of our overturn. How she had happened to disappear, and who had supplied her place, and whence she did now return, were problems too knotty for me to solve. There stood my wife. That was the one thing certain among a heap of mysteries. Nothing remained but to help her into the coach, and plod on, through the journey of the day and the journey of life, as comfortably as we could. As the driver closed the door upon us, I heard him whisper to the three countrymen,—

"How do you suppose a fellow feels shut up in the cage with a she tiger?"

Of course this query could have no reference to my situation. Yet, unreasonable as it may appear, I confess that my feelings were not altogether so ecstatic as when I first called Mrs. Bullfrog mine. True, she was a sweet woman and an angel of a wife; but what if a Gorgon should return, amid the transports of our connubial bliss, and take the angel's place. I recollected the tale of a fairy, who half the time was a beautiful woman and half the time a hideous monster. Had I taken that very fairy to be the wife of my bosom? While such whims and chimeras were flitting across my fancy I began to look askance at Mrs. Bullfrog, almost expecting that the transformation would be wrought before my eyes.

To divert my mind, I took up the newspaper which had covered the little basket of refreshments, and which now lay at the bottom of the coach, blushing with a deep-red stain and emitting a potent spirituous fume from the contents of the broken bottle of Kalydor. The paper was two or three years old, but contained an article of several columns, in which I soon grew wonderfully interested. It was the report of a trial for breach of promise of marriage, giving the testimony in full, with fervid extracts from both the gentleman's and lady's amatory correspondence. The deserted damsel had personally appeared in court, and had borne energetic evidence to her lover's perfidy and the strength of her blighted affections. On the defendant's part there had been an attempt, though insufficiently sustained, to blast the plaintiff's character, and a plea, in mitigation of damages, on account of her unamiable temper. A horrible idea was suggested by the lady's name.

"Madam," said I, holding the newspaper before Mrs. Bullfrog's eyes,—and, though a small, delicate, and thin-visaged man, I feel assured that I looked very terrific,—"madam," repeated I, through my shut teeth, "were you the plaintiff in this cause?"

"Oh, my dear Mr. Bullfrog," replied my wife, sweetly, "I thought all the world knew that!"

"Horror! horror!" exclaimed I, sinking back on the seat.

Covering my face with both hands, I emitted a deep and deathlike groan, as if my tormented soul were rending me asunder—I, the most exquisitely fastidious of men, and whose wife was to have been the most delicate and refined of women, with all the fresh dew-drops glittering on her virgin rosebud of a heart!

I thought of the glossy ringlets and pearly teeth; I thought of the Kalydor; I thought of the coachman's bruised ear and bloody nose; I thought of the tender love secrets which she had whispered to the judge and jury and a thousand tittering auditors,—and gave another groan!

"Mr. Bullfrog," said my wife.

As I made no reply, she gently took my hands within her own, removed them from my face, and fixed her eyes steadfastly on mine.

"Mr. Bullfrog," said she, not unkindly, yet with all the decision of her strong character, "let me advise you to overcome this foolish weakness, and prove yourself, to the best of your ability, as good a husband as I will be a wife. You have discovered, perhaps, some little imperfections in your bride. Well, what did you expect? Women are not angels. If they were, they would go to heaven for husbands; or, at least, be more difficult in their choice on earth."

"But why conceal those imperfections?" interposed I, tremulously.

"Now, my love, are not you a most unreasonable little man?" said Mrs. Bullfrog, patting me on the cheek. "Ought a woman to disclose her frailties earlier than the wedding day? Few husbands, I assure you, make the discovery in such good season, and still fewer complain that these trifles are concealed too long. Well, what a strange man you are! Poh! you are joking."

"But the suit for breach of promise!" groaned I.

"Ah, and is that the rub?" exclaimed my wife. "Is it possible that you view that affair in an objectionable light? Mr. Bullfrog, I never could have dreamed it! Is it an objection that I have triumphantly defended myself against slander and vindicated my purity in a court of justice? Or do you complain because your wife has shown the proper spirit of a woman, and punished the villain who trifled with her affections?"

"But," persisted I, shrinking into a corner of the coach, however,—for I did not know precisely how much contradiction the proper spirit of a woman would endure,—"but, my love, would it not have been more dignified to treat the villain with the silent contempt he merited?"

"That is all very well, Mr. Bullfrog," said my wife, slyly; "but, in that case, where would have been the five thousand dollars which are to stock your dry goods store?"

"Mrs. Bullfrog, upon your honor," demanded I, as if my life hung upon her words, "is there no mistake about those five thousand dollars?"

"Upon my word and honor there is none," replied she. "The jury gave me every cent the rascal had; and I have kept it all for my dear Bullfrog."

"Then, thou dear woman," cried I, with an overwhelming gush of tenderness, "let me fold thee to my heart. The basis of matrimonial bliss is secure, and all thy little defects and frailties are forgiven. Nay, since the result has been so fortunate, I rejoice at the wrongs which drove thee to this blessed lawsuit. Happy Bullfrog that I am!"

MONSIEUR DU MIROIR

Than the gentleman above named, there is nobody in the whole circle of my acquaintance, whom I have more attentively studied, yet of whom I have less real knowledge, beneath the surface which it pleases him to present. Being anxious to discover who and what he really is, and how connected with me, and what are to be the results to him and to myself of the joint interest which, without any choice on my part, seems to be permanently established between us,—and incited, furthermore, by the propensities of a student of human nature, though doubtful whether Monsieur du Miroir have aught of humanity but the figure,—I have determined to place a few of his remarkable points before the public, hoping to be favored with some clew to the explanation of his character. Nor let the reader condemn any part of the narrative as frivolous, since a subject of such grave reflection diffuses its importance through the minutest particulars; and there is no judging beforehand what odd little circumstance may do the office of a blind man's dog among the perplexities of this dark investigation; and however extraordinary, marvellous, preternatural, and utterly incredible some of the meditated disclosures may appear, I pledge my honor to maintain as sacred a regard to fact as if my testimony were given on oath and involved the dearest interests of the personage in question. Not that there is matter for a criminal accusation against Monsieur du Miroir, nor am I the man to bring it forward if there were. The chief that I complain of is his impenetrable mystery, which is no better than nonsense if it conceal anything good, and much worse in the contrary case.

But if undue partialities could be supposed to influence me, Monsieur du Miroir might hope to profit rather than to suffer by them, for in the whole of our long intercourse we have seldom had the slightest disagreement; and, moreover, there are reasons for supposing him a near relative of mine, and consequently entitled to the best word that I can give him. He bears undisputably a strong personal resemblance to myself, and generally puts on mourning at the funerals of the family. On the other hand, his name would indicate a French descent; in which case, infinitely preferring that my blood should flow from a bold British and pure Puritan source, I beg leave to disclaim all kindred with Monsieur du Miroir. Some genealogists trace his origin to Spain, and dub him a knight of the order of the CABALLEROS DE LOS ESPEJOZ, one of whom was overthrown by Don Quixote. But what says Monsieur du Miroir himself of his paternity and his fatherland? Not a word did he ever say about the matter; and herein, perhaps, lies one of his most especial reasons for maintaining such a vexatious mystery, that he lacks the faculty of speech to expound it. His lips are sometimes seen to move; his eyes and countenance are alive with shifting expression, as if corresponding by visible hieroglyphics to his modulated breath; and anon he will seem to pause with as satisfied an air as if he had been talking excellent sense. Good sense or bad, Monsieur du Miroir is the sole judge of his own conversational powers, never having whispered so much as a syllable that reached the ears of any other auditor. Is he really dumb? or is all the world deaf? or is it merely a piece of my friend's waggery, meant for nothing but to make fools of us? If so he has the joke all to himself.

This dumb devil which possesses Monsieur du Miroir is, I am persuaded, the sole reason that he does not make me the most flattering protestations of friendship. In many particulars—indeed, as to all his cognizable and not preternatural points, except that, once in a great while, I speak a word or two —there exists the greatest apparent sympathy between us. Such is his confidence in my taste that he goes astray from the general fashion and copies all his dresses after mine. I never try on a new garment without expecting to meet Monsieur du Miroir in one of the same pattern. He has duplicates of all my waistcoats and cravats, shirt bosoms of precisely a similar plait, and an old coat for private wear, manufactured, I suspect, by a Chinese tailor, in exact imitation of a beloved old coat of mine, with a facsimile, stitch by stitch, of a patch upon the elbow. In truth, the singular and minute coincidences that occur, both in the accidents of the passing day and the serious events of our lives, remind me of those doubtful legends of lovers, or twin children, twins of fate, who have lived, enjoyed, suffered, and died in unison, each faithfully repeating the last tremor of the other's breath, though separated by vast tracts of sea and land. Strange to say, my incommodities belong equally to my companion, though the burden is nowise alleviated by his participation. The other morning, after a night of torment from the toothache, I met Monsieur du Miroir with such a swollen anguish in his cheek that my own pangs were redoubled, as were also his, if I might judge by a fresh contortion of his visage. All the inequalities of my spirits are communicated to him, causing the unfortunate Monsieur du Miroir to mope and scowl through a whole summer's day, or to laugh as long, for no better reason than the gay or gloomy crotchets of my brain. Once we were joint sufferers of a three months' sickness, and met like mutual ghosts in the first days of convalescence. Whenever I have been in love, Monsieur du Miroir has looked passionate and tender; and never did my mistress discard me but this too susceptible gentleman grew lackadaisical. His temper, also, rises to blood heat, fever heat, or boiling water heat, according to the measure of any wrong which might seem to have fallen entirely on myself. I have sometimes been calmed down by the sight of my own inordinate wrath depicted on his frowning brow. Yet, however prompt in taking up my quarrels, I cannot call to mind that he ever struck a downright blow in my behalf; nor, in fact, do I perceive that any real and tangible good has resulted from his constant interference in my affairs; so that, in my distrustful moods, I am apt to suspect Monsieur du Miroir's sympathy to be mere outward show, not a whit better nor worse than other people's sympathy. Nevertheless, as mortal man must have something in the guise of sympathy,—and whether the true metal or merely copperwashed, is of less moment,—I choose rather to content myself with Monsieur du Miroir's such as it is than to seek the sterling coin, and perhaps miss even the counterfeit.

In my age of vanities I have often seen him in the ball room, and might again were I to seek him there. We have encountered each other at the Tremont Theatre, where, however, he took his seat neither in the dress circle, pit, nor upper regions, nor threw a single glance at the stage, though the brightest star, even Fanny Kemble herself, might be culminating there. No; this whimsical friend of mine chose to linger in the saloon, near one of the large looking-glasses which throw back their pictures of the illuminated room. He is so full of these unaccountable eccentricities that I never like to notice Monsieur du Miroir, nor to acknowledge the slightest connection with him, in places of public resort. He, however, has no scruple about claiming my acquaintance, even when his common sense, if he had any, might teach him that I would as willingly exchange a nod with the Old Nick. It was but the other day that he got into a large brass kettle at the entrance of a hardware store, and thrust his head, the moment afterwards, into a bright, new warming pan, whence he gave me a most merciless look of recognition. He smiled, and so did I; but these childish tricks make decent people rather shy of Monsieur du Miroir, and subject him to more dead cuts than any other gentleman in town.

One of this singular person's most remarkable peculiarities is his fondness for water, wherein he excels any temperance man whatever. His pleasure, it must be owned, is not so much to drink it (in which respect a very moderate quantity will answer his occasions) as to souse himself over head and ears wherever he may meet with it. Perhaps he is a merman, or born of a mermaid's marriage with a mortal, and thus amphibious by hereditary right, like the children which the old river deities, or nymphs of fountains, gave to earthly love. When no cleaner bathing-place happened to be at hand, I have seen the foolish fellow in a horse pond. Sometimes he refreshes himself in the trough of a town pump, without caring what the people think about him. Often, while carefully picking my way along the street after a heavy shower, I have been scandalized to see Monsieur du Miroir, in full dress, paddling from one mud puddle to another, and plunging into filthy depths of each. Seldom have I peeped into a well without discerning this ridiculous gentleman at the bottom, whence he gazes up, as through a long telescopic tube, and probably makes discoveries among the stars by daylight. Wandering along lonesome paths or in pathless forests, when I have come to virgin fountains, of which it would have been pleasant to deem myself the first discoverer, I have started to find Monsieur du Miroir there before me. The solitude seemed lonelier for his presence. I have leaned from a precipice that frowns over Lake George, which the French call Nature's font of sacramental water, and used it in their log churches here and their cathedrals beyond the sea, and seen him far below in that pure element. At Niagara, too, where I would gladly have forgotten both myself and him, I could not help observing my companion in the smooth water on the very verge of the cataract just above the Table Rock. Were I to reach the sources of the Nile, I should expect to meet him there. Unless he be another Ladurlad, whose garments the depths of ocean could not moisten, it is difficult to conceive how he keeps himself in any decent pickle; though I am bound to confess that his clothes seem always as dry and comfortable as my own. But, as a friend, I could wish that he would not so often expose himself in liquor.

All that I have hitherto related may be classed among those little personal oddities which agreeably diversify the surface of society, and, though they may sometimes annoy us, yet keep our daily intercourse fresher and livelier than if they were done away. By an occasional hint, however, I have endeavored to pave the way for stranger things to come, which, had they been disclosed at once, Monsieur du Miroir might have been deemed a shadow, and myself a person of no veracity, and this truthful history a fabulous legend. But, now that the reader knows me worthy of his confidence, I will begin to make him stare.

To speak frankly, then, I could bring the most astounding proofs that Monsieur du Miroir is at least a conjurer, if not one of that unearthly tribe with whom conjurers deal. He has inscrutable methods of conveying himself from place to place with the rapidity of the swiftest steamboat or rail car. Brick walls and oaken doors and iron bolts are no impediment to his passage. Here in my chamber, for instance, as the evening deepens into night, I sit alone—the key turned and withdrawn from the lock, the keyhole stuffed with paper to keep out a peevish little blast of wind. Yet, lonely as I seem, were I to lift one of the lamps and step five paces eastward, Monsieur du Miroir would be sure to meet me with a lamp also in his hand; and were I to take the stage-coach to-morrow, without giving him the least hint of my design, and post onward till the week's end, at whatever hotel I might find myself I should expect to share my private apartment with this inevitable Monsieur du Miroir. Or, out of a mere wayward fantasy, were I to go by moonlight and stand beside the stone font of the Shaker Spring at Canterbury, Monsieur du Miroir would set forth on the same fool's errand, and would not fail to meet me there. Shall I heighten the reader's wonder? While writing these latter sentences, I happened to glance towards the large, round globe of one of the brass andirons, and lo! a miniature apparition of Monsieur du Miroir, with his face widened and grotesquely contorted, as if he were making fun of my amazement! But he has played so many of these jokes that they begin to lose their effect. Once, presumptuous that he was, he stole into the heaven of a young lady's eyes; so that, while I gazed and was dreaming only of herself, I found him also in my dream. Years have so changed him since that he need never hope to enter those heavenly orbs again.

From these veritable statements it will be readily concluded that, had Monsieur du Miroir played such pranks in old witch times, matters might have gone hard with him; at least, if the constable and posse comitatus could have executed a warrant, or the jailer had been cunning enough to keep him. But it has often occurred to me as a very singular circumstance, and as betokening either a temperament morbidly suspicious or some weighty cause of apprehension, that he never trusts himself within the grasp even of his most intimate friend. If you step forward to meet him, he readily advances; if you offer him your hand, he extends his own with an air of the utmost frankness; but, though you calculate upon a hearty shake, you do not get hold of his little finger. Ah, this Monsieur du Miroir is a slippery fellow!

These truly are matters of special admiration. After vainly endeavoring, by the strenuous exertion of my own wits, to gain a satisfactory insight into the character of Monsieur du Miroir, I had recourse to certain wise men, and also to books of abstruse philosophy, seeking who it was that haunted me, and why. I heard long lectures, and read huge volumes with little profit beyond the knowledge that many former instances are recorded, in successive ages, of similar connections between ordinary mortals and beings possessing the attributes of Monsieur du Miroir. Some now alive, perhaps, besides myself have such attendants. Would that Monsieur du Miroir could be persuaded to transfer his attachment to one of those, and allow some other of his race to assume the situation that he now holds in regard to me! If I must needs have so intrusive an intimate, who stares me in the face in my closest privacy and follows me even to my bed chamber, I should prefer—scandal apart—the laughing bloom of a young girl to the dark and bearded gravity of my present companion. But such desires are never to be gratified. Though the members of Monsieur du Miroir's family have been accused, perhaps justly, of visiting their friends often in splendid halls, and seldom in darksome dungeons, yet they exhibit a rare constancy to the objects of their first attachment, however unlovely in person or unamiable in disposition—however unfortunate, or even infamous, and deserted by all the world besides. So will it be with my associate. Our fates appear inseparably blended. It is my belief, as I find him mingling with my earliest recollections, that we came into existence together, as my shadow follows me into the sunshine, and that hereafter, as heretofore, the brightness or gloom of my fortunes will shine upon or darken the face of Monsieur du Miroir. As we have been young together, and as it is now near the summer noon with both of us, so, if long life be granted, shall each count his own wrinkles on the other's brow and his white hairs on the other's head. And when the coffin lid shall have closed over me, and that face and form, which, more truly than the lover swears it to his beloved, are the sole light of his existence,—when they shall be laid in that dark chamber, whither his swift and secret footsteps cannot bring him,—then what is to become of poor Monsieur du Miroir? Will he have the fortitude, with my other friends, to take a last look at my pale countenance? Will he walk foremost in the funeral train? Will he come often and haunt around my grave, and weed away the nettles, and plant flowers amid the verdure, and scrape the moss out of the letters of my burial stone? Will he linger where I have lived, to remind the neglectful world of one who staked much to win a name, but will not then care whether he lost or won?

Not thus will he prove his deep fidelity. Oh, what terror, if this friend of mine, after our last farewell, should step into the crowded street, or roam along our old frequented path by the still waters, or sit down in the domestic circle where our faces are most familiar and beloved! No; but when the rays of heaven shall bless me no more, nor the thoughtful lamplight gleam upon my studies, nor the cheerful fireside gladden the meditative man, then, his task fulfilled, shall this mysterious being vanish from the earth forever. He will pass to the dark realm of nothingness, but will not find me there.

There is something fearful in bearing such a relation to a creature so imperfectly known, and in the idea that, to a certain extent, all which concerns myself will be reflected in its consequences upon him. When we feel that another is to share the selfsame fortune with ourselves, we judge more severely of our prospects, and withhold our confidence from that delusive magic which appears to shed an infallibility of happiness over our own pathway. Of late years, indeed, there has been much to sadden my intercourse with Monsieur du Miroir. Had not our union been a necessary condition of our life, we must have been estranged ere now. In early youth, when my affections were warm and free, I loved him well, and could always spend a pleasant hour in his society, chiefly because it gave me an excellent opinion of myself. Speechless as he was, Monsieur du Miroir had then a most agreeable way of calling me a handsome fellow; and I, of course, returned the compliment; so that, the more we kept each other's company, the greater coxcombs we mutually grew. But neither of us need apprehend any such misfortune now. When we chance to meet,—for it is chance oftener than design,—each glances sadly at the other's forehead, dreading wrinkles there; and at our temples, whence the hair is thinning away too early; and at the sunken eyes, which no longer shed a gladsome light over the whole face. I involuntarily peruse him as a record of my heavy youth, which has been wasted in sluggishness for lack to hope and impulse, or equally thrown away in toil that had no wise motive and has accomplished no good end. I perceive that the tranquil gloom of a disappointed soul has darkened through his countenance, where the blackness of the future seems to mingle with the shadows of the past, giving him the aspect of a fated man. Is it too wild a thought that my fate may have assumed this image of myself, and therefore haunts me with such inevitable pertinacity, originating every act which it appears to imitate, while it deludes me by pretending to share the events of which it is merely the emblem and the prophecy? I must banish this idea, or it will throw too deep an awe round my companion. At our next meeting, especially if it be at midnight or in solitude, I fear that I shall glance aside and shudder; in which case, as Monsieur du Miroir is extremely sensitive to ill treatment, he also will avert his eyes and express horror or disgust.

But no; this is unworthy of me. As of old I sought his society for the bewitching dreams of woman's love which he inspired and because I fancied a bright fortune in his aspect, so now will I hold daily and long communion with him for the sake of the stern lessons that he will teach my manhood. With folded arms we will sit face to face, and lengthen out our silent converse till a wiser cheerfulness shall have been wrought from the very texture of despondency. He will say, perhaps indignantly, that it befits only him to mourn for the decay of outward grace, which, while he possessed it, was his all. But have not you, he will ask, a treasure in reserve, to which every year may add far more value than age or death itself can snatch from that miserable clay? He will tell me that though the bloom of life has been nipped with a frost, yet the soul must not sit shivering in its cell, but bestir itself manfully, and kindle a genial warmth from its own exercise against the autumnal and the wintry atmosphere. And I, in return, will bid him be of good cheer, nor take it amiss that I must blanch his locks and wrinkle him up like a wilted apple, since it shall be my endeavor so to beautify his face with intellect and mild benevolence that he shall profit immensely by the change. But here a smile will glimmer somewhat sadly over Monsieur du Miroir's visage.

When this subject shall have been sufficiently discussed we may take up others as important. Reflecting upon his power of following me to the remotest regions and into the deepest privacy, I will compare the attempt to escape him to the hopeless race that men sometimes run with memory, or their own hearts, or their moral selves, which, though burdened with cares enough to crush an elephant, will never be one step behind. I will be self-contemplative, as Nature bids me, and make him the picture or visible type of what I muse upon, that my mind may not wander so vaguely as heretofore, chasing its own shadow through a chaos and catching only the monsters that abide there. Then we will turn our thoughts to the spiritual world, of the reality of which my companions shall furnish me an illustration, if not an argument; for, as we have only the testimony of the eye to Monsieur du Miroir's existence, while all the other senses would fail to inform us that such a figure stands within arm's length, wherefore should there not be beings innumerable close beside us, and filling heaven and earth with their multitude, yet of whom no corporeal perception can take cognizance? A blind man might as reasonably deny that Monsieur du Miroir exists as we, because the Creator has hitherto withheld the spiritual perception, can therefore contend that there are no spirits. Oh, there are! And, at this moment, when the subject of which I write has grown strong within me and surrounded itself with those solemn and awful associations which might have seemed most alien to it, I could fancy that Monsieur du Miroir himself is a wanderer from the spiritual world, with nothing human except his delusive garment of visibility. Methinks I should tremble now were his wizard power of gliding through all impediments in search of me to place him suddenly before my eyes.

Ha! What is yonder? Shape of mystery, did the tremor of my heartstrings vibrate to thine own, and call thee from thy home among the dancers of the northern lights, and shadows flung from departed sunshine, and giant spectres that appear on clouds at daybreak and affright the climber of the Alps? In truth it startled me, as I threw a wary glance eastward across the chamber, to discern an unbidden guest with his eyes bent on mine. The identical MONSIEUR DU MIROIR! Still there he sits and returns my gaze with as much of awe and curiosity as if he, too, had spent a solitary evening in fantastic musings and made me his theme. So inimitably does he counterfeit that I could almost doubt which of us is the visionary form, or whether each be not the other's mystery, and both twin brethren of one fate in mutually reflected spheres. O friend, canst thou not hear and answer me? Break down the barrier between us! Grasp my hand! Speak! Listen! A few words, perhaps, might satisfy the feverish yearning of my soul for some master thought that should guide me through this labyrinth of life, teaching wherefore I was born, and how to do my task on earth, and what is death. Alas! Even that unreal image should forget to ape me and smile at these vain questions. Thus do mortals deify, as it were, a mere shadow of themselves, a spectre of human reason, and ask of that to unveil the mysteries which Divine Intelligence has revealed so far as needful to our guidance, and hid the rest.

Farewell, Monsieur du Miroir. Of you, perhaps, as of many men, it may be doubted whether you are the wiser, though your whole business is REFLECTION.

THE HALL OF FANTASY

It has happened to me, on various occasions, to find myself in a certain edifice which would appear to have some of the characteristics of a public exchange. Its interior is a spacious hall, with a pavement of white marble. Overhead is a lofty dome, supported by long rows of pillars of fantastic architecture, the idea of which was probably taken from the Moorish ruins of the Alhambra, or perhaps from some enchanted edifice in the Arabian tales. The windows of this hall have a breadth and grandeur of design and an elaborateness of workmanship that have nowhere been equalled except in the Gothic cathedrals of the old world. Like their prototypes, too, they admit the light of heaven only through stained and pictured glass, thus filling the hall with many-colored radiance and painting its marble floor with beautiful or grotesque designs; so that its inmates breathe, as it were, a visionary atmosphere, and tread upon the fantasies of poetic minds. These peculiarities, combining a wilder mixture of styles than even an American architect usually recognizes as allowable,—Grecian, Gothic, Oriental, and nondescript,—cause the whole edifice to give the impression of a dream, which might be dissipated and shattered to fragments by merely stamping the foot upon the pavement. Yet, with such modifications and repairs as successive ages demand, the Hall of Fantasy is likely to endure longer than the most substantial structure that ever cumbered the earth.

It is not at all times that one can gain admittance into this edifice, although most persons enter it at some period or other of their lives; if not in their waking moments, then by the universal passport of a dream. At my last visit I wandered thither unawares while my mind was busy with an idle tale, and was startled by the throng of people who seemed suddenly to rise up around me.

"Bless me! Where am I?" cried I, with but a dim recognition of the place.

"You are in a spot," said a friend who chanced to be near at hand, "which occupies in the world of fancy the same position which the Bourse, the Rialto, and the Exchange do in the commercial world. All who have affairs in that mystic region, which lies above, below, or beyond the actual, may here meet and talk over the business of their dreams."

"It is a noble hall," observed I.

"Yes," he replied. "Yet we see but a small portion of the edifice. In its upper stories are said to be apartments where the inhabitants of earth may hold converse with those of the moon; and beneath our feet are gloomy cells, which communicate with the infernal regions, and where monsters and chimeras are kept in confinement and fed with all unwholesomeness."

In niches and on pedestals around about the hall stood the statues or busts of men who in every age have been rulers and demigods in the realms of imagination and its kindred regions. The grand old countenance of Homer; the shrunken and decrepit form but vivid face of Æsop; the dark presence of Dante; the wild Ariosto; Rabelais' smile of deep-wrought mirth; the profound, pathetic humor of Cervantes; the all-glorious Shakespeare; Spenser, meet guest for an allegoric structure; the severe divinity of Milton; and Bunyan, moulded of homeliest clay, but instinct with celestial fire,—were those that chiefly attracted my eye. Fielding, Richardson, and Scott occupied conspicuous pedestals. In an obscure and shadowy niche was deposited the bust of our countryman, the author of Arthur Mervyn.

"Besides these indestructible memorials of real genius," remarked my companion, "each century has erected statues of its own ephemeral favorities in wood."

"I observe a few crumbling relics of such," said I. "But ever and anon, I suppose, Oblivion comes with her huge broom and sweeps them all from the marble floor. But such will never be the fate of this fine statue of Goethe."

"Nor of that next to it—Emanuel Swedenborg," said he. "Were ever two men of transcendent imagination more unlike?"

In the centre of the hall springs an ornamental fountain, the water of which continually throws itself into new shapes and snatches the most diversified hues from the stained atmosphere around. It is impossible to conceive what a strange vivacity is imparted to the scene by the magic dance of this fountain, with its endless transformations, in which the imaginative beholder may discern what form he will. The water is supposed by some to flow from the same source as the Castalian spring, and is extolled by others as uniting the virtues of the Fountain of Youth with those of many other enchanted wells long celebrated in tale and song. Having never tasted it, I can bear no testimony to its quality.

"Did you ever drink this water?" I inquired of my friend.

"A few sips now and then," answered he. "But there are men here who make it their constant beverage—or, at least, have the credit of doing so. In some instances it is known to have intoxicating qualities."

"Pray let us look at these water drinkers," said I.

So we passed among the fantastic pillars till we came to a spot where a number of persons were clustered together in the light of one of the great stained windows, which seemed to glorify the whole group as well as the marble that they trod on. Most of them were men of broad foreheads, meditative countenances, and thoughtful, inward eyes; yet it required but a trifle to summon up mirth, peeping out from the very midst of grave and lofty musings. Some strode about, or leaned against the pillars of the hall, alone and in silence; their faces wore a rapt expression, as if sweet music were in the air around them or as if their inmost souls were about to float away in song. One or two, perhaps, stole a glance at the by-standers, to watch if their poetic absorption were observed. Others stood talking in groups, with a liveliness of expression, a ready smile, and a light, intellectual laughter, which showed how rapidly the shafts of wit were glancing to and fro among them.

A few held higher converse, which caused their calm and melancholy souls to beam moonlight from their eyes. As I lingered near them,—for I felt an inward attraction towards these men, as if the sympathy of feeling, if not of genius, had united me to their order,—my friend mentioned several of their names. The world has likewise heard those names; with some it has been familiar for years; and others are daily making their way deeper into the universal heart.

"Thank Heaven," observed I to my companion, as we passed to another part of the hall, "we have done with this techy, wayward, shy, proud, unreasonable set of laurel gatherers. I love them in their works, but have little desire to meet them elsewhere."

"You have adopted an old prejudice, I see," replied my friend, who was familiar with most of these worthies, being himself a student of poetry, and not without the poetic flame. "But, so far as my experience goes, men of genius are fairly gifted with the social qualities; and in this age there appears to be a fellow-feeling among them which had not heretofore been developed. As men, they ask nothing better than to be on equal terms with their fellow-men; and as authors, they have thrown aside their proverbial jealousy, and acknowledge a generous brotherhood."

"The world does not think so," answered I. "An author is received in general society pretty much as we honest citizens are in the Hall of Fantasy. We gaze at him as if he had no business among us, and question whether he is fit for any of our pursuits."

"Then it is a very foolish question," said he. "Now here are a class of men whom we may daily meet on Change. Yet what poet in the hall is more a fool of fancy than the sagest of them?"

He pointed to a number of persons, who, manifest as the fact was, would have deemed it an insult to be told that they stood in the Hall of Fantasy. Their visages were traced into wrinkles and furrows, each of which seemed the record of some actual experience in life. Their eyes had the shrewd, calculating glance which detects so quickly and so surely all that it concerns a man of business to know about the characters and purposes of his fellow-men. Judging them as they stood, they might be honored and trusted members of the Chamber of Commerce, who had found the genuine secret of wealth, and whose sagacity gave them the command of fortune. There was a character of detail and matter of fact in their talk which concealed the extravagance of its purport, insomuch that the wildest schemes had the aspect of every-day realities. Thus the listener was not startled at the idea of cities to be built, as if by magic, in the heart of pathless forests; and of streets to be laid out where now the sea was tossing; and of mighty rivers to be stayed in their courses in order to turn the machinery of a cotton mill. It was only by an effort, and scarcely then, that the mind convinced itself that such speculations were as much matter of fantasy as the old dream of Eldorado, or as Mammon's Cave, or any other vision of gold ever conjured up by the imagination of needy poet or romantic adventurer.

"Upon my word," said I, "it is dangerous to listen to such dreamers as these. Their madness is contagious."

"Yes," said my friend, "because they mistake the Hall of Fantasy for actual brick and mortar, and its purple atmosphere for unsophisticated sunshine. But the poet knows his whereabout, and therefore is less likely to make a fool of himself in real life."

"Here again," observed I, as we advanced a little farther, "we see another order of dreamers, peculiarly characteristic, too, of the genius of our country."

These were the inventors of fantastic machines. Models of their contrivances were placed against some of the pillars of the hall, and afforded good emblems of the result generally to be anticipated from an attempt to reduce daydreams to practice. The analogy may hold in morals as well as physics; for instance, here was the model of a railroad through the air and a tunnel under the sea. Here was a machine—stolen, I believe—for the distillation of heat from moonshine; and another for the condensation of morning mist into square blocks of granite, wherewith it was proposed to rebuild the entire Hall of Fantasy. One man exhibited a sort of lens whereby he had succeeded in making sunshine out of a lady's smile; and it was his purpose wholly to irradiate the earth by means of this wonderful invention.

"It is nothing new," said I; "for most of our sunshine comes from woman's smile already."

"True," answered the inventor; "but my machine will secure a constant supply for domestic use; whereas hitherto it has been very precarious."

Another person had a scheme for fixing the reflections of objects in a pool of water, and thus taking the most lifelike portraits imaginable; and the same gentleman demonstrated the practicability of giving a permanent dye to ladies' dresses, in the gorgeous clouds of sunset. There were at least fifty kinds of perpetual motion, one of which was applicable to the wits of newspaper editors and writers of every description. Professor Espy was here, with a tremendous storm in a gum-elastic bag. I could enumerate many more of these Utopian inventions; but, after all, a more imaginative collection is to be found in the patent office at Washington.

Turning from the inventors we took a more general survey of the inmates of the hall. Many persons were present whose right of entrance appeared to consist in some crotchet of the brain, which, so long as it might operate, produced a change in their relation to the actual world. It is singular how very few there are who do not occasionally gain admittance on such a score, either in abstracted musings, or momentary thoughts, or bright anticipations, or vivid remembrances; for even the actual becomes ideal, whether in hope or memory, and beguiles the dreamer into the Hall of Fantasy. Some unfortunates make their whole abode and business here, and contract habits which unfit them for all the real employments of life. Others—but these are few—possess the faculty, in their occasional visits, of discovering a purer truth than the world can impart among the lights and shadows of these pictured windows.

And with all its dangerous influences, we have reason to thank God that there is such a place of refuge from the gloom and chillness of actual life. Hither may come the prisoner, escaping from his dark and narrow cell and cankerous chain, to breathe free air in this enchanted atmosphere. The sick man leaves his weary pillow, and finds strength to wander hither, though his wasted limbs might not support him even to the threshold of his chamber. The exile passes through the Hall of Fantasy to revisit his native soil. The burden of years rolls down from the old man's shoulders the moment that the door uncloses. Mourners leave their heavy sorrows at the entrance, and here rejoin the lost ones whose faces would else be seen no more, until thought shall have become the only fact. It may be said, in truth, that there is but half a life—the meaner and earthlier half—for those who never find their way into the hall. Nor must I fail to mention that in the observatory of the edifice is kept that wonderful perspective glass, through which the shepherds of the Delectable Mountains showed Christian the far-off gleam of the Celestial City. The eye of Faith still loves to gaze through it.

"I observe some men here," said I to my friend, "who might set up a strong claim to be reckoned among the most real personages of the day."

"Certainly," he replied. "If a man be in advance of his age, he must be content to make his abode in this hall until the lingering generations of his fellow-men come up with him. He can find no other shelter in the universe. But the fantasies of one day are the deepest realities of a future one."

"It is difficult to distinguish them apart amid the gorgeous and bewildering light of this hall," rejoined I. "The white sunshine of actual life is necessary in order to test them. I am rather apt to doubt both men and their reasonings till I meet them in that truthful medium."

"Perhaps your faith in the ideal is deeper than you are aware," said my friend. "You are at least a democrat; and methinks no scanty share of such faith is essential to the adoption of that creed."

Among the characters who had elicited these remarks were most of the noted reformers of the day, whether in physics, politics, morals, or religion. There is no surer method of arriving at the Hall of Fantasy than to throw one's self into the current of a theory; for, whatever landmarks of fact may be set up along the stream, there is a law of nature that impels it thither. And let it be so; for here the wise head and capacious heart may do their work; and what is good and true becomes gradually hardened into fact, while error melts away and vanishes among the shadows of the hall. Therefore may none who believe and rejoice in the progress of mankind be angry with me because I recognized their apostles and leaders amid the fantastic radiance of those pictured windows. I love and honor such men as well as they.

It would be endless to describe the herd of real or self-styled reformers that peopled this place of refuge. They were the representatives of an unquiet period, when mankind is seeking to cast off the whole tissue of ancient custom like a tattered garment. Many of them had got possession of some crystal fragment of truth, the brightness of which so dazzled them that they could see nothing else in the wide universe. Here were men whose faith had embodied itself in the form of a potato; and others whose long beards had a deep spiritual significance. Here was the abolitionist, brandishing his one idea like an iron flail. In a word, there were a thousand shapes of good and evil, faith and infidelity, wisdom and nonsense—a most incongruous throng.

Yet, withal, the heart of the stanchest conservative, unless he abjured his fellowship with man, could hardly have helped throbbing in sympathy with the spirit that pervaded these innumerable theorists. It was good for the man of unquickened heart to listen even to their folly. Far down beyond the fathom of the intellect the soul acknowledged that all these varying and conflicting developments of humanity were united in one sentiment. Be the individual theory as wild as fancy could make it, still the wiser spirit would recognize the struggle of the race after a better and purer life than had yet been realized on earth. My faith revived even while I rejected all their schemes. It could not be that the world should continue forever what it has been; a soil where Happiness is so rare a flower and Virtue so often a blighted fruit; a battlefield where the good principle, with its shield flung above its head, can hardly save itself amid the rush of adverse influences. In the enthusiasm of such thoughts I gazed through one of the pictured windows, and, behold! the whole external world was tinged with the dimly glorious aspect that is peculiar to the Hall of Fantasy, insomuch that it seemed practicable at that very instant to realize some plan for the perfection of mankind. But, alas! if reformers would understand the sphere in which their lot is cast they must cease to look through pictured windows. Yet they not only use this medium, but mistake it for the whitest sunshine.

"Come," said I to my friend, starting from a deep reverie, "let us hasten hence or I shall be tempted to make a theory, after which there is little hope of any man."

"Come hither, then," answered he. "Here is one theory that swallows up and annihilates all others."

He led me to a distant part of the hall where a crowd of deeply attentive auditors were assembled round an elderly man of plain, honest, trustworthy aspect. With an earnestness that betokened the sincerest faith in his own doctrine, he announced that the destruction of the world was close at hand.

"It is Father Miller himself!" exclaimed I.

"No less a man," said my friend; "and observe how picturesque a contrast between his dogma and those of the reformers whom we have just glanced at. They look for the earthly perfection of mankind, and are forming schemes which imply that the immortal spirit will be connected with a physical nature for innumerable ages of futurity. On the other hand, here comes good Father Miller, and with one puff of his relentless theory scatters all their dreams like so many withered leaves upon the blast."

"It is, perhaps, the only method of getting mankind out of the various perplexities into which they have fallen," I replied. "Yet I could wish that the world might be permitted to endure until some great moral shall have been evolved. A riddle is propounded. Where is the solution? The sphinx did not slay herself until her riddle had been guessed. Will it not be so with the world? Now, if it should be burned to-morrow morning, I am at a loss to know what purpose will have been accomplished, or how the universe will be wiser or better for our existence and destruction."

"We cannot tell what mighty truths may have been embodied in act through the existence of the globe and its inhabitants," rejoined my companion. "Perhaps it may be revealed to us after the fall of the curtain over our castastrophe; or not impossibly, the whole drama, in which we are involuntary actors, may have been performed for the instruction of another set of spectators. I cannot perceive that our own comprehension of it is at all essential to the matter. At any rate, while our view is so ridiculously narrow and superficial it would be absurd to argue the continuance of the world from the fact that it seems to have existed hitherto in vain."

"The poor old earth," murmured I. "She has faults enough, in all conscience, but I cannot bear to have her perish."

"It is no great matter," said my friend. "The happiest of us has been weary of her many a time and oft."

"I doubt it," answered I, pertinaciously; "the root of human nature strikes down deep into this earthly soil, and it is but reluctantly that we submit to be transplanted, even for a higher cultivation in heaven. I query whether the destruction of the earth would gratify any one individual, except perhaps some embarrassed man of business whose notes fall due a day after the day of doom."

Then methought I heard the expostulating cry of a multitude against the consummation prophesied by Father Miller. The lover wrestled with Providence for his foreshadowed bliss. Parents entreated that the earth's span of endurance might be prolonged by some seventy years, so that their new-born infant should not be defrauded of his lifetime. A youthful poet murmured because there would be no posterity to recognize the inspiration of his song. The reformers, one and all, demanded a few thousand years to test their theories, after which the universe might go to wreck. A mechanician, who was busied with an improvement of the steam-engine, asked merely time to perfect his model. A miser insisted that the world's destruction would be a personal wrong to himself, unless he should first be permitted to add a specified sum to his enormous heap of gold. A little boy made dolorous inquiry whether the last day would come before Christmas, and thus deprive him of his anticipated dainties. In short, nobody seemed satisfied that this mortal scene of things should have its close just now. Yet, it must be confessed, the motives of the crowd for desiring its continuance were mostly so absurd that unless infinite Wisdom had been aware of much better reasons, the solid earth must have melted away at once.

For my own part, not to speak of a few private and personal ends, I really desired our old mother's prolonged existence for her own dear sake.

"The poor old earth!" I repeated. "What I should chiefly regret in her destruction would be that very earthliness which no other sphere or state of existence can renew or compensate. The fragrance of flowers and of new-mown hay; the genial warmth of sunshine and the beauty of a sunset among clouds; the comfort and cheerful glow of the fireside; the deliciousness of fruits and of all good cheer; the magnificence of mountains and seas and cataracts, and the softer charm of rural scenery; even the fast falling snow and the gray atmosphere through which it descends,—all these and innumerable other enjoyable things of earth must perish with her. Then the country frolics; the homely humor; the broad, open-mouthed roar of laughter, in which body and soul conjoin so heartily! I fear that no other world can show us anything just like this. As for purely moral enjoyments, the good will find them in every state of being. But where the material and the moral exist together, what is to happen then? And then our mute four-footed friends and the winged songsters of our woods! Might it not be lawful to regret them, even in the hallowed groves of paradise?"

"You speak like the very spirit of earth, imbued with a scent of freshly turned soil," exclaimed my friend.

"It is not that I so much object to giving up these enjoyments on my own account," continued I, "but I hate to think that they will have been eternally annihilated from the list of joys."

"Nor need they be," he replied. "I see no real force in what you say. Standing in this Hall of Fantasy, we perceive what even the earth-clogged intellect of man can do in creating circumstances which, though we call them shadowy and visionary, are scarcely more so than those that surround us in actual life. Doubt not then that man's disembodied spirit may recreate time and the world for itself, with all their peculiar enjoyments, should there still be human yearnings amid life eternal and infinite. But I doubt whether we shall be inclined to play such a poor scene over again."

"Oh, you are ungrateful to our mother earth!" rejoined I. "Come what may, I never will forget her! Neither will it satisfy me to have her exist merely in idea. I want her great, round, solid self to endure interminably, and still to be peopled with the kindly race of man, whom I uphold to be much better than he thinks himself. Nevertheless, I confide the whole matter to Providence, and shall endeavor so to live that the world may come to an end at any moment without leaving me at a loss to find foothold somewhere else."

"It is an excellent resolve," said my companion, looking at his watch. "But come; it is the dinner hour. Will you partake of my vegetable diet?"

A thing so matter-of-fact as an invitation to dinner, even when the fare was to be nothing more substantial than vegetables and fruit, compelled us forthwith to remove from the Hall of Fantasy. As we passed out of the portal we met the spirits of several persons who had been sent thither in magnetic sleep. I looked back among the sculptured pillars and at the transformations of the gleaming fountain, and almost desired that the whole of life might be spent in that visionary scene where the actual world, with its hard angles, should never rub against me, and only be viewed through the medium of pictured windows. But for those who waste all their days in the Hall of Fantasy, good Father Miller's prophecy is already accomplished, and the solid earth has come to an untimely end. Let us be content, therefore, with merely an occasional visit, for the sake of spiritualizing the grossness of this actual life, and prefiguring to ourselves a state in which the Idea shall be all in all.

THE CELESTIAL RAILROAD

Not a great while ago, passing through the gate of dreams, I visited that region of the earth in which lies the famous City of Destruction. It interested me much to learn that by the public spirit of some of the inhabitants a railroad has recently been established between this populous and flourishing town and the Celestial City. Having a little time upon my hands, I resolved to gratify a liberal curiosity by making a trip thither. Accordingly, one fine morning after paying my bill at the hotel, and directing the porter to stow my luggage behind a coach, I took my seat in the vehicle and set out for the station-house. It was my good fortune to enjoy the company of a gentleman—one Mr. Smooth-it-away—who, though he had never actually visited the Celestial City, yet seemed as well acquainted with its laws, customs, policy, and statistics, as with those of the City of Destruction, of which he was a native townsman. Being, moreover, a director of the railroad corporation and one of its largest stockholders, he had it in his power to give me all desirable information respecting that praiseworthy enterprise.

Our coach rattled out of the city, and at a short distance from its outskirts passed over a bridge of elegant construction, but somewhat too slight, as I imagined, to sustain any considerable weight. On both sides lay an extensive quagmire, which could not have been more disagreeable, either to sight or smell, had all the kennels of the earth emptied their pollution there.

"This," remarked Mr. Smooth-it-away, "is the famous Slough of Despond—a disgrace to all the neighborhood; and the greater that it might so easily be converted into firm ground."

"I have understood," said I, "that efforts have been made for that purpose from time immemorial. Bunyan mentions that above twenty thousand cartloads of wholesome instructions had been thrown in here without effect."

"Very probably! And what effect could be anticipated from such unsubstantial stuff?" cried Mr. Smooth-it-away. "You observe this convenient bridge. We obtained a sufficient foundation for it by throwing into the slough some editions of books of morality; volumes of French philosophy and German rationalism; tracts, sermons, and essays of modern clergymen; extracts from

Plato, Confucius, and various Hindoo sages, together with a few ingenious commentaries upon texts of Scripture,—all of which by some scientific process, have been converted into a mass like granite. The whole bog might be filled up with similar matter."

It really seemed to me, however, that the bridge vibrated and heaved up and down in a very formidable manner; and, spite of Mr. Smooth-it-away's testimony to the solidity of its foundation, I should be loath to cross it in a crowded omnibus, especially if each passenger were encumbered with as heavy luggage as that gentleman and myself. Nevertheless we got over without accident, and soon found ourselves at the station-house. This very neat and spacious edifice is erected on the site of the little wicket gate, which formerly, as all old pilgrims will recollect, stood directly across the highway, and, by its inconvenient narrowness, was a great obstruction to the traveller of liberal mind and expansive stomach. The reader of John Bunyan will be glad to know that Christian's old friend Evangelist, who was accustomed to supply each pilgrim with a mystic roll, now presides at the ticket office. Some malicious persons it is true deny the identity of this reputable character with the Evangelist of old times, and even pretend to bring competent evidence of an imposture. Without involving myself in a dispute I shall merely observe that, so far as my experience goes, the square pieces of pasteboard now delivered to passengers are much more convenient and useful along the road than the antique roll of parchment. Whether they will be as readily received at the gate of the Celestial City I decline giving an opinion.

A large number of passengers were already at the station-house awaiting the departure of the cars. By the aspect and demeanor of these persons it was easy to judge that the feelings of the community had undergone a very favorable change in reference to the celestial pilgrimage. It would have done Bunyan's heart good to see it. Instead of a lonely and ragged man with a huge burden on his back, plodding along sorrowfully on foot while the whole city hooted after him, here were parties of the first gentry and most respectable people in the neighborhood setting forth towards the Celestial City as cheerfully as if the pilgrimage were merely a summer tour. Among the gentlemen were characters of deserved eminence—magistrates, politicians, and men of wealth, by whose example religion could not but be greatly recommended to their meaner brethren. In the ladies' apartment, too, I rejoiced to distinguish some of those flowers of fashionable society who are so well fitted to adorn the most elevated circles of the Celestial City. There was much pleasant conversation about the news of the day, topics of business and politics, or the lighter matters of amusement; while religion, though indubitably the main thing at heart, was thrown tastefully into the background. Even an infidel would have heard little or nothing to shock his sensibility.

One great convenience of the new method of going on pilgrimage I must not forget to mention. Our enormous burdens, instead of being carried on our shoulders as had been the custom of old, were all snugly deposited in the baggage car, and, as I was assured, would be delivered to their respective owners at the journey's end. Another thing, likewise, the benevolent reader will be delighted to understand. It may be remembered that there was an ancient feud between Prince Beelzebub and the keeper of the wicket gate, and that the adherents of the former distinguished personage were accustomed to shoot deadly arrows at honest pilgrims while knocking at the door. This dispute, much to the credit as well of the illustrious potentate above mentioned as of the worthy and enlightened directors of the railroad, has been pacifically arranged on the principle of mutual compromise. The prince's subjects are now pretty numerously employed about the station-house, some in taking care of the baggage, others in collecting fuel, feeding the engines, and such congenial occupations; and I can conscientiously affirm that persons more attentive to their business, more willing to accommodate, or more generally agreeable to the passengers, are not to be found on any railroad. Every good heart must surely exult at so satisfactory an arrangement of an immemorial difficulty.

"Where is Mr. Greatheart?" inquired I. "Beyond a doubt the directors have engaged that famous old champion to be chief conductor on the railroad?"

"Why, no," said Mr. Smooth-it-away, with a dry cough. "He was offered the situation of brakeman; but, to tell you the truth, our friend Greatheart has grown preposterously stiff and narrow in his old age. He has so often guided pilgrims over the road on foot that he considers it a sin to travel in any other fashion. Besides, the old fellow had entered so heartily into the ancient feud with Prince Beelzebub that he would have been perpetually at blows or ill language with some of the prince's subjects, and thus have embroiled us anew. So, on the whole, we were not sorry when honest Greatheart went off to the Celestial City in a huff and left us at liberty to choose a more suitable and accommodating man. Yonder comes the engineer of the train. You will probably recognize him at once."

The engine at this moment took its station in advance of the cars, looking, I must confess, much more like a sort of mechanical demon that would hurry us to the infernal regions than a laudable contrivance for smoothing our way to the Celestial City. On its top sat a personage almost enveloped in smoke and flame, which, not to startle the reader, appeared to gush from his own mouth and stomach as well as from the engine's brazen abdomen.

"Do my eyes deceive me?" cried I. "What on earth is this! A living creature? If so, he is own brother to the engine he rides upon!"

"Poh, poh, you are obtuse!" said Mr. Smooth-it-away, with a hearty laugh. "Don't you know Apollyon, Christian's old enemy, with whom he fought so fierce a battle in the Valley of Humiliation? He was the very fellow to manage the engine; and so we have reconciled him to the custom of going on pilgrimage, and engaged him as chief engineer."

"Bravo, bravo!" exclaimed I, with irrepressible enthusiasm; "this shows the liberality of the age; this proves, if anything can, that all musty prejudices are in a fair way to be obliterated. And how will Christian rejoice to hear of this happy transformation of his old antagonist! I promise myself great pleasure in informing him of it when we reach the Celestial City."

The passengers being all comfortably seated, we now rattled away merrily, accomplishing a greater distance in ten minutes than Christian probably trudged over in a day. It was laughable, while we glanced along, as it were, at the tail of a thunderbolt, to observe two dusty foot travellers in the old pilgrim guise, with cockle shell and staff, their mystic rolls of parchment in their hands and their intolerable burdens on their backs. The preposterous obstinacy of these honest people in persisting to groan and stumble along the difficult pathway rather than take advantage of modern improvements, excited great mirth among our wiser brotherhood. We greeted the two pilgrims with many pleasant gibes and a roar of laughter; whereupon they gazed at us with such woful and absurdly compassionate visages that our merriment grew tenfold more obstreperous. Apollyon also entered heartily into the fun, and contrived to flirt the smoke and flame of the engine, or of his own breath, into their faces, and envelop them in an atmosphere of scalding steam. These little practical jokes amused us mightily, and doubtless afforded the pilgrims the gratification of considering themselves martyrs.

At some distance from the railroad Mr. Smooth-it-away pointed to a large, antique edifice, which, he observed, was a tavern of long standing, and had formerly been a noted stopping-place for pilgrims. In Bunyan's road-book it is mentioned as the Interpreter's House.

"I have long had a curiosity to visit that old mansion," remarked I.

"It is not one of our stations, as you perceive," said my companion. "The keeper was violently opposed to the railroad; and well he might be, as the track left his house of entertainment on one side, and thus was pretty certain to deprive him of all his reputable customers. But the footpath still passes his door, and the old gentleman now and then receives a call from some simple traveller, and entertains him with fare as old-fashioned as himself."

Before our talk on this subject came to a conclusion we were rushing by the place where Christian's burden fell from his shoulders at the sight of the Cross. This served as a theme for Mr. Smooth-it-away, Mr. Live-for-the-world, Mr. Hide-sin-in-the-heart, Mr. Scaly-conscience, and a knot of gentlemen from the town of Shun-repentance, to descant upon the inestimable advantages resulting from the safety of our baggage. Myself, and all the passengers indeed, joined with great unanimity in this view of the matter; for our burdens were rich in many things esteemed precious throughout the world; and, especially, we each of us possessed a great variety of favorite Habits, which we trusted would not be out of fashion even in the polite circles of the Celestial City. It would have been a sad spectacle to see such an assortment of valuable articles tumbling into the sepulchre. Thus pleasantly conversing on the favorable circumstances of our position as compared with those of past pilgrims and of narrow-minded ones at the present day, we soon found ourselves at the foot of the Hill Difficulty. Through the very heart of this rocky mountain a tunnel has been constructed of most admirable architecture, with a lofty arch and a spacious double track; so that, unless the earth and rocks should chance to crumble down, it will remain an eternal monument of the builder's skill and enterprise. It is a great though incidental advantage that the materials from the heart of the Hill Difficulty have been employed in filling up the Valley of Humiliation, thus obviating the necessity of descending into that disagreeable and unwholesome hollow.

"This is a wonderful improvement, indeed," said I. "Yet I should have been glad of an opportunity to visit the Palace Beautiful and be introduced to the charming young ladies—Miss Prudence, Miss Piety, Miss Charity, and the rest—who have the kindness to entertain pilgrims there."

"Young ladies!" cried Mr. Smooth-it-away, as soon as he could speak for laughing. "And charming young ladies! Why, my dear fellow, they are old maids, every soul of them—prim, starched, dry, and angular; and not one of them, I will venture to say, has altered so much as the fashion of her gown since the days of Christian's pilgrimage."

"Ah, well," said I, much comforted, "then I can very readily dispense with their acquaintance."

The respectable Apollyon was now putting on the steam at a prodigious rate, anxious, perhaps, to get rid of the unpleasant reminiscences connected with the spot where he had so disastrously encountered Christian. Consulting Mr. Bunyan's road-book, I perceived that we must now be within a few miles of the Valley of the Shadow of Death, into which doleful region, at our present speed, we should plunge much sooner than seemed at all desirable. In truth, I expected nothing better than to find myself in the ditch on one side or the quag on the other; but on communicating my apprehensions to Mr. Smooth-it-away, he assured me that the difficulties of this passage, even in its worst condition, had been vastly exaggerated, and that, in its present state of improvement, I might consider myself as safe as on any railroad in Christendom.

Even while we were speaking the train shot into the entrance of this dreaded Valley. Though I plead guilty to some foolish palpitations of the heart during our headlong rush over the causeway here constructed, yet it were unjust to withhold the highest encomiums on the boldness of its original conception and the ingenuity of those who executed it. It was gratifying, likewise, to observe how much care had been taken to dispel the everlasting gloom and supply the defect of cheerful sunshine, not a ray of which has ever penetrated among these awful shadows. For this purpose, the inflammable gas which exudes plentifully from the soil is collected by means of pipes, and thence communicated to a quadruple row of lamps along the whole extent of the passage. Thus a radiance has been created even out of the fiery and sulphurous curse that rests forever upon the valley—a radiance hurtful, however, to the eyes, and somewhat bewildering, as I discovered by the changes which it wrought in the visages of my companions. In this respect, as compared with natural daylight, there is the same difference as between truth and falsehood; but if the reader have ever travelled through the dark Valley, he will have learned to be thankful for any light that he could get—if not from the sky above, then from the blasted soil beneath. Such was the red brilliancy of these lamps that they appeared to build walls of fire on both sides of the track, between which we held our course at lightning speed, while a reverberating thunder filled the Valley with its echoes. Had the engine run off the track,—a catastrophe, it is whispered, by no means unprecedented,—the bottomless pit, if there be any such place, would undoubtedly have received us. Just as some dismal fooleries of this nature had made my heart quake there came a tremendous shriek, careering along the valley as if a thousand devils had burst their lungs to utter it, but which proved to be merely the whistle of the engine on arriving at a stopping-place.

The spot where we had now paused is the same that our friend Bunyan—a truthful man, but infected with many fantastic notions—has designated, in terms plainer than I like to repeat, as the mouth of the infernal region. This, however, must be a mistake, inasmuch as Mr. Smooth-it-away, while we remained in the smoky and lurid cavern, took occasion to prove that Tophet has not even a metaphorical existence. The place, he assured us, is no other than the crater of a half-extinct volcano, in which the directors had caused forges to be set up for the manufacture of railroad iron. Hence, also, is obtained a plentiful supply of fuel for the use of the engines. Whoever had gazed into the dismal obscurity of the broad cavern mouth, whence ever and anon darted huge tongues of dusky flame, and had seen the strange, half-shaped monsters, and visions of faces horribly grotesque, into which the smoke seemed to wreathe itself, and had heard the awful murmurs, and shrieks, and deep, shuddering whispers of the blast, sometimes forming themselves into words almost articulate, would have seized upon Mr. Smooth-it-away's comfortable explanation as greedily as we did. The inhabitants of the cavern, moreover, were unlovely personages, dark, smoke-begrimed, generally deformed, with misshapen feet, and a glow of dusky redness in their eyes as if their hearts had caught fire and were blazing out of the upper windows. It struck me as a peculiarity that the laborers at the forge and those who brought fuel to the engine, when they began to draw short breath, positively emitted smoke from their mouth and nostrils.

Among the idlers about the train, most of whom were puffing cigars which they had lighted at the flame of the crater, I was perplexed to notice several who, to my certain knowledge, had heretofore set forth by railroad for the Celestial City. They looked dark, wild, and smoky, with a singular resemblance, indeed, to the native inhabitants, like whom, also, they had a disagreeable propensity to ill-natured gibes and sneers, the habit of which had wrought a settled contortion of their visages. Having been on speaking terms with one of these persons,—an indolent, good-for-nothing fellow, who went by the name of Take-it-easy,—I called him, and inquired what was his business there.

"Did you not start," said I, "for the Celestial City?"

"That's a fact," said Mr. Take-it-easy, carelessly puffing some smoke into my eyes. "But I heard such bad accounts that I never took pains to climb the hill on which the city stands. No business doing, no fun going on, nothing to drink, and no smoking allowed, and a thrumming of church music from morning till night. I would not stay in such a place if they offered me house room and living free."

"But, my good Mr. Take-it-easy," cried I, "why take up your residence here, of all places in the world?"

"Oh," said the loafer, with a grin, "it is very warm hereabouts, and I meet with plenty of old acquaintances, and altogether the place suits me. I hope to see you back again some day soon. A pleasant journey to you."

While he was speaking the bell of the engine rang, and we dashed away after dropping a few passengers, but receiving no new ones. Rattling onward through the Valley, we were dazzled with the fiercely gleaming gas lamps, as before. But sometimes, in the dark of intense brightness, grim faces, that bore the aspect and expression of individual sins, or evil passions, seemed to thrust themselves through the veil of light, glaring upon us, and stretching forth a great, dusky hand, as if to impede our progress. I almost thought that they were my own sins that appalled me there. These were freaks of imagination—nothing more, certainly—mere delusions, which I ought to be heartily ashamed of; but all through the Dark Valley I was tormented, and pestered, and dolefully bewildered with the same kind of waking dreams. The mephitic gases of that region intoxicate the brain. As the light of natural day, however, began to struggle with the glow of the lanterns, these vain imaginations lost their vividness, and finally vanished with the first ray of sunshine that greeted our escape from the Valley of the Shadow of Death. Ere we had gone a mile beyond it I could wellnigh have taken my oath that this whole gloomy passage was a dream.

At the end of the valley, as John Bunyan mentions, is a cavern, where, in his days, dwelt two cruel giants, Pope and Pagan, who had strown the ground about their residence with the bones of slaughtered pilgrims. These vile old troglodytes are no longer there; but into their deserted cave another terrible giant has thrust himself, and makes it his business to seize upon honest travellers and fatten them for his table with plentiful meals of smoke, mist, moonshine, raw potatoes, and sawdust. He is a German by birth, and is called Giant Transcendentalist; but as to his form, his features, his substance, and his nature generally, it is the chief peculiarity of this huge miscreant that neither he for himself, nor anybody for him, has ever been able to describe them. As we rushed by the cavern's mouth we caught a hasty glimpse of him, looking somewhat like an ill-proportioned figure, but considerably more like a heap of fog and duskiness. He shouted after us, but in so strange a phraseology that we knew not what he meant, nor whether to be encouraged or affrighted.

It was late in the day when the train thundered into the ancient city of Vanity, where Vanity Fair is still at the height of prosperity, and exhibits an epitome of whatever is brilliant, gay, and fascinating beneath the sun. As I purposed to make a considerable stay here, it gratified me to learn that there is no longer the want of harmony between the town's-people and pilgrims, which impelled the former to such lamentably mistaken measures as the persecution of Christian and the fiery martyrdom of Faithful. On the contrary, as the new railroad brings with it great trade and a constant influx of strangers, the lord of Vanity Fair is its chief patron, and the capitalists of the city are among the largest stockholders. Many passengers stop to take their pleasure or make their profit in the Fair, instead of going onward to the Celestial City. Indeed, such are the charms of the place that people often affirm it to be the true and only heaven; stoutly contending that there is no other, that those who seek further are mere dreamers, and that, if the fabled brightness of the Celestial City lay but a bare mile beyond the gates of Vanity, they would not be fools enough to go thither. Without subscribing to these perhaps exaggerated encomiums, I can truly say that my abode in the city was mainly agreeable, and my intercourse with the inhabitants productive of much amusement and instruction.

Being naturally of a serious turn, my attention was directed to the solid advantages derivable from a residence here, rather than to the effervescent pleasures which are the grand object with too many visitants. The Christian reader, if he have had no accounts of the city later than Bunyan's time, will be surprised to hear that almost every street has its church, and that the reverend clergy are nowhere held in higher respect than at Vanity Fair. And well do they deserve such honorable estimation; for the maxims of wisdom and virtue which fall from their lips come from as deep a spiritual source, and tend to as lofty a religious aim, as those of the sagest philosophers of old. In justification of this high praise I need only mention the names of the Rev.

Mr. Shallow-deep, the Rev. Mr. Stumble-at-truth, that fine old clerical character the Rev. Mr. This-to-day, who expects shortly to resign his pulpit to the Rev. Mr. That-to-morrow; together with the Rev. Mr. Bewilderment, the Rev. Mr. Clog-the-spirit, and, last and greatest, the Rev. Dr. Wind-of-doctrine. The labors of these eminent divines are aided by those of innumerable lecturers, who diffuse such a various profundity, in all subjects of human or celestial science, that any man may acquire an omnigenous erudition without the trouble of even learning to read. Thus literature is etherealized by assuming for its medium the human voice; and knowledge, depositing all its heavier particles, except, doubtless, its gold, becomes exhaled into a sound, which forthwith steals into the ever-open ear of the community. These ingenious methods constitute a sort of machinery, by which thought and study are done to every person's hand without his putting himself to the slightest inconvenience in the matter. There is another species of machine for the wholesale manufacture of individual morality. This excellent result is effected by societies for all manner of virtuous purposes, with which a man has merely to connect himself, throwing, as it were, his quota of virtue into the common stock, and the president and directors will take care that the aggregate amount be well applied. All these, and other wonderful improvements in ethics, religion, and literature, being made plain to my comprehension by the ingenious Mr. Smooth-it-away, inspired me with a vast admiration of Vanity Fair.

It would fill a volume, in an age of pamphlets, were I to record all my observations in this great capital of human business and pleasure. There was an unlimited range of society—the powerful, the wise, the witty, and the famous in every walk of life; princes, presidents, poets, generals, artists, actors, and philanthropists,—all making their own market at the fair, and deeming no price too exorbitant for such commodities as hit their fancy. It was well worth one's while, even if he had no idea of buying or selling, to loiter through the bazaars and observe the various sorts of traffic that were going forward.

Some of the purchasers, I thought, made very foolish bargains. For instance, a young man having inherited a splendid fortune, laid out a considerable portion of it in the purchase of diseases, and finally spent all the rest for a heavy lot of repentance and a suit of rags. A very pretty girl bartered a heart as clear as crystal, and which seemed her most valuable possession, for another jewel of the same kind, but so worn and defaced as to be utterly worthless. In one shop there were a great many crowns of laurel and myrtle, which soldiers, authors, statesmen, and various other people pressed eagerly to buy; some purchased these paltry wreaths with their lives, others by a toilsome servitude of years, and many sacrificed whatever was most valuable, yet finally slunk away without the crown. There was a sort of stock or scrip, called Conscience, which seemed to be in great demand, and would purchase almost anything. Indeed, few rich commodities were to be obtained without paying a heavy sum in this particular stock, and a man's business was seldom very lucrative unless he knew precisely when and how to throw his hoard of conscience into the market. Yet as this stock was the only thing of permanent value, whoever parted with it was sure to find himself a loser in the long run. Several of the speculations were of a questionable character. Occasionally a member of Congress recruited his pocket by the sale of his constituents; and

I was assured that public officers have often sold their country at very moderate prices. Thousands sold their happiness for a whim. Gilded chains were in great demand, and purchased with almost any sacrifice. In truth, those who desired, according to the old adage, to sell anything valuable for a song, might find customers all over the Fair; and there were innumerable messes of pottage, piping hot, for such as chose to buy them with their birthrights. A few articles, however, could not be found genuine at Vanity Fair. If a customer wished to renew his stock of youth the dealers offered him a set of false teeth and an auburn wig; if he demanded peace of mind, they recommended opium or a brandy bottle.

Tracts of land and golden mansions, situate in the Celestial City, were often exchanged, at very disadvantageous rates, for a few years' lease of small, dismal, inconvenient tenements in Vanity Fair. Prince Beelzebub himself took great interest in this sort of traffic, and sometimes condescended to meddle with smaller matters. I once had the pleasure to see him bargaining with a miser for his soul, which, after much ingenious skirmishing on both sides, his highness succeeded in obtaining at about the value of sixpence. The prince remarked with a smile, that he was a loser by the transaction.

Day after day, as I walked the streets of Vanity, my manners and deportment became more and more like those of the inhabitants. The place began to seem like home; the idea of pursuing my travels to the Celestial City was almost obliterated from my mind. I was reminded of it, however, by the sight of the same pair of simple pilgrims at whom we had laughed so heartily when Apollyon puffed smoke and steam into their faces at the commencement of our journey. There they stood amidst the densest bustle of Vanity; the dealers offering them their purple and fine linen and jewels, the men of wit and humor gibing at them, a pair of buxom ladies ogling them askance, while the benevolent Mr. Smooth-it-away whispered some of his wisdom at their elbows, and pointed to a newly-erected temple; but there were these worthy simpletons, making the scene look wild and monstrous, merely by their sturdy repudiation of all part in its business or pleasures.

One of them—his name was Stick-to-the-right—perceived in my face, I suppose, a species of sympathy and almost admiration, which, to my own great surprise, I could not help feeling for this pragmatic couple. It prompted him to address me.

"Sir," inquired he, with a sad, yet mild and kindly voice, "do you call yourself a pilgrim?"

"Yes," I replied, "my right to that appellation is indubitable. I am merely a sojourner here in Vanity Fair, being bound to the Celestial City by the new railroad."

"Alas, friend," rejoined Mr. Stick-to-the-right, "I do assure you, and beseech you to receive the truth of my words, that that whole concern is a bubble. You may travel on it all your lifetime, were you to live thousands of years, and yet never get beyond the limits of Vanity Fair. Yea, though you should deem yourself entering the gates of the blessed city, it will be nothing but a miserable delusion."

"The Lord of the Celestial City," began the other pilgrim, whose name was Mr. Foot-it-to-heaven, "has refused, and will ever refuse, to grant an act of incorporation for this railroad; and unless that be obtained, no passenger can ever hope to enter his dominions. Wherefore every man who buys a ticket must lay his account with losing the purchase money, which is the value of his own soul."

"Poh, nonsense!" said Mr. Smooth-it-away, taking my arm and leading me off, "these fellows ought to be indicted for a libel. If the law stood as it once did in Vanity Fair we should see them grinning through the iron bars of the prison window."

This incident made a considerable impression on my mind, and contributed with other circumstances to indispose me to a permanent residence in the city of Vanity; although, of course, I was not simple enough to give up my original plan of gliding along easily and commodiously by railroad. Still, I grew anxious to be gone. There was one strange thing that troubled me. Amid the occupations or amusements of the Fair, nothing was more common than for a person —whether at feast, theatre, or church, or trafficking for wealth and honors, or whatever he might be doing, and however unseasonable the interruption— suddenly to vanish like a soap bubble, and be never more seen of his fellows; and so accustomed were the latter to such little accidents that they went on with their business as quietly as if nothing had happened. But it was otherwise with me.

Finally, after a pretty long residence at the Fair, I resumed my journey towards the Celestial City, still with Mr. Smooth-it-away at my side. At a short distance beyond the suburbs of Vanity we passed the ancient silver mine, of which Demas was the first discoverer, and which is now wrought to great advantage, supplying nearly all the coined currency of the world. A little further onward was the spot where Lot's wife had stood forever under the semblance of a pillar of salt. Curious travellers have long since carried it away piecemeal. Had all regrets been punished as rigorously as this poor dame's were, my yearning for the relinquished delights of Vanity Fair might have produced a similar change in my own corporeal substance, and left me a warning to future pilgrims.

The next remarkable object was a large edifice, constructed of mossgrown stone, but in a modern and airy style of architecture. The engine came to a pause in its vicinity, with the usual tremendous shriek.

"This was formerly the castle of the redoubted giant Despair," observed Mr. Smooth-it-way; "but since his death Mr. Flimsy-faith has repaired it, and keeps an excellent house of entertainment here. It is one of our stopping-places."

"It seems but slightly put together," remarked I, looking at the frail yet ponderous walls. "I do not envy Mr. Flimsy-faith his habitation. Some day it will thunder down upon the heads of the occupants."

"We shall escape at all events," said Mr. Smooth-it-away, "for Apollyon is putting on the steam again."

The road now plunged into a gorge of the Delectable Mountains, and traversed the field where in former ages the blind men wandered and stumbled among the tombs. One of these ancient tombstones had been thrust across the track by some malicious person, and gave the train of cars a terrible jolt. Far up the rugged side of a mountain I perceived a rusty iron door, half overgrown with bushes and creeping plants, but with smoke issuing from its crevices.

"Is that," inquired I, "the very door in the hill-side which the shepherds assured Christian was a by-way to hell?"

"That was a joke on the part of the shepherds," said Mr. Smooth-it-away, with a smile. "It is neither more nor less than the door of a cavern which they use as a smoke-house for the preparation of mutton hams."

My recollections of the journey are now, for a little space, dim and confused, inasmuch as a singular drowsiness here overcame me, owing to the fact that we were passing over the enchanted ground, the air of which encourages a disposition to sleep. I awoke, however, as soon as we crossed the borders of the pleasant land of Beulah. All the passengers were rubbing their eyes, comparing watches, and congratulating one another on the prospect of arriving so seasonably at the journey's end. The sweet breezes of this happy clime came refreshingly to our nostrils; we beheld the glimmering gush of silver fountains, overhung by trees of beautiful foliage and delicious fruit, which were propagated by grafts from the celestial gardens. Once, as we dashed onward like a hurricane, there was a flutter of wings and the bright appearance of an angel in the air, speeding forth on some heavenly mission. The engine now announced the close vicinity of the final station-house by one last and horrible scream, in which there seemed to be distinguishable every kind of wailing and woe, and bitter fierceness of wrath, all mixed up with the wild laughter of a devil or a madman. Throughout our journey, at every stopping-place, Apollyon had exercised his ingenuity in screwing the most abominable sounds out of the whistle of the steam-engine; but in this closing effort he outdid himself and created an infernal uproar, which, besides disturbing the peaceful inhabitants of Beulah, must have sent its discord even through the celestial gates.

While the horrid clamor was still ringing in our ears we heard an exulting strain, as if a thousand instruments of music, with height and depth and sweetness in their tones, at once tender and triumphant, were struck in unison, to greet the approach of some illustrious hero, who had fought the good fight and won a glorious victory, and was come to lay aside his battered arms forever. Looking to ascertain what might be the occasion of this glad harmony, I perceived, on alighting from the cars, that a multitude of shining ones had assembled on the other side of the river, to welcome two poor pilgrims, who were just emerging from its depths. They were the same whom Apollyon and ourselves had persecuted with taunts, and gibes, and scalding steam, at the commencement of our journey—the same whose unworldly aspect and impressive words had stirred my conscience amid the wild revellers of Vanity Fair.

"How amazingly well those men have got on," cried I to Mr. Smooth-it-away. "I wish we were secure of as good a reception."

"Never fear, never fear!" answered my friend. "Come, make haste; the ferry boat will be off directly, and in three minutes you will be on the other side of the river. No doubt you will find coaches to carry you up to the city gates."

A steam ferry boat, the last improvement on this important route, lay at the river side, puffing, snorting, and emitting all those other disagreeable utterances which betoken the departure to be immediate. I hurried on board with the rest of the passengers, most of whom were in great perturbation: some bawling out for their baggage; some tearing their hair and exclaiming that the boat would explode or sink; some already pale with the heaving of the stream; some gazing affrighted at the ugly aspect of the steersman; and some still dizzy with the slumberous influences of the Enchanted Ground. Looking back to the shore, I was amazed to discern Mr. Smooth-it-away waving his hand in token of farewell.

"Don't you go over to the Celestial City?" exclaimed I.

"Oh, no!" answered he with a queer smile, and that same disagreeable contortion of visage which I had remarked in the inhabitants of the Dark Valley. "Oh, no! I have come thus far only for the sake of your pleasant company. Good-by! We shall meet again."

And then did my excellent friend Mr. Smooth-it-away laugh outright, in the midst of which cachinnation a smoke-wreath issued from his mouth and nostrils, while a twinkle of lurid flame darted out of either eye, proving indubitably that his heart was all of a red blaze. The impudent fiend! To deny the existence of Tophet, when he felt its fiery tortures raging within his breast. I rushed to the side of the boat, intending to fling myself on shore; but the wheels, as they began their revolutions, threw a dash of spray over me so cold—so deadly cold, with the chill that will never leave those waters until Death be drowned in his own river—that with a shiver and a heartquake I awoke. Thank Heaven it was a Dream!

THE PROCESSION OF LIFE

Life figures itself to me as a festal or funereal procession. All of us have our places, and are to move onward under the direction of the Chief Marshal. The grand difficulty results from the invariably mistaken principles on which the deputy marshals seek to arrange this immense concourse of people, so much more numerous than those that train their interminable length through streets and highways in times of political excitement. Their scheme is ancient, far beyond the memory of man or even the record of history, and has hitherto been very little modified by the innate sense of something wrong, and the dim perception of better methods, that have disquieted all the ages through which the procession has taken its march. Its members are classified by the merest external circumstances, and thus are more certain to be thrown out of their true positions than if no principle of arrangement were attempted. In one part of the procession we see men of landed estate or moneyed capital gravely keeping each other company, for the preposterous reason that they chance to have a similar standing in the tax-gatherer's book. Trades and professions march together with scarcely a more real bond of union. In this manner, it cannot be denied, people are disentangled from the mass and separated into various classes according to certain apparent relations; all have some artificial badge which the world, and themselves among the first, learn to consider as a genuine characteristic. Fixing our attention on such outside shows of similarity or difference, we lose sight of those realities by which nature, fortune, fate, or Providence has constituted for every man a brotherhood, wherein it is one great office of human wisdom to classify him. When the mind has once accustomed itself to a proper arrangement of the Procession of Life, or a true classification of society, even though merely speculative, there is thenceforth a satisfaction which pretty well suffices for itself without the aid of any actual reformation in the order of march.

For instance, assuming to myself the power of marshalling the aforesaid procession, I direct a trumpeter to send forth a blast loud enough to be heard from hence to China; and a herald, with world-pervading voice, to make proclamation for a certain class of mortals to take their places. What shall be their principle of union? After all, an external one, in comparison with many that might be found, yet far more real than those which the world has selected for a similar purpose. Let all who are afflicted with like physical diseases form themselves into ranks.

Our first attempt at classification is not very successful. It may gratify the pride of aristocracy to reflect that disease, more than any other circumstance of human life, pays due observance to the distinctions which rank and wealth, and poverty and lowliness, have established among mankind. Some maladies are rich and precious, and only to be acquired by the right of inheritance or purchased with gold. Of this kind is the gout, which serves as a bond of brotherhood to the purple-visaged gentry, who obey the herald's voice, and painfully hobble from all civilized regions of the globe to take their post in the grand procession. In mercy to their toes, let us hope that the march may not be long. The Dyspeptics, too, are people of good standing in the world. For them the earliest salmon is caught in our eastern rivers, and the shy woodcock stains the dry leaves with his blood in his remotest haunts, and the turtle comes from the far Pacific Islands to be gobbled up in soup. They can afford to flavor all their dishes with indolence, which, in spite of the general opinion, is a sauce more exquisitely piquant than appetite won by exercise. Apoplexy is another highly respectable disease. We will rank together all who have the symptom of dizziness in the brain, and as fast as any drop by the way supply their places with new members of the board of aldermen.

On the other hand, here come whole tribes of people whose physical lives are but a deteriorated variety of life, and themselves a meaner species of mankind; so sad an effect has been wrought by the tainted breath of cities, scanty and unwholesome food, destructive modes of labor, and the lack of those moral supports that might partially have counteracted such bad influences. Behold here a train of house painters, all afflicted with a peculiar sort of colic. Next in place we will marshal those workmen in cutlery, who have breathed a fatal disorder into their lungs with the impalpable dust of steel. Tailors and shoemakers, being sedentary men, will chiefly congregate into one part of the procession and march under similar banners of disease; but among them we may observe here and there a sickly student, who has left his health between the leaves of classic volumes; and clerks, likewise, who have caught their deaths on high official stools; and men of genius too, who have written sheet after sheet with pens dipped in their heart's blood. These are a wretched, quaking, short-breathed set. But what is this cloud of pale-cheeked, slender girls, who disturb the ear with the multiplicity of their short, dry coughs? They are seamstresses, who have plied the daily and nightly needle in the service of master tailors and close-fisted contractors, until now it is almost time for each to hem the borders of her own shroud. Consumption points their place in the procession. With their sad sisterhood are intermingled many youthful maidens who have sickened in aristocratic mansions, and for whose aid science has unavailingly searched its volumes, and whom breathless love has watched. In our ranks the rich maiden and the poor seamstress may walk arm in arm. We might find innumerable other instances, where the bond of mutual disease—not to speak of nation-sweeping pestilence—embraces high and low, and makes the king a brother of the clown. But it is not hard to own that disease is the natural aristocrat. Let him keep his state, and have his established orders of rank, and wear his royal mantle of the color of a fever flush; and let the noble and wealthy boast their own physical infirmities, and display their symptoms as the badges of high station. All things considered, these are as proper subjects of human pride as any relations of human rank that men can fix upon.

Sound again, thou deep-breathed trumpeter! and herald, with thy voice of might, shout forth another summons that shall reach the old baronial castles of Europe, and the rudest cabin of our western wilderness! What class is next to take its place in the procession of mortal life? Let it be those whom the gifts of intellect have united in a noble brotherhood.

Ay, this is a reality, before which the conventional distinctions of society melt away like a vapor when we would grasp it with the hand. Were Byron now alive, and Burns, the first would come from his ancestral abbey, flinging aside, although unwillingly, the inherited honors of a thousand years, to take the arm of the mighty peasant who grew immortal while he stooped behind his plough. These are gone; but the hall, the farmer's fireside, the hut, perhaps the palace, the counting-room, the workshop, the village, the city, life's high places and low ones, may all produce their poets, whom a common temperament pervades like an electric sympathy. Peer or ploughman, we will muster them pair by pair and shoulder to shoulder. Even society, in its most artificial state, consents to this arrangement. These factory girls from Lowell shall mate themselves with the pride of drawing-rooms and literary circles, the bluebells in fashion's nosegay, the Sapphos, and Montagues, and Nortons of the age. Other modes of intellect bring together as strange companies. Silk-gowned professor of languages, give your arm to this sturdy blacksmith, and deem yourself honored by the conjunction, though you behold him grimy from the anvil. All varieties of human speech are like his mother tongue to this rare man. Indiscriminately let those take their places, of whatever rank they come, who possess the kingly gifts to lead armies or to sway a people—Nature's generals, her lawgivers, her kings, and with them also the deep philosophers who think the thought in one generation that is to revolutionize society in the next. With the hereditary legislator in whom eloquence is a far-descended attainment—a rich echo repeated by powerful voices from Cicero downward—we will match some wondrous backwoodsman, who has caught a wild power of language from the breeze among his native forest boughs. But we may safely leave these brethren and sisterhood to settle their own congenialities. Our ordinary distinctions become so trifling, so impalpable, so ridiculously visionary, in comparison with a classification founded on truth, that all talk about the matter is immediately a common place.

Yet the longer I reflect the less am I satisfied with the idea of forming a separate class of mankind on the basis of high intellectual power. At best it is but a higher development of innate gifts common to all. Perhaps, moreover, he whose genius appears deepest and truest excels his fellows in nothing save the knack of expression; he throws out occasionally a lucky hint at truths of which every human soul is profoundly, though unutterably, conscious. Therefore, though we suffer the brotherhood of intellect to march onward together, it may be doubted whether their peculiar relation will not begin to vanish as soon as the procession shall have passed beyond the circle of this present world. But we do not classify for eternity.

And next, let the trumpet pour forth a funereal wail, and the herald's voice give breath in one vast cry to all the groans and grievous utterances that are audible throughout the earth. We appeal now to the sacred bond of sorrow, and summon the great multitude who labor under similar afflictions to take their places in the march.

How many a heart that would have been insensible to any other call has responded to the doleful accents of that voice! It has gone far and wide, and high and low, and left scarcely a mortal roof unvisited. Indeed, the principle is only too universal for our purpose, and, unless we limit it, will quite break up our classification of mankind, and convert the whole procession into a funeral train. We will therefore be at some pains to discriminate. Here comes a lonely rich man; he has built a noble fabric for his dwelling-house, with a front of stately architecture and marble floors and doors of precious woods; the whole structure is as beautiful as a dream and as substantial as the native rock. But the visionary shapes of a long posterity, for whose home this mansion was intended, have faded into nothingness since the death of the founder's only son. The rich man gives a glance at his sable garb in one of the splendid mirrors of his drawing-room, and descending a flight of lofty steps instinctively offers his arm to yonder poverty stricken widow in the rusty black bonnet, and with a check apron over her patched gown. The sailor boy, who was her sole earthly stay, was washed overboard in a late tempest. This couple from the palace and the almshouse are but the types of thousands more who represent the dark tragedy of life and seldom quarrel for the upper parts. Grief is such a leveller, with its own dignity and its own humility, that the noble and the peasant, the beggar and the monarch, will waive their pretensions to external rank without the officiousness of interference on our part. If pride—the influence of the world's false distinctions—remain in the heart, then sorrow lacks the earnestness which makes it holy and reverend. It loses its reality and becomes a miserable shadow. On this ground we have an opportunity to assign over multitudes who would willingly claim places here to other parts of the procession. If the mourner have anything dearer than his grief he must seek his true position elsewhere. There are so many unsubstantial sorrows which the necessity of our mortal state begets on idleness, that an observer, casting aside sentiment, is sometimes led to question whether there be any real woe, except absolute physical suffering and the loss of closest friends. A crowd who exhibit what they deem to be broken hearts—and among them many lovelorn maids and bachelors, and men of disappointed ambition in arts or politics, and the poor who were once rich, or who have sought to be rich in vain—the great majority of these may ask admittance into some other fraternity. There is no room here. Perhaps we may institute a separate class where such unfortunates will naturally fall into the procession. Meanwhile let them stand aside and patiently await their time.

If our trumpeter can borrow a note from the doomsday trumpet blast, let him sound it now. The dread alarum should make the earth quake to its centre, for the herald is about to address mankind with a summons to which even the purest mortal may be sensible of some faint responding echo in his breast. In many bosoms it will awaken a still small voice more terrible than its own reverberating uproar.

The hideous appeal has swept around the globe. Come, all ye guilty ones, and rank yourselves in accordance with the brotherhood of crime. This, indeed, is an awful summons. I almost tremble to look at the strange partnerships that begin to be formed, reluctantly, but by the invincible necessity of like to like in this part of the procession. A forger from the state prison seizes the arm of a distinguished financier. How indignantly does the latter plead his fair reputation upon 'Change, and insist that his operations, by their magnificence of scope, were removed into quite another sphere of morality than those of his pitiful companion! But let him cut the connection if he can. Here comes a murderer with his clanking chains, and pairs himself—horrible to tell—with as pure and upright a man, in all observable respects, as ever partook of the consecrated bread and wine. He is one of those, perchance the most hopeless of all sinners, who practise such an exemplary system of outward duties, that even a deadly crime may be hidden from their own sight and remembrance, under this unreal frostwork. Yet he now finds his place. Why do that pair of flaunting girls, with the pert, affected laugh and the sly leer at the by-standers, intrude themselves into the same rank with yonder decorous matron, and that somewhat prudish maiden? Surely these poor creatures, born to vice as their sole and natural inheritance, can be no fit associates for women who have been guarded round about by all the proprieties of domestic life, and who could not err unless they first created the opportunity. Oh, no; it must be merely the impertinence of those unblushing hussies; and we can only wonder how such respectable ladies should have responded to a summons that was not meant for them.

We shall make short work of this miserable class, each member of which is entitled to grasp any other member's hand, by that vile degradation wherein guilty error has buried all alike. The foul fiend to whom it properly belongs must relieve us of our loathsome task. Let the bond servants of sin pass on. But neither man nor woman, in whom good predominates, will smile or sneer, nor bid the Rogues' March be played, in derision of their array. Feeling within their breasts a shuddering sympathy, which at least gives token of the sin that might have been, they will thank God for any place in the grand procession of human existence, save among those most wretched ones. Many, however, will be astonished at the fatal impulse that drags them thitherward. Nothing is more remarkable than the various deceptions by which guilt conceals itself from the perpetrator's conscience, and oftenest, perhaps, by the splendor of its garments. Statesmen, rulers, generals, and all men who act over an extensive sphere, are most liable to be deluded in this way; they commit wrong, devastation, and murder, on so grand a scale, that it impresses them as speculative rather than actual; but in our procession we find them linked in detestable conjunction with the meanest criminals whose deeds have the vulgarity of petty details. Here the effect of circumstance and accident is done away, and a man finds his rank according to the spirit of his crime, in whatever shape it may have been developed.

We have called the Evil; now let us call the Good. The trumpet's brazen throat should pour heavenly music over the earth, and the herald's voice go forth with the sweetness of an angel's accents, as if to summon each upright man to his reward. But how is this? Does none answer to the call? Not one: for the just, the pure, the true, and all who might most worthily obey it, shrink sadly back, as most conscious of error and imperfection. Then let the summons be to those whose pervading principle is Love. This classification will embrace all the truly good, and none in whose souls there exists not something that may expand itself into a heaven, both of well-doing and felicity.

The first that presents himself is a man of wealth, who has bequeathed the bulk of his property to a hospital; his ghost, methinks, would have a better right here than his living body. But here they come, the genuine benefactors of their race. Some have wandered about the earth with pictures of bliss in their imagination, and with hearts that shrank sensitively from the idea of pain and woe, yet have studied all varieties of misery that human nature can endure. The prison, the insane asylum, the squalid chamber of the almshouse, the manufactory where the demon of machinery annihilates the human soul, and the cotton field where God's image becomes a beast of burden; to these and every other scene where man wrongs or neglects his brother, the apostles of humanity have penetrated. This missionary, black with India's burning sunshine, shall give his arm to a pale-faced brother who has made himself familiar with the infected alleys and loathsome haunts of vice in one of our own cities. The generous founder of a college shall be the partner of a maiden lady of narrow substance, one of whose good deeds it has been to gather a little school of orphan children. If the mighty merchant whose benefactions are reckoned by thousands of dollars deem himself worthy, let him join the procession with her whose love has proved itself by watchings at the sick-bed, and all those lowly offices which bring her into actual contact with disease and wretchedness. And with those whose impulses have guided them to benevolent actions, we will rank others to whom Providence has assigned a different tendency and different powers. Men who have spent their lives in generous and holy contemplation for the human race; those who, by a certain heavenliness of spirit, have purified the atmosphere around them, and thus supplied a medium in which good and high things may be projected and performed—give to these a lofty place among the benefactors of mankind, although no deed, such as the world calls deeds, may be recorded of them. There are some individuals of whom we cannot conceive it proper that they should apply their hands to any earthly instrument, or work out any definite act; and others, perhaps not less high, to whom it is an essential attribute to labor in body as well as spirit for the welfare of their brethren. Thus, if we find a spiritual sage whose unseen, inestimable influence has exalted the moral standard of mankind, we will choose for his companion some poor laborer who has wrought for love in the potato field of a neighbor poorer than himself.

We have summoned this various multitude—and, to the credit of our nature, it is a large one—on the principle of Love. It is singular, nevertheless, to remark the shyness that exists among many members of the present class, all of whom we might expect to recognize one another by the freemasonry of mutual goodness, and to embrace like brethren, giving God thanks for such various specimens of human excellence. But it is far otherwise. Each sect surrounds its own righteousness with a hedge of thorns. It is difficult for the good Christian to acknowledge the good Pagan; almost impossible for the good Orthodox to grasp the hand of the good Unitarian, leaving to their Creator to settle the matters in dispute, and giving their mutual efforts strongly and trustingly to whatever right thing is too evident to be mistaken. Then again, though the heart be large, yet the mind is often of such moderate dimensions as to be exclusively filled up with one idea. When a good man has long devoted himself to a particular kind of beneficence—to one species of reform—he is apt to become narrowed into the limits of the path wherein he treads, and to fancy that there is no other good to be done on earth but that selfsame good to which he has put his hand, and in the very mode that best suits his own conceptions. All else is worthless. His scheme must be wrought out by the united strength of the whole world's stock of love, or the world is no longer worthy of a position in the universe. Moreover, powerful Truth, being the rich grape juice expressed from the vineyard of the ages, has an intoxicating quality, when imbibed by any save a powerful intellect, and often, as it were, impels the quaffer to quarrel in his cups. For such reasons, strange to say, it is harder to contrive a friendly arrangement of these brethren of love and righteousness, in the procession of life, than to unite even the wicked, who, indeed, are chained together by their crimes. The fact is too preposterous for tears, too lugubrious for laughter.

But, let good men push and elbow one another as they may during their earthly march, all will be peace among them when the honorable array of their procession shall tread on heavenly ground. There they will doubtless find that they have been working each for the other's cause, and that every well-delivered stroke, which, with an honest purpose any mortal struck, even for a narrow object, was indeed stricken for the universal cause of good. Their own view may be bounded by country, creed, profession, the diversities of individual character—but above them all is the breadth of Providence. How many who have deemed themselves antagonists will smile hereafter, when they look back upon the world's wide harvest field, and perceive that, in unconscious brotherhood, they were helping to bind the selfsame sheaf!

But, come! The sun is hastening westward, while the march of human life, that never paused before, is delayed by our attempt to rearrange its order. It is desirable to find some comprehensive principle, that shall render our task easier by bringing thousands into the ranks where hitherto we have brought one. Therefore let the trumpet, if possible, split its brazen throat with a louder note than ever, and the herald summon all mortals, who, from whatever cause, have lost, or never found, their proper places in the world.

Obedient to this call, a great multitude come together, most of them with a listless gait, betokening weariness of soul, yet with a gleam of satisfaction in their faces, at a prospect of at length reaching those positions which, hitherto, they have vainly sought. But here will be another disappointment; for we can attempt no more than merely to associate in one fraternity all who are afflicted with the same vague trouble. Some great mistake in life is the chief condition of admittance into this class. Here are members of the learned professions, whom Providence endowed with special gifts for the plough, the forge, and the wheelbarrow, or for the routine of unintellectual business. We will assign to them, as partners in the march, those lowly laborers and handicraftsmen, who have pined, as with a dying thirst, after the unattainable fountains of knowledge. The latter have lost less than their companions; yet more, because they deem it infinite. Perchance the two species of unfortunates may comfort one another. Here are Quakers with the instinct of battle in them; and men of war who should have worn the broad brim. Authors shall be ranked here whom some freak of Nature, making game of her poor children, had imbued with the confidence of genius and strong desire of fame, but has favored with no corresponding power; and others, whose lofty gifts were unaccompanied with the faculty of expression, or any of that earthly machinery by which ethereal endowments must be manifested to mankind. All these, therefore, are melancholy laughing-stocks. Next, here are honest and well intentioned persons, who by a want of tact—by inaccurate perceptions—by a distorting imagination—have been kept continually at cross purposes with the world and bewildered upon the path of life. Let us see if they can confine themselves within the line of our procession. In this class, likewise, we must assign places to those who have encountered that worst of ill success, a higher fortune than their abilities could vindicate; writers, actors, painters, the pets of a day, but whose laurels wither unrenewed amid their hoary hair; politicians, whom some malicious contingency of affairs has thrust into conspicuous station, where, while the world stands gazing at them, the dreary consciousness of imbecility makes them curse their birth hour. To such men, we give for a companion him whose rare talents, which perhaps require a Revolution for their exercise, are buried in the tomb of sluggish circumstances.

Not far from these, we must find room for one whose success has been of the wrong kind; the man who should have lingered in the cloisters of a university, digging new treasures out of the Herculaneum of antique lore, diffusing depth and accuracy of literature throughout his country, and thus making for himself a great and quiet fame. But the outward tendencies around him have proved too powerful for his inward nature, and have drawn him into the arena of political tumult, there to contend at disadvantage, whether front to front, or side by side, with the brawny giants of actual life. He becomes, it may be, a name for brawling parties to bandy to and fro, a legislator of the Union; a governor of his native state; an ambassador to the courts of kings or queens; and the world may deem him a man of happy stars. But not so the wise; and not so himself, when he looks through his experience, and sighs to miss that fitness, the one invaluable touch which makes all things true and real. So much achieved, yet how abortive is his life! Whom shall we choose for his companion? Some weak framed blacksmith, perhaps, whose delicacy of muscle might have suited a tailor's shopboard better than the anvil.

Shall we bid the trumpet sound again? It is hardly worth the while. There remain a few idle men of fortune, tavern and grog-shop loungers, lazzaroni, old bachelors, decaying maidens, and people of crooked intellect or temper, all of whom may find their like, or some tolerable approach to it, in the plentiful diversity of our latter class. There too, as his ultimate destiny, must we rank the dreamer, who, all his life long, has cherished the idea that he was peculiarly apt for something, but never could determine what it was; and there the most unfortunate of men, whose purpose it has been to enjoy life's pleasures, but to avoid a manful struggle with its toil and sorrow. The remainder, if any, may connect themselves with whatever rank of the procession they shall find best adapted to their tastes and consciences. The worst possible fate would be to remain behind, shivering in the solitude of time, while all the world is on the move towards eternity. Our attempt to classify society is now complete. The result may be anything but perfect; yet better—to give it the very lowest praise—than the antique rule of the herald's office, or the modern one of the tax-gatherer, whereby the accidents and superficial attributes, with which the real nature of individuals has least to do, are acted upon as the deepest characteristics of mankind. Our task is done! Now let the grand procession move!

Yet pause a while! We had forgotten the Chief Marshal.

Hark! That world-wide swell of solemn music, with the clang of a mighty bell breaking forth through its regulated uproar, announces his approach. He comes; a severe, sedate, immovable, dark rider, waving his truncheon of universal sway, as he passes along the lengthened line, on the pale horse of the Revelation. It is Death! Who else could assume the guidance of a procession that comprehends all humanity? And if some, among these many millions, should deem themselves classed amiss, yet let them take to their hearts the comfortable truth, that Death levels us all into one great brotherhood, and that another state of being will surely rectify the wrong of this. Then breathe thy wail upon the earth's wailing wind, thou band of melancholy music, made up of every sigh that the human heart, unsatisfied, has uttered! There is yet triumph in thy tones. And now we move! Beggars in their rags, and Kings trailing the regal purple in the dust; the Warrior's gleaming helmet; the Priest in his sable robe; the hoary Grandsire, who has run life's circle and come back to childhood; the ruddy School-boy with his golden curls, frisking along the march; the Artisan's stuff jacket; the Noble's star-decorated coat;—the whole presenting a motley spectacle, yet with a dusky grandeur brooding over it. Onward, onward, into that dimness where the lights of Time, which have blazed along the procession, are flickering in their sockets! And whither! We know not; and Death, hitherto our leader, deserts us by the wayside, as the tramp of our innumerable footsteps echoes beyond his sphere. He knows not, more than we, our destined goal. But God, who made us, knows, and will not leave us on our toilsome and doubtful march, either to wander in infinite uncertainty, or perish by the way!

FEATHERTOP: A MORALIZED LEGEND

"Dickon," cried Mother Rigby, "a coal for my pipe!"

The pipe was in the old dame's mouth when she said these words. She had thrust it there after filling it with tobacco, but without stooping to light it at the hearth, where indeed there was no appearance of a fire having been kindled that morning. Forthwith, however, as soon as the order was given, there was an intense red glow out of the bowl of the pipe, and a whiff of smoke from Mother Rigby's lips. Whence the coal came, and how brought thither by an invisible hand, I have never been able to discover.

"Good!" quoth Mother Rigby, with a nod of her head. "Thank ye, Dickon! And now for making this scarecrow. Be within call, Dickon, in case I need you again."

The good woman had risen thus early (for as yet it was scarcely sunrise) in order to set about making a scarecrow, which she intended to put in the middle of her corn-patch. It was now the latter week of May, and the crows and blackbirds had already discovered the little, green, rolled-up leaf of the Indian corn just peeping out of the soil. She was determined, therefore, to contrive as lifelike a scarecrow as ever was seen, and to finish it immediately, from top to toe, so that it should begin its sentinel's duty that very morning. Now Mother Rigby (as everybody must have heard) was one of the most cunning and potent witches in New England, and might, with very little trouble, have made a scarecrow ugly enough to frighten the minister himself. But on this occasion, as she had awakened in an uncommonly pleasant humor, and was further dulcified by her pipe of tobacco, she resolved to produce something fine, beautiful, and splendid, rather than hideous and horrible.

"I don't want to set up a hobgoblin in my own cornpatch, and almost at my own doorstep," said Mother Rigby to herself, puffing out a whiff of smoke; "I could do it if I pleased, but I'm tried of doing marvellous things, and so I'll keep within the bounds of every-day business just for variety's sake. Besides, there is no use in scaring the little children for a mile roundabout, though 't is true I'm a witch."

It was settled, therefore, in her own mind, that the scarecrow should represent a fine gentleman of the period, so far as the materials at hand would allow. Perhaps it may be as well to enumerate the chief of the articles that went to the composition of this figure.

The most important item of all, probably, although it made so little show, was a certain broomstick, on which Mother Rigby had taken many an airy gallop at midnight, and which now served the scarecrow by way of a spinal column, or, as the unlearned phrase it, a backbone. One of its arms was a disabled flail which used to be wielded by Goodman Rigby, before his spouse worried him out of this troublesome world; the other, if I mistake not, was composed of the pudding stick and a broken rung of a chair, tied loosely together at the elbow. As for its legs, the right was a hoe handle, and the left an undistinguished and miscellaneous stick from the woodpile. Its lungs, stomach, and other affairs of that kind were nothing better than a meal bag stuffed with straw. Thus we have made out the skeleton and entire corporosity of the scarecrow, with the exception of its head; and this was admirably supplied by a somewhat withered and shrivelled pumpkin, in which Mother Rigby cut two holes for the eyes, and a slit for the mouth, leaving a bluish-colored knob in the middle to pass for a nose. It was really quite a respectable face.

"I've seen worse ones on human shoulders, at any rate," said Mother Rigby. "And many a fine gentleman has a pumpkin head, as well as my scarecrow."

But the clothes, in this case, were to be the making of the man. So the good old woman took down from a peg an ancient plum-colored coat of London make, and with relics of embroidery on its seams, cuffs, pocket-flaps, and button-holes, but lamentably worn and faded, patched at the elbows, tattered at the skirts, and threadbare all over. On the left breast was a round hole, whence either a star of nobility had been rent away, or else the hot heart of some former wearer had scorched it through and through. The neighbors said that this rich garment belonged to the Black Man's wardrobe, and that he kept it at Mother Rigby's cottage for the convenience of slipping it on whenever he wished to make a grand appearance at the governor's table. To match the coat there was a velvet waistcoat of very ample size, and formerly embroidered with foliage that had been as brightly golden as the maple leaves in October, but which had now quite vanished out of the substance of the velvet. Next came a pair of scarlet breeches, once worn by the French governor of Louisbourg, and the knees of which had touched the lower step of the throne of Louis le Grand. The Frenchman had given these small clothes to an Indian powwow, who parted with them to the old witch for a gill of strong waters, at one of their dances in the forest. Furthermore, Mother Rigby produced a pair of silk stockings and put them on the figure's legs, where they showed as unsubstantial as a dream, with the wooden reality of the two sticks making itself miserably apparent through the holes. Lastly, she put her dead husband's wig on the bare scalp of the pumpkin, and surmounted the whole with a dusty three-cornered hat, in which was stuck the longest tail feather of a rooster.

Then the old dame stood the figure up in a corner of her cottage and chuckled to behold its yellow semblance of a visage, with its nobby little nose thrust into the air. It had a strangely self-satisfied aspect, and seemed to say, "Come look at me!"

"And you are well worth looking at, that's a fact!" quoth Mother Rigby, in admiration at her own handiwork. "I've made many a puppet since I've been a witch, but methinks this is the finest of them all. 'T is almost too good for a scarecrow. And, by the by, I'll just fill a fresh pipe of tobacco and then take him out to the corn-patch."

While filling her pipe the old woman continued to gaze with almost motherly affection at the figure in the corner. To say the truth, whether it were chance, or skill, or downright witchcraft, there was something wonderfully human in this ridiculous shape, bedizened with its tattered finery; and as for the countenance, it appeared to shrivel its yellow surface into a grin—a funny kind of expression betwixt scorn and merriment, as if it understood itself to be a jest at mankind. The more Mother Rigby looked the better she was pleased.

"Dickon," cried she sharply, "another coal for my pipe!"

Hardly had she spoken, than, just as before, there was a red-glowing coal on the top of the tobacco. She drew in a long whiff and puffed it forth again into the bar of morning sunshine which struggled through the one dusty pane of her cottage window. Mother Rigby always liked to flavor her pipe with a coal of fire from the particular chimney corner whence this had been brought. But where that chimney corner might be, or who brought the coal from it,—further than that the invisible messenger seemed to respond to the name of Dickon,—I cannot tell.

"That puppet yonder," thought Mother Rigby, still with her eyes fixed on the scarecrow, "is too good a piece of work to stand all summer in a corn-patch, frightening away the crows and blackbirds. He's capable of better things. Why, I've danced with a worse one, when partners happened to be scarce, at our witch meetings in the forest! What if I should let him take his chance among the other men of straw and empty fellows who go bustling about the world?"

The old witch took three or four more whiffs of her pipe and smiled.

"He'll meet plenty of his brethren at every street corner!" continued she. "Well; I didn't mean to dabble in witchcraft to-day, further than the lighting of my pipe, but a witch I am, and a witch I'm likely to be, and there's no use trying to shirk it. I'll make a man of my scarecrow, were it only for the joke's sake!"

While muttering these words, Mother Rigby took the pipe from her own mouth and thrust it into the crevice which represented the same feature in the pumpkin visage of the scarecrow.

"Puff, darling, puff!" said she. "Puff away, my fine fellow! your life depends on it!"

This was a strange exhortation, undoubtedly, to be addressed to a mere thing of sticks, straw, and old clothes, with nothing better than a shrivelled pumpkin for a head,—as we know to have been the scarecrow's case. Nevertheless, as we must carefully hold in remembrance, Mother Rigby was a witch of singular power and dexterity; and, keeping this fact duly before our minds, we shall see nothing beyond credibility in the remarkable incidents of our story. Indeed, the great difficulty will be at once got over, if we can only bring ourselves to believe that, as soon as the old dame bade him puff, there came a whiff of smoke from the scarecrow's mouth. It was the very feeblest of whiffs, to be sure; but it was followed by another and another, each more decided than the preceding one.

"Puff away, my pet! puff away, my pretty one!" Mother Rigby kept repeating, with her pleasantest smile. "It is the breath of life to ye; and that you may take my word for."

Beyond all question the pipe was bewitched. There must have been a spell either in the tobacco or in the fiercely-glowing coal that so mysteriously burned on top of it, or in the pungently-aromatic smoke which exhaled from the kindled weed. The figure, after a few doubtful attempts, at length blew forth a volley of smoke extending all the way from the obscure corner into the bar of sunshine. There it eddied and melted away among the motes of dust. It seemed a convulsive effort; for the two or three next whiffs were fainter, although the coal still glowed and threw a gleam over the scarecrow's visage. The old witch clapped her skinny hands together, and smiled encouragingly upon her handiwork. She saw that the charm worked well. The shrivelled, yellow face, which heretofore had been no face at all, had already a thin, fantastic haze, as it were of human likeness, shifting to and fro across it; sometimes vanishing entirely, but growing more perceptible than ever with the next whiff from the pipe. The whole figure, in like manner, assumed a show of life, such as we impart to ill-defined shapes among the clouds, and half deceive ourselves with the pastime of our own fancy.

If we must needs pry closely into the matter, it may be doubted whether there was any real change, after all, in the sordid, wornout, worthless, and ill-jointed substance of the scarecrow; but merely a spectral illusion, and a cunning effect of light and shade so colored and contrived as to delude the eyes of most men. The miracles of witchcraft seem always to have had a very shallow subtlety; and, at least, if the above explanation do not hit the truth of the process, I can suggest no better.

"Well puffed, my pretty lad!" still cried old Mother Rigby. "Come, another good stout whiff, and let it be with might and main. Puff for thy life, I tell thee! Puff out of the very bottom of thy heart, if any heart thou hast, or any bottom to it! Well done, again! Thou didst suck in that mouthful as if for the pure love of it."

And then the witch beckoned to the scarecrow, throwing so much magnetic potency into her gesture that it seemed as if it must inevitably be obeyed, like the mystic call of the loadstone when it summons the iron.

"Why lurkest thou in the corner, lazy one?" said she. "Step forth! Thou hast the world before thee!"

Upon my word, if the legend were not one which I heard on my grandmother's knee, and which had established its place among things credible before my childish judgment could analyze its probability, I question whether I should have the face to tell it now.

In obedience to Mother Rigby's word, and extending its arm as if to reach her outstretched hand, the figure made a step forward—a kind of hitch and jerk, however, rather than a step—then tottered and almost lost its balance. What could the witch expect? It was nothing, after all, but a scarecrow stuck upon two sticks. But the strong-willed old beldam scowled, and beckoned, and flung the energy of her purpose so forcibly at this poor combination of rotten wood, and musty straw, and ragged garments, that it was compelled to show itself a man, in spite of the reality of things. So it stepped into the bar of sunshine. There it stood—poor devil of a contrivance that it was!—with only the thinnest vesture of human similitude about it, through which was evident the stiff, rickety, incongruous, faded, tattered, good-for-nothing patchwork of its substance, ready to sink in a heap upon the floor, as conscious of its own unworthiness to be erect. Shall I confess the truth? At its present point of vivification, the scarecrow reminds me of some of the lukewarm and abortive characters, composed of heterogeneous materials, used for the thousandth time, and never worth using, with which romance writers (and myself, no doubt, among the rest) have so over-peopled the world of fiction.

But the fierce old hag began to get angry and show a glimpse of her diabolic nature (like a snake's head, peeping with a hiss out of her bosom), at this pusillanimous behavior of the thing which she had taken the trouble to put together.

"Puff away, wretch!" cried she, wrathfully. "Puff, puff, puff, thou thing of straw and emptiness! thou rag or two! thou meal bag! thou pumpkin head! thou nothing! Where shall I find a name vile enough to call thee by? Puff, I say, and suck in thy fantastic life along with the smoke! else I snatch the pipe from thy mouth and hurl thee where that red coal came from."

Thus threatened, the unhappy scarecrow had nothing for it but to puff away for dear life. As need was, therefore, it applied itself lustily to the pipe, and sent forth such abundant volleys of tobacco smoke that the small cottage kitchen became all vaporous. The one sunbeam struggled mistily through, and could but imperfectly define the image of the cracked and dusty window pane on the opposite wall. Mother Rigby, meanwhile, with one brown arm akimbo and the other stretched towards the figure, loomed grimly amid the obscurity with such port and expression as when she was wont to heave a ponderous nightmare on her victims and stand at the bedside to enjoy their agony. In fear and trembling did this poor scarecrow puff. But its efforts, it must be acknowledged, served an excellent purpose; for, with each successive whiff, the figure lost more and more of its dizzy and perplexing tenuity and seemed to take denser substance. Its very garments, moreover, partook of the magical change, and shone with the gloss of novelty and glistened with the skilfully embroidered gold that had long ago been rent away. And, half revealed among the smoke, a yellow visage bent its lustreless eyes on Mother Rigby.

At last the old witch clinched her fist and shook it at the figure. Not that she was positively angry, but merely acting on the principle—perhaps untrue, or not the only truth, though as high a one as Mother Rigby could be expected to attain—that feeble and torpid natures, being incapable of better inspiration, must be stirred up by fear. But here was the crisis. Should she fail in what she now sought to effect, it was her ruthless purpose to scatter the miserable simulacre into its original elements.

"Thou hast a man's aspect," said she, sternly. "Have also the echo and mockery of a voice! I bid thee speak!"

The scarecrow gasped, struggled, and at length emitted a murmur, which was so incorporated with its smoky breath that you could scarcely tell whether it were indeed a voice or only a whiff of tobacco. Some narrators of this legend hold the opinion that Mother Rigby's conjurations and the fierceness of her will had compelled a familiar spirit into the figure, and that the voice was his.

"Mother," mumbled the poor stifled voice, "be not so awful with me! I would fain speak; but being without wits, what can I say?"

"Thou canst speak, darling, canst thou?" cried Mother Rigby, relaxing her grim countenance into a smile. "And what shalt thou say, quotha! Say, indeed! Art thou of the brotherhood of the empty skull, and demandest of me what thou shalt say? Thou shalt say a thousand things, and saying them a thousand times over, thou shalt still have said nothing! Be not afraid, I tell thee! When thou comest into the world (whither I purpose sending thee forwith) thou shalt not lack the wherewithal to talk. Talk! Why, thou shall babble like a mill-stream, if thou wilt. Thou hast brains enough for that, I trow!"

"At your service, mother," responded the figure.

"And that was well said, my pretty one," answered Mother Rigby. "Then thou speakest like thyself, and meant nothing. Thou shalt have a hundred such set phrases, and five hundred to the boot of them. And now, darling, I have taken so much pains with thee and thou art so beautiful, that, by my troth, I love thee better than any witch's puppet in the world; and I've made them of all sorts—clay, wax, straw, sticks, night fog, morning mist, sea foam, and chimney smoke. But thou art the very best. So give heed to what I say."

"Yes, kind mother," said the figure, "with all my heart!"

"With all thy heart!" cried the old witch, setting her hands to her sides and laughing loudly. "Thou hast such a pretty way of speaking. With all thy heart! And thou didst put thy hand to the left side of thy waistcoat as if thou really hadst one!"

So now, in high good humor with this fantastic contrivance of hers, Mother

Rigby told the scarecrow that it must go and play its part in the great world, where not one man in a hundred, she affirmed, was gifted with more real substance than itself. And, that he might hold up his head with the best of them, she endowed him, on the spot, with an unreckonable amount of wealth. It consisted partly of a gold mine in Eldorado, and of ten thousand shares in a broken bubble, and of a half a million acres of vineyard at the North Pole, and of a castle in the air, and a chateau in Spain, together with all the rents and income therefrom accruing. She further made over to him the cargo of a certain ship, laden with salt of Cadiz, which she herself, by her necromantic arts, had caused to founder, ten years before, in the deepest part of mid-ocean. If the salt were not dissolved, and could be brought to market, it would fetch a pretty penny among the fishermen. That he might not lack ready money, she gave him a copper farthing of Birmingham manufacture, being all the coin she had about her, and likewise a great deal of brass, which she applied to his forehead, thus making it yellower than ever.

"With that brass alone," quoth Mother Rigby, "thou canst pay thy way all over the earth. Kiss me, pretty darling! I have done my best for thee."

Furthermore, that the adventurer might lack no possible advantage towards a fair start in life, this excellent old dame gave him a token by which he was to introduce himself to a certain magistrate, member of the council, merchant, and elder of the church (the four capacities constituting but one man), who stood at the head of society in the neighboring metropolis. The token was neither more nor less than a single word, which Mother Rigby whispered to the scarecrow, and which the scarecrow was to whisper to the merchant.

"Gouty as the old fellow is, he'll run thy errands for thee, when once thou hast given him that word in his ear," said the old witch. "Mother Rigby knows the worshipful Justice Gookin, and the worshipful Justice knows Mother Rigby!"

Here the witch thrust her wrinkled face close to the puppet's, chuckling irrepressibly, and fidgeting all through her system, with delight at the idea which she meant to communicate.

"The worshipful Master Gookin," whispered she, "hath a comely maiden to his daughter. And hark ye, my pet! Thou hast a fair outside, and a pretty wit enough of thine own. Yea, a pretty wit enough. Thou wilt think better of it when thou hast seen more of other people's wits. Now, with thy outside and thy inside, thou art the very man to win a young girl's heart. Never doubt it! I tell thee it shall be so. Put but a bold face on the matter, sigh, smile, flourish thy hat, thrust forth thy leg like a dancing-master, put thy right hand to the left side of thy waistcoat, and pretty Polly Gookin is thine own!"

All this while the new creature had been sucking in and exhaling the vapory fragrance of his pipe, and seemed now to continue this occupation as much for the enjoyment it afforded as because it was an essential condition of his existence. It was wonderful to see how exceedingly like a human being it behaved. Its eyes (for it appeared to possess a pair) were bent on Mother Rigby, and at suitable junctures it nodded or shook its head. Neither did it lack words proper for the occasion: "Really! Indeed! Pray tell me! Is it possible! Upon my word! By no means! Oh! Ah! Hem!" and other such weighty utterances as imply attention, inquiry, acquiescence, or dissent on the part of the auditor. Even had you stood by and seen the scarecrow made, you could scarcely have resisted the conviction that it perfectly understood the cunning counsels which the old witch poured into its counterfeit of an ear. The more earnestly it applied its lips to the pipe, the more distinctly was its human likeness stamped among visible realities, the more sagacious grew its expression, the more lifelike its gestures and movements, and the more intelligibly audible its voice. Its garments, too, glistened so much the brighter with an illusory magnificence. The very pipe, in which burned the spell of all this wonderwork, ceased to appear as a smoke-blackened earthen stump, and became a meerschaum, with painted bowl and amber mouthpiece.

It might be apprehended, however, that as the life of the illusion seemed identical with the vapor of the pipe, it would terminate simultaneously with the reduction of the tobacco to ashes. But the beldam foresaw the difficulty.

"Hold thou the pipe, my precious one," said she, "while I fill it for thee again."

It was sorrowful to behold how the fine gentleman began to fade back into a scarecrow while Mother Rigby shook the ashes out of the pipe and proceeded to replenish it from her tobacco-box.

"Dickon," cried she, in her high, sharp tone, "another coal for this pipe!"

No sooner said than the intensely red speck of fire was glowing within the pipe-bowl; and the scarecrow, without waiting for the witch's bidding, applied the tube to his lips and drew in a few short, convulsive whiffs, which soon, however, became regular and equable.

"Now, mine own heart's darling," quoth Mother Rigby, "whatever may happen to thee, thou must stick to thy pipe. Thy life is in it; and that, at least, thou knowest well, if thou knowest nought besides. Stick to thy pipe, I say! Smoke, puff, blow thy cloud; and tell the people, if any question be made, that it is for thy health, and that so the physician orders thee to do. And, sweet one, when thou shalt find thy pipe getting low, go apart into some corner, and (first filling thyself with smoke) cry sharply, 'Dickon, a fresh pipe of tobacco!' and, 'Dickon, another coal for my pipe!' and have it into thy pretty mouth as speedily as may be. Else, instead of a gallant gentleman in a gold-laced coat, thou wilt be but a jumble of sticks and tattered clothes, and a bag of straw, and a withered pumpkin! Now depart, my treasure, and good luck go with thee!"

"Never fear, mother!" said the figure, in a stout voice, and sending forth a courageous whiff of smoke, "I will thrive, if an honest man and a gentleman may!"

"Oh, thou wilt be the death of me!" cried the old witch, convulsed with laughter. "That was well said. If an honest man and a gentleman may! Thou playest thy part to perfection. Get along with thee for a smart fellow; and I will wager on thy head, as a man of pith and substance, with a brain and what they call a heart, and all else that a man should have, against any other thing on two legs. I hold myself a better witch than yesterday, for thy sake. Did not I make thee? And I defy any witch in New England to make such another! Here; take my staff along with thee!"

The staff, though it was but a plain oaken stick, immediately took the aspect of a gold-headed cane.

"That gold head has as much sense in it as thine own," said Mother Rigby, "and it will guide thee straight to worshipful Master Gookin's door. Get thee gone, my pretty pet, my darling, my precious one, my treasure; and if any ask thy name, it is Feathertop. For thou hast a feather in thy hat, and I have thrust a handful of feathers into the hollow of thy head, and thy wig, too, is of the fashion they call Feathertop,—so be Feathertop thy name!"

And, issuing from the cottage, Feathertop strode manfully towards town. Mother Rigby stood at the threshold, well pleased to see how the sunbeams glistened on him, as if all his magnificence were real, and how diligently and lovingly he smoked his pipe, and how handsomely he walked, in spite of a little stiffness of his legs. She watched him until out of sight, and threw a witch benediction after her darling, when a turn of the road snatched him from her view.

Betimes in the forenoon, when the principal street of the neighboring town was just at its acme of life and bustle, a stranger of very distinguished figure was seen on the sidewalk. His port as well as his garments betokened nothing short of nobility. He wore a richly-embroidered plum-colored coat, a waistcoat of costly velvet, magnificently adorned with golden foliage, a pair of splendid scarlet breeches, and the finest and glossiest of white silk stockings. His head was covered with a peruke, so daintily powdered and adjusted that it would have been sacrilege to disorder it with a hat; which, therefore (and it was a gold-laced hat, set off with a snowy feather), he carried beneath his arm. On the breast of his coat glistened a star. He managed his gold-headed cane with an airy grace, peculiar to the fine gentlemen of the period; and, to give the highest possible finish to his equipment, he had lace ruffles at his wrist, of a most ethereal delicacy, sufficiently avouching how idle and aristocratic must be the hands which they half concealed.

It was a remarkable point in the accoutrement of this brilliant personage that he held in his left hand a fantastic kind of a pipe, with an exquisitely painted bowl and an amber mouthpiece. This he applied to his lips as often as every five or six paces, and inhaled a deep whiff of smoke, which, after being retained a moment in his lungs, might be seen to eddy gracefully from his mouth and nostrils.

As may well be supposed, the street was all astir to find out the stranger's name.

"It is some great nobleman, beyond question," said one of the towns-people. "Do you see the star at his breast?"

"Nay; it is too bright to be seen," said another. "Yes; he must needs be a nobleman, as you say. But by what conveyance, think you, can his lordship have voyaged or travelled hither? There has been no vessel from the old country for a month past; and if he have arrived overland from the southward, pray where are his attendants and equipage?"

"He needs no equipage to set off his rank," remarked a third. "If he came among us in rags, nobility would shine through a hole in his elbow. I never saw such dignity of aspect. He has the old Norman blood in his veins, I warrant him."

"I rather take him to be a Dutchman, or one of your high Germans," said another citizen. "The men of those countries have always the pipe at their mouths."

"And so has a Turk," answered his companion. "But, in my judgment, this stranger hath been bred at the French court, and hath there learned politeness and grace of manner, which none understand so well as the nobility of France. That gait, now! A vulgar spectator might deem it stiff—he might call it a hitch and jerk—but, to my eye, it hath an unspeakable majesty, and must have been acquired by constant observation of the deportment of the Grand Monarque. The stranger's character and office are evident enough. He is a French ambassador, come to treat with our rulers about the cession of Canada."

"More probably a Spaniard," said another, "and hence his yellow complexion; or, most likely, he is from the Havana, or from some port on the Spanish main, and comes to make investigation about the piracies which our government is thought to connive at. Those settlers in Peru and Mexico have skins as yellow as the gold which they dig out of their mines."

"Yellow or not," cried a lady, "he is a beautiful man!—so tall, so slender! such a fine, noble face, with so well-shaped a nose, and all that delicacy of expression about the mouth! And, bless me, how bright his star is! It positively shoots out flames!"

"So do your eyes, fair lady," said the stranger, with a bow and a flourish of his pipe; for he was just passing at the instant. "Upon my honor, they have quite dazzled me."

"Was ever so original and exquisite a compliment?" murmured the lady, in an ecstasy of delight.

Amid the general admiration excited by the stranger's appearance, there were only two dissenting voices. One was that of an impertinent cur, which, after snuffing at the heels of the glistening figure, put its tail between its legs and skulked into its master's back yard, vociferating an execrable howl. The other dissentient was a young child, who squalled at the fullest stretch of his lungs, and babbled some unintelligible nonsense about a pumpkin.

Feathertop meanwhile pursued his way along the street. Except for the few complimentary words to the lady, and now and then a slight inclination of the head in requital of the profound reverences of the bystanders, he seemed wholly absorbed in his pipe. There needed no other proof of his rank and consequence than the perfect equanimity with which he comported himself, while the curiosity and admiration of the town swelled almost into clamor around him. With a crowd gathering behind his footsteps, he finally reached the mansion-house of the worshipful Justice Gookin, entered the gate, ascended the steps of the front door, and knocked. In the interim, before his summons was answered, the stranger was observed to shake the ashes out of his pipe.

"What did he say in that sharp voice?" inquired one of the spectators.

"Nay, I know not," answered his friend. "But the sun dazzles my eyes strangely. How dim and faded his lordship looks all of a sudden! Bless my wits, what is the matter with me?"

"The wonder is," said the other, "that his pipe, which was out only an instant ago, should be all alight again, and with the reddest coal I ever saw. There is something mysterious about this stranger. What a whiff of smoke was that! Dim and faded did you call him? Why, as he turns about the star on his breast is all ablaze."

"It is, indeed," said his companion; "and it will go near to dazzle pretty Polly Gookin, whom I see peeping at it out of the chamber window."

The door being now opened, Feathertop turned to the crowd, made a stately bend of his body like a great man acknowledging the reverence of the meaner sort, and vanished into the house. There was a mysterious kind of a smile, if it might not better be called a grin or grimace, upon his visage; but, of all the throng that beheld him, not an individual appears to have possessed insight enough to detect the illusive character of the stranger except a little child and a cur dog.

Our legend here loses somewhat of its continuity, and, passing over the preliminary explanation between Feathertop and the merchant, goes in quest of the pretty Polly Gookin. She was a damsel of a soft, round figure, with light hair and blue eyes, and a fair, rosy face, which seemed neither very shrewd nor very simple. This young lady had caught a glimpse of the glistening stranger while standing at the threshold, and had forthwith put on a laced cap, a string of beads, her finest kerchief, and her stiffest damask petticoat in preparation for the interview. Hurrying from her chamber to the parlor, she had ever since been viewing herself in the large looking-glass and practising pretty airs—now a smile, now a ceremonious dignity of aspect, and now a softer smile than the former, kissing her hand likewise, tossing her head, and managing her fan; while within the mirror an unsubstantial little maid repeated every gesture and did all the foolish things that Polly did, but without making her ashamed of them. In short, it was the fault of pretty Polly's ability rather than her will if she failed to be as complete an artifice as the illustrious Feathertop himself; and, when she thus tampered with her own simplicity, the witch's phantom might well hope to win her.

No sooner did Polly hear her father's gouty footsteps approaching the parlor door, accompanied with the stiff clatter of Feathertop's high-heeled shoes, than she seated herself bolt upright and innocently began warbling a song.

"Polly! daughter Polly!" cried the old merchant. "Come hither, child."

Master Gookin's aspect, as he opened the door, was doubtful and troubled.

"This gentleman," continued he, presenting the stranger, "is the Chevalier Feathertop,—nay, I beg his pardon, my Lord Feathertop,—who hath brought me a token of remembrance from an ancient friend of mine. Pay your duty to his lordship, child, and honor him as his quality deserves."

After these few words of introduction, the worshipful magistrate immediately quitted the room. But, even in that brief moment, had the fair Polly glanced aside at her father instead of devoting herself wholly to the brilliant guest, she might have taken warning of some mischief nigh at hand. The old man was nervous, fidgety, and very pale. Purposing a smile of courtesy, he had deformed his face with a sort of galvanic grin, which, when Feathertop's back was turned, he exchanged for a scowl, at the same time shaking his fist and stamping his gouty foot—an incivility which brought its retribution along with it. The truth appears to have been that Mother Rigby's word of introduction, whatever it might be, had operated far more on the rich merchant's fears than on his good will. Moreover, being a man of wonderfully acute observation, he had noticed that these painted figures on the bowl of Feathertop's pipe were in motion. Looking more closely, he became convinced that these figures were a party of little demons, each duly provided with horns and a tail, and dancing hand in hand, with gestures of diabolical merriment, round the circumference of the pipe bowl. As if to confirm his suspicions, while Master Gookin ushered his guest along a dusky passage from his private room to the parlor, the star on Feathertop's breast had scintillated actual flames, and threw a flickering gleam upon the wall, the ceiling, and the floor.

With such sinister prognostics manifesting themselves on all hands, it is not to be marvelled at that the merchant should have felt that he was committing his daughter to a very questionable acquaintance. He cursed, in his secret soul, the insinuating elegance of Feathertop's manners, as this brilliant personage bowed, smiled, put his hand on his heart, inhaled a long whiff from his pipe, and enriched the atmosphere with the smoky vapor of a fragrant and visible sigh. Gladly would poor Master Gookin have thrust his dangerous guest into the street; but there was a constraint and terror within him. This respectable old gentleman, we fear, at an earlier period of life, had given some pledge or other to the evil principle, and perhaps was now to redeem it by the sacrifice of his daughter.

It so happened that the parlor door was partly of glass, shaded by a silken curtain, the folds of which hung a little awry. So strong was the merchant's interest in witnessing what was to ensue between the fair Polly and the gallant Feathertop that, after quitting the room, he could by no means refrain from peeping through the crevice of the curtain.

But there was nothing very miraculous to be seen; nothing—except the trifles previously noticed—to confirm the idea of a supernatural peril environing the pretty Polly. The stranger it is true was evidently a thorough and practised man of the world, systematic and self-possessed, and therefore the sort of a person to whom a parent ought not to confide a simple, young girl without due watchfulness for the result. The worthy magistrate, who had been conversant with all degrees and qualities of mankind, could not but perceive every motion and gesture of the distinguished Feathertop came in its proper place; nothing had been left rude or native in him; a well-digested conventionalism had incorporated itself thoroughly with his substance and transformed him into a work of art. Perhaps it was this peculiarity that invested him with a species of ghastliness and awe. It is the effect of anything completely and consummately artificial, in human shape, that the person impresses us as an unreality and as having hardly pith enough to cast a shadow upon the floor. As regarded Feathertop, all this resulted in a wild, extravagant, and fantastical impression, as if his life and being were akin to the smoke that curled upward from his pipe.

But pretty Polly Gookin felt not thus. The pair were now promenading the room: Feathertop with his dainty stride and no less dainty grimace; the girl with a native maidenly grace, just touched, not spoiled, by a slightly affected manner, which seemed caught from the perfect artifice of her companion. The longer the interview continued, the more charmed was pretty Polly, until, within the first quarter of an hour (as the old magistrate noted by his watch), she was evidently beginning to be in love. Nor need it have been witchcraft that subdued her in such a hurry; the poor child's heart, it may be, was so very fervent that it melted her with its own warmth as reflected from the hollow semblance of a lover. No matter what Feathertop said, his words found depth and reverberation in her ear; no matter what he did, his action was heroic to her eye. And by this time it is to be supposed there was a blush on Polly's cheek, a tender smile about her mouth, and a liquid softness in her glance; while the star kept coruscating on Feathertop's breast, and the little demons careered with more frantic merriment than ever about the circumference of his pipe bowl. O pretty Polly Gookin, why should these imps rejoice so madly that a silly maiden's heart was about to be given to a shadow! Is it so unusual a misfortune, so rare a triumph?

By and by Feathertop paused, and throwing himself into an imposing attitude, seemed to summon the fair girl to survey his figure and resist him longer if she could. His star, his embroidery, his buckles glowed at that instant with unutterable splendor; the picturesque hues of his attire took a richer depth of coloring; there was a gleam and polish over his whole presence betokening the perfect witchery of well-ordered manners. The maiden raised her eyes and suffered them to linger upon her companion with a bashful and admiring gaze. Then, as if desirous of judging what value her own simple comeliness might have side by side with so much brilliancy, she cast a glance towards the full-length looking-glass in front of which they happened to be standing. It was one of the truest plates in the world and incapable of flattery. No sooner did the images therein reflected meet Polly's eye than she shrieked, shrank from the stranger's side, gazed at him for a moment in the wildest dismay, and sank insensible upon the floor. Feathertop likewise had looked towards the mirror, and there beheld, not the glittering mockery of his outside show, but a picture of the sordid patchwork of his real composition, stripped of all witchcraft.

The wretched simulacrum! We almost pity him. He threw up his arms with an expression of despair that went further than any of his previous manifestations towards vindicating his claims to be reckoned human; for, perchance the only time since this so often empty and deceptive life of mortals began its course, an illusion had seen and fully recognized itself.

Mother Rigby was seated by her kitchen hearth in the twilight of this eventful day, and had just shaken the ashes out of a new pipe, when she heard a hurried tramp along the road. Yet it did not seem so much the tramp of human footsteps as the clatter of sticks or the rattling of dry bones.

"Ha!" thought the old witch, "what step is that? Whose skeleton is out of its grave now, I wonder?"

A figure burst headlong into the cottage door. It was Feathertop! His pipe was still alight; the star still flamed upon his breast; the embroidery still glowed upon his garments; nor had he lost, in any degree or manner that could be estimated, the aspect that assimilated him with our mortal brotherhood. But yet, in some indescribable way (as is the case with all that has deluded us when once found out), the poor reality was felt beneath the cunning artifice.

"What has gone wrong?" demanded the witch. "Did yonder sniffling hypocrite thrust my darling from his door? The villain! I'll set twenty fiends to torment him till he offer thee his daughter on his bended knees!"

"No, mother," said Feathertop despondingly; "it was not that."

"Did the girl scorn my precious one?" asked Mother Rigby, her fierce eyes glowing like two coals of Tophet. "I'll cover her face with pimples! Her nose shall be as red as the coal in thy pipe! Her front teeth shall drop out! In a week hence she shall not be worth thy having!"

"Let her alone, mother," answered poor Feathertop; "the girl was half won; and methinks a kiss from her sweet lips might have made me altogether human.

But," he added, after a brief pause and then a howl of self-contempt, "I've seen myself, mother! I've seen myself for the wretched, ragged, empty thing I am! I'll exist no longer!"

Snatching the pipe from his mouth, he flung it with all his might against the chimney, and at the same instant sank upon the floor, a medley of straw and tattered garments, with some sticks protruding from the heap, and a shrivelled pumpkin in the midst. The eyeholes were now lustreless; but the rudely-carved gap, that just before had been a mouth, still seemed to twist itself into a despairing grin, and was so far human.

"Poor fellow!" quoth Mother Rigby, with a rueful glance at the relics of her ill-fated contrivance. "My poor, dear, pretty Feathertop! There are thousands upon thousands of coxcombs and charlatans in the world, made up of just such a jumble of wornout, forgotten, and good-for-nothing trash as he was! Yet they live in fair repute, and never see themselves for what they are. And why should my poor puppet be the only one to know himself and perish for it?"

While thus muttering, the witch had filled a fresh pipe of tobacco, and held the stem between her fingers, as doubtful whether to thrust it into her own mouth or Feathertop's.

"Poor Feathertop!" she continued. "I could easily give him another chance and send him forth again to-morrow. But no; his feelings are too tender, his sensibilities too deep. He seems to have too much heart to bustle for his own advantage in such an empty and heartless world. Well! well! I'll make a scarecrow of him after all. 'T is an innocent and useful vocation, and will suit my darling well; and, if each of his human brethren had as fit a one, 't would be the better for mankind; and as for this pipe of tobacco, I need it more than he."

So saying, Mother Rigby put the stem between her lips. "Dickon!" cried she, in her high, sharp tone, "another coal for my pipe!"

THE NEW ADAM AND EVE

We who are born into the world's artificial system can never adequately know how little in our present state and circumstances is natural, and how much is merely the interpolation of the perverted mind and heart of man. Art has become a second and stronger nature; she is a stepmother, whose crafty tenderness has taught us to despise the bountiful and wholesome ministrations of our true parent. It is only through the medium of the imagination that we can lessen those iron fetters, which we call truth and reality, and make ourselves even partially sensible what prisoners we are. For instance, let us conceive good Father Miller's interpretation of the prophecies to have proved true. The Day of Doom has burst upon the globe and swept away the whole race of men. From cities and fields, sea-shore and midland mountain region, vast continents, and even the remotest islands of the ocean, each living thing is gone. No breath of a created being disturbs this earthly atmosphere. But the abodes of man, and all that he has accomplished, the footprints of his wanderings and the results of his toil, the visible symbols of his intellectual cultivation and moral progress—in short, everything physical that can give evidence of his present position—shall remain untouched by the hand of destiny. Then, to inherit and repeople this waste and deserted earth, we will suppose a new Adam and a new Eve to have been created, in the full development of mind and heart, but with no knowledge of their predecessors nor of the diseased circumstances that had become encrusted around them. Such a pair would at once distinguish between art and nature. Their instincts and intuitions would immediately recognize the wisdom and simplicity of the latter; while the former with its elaborate perversities, would offer them a continual succession of puzzles.

Let us attempt in a mood half sportive and half thoughtful, to track these imaginary heirs of our mortality through their first day's experience. No longer ago than yesterday the flame of human life was extinguished; there has been a breathless night; and now another morn approaches expecting to find the earth no less desolate than at eventide.

It is dawn. The east puts on its immemorial blush, although no human eye is gazing at it; for all the phenomena of the natural world renew themselves, in spite of the solitude that now broods around the globe. There is still beauty of earth, sea, and sky for beauty's sake. But soon there are to be spectators. Just when the earliest sunshine gilds earth's mountain tops, two beings have come into life, not in such an Eden as bloomed to welcome our first parents, but in the heart of a modern city. They find themselves in existence, and gazing into one another's eyes. Their emotion is not astonishment; nor do they perplex themselves with efforts to discover what, and whence, and why they are. Each is satisfied to be, because the other exists likewise; and their first consciousness is of calm and mutual enjoyment, which seems not to have been the birth of that very moment, but prolonged from a past eternity. Thus content with an inner sphere which they inhabit together, it is not immediately that the outward world can obtrude itself upon their notice.

Soon, however, they feel the invincible necessity of this earthly life, and begin to make acquaintance with the objects and circumstances that surround them. Perhaps no other stride so vast remains to be taken as when they first turn from the reality of their mutual glance to the dreams and shadows that perplex them everywhere else.

"Sweetest Eve, where are we?" exclaims the new Adam; for speech, or some equivalent mode of expression, is born with them, and comes just as natural as breath. "Methinks I do not recognize this place."

"Nor I, dear Adam," replies the new Eve. "And what a strange place too! Let me come closer to thy side and behold thee only; for all other sights trouble and perplex my spirit."

"Nay, Eve," replies Adam, who appears to have the stronger tendency towards the material world; "it were well that we gain some insight into these matters. We are in an odd situation here. Let us look about us."

Assuredly there are sights enough to throw the new inheritors of earth into a state of hopeless perplexity. The long lines of edifices, their windows glittering in the yellow sunrise, and the narrow street between, with its barren pavement tracked and battered by wheels that have now rattled into an irrevocable past! The signs, with their unintelligible hieroglyphics! The squareness and ugliness, and regular or irregular deformity of everything that meets the eye! The marks of wear and tear, and unrenewed decay, which distinguish the works of man from the growth of nature! What is there in all this capable of the slightest significance to minds that know nothing of the artificial system which is implied in every lamp post and each brick of the houses? Moreover, the utter loneliness and silence, in a scene that originally grew out of noise and bustle, must needs impress a feeling of desolation even upon Adam and Eve, unsuspicious as they are of the recent extinction of human existence. In a forest, solitude would be life; in a city, it is death.

The new Eve looks round with a sensation of doubt and distrust, such as a city dame, the daughter of numberless generations of citizens, might experience if suddenly transported to the garden of Eden. At length her downcast eye discovers a small tuft of grass, just beginning to sprout among the stones of the pavement; she eagerly grasps it, and is sensible that this little herb awakens some response within her heart. Nature finds nothing else to offer her. Adam, after staring up and down the street without detecting a single object that his comprehension can lay hold of, finally turns his forehead to the sky. There, indeed, is something which the soul within him recognizes.

"Look up yonder, mine own Eve," he cries; "surely we ought to dwell among those gold-tinged clouds or in the blue depths beyond them. I know not how nor when, but evidently we have strayed away from our home; for I see nothing hereabouts that seems to belong to us."

"Can we not ascend thither?" inquires Eve.

"Why not?" answers Adam hopefully. "But no; something drags us down in spite of our best efforts. Perchance we may find a path hereafter."

In the energy of new life it appears no such impracticable feat to climb into the sky. But they have already received a woful lesson, which may finally go far towards reducing them to the level of the departed race, when they acknowledge the necessity of keeping the beaten track of earth. They now set forth on a ramble through the city, in the hope of making their escape from this uncongenial sphere. Already in the fresh elasticity of their spirits they have found the idea of weariness. We will watch them as they enter some of the shops and public or private edifices; for every door, whether of alderman or beggar, church or hall of state, has been flung wide open by the same agency that swept away the inmates.

It so happens—and not unluckily for an Adam and Eve who are still in the costume that might better have befitted Eden—it so happens that their first visit is to a fashionable dry goods store. No courteous and importunate attendants hasten to receive their orders; no throng of ladies are tossing over the rich Parisian fabrics. All is deserted; trade is at a stand-still, and not even an echo of the national watchword, "Go ahead!" disturbs the quiet of the new customers. But specimens of the latest earthly fashions, silks of every shade, and whatever is most delicate or splendid for the decoration of the human form, lie scattered around, profusely as bright autumnal leaves in a forest. Adam looks at a few of the articles but throws them carelessly aside with whatever exclamation may correspond to "Pish!" or "Pshaw!" in the new vocabulary of nature. Eve, however,—be it said without offence to her native modesty,—examines these treasures of her sex with somewhat livelier interest. A pair of corsets chance to lie upon the counter; she inspects them curiously, but knows not what to make of them. Then she handles a fashionable silk with dim yearnings, thoughts that wander hither and thither, instincts groping in the dark.

"On the whole, I do not like it," she observes, laying the glossy fabric upon the counter. "But, Adam, it is very strange. What can these things mean? Surely I ought to know; yet they put me in a perfect maze."

"Poh! my dear Eve, why trouble thy little head about such nonsense?" cries Adam, in a fit of impatience. "Let us go somewhere else. But stay; how very beautiful! My loveliest Eve, what a charm you have imparted to that robe by merely throwing it over your shoulders!"

For Eve, with the taste that nature moulded into her composition, has taken a remnant of exquisite silver gauze and drawn it around her form, with an effect that gives Adam his first idea of the witchery of dress. He beholds his spouse in a new light and with renewed admiration; yet is hardly reconciled to any other attire than her own golden locks. However, emulating Eve's example, he makes free with a mantle of blue velvet, and puts it on so picturesquely that it might seem to have fallen from heaven upon his stately figure. Thus garbed they go in search of new discoveries.

They next wander into a church, not to make a display of their fine clothes, but attracted by its spire, pointing upwards to the sky, whither they have already yearned to climb. As they enter the portal, a clock, which it was the last earthly act of the sexton to wind up, repeats the hour in deep reverberating tones; for Time has survived his former progeny, and, with the iron tongue that man gave him, is now speaking to his two grandchildren. They listen, but understand him not. Nature would measure time by the succession of thoughts and acts which constitute real life, and not by hours of emptiness. They pass up the church aisle, and raise their eyes to the ceiling. Had our Adam and Eve become mortal in some European city, and strayed into the vastness and sublimity of an old cathedral, they might have recognized the purpose for which the deep-souled founders reared it. Like the dim awfulness of an ancient forest, its very atmosphere would have incited them to prayer. Within the snug walls of a metropolitan church there can be no such influence.

Yet some odor of religion is still lingering here, the bequest of pious souls, who had grace to enjoy a foretaste of immortal life. Perchance they breathe a prophecy of a better world to their successors, who have become obnoxious to all their own cares and calamities in the present one.

"Eve, something impels me to look upward," says Adam; "but it troubles me to see this roof between us and the sky. Let us go forth and perhaps we shall discern a Great Face looking down upon us."

"Yes; a Great Face, with a beam of love brightening over it like sunshine," responds Eve. "Surely we have seen such a countenance somewhere."

They go out of the church and kneeling at its threshold give way to the spirit's natural instinct of adoration towards a beneficent Father. But, in truth, their life thus far has been a continual prayer. Purity and simplicity hold converse at every moment with their Creator.

We now observe them entering a Court of Justice. But what remotest conception can they attain of the purposes of such an edifice? How should the idea occur to them that human brethren, of like nature with themselves, and originally included in the same law of love which is their only rule of life, should ever need an outward enforcement of the true voice within their souls? And what, save a woful experience, the dark result of many centuries, could teach them the sad mysteries of crime? O Judgment Seat, not by the pure in heart wast thou established, nor in the simplicity of nature; but by hard and wrinkled men, and upon the accumulated heap of earthly wrong. Thou art the very symbol of man's perverted state.

On as fruitless an errand our wanderers next visit a Hall of Legislation, where Adam places Eve in the Speaker's chair, unconscious of the moral which he thus exemplifies. Man's intellect, moderated by Woman's tenderness and moral sense! Were such the legislation of the world there would be no need of State Houses, Capitols, Halls of Parliament, nor even of those little assemblages of patriarchs beneath the shadowy trees, by whom freedom was first interpreted to mankind on our native shores.

Whither go they next? A perverse destiny seems to perplex them with one after another of the riddles which mankind put forth to the wandering universe, and left unsolved in their own destruction. They enter an edifice of stern gray stone standing insulated in the midst of others, and gloomy even in the sunshine, which it barely suffers to penetrate through its iron-grated windows. It is a prison. The jailer has left his post at the summons of a stronger authority than the sheriff's. But the prisoners? Did the messenger of fate, when he shook open all the doors, respect the magistrate's warrant and the judge's sentence, and leave the inmates of the dungeons to be delivered by due course of earthly law? No; a new trial has been granted in a higher court, which may set judge, jury, and prisoner at its bar all in a row, and perhaps find one no less guilty than another. The jail, like the whole earth, is now a solitude, and has thereby lost something of its dismal gloom. But here are the narrow cells, like tombs, only drearier and deadlier, because in these the immortal spirit was buried with the body. Inscriptions appear on the walls, scribbled with a pencil or scratched with a rusty nail; brief words of agony, perhaps, or guilt's desperate defiance to the world, or merely a record of a date by which the writer strove to keep up with the march of life. There is not a living eye that could now decipher these memorials.

Nor is it while so fresh from their Creator's hand that the new denizens of earth—no, nor their descendants for a thousand years—could discover that this edifice was a hospital for the direst disease which could afflict their predecessors. Its patients bore the outward marks of that leprosy with which all were more or less infected. They were sick—and so were the purest of their brethren—with the plague of sin. A deadly sickness, indeed! Feeling its symptoms within the breast, men concealed it with fear and shame, and were only the more cruel to those unfortunates whose pestiferous sores were flagrant to the common eye. Nothing save a rich garment could ever hide the plague spot. In the course of the world's lifetime, every remedy was tried for its cure and extirpation except the single one, the flower that grew in heaven and was sovereign for all the miseries of earth. Man never had attempted to cure sin by LOVE! Had he but once made the effort it might well have happened that there would have been no more need of the dark lazar house into which Adam and Eve have wandered. Hasten forth with your native innocence, lest the damps of these still conscious walls infect you likewise, and thus another fallen race be propagated!

Passing from the interior of the prison into the space within its outward wall, Adam pauses beneath a structure of the simplest contrivance, yet altogether unaccountable to him. It consists merely of two upright posts, supporting a transverse beam, from which dangles a cord.

"Eve, Eve!" cries Adam, shuddering with a nameless horror. "What can this thing be?"

"I know not," answers Eve; "but Adam, my heart is sick! There seems to be no more sky—no more sunshine!"

Well might Adam shudder and poor Eve be sick at heart; for this mysterious object was the type of mankind's whole system in regard to the great difficulties which God had given to be solved—a system of fear and vengeance, never successful, yet followed to the last. Here, on the morning when the final summons came, a criminal—one criminal, where none were guiltless—had died upon the gallows. Had the world heard the footfall of its own approaching doom, it would have been no inappropriate act thus to close the record of its deeds by one so characteristic.

The two pilgrims now hurry from the prison. Had they known how the former inhabitants of earth were shut up in artificial error and cramped and chained by their perversions, they might have compared the whole moral world to a prison house, and have deemed the removal of the race a general jail delivery.

They next enter, unannounced, but they might have rung at the door in vain, a private mansion, one of the stateliest in Beacon Street. A wild and plaintive strain of music is quivering through the house, now rising like a solemn organ peal, and now dying into the faintest murmur, as if some spirit that had felt an interest in the departed family were bemoaning itself in the solitude of hall and chamber. Perhaps a virgin, the purest of mortal race, has been left behind to perform a requiem for the whole kindred of humanity. Not so. These are the tones of an Æolian harp, through which Nature pours the harmony that lies concealed in her every breath, whether of summer breeze or tempest. Adam and Eve are lost in rapture unmingled with surprise. The passing wind, that stirred the harp strings, has been hushed, before they can think of examining the splendid furniture, the gorgeous carpets, and the architecture of the rooms. These things amuse their unpractised eyes, but appeal to nothing within their hearts. Even the pictures upon the walls scarcely excite a deeper interest; for there is something radically artificial and deceptive in painting with which minds in the primal simplicity cannot sympathize. The unbidden guests examine a row of family portraits, but are too dull to recognize them as men and women, beneath the disguise of a preposterous garb, and with features and expression debased, because inherited through ages of moral and physical decay.

Chance, however, presents them with pictures of human beauty, fresh from the hand of Nature. As they enter a magnificent apartment they are astonished, but not affrighted, to perceive two figures advancing to meet them. Is it not awful to imagine that any life save their own, should remain in the wide world?

"How is this?" exclaims Adam. "My beautiful Eve, are you in two places at once?"

"And you, Adam!" answers Eve, doubtful, yet delighted. "Surely that noble and lovely form is yours. Yet here you are by my side. I am content with one,—methinks there should not be two."

This miracle is wrought by a tall looking-glass, the mystery of which they soon fathom, because Nature creates a mirror for the human face in every pool of water, and for her own great features in waveless lakes. Pleased and satisfied with gazing at themselves, they now discover the marble statue of a child in a corner of the room so exquisitely idealized that it is almost worthy to be the prophetic likeness of their first born. Sculpture, in its highest excellence, is more genuine than painting, and might seem to be evolved from a natural germ, by the same law as a leaf or flower. The statue of the child impresses the solitary pair as if it were a companion; it likewise hints at secrets both of the past and future.

"My husband!" whispers Eve.

"What would you say, dearest Eve?" inquires Adam.

"I wonder if we are alone in the world," she continues, with a sense of something like fear at the thought of other inhabitants. "This lovely little form! Did it ever breathe? Or is it only the shadow of something real, like our pictures in the mirror?"

"It is strange!" replies Adam, pressing his hand to his brow. "There are mysteries all around us. An idea flits continually before me—would that I could seize it! Eve, Eve, are we treading in the footsteps of beings that bore a likeness to ourselves? If so, whither are they gone?—and why is their world so unfit for our dwelling place?"

"Our great Father only knows," answers Eve. "But something tells me that we shall not always be alone. And how sweet if other beings were to visit us in the shape of this fair image!"

Then they wander through the house, and everywhere find tokens of human life, which now, with the idea recently suggested, excite a deeper curiosity in their bosoms. Woman has here left traces of her delicacy and refinement, and of her gentle labors. Eve ransacks a work-basket and instinctively thrusts the rosy tip of her finger into a thimble. She takes up a piece of embroidery, glowing with mimic flowers, in one of which a fair damsel of the departed race has left her needle. Pity that the Day of Doom should have anticipated the completion of such a useful task! Eve feels almost conscious of the skill to finish it. A pianoforte has been left open. She flings her hand carelessly over the keys, and strikes out a sudden melody, no less natural than the strains of the Æolian harp, but joyous with the dance of her yet unburdened life. Passing through a dark entry they find a broom behind the door; and Eve, who comprises the whole nature of womanhood, has a dim idea that it is an instrument proper for her hand. In another apartment they behold a canopied bed, and all the appliances of luxurious repose. A heap of forest leaves would be more to the purpose. They enter the nursery, and are perplexed with the sight of little gowns and caps, tiny shoes, and a cradle, amid the drapery of which is still to be seen the impress of a baby's form. Adam slightly notices these trifles; but Eve becomes involved in a fit of mute reflection from which it is hardly possible to rouse her.

By a most unlucky arrangement there was to have been a grand dinner party in this mansion on the very day when the whole human family, including the invited guests, were summoned to the unknown regions of illimitable space. At the moment of fate, the table was actually spread, and the company on the point of sitting down. Adam and Eve come unbidden to the banquet; it has now been some time cold, but otherwise furnishes them with highly favorable specimens of the gastronomy of their predecessors. But it is difficult to imagine the perplexity of the unperverted couple, in endeavoring to find proper food for their first meal, at a table where the cultivated appetites of a fashionable party were to have been gratified. Will Nature teach them the mystery of a plate of turtle soup? Will she embolden them to attack a haunch of venison? Will she initiate them into the merits of a Parisian pasty, imported by the last steamer that ever crossed the Atlantic? Will she not, rather, bid them turn with disgust from fish, fowl, and flesh, which, to their pure nostrils, steam with a loathsome odor of death and corruption?— Food? The bill of fare contains nothing which they recognize as such.

Fortunately, however, the dessert is ready upon a neighboring table. Adam, whose appetite and animal instincts are quicker than those of Eve, discovers this fitting banquet.

"Here, dearest Eve," he exclaims, "here is food."

"Well," answered she, with the germ of a housewife stirring within her, "we have been so busy today, that a picked-up dinner must serve."

So Eve comes to the table and receives a red-cheeked apple from her husband's hand in requital of her predecessor's fatal gift to our common grandfather. She eats it without sin, and, let us hope, with no disastrous consequences to her future progeny. They make a plentiful, yet temperate, meal of fruit, which, though not gathered in paradise, is legitimately derived from the seeds that were planted there. Their primal appetite is satisfied.

"What shall we drink, Eve?" inquires Adam.

Eve peeps among some bottles and decanters, which, as they contain fluids, she naturally conceives must be proper to quench thirst. But never before did claret, hock, and madeira, of rich and rare perfume, excite such disgust as now.

"Pah!" she exclaims, after smelling at various wines. "What stuff is here? The beings who have gone before us could not have possessed the same nature that we do: for neither their hunger nor thirst were like our own."

"Pray hand me yonder bottle," says Adam. "If it be drinkable by any manner of mortal, I must moisten my throat with it."

After some remonstrances she takes up a champagne bottle, but is frightened by the sudden explosion of the cork, and drops it upon the floor. There the untasted liquor effervesces. Had they quaffed it they would have experienced that brief delirium whereby, whether excited by moral or physical causes, man sought to recompense himself for the calm, lifelong joys which he had lost by his revolt from Nature. At length in a refrigerator, Eve finds a glass pitcher of water, pure, cold, and bright as ever gushed from a fountain among the hills. Both drink; and such refreshment does it bestow, that they question one another if this precious liquid be not identical with the stream of life within them.

"And now," observes Adam, "we must again try to discover what sort of a world this is, and why we have been sent hither."

"Why? to love one another," cried Eve. "Is not that employment enough?"

"Truly is it," answers Adam, kissing her; "but still—I know not—something tells us there is labor to be done. Perhaps our allotted task is no other than to climb into the sky, which is so much more beautiful than earth."

"Then would we were there now," murmurs Eve, "that no task or duty might come between us!"

They leave the hospitable mansion, and we next see them passing down State Street. The clock on the old State House points to high noon, when the Exchange should be in its glory and present the liveliest emblem of what was the sole business of life, as regarded a multitude of the foregone worldlings. It is over now. The Sabbath of eternity has shed its stillness along the street. Not even a newsboy assails the two solitary passers-by with an extra penny paper from the office of the Times or Mail, containing a full account of yesterday's terrible catastrophe. Of all the dull times that merchants and speculators have known, this is the very worst; for, so far as they were concerned, creation itself has taken the benefit of the bankrupt act. After all, it is a pity. Those mighty capitalists who had just attained the wished-for wealth! Those shrewd men of traffic who had devoted so many years to the most intricate and artificial of sciences, and had barely mastered it when the universal bankruptcy was announced by peal of trumpet! Can they have been so incautious as to provide no currency of the country whither they have gone, nor any bills of exchange, or letters of credit from the needy on earth to the cash keepers of heaven?

Adam and Eve enter a bank. Start not, ye whose funds are treasured there! You will never need them now. Call not for the police. The stones of the street and the coin of the vaults are of equal value to this simple pair. Strange sight! They take up the bright gold in handfuls and throw it sportively into the air for the sake of seeing the glittering worthlessness descend again in a shower. They know not that each of those small yellow circles was once a magic spell, potent to sway men's hearts and mystify their moral sense. Here let them pause in the investigation of the past. They have discovered the mainspring, the life, the very essence of the system that had wrought itself into the vitals of mankind, and choked their original nature in its deadly gripe. Yet how powerless over these young inheritors of earth's hoarded wealth! And here, too, are huge packages of bank-notes, those talismanic slips of paper which once had the efficacy to build up enchanted palaces like exhalations, and work all kinds of perilous wonders, yet were themselves but the ghosts of money, the shadows of a shade. How like is this vault to a magician's cave when the all-powerful wand is broken, and the visionary splendor vanished, and the floor strown with fragments of shattered spells, and lifeless shapes, once animated by demons!

"Everywhere, my dear Eve," observes Adam, "we find heaps of rubbish of one kind or another. Somebody, I am convinced, has taken pains to collect them, but for what purpose? Perhaps, hereafter, we shall be moved to do the like. Can that be our business in the world?"

"Oh no, no, Adam!" answers Eve. "It would be better to sit down quietly and look upward to the sky."

They leave the bank, and in good time; for had they tarried later they would probably have encountered some gouty old goblin of a capitalist, whose soul could not long be anywhere save in the vault with his treasure.

Next they drop into a jeweller's shop. They are pleased with the glow of gems; and Adam twines a string of beautiful pearls around the head of Eve, and fastens his own mantle with a magnificent diamond brooch. Eve thanks him, and views herself with delight in the nearest looking-glass. Shortly afterward, observing a bouquet of roses and other brilliant flowers in a vase of water, she flings away the inestimable pearls, and adorns herself with these lovelier gems of nature. They charm her with sentiment as well as beauty.

"Surely they are living beings," she remarks to Adam.

"I think so," replies Adam, "and they seem to be as little at home in the world as ourselves."

We must not attempt to follow every footstep of these investigators whom their Creator has commissioned to pass unconscious judgment upon the works and ways of the vanished race. By this time, being endowed with quick and accurate perceptions, they begin to understand the purpose of the many things around them. They conjecture, for instance, that the edifices of the city were erected, not by the immediate hand that made the world, but by beings somewhat similar to themselves, for shelter and convenience. But how will they explain the magnificence of one habitation as compared with the squalid misery of another? Through what medium can the idea of servitude enter their minds? When will they comprehend the great and miserable fact—the evidences of which appeal to their senses everywhere—that one portion of earth's lost inhabitants was rolling in luxury while the multitude was toiling for scanty food? A wretched change, indeed, must be wrought in their own hearts ere they can conceive the primal decree of Love to have been so completely abrogated, that a brother should ever want what his brother had. When their intelligence shall have reached so far, Earth's new progeny will have little reason to exult over her old rejected one.

Their wanderings have now brought them into the suburbs of the city. They stand on a grassy brow of a hill at the foot of a granite obelisk which points its great finger upwards, as if the human family had agreed, by a visible symbol of age-long endurance, to offer some high sacrifice of thanksgiving or supplication. The solemn height of the monument, its deep simplicity, and the absence of any vulgar and practical use, all strengthen its effect upon Adam and Eve, and leave them to interpret it by a purer sentiment than the builders thought of expressing.

"Eve, it is a visible prayer," observed Adam.

"And we will pray too," she replies.

Let us pardon these poor children of neither father nor mother for so absurdly mistaking the purport of the memorial which man founded and woman finished on far-famed Bunker Hill. The idea of war is not native to their souls. Nor have they sympathies for the brave defenders of liberty, since oppression is one of their unconjectured mysteries. Could they guess that the green sward on which they stand so peacefully was once strewn with human corpses and purple with their blood, it would equally amaze them that one generation of men should perpetrate such carnage, and that a subsequent generation should triumphantly commemorate it.

With a sense of delight they now stroll across green fields and along the margin of a quiet river. Not to track them too closely, we next find the wanderers entering a Gothic edifice of gray stone where the by-gone world has left whatever it deemed worthy of record, in the rich library of Harvard University.

No student ever yet enjoyed such solitude and silence as now broods within its deep alcoves. Little do the present visitors understand what opportunities are thrown away upon them. Yet Adam looks anxiously at the long rows of volumes, those storied heights of human lore, ascending one above another from floor to ceiling. He takes up a bulky folio. It opens in his hands as if spontaneously to impart the spirit of its author to the yet unworn and untainted intellect of the fresh-created mortal. He stands poring over the regular columns of mystic characters, seemingly in studious mood; for the unintelligible thought upon the page has a mysterious relation to his mind, and makes itself felt as if it were a burden flung upon him. He is even painfully perplexed, and grasps vainly at he knows not what. O Adam, it is too soon, too soon by at least five thousand years, to put on spectacles and bury yourself in the alcoves of a library!

"What can this be?" he murmurs at last. "Eve, methinks nothing is so desirable as to find out the mystery of this big and heavy object with its thousand thin divisions. See! it stares me in the face as if it were about to speak!"

Eve, by a feminine instinct, is dipping into a volume of fashionable poetry, the production certainly of the most fortunate of earthly bards, since his lay continues in vogue when all the great masters of the lyre have passed into oblivion. But let not his ghost be too exultant! The world's one lady tosses the book upon the floor and laughs merrily at her husband's abstracted mien.

"My dear Adam," cried she, "you look pensive and dismal. Do fling down that stupid thing; for even if it should speak it would not be worth attending to. Let us talk with one another, and with the sky, and the green earth, and its trees and flowers. They will teach us better knowledge than we can find here."

"Well, Eve, perhaps you are right," replies Adam, with a sort of sigh. "Still I cannot help thinking that the interpretation of the riddles amid which we have been wandering all day long might here be discovered."

"It may be better not to seek the interpretation," persists Eve. "For my part, the air of this place does not suit me. If you love me, come away!"

She prevails, and rescues him from the mysterious perils of the library. Happy influence of woman! Had he lingered there long enough to obtain a clue to its treasures—as was not impossible, his intellect being of human structure, indeed, but with an untransmitted vigor and acuteness,—had he then and there become a student, the annalist of our poor world would soon have recorded the downfall of a second Adam. The fatal apple of another Tree of Knowledge would have been eaten. All the perversions, and sophistries, and false wisdom so aptly mimicking the true—all the narrow truth, so partial that it becomes more deceptive than falsehood—all the wrong principles and worse practice, the pernicious examples and mistaken rules of life—all the specious theories which turn earth into cloudland and men into shadows—all the sad experience which it took mankind so many ages to accumulate, and from which they never drew a moral for their future guidance,—the whole heap of this disastrous lore would have tumbled at once upon Adam's head. There would have been nothing left for him but to take up the already abortive experiment of life where we had dropped it, and toil onward with it a little further.

But, blessed in his ignorance, he may still enjoy a new world in our wornout one. Should he fall short of good, even as far as we did, he has at least the freedom—no worthless one—to make errors for himself. And his literature, when the progress of centuries shall create it, will be no interminably repeated echo of our own poetry and reproduction of the images that were moulded by our great fathers of song and fiction, but a melody never yet heard on earth, and intellectual forms unbreathed upon by our conceptions. Therefore let the dust of ages gather upon the volumes of the library, and in due season the roof of the edifice crumble down upon the whole. When the second Adam's descendants shall have collected as much rubbish of their own, it will be time enough to dig into our ruins and compare the literary advancement of two independent races.

But we are looking forward too far. It seems to be the vice of those who have a long past behind them. We will return to the new Adam and Eve, who, having no reminiscences save dim and fleeting visions of a preëxistence, are content to live and be happy in the present.

The day is near its close when these pilgrims, who derive their being from no dead progenitors, reach the cemetery of Mount Auburn. With light hearts—for earth and sky now gladden each other with beauty—they tread along the winding paths, among marble pillars, mimic temples, urns, obelisks, and sarcophagi, sometimes pausing to contemplate these fantasies of human growth, and sometimes to admire the flowers wherewith Nature converts decay to loveliness. Can death, in the midst of his old triumphs, make them sensible that they have taken up the heavy burden of mortality which a whole species had thrown down? Dust kindred to their own has never lain in the grave. Will they then recognize, and so soon, that Time and the elements have an indefeasible claim upon their bodies? Not improbably they may. There must have been shadows enough, even amid the primal sunshine of their existence, to suggest the thought of the soul's incongruity with its circumstances. They have already learned that something is to be thrown aside. The idea of Death is in them, or not far off. But, were they to choose a symbol for him, it would be the butterfly soaring upward, or the bright angel beckoning them aloft, or the child asleep, with soft dreams visible through her transparent purity.

Such a Child, in whitest marble, they have found among the monuments of Mount Auburn.

"Sweetest Eve," observes Adam, while hand in hand they contemplate this beautiful object, "yonder sun has left us, and the whole world is fading from our sight. Let us sleep as this lovely little figure is sleeping. Our Father only knows whether what outward things we have possessed to-day are to be snatched from us forever. But should our earthly life be leaving us with the departing light, we need not doubt that another morn will find us somewhere beneath the smile of God. I feel that he has imparted the boon of existence never to be resumed."

"And no matter where we exist," replies Eve, "for we shall always be together."

EGOTISM;[1] OR, THE BOSOM SERPENT

(FROM THE UNPUBLISHED "ALLEGORIES OF THE HEART.")

"Here he comes!" shouted the boys along the street. "Here comes the man with a snake in his bosom!"

This outcry, saluting Herkimer's ears as he was about to enter the iron gate of the Elliston mansion, made him pause. It was not without a shudder that he found himself on the point of meeting his former acquaintance, whom he had known in the glory of youth, and whom now after an interval of five years, he was to find the victim either of a diseased fancy or a horrible physical misfortune.

"A snake in his bosom!" repeated the young sculptor to himself. "It must be he. No second man on earth has such a bosom friend. And now, my poor Rosina, Heaven grant me wisdom to discharge my errand aright! Woman's faith must be strong indeed since thine has not yet failed."

Thus musing, he took his stand at the entrance of the gate and waited until the personage so singularly announced should make his appearance. After an instant or two he beheld the figure of a lean man, of unwholesome look, with glittering eyes and long black hair, who seemed to imitate the motion of a snake; for, instead of walking straight forward with open front, he undulated along the pavement in a curved line. It may be too fanciful to say that something, either in his moral or material aspect, suggested the idea that a miracle had been wrought by transforming a serpent into a man, but so imperfectly that the snaky nature was yet hidden, and scarcely hidden, under the mere outward guise of humanity. Herkimer remarked that his complexion had a greenish tinge over its sickly white, reminding him of a species of marble out of which he had once wrought a head of Envy, with her snaky locks.

The wretched being approached the gate, but, instead of entering, stopped short and fixed the glitter of his eye full upon the compassionate yet steady countenance of the sculptor.

"It gnaws me! It gnaws me!" he exclaimed.

And then there was an audible hiss, but whether it came from the apparent lunatic's own lips, or was the real hiss of a serpent, might admit of a discussion. At all events, it made Herkimer shudder to his heart's core.

"Do you know me, George Herkimer?" asked the snake-possessed.

Herkimer did know him; but it demanded all the intimate and practical acquaintance with the human face, acquired by modelling actual likenesses in clay, to recognize the features of Roderick Elliston in the visage that now met the sculptor's gaze. Yet it was he. It added nothing to the wonder to reflect that the once brilliant young man had undergone this odious and fearful change during the no more than five brief years of Herkimer's abode at Florence. The possibility of such a transformation being granted, it was as easy to

[1]The physical fact, to which it is here attempted to give a moral signification, has been known to occur in more than one instance.

conceive it effected in a moment as in an age. Inexpressibly shocked and startled, it was still the keenest pang when Herkimer remembered that the fate of his cousin Rosina, the ideal of gentle womanhood, was indissolubly interwoven with that of a being whom Providence seemed to have unhumanized.

"Elliston! Roderick!" cried he, "I had heard of this; but my conception came far short of the truth. What has befallen you? Why do I find you thus?"

"Oh, 't is a mere nothing! A snake! A snake! The commonest thing in the world. A snake in the bosom—that's all," answered Roderick Elliston. "But how is your own breast?" continued he, looking the sculptor in the eye with the most acute and penetrating glance that it had ever been his fortune to encounter. "All pure and wholesome? No reptile there? By my faith and conscience, and by the devil within me, here is a wonder! A man without a serpent in his bosom!"

"Be calm, Elliston," whispered George Herkimer, laying his hand upon the shoulder of the snake-possessed. "I have crossed the ocean to meet you. Listen! Let us be private. I bring a message from Rosina—from your wife!"

"It gnaws me! It gnaws me!" muttered Roderick.

With this exclamation, the most frequent in his mouth, the unfortunate man clutched both hands upon his breast as if an intolerable sting or torture impelled him to rend it open and let out the living mischief, even should it be intertwined with his own life. He then freed himself from Herkimer's grasp by a subtle motion, and, gliding through the gate, took refuge in his antiquated family residence. The sculptor did not pursue him. He saw that no available intercourse could be expected at such a moment, and was desirous, before another meeting, to inquire closely into the nature of Roderick's disease and the circumstances that had reduced him to so lamentable a condition. He succeeded in obtaining the necessary information from an eminent medical gentleman.

Shortly after Elliston's separation from his wife—now nearly four years ago—his associates had observed a singular gloom spreading over his daily life, like those chill, gray mists that sometimes steal away the sunshine from a summer's morning. The symptoms caused them endless perplexity. They knew not whether ill health were robbing his spirits of elasticity, or whether a canker of the mind was gradually eating, as such cankers do, from his moral system into the physical frame, which is but the shadow of the former. They looked for the root of this trouble in his shattered schemes of domestic bliss,—wilfully shattered by himself,—but could not be satisfied of its existence there. Some thought that their once brilliant friend was in an incipient stage of insanity, of which his passionate impulses had perhaps been the forerunners; others prognosticated a general blight and gradual decline. From Roderick's own lips they could learn nothing. More than once, it is true, he had been heard to say, clutching his hands convulsively upon his breast,—"It gnaws me! It gnaws me!"—but, by different auditors, a great diversity of explanation was assigned to this ominous expression. What could it be that gnawed the breast of Roderick Elliston? Was it sorrow? Was it merely the tooth of physical disease? Or, in his reckless course, often verging upon profligacy, if not plunging into its depths, had he been guilty of some deed which made his bosom a prey to the deadlier fangs of remorse? There was plausible ground for each of these conjectures; but it must not be concealed that more than one elderly gentleman, the victim of good cheer and slothful habits, magisterially pronounced the secret of the whole matter to be Dyspepsia!

Meanwhile, Roderick seemed aware how generally he had become the subject of curiosity and conjecture, and, with a morbid repugnance to such notice, or to any notice whatsoever, estranged himself from all companionship. Not merely the eye of man was a horror to him; not merely the light of a friend's countenance; but even the blessed sunshine, likewise, which in its universal beneficence typifies the radiance of the Creator's face, expressing his love for all the creatures of his hand. The dusky twilight was now too transparent for Roderick Elliston; the blackest midnight was his chosen hour to steal abroad; and if ever he were seen, it was when the watchman's lantern gleamed upon his figure, gliding along the street, with his hands clutched upon his bosom, still muttering, "It gnaws me! It gnaws me!" What could it be that gnawed him?

After a time, it became known that Elliston was in the habit of resorting to all the noted quacks that infested the city, or whom money would tempt to journey thither from a distance. By one of these persons, in the exultation of a supposed cure, it was proclaimed far and wide, by dint of handbills and little pamphlets on dingy paper, that a distinguished gentleman, Roderick Elliston, Esq., had been relieved of a SNAKE in his stomach! So here was the monstrous secret, ejected from its lurking place into public view, in all its horrible deformity. The mystery was out; but not so the bosom serpent. He, if it were anything but a delusion, still lay coiled in his living den. The empiric's cure had been a sham, the effect, it was supposed, of some stupefying drug which more nearly caused the death of the patient than of the odious reptile that possessed him. When Roderick Elliston regained entire sensibility, it was to find his misfortune the town talk—the more than nine days' wonder and horror—while, at his bosom, he felt the sickening motion of a thing alive, and the gnawing of that restless fang which seemed to gratify at once a physical appetite and a fiendish spite.

He summoned the old black servant, who had been bred up in his father's house, and was a middle-aged man while Roderick lay in his cradle.

"Scipio!" he began; and then paused, with his arms folded over his heart. "What do people say of me, Scipio."

"Sir! my poor master! that you had a serpent in your bosom," answered the servant with hesitation.

"And what else?" asked Roderick, with a ghastly look at the man.

"Nothing else, dear master," replied Scipio, "only that the doctor gave you a powder, and that the snake leaped out upon the floor."

"No, no!" muttered Roderick to himself, as he shook his head, and pressed his hands with a more convulsive force upon his breast, "I feel him still. It gnaws me! It gnaws me!"

From this time the miserable sufferer ceased to shun the world, but rather solicited and forced himself upon the notice of acquaintances and strangers. It was partly the result of desperation on finding that the cavern of his own bosom had not proved deep and dark enough to hide the secret, even while it was so secure a fortress for the loathsome fiend that had crept into it. But still more, this craving for notoriety was a symptom of the intense morbidness which now pervaded his nature. All persons chronically diseased are egotists, whether the disease be of the mind or body; whether it be sin, sorrow, or merely the more tolerable calamity of some endless pain, or mischief among the cords of mortal life. Such individuals are made acutely conscious of a self, by the torture in which it dwells. Self, therefore, grows to be so prominent an object with them that they cannot but present it to the face of every casual passer-by. There is a pleasure—perhaps the greatest of which the sufferer is susceptible—in displaying the wasted or ulcerated limb, or the cancer in the breast; and the fouler the crime, with so much the more difficulty does the perpetrator prevent it from thrusting up its snakelike head to frighten the world; for it is that cancer, or that crime, which constitutes their respective individuality. Roderick Elliston, who, a little while before, had held himself so scornfully above the common lot of men, now paid full allegiance to this humiliating law. The snake in his bosom seemed the symbol of a monstrous egotism to which everything was referred, and which he pampered, night and day, with a continual and exclusive sacrifice of devil worship.

He soon exhibited what most people considered indubitable tokens of insanity. In some of his moods, strange to say, he prided and gloried himself on being marked out from the ordinary experience of mankind, by the possession of a double nature, and a life within a life. He appeared to imagine that the snake was a divinity,—not celestial, it is true, but darkly infernal,—and that he thence derived an eminence and a sanctity, horrid, indeed, yet more desirable than whatever ambition aims at. Thus he drew his misery around him like a regal mantle, and looked down triumphantly upon those whose vitals nourished no deadly monster. Oftener, however, his human nature asserted its empire over him in the shape of a yearning for fellowship. It grew to be his custom to spend the whole day in wandering about the streets, aimlessly, unless it might be called an aim to establish a species of brotherhood between himself and the world. With cankered ingenuity, he sought out his own disease in every breast. Whether insane or not, he showed so keen a perception of frailty, error, and vice, that many persons gave him credit for being possessed not merely with a serpent, but with an actual fiend, who imparted this evil faculty of recognizing whatever was ugliest in man's heart.

For instance, he met an individual, who, for thirty years, had cherished a hatred against his own brother. Roderick, amidst the throng of the street, laid his hand on this man's chest, and looking full into his forbidding face,—

"How is the snake to-day?" he inquired, with a mock expression of sympathy.

"The snake!" exclaimed the brother hater—"what do you mean?"

"The snake! The snake! Does he gnaw you?" persisted Roderick. "Did you take counsel with him this morning when you should have been saying your prayers? Did he sting, when you thought of your brother's health, wealth, and good repute? Did he caper for joy, when you remembered the profligacy of his only son? And whether he stung, or whether he frolicked, did you feel his poison throughout your body and soul, converting everything to sourness and bitterness? That is the way of such serpents. I have learned the whole nature of them from my own!"

"Where is the police?" roared the object of Roderick's persecution, at the same time giving an instinctive clutch to his breast. "Why is this lunatic allowed to go at large?"

"Ha, ha!" chuckled Roderick, releasing his grasp of the man. "His bosom serpent has stung him then!"

Often it pleased the unfortunate young man to vex people with a lighter satire, yet still characterized by somewhat of snakelike virulence. One day he encountered an ambitious statesman, and gravely inquired after the welfare of his boa constrictor; for of that species, Roderick affirmed, this gentleman's serpent must needs be, since its appetite was enormous enough to devour the whole country and constitution. At another time, he stopped a close-fisted old fellow, of great wealth, but who skulked about the city in the guise of a scarecrow, with a patched blue surtout, brown hat, and mouldy boots, scraping pence together, and picking up rusty nails. Pretending to look earnestly at this respectable person's stomach, Roderick assured him that his snake was a copper-head, and had been generated by the immense quantities of that base metal, with which he daily defiled his fingers. Again, he assaulted a man of rubicund visage, and told him that few bosom serpents had more of the devil in them than those that breed in the vats of a distillery. The next whom Roderick honored with his attention was a distinguished clergyman, who happened just then to be engaged in a theological controversy, where human wrath was more perceptible than divine inspiration.

"You have swallowed a snake in a cup of sacramental wine," quoth he.

"Profane wretch!" exclaimed the divine; but, nevertheless, his hand stole to his breast.

He met a person of sickly sensibility, who, on some early disappointment, had retired from the world, and thereafter held no intercourse with his fellow-men, but brooded sullenly or passionately over the irrevocable past. This man's very heart, if Roderick might be believed, had been changed into a serpent, which would finally torment both him and itself to death. Observing a married couple, whose domestic troubles were matter of notoriety, he condoled with both on having mutually taken a house adder to their bosoms. To an envious author, who depreciated works which he could never equal, he said that his snake was the slimiest and filthiest of all the reptile tribe, but was fortunately without a sting. A man of impure life, and a brazen face, asking Roderick if there were any serpent in his breast, he told him that there was, and of the same species that once tortured Don Rodrigo, the Goth. He took a fair young girl by the hand, and gazing sadly into her eyes, warned her that she cherished a serpent of the deadliest kind within her gentle breast; and the world found the truth of those ominous words, when, a few months afterwards, the poor girl died of love and shame. Two ladies, rivals in fashionable life, who tormented one another with a thousand little stings of womanish spite, were given to understand that each of their hearts was a nest of diminutive snakes, which did quite as much mischief as one great one.

But nothing seemed to please Roderick better than to lay hold of a person infected with jealousy, which he represented as an enormous green reptile, with an ice-cold length of body, and the sharpest sting of any snake save one.

"And what one is that?" asked a by-stander, overhearing him.

It was a dark-browed man who put the question; he had an evasive eye, which in the course of a dozen years had looked no mortal directly in the face. There was an ambiguity about this person's character,—a stain upon his reputation,—yet none could tell precisely of what nature, although the city gossips, male and female, whispered the most atrocious surmises. Until a recent period he had followed the sea, and was, in fact, the very shipmaster whom George Herkimer had encountered, under such singular circumstances, in the Grecian Archipelago.

"What bosom serpent has the sharpest sting?" repeated this man; but he put the question as if by a reluctant necessity, and grew pale while he was uttering it.

"Why need you ask?" replied Roderick, with a look of dark intelligence. "Look into your own breast. Hark! my serpent bestirs himself! He acknowledges the presence of a master fiend!"

And then, as the by-standers afterwards affirmed, a hissing sound was heard, apparently in Roderick Elliston's breast. It was said, too, that an answering hiss came from the vitals of the shipmaster, as if a snake were actually lurking there and had been aroused by the call of its brother reptile. If there were in fact any such sound, it might have been caused by a malicious exercise of ventriloquism on the part of Roderick.

Thus making his own actual serpent—if a serpent there actually was in his bosom—the type of each man's fatal error, or hoarded sin, or unquiet conscience, and striking his sting so unremorsefully into the sorest spot, we may well imagine that Roderick became the pest of the city. Nobody could elude him—none could withstand him. He grappled with the ugliest truth that he could lay his hand on, and compelled his adversary to do the same. Strange spectacle in human life where it is the instinctive effort of one and all to hide those sad realities, and leave them undisturbed beneath a heap of superficial topics which constitute the materials of intercourse between man and man! It was not to be tolerated that Roderick Elliston should break through the tacit compact by which the world has done its best to secure repose without relinquishing evil. The victims of his malicious remarks, it is true, had brothers enough to keep them in countenance; for, by Roderick's theory, every mortal bosom harbored either a brood of small serpents or one overgrown monster that had devoured all the rest. Still the city could not bear this new apostle. It was demanded by nearly all, and particularly by the most respectable inhabitants, that Roderick should no longer be permitted to violate the received rules of decorum by obtruding his own bosom serpent to the public gaze, and dragging those of decent people from their lurking places.

Accordingly, his relatives interfered and placed him in a private asylum for the insane. When the news was noised abroad, it was observed that many persons walked the streets with freer countenances and covered their breasts less carefully with their hands.

His confinement, however, although it contributed not a little to the peace of the town, operated unfavorably upon Roderick himself. In solitude his melancholy grew more black and sullen. He spent whole days—indeed, it was his sole occupation—in communing with the serpent. A conversation was sustained, in which, as it seemed, the hidden monster bore a part, though unintelligibly to the listeners, and inaudible except in a hiss. Singular as it may appear, the sufferer had now contracted a sort of affection for his tormentor, mingled, however, with the intensest loathing and horror. Nor were such discordant emotions incompatible. Each, on the contrary, imparted strength and poignancy to its opposite. Horrible love—horrible antipathy—embracing one another in his bosom, and both concentrating themselves upon a being that had crept into his vitals or been engendered there, and which was nourished with his food, and lived upon his life, and was as intimate with him as his own heart, and yet was the foulest of all created things! But not the less was it the true type of a morbid nature.

Sometimes, in his moments of rage and bitter hatred against the snake and himself, Roderick determined to be the death of him, even at the expense of his own life. Once he attempted it by starvation; but, while the wretched man was on the point of famishing, the monster seemed to feed upon his heart, and to thrive and wax gamesome, as if it were his sweetest and most congenial diet. Then he privily took a dose of active poison, imagining that it would not fail to kill either himself or the devil that possessed him, or both together. Another mistake; for if Roderick had not yet been destroyed by his own poisoned heart nor the snake by gnawing it, they had little to fear from arsenic or corrosive sublimate. Indeed, the venomous pest appeared to operate as an antidote against all other poisons. The physicians tried to suffocate the fiend with tobacco smoke. He breathed it as freely as if it were his native atmosphere. Again, they drugged their patient with opium and drenched him with intoxicating liquors, hoping that the snake might thus be reduced to stupor and perhaps be ejected from the stomach. They succeeded in rendering Roderick insensible; but, placing their hands upon his breast, they were inexpressibly horror stricken to feel the monster wriggling, twining, and darting to and fro within his narrow limits, evidently enlivened by the opium or alcohol, and incited to unusual feats of activity. Thenceforth they gave up all attempts at cure or palliation. The doomed sufferer submitted to his fate, resumed his former loathsome affection for the bosom fiend, and spent whole miserable days before a looking-glass, with his mouth wide open, watching, in hope and horror, to catch a glimpse of the snake's head far down within his throat. It is supposed that he succeeded; for the attendants once heard a frenzied shout, and, rushing into the room, found Roderick lifeless upon the floor.

He was kept but little longer under restraint. After minute investigation, the medical directors of the asylum decided that his mental disease did not amount to insanity, nor would warrant his confinement, especially as its influence upon his spirits was unfavorable, and might produce the evil which it was meant to remedy. His eccentricities were doubtless great; he had habitually violated many of the customs and prejudices of society; but the world was not, without surer ground, entitled to treat him as a madman. On this decision of such competent authority Roderick was released, and had returned to his native city the very day before his encounter with George Herkimer.

As soon as possible after learning these particulars the sculptor, together with a sad and tremulous companion, sought Elliston at his own house. It was a large, sombre edifice of wood, with pilasters and a balcony, and was divided from one of the principal streets by a terrace of three elevations, which was ascended by successive flights of stone steps. Some immense old elms almost concealed the front of the mansion. This spacious and once magnificent family residence was built by a grandee of the race early in the past century, at which epoch, land being of small comparative value, the garden and other grounds had formed quite an extensive domain. Although a portion of the ancestral heritage had been alienated, there was still a shadowy enclosure in the rear of the mansion where a student, or a dreamer, or a man of stricken heart might lie all day upon the grass, amid the solitude of murmuring boughs, and forget that a city had grown up around him.

Into this retirement the sculptor and his companion were ushered by Scipio, the old black servant, whose wrinkled visage grew almost sunny with intelligence and joy as he paid his humble greetings to one of the two visitors.

"Remain in the arbor," whispered the sculptor to the figure that leaned upon his arm. "You will know whether, and when, to make your appearance."

"God will teach me," was the reply. "May He support me too!"

Roderick was reclining on the margin of a fountain which gushed into the fleckered sunshine with the same clear sparkle and the same voice of airy quietude as when trees of primeval growth flung their shadows across its bosom. How strange is the life of a fountain!—born at every moment, yet of an age coeval with the rocks, and far surpassing the venerable antiquity of a forest.

"You are come! I have expected you," said Elliston, when he became aware of the sculptor's presence.

His manner was very different from that of the preceding day—quiet, courteous, and, as Herkimer thought, watchful both over his guest and himself. This unnatural restraint was almost the only trait that betokened anything amiss. He had just thrown a book upon the grass, where it lay half opened, thus disclosing itself to be a natural history of the serpent tribe, illustrated by lifelike plates. Near it lay that bulky volume, the Ductor Dubitantium of Jeremy Taylor, full of cases of conscience, and in which most men, possessed of a conscience, may find something applicable to their purpose.

"You see," observed Elliston, pointing to the book of serpents, while a smile gleamed upon his lips, "I am making an effort to become better acquainted with my bosom friend; but I find nothing satisfactory in this volume. If I mistake not, he will prove to be *sui generis,* and akin to no other reptile in creation."

"Whence came this strange calamity?" inquired the sculptor.

"My sable friend Scipio has a story," replied Roderick, "of a snake that had lurked in this fountain—pure and innocent as it looks—ever since it was known to the first settlers. This insinuating personage once crept into the vitals of my great grandfather and dwelt there many years, tormenting the old gentleman beyond mortal endurance. In short it is a family peculiarity. But, to tell you the truth, I have no faith in this idea of the snake's being an heirloom. He is my own snake, and no man's else."

"But what was his origin?" demanded Herkimer.

"Oh, there is poisonous stuff in any man's heart sufficient to generate a brood of serpents," said Elliston with a hollow laugh. "You should have heard my homilies to the good town's-people. Positively, I deem myself fortunate in having bred but a single serpent. You, however, have none in your bosom, and therefore cannot sympathize with the rest of the world. It gnaws me! It gnaws me!"

With this exclamation Roderick lost his self-control and threw himself upon the grass, testifying his agony by intricate writhings, in which Herkimer could not but fancy a resemblance to the motions of a snake. Then, likewise, was heard that frightful hiss, which often ran through the sufferer's speech, and crept between the words and syllables without interrupting their succession.

"This is awful indeed!" exclaimed the sculptor—"an awful infliction, whether it be actual or imaginary. Tell me, Roderick Elliston, is there any remedy for this loathsome evil?"

"Yes, but an impossible one," muttered Roderick, as he lay wallowing with his face in the grass. "Could I for one instant forget myself, the serpent might not abide within me. It is my diseased self-contemplation that has engendered and nourished him."

"Then forget yourself, my husband," said a gentle voice above him; "forget yourself in the idea of another!"

Rosina had emerged from the arbor, and was bending over him with the shadow of his anguish reflected in her countenance, yet so mingled with hope and unselfish love that all anguish seemed but an earthly shadow and a dream. She touched Roderick with her hand. A tremor shivered through his frame. At that moment, if report be trustworthy, the sculptor beheld a waving motion through the grass, and heard a tinkling sound, as if something had plunged into the fountain. Be the truth as it might, it is certain that Roderick Elliston sat up like a man renewed, restored to his right mind, and rescued from the fiend which had so miserably overcome him in the battle-field of his own breast.

"Rosina!" cried he, in broken and passionate tones, but with nothing of the wild wail that had haunted his voice so long, "forgive! forgive!"

Her happy tears bedewed his face.

"The punishment has been severe," observed the sculptor. "Even Justice might now forgive; how much more a woman's tenderness! Roderick Elliston, whether the serpent was a physical reptile, or whether the morbidness of your nature suggested that symbol to your fancy, the moral of the story is not the less true and strong. A tremendous Egotism, manifesting itself in your case in the form of jealousy, is as fearful a fiend as ever stole into the human heart. Can a breast, where it has dwelt so long, be purified?"

"Oh yes," said Rosina with a heavenly smile. "The serpent was but a dark fantasy, and what it typified was as shadowy as itself. The past, dismal as it seems, shall fling no gloom upon the future. To give it its due importance we must think of it but as an anecdote in our Eternity."

THE CHRISTMAS BANQUET

(FROM THE UNPUBLISHED "ALLEGORIES OF THE HEART.")

"I have here attempted," said Roderick, unfolding a few sheets of manuscript, as he sat with Rosina and the sculptor in the summer-house,—"I have attempted to seize hold of a personage who glides past me occasionally, in my walk through life. My former sad experience, as you know, has gifted me with some degree of insight into the gloomy mysteries of the human heart, through which I have wandered like one astray in a dark cavern, with his torch fast flickering to extinction. But this man, this class of men, is a hopeless puzzle."

"Well, but propound him," said the sculptor. "Let us have an idea of him, to begin with."

"Why, indeed," replied Roderick, "he is such a being as I could conceive you to carve out of marble, and some yet unrealized perfection of human science to endow with an exquisite mockery of intellect; but still there lacks the last inestimable touch of a divine Creator. He looks like a man; and, perchance, like a better specimen of man than you ordinarily meet. You might esteem him wise; he is capable of cultivation and refinement, and has at least an external conscience, but the demands that spirit makes upon spirit are precisely those to which he cannot respond. When at last you come close to him you find him chill and unsubstantial—a mere vapor."

"I believe," said Rosina, "I have a glimmering idea of what you mean."

"Then be thankful," answered her husband, smiling; "but do not anticipate any further illumination from what I am about to read. I have here imagined such a man to be—what, probably, he never is—conscious of the deficiency in his spiritual organization. Methinks the result would be a sense of cold unreality wherewith he would go shivering through the world, longing to exchange his load of ice for any burden of real grief that fate could fling upon a human being."

Contenting himself with this preface, Roderick began to read.

In a certain old gentleman's last will and testament there appeared a bequest, which, as his final thought and deed, was singularly in keeping with a long life of melancholy eccentricity. He devised a considerable sum for establishing a fund, the interest of which was to be expended, annually forever, in preparing a Christmas Banquet for ten of the most miserable persons that could be found. It seemed not to be the testator's purpose to make these half a score of sad hearts merry, but to provide that the stern or fierce expression of human discontent should not be drowned, even for that one holy and joyful day, amid the acclamations of festal gratitude which all Christendom sends up. And he desired, likewise, to perpetuate his own remonstrance against the earthly course of Providence, and his sad and sour dissent from those systems of religion or philosophy which either find sunshine in the world or draw it down from heaven.

The task of inviting the guests, or of selecting among such as might advance their claims to partake of this dismal hospitality, was confided to the two trustees or stewards of the fund. These gentlemen, like their deceased friend, were sombre humorists, who made it their principal occupation to number the sable threads in the web of human life, and drop all the golden ones out of the reckoning. They performed their present office with integrity and judgment. The aspect of the assembled company on the day of the first festival might not, it is true, have satisfied every beholder that these were especially the individuals, chosen forth from all the world, whose griefs were worthy to stand as indicators of the mass of human suffering. Yet, after due consideration, it could not be disputed that here was a variety of hopeless discomfort, which, if it sometimes arose from causes apparently inadequate, was thereby only the shrewder imputation against the nature and mechanism of life.

The arrangements and decorations of the banquet were probably intended to signify that death in life which had been the testator's definition of existence. The hall, illuminated by torches, was hung round with curtains of deep and dusky purple, and adorned with branches of cypress and wreaths of artificial flowers, imitative of such as used to be strown over the dead. A sprig of parsley was laid by every plate. The main reservoir of wine was a sepulchral urn of silver, whence the liquor was distributed around the table in small vases, accurately copied from those that held the tears of ancient mourners. Neither had the stewards—if it were their taste that arranged these details—forgotten the fantasy of the old Egyptians, who seated a skeleton at every festive board, and mocked their own merriment with the imperturbable grin of a death's head. Such a fearful guest, shrouded in a black mantle, sat now at the head of the table. It was whispered, I know not with what truth, that the testator himself had once walked the visible world with the machinery of that same skeleton, and that it was one of the stipulations of his will that he should thus be permitted to sit, from year to year, at the banquet which he had instituted. If so, it was perhaps covertly implied that he had cherished no hopes of bliss beyond the grave to compensate for the evils which he felt or imagined here. And if, in their bewildered conjectures as to the purpose of earthly existence, the banqueters should throw aside the veil, and cast an inquiring glance at this figure of death, as seeking thence the solution otherwise unattainable, the only reply would be a stare of the vacant eye caverns and a grin of the skeleton jaws. Such was the response that the dead man had fancied himself to receive when he asked of Death to solve the riddle of his life; and it was his desire to repeat it when the guests of his dismal hospitality should find themselves perplexed with the same question.

"What means that wreath?" asked several of the company, while viewing the decorations of the table.

They alluded to a wreath of cypress which was held on high by a skeleton arm, protruding from within the black mantle.

"It is a crown," said one of the stewards, "not for the worthiest, but for the wofulest, when he shall prove his claim to it."

The guest earliest bidden to the festival was a man of soft and gentle character, who had not energy to struggle against the heavy despondency to which his temperament rendered him liable; and therefore with nothing outwardly to excuse him from happiness, he had spent a life of quiet misery that made his blood torpid, and weighed upon his breath, and sat like a ponderous night fiend upon every throb of his unresisting heart. His wretchedness seemed as deep as his original nature, if not identical with it. It was the misfortune of a second guest to cherish within his bosom a diseased heart, which had become so wretchedly sore that the continual and unavoidable rubs of the world, the blow of an enemy, the careless jostle of a stranger, and even the faithful and loving touch of a friend, alike made ulcers in it. As is the habit of people thus afflicted, he found his chief employment in exhibiting these miserable sores to any who would give themselves the pain of viewing them. A third guest was a hypochondriac, whose imagination wrought necromancy in its outward and inward world, and caused him to see monstrous faces in the household fire, and dragons in the clouds of sunset, and fiends in the guise of beautiful women, and something ugly or wicked beneath all the pleasant surfaces of nature. His neighbor at table was one who, in his early youth, had trusted mankind too much, and hoped too highly in their behalf, and, in meeting with many disappointments, had become desperately soured. For several years back this misanthrope had employed himself in accumulating motives for hating and despising his race—such as murder, lust, treachery, ingratitude, faithlessness of trusted friends, instinctive vices of children, impurity of women, hidden guilt in men of saintlike aspect—and, in short, all manner of black realities that sought to decorate themselves with outward grace or glory. But at every atrocious fact that was added to his catalogue, at every increase of the sad knowledge which he spent his life to collect, the native impulses of the poor man's loving and confiding heart made him groan with anguish. Next, with his heavy brow bent downward, there stole into the hall a man naturally earnest and impassioned, who, from his immemorial infancy, had felt the consciousness of a high message to the world; but, essaying to deliver it, had found either no voice or form of speech, or else no ears to listen. Therefore his whole life was a bitter questioning of himself—"Why have not men acknowledged my mission? Am I not a self-deluding fool? What business have I on earth? Where is my grave?" Throughout the festival, he quaffed frequent draughts from the sepulchral urn of wine, hoping thus to quench the celestial fire that tortured his own breast and could not benefit his race.

Then there entered, having flung away a ticket for a ball, a gay gallant of yesterday, who had found four or five wrinkles in his brow, and more gray hairs than he could well number on his head. Endowed with sense and feeling, he had nevertheless spent his youth in folly, but had reached at last that dreary point in life where Folly quits us of her own accord, leaving us to make friends with Wisdom if we can. Thus, cold and desolate, he had come to seek Wisdom at the banquet, and wondered if the skeleton were she. To eke out the company, the stewards had invited a distressed poet from his home in the almshouse, and a melancholy idiot from the street corner. The latter had just the glimmering of sense that was sufficient to make him conscious of a vacancy, which the poor fellow, all his life long, had mistily sought to fill up with intelligence, wandering up and down the streets, and groaning miserably because his attempts were ineffectual. The only lady in the hall was one who had fallen short of absolute and perfect beauty, merely by the trifling defect of a slight cast in her left eye. But this blemish, minute as it was, so shocked the pure ideal of her soul, rather than her vanity, that she passed her life in solitude, and veiled her countenance even from her own gaze. So the skeleton sat shrouded at one end of the table and this poor lady at the other.

One other guest remains to be described. He was a young man of smooth brow, fair cheek, and fashionable mien. So far as his exterior developed him, he might much more suitably have found a place at some merry Christmas table, than have been numbered among the blighted, fate-stricken, fancy-tortured set of ill-starred banqueters. Murmurs arose among the guests as they noted the glance of general scrutiny which the intruder threw over his companions. What had he to do among them? Why did not the skeleton of the dead founder of the feast unbend its rattling joints, arise, and motion the unwelcome stranger from the board?

"Shameful!" said the morbid man, while a new ulcer broke out in his heart. "He comes to mock us,—we shall be the jest of his tavern friends!—he will make a farce of our miseries, and bring it out upon the stage!"

"Oh, never mind him!" said the hypochondriac, smiling sourly. "He shall feast from yonder tureen of viper soup; and if there is a fricassee of scorpions on the table, pray let him have his share of it. For the dessert, he shall taste the apples of Sodom. Then, if he like our Christmas fare, let him return again next year!"

"Trouble him not," murmured the melancholy man, with gentleness. "What matters it whether the consciousness of misery come a few years sooner or later? If this youth deem himself happy now, yet let him sit with us for the sake of the wretchedness to come."

The poor idiot approached the young man with that mournful aspect of vacant inquiry which his face continually wore, and which caused people to say that he was always in search of his missing wits. After no little examination he touched the stranger's hand, but immediately drew back his own, shaking his head and shivering.

"Cold, cold, cold!" muttered the idiot.

The young man shivered too, and smiled.

"Gentlemen,—and you, madam,"—said one of the stewards of the festival, "do not conceive so ill either of our caution or judgment as to imagine that we have admitted this young stranger—Gervayse Hastings by name—without a full investigation and thoughtful balance of his claims. Trust me, not a guest at the table is better entitled to his seat."

The steward's guaranty was perforce satisfactory. The company, therefore, took their places and addressed themselves to the serious business of the feast, but were soon disturbed by the hypochondriac, who thrust back his chair complaining that a dish of stewed toads and vipers was set before him, and that there was green ditch water in his cup of wine. This mistake being amended, he quietly resumed his seat. The wine, as it flowed freely from the sepulchral urn, seemed to come imbued with all gloomy inspirations; so that its influence was not to cheer, but either to sink the revellers into a deeper melancholy or elevate their spirits to an enthusiasm of wretchedness. The conversation was various. They told sad stories about people who might have been worthy guests at such a festival as the present. They talked of grisly incidents in human history; of strange crimes, which, if truly considered, were but convulsions of agony; of some lives that had been altogether wretched, and of others, which, wearing a general semblance of happiness, had yet been deformed sooner or later by misfortune, as by the intrusion of a grim face at a banquet; of death-bed scenes, and what dark intimations might be gathered from the words of dying men; of suicide, and whether the more eligible mode were by halter, knife, poison, drowning, gradual starvation, or the fumes of charcoal. The majority of the guests, as is the custom with people thoroughly and profoundly sick at heart, were anxious to make their own woes the theme of discussion, and prove themselves most excellent in anguish. The misanthropist went deep into the philosophy of evil, and wandered about in the darkness, with now and then a gleam of discolored light hovering on ghastly shapes and horrid scenery. Many a miserable thought, such as men have stumbled upon from age to age, did he now rake up again, and gloat over it as an inestimable gem, a diamond, a treasure far preferable to those bright, spiritual revelations of a better world, which are like precious stones from heaven's pavement. And then, amid his lore of wretchedness he hid his face and wept.

It was a festival at which the woful man of Uz might suitably have been a guest, together with all, in each succeeding age, who have tasted deepest of the bitterness of life. And be it said, too, that every son or daughter of woman, however favored with happy fortune, might, at one sad moment or another, have claimed the privilege of a stricken heart, to sit down at this table. But, throughout the feast, it was remarked that the young stranger, Gervayse Hastings, was unsuccessful in his attempts to catch its pervading spirit. At any deep, strong thought that found utterance, and which was torn out, as it were, from the saddest recesses of human consciousness, he looked mystified and bewildered; even more than the poor idiot, who seemed to grasp at such things with his earnest heart, and thus occasionally to comprehend them. The young man's conversation was of a colder and lighter kind, often brilliant, but lacking the powerful characteristics of a nature that had been developed by suffering.

"Sir," said the misanthropist, bluntly, in reply to some observation by Gervayse Hastings, "pray do not address me again. We have no right to talk together. Our minds have nothing in common. By what claim you appear at this banquet I cannot guess; but methinks, to a man who could say what you have just now said, my companions and myself must seem no more than shadows flickering on the wall. And precisely such a shadow are you to us."

The young man smiled and bowed, but drawing himself back in his chair, he buttoned his coat over his breast, as if the banqueting hall were growing chill. Again the idiot fixed his melancholy stare upon the youth and murmured, "Cold, cold, cold!"

The banquet drew to its conclusion, and the guests departed. Scarcely had they stepped across the threshold of the hall, when the scene that had there passed seemed like the vision of a sick fancy, or an exhalation from a stagnant heart. Now and then, however, during the year that ensued, these melancholy people caught glimpses of one another, transient, indeed, but enough to prove that they walked the earth with the ordinary allotment of reality. Sometimes a pair of them came face to face, while stealing through the evening twilight, enveloped in their sable cloaks. Sometimes they casually met in churchyards. Once, also, it happened that two of the dismal banqueters mutually started at recognizing each other in the noonday sunshine of a crowded street, stalking there like ghosts astray. Doubtless they wondered why the skeleton did not come abroad at noonday too.

But whenever the necessity of their affairs compelled these Christmas guests into the bustling world, they were sure to encounter the young man who had so unaccountably been admitted to the festival. They saw him among the gay and fortunate; they caught the sunny sparkle of his eye; they heard the light and careless tones of his voice, and muttered to themselves with such indignation as only the aristocracy of wretchedness could kindle—"The traitor! The vile impostor! Providence, in its own good time, may give him a right to feast among us!" But the young man's unabashed eye dwelt upon their gloomy figures as they passed him, seeming to say, perchance with somewhat of a sneer, "First know my secret!—then, measure your claims with mine!"

The step of Time stole onward, and soon brought merry Christmas round again, with glad and solemn worship in the churches, and sports, games, festivals, and everywhere the bright face of Joy beside the household fire. Again likewise the hall, with its curtains of dusky purple, was illuminated by the death torches gleaming on the sepulchral decorations of the banquet. The veiled skeleton sat in state, lifting the cypress wreath above its head, as the guerdon of some guest illustrious in the qualifications which there claimed precedence. As the stewards deemed the world inexhaustible in misery, and were desirous of recognizing it in all its forms, they had not seen fit to reassemble the company of the former year. New faces now threw their gloom across the table.

There was a man of nice conscience, who bore a blood stain in his heart—the death of a fellow-creature—which, for his more exquisite torture, had chanced with such a peculiarity of circumstances, that he could not absolutely determine whether his will had entered into the deed or not. Therefore, his whole life was spent in the agony of an inward trial for murder, with a continual sifting of the details of his terrible calamity, until his mind had no longer any thought, nor his soul any emotion, disconnected with it. There was a mother, too—a mother once, but a desolation now—who, many years before, had gone out on a pleasure party, and, returning, found her infant smothered in its little bed. And ever since she had been tortured with the fantasy that her buried baby lay smothering in its coffin. Then there was an aged lady, who had lived from time immemorial with a constant tremor quivering through her frame. It was terrible to discern her dark shadow tremulous upon the wall; her lips, likewise, were tremulous; and the expression of her eye seemed to indicate that her soul was trembling too. Owing to the bewilderment and confusion which made almost a chaos of her intellect, it was impossible to discover what dire misfortune had thus shaken her nature to its depths; so that the stewards had admitted her to the table, not from any acquaintance with her history, but on the safe testimony of her miserable aspect. Some surprise was expressed at the presence of a bluff, red-faced gentleman, a certain Mr. Smith, who had evidently the fat of many a rich feast within him, and the habitual twinkle of whose eye betrayed a disposition to break forth into uproarious laughter for little cause or none. It turned out, however, that with the best possible flow of spirits, our poor friend was afflicted with a physical disease of the heart, which threatened instant death on the slightest cachinnatory indulgence, or even that titillation of the bodily frame produced by merry thoughts. In this dilemma he had sought admittance to the banquet, on the ostensible plea of his irksome and miserable state, but, in reality, with the hope of imbibing a life-preserving melancholy.

A married couple had been invited from a motive of bitter humor, it being well understood that they rendered each other unutterably miserable whenever they chanced to meet, and therefore must necessarily be fit associates at the festival. In contrast with these was another couple, still unmarried, who had interchanged their hearts in early life, but had been divided by circumstances as impalpable as morning mist, and kept apart so long that their spirits now found it impossible to meet. Therefore yearning for communion, yet shrinking from one another and choosing none beside, they felt themselves companionless in life, and looked upon eternity as a boundless desert. Next to the skeleton sat a mere son of earth—a hunter of the Exchange—a gatherer of shining dust—a man whose life's record was in his ledger, and whose soul's prison house the vaults of the bank where he kept his deposits. This person had been greatly perplexed at his invitation, deeming himself one of the most fortunate men in the city; but the stewards persisted in demanding his presence, assuring him that he had no conception how miserable he was.

And now appeared a figure which we must acknowledge as our acquaintance of the former festival. It was Gervayse Hastings, whose presence had then caused so much question and criticism, and who now took his place with the composure of one whose claims were satisfactory to himself and must needs be allowed by others. Yet his easy and unruffled face betrayed no sorrow. The well-skilled beholders gazed a moment into his eyes and shook their heads, to miss the unuttered sympathy—the countersign, never to be falsified—of those whose hearts are cavern mouths, through which they descend into a region of illimitable woe and recognize other wanderers there.

"Who is this youth?" asked the man with a blood stain on his conscience. "Surely he has never gone down into the depths! I know all the aspects of those who have passed through the dark valley. By what right is he among us?"

"Ah, it is a sinful thing to come hither without a sorrow," murmured the aged lady, in accents that partook of the eternal tremor which pervaded her whole being. "Depart, young man! Your soul has never been shaken, and, therefore, I tremble so much the more to look at you."

"His soul shaken! No; I'll answer for it," said bluff Mr. Smith, pressing his hand upon his heart and making himself as melancholy as he could, for fear of a fatal explosion of laughter. "I know the lad well; he has as fair prospects as any young man about town, and has no more right among us miserable creatures than the child unborn. He never was miserable and probably never will be!"

"Our honored guests," interposed the stewards, "pray have patience with us, and believe, at least, that our deep veneration for the sacredness of this solemnity would preclude any wilful violation of it. Receive this young man to your table. It may not be too much to say that no guest here would exchange his own heart for the one that beats within that youthful bosom!"

"I'd call it a bargain, and gladly too," muttered Mr. Smith, with a perplexing mixture of sadness and mirthful conceit. "A plague upon their nonsense! My own heart is the only really miserable one in the company; it will certainly be the death of me at last!"

Nevertheless, as on the former occasion, the judgment of the stewards being without appeal, the company sat down. The obnoxious guest made no more attempt to obtrude his conversation on those about him, but appeared to listen to the table talk with peculiar assiduity, as if some inestimable secret, otherwise beyond his reach, might be conveyed in a casual word. And in truth, to those who could understand and value it, there was rich matter in the upgushings and outpourings of these initiated souls to whom sorrow had been a talisman, admitting them into spiritual depths which no other spell can open. Sometimes out of the midst of densest gloom there flashed a momentary radiance, pure as crystal, bright as the flame of stars, and shedding such a glow upon the mysteries of life that the guests were ready to exclaim, "Surely the riddle is on the point of being solved!" At such illuminated intervals the saddest mourners felt it to be revealed that mortal griefs are but shadowy and external; no more than the sable robes voluminously shrouding a certain divine reality, and thus indicating what might otherwise be altogether invisible to mortal eye.

"Just now," remarked the trembling old woman, "I seemed to see beyond the outside. And then my everlasting tremor passed away!"

"Would that I could dwell always in these momentary gleams of light!" said the man of stricken conscience. "Then the blood stain in my heart would be washed clean away."

This strain of conversation appeared so unintelligibly absurd to good Mr. Smith, that he burst into precisely the fit of laughter which his physicians had warned him against, as likely to prove instantaneously fatal. In effect, he fell back in his chair a corpse, with a broad grin upon his face, while his ghost, perchance, remained beside it bewildered at its unpremeditated exit. This catastrophe of course broke up the festival.

"How is this? You do not tremble?" observed the tremulous old woman to Gervayse Hastings, who was gazing at the dead man with singular intentness. "Is it not awful to see him so suddenly vanish out of the midst of life—this man of flesh and blood, whose earthly nature was so warm and strong? There is a never-ending tremor in my soul, but it trembles afresh at this! And you are calm!"

"Would that he could teach me somewhat!" said Gervayse Hastings, drawing a long breath. "Men pass before me like shadows on the wall; their actions, passions, feelings, are flickerings of the light, and then they vanish! Neither the corpse, nor yonder skeleton, nor this old woman's everlasting tremor, can give me what I seek."

And then the company departed.

We cannot linger to narrate, in such detail, more circumstances of these singular festivals, which, in accordance with the founder's will, continued to be kept with the regularity of an established institution. In process of time the stewards adopted the custom of inviting, from far and near, those individuals whose misfortunes were prominent above other men's, and whose mental and moral development might, therefore, be supposed to possess a corresponding interest. The exiled noble of the French Revolution, and the broken soldier of the Empire, were alike represented at the table. Fallen monarchs, wandering about the earth, have found places at that forlorn and miserable feast. The statesman, when his party flung him off, might, if he chose it, be once more a great man for the space of a single banquet. Aaron Burr's name appears on the record at a period when his ruin—the profoundest and most striking, with more of moral circumstance in it than that of almost any other man—was complete in his lonely age. Stephen Girard, when his wealth weighed upon him like a mountain, once sought admittance of his own accord. It is not probable, however, that these men had any lesson to teach in the lore of discontent and misery which might not equally well have been studied in the common walks of life. Illustrious unfortunates attract a wider sympathy, not because their griefs are more intense, but because, being set on lofty pedestals, they the better serve mankind as instances and by-words of calamity.

It concerns our present purpose to say that, at each successive festival, Gervayse Hastings showed his face, gradually changing from the smooth beauty of his youth to the thoughtful comeliness of manhood, and thence to the bald impressive dignity of age. He was the only individual invariably present. Yet on every occasion there were murmurs, both from those who knew his character and position, and from them whose hearts shrank back as denying his companionship in their mystic fraternity.

"Who is this impassive man?" had been asked a hundred times. "Has he suffered? Has he sinned? There are no traces of either. Then wherefore is he here?"

"You must inquire of the stewards, or of himself," was the constant reply. "We seem to know him well here in our city, and know nothing of him but what is creditable and fortunate. Yet hither he comes, year after year, to this gloomy banquet, and sits among the guests like a marble statue. Ask yonder skeleton; perhaps that may solve the riddle."

It was in truth a wonder. The life of Gervayse Hastings was not merely a prosperous, but a brilliant one. Everything had gone well with him. He was wealthy, far beyond the expenditure that was required by habits of magnificence, a taste of rare purity and cultivation, a love of travel, a scholar's instinct to collect a splendid library, and, moreover, what seemed a magnificent liberality to the distressed. He had sought happiness, and not vainly, if a lovely and tender wife and children of fair promise could insure it. He had, besides, ascended above the limit which separates the obscure from the distinguished, and had won a stainless reputation in affairs of the widest public importance. Not that he was a popular character, or had within him the mysterious attributes which are essential to that species of success. To the public he was a cold abstraction, wholly destitute of those rich hues of personality, that living warmth, and the peculiar faculty of stamping his own heart's impression on a multitude of hearts by which the people recognize their favorites. And it must be owned that, after his most intimate associates had done their best to know him thoroughly and love him warmly, they were startled to find how little hold he had upon their affections. They approved, they admired, but still in those moments when the human spirit most craves reality they shrank back from Gervayse Hastings, as powerless to give them what they sought. It was the feeling of distrustful regret with which we should draw back the hand after extending it, in an illusive twilight, to grasp the hand of a shadow upon the wall.

As the superficial fervency of youth decayed, this peculiar effect of Gervayse Hastings's character grew more perceptible. His children, when he extended his arms, came coldly to his knees, but never climbed them of their own accord. His wife wept secretly, and almost adjudged herself a criminal, because she shivered in the chill of his bosom. He, too, occasionally appeared not unconscious of the chillness of his moral atmosphere, and willing, if it might be so, to warm himself at a kindly fire. But age stole onward and benumbed him more and more. As the hoarfrost began to gather on him his wife went to her grave, and was doubtless warmer there; his children either died or were scattered to different homes of their own; and old Gervayse Hastings, unscathed by grief—alone, but needing no companionship, continued his steady walk through life, and still on every Christmas day attended at the dismal banquet. His privilege as a guest had become prescriptive now. Had he claimed the head of the table, even the skeleton would been ejected from its seat.

Finally, at the merry Christmas tide, when he had numbered fourscore years complete, this pale, high-browed, marble-featured old man once more entered the long-frequented hall, with the same impassive aspect that had called forth so much dissatisfied remark at his first attendance. Time, except in matters merely external, had done nothing for him, either of good or evil. As he took his place he threw a calm, inquiring glance around the table, as if to ascertain whether any guest had yet appeared, after so many unsuccessful banquets, who might impart to him the mystery—the deep, warm secret—the life within the life—which, whether manifested in joy or sorrow, is what gives substance to a world of shadows.

"My friends," said Gervayse Hastings, assuming a position which his long conversance with the festival caused to appear natural, "you are welcome! I drink to you all in this cup of sepulchral wine."

The guests replied courteously, but still in a manner that proved them unable to receive the old man as a member of their sad fraternity. It may be well to give the reader an idea of the present company at the banquet.

One was formerly a clergyman, enthusiastic in his profession, and apparently of the genuine dynasty of those old Puritan divines whose faith in their calling, and stern exercise of it, had placed them among the mighty of the earth. But, yielding to the speculative tendency of the age, he had gone astray from the firm foundation of an ancient faith, and wandered into a cloud region, where everything was misty and deceptive, ever mocking him with a semblance of reality, but still dissolving when he flung himself upon it for support and rest. His instinct and early training demanded something steadfast; but, looking forward, he beheld vapors piled on vapors, and behind him an impassable gulf between the man of yesterday and to-day, on the borders of which he paced to and fro, sometimes wringing his hands in agony, and often making his own woe a theme of scornful merriment. This surely was a miserable man. Next there was a theorist—one of a numerous tribe, although he deemed himself unique since the creation—a theorist who had conceived a plan, by which all the wretchedness of earth, moral and physical, might be done away, and the bliss of the millennium at once accomplished. But, the incredulity of mankind debarring him from action, he was smitten with as much grief as if the whole mass of woe which he was denied the opportunity to remedy were crowded into his own bosom. A plain old man in black attracted much of the company's notice, on the supposition that he was no other than Father Miller, who, it seemed, had given himself up to despair at the tedious delay of the final conflagration. Then there was a man distinguished for native pride and obstinacy, who, a little while before, had possessed immense wealth, and held the control of a vast moneyed interest which he had wielded in the same spirit as a despotic monarch would wield the power of his empire, carrying on a tremendous moral warfare, the roar and tremor of which was felt at every fireside in the land. At length came a crushing ruin—a total overthrow of fortune, power, and character—the effect of which on his imperious, and, in many respects, noble and lofty nature, might have entitled him to a place, not merely at our festival, but among the peers of Pandemonium.

There was a modern philanthropist, who had become so deeply sensible of the calamities of thousands and millions of his fellow-creatures, and of the impracticableness of any general measures for their relief, that he had no heart to do what little good lay immediately within his power, but contented himself with being miserable for sympathy. Near him sat a gentleman in a predicament hitherto unprecedented, but of which the present epoch probably affords numerous examples. Ever since he was of capacity to read a newspaper, this person had prided himself on his consistent adherence to one political party, but, in the confusion of these latter days, had got bewildered and knew not whereabouts his party was. This wretched condition, so morally desolate and disheartening to a man who has long accustomed himself to merge his individuality in the mass of a great body, can only be conceived by such as have experienced it. His next companion was a popular orator who had lost his voice, and—as it was pretty much all that he had to lose—had fallen into a state of hopeless melancholy. The table was likewise graced by two of the gentler sex: one, a half-starved, consumptive seamstress, the representative of thousands just as wretched; the other, a woman of unemployed energy, who found herself in the world with nothing to achieve, nothing to enjoy, and nothing even to suffer. She had, therefore, driven herself to the verge of madness by dark broodings over the wrongs of her sex, and its exclusion from a proper field of action. The roll of guests being thus complete, a side table had been set for three or four disappointed office seekers, with hearts as sick as death, whom the stewards had admitted partly because their calamities really entitled them to entrance here, and partly that they were in especial need of a good dinner. There was likewise a homeless dog, with his tail between his legs, licking up the crumbs and gnawing the fragments of the feast,—such a melancholy cur as one sometimes sees about the streets without a master, and willing to follow the first that will accept his service.

In their own way, these were as wretched a set of people as ever had assembled at the festival. There they sat, with the veiled skeleton of the founder holding aloft the cypress wreath at one end of the table, and at the other, wrapped in furs, the withered figure of Gervayse Hastings, stately, calm, and cold, impressing the company with awe, yet so little interesting their sympathy that he might have vanished into thin air without their once exclaiming, "Whither is he gone?"

"Sir," said the philanthropist, addressing the old man, "you have been so long a guest at this annual festival, and have thus been conversant with so many varieties of human affliction, that, not improbably, you have thence derived some great and important lessons. How blessed were your lot could you reveal a secret by which all this mass of woe might be removed!"

"I know of but one misfortune," answered Gervayse Hastings, quietly, "and that is my own."

"Your own!" rejoined the philanthropist. "And looking back on your serene and prosperous life, how can you claim to be the sole unfortunate of the human race?"

"You will not understand it," replied Gervayse Hastings, feebly, and with a singular inefficiency of pronunciation, and sometimes putting one word for another. "None have understood it—not even those who experience the like. It is a chilliness—a want of earnestness—a feeling as if what should be my heart were a thing of vapor—a haunting perception of unreality! Thus seeming to possess all that other men have—all that men aim at—I have really possessed nothing, neither joy nor griefs. All things, all persons—as was truly said to me at this table long and long ago—have been like shadows flickering on the wall. It was so with my wife and children—with those who seemed my friends: it is so with yourselves, whom I see now before me. Neither have I myself any real existence, but am a shadow like the rest."

"And how is it with your views of a future life?" inquired the speculative clergyman.

"Worse than with you," said the old man, in a hollow and feeble tone; "for I cannot conceive it earnestly enough to feel either hope or fear. Mine—mine is the wretchedness! This cold heart—this unreal life! Ah! it grows colder still."

It so chanced that at this juncture the decayed ligaments of the skeleton gave way, and the dry bones fell together in a heap, thus causing the dusty wreath of cypress to drop upon the table. The attention of the company being thus diverted for a single instant from Gervayse Hastings, they perceived, on turning again towards him, that the old man had undergone a change. His shadow had ceased to flicker on the wall.

"Well, Rosina, what is your criticism?" asked Roderick as he rolled up the manuscript.

"Frankly, your success is by no means complete," replied she. "It is true, I have an idea of the character you endeavor to describe; but it is rather by dint of my own thought than your expression."

"That is unavoidable," observed the sculptor, "because the characteristics are all negative. If Gervayse Hastings could have imbibed one human grief at the gloomy banquet, the task of describing him would have been infinitely easier. Of such persons—and we do meet with these moral monsters now and then—it is difficult to conceive how they came to exist here, or what there is in them capable of existence hereafter. They seem to be on the outside of everything; and nothing wearies the soul more than an attempt to comprehend them within its grasp."

DROWNE'S WOODEN IMAGE

One sunshiny morning, in the good old times of the town of Boston, a young carver in wood, well known by the name of Drowne, stood contemplating a large oaken log, which it was his purpose to convert into the figure-head of a vessel. And while he discussed within his own mind what sort of shape or similitude it were well to bestow upon this excellent piece of timber, there came into Drowne's workshop a certain Captain Hunnewell, owner and commander of the good brig called the Cynosure, which had just returned from her first voyage to Fayal.

"Ah! that will do, Drowne, that will do!" cried the jolly captain, tapping the log with his rattan. "I bespeak this very piece of oak for the figure-head of the Cynosure. She has shown herself the sweetest craft that ever floated, and I mean to decorate her prow with the handsomest image that the skill of man can cut out of timber. And, Drowne, you are the fellow to execute it."

"You give me more credit than I deserve, Captain Hunnewell," said the carver, modestly, yet as one conscious of eminence in his art. "But, for the sake of the good brig, I stand ready to do my best. And which of these designs do you prefer? Here,"—pointing to a staring, half-length figure, in a white wig and scarlet coat,—"here is an excellent model, the likeness of our gracious king. Here is the valiant Admiral Vernon. Or, if you prefer a female figure, what say you to Britannia with the trident?"

"All very fine, Drowne; all very fine," answered the mariner. "But as nothing like the brig ever swam the ocean, so I am determined she shall have such a figure-head as old Neptune never saw in his life. And what is more, as there is a secret in the matter, you must pledge your credit not to betray it."

"Certainly," said Drowne, marvelling, however, what possible mystery there could be in reference to an affair so open, of necessity, to the inspection of all the world as the figure-head of a vessel. "You may depend, captain, on my being as secret as the nature of the case will permit."

Captain Hunnewell then took Drowne by the button, and communicated his wishes in so low a tone that it would be unmannerly to repeat what was evidently intended for the carver's private ear. We shall, therefore, take the opportunity to give the reader a few desirable particulars about Drowne himself.

He was the first American who is known to have attempted—in a very humble line, it is true—that art in which we can now reckon so many names already distinguished, or rising to distinction. From his earliest boyhood he had exhibited a knack—for it would be too proud a word to call it genius—a knack, therefore, for the imitation of the human figure in whatever material came most readily to hand. The snows of a New England winter had often supplied him with a species of marble as dazzlingly white, at least, as the Parian or the Carrara, and if less durable, yet sufficiently so to correspond with any claims to permanent existence possessed by the boy's frozen statues. Yet they won admiration from maturer judges than his school-fellows, and were indeed, remarkably clever, though destitute of the native warmth that might have made the snow melt beneath his hand. As he advanced in life, the young man adopted pine and oak as eligible materials for the display of his skill, which now began to bring him a return of solid silver as well as the empty praise that had been an apt reward enough for his productions of evanescent snow. He became noted for carving ornamental pump heads, and wooden urns for gate posts, and decorations, more grotesque than fanciful, for mantelpieces. No apothecary would have deemed himself in the way of obtaining custom without setting up a gilded mortar, if not a head of Galen or Hippocrates, from the skilful hand of Drowne.

But the great scope of his business lay in the manufacture of figure-heads for vessels. Whether it were the monarch himself, or some famous British admiral or general, or the governor of the province, or perchance the favorite daughter of the ship-owner, there the image stood above the prow, decked out in gorgeous colors, magnificently gilded, and staring the whole world out of countenance, as if from an innate consciousness of its own superiority. These specimens of native sculpture had crossed the sea in all directions, and been not ignobly noticed among the crowded shipping of the Thames and wherever else the hardy mariners of New England had pushed their adventures. It must be confessed that a family likeness pervaded these respectable progeny of Drowne's skill; that the benign countenance of the king resembled those of his subjects, and that Miss Peggy Hobart, the merchant's daughter, bore a remarkable similitude to Britannia, Victory, and other ladies of the allegoric sisterhood; and, finally, that they all had a kind of wooden aspect which proved an intimate relationship with the unshaped blocks of timber in the carver's workshop. But at least there was no inconsiderable skill of hand, nor a deficiency of any attribute to render them really works of art, except that deep quality, be it of soul or intellect, which bestows life upon the lifeless and warmth upon the cold, and which, had it been present, would have made Drowne's wooden image instinct with spirit.

The captain of the Cynosure had now finished his instructions.

"And Drowne," said he, impressively, "you must lay aside all other business and set about this forthwith. And as to the price, only do the job in first-rate style, and you shall settle that point yourself."

"Very well, captain," answered the carver, who looked grave and somewhat perplexed, yet had a sort of smile upon his visage; "depend upon it, I'll do my utmost to satisfy you."

From that moment the men of taste about Long Wharf and the Town Dock who were wont to show their love for the arts by frequent visits to Drowne's workshop, and admiration of his wooden images, began to be sensible of a mystery in the carver's conduct. Often he was absent in the daytime. Sometimes, as might be judged by gleams of light from the shop windows, he was at work until a late hour of the evening; although neither knock nor voice, on such occasions, could gain admittance for a visitor, or elicit any word of response. Nothing remarkable, however, was observed in the shop at those hours when it was thrown open. A fine piece of timber, indeed, which Drowne was known to have reserved for some work of especial dignity, was seen to be gradually assuming shape. What shape it was destined ultimately to take was a problem to his friends and a point on which the carver himself preserved a rigid silence. But day after day, though Drowne was seldom noticed in the act of working upon it, this rude form began to be developed until it became evident to all observers that a female figure was growing into mimic life. At each new visit they beheld a larger pile of wooden chips and a nearer approximation to something beautiful. It seemed as if the hamadryad of the oak had sheltered herself from the unimaginative world within the heart of her native tree, and that it was only necessary to remove the strange shapelessness that had incrusted her, and reveal the grace and loveliness of a divinity. Imperfect as the design, the attitude, the costume, and especially the face of the image still remained, there was already an effect that drew the eye from the wooden cleverness of Drowne's earlier productions and fixed it upon the tantalizing mystery of this new project.

Copley, the celebrated painter, then a young man and a resident of Boston, came one day to visit Drowne; for he had recognized so much of moderate ability in the carver as to induce him, in the dearth of professional sympathy, to cultivate his acquaintance. On entering the shop, the artist glanced at the inflexible image of king, commander, dame, and allegory, that stood around, on the best of which might have been bestowed the questionable praise that it looked as if a living man had here been changed to wood, and that not only the physical, but the intellectual and spiritual part, partook of the stolid transformation. But in not a single instance did it seem as if the wood were imbibing the ethereal essence of humanity. What a wide distinction is here! and how far would the slightest portion of the latter merit have outvalued the utmost degree of the former!

"My friend Drowne," said Copley, smiling to himself, but alluding to the mechanical and wooden cleverness that so invariably distinguished the images, "you are really a remarkable person! I have seldom met with a man in your line of business that could do so much; for one other touch might make this figure of General Wolfe, for instance, a breathing and intelligent human creature."

"You would have me think that you are praising me highly, Mr. Copley," answered Drowne, turning his back upon Wolfe's image in apparent disgust. "But there has come a light into my mind. I know, what you know as well, that the one touch which you speak of as deficient is the only one that would be truly valuable, and that without it these works of mine are no better than worthless abortions. There is the same difference between them and the works of an inspired artist as between a sign-post daub and one of your best pictures."

"This is strange," cried Copley, looking him in the face, which now, as the painter fancied, had a singular depth of intelligence, though hitherto it had not given him greatly the advantage over his own family of wooden images. "What has come over you? How is it that, possessing the idea which you have now uttered, you should produce only such works as these?"

The carver smiled, but made no reply. Copley turned again to the images, conceiving that the sense of deficiency which Drowne had just expressed, and which is so rare in a merely mechanical character, must surely imply a genius, the tokens of which had heretofore been overlooked. But no; there was not a trace of it. He was about to withdraw when his eyes chanced to fall upon a half-developed figure which lay in a corner of the workshop, surrounded by scattered chips of oak. It arrested him at once.

"What is here? Who has done this?" he broke out, after contemplating it in speechless astonishment for an instant. "Here is the divine, the life-giving touch. What inspired hand is beckoning this wood to arise and live? Whose work is this?"

"No man's work," replied Drowne. "The figure lies within the block of oak, and it is my business to find it."

"Drowne," said the true artist, grasping the carver fervently by the hand, "you are a man of genius!"

As Copley departed, happening to glance backward from the threshold, he beheld Drowne bending over the half-created shape, and stretching forth his arms as if he would have embraced and drawn it to his heart; while, had such a miracle been possible, his countenance expressed passion enough to communicate warmth and sensibility to the lifeless oak.

"Strange enough!" said the artist to himself. "Who would have looked for a modern Pygmalion in the person of a Yankee mechanic!"

As yet, the image was but vague in its outward presentment; so that, as in the cloud shapes around the western sun, the observer rather felt, or was led to imagine, than really saw what was intended by it. Day by day, however, the work assumed greater precision, and settled its irregular and misty outline into distincter grace and beauty. The general design was now obvious to the common eye. It was a female figure, in what appeared to be a foreign dress; the gown being laced over the bosom, and opening in front so as to disclose a skirt or petticoat, the folds and inequalities of which were admirably represented in the oaken substance. She wore a hat of singular gracefulness, and abundantly laden with flowers, such as never grew in the rude soil of New England, but which, with all their fanciful luxuriance, had a natural truth that it seemed impossible for the most fertile imagination to have attained without copying from real prototypes. There were several little appendages to this dress, such as a fan, a pair of earrings, a chain about the neck, a watch in the bosom, and a ring upon the finger, all of which would have been deemed beneath the dignity of sculpture. They were put on, however, with as much taste as a lovely woman might have shown in her attire, and could therefore have shocked none but a judgment spoiled by artistic rules.

The face was still imperfect; but gradually, by a magic touch, intelligence and sensibility brightened through the features, with all the effect of light gleaming forth from within the solid oak. The face became alive. It was a beautiful, though not precisely regular and somewhat haughty aspect, but with a certain piquancy about the eyes and mouth, which, of all expressions, would have seemed the most impossible to throw over a wooden countenance. And now, so far as carving went, this wonderful production was complete.

"Drowne," said Copley, who had hardly missed a single day in his visits to the carver's workshop, "if this work were in marble it would make you famous at once; nay, I would almost affirm that it would make an era in the art. It is as ideal as an antique statue, and yet as real as any lovely woman whom one meets at a fireside or in the street. But I trust you do not mean to desecrate this exquisite creature with paint, like those staring kings and admirals yonder?"

"Not paint her!" exclaimed Captain Hunnewell, who stood by; "not paint the figure-head of the Cynosure! And what sort of a figure should I cut in a foreign port with such an unpainted oaken stick as this over my prow! She must, and she shall, be painted to the life, from the topmost flower in her hat down to the silver spangles on her slippers."

"Mr. Copley," said Drowne, quietly, "I know nothing of marble statuary, and nothing of the sculptor's rules of art; but of this wooden image, this work of my hands, this creature of my heart,"—and here his voice faltered and choked in a very singular manner,—"of this—of her—I may say that I know something. A well-spring of inward wisdom gushed within me as I wrought upon the oak with my whole strength, and soul, and faith. Let others do what they may with marble, and adopt what rules they choose. If I can produce my desired effect by painted wood, those rules are not for me, and I have a right to disregard them."

"The very spirit of genius," muttered Copley to himself. "How otherwise should this carver feel himself entitled to transcend all rules, and make me ashamed of quoting them?"

He looked earnestly at Drowne, and again saw that expression of human love which, in a spiritual sense, as the artist could not help imagining, was the secret of the life that had been breathed into this block of wood.

The carver, still in the same secrecy that marked all his operations upon this mysterious image, proceeded to paint the habiliments in their proper colors, and the countenance with Nature's red and white. When all was finished he threw open his workshop, and admitted the towns-people to behold what he had done. Most persons, at their first entrance, felt impelled to remove their hats, and pay such reverence as was due to the richly-dressed and beautiful young lady who seemed to stand in a corner of the room, with oaken chips and shavings scattered at her feet. Then came a sensation of fear; as if, not being actually human, yet so like humanity, she must therefore be something preternatural. There was, in truth, an indefinable air and expression that might reasonably induce the query, Who and from what sphere this daughter of the oak should be? The strange, rich flowers of Eden on her head; the complexion, so much deeper and more brilliant than those of our native beauties; the foreign, as it seemed, and fantastic garb, yet not too fantastic to be worn decorously in the street; the delicately-wrought embroidery of the skirt; the broad gold chain about her neck; the curious ring upon her finger; the fan, so exquisitely sculptured in open work, and painted to resemble pearl and ebony;—where could Drowne, in his sober walk of life, have beheld the vision here so matchlessly embodied! And then her face! In the dark eyes, and around the voluptuous mouth, there played a look made up of pride, coquetry, and a gleam of mirthfulness, which impressed Copley with the idea that the image was secretly enjoying the perplexing admiration of himself and other beholders.

"And will you," said he to the carver, "permit this masterpiece to become the figure-head of a vessel? Give the honest captain yonder figure of Britannia—it will answer his purpose far better—and send this fairy queen to England, where, for aught I know, it may bring you a thousand pounds."

"I have not wrought it for money," said Drowne.

"What sort of a fellow is this!" thought Copley. "A Yankee, and throw away the chance of making his fortune! He has gone mad; and thence has come this gleam of genius."

There was still further proof of Drowne's lunacy, if credit were due to the rumor that he had been seen kneeling at the feet of the oaken lady, and gazing with a lover's passionate ardor into the face that his own hands had created. The bigots of the day hinted that it would be no matter of surprise if an evil spirit were allowed to enter this beautiful form, and seduce the carver to destruction.

The fame of the image spread far and wide. The inhabitants visited it so universally, that after a few days of exhibition there was hardly an old man or a child who had not become minutely familiar with its aspect. Even had the story of Drowne's wooden image ended here, its celebrity might have been prolonged for many years by the reminiscences of those who looked upon it in their childhood, and saw nothing else so beautiful in after life. But the town was now astounded by an event, the narrative of which has formed itself into one of the most singular legends that are yet to be met with in the traditionary chimney corners of the New England metropolis, where old men and women sit dreaming of the past, and wag their heads at the dreamers of the present and the future.

One fine morning, just before the departure of the Cynosure on her second voyage to Fayal, the commander of that gallant vessel was seen to issue from his residence in Hanover Street. He was stylishly dressed in a blue broadcloth coat, with gold lace at the seams and button-holes, an embroidered scarlet waist-coat, a triangular hat, with a loop and broad binding of gold, and wore a silver-hilted hanger at his side. But the good captain might have been arrayed in the robes of a prince or the rags of a beggar, without in either case attracting notice, while obscured by such a companion as now leaned on his arm. The people in the street started, rubbed their eyes, and either leaped aside from their path, or stood as if transfixed to wood or marble in astonishment.

"Do you see it?—do you see it?" cried one, with tremulous eagerness. "It is the very same!"

"The same?" answered another, who had arrived in town only the night before. "Who do you mean? I see only a sea-captain in his shore-going clothes, and a young lady in a foreign habit, with a bunch of beautiful flowers in her hat. On my word, she is as fair and bright a damsel as my eyes have looked on this many a day!"

"Yes; the same!—the very same!" repeated the other. "Drowne's wooden image has come to life!"

Here was a miracle indeed! Yet, illuminated by the sunshine, or darkened by the alternate shade of the houses, and with its garments fluttering lightly in the morning breeze, there passed the image along the street. It was exactly and minutely the shape, the garb, and the face which the towns-people had so recently thronged to see and admire. Not a rich flower upon her head, not a single leaf, but had had its prototype in Drowne's wooden workmanship, although now their fragile grace had become flexible, and was shaken by every footstep that the wearer made. The broad gold chain upon the neck was identical with the one represented on the image, and glistened with the motion imparted by the rise and fall of the bosom which it decorated. A real diamond sparkled on her finger. In her right hand she bore a pearl and ebony fan, which she flourished with a fantastic and bewitching coquetry, that was likewise expressed in all her movements as well as in the style of her beauty and the attire that so well harmonized with it. The face with its brilliant depth of complexion had the same piquancy of mirthful mischief that was fixed upon the countenance of the image, but which was here varied and continually shifting, yet always essentially the same, like the sunny gleam upon a bubbling fountain. On the whole, there was something so airy and yet so real in the figure, and withal so perfectly did it represent Drowne's image, that people knew not whether to suppose the magic wood etherealized into a spirit or warmed and softened into an actual woman.

"One thing is certain," muttered a Puritan of the old stamp, "Drowne has sold himself to the devil; and doubtless this gay Captain Hunnewell is a party to the bargain."

"And I," said a young man who overheard him, "would almost consent to be the third victim, for the liberty of saluting those lovely lips."

"And so would I," said Copley, the painter, "for the privilege of taking her picture."

The image, or the apparition, whichever it might be, still escorted by the bold captain, proceeded from Hanover Street through some of the cross lanes that make this portion of the town so intricate, to Ann Street, thence into Dock Square, and so downward to Drowne's shop, which stood just on the water's edge. The crowd still followed, gathering volume as it rolled along. Never had a modern miracle occurred in such broad daylight, nor in the presence of such a multitude of witnesses. The airy image, as if conscious that she was the object of the murmurs and disturbance that swelled behind her, appeared slightly vexed and flustered, yet still in a manner consistent with the light vivacity and sportive mischief that were written in her countenance. She was observed to flutter her fan with such vehement rapidity that the elaborate delicacy of its workmanship gave way, and it remained broken in her hand.

Arriving at Drowne's door, while the captain threw it open, the marvellous apparition paused an instant on the threshold, assuming the very attitude of the image, and casting over the crowd that glance of sunny coquetry which all remembered on the face of the oaken lady. She and her cavalier then disappeared.

"Ah!" murmured the crowd, drawing a deep breath, as with one vast pair of lungs.

"The world looks darker now that she has vanished," said some of the young men.

But the aged, whose recollections dated as far back as witch times, shook their heads, and hinted that our forefathers would have thought it a pious deed to burn the daughter of the oak with fire.

"If she be other than a bubble of the elements," exclaimed Copley, "I must look upon her face again."

He accordingly entered the shop; and there, in her usual corner, stood the image, gazing at him, as it might seem, with the very same expression of mirthful mischief that had been the farewell look of the apparition when, but a moment before, she turned her face towards the crowd. The carver stood beside his creation mending the beautiful fan, which by some accident was broken in her hand. But there was no longer any motion in the lifelike image, nor any real woman in the workshop, nor even the witchcraft of a sunny shadow, that might have deluded people's eyes as it flitted along the street. Captain Hunnewell, too, had vanished. His hoarse sea-breezy tones, however, were audible on the other side of a door that opened upon the water.

"Sit down in the stern sheets, my lady," said the gallant captain. "Come, bear a hand, you lubbers, and set us on board in the turning of a minute-glass."

And then was heard the stroke of oars.

"Drowne," said Copley with a smile of intelligence, "you have been a truly fortunate man. What painter or statuary ever had such a subject! No wonder that she inspired a genius into you, and first created the artist who afterwards created her image."

Drowne looked at him with a visage that bore the traces of tears, but from which the light of imagination and sensibility, so recently illuminating it, had departed. He was again the mechanical carver that he had been known to be all his lifetime.

"I hardly understand what you mean, Mr. Copley," said he, putting his hand to his brow. "This image! Can it have been my work? Well, I have wrought it in a kind of dream; and now that I am broad awake I must set about finishing yonder figure of Admiral Vernon."

And forthwith he employed himself on the stolid countenance of one of his wooden progeny, and completed it in his own mechanical style, from which he was never known afterwards to deviate. He followed his business industriously for many years, acquired a competence, and in the latter part of his life attained to a dignified station in the church, being remembered in records and traditions as Deacon Drowne, the carver. One of his productions, an Indian chief, gilded all over, stood during the better part of a century on the cupola of the Province House, bedazzling the eyes of those who looked upward, like an angel of the sun. Another work of the good deacon's hand—a reduced likeness of his friend Captain Hunnewell, holding a telescope and quadrant—may be seen to this day, at the corner of Broad and State streets, serving in the useful capacity of sign to the shop of a nautical instrument maker. We know not how to account for the inferiority of this quaint old figure, as compared with the recorded excellence of the Oaken Lady, unless on the supposition that in every human spirit there is imagination, sensibility, creative power, genius, which, according to circumstances, may either be developed in this world, or shrouded in a mask of dulness until another state of being. To our friend Drowne there came a brief season of excitement, kindled by love. It rendered him a genius for that one occasion, but, quenched in disappointment, left him again the mechanical carver in wood, without the power even of appreciating the work that his own hands had wrought. Yet who can doubt that the very highest state to which a human spirit can attain, in its loftiest aspirations, is its truest and most natural state, and that Drowne was more consistent with himself when he wrought the admirable figure of the mysterious lady, than when he perpetrated a whole progeny of blockheads?

There was a rumor in Boston, about this period, that a young Portuguese lady of rank, on some occasion of political or domestic disquietude, had fled from her home in Fayal and put herself under the protection of Captain Hunnewell, on board of whose vessel, and at whose residence, she was sheltered until a change of affairs. This fair stranger must have been the original of Drowne's Wooden Image.

THE INTELLIGENCE OFFICE

A grave figure, with a pair of mysterious spectacles on his nose and a pen behind his ear, was seated at a desk in the corner of a metropolitan office. The apartment was fitted up with a counter, and furnished with an oaken cabinet and a chair or two, in simple and business-like style. Around the walls were stuck advertisements of articles lost, or articles wanted, or articles to be disposed of; in one or another of which classes were comprehended nearly all the conveniences, or otherwise, that the imagination of man has contrived. The interior of the room was thrown into shadow, partly by the tall edifices that rose on the opposite side of the street, and partly by the immense show bills of blue and crimson paper that were expanded over each of the three windows. Undisturbed by the tramp of feet, the rattle of wheels, the hum of voices, the shout of the city crier, the scream of the newsboys, and other tokens of the multitudinous life that surged along in front of the office, the figure at the desk pored diligently over a folio volume, of ledger-like size and aspect. He looked like the spirit of a record—the soul of his own great volume—made visible in mortal shape.

But scarcely an instant elapsed without the appearance at the door of some individual from the busy population whose vicinity was manifested by so much buzz, and clatter, and outcry. Now, it was a thriving mechanic in quest of a tenement that should come within his moderate means of rent; now, a ruddy Irish girl from the banks of Killarney, wandering from kitchen to kitchen of our land, while her heart still hung in the peat smoke of her native cottage; now, a single gentleman looking out for economical board; and now—for this establishment offered an epitome of worldly pursuits—it was a faded beauty inquiring for her lost bloom; or Peter Schlemihl for his lost shadow; or an author of ten years' standing for his vanished reputation; or a moody man for yesterday's sunshine.

At the next lifting of the latch there entered a person with his hat awry upon his head, his clothes perversely ill suited to his form, his eyes staring in directions opposite to their intelligence, and a certain odd unsuitableness pervading his whole figure. Wherever he might chance to be, whether in palace or cottage, church or market, on land or sea, or even at his own fireside, he must have worn the characteristic expression of a man out of his right place.

"This," inquired he, putting his question in the form of an assertion, "this is the Central Intelligence Office?"

"Even so," answered the figure at the desk, turning another leaf of his volume; he then looked the applicant in the face and said briefly, "Your business?"

"I want," said the latter, with tremulous earnestness, "a place!"

"A place! and of what nature?" asked the Intelligencer. "There are many vacant, or soon to be so, some of which will probably suit, since they range from that of a footman up to a seat at the council board, or in the cabinet, or a throne, or a presidential chair."

The stranger stood pondering before the desk with an unquiet, dissatisfied air—a dull, vague pain of heart, expressed by a slight contortion of the brow—an earnestness of glance, that asked and expected, yet continually wavered as if distrusting. In short, he evidently wanted, not in a physical or intellectual sense, but with an urgent moral necessity that is the hardest of all things to satisfy, since it knows not its own object.

"Ah, you mistake me!" said he at length, with a gesture of nervous impatience. "Either of the places you mention, indeed, might answer my purpose; or, more probably, none of them. I want my place! my own place! my true place in the world! my proper sphere! my thing to do, which nature intended me to perform when she fashioned me thus awry, and which I have vainly sought all my lifetime! Whether it be a footman's duty or a king's is of little consequence, so it be naturally mine. Can you help me here?"

"I will enter your application," answered the Intelligencer, at the same time writing a few lines in his volume. "But to undertake such a business, I tell you frankly, is quite apart from the ground covered by my official duties. Ask for something specific, and it may doubtless be negotiated for you on your compliance with the conditions. But were I to go further, I should have the whole population of the city upon my shoulders; since far the greater proportion of them are, more or less, in your predicament."

The applicant sank into a fit of despondency, and passed out of the door without again lifting his eyes; and, if he died of the disappointment, he was probably buried in the wrong tomb, inasmuch as the fatality of such people never deserts them, and whether alive or dead they are invariably out of place.

Almost immediately another foot was heard on the threshold. A youth entered hastily, and threw a glance around the office to ascertain whether the man of intelligence was alone. He then approached close to the desk, blushed like a maiden, and seemed at a loss how to broach his business.

"You come upon an affair of the heart," said the official personage, looking into him through his mysterious spectacles. "State it in as few words as may be."

"You are right," replied the youth. "I have a heart to dispose of."

"You seek an exchange?" said the Intelligencer. "Foolish youth, why not be contented with your own?"

"Because," exclaimed the young man, losing his embarrassment in a passionate glow, "because my heart burns me with an intolerable fire; it tortures me all day long with yearnings for I know not what, and feverish throbbings, and the pangs of a vague sorrow; and it awakens me in the night-time with a quake when there is nothing to be feared. I cannot endure it any longer. It were wiser to throw away such a heart, even if it brings me nothing in return."

"Oh, very well," said the man of office, making an entry in his volume. "Your affair will be easily transacted. This species of brokerage makes no inconsiderable part of my business, and there is always a large assortment of the article to select from. Herein, if I mistake not, comes a pretty fair sample."

Even as he spoke the door was gently and slowly thrust ajar, affording a glimpse of the slender figure of a young girl, who, as she timidly entered, seemed to bring the light and cheerfulness of the outer atmosphere into the somewhat gloomy apartment. We know not her errand there, nor can we reveal whether the young man gave up his heart into her custody. If so, the arrangement was neither better nor worse than in ninety-nine cases out of a hundred, where the parallel sensibilities of a similar age, importunate affections, and the easy satisfaction of characters not deeply conscious of themselves, supply the place of any profounder sympathy.

Not always, however, was the agency of the passions and affections an office of so little trouble. It happened rarely, indeed, in proportion to the cases that came under an ordinary rule, but still it did happen—that a heart was occasionally brought hither of such exquisite material, so delicately attempered, and so curiously wrought, that no other heart could be found to match it. It might almost be considered a misfortune, in a worldly point of view, to be the possessor of such a diamond of the purest water; since in any reasonable probability it could only be exchanged for an ordinary pebble, or a bit of cunningly-manufactured glass, or, at least, for a jewel of native richness, but ill set, or with some fatal flaw, or an earthy vein running through its central lustre. To choose another figure, it is sad that hearts which have their well-spring in the infinite, and contain inexhaustible sympathies, should ever be doomed to pour themselves into shallow vessels, and thus lavish their rich affections on the ground. Strange that the finer and deeper nature, whether in man or woman, while possessed of every other delicate instinct, should so often lack that most invaluable one of preserving itself from contamination with what is of a baser kind! Sometimes, it is true, the spiritual fountain is kept pure by a wisdom within itself, and sparkles into the light of heaven without a stain from the earthy strata through which it had gushed upward. And sometimes, even here on earth, the pure mingles with the pure, and the inexhaustible is recompensed with the infinite. But these miracles, though he should claim the credit of them, are far beyond the scope of such a superficial agent in human affairs as the figure in the mysterious spectacles.

Again the door was opened, admitting the bustle of the city with a fresher reverberation into the Intelligence Office. Now entered a man of woe-begone and downcast look; it was such an aspect as if he had lost the very soul out of his body, and had traversed all the world over, searching in the dust of the highways, and along the shady footpaths, and beneath the leaves of the forest, and among the sands of the sea-shore, in hopes to recover it again. He had bent an anxious glance along the pavement of the street as he came hitherward; he looked also in the angle of the doorstep, and upon the floor of the room; and, finally, coming up to the man of Intelligence, he gazed through the inscrutable spectacles which the latter wore, as if the lost treasure might be hidden within his eyes.

"I have lost"—he began; and then he paused.

"Yes," said the Intelligencer, "I see that you have lost—but what?"

"I have lost a precious jewel!" replied the unfortunate person, "the like of which is not to be found among any prince's treasures. While I possessed it, the contemplation of it was my sole and sufficient happiness. No price should have purchased it of me; but it has fallen from my bosom where I wore it in my careless wanderings about the city."

After causing the stranger to describe the marks of his lost jewel, the Intelligencer opened a drawer of the oaken cabinet which has been mentioned as forming a part of the furniture of the room. Here were deposited whatever articles had been picked up in the streets, until the right owners should claim them. It was a strange and heterogeneous collection. Not the least remarkable part of it was a great number of wedding-rings, each one of which had been riveted upon the finger with holy vows, and all the mystic potency that the most solemn rites could attain, but had, nevertheless, proved too slippery for the wearer's vigilance. The gold of some was worn thin, betokening the attrition of years of wedlock; others, glittering from the jeweller's shop, must have been lost within the honeymoon. There were ivory tablets, the leaves scribbled over with sentiments that had been the deepest truths of the writer's earlier years, but which were now quite obliterated from his memory. So scrupulously were articles preserved in this depository, that not even withered flowers were rejected; white roses, and blush roses, and moss roses, fit emblems of virgin purity and shamefacedness, which had been lost or flung away, and trampled into the pollution of the streets; locks of hair—the golden and the glossy dark—

the long tresses of woman and the crisp curls of man, signified that lovers were now and then so heedless of the faith intrusted to them as to drop its symbol from the treasure place of the bosom. Many of these things were imbued with perfumes, and perhaps a sweet scent had departed from the lives of their former possessors ever since they had so wilfully or negligently lost them. Here were gold pencil cases, little ruby hearts with golden arrows through them, bosom-pins, pieces of coin, and small articles of every description, comprising nearly all that have been lost since a long time ago. Most of them, doubtless, had a history and a meaning, if there were time to search it out and room to tell it. Whoever has missed anything valuable, whether out of his heart, mind, or pocket, would do well to make inquiry at the Central Intelligence Office.

And in the corner of one of the drawers of the oaken cabinet, after considerable research, was found a great pearl, looking like the soul of celestial purity congealed and polished.

"There is my jewel! my very pearl!" cried the stranger, almost beside himself with rapture. "It is mine! Give it me, this moment! or I shall perish!"

"I perceive," said the Man of Intelligence, examining it more closely, "that this is the Pearl of Great Price."

"The very same," answered the stranger. "Judge, then, of my misery at losing it out of my bosom! Restore it to me! I must not live without it an instant longer."

"Pardon me," rejoined the Intelligencer, calmly. "You ask what is beyond my duty. This pearl, as you well know, is held upon a peculiar tenure; and having once let it escape from your keeping, you have no greater claim to it—nay, not so great—as any other person. I cannot give it back."

Nor could the entreaties of the miserable man—who saw before his eyes the jewel of his life without the power to reclaim it—soften the heart of this stern being, impassive to human sympathy, though exercising such an apparent influence over human fortunes. Finally the loser of the inestimable pearl clutched his hands among his hair, and ran madly forth into the world, which was affrighted at his desperate looks. There passed him on the doorstep a fashionable young gentleman, whose business was to inquire for a damask rosebud, the gift of his lady love, which he had lost out of his button-hole within an hour after receiving it. So various were the errands of those who visited this Central Office, where all human wishes seemed to be made known, and so far as destiny would allow, negotiated to their fulfilment.

The next that entered was a man beyond the middle age, bearing the look of one who knew the world and his own course in it. He had just alighted from a handsome private carriage, which had orders to wait in the street while its owner transacted his business. This person came up to the desk with a quick, determined step, and looked the Intelligencer in the face with a resolute eye; though, at the same time, some secret trouble gleamed from it in red and dusky light.

"I have an estate to dispose of," said he, with a brevity that seemed characteristic.

"Describe it," said the Intelligencer.

The applicant proceeded to give the boundaries of his property, its nature, comprising tillage, pasture, woodland, and pleasure grounds, in ample circuit;

together with a mansion-house, in the construction of which it had been his object to realize a castle in the air, hardening its shadowy walls into granite, and rendering its visionary splendor perceptible to the awakened eye. Judging from his description, it was beautiful enough to vanish like a dream, yet substantial enough to endure for centuries. He spoke, too, of the gorgeous furniture, the refinements of upholstery, and all the luxurious artifices that combined to render this a residence where life might flow onward in a stream of golden days, undisturbed by the ruggedness which fate loves to fling into it.

"I am a man of strong will," said he, in conclusion, "and at my first setting out in life, as a poor, unfriended youth, I resolved to make myself the possessor of such a mansion and estate as this, together with the abundant revenue necessary to uphold it. I have succeeded to the extent of my utmost wish. And this is the estate which I have now concluded to dispose of."

"And your terms?" asked the Intelligencer, after taking down the particulars with which the stranger had supplied him.

"Easy, abundantly easy!" answered the successful man, smiling, but with a stern and almost frightful contraction of the brow, as if to quell an inward pang. "I have been engaged in various sorts of business—a distiller, a trader to Africa, an East India merchant, a speculator in the stocks—and, in the course of these affairs, have contracted an incumbrance of a certain nature. The purchaser of the estate shall merely be required to assume this burden to himself."

"I understand you," said the man of Intelligence, putting his pen behind his ear. "I fear that no bargain can be negotiated on these conditions. Very probably the next possessor may acquire the estate with a similar incumbrance, but it will be of his own contracting, and will not lighten your burden in the least."

"And am I to live on," fiercely exclaimed the stranger, "with the dirt of these accursed acres and the granite of this infernal mansion crushing down my soul? How, if I should turn the edifice into an alms-house or a hospital, or tear it down and build a church?"

"You can at least make the experiment," said the Intelligencer; "but the whole matter is one which you must settle for yourself."

The man of deplorable success withdrew, and got into his coach, which rattled off lightly over the wooden pavements, though laden with the weight of much land, a stately house, and ponderous heaps of gold, all compressed into an evil conscience.

There now appeared many applicants for places; among the most noteworthy of whom was a small, smoke-dried figure, who gave himself out to be one of the bad spirits that had waited upon Doctor Faustus in his laboratory. He pretended to show a certificate of character, which, he averred, had been given him by that famous necromancer, and countersigned by several masters whom he had subsequently served.

"I am afraid, my good friend," observed the Intelligencer, "that your chance of getting a service is but poor. Nowadays, men act the evil spirit for themselves and their neighbors, and play the part more effectually than ninety-nine out of a hundred of your fraternity."

But, just as the poor fiend was assuming a vaporous consistency, being about to vanish through the floor in sad disappointment and chagrin, the editor of a political newspaper chanced to enter the office in quest of a scribbler of party paragraphs. The former servant of Doctor Faustus, with some misgivings as to his sufficiency of venom, was allowed to try his hand in this capacity. Next appeared, likewise seeking a service, the mysterious man in Red, who had aided Bonaparte in his ascent to imperial power. He was examined as to his qualifications by an aspiring politician, but finally rejected, as lacking familiarity with the cunning tactics of the present day.

People continued to succeed each other with as much briskness as if everybody turned aside, out of the roar and tumult of the city, to record here some want, or superfluity, or desire. Some had goods or possessions, of which they wished to negotiate the sale. A China merchant had lost his health by a long residence in that wasting climate. He very liberally offered his disease, and his wealth along with it, to any physician who would rid him of both together. A soldier offered his wreath of laurels for as good a leg as that which it had cost him on the battle-field. One poor weary wretch desired nothing but to be accommodated with any creditable method of laying down his life; for misfortune and pecuniary troubles had so subdued his spirits that he could no longer conceive the possibility of happiness, nor had the heart to try for it. Nevertheless, happening to overhear some conversation in the Intelligence Office respecting wealth to be rapidly accumulated by a certain mode of speculation, he resolved to live out this one other experiment of better fortune. Many persons desired to exchange their youthful vices for others better suited to the gravity of advancing age; a few, we are glad to say, made earnest efforts to exchange vice for virtue, and, hard as the bargain was, succeeded in effecting it. But it was remarkable that what all were the least willing to give up, even on the most advantageous terms, were the habits, the oddities, the characteristic traits, the little ridiculous indulgences, somewhere between faults and follies, of which nobody but themselves could understand the fascination.

The great folio, in which the Man of Intelligence recorded all these freaks of idle hearts, and aspirations of deep hearts, and desperate longings of miserable hearts, and evil prayers of perverted hearts, would be curious reading were it possible to obtain it for publication. Human character in its individual developments—human nature in the mass—may best be studied in its wishes; and this was the record of them all. There was an endless diversity of mode and circumstance, yet withal such a similarity in the real ground-work, that any one page of the volume—whether written in the days before the Flood, or the yesterday that is just gone by, or to be written on the morrow that is close at hand, or a thousand ages hence—might serve as a specimen of the whole. Not but that there were wild sallies of fantasy that could scarcely occur to more than one man's brain, whether reasonable or lunatic. The strangest wishes—yet most incident to men who had gone deep into scientific pursuits, and attained a high intellectual stage, though not the loftiest—were to contend with Nature, and wrest from her some secret or some power which she had seen fit to withhold from mortal grasp. She loves to delude her aspiring students, and mock them with mysteries that seem but just beyond their utmost reach. To concoct new minerals, to produce new forms of vegetable life, to create an insect, if nothing higher in the living scale, is a sort of wish that has often revelled in the breast of a man of science. An astronomer, who lived far more among the distant worlds of space than in this lower sphere, recorded a wish to behold the opposite side of the moon, which, unless the system of the firmament be reversed, she can never turn towards the earth. On the same page of the volume was written the wish of a little child to have the stars for playthings.

The most ordinary wish, that was written down with wearisome recurrence, was, of course, for wealth, wealth, wealth, in sums from a few shillings up to unreckonable thousands. But in reality this often-repeated expression covered as many different desires. Wealth is the golden essence of the outward world, embodying almost everything that exists beyond the limits of the soul; and therefore it is the natural yearning for the life in the midst of which we find ourselves, and of which gold is the condition of enjoyment, that men abridge into this general wish. Here and there, it is true, the volume testified to some heart so perverted as to desire gold for its own sake. Many wished for power; a strange desire indeed, since it is but another form of slavery. Old people wished for the delights of youth; a fop, for a fashionable coat; an idle reader, for a new novel; a versifier, for a rhyme to some stubborn word; a painter, for Titian's secret of coloring; a prince, for a cottage; a republican, for a kingdom and a palace; a libertine for his neighbor's wife; a man of palate, for green peas; and a poor man, for a crust of bread. The ambitious desires of public men, elsewhere so craftily concealed, were here expressed openly and boldly, side by side with the unselfish wishes of the philanthropist for the welfare of the race, so beautiful, so comforting, in contrast with the egotism that continually weighed self against the world. Into the darker secrets of the Book of Wishes we will not penetrate.

It would be an instructive employment for a student of mankind, perusing this volume carefully and comparing its records with men's perfected designs, as expressed in their deeds and daily life, to ascertain how far the one accorded with the other. Undoubtedly, in most cases, the correspondence would be found remote. The holy and generous wish, that rises like incense from a pure heart towards heaven, often lavishes its sweet perfume on the blast of evil times. The foul, selfish, murderous wish, that steams forth from a corrupted heart, often passes into the spiritual atmosphere without being concreted into an earthly deed. Yet this volume is probably truer, as a representation of the human heart, than is the living drama of action as it evolves around us. There is more of good and more of evil in it; more redeeming points of the bad and more errors of the virtuous; higher upsoarings, and baser degradation of the soul; in short, a more perplexing amalgamation of vice and virtue than we witness in the outward world. Decency and external conscience often produce a far fairer outside than is warranted by the stains within. And be it owned, on the other hand, that a man seldom repeats to his nearest friend, any more than he realizes in act, the purest wishes, which, at some blessed time or other, have arisen from the depths of his nature and witnessed for him in this volume. Yet there is enough on every leaf to make the good man shudder for his own wild and idle wishes, as well as for the sinner, whose whole life is the incarnation of a wicked desire.

But again the door is opened, and we hear the tumultuous stir of the world—a deep and awful sound, expressing in another form some portion of what is written in the volume that lies before the Man of Intelligence. A grandfatherly personage tottered hastily into the office, with such an earnestness in his infirm alacrity that his white hair floated backward as he hurried up to the desk, while his dim eyes caught a momentary lustre from his vehemence of purpose. This venerable figure explained that he was in search of To-Morrow.

"I have spent all my life in pursuit of it," added the sage old gentleman, "being assured that To-Morrow has some vast benefit or other in store for me. But I am now getting a little in years, and must make haste; for, unless I overtake To-Morrow soon, I begin to be afraid it will finally escape me."

"This fugitive To-Morrow, my venerable friend," said the Man of Intelligence, "is a stray child of Time, and is flying from his father into the region of the infinite. Continue your pursuit, and you will doubtless come up with him; but as to the earthly gifts which you expect, he has scattered them all among a throng of Yesterdays."

Obliged to content himself with this enigmatical response, the grandsire hastened forth with a quick clatter of his staff upon the floor; and, as he disappeared, a little boy scampered through the door in chase of a butterfly which had got astray amid the barren sunshine of the city. Had the old gentleman been shrewder, he might have detected To-Morrow under the semblance of that gaudy insect. The golden butterfly glistened through the shadowy apartment, and brushed its wings against the Book of Wishes, and fluttered forth again with the child still in pursuit.

A man now entered, in neglected attire, with the aspect of a thinker, but somewhat too rough-hewn and brawny for a scholar. His face was full of sturdy vigor, with some finer and keener attribute beneath. Though harsh at first, it was tempered with the glow of a large, warm heart, which had force enough to heat his powerful intellect through and through. He advanced to the Intelligencer and looked at him with a glance of such stern sincerity that perhaps few secrets were beyond its scope.

"I seek for Truth," said he.

"It is precisely the most rare pursuit that has ever come under my cognizance," replied the Intelligencer, as he made the new inscription in his volume. "Most men seek to impose some cunning falsehood upon themselves for truth. But I can lend no help to your researches. You must achieve the miracle for yourself. At some fortunate moment you may find Truth at your side, or perhaps she may be mistily discerned far in advance, or possibly behind you."

"Not behind me," said the seeker; "for I have left nothing on my track without a thorough investigation. She flits before me, passing now through a naked solitude, and now mingling with the throng of a popular assembly, and now writing with the pen of a French philosopher, and now standing at the altar of an old cathedral, in the guise of a Catholic priest, performing the high mass. Oh weary search! But I must not falter; and surely my heart-deep quest of Truth shall avail at last."

He paused and fixed his eyes upon the Intelligencer with a depth of investigation that seemed to hold commerce with the inner nature of this being, wholly regardless of his external development.

"And what are you?" said he. "It will not satisfy me to point to this fantastic show of an Intelligence Office and this mockery of business. Tell me what is beneath it, and what your real agency in life, and your influence upon mankind."

"Yours is a mind," answered the Man of Intelligence, "before which the forms and fantasies that conceal the inner idea from the multitude vanish at once and leave the naked reality beneath. Know, then, the secret. My agency in worldly action, my connection with the press, and tumult, and intermingling, and development of human affairs, is merely delusive. The desire of man's heart does for him whatever I seem to do. I am no minister of action, but the Recording Spirit."

What further secrets were then spoken remains a mystery, inasmuch as the roar of the city, the bustle of human business, the outcry of the jostling masses, the rush and tumult of man's life in its noisy and brief career, arose so high that it drowned the words of these two talkers; and whether they stood talking in the moon, or in Vanity Fair, or in a city of this actual world, is more than I can say.

ROGER MALVIN'S BURIAL

One of the few incidents of Indian warfare naturally susceptible of the moonlight of romance was that expedition undertaken for the defence of the frontiers in the year 1725, which resulted in the well-remembered "Lovell's Fight." Imagination, by casting certain circumstances judicially into the shade, may see much to admire in the heroism of a little band who gave battle to twice their number in the heart of the enemy's country. The open bravery displayed by both parties was in accordance with civilized ideas of valor; and chivalry itself might not blush to record the deeds of one or two individuals. The battle, though so fatal to those who fought, was not unfortunate in its consequences to the country; for it broke the strength of a tribe and conduced to the peace which subsisted during several ensuing years. History and tradition are unusually minute in their memorials of this affair; and the captain of a scouting party of frontier men has acquired as actual a military renown as many a victorious leader of thousands. Some of the incidents contained in the following pages will be recognized, notwithstanding the substitution of fictitious names, by such as have heard, from old men's lips, the fate of the few combatants who were in a condition to retreat after "Lovell's Fight."

The early sunbeams hovered cheerfully upon the tree-tops, beneath which two weary and wounded men had stretched their limbs the night before. Their bed of withered oak leaves was strewn upon the small level space, at the foot of a rock, situated near the summit of one of the gentle swells by which the face of the country is there diversified. The mass of granite, rearing its smooth, flat surface fifteen or twenty feet above their heads, was not unlike a gigantic gravestone, upon which the veins seemed to form an inscription in forgotten characters. On a tract of several acres around this rock, oaks and other hard-wood trees had supplied the place of the pines, which were the usual growth of the land; and a young and vigorous sapling stood close beside the travellers.

The severe wound of the elder man had probably deprived him of sleep; for, so soon as the first ray of sunshine rested on the top of the highest tree, he reared himself painfully from his recumbent posture and sat erect. The deep lines of his countenance and the scattered gray of his hair marked him as past the middle age; but his muscular frame would, but for the effects of his wound, have been as capable of sustaining fatigue as in the early vigor of life. Languor and exhaustion now sat upon his haggard features; and the despairing glance which he sent forward through the depths of the forest proved his own conviction that his pilgrimage was at an end. He next turned his eyes to the companion who reclined by his side. The youth—for he had scarcely attained the years of manhood—lay, with his head upon his arm, in the embrace of an unquiet sleep, which a thrill of pain from his wounds seemed each moment on the point of breaking. His right hand grasped a musket; and, to judge from the violent action of his features, his slumbers were bringing back a vision of the conflict of which he was one of the few survivors. A shout—deep and loud in his dreaming fancy—found its way in an imperfect murmur to his lips; and, starting even at the slight sound of his own voice, he suddenly awoke. The first act of reviving recollection was to make anxious inquiries respecting the condition of his wounded fellow-traveller. The latter shook his head.

"Reuben, my boy," said he, "this rock beneath which we sit will serve for an old hunter's gravestone. There is many and many a long mile of howling wilderness before us yet; nor would it avail me anything if the smoke of my own chimney were but on the other side of that swell of land. The Indian bullet was deadlier than I thought."

"You are weary with our three days' travel," replied the youth, "and a little longer rest will recruit you. Sit you here while I search the woods for the herbs and roots that must be our sustenance; and, having eaten, you shall lean on me, and we will turn our faces homeward. I doubt not that, with my help, you can attain to some one of the frontier garrisons."

"There is not two days' life in me, Reuben," said the other, calmly, "and I will no longer burden you with my useless body, when you can scarcely support your own. Your wounds are deep and your strength is failing fast; yet, if you hasten onward alone, you may be preserved. For me there is no hope, and I will await death here."

"If it must be so, I will remain and watch by you," said Reuben, resolutely.

"No, my son, no," rejoined his companion. "Let the wish of a dying man have weight with you; give me one grasp of your hand, and get you hence. Think you that my last moments will be eased by the thought that I leave you to die a more lingering death? I have loved you like a father, Reuben; and at a time like this I should have something of a father's authority. I charge you to be gone that I may die in peace."

"And because you have been a father to me, should I therefore leave you to perish and to lie unburied in the wilderness?" exclaimed the youth. "No; if your end be in truth approaching, I will watch by you and receive your parting words. I will dig a grave here by the rock, in which, if my weakness overcome me, we will rest together; or, if Heaven gives me strength, I will seek my way home."

"In the cities and wherever men dwell," replied the other, "they bury their dead in the earth; they hide them from the sight of the living; but here, where no step may pass perhaps for a hundred years, wherefore should I not rest beneath the open sky, covered only by the oak leaves when the autumn winds shall strew them? And for a monument, here is this gray rock, on which my dying hand shall carve the name of Roger Malvin; and the traveller in days to come will know that here sleeps a hunter and a warrior. Tarry not, then, for a folly like this, but hasten away, if not for your own sake, for hers who will else be desolate."

Malvin spoke the last few words in a faltering voice, and their effect upon his companion was strongly visible. They reminded him that there were other and less questionable duties than that of sharing the fate of a man whom his death could not benefit. Nor can it be affirmed that no selfish feeling strove to enter Reuben's heart, though the consciousness made him more earnestly resist his companion's entreaties.

"How terrible to wait the slow approach of death in this solitude!" exclaimed he. "A brave man does not shrink in the battle; and, when friends stand round the bed, even women may die composedly; but here"—

"I shall not shrink even here, Reuben Bourne," interrupted Malvin. "I am a man of no weak heart, and, if I were, there is a surer support than that of earthly friends. You are young, and life is dear to you. Your last moments will need comfort far more than mine; and when you have laid me in the earth, and are alone, and night is settling on the forest, you will feel all the bitterness of the death that may now be escaped. But I will urge no selfish motive to your generous nature. Leave me for my sake, that, having said a prayer for your safety, I may have space to settle my account undisturbed by worldly sorrows."

"And your daughter,—how shall I dare to meet her eye?" exclaimed Reuben. "She will ask the fate of her father, whose life I vowed to defend with my own. Must I tell her that he travelled three days' march with me from the field of battle and that then I left him to perish in the wilderness? Were it not better to lie down and die by your side than to return safe and say this to Dorcas?"

"Tell my daughter," said Roger Malvin, "that, though yourself sore wounded, and weak, and weary, you led my tottering footsteps many a mile, and left me only at my earnest entreaty, because I would not have your blood upon my soul. Tell her that through pain and danger you were faithful, and that, if your lifeblood could have saved me, it would have flowed to its last drop; and tell her that you will be something dearer than a father, and that my blessing is with you both, and that my dying eyes can see a long and pleasant path in which you will journey together."

As Malvin spoke he almost raised himself from the ground, and the energy of his concluding words seemed to fill the wild and lonely forest with a vision of happiness; but, when he sank exhausted upon his bed of oak leaves, the light which had kindled in Reuben's eye was quenched. He felt as if it were both sin and folly to think of happiness at such a moment. His companion watched his changing countenance, and sought with generous art to wile him to his own good.

"Perhaps I deceive myself in regard to the time I have to live," he resumed. "It may be that, with speedy assistance, I might recover of my wound. The foremost fugitives must, ere this, have carried tidings of our fatal battle to the frontiers, and parties will be out to succor those in like condition with ourselves. Should you meet one of these and guide them hither, who can tell but that I may sit by my own fireside again?"

A mournful smile strayed across the features of the dying man as he insinuated that unfounded hope,—which, however, was not without its effect on Reuben. No merely selfish motive, nor even the desolate condition of Dorcas, could have induced him to desert his companion at such a moment—but his wishes seized on the thought that Malvin's life might be preserved, and his sanguine nature heightened almost to certainty the remote possibility of procuring human aid.

"Surely there is reason, weighty reason, to hope that friends are not far distant," he said, half aloud. "There fled one coward, unwounded, in the beginning of the fight, and most probably he made good speed. Every true man on the frontier would shoulder his musket at the news; and, though no party may range so far into the woods as this, I shall perhaps encounter them in one day's march. Counsel me faithfully," he added, turning to Malvin, in distrust of his own motives. "Were your situation mine, would you desert me while life remained?"

"It is now twenty years," replied Roger Malvin,—sighing, however, as he secretly acknowledged the wide dissimilarity between the two cases,—"it is now twenty years since I escaped with one dear friend from Indian captivity near Montreal. We journeyed many days through the woods, till at length overcome with hunger and weariness, my friend lay down and besought me to leave him; for he knew that, if I remained, we both must perish; and, with but little hope of obtaining succor, I heaped a pillow of dry leaves beneath his head and hastened on."

"And did you return in time to save him?" asked Reuben, hanging on Malvin's words as if they were to be prophetic of his own success.

"I did," answered the other. "I came upon the camp of a hunting party before sunset of the same day. I guided them to the spot where my comrade was expecting death; and he is now a hale and hearty man upon his own farm, far within the frontiers, while I lie wounded here in the depths of the wilderness."

This example, powerful in affecting Reuben's decision, was aided, unconsciously to himself, by the hidden strength of many another motive. Roger Malvin perceived that the victory was nearly won.

"Now, go, my son, and Heaven prosper you!" he said. "Turn not back with your friends when you meet them, lest your wounds and weariness overcome you; but send hitherward two or three, that may be spared, to search for me; and believe me, Reuben, my heart will be lighter with every step you take towards home." Yet there was, perhaps, a change both in his countenance and voice as he spoke thus; for, after all, it was a ghastly fate to be left expiring in the wilderness.

Reuben Bourne, but half convinced that he was acting rightly, at length raised himself from the ground and prepared himself for his departure. And first, though contrary to Malvin's wishes, he collected a stock of roots and herbs, which had been their only food during the last two days. This useless supply he placed within reach of the dying man, for whom, also, he swept together a bed of dry oak leaves. Then climbing to the summit of the rock, which on one side was rough and broken, he bent the oak sapling downward, and bound his handkerchief to the topmost branch. This precaution was not unnecessary to direct any who might come in search of Malvin; for every part of the rock, except its broad, smooth front, was concealed at a little distance by the dense undergrowth of the forest. The handkerchief had been the bandage of a wound upon Reuben's arm; and, as he bound it to the tree, he vowed by the blood that stained it that he would return, either to save his companion's life or to lay his body in the grave. He then descended, and stood, with downcast eyes, to receive Roger Malvin's parting words.

The experience of the latter suggested much and minute advice respecting the youth's journey through the trackless forest. Upon this subject he spoke with calm earnestness, as if he were sending Reuben to the battle or the chase while he himself remained secure at home, and not as if the human countenance that was about to leave him were the last he would ever behold. But his firmness was shaken before he concluded.

"Carry my blessing to Dorcas, and say that my last prayer shall be for her and you. Bid her to have no hard thoughts because you left me here,"—Reuben's heart smote him,—"for that your life would not have weighed with you if its sacrifice could have done me good. She will marry you after she has mourned a little while for her father; and Heaven grant you long and happy days, and may your children's children stand round your death bed! And, Reuben," added he, as the weakness of mortality made its way at last, "return, when your wounds are healed and your weariness refreshed,—return to this wild rock, and lay my bones in the grave, and say a prayer over them."

An almost superstitious regard, arising perhaps from the customs of the Indians, whose war was with the dead as well as the living, was paid by the frontier inhabitants to the rites of sepulture; and there are many instances of the sacrifice of life in the attempt to bury those who had fallen by the "sword of the wilderness." Reuben, therefore, felt the full importance of the promise which he most solemnly made to return and perform Roger Malvin's obsequies. It was remarkable that the latter, speaking his whole heart in his parting words, no longer endeavored to persuade the youth that even the speediest succor might avail to the preservation of his life. Reuben was internally convinced that he should see Malvin's living face no more. His generous nature would fain have delayed him, at whatever risk, till the dying scene were past; but the desire of existence and the hope of happiness had strengthened in his heart, and he was unable to resist them.

"It is enough," said Roger Malvin, having listened to Reuben's promise. "Go, and God speed you!"

The youth pressed his hand in silence, turned, and was departing. His slow and faltering steps, however, had borne him but a little way before Malvin's voice recalled him.

"Reuben, Reuben," said he, faintly; and Reuben returned and knelt down by the dying man.

"Raise me, and let me lean against the rock," was his last request. "My face will be turned towards home, and I shall see you a moment longer as you pass among the trees."

Reuben, having made the desired alteration in his companion's posture, again began his solitary pilgrimage. He walked more hastily at first than was consistent with his strength; for a sort of guilty feeling, which sometimes torments men in their most justifiable acts, caused him to seek concealment from Malvin's eyes; but after he had trodden far upon the rustling forest leaves he crept back, impelled by a wild and painful curiosity, and, sheltered by the earthy roots of an uptorn tree, gazed earnestly at the desolate man. The morning sun was unclouded, and the trees and shrubs imbibed the sweet air of the month of May; yet there seemed a gloom on Nature's face, as if she sympathized with mortal pain and sorrow. Roger Malvin's hands were uplifted in a fervent prayer, some of the words of which stole through the stillness of the woods and entered Reuben's heart, torturing it with an unutterable pang. They were the broken accents of a petition for his own happiness and that of Dorcas; and, as the youth listened, conscience, or something in its similitude, pleaded strongly with him to return and lie down again by the rock. He felt how hard was the doom of the kind and generous being whom he had deserted in his extremity. Death would come like the slow approach of a corpse, stealing gradually towards him through the forest, and showing its ghastly and motionless features from behind a nearer and yet a nearer tree. But such must have been Reuben's own fate had he tarried another sunset; and who shall impute blame to him if he shrink from so useless a sacrifice? As he gave a parting look, a breeze waved the little banner upon the sapling oak and reminded Reuben of his vow.

Many circumstances combined to retard the wounded traveller in his way to the frontiers. On the second day the clouds, gathering densely over the sky, precluded the possibility of regulating his course by the position of the sun; and he knew not but that every effort of his almost exhausted strength was removing him farther from the home he sought. His scanty sustenance was supplied by the berries and other spontaneous products of the forest. Herds of deer, it is true, sometimes bounded past him, and partridges frequently whirred up before his footsteps; but his ammunition had been expended in the fight, and he had no means of slaying them. His wounds, irritated by the constant exertion in which lay the only hope of life, wore away his strength and at intervals confused his reason. But, even in the wanderings of intellect, Reuben's young heart clung strongly to existence; and it was only through absolute incapacity of motion that he at last sank down beneath a tree, compelled there to await death.

In this situation he was discovered by a party who, upon the first intelligence of the fight, had been despatched to the relief of the survivors. They conveyed him to the nearest settlement, which chanced to be that of his own residence.

Dorcas, in the simplicity of the olden time, watched by the bedside of her wounded lover, and administered all those comforts that are in the sole gift of woman's heart and hand. During several days Reuben's recollection strayed drowsily among the perils and hardships through which he had passed, and he was incapable of returning definite answers to the inquiries with which many were eager to harass him. No authentic particulars of the battle had yet been circulated; nor could mothers, wives, and children tell whether their loved ones were detained by captivity or by the stronger chain of death. Dorcas nourished her apprehensions in silence till one afternoon when Reuben awoke from an unquiet sleep, and seemed to recognize her more perfectly than at any previous time. She saw that his intellect had become composed, and she could no longer restrain her filial anxiety.

"My father, Reuben?" she began; but the change in her lover's countenance made her pause.

The youth shrank as if with a bitter pain, and the blood gushed vividly into his wan and hollow cheeks. His first impulse was to cover his face; but, apparently with a desperate effort, he half raised himself and spoke vehemently, defending himself against an imaginary accusation.

"Your father was sore wounded in the battle, Dorcas; and he bade me not burden myself with him, but only to lead him to the lakeside, that he might quench his thirst and die. But I would not desert the old man in his extremity, and, though bleeding myself, I supported him; I gave him half my strength, and led him away with me. For three days we journeyed on together, and your father was sustained beyond my hopes, but, awaking at sunrise on the fourth day, I found him faint and exhausted; he was unable to proceed; his life had ebbed away fast; and"—

"He died!" exclaimed Dorcas, faintly.

Reuben felt it impossible to acknowledge that his selfish love of life had hurried him away before her father's fate was decided. He spoke not; he only bowed his head; and, between shame and exhaustion, sank back and hid his face in the pillow. Dorcas wept when her fears were thus confirmed; but the shock, as it had been long anticipated, was on that account the less violent.

"You dug a grave for my poor father in the wilderness, Reuben?" was the question by which her filial piety manifested itself.

"My hands were weak; but I did what I could," replied the youth in a smothered tone. "There stands a noble tombstone above his head; and I would to Heaven I slept as soundly as he!"

Dorcas, perceiving the wildness of his latter words, inquired no further at the time; but her heart found ease in the thought that Roger Malvin had not lacked such funeral rites as it was possible to bestow. The tale of Reuben's courage and fidelity lost nothing when she communicated it to her friends; and the poor youth, tottering from his sick chamber to breathe the sunny air, experienced from every tongue the miserable and humiliating torture of unmerited praise. All acknowledged that he might worthily demand the hand of the fair maiden to whose father he had been "faithful unto death;" and, as my tale is not of love, it shall suffice to say that in the space of a few months Reuben became the husband of Dorcas Malvin. During the marriage ceremony the bride was covered with blushes, but the bridegroom's face was pale.

There was now in the breast of Reuben Bourne an incommunicable thought —something which he was to conceal most heedfully from her whom he most loved and trusted. He regretted, deeply and bitterly, the moral cowardice that had restrained his words when he was about to disclose the truth to Dorcas; but pride, the fear of losing her affection, the dread of universal scorn, forbade him to rectify this falsehood. He felt that for leaving Roger Malvin he deserved no censure. His presence, the gratuitous sacrifice of his own life, would have added only another and a needless agony to the last moments of the dying man; but concealment had imparted to a justifiable act much of the secret effect of guilt; and Reuben, while reason told him that he had done right, experienced in no small degree the mental horrors which punish the perpetrator of undiscovered crime. By a certain association of ideas, he at times almost imagined himself a murderer. For years, also, a thought would occasionally recur, which, though he perceived all its folly and extravagance, he had not power to banish from his mind. It was a haunting and torturing fancy that his father-in-law was yet sitting at the foot of the rock, on the withered forest leaves, alive, and awaiting his pledged assistance. These mental deceptions, however, came and went, nor did he ever mistake them for realities; but in the calmest and clearest moods of his mind he was conscious that he had a deep vow unredeemed, and that an unburied corpse was calling to him out of the wilderness. Yet such was the consequence of his prevarication that he could not obey the call. It was now too late to require the assistance of Roger Malvin's friends in performing his long-deferred sepulture; and superstitious fears, of which none were more susceptible than the people of the outward settlements, forbade Reuben to go alone. Neither did he know where in the pathless and illimitable forest to seek that smooth and lettered rock at the base of which the body lay: his remembrance of every portion of his travel thence was indistinct, and the latter part had left no impression upon his mind. There was, however, a continual impulse, a voice audible only to himself, commanding him to go forth and redeem his vow; and he had a strange impression that, were he to make the trial, he would be led straight to Malvin's bones. But year after year that summons, unheard but felt, was disobeyed. His one secret thought became like a chain binding down his spirit and like a serpent gnawing into his heart; and he was transformed into a sad and downcast yet irritable man.

In the course of a few years after their marriage changes began to be visible in the external prosperity of Reuben and Dorcas. The only riches of the former had been his stout heart and strong arm; but the latter, her father's sole heiress, had made her husband master of a farm, under older cultivation, larger, and better stocked than most of the frontier establishments. Reuben Bourne, however, was a neglectful husbandman; and, while the lands of the other settlers became annually more fruitful, his deteriorated in the same proportion. The discouragements to agriculture were greatly lessened by the cessation of Indian war, during which men held the plough in one hand and the musket in the other, and were fortunate if the products of their dangerous labor were not destroyed, either in the field or in the barn, by the savage enemy. But Reuben did not profit by the altered condition of the country; nor can it be denied that his intervals of industrious attention to his affairs were but scantily rewarded with success. The irritability by which he had recently become distinguished was another cause of his declining prosperity, as it occasioned frequent quarrels in his unavoidable intercourse with the neighboring settlers. The results of these were innumerable lawsuits; for the people of New England, in the earliest stages and wildest circumstances of the country, adopted, whenever attainable, the legal mode of deciding their differences.

To be brief, the world did not go well with Reuben Bourne; and, though not till many years after his marriage, he was finally a ruined man, with but one remaining expedient against the evil fate that had pursued him. He was to throw sunlight into some deep recess of the forest, and seek subsistence from the virgin bosom of the wilderness.

The only child of Reuben and Dorcas was a son, now arrived at the age of fifteen years, beautiful in youth, and giving promise of a glorious manhood. He was peculiarly qualified for, and already began to excel in, the wild accomplishments of frontier life. His foot was fleet, his aim true, his apprehension quick, his heart glad and high; and all who anticipated the return of Indian war spoke of Cyrus Bourne as a future leader in the land. The boy was loved by his father with a deep and silent strength, as if whatever was good and happy in his own nature had been transferred to his child, carrying his affections with it. Even Dorcas, though loving and beloved, was far less dear to him; for Reuben's secret thoughts and insulated emotions had gradually made him a selfish man, and he could no longer love deeply except where he saw or imagined some reflection or likeness of his own mind. In Cyrus he recognized what he had himself been in other days; and at intervals he seemed to partake of the boy's spirit, and to be revived with a fresh and happy life. Reuben was accompanied by his son in the expedition, for the purpose of selecting a tract of land and felling and burning the timber, which necessarily preceded the removal of the household goods. Two months of autumn were thus occupied, after which Reuben Bourne and his young hunter returned to spend their last winter in the settlements.

It was early in the month of May that the little family snapped asunder whatever tendrils of affections had clung to inanimate objects, and bade farewell to the few who, in the blight of fortune, called themselves their friends. The sadness of the parting moment had, to each of the pilgrims, its peculiar alleviations. Reuben, a moody man, and misanthropic because unhappy, strode onward with his usual stern brow and downcast eye, feeling few regrets and disdaining to acknowledge any. Dorcas, while she wept abundantly over the broken ties by which her simple and affectionate nature had bound itself to everything, felt that the inhabitants of her inmost heart moved on with her, and that all else would be supplied wherever she might go. And the boy dashed one tear-drop from his eye, and thought of the adventurous pleasures of the untrodden forest.

Oh, who, in the enthusiasm of a daydream, has not wished that he were a wanderer in a world of summer wilderness, with one fair and gentle being hanging lightly on his arm? In youth his free and exulting step would know no barrier but the rolling ocean or the snow-topped mountains; calmer manhood would choose a home where Nature had strewn a double wealth in the vale of some transparent stream; and when hoary age, after long, long years of that pure life, stole on and found him there, it would find him the father of a race, the patriarch of a people, the founder of a mighty nation yet to be. When death, like the sweet sleep which we welcome after a day of happiness, came over him, his far descendants would mourn over the venerated dust. Enveloped by tradition in mysterious attributes, the men of future generations would call him godlike; and remote posterity would see him standing, dimly glorious, far up the valley of a hundred centuries.

The tangled and gloomy forest through which the personages of my tale were wandering differed widely from the dreamer's land of fantasy; yet there was something in their way of life that Nature asserted as her own, and the gnawing cares which went with them from the world were all that now obstructed their happiness. One stout and shaggy steed, the bearer of all their wealth, did not shrink from the added weight of Dorcas; although her hardy breeding sustained her, during the latter part of each day's journey, by her husband's side. Reuben and his son, their muskets on their shoulders and their axes slung behind them, kept an unwearied pace, each watching with a hunter's eye for the game that supplied their food. When hunger bade, they halted and prepared their meal on the bank of some unpolluted forest brook, which, as they knelt down with thirsty lips to drink, murmured a sweet unwillingness, like a maiden at love's first kiss. They slept beneath a hut of branches, and awoke at peep of light refreshed for the toils of another day. Dorcas and the boy went on joyously, and even Reuben's spirit shone at intervals with an outward gladness; but inwardly there was a cold, cold sorrow, which he compared to the snowdrifts lying deep in the glens and hollows of the rivulets while the leaves were brightly green above.

Cyrus Bourne was sufficiently skilled in the travel of the woods to observe that his father did not adhere to the course they had pursued in their expedition of the preceding autumn. They were now keeping farther to the north, striking out more directly from the settlements, and into a region of which savage beasts and savage men were as yet the sole possessors. The boy sometimes hinted his opinions upon the subject, and Reuben listened attentively, and once or twice altered the direction of their march in accordance with his son's counsel; but, having so done, he seemed ill at ease. His quick and wandering glances were sent forward, apparently in search of enemies lurking behind the tree trunks; and, seeing nothing there, he would cast his eyes backwards as if in fear of some pursuer. Cyrus, perceiving that his father gradually resumed the old direction, forbore to interfere; nor, though something began to weigh upon his heart, did his adventurous nature permit him to regret the increased length and the mystery of their way.

On the afternoon of the fifth day they halted, and made their simple encampment nearly an hour before sunset. The face of the country, for the last few miles, had been diversified by swells of land resembling huge waves of a petrified sea; and in one of the corresponding hollows, a wild and romantic spot, had the family reared their hut and kindled their fire. There is something chilling, and yet heart-warming, in the thought of these three, united by strong bands of love and insulated from all that breathe beside. The dark and gloomy pines looked down upon them, and, as the wind swept through their tops, a pitying sound was heard in the forest; or did those old trees groan in fear that men were come to lay the axe to their roots at last? Reuben and his son, while Dorcas made ready their meal, proposed to wander out in search of game, of which that day's march had afforded no supply. The boy, promising not to quit the vicinity of the encampment, bounded off with a step as light and elastic as that of the deer he hoped to slay; while his father, feeling a transient happiness as he gazed after him, was about to pursue an opposite direction. Dorcas, in the meanwhile, had seated herself near their fire of fallen branches, upon the mossgrown and mouldering trunk of a tree uprooted years before. Her employment, diversified by an occasional glance at the pot, now beginning to simmer over the blaze, was the perusal of the current year's Massachusetts Almanac, which, with the exception of an old black-letter Bible, comprised all the literary wealth of the family. None pay a greater regard to arbitrary divisions of time than those who are excluded from society; and Dorcas mentioned, as if the information were of importance, that it was now the twelfth of May. Her husband started.

"The twelfth of May! I should remember it well," muttered he, while many thoughts occasioned a momentary confusion in his mind. "Where am I? Whither am I wandering? Where did I leave him?"

Dorcas, too well accustomed to her husband's wayward moods to note any peculiarity of demeanor, now laid aside the almanac and addressed him in that mournful tone which the tender hearted appropriate to griefs long cold and dead.

"It was near this time of the month, eighteen years ago, that my poor father left this world for a better. He had a kind arm to hold his head and a kind voice to cheer him, Reuben, in his last moments; and the thought of the faithful care you took of him has comforted me many a time since. Oh, death would have been awful to a solitary man in a wild place like this!"

"Pray Heaven, Dorcas," said Reuben, in a broken voice,—"pray Heaven that neither of us three dies solitary and lies unburied in this howling wilderness!" And he hastened away, leaving her to watch the fire beneath the gloomy pines.

Reuben Bourne's rapid pace gradually slackened as the pang, unintentionally inflicted by the words of Dorcas, became less acute. Many strange reflections, however, thronged upon him; and, straying onward rather like a sleep walker than a hunter, it was attributable to no care of his own that his devious course kept him in the vicinity of the encampment. His steps were imperceptibly led almost in a circle; nor did he observe that he was on the verge of a tract of land heavily timbered, but not with pine-trees. The place of the latter was here supplied by oaks and other of the harder woods; and around their roots clustered a dense and bushy under-growth, leaving, however, barren spaces between the trees, thick strewn with withered leaves. Whenever the rustling of the branches or the creaking of the trunks made a sound, as if the forest were waking from slumber, Reuben instinctively raised the musket that rested on his arm, and cast a quick, sharp glance on every side; but, convinced by a partial observation that no animal was near, he would again give himself up to his thoughts. He was musing on the strange influence that had led him away from his premeditated course, and so far into the depths of the wilderness. Unable to penetrate to the secret place of his soul where his motives lay hidden, he believed that a supernatural voice had called him onward, and that a supernatural power had obstructed his retreat. He trusted that it was Heaven's intent to afford him an opportunity of expiating his sin; he hoped that he might find the bones so long unburied; and that, having laid the earth over them, peace would throw its sunlight into the sepulchre of his heart. From these thoughts he was aroused by a rustling in the forest at some distance from the spot to which he had wandered. Perceiving the motion of some object behind a thick veil of undergrowth, he fired, with the instinct of a hunter and the aim of a practised marksman. A low moan, which told his success, and by which even animals can express their dying agony, was unheeded by Reuben Bourne. What were the recollections now breaking upon him?

The thicket into which Reuben had fired was near the summit of a swell of land, and was clustered around the base of a rock, which, in the shape and smoothness of one of its surfaces, was not unlike a gigantic gravestone. As if reflected in a mirror, its likeness was in Reuben's memory. He even recognized the veins which seemed to form an inscription in forgotten characters: everything remained the same, except that a thick covert of bushes shrouded the lower part of the rock, and would have hidden Roger Malvin had he still been sitting there. Yet in the next moment Reuben's eye was caught by another change that time had effected since he last stood where he was now standing again behind the earthy roots of the uptorn tree. The sapling to which he had bound the bloodstained symbol of his vow had increased and strengthened into an oak, far indeed from its maturity, but with no mean spread of shadowy branches. There was one singularity observable in this tree which made Reuben tremble. The middle and lower branches were in luxuriant life, and an excess of vegetation had fringed the trunk almost to the ground; but a blight had apparently stricken the upper part of the oak, and the very topmost bough was withered, sapless, and utterly dead. Reuben remembered how the little banner had fluttered on that topmost bough, when it was green and lovely, eighteen years before. Whose guilt had blasted it?

Dorcas, after the departure of the two hunters, continued her preparations for their evening repast. Her sylvan table was the moss-covered trunk of a large fallen tree, on the broadest part of which she had spread a snow-white cloth and arranged what were left of the bright pewter vessels that had been her pride in the settlements. It had a strange aspect, that one little spot of homely comfort in the desolate heart of Nature. The sunshine yet lingered upon the higher branches of the trees that grew on rising ground; but the shadows of evening had deepened into the hollow where the encampment was made, and the firelight began to redden as it gleamed up the tall trunks of the pines or hovered on the dense and obscure mass of foliage that circled round the spot. The heart of Dorcas was not sad; for she felt that it was better to journey in the wilderness with two whom she loved than to be a lonely woman in a crowd that cared not for her. As she busied herself in arranging seats of mouldering wood, covered with leaves, for Reuben and her son, her voice danced through the gloomy forest in the measure of a song that she had learned in youth. The rude melody, the production of a bard who won no name, was descriptive of a winter evening in a frontier cottage, when, secured from savage inroad by the high-piled snow-drifts, the family rejoiced by their own fireside. The whole song possessed the nameless charm peculiar to unborrowed thought, but four continually-recurring lines shone out from the rest like the blaze of the hearth whose joys they celebrated. Into them, working magic with a few simple words, the poet had instilled the very essence of domestic love and household happiness, and they were poetry and picture joined in one. As Dorcas sang, the walls of her forsaken home seemed to encircle her; she no longer saw the gloomy pines, nor heard the wind which still, as she began each verse, sent a heavy breath through the branches, and died away in a hollow moan from the burden of the song. She was aroused by the report of a gun in the vicinity of the encampment; and either the sudden sound, or her loneliness by the glowing fire, caused her to tremble violently. The next moment she laughed in the pride of a mother's heart.

"My beautiful young hunter! My boy has slain a deer!" she exclaimed, recollecting that in the direction whence the shot proceeded Cyrus had gone to the chase.

She waited a reasonable time to hear her son's light step bounding over the rustling leaves to tell of his success. But he did not immediately appear; and she sent her cheerful voice among the trees in search of him.

"Cyrus! Cyrus!"

His coming was still delayed; and she determined, as the report had apparently been very near, to seek for him in person. Her assistance, also, might be necessary in bringing home the venison which she flattered herself he had obtained. She therefore set forward, directing her steps by the long-past sound, and singing as she went, in order that the boy might be aware of her approach and run to meet her. From behind the trunk of every tree, and from every hiding-place in the thick foliage of the undergrowth, she hoped to discover the countenance of her son, laughing with the sportive mischief that is born of affection. The sun was now beneath the horizon, and the light that came down among the leaves was sufficiently dim to create many illusions in her expecting fancy. Several times she seemed indistinctly to see his face gazing out from among the leaves; and once she imagined that he stood beckoning to her at the base of a craggy rock. Keeping her eyes on this object, however, it proved to be no more than the trunk of an oak fringed to the very ground with little branches, one of which, thrust out farther than the rest, was shaken by the breeze. Making her way round the foot of the rock, she suddenly found herself close to her husband, who had approached in another direction. Leaning upon the butt of his gun, the muzzle of which rested upon the withered leaves, he was apparently absorbed in the contemplation of some object at his feet.

"How is this Reuben? Have you slain the deer and fallen asleep over him?" exclaimed Dorcas, laughing cheerfully, on her first slight observation of his posture and appearance.

He stirred not, neither did he turn his eyes towards her; and a cold, shuddering fear, indefinite in its source and object, began to creep into her blood. She now perceived that her husband's face was ghastly pale, and his features were rigid, as if incapable of assuming any other expression than the strong despair which had hardened upon them. He gave not the slightest evidence that he was aware of her approach.

"For the love of Heaven, Reuben, speak to me!" cried Dorcas; and the strange sound of her own voice affrighted her even more than the dead silence.

Her husband started, stared into her face, drew her to the front of the rock, and pointed with his finger.

Oh, there lay the boy, asleep, but dreamless, upon the fallen forest leaves! His cheek rested upon his arm—his curled locks were thrown back from his brow—his limbs were slightly relaxed. Had a sudden weariness overcome the youthful hunter? Would his mother's voice arouse him? She knew that it was death.

"This broad rock is the gravestone of your near kindred, Dorcas," said her husband. "Your tears will fall at once over your father and your son."

She heard him not. With one wild shriek, that seemed to force its way from the sufferer's inmost soul, she sank insensible by the side of her dead boy. At that moment the withered topmost bough of the oak loosened itself in the stilly air, and fell in soft, light fragments upon the rock, upon the leaves, upon Reuben, upon his wife and child, and upon Roger Malvin's bones. Then Reuben's heart was stricken, and the tears gushed out like water from a rock. The vow that the wounded youth had made the blighted man had come to redeem. His sin was expiated,—the curse was gone from him; and in the hour when he had shed blood dearer to him than his own, a prayer, the first for years, went up to Heaven from the lips of Reuben Bourne.

P.'S CORRESPONDENCE

My unfortunate friend P. has lost the thread of his life by the interposition of long intervals of partially disordered reason. The past and present are jumbled together in his mind in a manner often productive of curious results, and which will be better understood after the perusal of the following letter than from any description that I could give. The poor fellow, without once stirring from the little whitewashed, iron-grated room to which he alludes in his first paragraph, is nevertheless a great traveller, and meets in his wanderings a variety of personages who have long ceased to be visible to any eye save his own. In my opinion, all this is not so much a delusion as a partly wilful and partly involuntary sport of the imagination, to which his disease has imparted such morbid energy that he beholds these spectral scenes and characters with no less distinctness than a play upon the stage, and with somewhat more of illusive credence. Many of his letters are in my possession, some based upon the same vagary as the present one, and others upon hypotheses not a whit short of it in absurdity. The whole form a series of correspondence, which, should fate seasonably remove my poor friend from what is to him a world of moonshine, I promise myself a pious pleasure in editing for the public eye. P. had always a hankering after literary reputation, and has made more than one unsuccessful effort to achieve it. It would not be a little odd if, after missing his object while seeking it by the light of reason, he should prove to have stumbled upon it in his misty excursions beyond the limits of sanity.

LONDON, February 29, 1845.

MY DEAR FRIEND,—Old associations cling to the mind with astonishing tenacity. Daily custom grows up about us like a stone wall, and consolidates itself into almost as material entity as mankind's strongest architecture. It is sometimes a serious question with me whether ideas be not really visible and tangible and endowed with all the other qualities of matter. Sitting as I do at this moment in my hired apartment, writing beside the hearth, over which hangs a print of Queen Victoria, listening to the muffled roar of the world's metropolis, and with a window at but five paces distant, through which, whenever I please, I can gaze out on actual London,—with all this positive certainty as to my whereabouts, what kind of notion, do you think, is just now perplexing my brain? Why,—would you believe it?—that all this time I am still an inhabitant of that wearisome little chamber—that whitewashed little chamber—that little chamber with its one small window, across which, from some inscrutable reason of taste or convenience, my landlord had placed a row of iron bars—that same little chamber, in short, whither your kindness has so often brought you to visit me! Will no length of time or breadth of space enfranchise me from that unlovely abode? I travel; but it seems to be like the snail, with my house upon my head. Ah, well! I am verging, I suppose, on that period of life when present scenes and events make but feeble impressions in comparison with those of yore; so that I must reconcile myself to be more and more the prisoner of Memory, who merely lets me hop about a little with her chain around my leg.

My letters of introduction have been of the utmost service, enabling me to make the acquaintance of several distinguished characters, who, until now, have seemed as remote from the sphere of my personal intercourse as the wits of Queen Anne's time or Ben Jonson's compotators at the Mermaid. One of the first of which I availed myself was the letter to Lord Byron. I found his lordship looking much older than I had anticipated, although, considering his former irregularities of life and the various wear and tear of his constitution, not older than a man on the verge of sixty reasonably may look. But I had invested his earthly frame, in my imagination, with the poet's spiritual immortality. He wears a brown wig, very luxuriantly curled, and extending down over his forehead. The expression of his eyes is concealed by spectacles. His early tendency to obesity having increased, Lord Byron is now enormously fat—so fat as to give the impression of a person quite overladen with his own flesh, and without sufficient vigor to diffuse his personal life through the great mass of corporeal substance which weighs upon him so cruelly. You gaze at the mortal heap; and, while it fills your eye with what purports to be Byron, you murmur within yourself, "For Heaven's sake, where is he?" Were I disposed to be caustic, I might consider this mass of earthly matter as the symbol, in a material shape, of those evil habits and carnal vices which unspiritualize man's nature and clog up his avenues of communication with the better life. But this would be too harsh; and, besides, Lord Byron's morals have been improving while his outward man has swollen to such unconscionable circumference. Would that he were leaner; for though he did me the honor to present his hand, yet it was so puffed out with alien substance that I could not feel as if I had touched the hand that wrote Childe Harold.

On my entrance his lordship apologized for not rising to receive me on the sufficient plea that the gout for several years past had taken up its constant residence in his right foot, which accordingly was swathed in many rolls of flannel and deposited upon a cushion. The other foot was hidden in the drapery of his chair. Do you recollect whether Byron's right or left foot was the deformed one?

The noble poet's reconciliation with Lady Byron is now, as you are aware, of ten years' standing; nor does it exhibit, I am assured, any symptom of breach or fracture. They are said to be, if not a happy, at least a contented, or at all events a quiet couple, descending the slope of life with that tolerable degree of mutual support which will enable them to come easily and comfortably to the bottom. It is pleasant to reflect how entirely the poet has redeemed his youthful errors in this particular. Her ladyship's influence, it rejoices me to add, has been productive of the happiest results upon Lord Byron in a religious point of view. He now combines the most rigid tenets of Methodism with the ultra doctrines of the Puseyites; the former being perhaps due to the convictions wrought upon his mind by his noble consort, while the latter are the embroidery and picturesque illumination demanded by his imaginative character. Much of whatever expenditure his increasing habits of thrift continue to allow him is bestowed in the reparation or beautifying of places of worship; and this nobleman, whose name was once considered a synonyme of the foul fiend, is now all but canonized as a saint in many pulpits of the metropolis and elsewhere. In politics, Lord Byron is an uncompromising conservative, and loses no opportunity, whether in the House of Lords or in private circles, of denouncing and repudiating the mischievous and anarchical notions of his earlier day. Nor does he fail to visit similar sins in other people with the sincerest vengeance which his somewhat blunted pen is capable of inflicting. Southey and he are on the most intimate terms. You are aware, that some little time before the death of Moore, Byron caused that brilliant but reprehensible man to be ejected from his house. Moore took the insult so much to heart that it is said to have been one great cause of the fit of illness which brought him to the grave. Others pretend that the lyrist died in a very happy state of mind, singing one of his own sacred melodies, and expressing his belief that it would be heard within the gate of paradise, and gain him instant and honorable admittance. I wish he may have found it so.

I failed not, as you may suppose in the course of conversation with Lord Byron, to pay the meed of homage due to a mighty poet, by allusions to passages in Childe Harold, and Manfred, and Don Juan, which have made so large a portion of the music of my life. My words, whether apt or otherwise, were at least warm with the enthusiasm of one worthy to discourse of immortal poesy. It was evident, however, that they did not go precisely to the right spot. I could perceive that there was some mistake or other, and was not a little angry with myself, and ashamed of my abortive attempt to throw back, from my own heart to the gifted author's ear, the echo of those strains that have resounded throughout the world. But by and by the secret peeped quietly out. Byron,—I have the information from his own lips, so that you need not hesitate to repeat it in literary circles,—Byron is preparing a new edition of his complete works, carefully corrected, expurgated, and amended, in accordance with his present creed of taste, morals, politics, and religion. It so happened that the very passages of highest inspiration to which I had alluded were among the condemned and rejected rubbish which it is his purpose to cast into the gulf of oblivion. To whisper you the truth, it appears to me that his passions having burned out, the extinction of their vivid and riotous flame has deprived Lord Byron of the illumination by which he not merely wrote, but was enabled to feel and comprehend what he had written. Positively he no longer understands his own poetry.

This became very apparent on his favoring me so far as to read a few specimens of Don Juan in the moralized version. Whatever is licentious, whatever disrespectful to the sacred mysteries of our faith, whatever morbidly melancholic or splenetically sportive, whatever assails settled constitutions of government or systems of society, whatever could wound the sensibility of any mortal, except a pagan, a republican, or a dissenter, has been unrelentingly blotted out, and its place supplied by unexceptionable verses in his lordship's later style. You may judge how much of the poem remains as hitherto published. The result is not so good as might be wished; in plain terms, it is a very sad affair indeed; for, though the torches kindled in Tophet have been extinguished, they leave an abominably ill odor, and are succeeded by no glimpses of hallowed fire. It is to be hoped, nevertheless, that this attempt on Lord Byron's part to atone for his youthful errors will at length induce the Dean of Westminster, or whatever churchman is concerned, to allow Thorwaldsen's statue of the poet its due niche in the grand old Abbey. His bones, you know, when brought from Greece, were denied sepulture among those of his tuneful brethren there.

What a vile slip of the pen was that! How absurd in me to talk about burying the bones of Byron, whom I have just seen alive, and incased in a big, round bulk of flesh! But, to say the truth, a prodigiously fat man always impresses me as a kind of hobgoblin; in the very extravagance of his mortal system I find something akin to the immateriality of a ghost. And then that ridiculous old story darted into my mind, how that Byron died of fever at Missolonghi, above twenty years ago. More and more I recognize that we dwell in a world of shadows; and, for my part, I hold it hardly worth the trouble, to attempt a distinction between shadows in the mind and shadows out of it. If there be any difference, the former are rather the more substantial.

Only think of my good fortune! The venerable Robert Burns—now, if I mistake not, in his eighty-seventh year—happens to be making a visit to London, as if on purpose to afford me an opportunity of grasping him by the hand. For upwards of twenty years past he has hardly left his quiet cottage in Ayrshire for a single night, and has only been drawn hither now by the irresistible persuasions of all the distinguished men in England. They wish to celebrate the patriarch's birthday by a festival. It will be the greatest literary triumph on record. Pray Heaven the little spirit of life within the aged bard's bosom may not be extinguished in the lustre of that hour! I have already had the honor of an introduction to him at the British Museum, where he was examining a collection of his own unpublished letters, interspersed with songs, which have escaped the notice of all his biographers.

Poh! Nonsense! What am I thinking of? How should Burns have been embalmed in biography when he is still a hearty old man?

The figure of the bard is tall and in the highest degree reverend, nor the less so that it is much bent by the burden of time. His white hair floats like a snow-drift around his face, in which are seen the furrows of intellect and passion, like the channels of headlong torrents that have foamed themselves away. The old gentleman is in excellent preservation considering his time of life. He has that crickety sort of liveliness—I mean the cricket's humor of chirping for any cause or none—which is perhaps the most favorable mood that can befall extreme old age. Our pride forbids us to desire it for ourselves, although we perceive it to be a beneficence of nature in the case of others. I was surprised to find it in Burns. It seems as if his ardent heart and brilliant imagination had both burned down to the last embers, leaving only a little flickering flame in one corner, which keeps dancing upward and laughing all by itself. He is no longer capable of pathos. At the request of Allan Cunningham, he attempted to sing his own song to Mary in Heaven; but it was evident that the feeling of those verses, so profoundly true and so simply expressed, was entirely beyond the scope of his present sensibilities; and, when a touch of it did partially awaken him, the tears immediately gushed into his eyes and his voice broke into a tremulous cackle. And yet he but indistinctly knew wherefore he was weeping. Ah, he must not think again of Mary in Heaven until he shake off the dull impediment of time and ascend to meet her there.

Burns then began to repeat Tam O'Shanter; but was so tickled with its wit and humor—of which, however, I suspect he had but a traditionary sense—that he soon burst into a fit of chirruping laughter, succeeded by a cough, which brought this not very agreeable exhibition to a close. On the whole, I would rather not have witnessed it. It is a satisfactory idea, however, that the last forty years of the peasant poet's life have been passed in competence and perfect comfort. Having been cured of his bardic improvidence for many a day past, and grown as attentive to the main chance as a canny Scotsman should be, he is now considered to be quite well off as to pecuniary circumstances. This, I suppose, is worth having lived so long for.

I took occasion to inquire of some of the countrymen of Burns in regard to the health of Sir Walter Scott. His condition, I am sorry to say, remains the same as for ten years past; it is that of a hopeless paralytic, palsied not more in body than in those nobler attributes of which the body is the instrument. And thus he vegetates from day to day and from year to year at that splendid fantasy of Abbotsford, which grew out of his brain, and became a symbol of the great romancer's tastes, feelings, studies, prejudices, and modes of intellect. Whether in verse, prose, or architecture, he could achieve but one thing, although that one in infinite variety. There he reclines, on a couch in his library, and is said to spend whole hours of every day in dictating tales to an amanuensis,—to an imaginary amanuensis; for it is not deemed worth any one's trouble now to take down what flows from that once brilliant fancy, every image of which was formerly worth gold and capable of being coined. Yet Cunningham, who has lately seen him, assures me that there is now and then a touch of the genius,—a striking combination of incident, or a picturesque trait of character, such as no other man alive could have hit off,—a glimmer from that ruined mind, as if the sun had suddenly flashed on a half-rusted helmet in the gloom of an ancient hall. But the plots of these romances become inextricably confused; the characters melt into one another; and the tale loses itself like the course of a stream flowing through muddy and marshy ground.

For my part, I can hardly regret that Sir Walter Scott had lost his consciousness of outward things before his works went out of vogue. It was good that he should forget his fame rather than that fame should first have forgotten him. Were he still a writer, and as brilliant a one as ever, he could no longer maintain anything like the same position in literature. The world, nowadays, requires a more earnest purpose, a deeper moral, and a closer and homelier truth than he was qualified to supply it with. Yet who can be to the present generation even what Scott has been to the past? I had expectations from a young man—one Dickens—who published a few magazine articles, very rich in humor, and not without symptoms of genuine pathos, but the poor fellow died shortly after commencing an odd series of sketches, entitled, I think, the Pickwick Papers. Not impossibly the world has lost more than it dreams of by the untimely death of this Mr. Dickens.

Whom do you think I met in Pall Mall the other day? You would not hit it in ten guesses. Why, no less a man than Napoleon Bonaparte, or all that is now left of him—that is to say, the skin, bones, and corporeal substance, little cocked hat, green coat, white breeches, and small sword, which are still known by his redoubtable name. He was attended only by two policemen, who walked quietly behind the phantasm of the old ex-emperor, appearing to have no duty in regard to him except to see that none of the light-fingered gentry should possess themselves of the star of the Legion of Honor. Nobody, save myself, so much as turned to look after him; nor, it grieves me to confess, could even I contrive to muster up any tolerable interest, even by all that the warlike spirit, formerly manifested within that now decrepit shape, had wrought upon our globe. There is no surer method of annihilating the magic influence of a great renown than by exhibiting the possessor of it in the decline, the overthrow, the utter degradation of his powers,—buried beneath his own mortality,—and lacking even the qualities of sense that enable the most ordinary men to bear themselves decently in the eye of the world. This is the state to which disease, aggravated by long endurance of a tropical climate, and assisted by old age,—for he is now above seventy,—has reduced Bonaparte. The British government has acted shrewdly in retransporting him from St. Helena to England. They should now restore him to Paris, and there let him once again review the relics of his armies. His eye is dull and rheumy; his nether lip hung down upon his chin. While I was observing him there chanced to be a little extra bustle in the street; and he, the brother of Cæsar and Hannibal,—the great captain who had veiled the world in battle smoke and tracked it round with bloody footsteps,—was seized with a nervous trembling, and claimed the protection of the two policemen by a cracked and dolorous cry. The fellows winked at one another, laughed aside, and, patting Napoleon on the back, took each an arm and led him away.

Death and fury! Ha, villain, how came you hither? Avaunt! or I fling my inkstand at your head. Tush, tush; it is all a mistake. Pray, my dear friend, pardon this little outbreak. The fact is, the mention of those two policemen, and their custody of Bonaparte, had called up the idea of that odious wretch—you remember him well—who was pleased to take such gratuitous and impertinent care of my person before I quitted New England. Forthwith up rose before my mind's eye that same little whitewashed room, with the iron-grated window,—strange that it should have been iron-grated!—where, in too easy compliance with the absurd wishes of my relatives, I have wasted several good years of my life. Positively it seemed to me that I was still sitting there, and that the keeper—not that he ever was my keeper neither, but only a kind of intrusive devil of a body servant—had just peeped in at the door. The rascal! I owe him an old grudge, and will find a time to pay it yet. Fie! fie! The mere thought of him has exceedingly discomposed me. Even now that hateful chamber—the iron-grated window, which blasted the blessed sunshine as it fell through the dusty panes and made it poison to my soul—looks more distinct to my view than does this my comfortable apartment in the heart of London. The reality—that which I know to be such—hangs like remnants of tattered scenery over the intolerably prominent illusion. Let us think of it no more.

You will be anxious to hear of Shelley. I need not say, what is known to all the world, that this celebrated poet has for many years past been reconciled to the Church of England. In his more recent works he has applied his fine powers to the vindication of the Christian faith, with an especial view to that particular development. Latterly, as you may not have heard, he has taken orders, and been inducted to a small country living in the gift of the lord chancellor. Just now, luckily for me, he has come to the metropolis to superintend the publication of a volume of discourses treating of the poetico-philosophical proofs of Christianity on the basis of the Thirty-Nine Articles. On my first introduction I felt no little embarrassment as to the manner of combining what I had to say to the author of Queen Mab, the Revolt of Islam, and Prometheus Unbound with such acknowledgments as might be acceptable to a Christian minister and zealous upholder of the established church. But Shelley soon placed me at my ease. Standing where he now does, and reviewing all his successive productions from a higher point, he assures me that there is a harmony, an order, a regular procession, which enables him to lay his hand upon any one of the earlier poems and say, "This is my work," with precisely the same complacency of conscience wherewithal he contemplates the volume of discourses above mentioned. They are like the successive steps of a staircase, the lowest of which, in the depth of chaos, is as essential to the support of the whole as the highest and final one resting upon the threshold of the heavens. I felt half inclined to ask him what would have been his fate had he perished on the lower steps of his staircase instead of building his way aloft into the celestial brightness.

How all this may be I neither pretend to understand nor greatly care, so long as Shelley has really climbed, as it seems he has, from a lower region to a loftier one. Without touching upon their religious merits, I consider the productions of his maturity superior, as poems, to those of his youth. They are warmer with human love, which has served as an interpreter between his mind and the multitude. The author has learned to dip his pen oftener into his heart, and has thereby avoided the faults into which a too exclusive use of fancy and intellect are wont to betray him. Formerly his page was often little other than a concrete arrangement of crystallizations, or even of icicles, as cold as they were brilliant. Now you take it to your heart, and are conscious of a heart warmth responsive to your own. In his private character Shelley can hardly have grown more gentle, kind, and affectionate, than his friends always represented him to be up to that disastrous night when he was drowned in the Mediterranean. Nonsense, again—sheer nonsense! What am I babbling about? I was thinking of that old figment of his being lost in the Bay of Spezzia, and washed ashore near Via Reggio, and burned to ashes on a funeral pyre, with wine, and spices, and frankincense; while Byron stood on the beach and beheld a flame of marvellous beauty rise heavenward from the dead poet's heart, and that his fire-purified relics were finally buried near his child in Roman earth. If all this happened three and twenty years ago, how could I have met the drowned, and burned, and buried man here in London only yesterday?

Before quitting the subject, I may mention that Dr. Reginald Heber, heretofore Bishop of Calcutta, but recently translated to a see in England, called on Shelley while I was with him. They appeared to be on terms of very cordial intimacy, and are said to have a joint poem in contemplation. What a strange, incongruous dream is the life of man!

Coleridge has at last finished his poem of Christabel. It will be issued entire by old John Murray in the course of the present publishing season. The poet, I hear, is visited with a troublesome affection of the tongue, which has put a period, or some lesser stop, to the life-long discourse that has hitherto been flowing from his lips. He will not survive it above a month unless his accumulation of ideas be sluiced off in some other way. Wordsworth died only a week or two ago. Heaven rest his soul, and grant that he may not have completed The Excursion! Methinks I am sick of everything he wrote except his Laodamia. It is very sad, this inconstancy of the mind to the poets whom it once worshipped. Southey is as hale as ever, and writes with his usual diligence. Old Gifford is still alive in the extremity of age, and with most pitiable decay of what little sharp and narrow intellect the devil had gifted him withal. One hates to allow such a man the privilege of growing old and infirm. It takes away our speculative license of kicking him.

Keats? No; I have not seen him except across a crowded street, with coaches, drays, horsemen, cabs, omnibuses, foot passengers, and divers other sensual obstructions intervening betwixt his small and slender figure and my eager glance. I would fain have met him on the sea-shore, or beneath a natural arch of forest trees, or the Gothic arch of an old cathedral, or among Grecian ruins, or at a glimmering fireside on the verge of evening, or at the twilight entrance of a cave, into the dreary depths of which he would have led me by the hand; anywhere, in short, save at Temple Bar, where his presence was blotted out by the porter-swollen bulks of these gross Englishmen. I stood and watched him fading away, fading away along the pavement, and could hardly tell whether he were an actual man or a thought that had slipped out of my mind and clothed itself in human form and habiliments merely to beguile me. At one moment he put his handkerchief to his lips, and withdrew it, I am almost certain, stained with blood. You never saw anything so fragile as his person. The truth is, Keats has all his life felt the effects of that terrible bleeding at the lungs caused by the article on his Endymion in the Quarterly Review, and which so nearly brought him to the grave. Ever since he has glided about the world like a ghost, sighing a melancholy tone in the ear of here and there a friend, but never sending forth his voice to greet the multitude. I can hardly think him a great poet. The burden of a mighty genius would never have been imposed upon shoulders so physically frail and a spirit so infirmly sensitive. Great poets should have iron sinews.

Yet Keats, though for so many years he has given nothing to the world, is understood to have devoted himself to the composition of an epic poem. Some passages of it have been communicated to the inner circle of his admirers, and impressed them as the loftiest strains that have been audible on earth since Milton's days. If I can obtain copies of these specimens, I will ask you to present them to James Russell Lowell, who seems to be one of the poet's most fervent and worthiest worshippers. The information took me by surprise. I had supposed that all Keats's poetic incense, without being embodied in human language, floated up to heaven and mingled with the songs of the immortal choristers, who, perhaps, were conscious of an unknown voice among them, and thought their melody the sweeter for it. But it is not so; he has positively written a poem on the subject of Paradise Regained, though in another sense than that which presented itself to the mind of Milton. In compliance, it may be imagined, with the dogma of those who pretend that all epic possibilities in the past history of the world are exhausted, Keats has thrown his poem forward into an indefinitely remote futurity. He pictures mankind amid the closing circumstances of the timelong warfare between good and evil. Our race is on the eve of its final triumph. Man is within the last stride of perfection; Woman, redeemed from the thraldom against which our sibyl uplifts so powerful and so sad a remonstrance, stands equal by his side, or communes for herself with angels; the Earth, sympathizing with her children's happier state, has clothed herself in such luxuriant and loving beauty as no eye ever witnessed since our first parents saw the sun rise over dewy Eden. Nor then indeed; for this is the fulfilment of what was then but a golden promise. But the picture has its shadows. There remains to mankind another peril—a last encounter with the evil principle. Should the battle go against us, we sink back into the slime and misery of ages. If we triumph—But it demands a poet's eye to contemplate the splendor of such a consummation and not to be dazzled.

To this great work Keats is said to have brought so deep and tender a spirit of humanity that the poem has all the sweet and warm interest of a village tale no less than the grandeur which befits so high a theme. Such, at least, is the perhaps partial representation of his friends; for I have not read or heard even a single line of the performance in question. Keats, I am told, withholds it from the press, under an idea that the age has not enough of spiritual insight to receive it worthily. I do not like this distrust; it makes me distrust the poet. The universe is waiting to respond to the highest word that the best child of time and immortality can utter. If it refuse to listen, it is because he mumbles and stammers, or discourses things unseasonable and foreign to the purpose.

I visited the House of Lords the other day to hear Canning, who, you know, is now a peer, with I forget what title. He disappointed me. Time blunts both point and edge, and does great mischief to men of his order of intellect. Then I stepped into the lower house and listened to a few words from Cobbett, who looked as earthy as a real clod-hopper, or rather as if he had lain a dozen years beneath the clods. The men whom I meet nowadays often impress me thus; probably because my spirits are not very good, and lead me to think much about graves, with the long grass upon them, and weather-worn epitaphs, and dry bones of people who made noise enough in their day, but now can only clatter, clatter, clatter when the sexton's spade disturbs them. Were it only possible to find out who are alive and who dead, it would contribute infinitely to my peace of mind. Every day of my life somebody comes and stares me in the face whom I had quietly blotted out of the tablet of living men, and trusted nevermore to be pestered with the sight or sound of him. For instance, going to Drury Lane Theatre a few evenings since, up rose before me, in the ghost of Hamlet's father, the bodily presence of the elder Kean, who did die, or ought to have died, in some drunken fit or other, so long ago that his fame is scarcely traditionary now. His powers are quite gone; he was rather the ghost of himself than the ghost of the Danish king.

In the stage box sat several elderly and decrepit people, and among them a stately ruin of a woman on a very large scale, with a profile—for I did not see her front face—that stamped itself into my brain as a seal impresses hot wax. By the tragic gesture with which she took a pinch of snuff, I was sure it must be Mrs. Siddons. Her brother, John Kemble, sat behind—a broken-down figure, but still with a kingly majesty about him. In lieu of all former achievements, Nature enables him to look the part of Lear far better than in the meridian of his genius. Charles Matthews was likewise there; but a paralytic affection has distorted his once mobile countenance into a most disagreeable one-sidedness, from which he could no more wrench it into proper form than he could rearrange the face of the great globe itself. It looks as if, for the joke's sake, the poor man had twisted his features into an expression at once the most ludicrous and horrible that he could contrive, and at that very moment, as a judgment for making himself so hideous, an avenging Providence had seen fit to petrify him. Since it is out of his own power, I would gladly assist him to change countenance, for his ugly visage haunts me both at noontide and nighttime. Some other players of the past generation were present, but none that greatly interested me. It behooves actors, more than all other men of publicity, to vanish from the scene betimes. Being at best but painted shadows flickering on the wall, and empty sounds that echo another's thought, it is a sad disenchantment when the colors begin to fade and the voice to croak with age.

What is there new in the literary way on your side of the water? Nothing of the kind has come under my inspection except a volume of poems published above a year ago by Dr. Channing. I did not before know that this eminent writer is a poet; nor does the volume alluded to exhibit any of the characteristics of the author's mind as displayed in his prose works; although some of the poems have a richness that is not merely of the surface, but glows still brighter the deeper and more faithfully you look into them. They seem carelessly wrought, however, like those rings and ornaments of the very purest gold, but of rude, native manufacture, which are found among the gold dust from Africa. I doubt whether the American public will accept them; it looks less to the assay of metal than to the neat and cunning manufacture. How slowly our literature grows up! Most of our writers of promise have come to untimely ends. There was that wild fellow, John Neal, who almost turned my boyish brain with his romances; he surely has long been dead, else he never could keep himself so quiet. Bryant has gone to his last sleep, with the Thanatopsis gleaming over him like a sculptured marble sepulchre by moonlight. Halleck, who used to write queer verses in the newspapers and published a Don Juanic poem called Fanny, is defunct as a poet, though averred to be exemplifying the metempsychosis as a man of business. Somewhat later there was Whittier, a fiery Quaker youth, to whom the muse had perversely assigned a battle trumpet, and who got himself lynched, ten years agone, in South Carolina. I remember, too, a lad just from college, Longfellow by name, who scattered some delicate verses to the winds, and went to Germany, and perished, I think, of intense application, at the University of Gottingen.

Willis—what a pity!—was lost, if I recollect rightly, in 1833, on his voyage to Europe, whither he was going to give us sketches of the world's sunny face. If these had lived, they might, one or all of them, have grown to be famous men.

And yet there is no telling; it may be as well that they have died. I was myself a young man of promise. Oh shattered brain, of broken spirit, where is the fulfilment of that promise? The sad truth is, that, when fate would gently disappoint the world, it takes away the hopefulest mortals in their youth; when it would laugh the world's hopes to scorn, it lets them live. Let me die upon this apothegm, for I shall never make a truer one.

What a strange substance is the human brain! Or rather,—for there is no need of generalizing the remark,—what an odd brain is mine! Would you believe it? Daily and nightly there come scraps of poetry humming in my intellectual ear—some as airy as bird notes, and some as delicately neat as parlor music, and a few as grand as organ peals—that seem just such verses as those departed poets would have written had not an inexorable destiny snatched them from their inkstands. They visit me in spirit, perhaps desiring to engage my services as the amanuensis of their posthumous productions, and thus secure the endless renown that they have forfeited by going hence too early. But I have my own business to attend to; and besides, a medical gentleman, who interests himself in some little ailments of mine, advises me not to make too free use of pen and ink. There are clerks enough out of employment who would be glad of such a job.

Good by! Are you alive or dead? and what are you about? Still scribbling for the Democratic? And do those infernal compositors and proof readers misprint your unfortunate productions as vilely as ever? It is too bad. Let every man manufacture his own nonsense, say I. Expect me home soon, and—to whisper you a secret—in company with the poet Campbell, who purposes to visit Wyoming and enjoy the shadow of the laurels that he planted there. Campbell is now an old man. He calls himself well, better than ever in his life, but looks strangely pale, and so shadow-like that one might almost poke a finger through his densest material. I tell him, by way of joke, that he is as dim and forlorn as Memory, though as unsubstantial as Hope.

Your true friend, P.

P.S.—Pray present my most respectful regards to our venerable and revered friend Mr. Brockden Brown. It gratifies me to learn that a complete edition of his works, in a double-columned octavo volume, is shortly to issue from the press at Philadelphia. Tell him that no American writer enjoys a more classic reputation on this side of the water. *Is* old Joel Barlow yet alive? Unconscionable man! Why, he must have nearly fulfilled his century. And *does* he meditate an epic on the war between Mexico and Texas with machinery contrived on the principle of the steam-engine, as being the nearest to celestial agency that our epoch can boast? How can he expect ever to rise again, if, while just sinking into his grave, he persists in burdening himself with such a ponderosity of leaden verses?

EARTH'S HOLOCAUST

Once upon a time—but whether in the time past or time to come is a matter of little or no moment—this wide world had become so overburdened with an accumulation of wornout trumpery that the inhabitants determined to rid themselves of it by a general bonfire. The site fixed upon at the representation of the insurance companies, and as being as central a spot as any other on the globe, was one of the broadest prairies of the West, where no human habitation would be endangered by the flames, and where a vast assemblage of spectators might commodiously admire the show. Having a taste for sights of this kind, and imagining, likewise, that the illumination of the bonfire might reveal some profundity of moral truth heretofore hidden in mist or darkness, I made it convenient to journey thither and be present. At my arrival, although the heap of condemned rubbish was as yet comparatively small, the torch had already been applied. Amid that boundless plain, in the dusk of the evening, like a far off star alone in the firmament, there was merely visible one tremulous gleam, whence none could have anticipated so fierce a blaze as was destined to ensue. With every moment, however, there came foot travellers, women holding up their aprons, men on horseback, wheelbarrows, lumbering baggage wagons, and other vehicles, great and small, and from far and near laden with articles that were judged fit for nothing but to be burned.

"What materials have been used to kindle the flame?" inquired I of a by-stander; for I was desirous of knowing the whole process of the affair from beginning to end.

The person whom I addressed was a grave man, fifty years old or thereabout, who had evidently come thither as a looker on. He struck me immediately as having weighed for himself the true value of life and its circumstances, and therefore as feeling little personal interest in whatever judgment the world might form of them. Before answering my question, he looked me in the face by the kindling light of the fire.

"Oh, some very dry combustibles," replied he, "and extremely suitable to the purpose—no other, in fact, than yesterday's newspapers, last month's magazines, and last year's withered leaves. Here now comes some antiquated trash that will take fire like a handful of shavings."

As he spoke some rough-looking men advanced to the verge of the bonfire, and threw in, as it appeared, all the rubbish of the herald's office—the blazonry of coat armor, the crests and devices of illustrious families, pedigrees that extended back, like lines of light, into the mist of the dark ages, together with stars, garters, and embroidered collars, each of which, as paltry a bawble as it might appear to the uninstructed eye, had once possessed vast significance, and was still, in truth, reckoned among the most precious of moral or material facts by the worshippers of the gorgeous past. Mingled with this confused heap, which was tossed into the flames by armfuls at once, were innumerable badges of knighthood, comprising those of all the European sovereignties, and

Napoleon's decoration of the Legion of Honor, the ribbons of which were entangled with those of the ancient order of St. Louis. There, too, were the medals of our own society of Cincinnati, by means of which, as history tells us, an order of hereditary knights came near being constituted out of the king quellers of the revolution. And besides, there were the patents of nobility of German counts and barons, Spanish grandees, and English peers, from the worm-eaten instruments signed by William the Conqueror down to the brand new parchment of the latest lord who has received his honors from the fair hand of Victoria.

At sight of the dense volumes of smoke, mingled with vivid jets of flame, that gushed and eddied forth from this immense pile of earthly distinctions, the multitude of plebeian spectators set up a joyous shout, and clapped their hands with an emphasis that made the welkin echo. That was their moment of triumph, achieved, after long ages, over creatures of the same clay and the same spiritual infirmities, who had dared to assume the privileges due only to Heaven's better workmanship. But now there rushed towards the blazing heap a grayhaired man, of stately presence, wearing a coat, from the breast of which a star, or other badge of rank, seemed to have been forcibly wrenched away. He had not the tokens of intellectual power in his face; but still there was the demeanor, the habitual and almost native dignity, of one who had been born to the idea of his own social superiority, and had never felt it questioned till that moment.

"People," cried he, gazing at the ruin of what was dearest to his eyes with grief and wonder, but nevertheless with a degree of stateliness,—"people, what have you done? This fire is consuming all that marked your advance from barbarism, or that could have prevented your relapse thither. We, the men of the privileged orders, were those who kept alive from age to age the old chivalrous spirit; the gentle and generous thought; the higher, the purer, the more refined and delicate life. With the nobles, too, you cast off the poet, the painter, the sculptor—all the beautiful arts; for we were their patrons, and created the atmosphere in which they flourish. In abolishing the majestic distinctions of rank, society loses not only its grace, but its steadfastness"—

More he would doubtless have spoken; but here there arose an outcry, sportive, contemptuous, and indignant, that altogether drowned the appeal of the fallen nobleman, insomuch that, casting one look of despair at his own half-burned pedigree, he shrunk back into the crowd, glad to shelter himself under his new-found insignificance.

"Let him thank his stars that we have not flung him into the same fire!" shouted a rude figure, spurning the embers with his foot. "And henceforth let no man dare to show a piece of musty parchment as his warrant for lording it over his fellows. If he have strength of arm, well and good; it is one species of superiority. If he have wit, wisdom, courage, force of character, let these attributes do for him what they may; but from this day forward no mortal must hope for place and consideration by reckoning up the mouldy bones of his ancestors. That nonsense is done away."

"And in good time," remarked the grave observer by my side, in a low voice, however, "if no worse nonsense comes in its place; but, at all events, this species of nonsense has fairly lived out its life."

There was little space to muse or moralize over the embers of this time-honored rubbish; for, before it was half burned out, there came another multitude from beyond the sea, bearing the purple robes of royalty, and the crowns, globes, and sceptres of emperors and kings. All these had been condemned as useless bawbles, playthings at best, fit only for the infancy of the world or rods to govern and chastise it in its nonage, but with which universal manhood at its full-grown stature could no longer brook to be insulted. Into such contempt had these regal insignia now fallen that the gilded crown and tinselled robes of the player king from Drury Lane Theatre had been thrown in among the rest, doubtless as a mockery of his brother monarchs on the great stage of the world. It was a strange sight to discern the crown jewels of England glowing and flashing in the midst of the fire. Some of them had been delivered down from the time of the Saxon princes; others were purchased with vast revenues, or perchance ravished from the dead brows of the native potentates of Hindostan; and the whole now blazed with a dazzling lustre, as if a star had fallen in that spot and been shattered into fragments. The splendor of the ruined monarchy had no reflection save in those inestimable precious stones. But enough on this subject. It were but tedious to describe how the Emperor of Austria's mantle was converted to tinder, and how the posts and pillars of the French throne became a heap of coals, which it was impossible to distinguish from those of any other wood. Let me add, however, that I noticed one of the exiled Poles stirring up the bonfire with the Czar of Russia's sceptre, which he afterwards flung into the flames.

"The smell of singed garments is quite intolerable here," observed my new acquaintance, as the breeze enveloped us in the smoke of a royal wardrobe. "Let us get to windward and see what they are doing on the other side of the bonfire."

We accordingly passed around, and were just in time to witness the arrival of a vast procession of Washingtonians,—as the votaries of temperance call themselves nowadays,—accompanied by thousands of the Irish disciples of Father Mathew, with that great apostle at their head. They brought a rich contribution to the bonfire—being nothing less than all the hogsheads and barrels of liquor in the world, which they rolled before them across the prairie.

"Now, my children," cried Father Mathew, when they reached the verge of the fire, "one shove more, and the work is done. And now let us stand off and see Satan deal with his own liquor."

Accordingly, having placed their wooden vessels within reach of the flames, the procession stood off at a safe distance, and soon beheld them burst into a blaze that reached the clouds and threatened to set the sky itself on fire. And well it might; for here was the whole world's stock of spirituous liquors, which, instead of kindling a frenzied light in the eyes of individual topers as of yore, soared upwards with a bewildering gleam that startled all mankind. It was the aggregate of that fierce fire which would otherwise have scorched the hearts of millions. Meantime numberless bottles of precious wine were flung into the blaze, which lapped up the contents as if it loved them, and grew, like other drunkards, the merrier and fiercer for what it quaffed. Never again will the insatiable thirst of the fire fiend be so pampered. Here were the treasures of famous bon vivants—liquors that had been tossed on ocean, and mellowed in the sun, and hoarded long in the recesses of the earth—the pale, the gold, the ruddy juice of whatever vineyards were most delicate—the entire vintage of Tokay—all mingling in one stream with the vile fluids of the common pothouse, and contributing to heighten the selfsame blaze. And while it rose in a gigantic spire that seemed to wave against the arch of the firmament and combine itself with the light of stars, the multitude gave a shout as if the broad earth were exulting in its deliverance from the curse of ages.

But the joy was not universal. Many deemed that human life would be gloomier than ever when that brief illumination should sink down. While the reformers were at work, I overheard muttered expostulations from several respectable gentlemen with red noses and wearing gouty shoes; and a ragged worthy, whose face looked like a hearth where the fire is burned out, now expressed his discontent more openly and boldly.

"What is this world good for," said the last toper, "now that we can never be jolly any more? What is to comfort the poor man in sorrow and perplexity? How is he to keep his heart warm against the cold winds of this cheerless earth? And what do you propose to give him in exchange for the solace that you take away? How are old friends to sit together by the fireside without a cheerful glass between them? A plague upon your reformation! It is a sad world, a cold world, a selfish world, a low world, not worth an honest fellow's living in, now that good fellowship is gone forever!"

This harangue excited great mirth among the bystanders; but, preposterous as was the sentiment, I could not help commiserating the forlorn condition of the last toper, whose boon companions had dwindled away from his side, leaving the poor fellow without a soul to countenance him in sipping his liquor, nor indeed any liquor to sip. Not that this was quite the true state of the case; for I had observed him at a critical moment filch a bottle of fourth-proof brandy that fell beside the bonfire and hide it in his pocket.

The spirituous and fermented liquors being thus disposed of, the zeal of the reformers next induced them to replenish the fire with all the boxes of tea and bags of coffee in the world. And now came the planters of Virginia, bringing their crops and tobacco. These, being cast upon the heap of inutility, aggregated it to the size of a mountain, and incensed the atmosphere with such potent fragrance that methought we should never draw pure breath again. The present sacrifice seemed to startle the lovers of the weed more than any that they had hitherto witnessed.

"Well, they've put my pipe out," said an old gentleman flinging it into the flames in a pet. "What is this world coming to? Everything rich and racy—all the spice of life—is to be condemned as useless. Now that they have kindled the bonfire, if these nonsensical reformers would fling themselves into it, all would be well enough!"

"Be patient," responded a stanch conservative; "it will come to that in the end. They will first fling us in, and finally themselves."

From the general and systematic measures of reform I now turned to consider the individual contributions to this memorable bonfire. In many instances these were of a very amusing character. One poor fellow threw in his empty purse, and another a bundle of counterfeit or insolvable bank notes. Fashionable ladies threw in their last season's bonnets, together with heaps of ribbons, yellow lace, and much other half-worn milliner's ware, all of which proved even more evanescent in the fire than it had been in the fashion. A multitude of lovers of both sexes—discarded maids or bachelors and couples mutually weary of one another—tossed in bundles of perfumed letters and enamored sonnets. A hack politician, being deprived of bread by the loss of office, threw in his teeth, which happened to be false ones. The Rev. Sydney Smith—having voyaged across the Atlantic for that sole purpose—came up to the bonfire with a bitter grin and threw in certain repudiated bonds, fortified though they were with the broad seal of a sovereign state. A little boy of five years old, in the premature manliness of the present epoch, threw in his playthings; a college graduate his diploma; an apothecary, ruined by the spread of homœopathy, his whole stock of drugs and medicines; a physician his library; a parson his old sermons; and a fine gentleman of the old school his code of manners, which he had formerly written down for the benefit of the next generation. A widow, resolving on a second marriage, slyly threw in her dead husband's miniature. A young man, jilted by his mistress, would willingly have flung his own desperate heart into the flames, but could find no means to wrench it out of his bosom. An American author, whose works were neglected by the public, threw his pen and paper into the bonfire, and betook himself to some less discouraging occupation. It somewhat startled me to overhear a number of ladies, highly respectable in appearance, proposing to fling their gowns and petticoats into the flames, and assume the garb, together with the manners, duties, offices, and responsibilities, of the opposite sex.

What favor was accorded to this scheme I am unable to say, my attention being suddenly drawn to a poor, deceived, and half-delirious girl, who, exclaiming that she was the most worthless thing alive or dead, attempted to cast herself into the fire amid all that wrecked and broken trumpery of the world. A good man, however, ran to her rescue.

"Patience, my poor girl!" said he, as he drew her back from the fierce embrace of the destroying angel. "Be patient, and abide Heaven's will. So long as you possess a living soul, all may be restored to its first freshness. These things of matter and creations of human fantasy are fit for nothing but to be burned when once they have had their day; but your day is eternity!"

"Yes," said the wretched girl, whose frenzy seemed now to have sunk down into deep despondency,—"yes and the sunshine is blotted out of it!"

It was now rumored among the spectators that all the weapons and munitions of war were to be thrown into the bonfire, with the exception of the world's stock of gunpowder, which, as the safest mode of disposing of it, had already been drowned in the sea. This intelligence seemed to awaken great diversity of opinion. The hopeful philanthropist esteemed it a token that the millennium was already come; while persons of another stamp, in whose view mankind was a breed of bulldogs, prophesied that all the old stoutness, fervor, nobleness, generosity, and magnanimity of the race would disappear,—these qualities, as they affirmed, requiring blood for their nourishment. They comforted themselves, however, in the belief that the proposed abolition of war was impracticable for any length of time together.

Be that as it might, numberless great guns, whose thunder had long been the voice of battle,—the artillery of the Armada, the battering trains of Marlborough, and the adverse cannon of Napoleon and Wellington,—were trundled into the midst of the fire. By the continual addition of dry combustibles, it had now waxed so intense that neither brass nor iron could withstand it. It was wonderful to behold how these terrible instruments of slaughter melted away like playthings of wax. Then the armies of the earth wheeled around the mighty furnace, with their military music playing triumphant marches, and flung in their muskets and swords. The standard-bearers, likewise, cast one look upward at their banners, all tattered with shot holes and inscribed with the names of victorious fields; and, giving them a last flourish on the breeze, they lowered them into the flame, which snatched them upward in its rush towards the clouds. This ceremony being over, the world was left without a single weapon in its hands, except possibly a few old king's arms and rusty swords and other trophies of the Revolution in some of our state armories. And now the drums were beaten and the trumpets brayed all together, as a prelude to the proclamation of universal and eternal peace and the announcement that glory was no longer to be won by blood, but that it would henceforth be the contention of the human race to work out the greatest mutual good, and that beneficence, in the future annals of the earth, would claim the praise of valor. The blessed tidings were accordingly promulgated, and caused infinite rejoicings among those who had stood aghast at the horror and absurdity of war.

But I saw a grim smile pass over the seared visage of a stately old commander,—by his warworn figure and rich military dress, he might have been one of Napoleon's famous marshals,—who, with the rest of the world's soldiery, had just flung away the sword that had been familiar to his right hand for half a century.

"Ay! ay!" grumbled he. "Let them proclaim what they please; but, in the end, we shall find that all this foolery has only made more work for the armorers and cannon founders."

"Why, sir," exclaimed I, in astonishment, "do you imagine that the human race will ever so far return on the steps of its past madness as to weld another sword or cast another cannon?"

"There will be no need," observed, with a sneer, one who neither felt benevolence nor had faith in it. "When Cain wished to slay his brother, he was at no loss for a weapon."

"We shall see," replied the veteran commander. "If I am mistaken, so much the better; but in my opinion, without pretending to philosophize about the matter, the necessity of war lies far deeper than these honest gentlemen suppose. What! is there a field for all the petty disputes of individuals? and shall there be no great law court for the settlement of national difficulties? The battle field is the only court where such suits can be tried."

"You forget, general," rejoined I, "that, in this advanced stage of civilization, Reason and Philanthropy combined will constitute just such a tribunal as is requisite."

"Ah, I had forgotten that, indeed!" said the old warrior, as he limped away.

The fire was now to be replenished with materials that had hitherto been considered of even greater importance to the well being of society than the warlike munitions which we had already seen consumed. A body of reformers had travelled all over the earth in quest of the machinery by which the different nations were accustomed to inflict the punishment of death. A shudder passed through the multitude as these ghastly emblems were dragged forward. Even the flames seemed at first to shrink away, displaying the shape and murderous contrivance of each in a full blaze of light, which of itself was sufficient to convince mankind of the long and deadly error of human law. Those old implements of cruelty; those horrible monsters of mechanism; those inventions which seemed to demand something worse than man's natural heart to contrive, and which had lurked in the dusky nooks of ancient prisons, the subject of terror-stricken legend,—were now brought forth to view. Headsmen's axes, with the rust of noble and royal blood upon them, and a vast collection of halters that had choked the breath of plebeian victims, were thrown in together. A shout greeted the arrival of the guillotine, which was thrust forward on the same wheels that had borne it from one to another of the blood-stained streets of Paris. But the loudest roar of applause went up, telling the distant sky of the triumph of the earth's redemption, when the gallows made its appearance. An ill-looking fellow, however, rushed forward, and, putting himself in the path of the reformers, bellowed hoarsely, and fought with brute fury to stay their progress.

It was little matter of surprise, perhaps, that the executioner should thus do his best to vindicate and uphold the machinery by which he himself had his livelihood and worthier individuals their death; but it deserved special note that men of a far different sphere—even of that consecrated class in whose guardianship the world is apt to trust its benevolence—were found to take the hangman's view of the question.

"Stay, my brethren!" cried one of them. "You are misled by a false philanthropy; you know not what you do. The gallows is a Heaven-ordained instrument. Bear it back, then, reverently, and set it up in its old place, else the world will fall to speedy ruin and desolation!"

"Onward! onward!" shouted a leader in the reform. "Into the flames with the accursed instrument of man's blood policy! How can human law inculcate benevolence and love while it persists in setting up the gallows as its chief symbol? One heave more, good friends, and the world will be redeemed from its greatest error."

A thousand hands, that nevertheless loathed the touch, now lent their assistance, and thrust the ominous burden far, far into the centre of the raging furnace. There its fatal and abhorred image was beheld, first black, then a red coal, then ashes.

"That was well done!" exclaimed I.

"Yes, it was well done," replied, but with less enthusiasm than I expected, the thoughtful observer who was still at my side; "well done, if the world be good enough for the measure. Death, however, is an idea that cannot easily be dispensed with in any condition between the primal innocence and that other purity and perfection which perchance we are destined to attain after travelling round the full circle: but, at all events, it is well that the experiment should now be tried."

"Too cold! too cold!" impatiently exclaimed the young and ardent leader in this triumph. "Let the heart have its voice here as well as the intellect. And as for ripeness, and as for progress, let mankind always do the highest, kindest, noblest thing that, at any given period, it has attained the perception of; and surely that thing cannot be wrong nor wrongly timed."

I know not whether it were the excitement of the scene, or whether the good people around the bonfire were really growing more enlightened every instant; but they now proceeded to measures in the full length of which I was hardly prepared to keep them company. For instance, some threw their marriage certificates into the flames, and declared themselves candidates for a higher, holier, and more comprehensive union than that which had subsisted from the birth of time under the form of the connubial tie. Others hastened to the vaults of banks and to the coffers of the rich,—all of which were open to the first comer on this fated occasion,—and brought entire bales of paper money to enliven the blaze, and tons of coin to be melted down by its intensity. Henceforth, they said, universal benevolence, uncoined and exhaustless, was to be the golden currency of the world. At this intelligence the bankers and speculators in the stocks grew pale, and a pickpocket, who had reaped a rich harvest among the crowd, fell down in a deadly fainting fit. A few men of business burned their daybooks and ledgers, the notes and obligations of their creditors, and all other evidences of debts due to themselves; while perhaps a somewhat larger number satisfied their zeal for reform with the sacrifice of any uncomfortable recollection of their own indebtment. There was then a cry that the period was arrived when the title deeds of landed property should be given to the flames, and the whole soil of the earth revert to the public, from whom it had been wrongfully abstracted and most unequally distributed among individuals. Another party demanded that all written constitutions, set forms of government, legislative acts, statute books, and everything else on which human invention had endeavored to stamp its arbitrary laws, should at once be destroyed, leaving the consummated world as free as the man first created.

Whether any ultimate action was taken with regard to these propositions is beyond my knowledge; for, just then, some matters were in progress that concerned my sympathies more nearly.

"See! see! What heaps of books and pamphlets!" cried a fellow, who did not seem to be a lover of literature. "Now we shall have a glorious blaze!"

"That's just the thing!" said a modern philosopher. "Now we shall get rid of the weight of dead men's thought, which has hitherto pressed so heavily on the living intellect that it has been incompetent to any effectual self-exertion. Well done, my lads! Into the fire with them! Now you are enlightening the world indeed!"

"But what is to become of the trade?" cried a frantic bookseller.

"Oh, by all means, let them accompany their merchandise," coolly observed an author. "It will be a noble funeral pile!"

The truth was, that the human race had now reached a stage of progress so far beyond what the wisest and wittiest men of former ages had ever dreamed of that it would have been a manifest absurdity to allow the earth to be any longer encumbered with their poor achievements in the literary line. Accordingly a thorough and searching investigation had swept the booksellers' shops, hawkers' stands, public, and private libraries, and even the little book-shelf by the country fireside, and had brought the world's entire mass of printed paper, bound or in sheets, to swell the already mountain bulk of our illustrious bonfire. Thick, heavy folios, containing the labors of lexicographers, commentators and encyclopedists, were flung in, and falling among the embers with a leaden thump, smouldered away to ashes like rotten wood. The small, richly gilt French tomes of the last age, with the hundred volumes of Voltaire among them, went off in a brilliant shower of sparkles and little jets of flame; while the current literature of the same nation burned red and blue, and threw an infernal light over the visages of the spectators, converting them all to the aspect of party-colored fiends. A collection of German stories emitted a scent of brimstone. The English standard authors made excellent fuel, generally exhibiting the properties of sound oak logs. Milton's works, in particular, sent up a powerful blaze, gradually reddening into a coal, which promised to endure longer than almost any other material of the pile. From Shakespeare there gushed a flame of such marvellous splendor that men shaded their eyes as against the sun's meridian glory; nor even when the works of his own elucidators were flung upon him did he cease to flash forth a dazzling radiance from beneath the ponderous heap. It is my belief that he is blazing as fervidly as ever.

"Could a poet but light a lamp at that glorious flame," remarked I, "he might then consume the midnight oil to some good purpose."

"That is the very thing which modern poets have been too apt to do, or at least to attempt," answered a critic. "The chief benefit to be expected from this conflagration of past literature undoubtedly is, that writers will henceforth be compelled to light their lamps at the sun or stars."

"If they can reach so high," said I; "but that task requires a giant, who may afterwards distribute the light among inferior men. It is not every one that can steal the fire from heaven like Prometheus; but, when once he had done the deed, a thousand hearths were kindled by it."

It amazed me much to observe how indefinite was the proportion between the physical mass of any given author and the property of brilliant and long-continued combustion. For instance, there was not a quarto volume of the last century—nor, indeed, of the present—that could compete in that particular with a child's little gilt-covered book, containing Mother Goose's Melodies. The Life and Death of Tom Thumb outlasted the biography of Marlborough. An epic, indeed a dozen of them, was converted to white ashes before the single sheet of an old ballad was half consumed. In more than one case, too, when volumes of applauded verse proved incapable of anything better than a stifling smoke, an unregarded ditty of some nameless bard—perchance in the corner of a newspaper—soared up among the stars with a flame as brilliant as their own. Speaking of the properties of flame, methought Shelley's poetry emitted a purer light than almost any other productions of his day, contrasting beautifully with the fitful and lurid gleams and gushes of black vapor that flashed and eddied from the volumes of Lord Byron. As for Tom Moore, some of his songs diffused an odor like a burning pastil.

I felt particular interest in watching the combustion of American authors, and scrupulously noted by my watch the precise number of moments that changed most of them from shabbily-printed books to indistinguishable ashes. It would be invidious, however, if not perilous, to betray these awful secrets; so that I shall content myself with observing that it was not invariably the writer most frequent in the public mouth that made the most splendid appearance in the bonfire. I especially remember that a great deal of excellent inflammability was exhibited in a thin volume of poems by Ellery Channing; although, to speak the truth, there were certain portions that hissed and spluttered in a very disagreeable fashion. A curious phenomenon occurred in reference to several writers, native as well as foreign. Their books, though of highly respectable figure, instead of bursting into a blaze, or even smouldering out their substance in smoke, suddenly melted away in a manner that proved them to be ice.

If it be no lack of modesty to mention my own works, it must here be confessed that I looked for them with fatherly interest, but in vain. Too probably they were changed to vapor by the first action of the heat; at best, I can only hope that, in their quiet way, they contributed a glimmering spark or two to the splendor of the evening.

"Alas! and woe is me!" thus bemoaned himself a heavy-looking gentleman in green spectacles. "The world is utterly ruined, and there is nothing to live for any longer. The business of my life is snatched from me. Not a volume to be had for love or money!"

"This," remarked the sedate observer beside me, "is a bookworm—one of those men who are born to gnaw dead thoughts. His clothes, you see, are covered with the dust of libraries. He has no inward fountain of ideas; and, in good earnest, now that the old stock is abolished, I do not see what is to become of the poor fellow. Have you no word of comfort for him?"

"My dear sir," said I to the desperate bookworm, "is not Nature better than a book? Is not the human heart deeper than any system of philosophy? Is not life replete with more instruction than past observers have found it possible to write down in maxims? Be of good cheer. The great book of Time is still spread wide open before us; and, if we read it aright, it will be to us a volume of eternal truth."

"Oh, my books, my books, my precious printed books!" reiterated the forlorn bookworm. "My only reality was a bound volume; and now they will not leave me even a shadowy pamphlet!"

In fact, the last remnant of the literature of all the ages was now descending upon the blazing heap in the shape of a cloud of pamphlets from the press of the New World. These likewise were consumed in the twinkling of an eye, leaving the earth, for the first time since the days of Cadmus, free from the plague of letters—an enviable field for the authors of the next generation.

"Well, and does anything remain to be done?" inquired I somewhat anxiously. "Unless we set fire to the earth itself, and then leap boldly off into infinite space, I know not that we can carry reform to any farther point."

"You are vastly mistaken, my good friend," said the observer. "Believe me, the fire will not be allowed to settle down without the addition of fuel that will startle many persons who have lent a willing hand thus far."

Nevertheless there appeared to be a relaxation of effort for a little time, during which, probably, the leaders of the movement were considering what should be done next. In the interval, a philosopher threw his theory into the flames,—a sacrifice which, by those who knew how to estimate it, was pronounced the most remarkable that had yet been made. The combustion, however, was by no means brilliant. Some indefatigable people, scorning to take a moment's ease, now employed themselves in collecting all the withered leaves and fallen boughs of the forest, and thereby recruited the bonfire to a greater height than ever. But this was mere by-play.

"Here comes the fresh fuel that I spoke of," said my companion.

To my astonishment, the persons who now advanced into the vacant space around the mountain fire bore surplices and other priestly garments, mitres, crosiers, and a confusion of Popish and Protestant emblems, with which it seemed their purpose to consummate the great act of faith. Crosses from the spires of old cathedrals were cast upon the heap with as little remorse as if the reverence of centuries, passing in long array beneath the lofty towers, had not looked up to them as the holiest of symbols. The font in which infants were consecrated to God, the sacramental vessels whence piety received the hallowed draught, were given to the same destruction. Perhaps it most nearly touched my heart to see among these devoted relics fragments of the humble communion tables and undecorated pulpits which I recognized as having been torn from the meeting-houses of New England. Those simple edifices might have been permitted to retain all of sacred embellishment that their Puritan founders had bestowed, even though the mighty structure of St. Peter's had sent its spoils to the fire of this terrible sacrifice. Yet I felt that these were but the externals of religion, and might most safely be relinquished by spirits that best knew their deep significance.

"All is well," said I, cheerfully. "The woodpaths shall be the aisles of our cathedral,—the firmament itself shall be its ceiling. What needs an earthly roof between the Deity and his worshippers? Our faith can well afford to lose all the drapery that even the holiest men have thrown around it, and be only the more sublime in its simplicity."

"True," said my companion; "but will they pause here?"

The doubt implied in his question was well founded. In the general destruction of books already described, a holy volume, that stood apart from the catalogue of human literature, and yet, in one sense, was at its head, had been spared. But the Titan of innovation,—angel or fiend, double in his nature, and capable of deeds befitting both characters,—at first shaking down only the old and rotten shapes of things, had now, as it appeared, laid his terrible hand upon the main pillars which supported the whole edifice of our moral and spiritual state. The inhabitants of the earth had grown too enlightened to define their faith within a form of words, or to limit the spiritual by any analogy to our material existence. Truths which the heavens trembled at were now but a fable of the world's infancy. Therefore, as the final sacrifice of human error, what else remained to be thrown upon the embers of that awful pile except the book which, though a celestial revelation to past ages, was but a voice from a lower sphere as regarded the present race of man? It was done! Upon the blazing heap of falsehood and wornout truth—things that the earth had never needed, or had ceased to need, or had grown childishly weary of—fell the ponderous church Bible, the great old volume that had lain so long on the cushion of the pulpit, and whence the pastor's solemn voice had given holy utterance on so many a Sabbath day. There, likewise, fell the family Bible, which the long-buried patriarch had read to his children,—in prosperity or sorrow, by the fireside and in the summer shade of trees,—and had bequeathed downward as the heirloom of generations. There fell the bosom Bible, the little volume that had been the soul's friend of some sorely-tried child of dust, who thence took courage, whether his trial were for life or death, steadfastly confronting both in the strong assurance of immortality.

All these were flung into the fierce and riotous blaze; and then a mighty wind came roaring across the plain with a desolate howl, as if it were the angry lamentation of the earth for the loss of heaven's sunshine; and it shook the gigantic pyramid of flame and scattered the cinders of half-consumed abominations around upon the spectators.

"This is terrible!" said I, feeling that my cheek grew pale, and seeing a like change in the visages about me.

"Be of good courage yet," answered the man with whom I had so often spoken. He continued to gaze steadily at the spectacle with a singular calmness, as if it concerned him merely as an observer. "Be of good courage, nor yet exult too much; for there is far less both of good and evil in the effect of this bonfire than the world might be willing to believe."

"How can that be?" exclaimed I, impatiently. "Has it not consumed everything? Has it not swallowed up or melted down every human or divine appendage of our mortal state that had substance enough to be acted on by fire? Will there be anything left us to-morrow morning better or worse than a heap of embers and ashes?"

"Assuredly there will," said my grave friend. "Come hither to-morrow morning, or whenever the combustible portion of the pile shall be quite burned out, and you will find among the ashes everything really valuable that you have seen cast into the flames. Trust me, the world of to-morrow will again enrich itself with the gold and diamonds which have been cast off by the world of to-day. Not a truth is destroyed nor buried so deep among the ashes but it will be raked up at last."

This was a strange assurance. Yet I felt inclined to credit it, the more especially as I beheld among the wallowing flames a copy of the Holy Scriptures, the pages of which, instead of being blackened into tinder, only assumed a more dazzling whiteness as the finger marks of human imperfection were purified away. Certain marginal notes and commentaries, it is true, yielded to the intensity of the fiery test, but without detriment to the smallest syllable that had flamed from the pen of inspiration.

"Yes; there is the proof of what you say," answered I, turning to the observer; "but if only what is evil can feel the action of the fire, then, surely, the conflagration has been of inestimable utility. Yet, if I understand aright, you intimate a doubt whether the world's expectation of benefit would be realized by it."

"Listen to the talk of these worthies," said he, pointing to a group in front of the blazing pile; "possibly they may teach you something useful without intending it."

The persons whom he indicated consisted of that brutal and most earthy figure who had stood forth so furiously in defence of the gallows,—the hangman, in short,—together with the last thief and the last murderer, all three of whom were clustered about the last toper. The latter was liberally passing the brandy bottle, which he had rescued from the general destruction of wines and spirits. This little convivial party seemed at the lowest pitch of despondency, as considering that the purified world must needs be utterly unlike the sphere that they had hitherto known, and therefore but a strange and desolate abode for gentlemen of their kidney.

"The best counsel for all of us is," remarked the hangman, "that, as soon as we have finished the last drop of liquor, I help you, my three friends, to a comfortable end upon the nearest tree, and then hang myself on the same bough. This is no world for us any longer."

"Poh, poh, my good fellows!" said a dark-complexioned personage, who now joined the group,—his complexion was indeed fearfully dark, and his eyes glowed with a redder light than that of the bonfire; "be not so cast down, my dear friends; you shall see good days yet. There's one thing that these wiseacres have forgotten to throw into the fire, and without which all the rest of the conflagration is just nothing at all; yes, though they had burned the earth itself to a cinder."

"And what may that be?" eagerly demanded the last murderer.

"What but the human heart itself?" said the dark-visaged stranger, with a portentous grin. "And, unless they hit upon some method of purifying that foul cavern, forth from it will reissue all the shapes of wrong and misery—the same old shapes or worse ones—which they have taken such a vast deal of trouble to consume to ashes. I have stood by this livelong night and laughed in my sleeve at the whole business. Oh, take my word for it, it will be the old world yet!"

This brief conversation supplied me with a theme for lengthened thought. How sad a truth, if true it were, that man's agelong endeavor for perfection had served only to render him the mockery of the evil principle, from the fatal circumstance of an error at the very root of the matter! The heart, the heart,—there was the little yet boundless sphere wherein existed the original wrong of which the crime and misery of this outward world were merely types. Purify that inward sphere, and the many shapes of evil that haunt the outward, and which now seem almost our only realities, will turn to shadowy phantoms and vanish of their own accord; but if we go no deeper than the intellect, and strive, with merely that feeble instrument, to discern and rectify what is wrong, our whole accomplishment will be a dream, so unsubstantial that it matters little whether the bonfire, which I have so faithfully described, were what we choose to call a real event and a flame that would scorch the finger, or only a phosphoric radiance and a parable of my own brain.

PASSAGES FROM A RELINQUISHED WORK

AT HOME

From infancy I was under the guardianship of a village parson, who made me the subject of daily prayer and the sufferer of innumerable stripes, using no distinction, as to these marks of paternal love, between myself and his own three boys. The result, it must be owned, has been very different in their cases and mine, they being all respectable men and well settled in life; the eldest as the successor to his father's pulpit, the second as a physician, and the third as a partner in a wholesale shoe store; while I, with better prospects than either of them, have run the course which this volume will describe. Yet there is room for doubt whether I should have been any better contented with such success as theirs than with my own misfortunes—at least, till after my experience of the latter had made it too late for another trial.

My guardian had a name of considerable eminence, and fitter for the place it occupies in ecclesiastical history than for so frivolous a page as mine. In his own vicinity, among the lighter part of his hearers, he was called Parson Thumpcushion, from the very forcible gestures with which he illustrated his doctrines. Certainly, if his powers as a preacher were to be estimated by the damage done to his pulpit furniture, none of his living brethren, and but few dead ones, would have been worthy even to pronounce a benediction after him. Such pounding and expounding the moment he began to grow warm, such slapping with his open palm, thumping with his closed fist, and banging with the whole weight of the great Bible, convinced me that he held, in imagination, either the Old Nick or some Unitarian infidel at bay, and belabored his unhappy cushion as proxy for those abominable adversaries. Nothing but this exercise of the body while delivering his sermons could have supported the good parson's health under the mental toil which they cost him in composition.

Though Parson Thumpcushion had an upright heart, and some called it a warm one, he was invariably stern and severe, on principle, I suppose, to me. With late justice, though early enough, even now, to be tinctured with generosity, I acknowledge him to have been a good and wise man after his own fashion. If his management failed as to myself, it succeeded with his three sons; nor, I must frankly say, could any mode of education with which it was possible for him to be acquainted have made me much better than what I was or led me to a happier fortune than the present. He could neither change the nature that God gave me nor adapt his own inflexible mind to my peculiar character. Perhaps it was my chief misfortune that I had neither father nor mother alive; for parents have an instinctive sagacity in regard to the welfare of their children, and the child feels a confidence both in the wisdom and affection of his parents which he cannot transfer to any delegate of their duties, however conscientious. An orphan's fate is hard, be he rich or poor. As for Parson Thumpcushion, whenever I see the old gentleman in my dreams he looks kindly and sorrowfully at me, holding out his hand as if each had something to forgive. With such kindness and such forgiveness, but without the sorrow, may our next meeting be!

I was a youth of gay and happy temperament, with an incorrigible levity of spirit, of no vicious propensities, sensible enough, but wayward and fanciful. What a character was this to be brought in contact with the stern old Pilgrim spirit of my guardian! We were at variance on a thousand points; but our chief and final dispute arose from the pertinacity with which he insisted on my adopting a particular profession; while I, being heir to a moderate competence, had avowed my purpose of keeping aloof from the regular business of life. This would have been a dangerous resolution anywhere in the world; it was fatal in New England. There is a grossness in the conceptions of my countrymen; they will not be convinced that any good thing may consist with what they call idleness; they can anticipate nothing but evil of a young man who neither studies physic, law, nor gospel, nor opens a store, nor takes to farming but manifests an incomprehensible disposition to be satisfied with what his father left him. The principle is excellent in its general influence, but miserable in its effect on the few that violate it. I had a quick sensitiveness to public opinion, and felt as if it ranked me with the tavern haunters and town paupers,—with the drunken poet who hawked his own Fourth of July odes, and the broken soldier who had been good for nothing since last war. The consequence of all this was a piece of light-hearted desperation.

I do not over-estimate my notoriety when I take it for granted that many of my readers must have heard of me in the wild way of life which I adopted. The idea of becoming a wandering story teller had been suggested, a year or two before, by an encounter with several merry vagabonds in a showman's wagon, where they and I had sheltered ourselves during a summer shower. The project was not more extravagant than most which a young man forms. Stranger ones are executed every day; and, not to mention my prototypes in the East, and the wandering orators and poets whom my own ears have heard, I had the example of one illustrious itinerant in the other hemisphere,—of Goldsmith, who planned and performed his travels through France and Italy on a less promising scheme than mine. I took credit to myself for various qualifications, mental and personal, suited to the undertaking. Besides, my mind had latterly tormented me for employment, keeping up an irregular activity even in sleep, and making me conscious that I must toil, if it were but in catching butterflies. But my chief motives were, discontent with home and a bitter grudge against Parson Thumpcushion, who would rather have laid me in my father's tomb than seen me either a novelist or an actor, two characters which I thus hit upon a method of uniting. After all it was not half so foolish as if I had written romances instead of reciting them.

The following pages will contain a picture of my vagrant life, intermixed with specimens, generally brief and slight, of that great mass of fiction to which I gave existence, and which has vanished like cloud shapes. Besides the occasions when I sought a pecuniary reward, I was accustomed to exercise my narrative faculty wherever chance had collected a little audience idle enough to listen. These rehearsals were useful in testing the strong points of my stories; and, indeed, the flow of fancy soon came upon me so abundantly that its indulgence was its own reward, though the hope of praise also became a powerful incitement. Since I shall never feel the warm gush of new thought as I did then, let me beseech the reader to believe that my tales were not always so cold as he may find them now. With each specimen will be given a sketch of the circumstances in which the story was told. Thus my airdrawn pictures will be set in frames perhaps more valuable than the pictures themselves, since they will be embossed with groups of characteristic figures, amid the lake and mountain scenery, the villages and fertile fields, of our native land. But I write the book for the sake of its moral, which many a dreaming youth may profit by, though it is the experience of a wandering story teller.

A FLIGHT IN THE FOG

I set out on my rambles one morning in June about sunrise. The day promised to be fair, though at that early hour a heavy mist lay along the earth and settled in minute globules on the folds of my clothes, so that I looked precisely as if touched with a hoar-frost. The sky was quite obscured, and the trees and houses invisible till they grew out of the fog as I came close upon them. There is a hill towards the west whence the road goes abruptly down, holding a level course through the village and ascending an eminence on the other side, behind which it disappears. The whole view comprises an extent of half a mile. Here I paused and, while gazing through the misty veil, it partially rose and swept away with so sudden an effect that a gray cloud seemed to have taken the aspect of a small white town. A thin vapor being still diffused through the atmosphere, the wreaths and pillars of fog, whether hung in air or based on earth, appeared not less substantial than the edifices, and gave their own indistinctness to the whole. It was singular that such an unromantic scene should look so visionary.

Half of the parson's dwelling was a dingy white house, and half of it was a cloud; but Squire Moody's mansion, the grandest in the village, was wholly visible, even the lattice work of the balcony under the front window; while in another place only two red chimneys were seen above the mist, appertaining to my own paternal residence, then tenanted by strangers. I could not remember those with whom I had dwelt there, not even my mother. The brick edifice of the bank was in the clouds; the foundations of what was to be a great block of buildings had vanished, ominously, as it proved; the dry goods store of Mr. Nightingale seemed a doubtful concern; and Dominicus Pike's tobacco manufactory an affair of smoke, except the splendid image of an Indian chief in front. The white spire of the meeting-house ascended out of the densest heap of vapor, as if that shadowy base were its only support; or, to give a truer interpretation, the steeple was the emblem of Religion, enveloped in mystery below, yet pointing to a cloudless atmosphere, and catching the brightness of the east on its gilded vane.

As I beheld these objects, and the dewy street, with grassy intervals and a border of trees between the wheel track and the sidewalks, all so indistinct, and not to be traced without an effort, the whole seemed more like memory than reality. I would have imagined that years had already passed, and I was far away, contemplating that dim picture of my native place which I should retain in my mind through the mist of time. No tears fell from my eyes among the dewdrops of the morning; nor does it occur to me that I heaved a sigh. In truth, I had never felt such a delicious excitement, nor known what freedom was, till that moment when I gave up my home and took the whole world in exchange, fluttering the wings of my spirit as if I would have flown from one star to another through the universe. I waved my hand towards the dusky village, bade it a joyous farewell, and turned away to follow any path but that which might lead me back. Never was Childe Harold's sentiment adopted in a spirit more unlike his own.

Naturally enough, I thought of Don Quixote. Recollecting how the knight and Sancho had watched for auguries when they took the road to Toboso, I began, between jest and earnest, to feel a similar anxiety. It was gratified, and by a more poetical phenomenon than the braying of the dappled ass or the neigh of Rosinante. The sun, then just above the horizon, shone faintly through the fog, and formed a species of rainbow in the west, bestriding my intended road like a gigantic portal. I had never known before that a bow could be generated between the sunshine and the morning mist. It had no brilliancy, no perceptible hues, but was a mere unpainted framework, as white and ghostlike as the lunar rainbow, which is deemed ominous of evil. But, with a light heart to which all omens were propitious, I advanced beneath the misty archway of futurity.

I had determined not to enter on my profession within a hundred miles of home, and then to cover myself with a fictitious name. The first precaution was reasonable enough, as otherwise Parson Thumpcushion might have put an untimely catastrophe to my story; but as nobody would be much affected by my disgrace, and all was to be suffered in my own person, I know not why I cared about a name. For a week or two I travelled almost at random, seeking hardly any guidance except the whirling of a leaf at some turn of the road, or the green bough that beckoned me, or the naked branch that pointed its withered finger onward. All my care was to be farther from home each night than the preceding morning.

A FELLOW-TRAVELLER

One day at noontide, when the sun had burst suddenly out of a cloud and threatened to dissolve me, I looked round for shelter, whether of tavern, cottage, barn, or shady tree. The first which offered itself was a wood—not a forest, but a trim plantation of young oaks, growing just thick enough to keep the mass of sunshine out, while they admitted a few straggling beams, and thus produced the most cheerful gloom imaginable. A brook, so small and clear, and apparently so cool, that I wanted to drink it up, ran under the road through a little arch of stone without once meeting the sun in its passage from the shade on one side to the shade on the other. As there was a stepping-place over the stone wall, and a path along the rivulet, I followed it and discovered its source—a spring gushing out of an old barrel.

In this pleasant spot I saw a light pack suspended from the branch of a tree, a stick leaning against the trunk, and a person seated on the grassy verge of the spring, with his back towards me. He was a slender figure, dressed in black broadcloth, which was none of the finest nor very fashionably cut. On hearing my footsteps he started up rather nervously, and, turning round, showed the face of a young man about my own age, with his finger in a volume which he had been reading till my intrusion. His book was evidently a pocket Bible. Though I piqued myself at that period on my great penetration into people's characters and pursuits, I could not decide whether this young man in black were an unfledged divine from Andover, a college student, or preparing for college at some academy. In either case I would quite as willingly have found a merrier companion; such, for instance, as the comedian with whom Gil Blas shared his dinner beside a fountain in Spain.

After a nod which was duly returned, I made a goblet of oak leaves, filled and emptied it two or three times, and then remarked, to hit the stranger's classical associations, that this beautiful fountain ought to flow from an urn instead of an old barrel. He did not show that he understood the allusion, and replied very briefly, with a shyness that was quite out of place between persons who met in such circumstances. Had he treated my next observation in the same way, we should have parted without another word.

"It is very singular," said I,—"though doubtless there are good reasons for it,—that Nature should provide drink so abundantly, and lavish it everywhere by the roadside, but so seldom anything to eat. Why should we not find a loaf of bread on this tree as well as a barrel of good liquor at the foot of it?"

"There is a loaf of bread on the tree," replied the stranger, without even smiling at a coincidence which made me laugh. "I have something to eat in my bundle; and, if you can make a dinner with me, you shall be welcome."

"I accept your offer with pleasure," said I. "A pilgrim such as I am must not refuse a providential meal."

The young man had risen to take his bundle from the branch of the tree, but now turned round and regarded me with great earnestness, coloring deeply at the same time. However, he said nothing, and produced part of a loaf of bread and some cheese, the former being evidently home-baked, though some days out of the oven. The fare was good enough, with a real welcome, such as his appeared to be. After spreading these articles on the stump of a tree, he proceeded to ask a blessing on our food, an unexpected ceremony, and quite an impressive one at our woodland table, with the fountain gushing beside us and the bright sky glimmering through the boughs; nor did his brief petition affect me less because his embarrassment made his voice tremble. At the end of the meal he returned thanks with the same tremulous fervor.

He felt a natural kindness for me after thus relieving my necessities, and showed it by becoming less reserved. On my part, I professed never to have relished a dinner better; and, in requital of the stranger's hospitality, solicited the pleasure of his company to supper.

"Where? At your home?" asked he.

"Yes," said I, smiling.

"Perhaps our roads are not the same," observed he.

"Oh, I can take any road but one, and yet not miss my way," answered I. "This morning I breakfasted at home; I shall sup at home to-night; and a moment ago I dined at home. To be sure, there was a certain place which I called home; but I have resolved not to see it again till I have been quite round the globe and enter the street on the east as I left it on the west. In the meantime, I have a home everywhere or nowhere, just as you please to take it."

"Nowhere, then; for this transitory world is not our home," said the young man, with solemnity. "We are all pilgrims and wanderers; but it is strange that we two should meet."

I inquired the meaning of this remark, but could obtain no satisfactory reply. But we had eaten salt together, and it was right that we should form acquaintance after that ceremony as the Arabs of the desert do, especially as he had learned something about myself, and the courtesy of the country entitled me to as much information in return. I asked whither he was travelling.

"I do not know," said he; "but God knows."

"That is strange!" exclaimed I; "not that God should know it, but that you should not. And how is your road to be pointed out?"

"Perhaps by an inward conviction," he replied, looking sideways at me to discover whether I smiled; "perhaps by an outward sign."

"Then, believe me," said I, "the outward sign is already granted you, and the inward conviction ought to follow. We are told of pious men in old times who committed themselves to the care of Providence, and saw the manifestation of its will in the slightest circumstances, as in the shooting of a star, the flight of a bird, or the course taken by some brute animal. Sometimes even a stupid ass was their guide. May not I be as good a one?"

"I do not know," said the pilgrim, with perfect simplicity.

We did, however, follow the same road, and were not overtaken, as I partly apprehended, by the keepers of any lunatic asylum in pursuit of a stray patient. Perhaps the stranger felt as much doubt of my sanity as I did of his, though certainly with less justice, since I was fully aware of my own extravagances, while he acted as wildly and deemed it heavenly wisdom. We were a singular couple, strikingly contrasted, yet curiously assimilated, each of us remarkable enough by himself, and doubly so in the other's company. Without any formal compact, we kept together day after day till our union appeared permanent. Even had I seen nothing to love and admire in him, I could never have thought of deserting one who needed me continually; for I never knew a person, not even a woman, so unfit to roam the world in solitude as he was—so painfully shy, so easily discouraged by slight obstacles, and so often depressed by a weight within himself.

I was now far from my native place, but had not yet stepped before the public. A slight tremor seized me whenever I thought of relinquishing the immunities of a private character, and giving every man, and for money too, the right, which no man yet possessed, of treating me with open scorn. But about a week after contracting the above alliance I made my bow to an audience of nine persons, seven of whom hissed me in a very disagreeable manner, and not without good cause. Indeed, the failure was so signal that it would have been mere swindling to retain the money, which had been paid on my implied contract to give its value of amusement. So I called in the door-keeper, bade him refund the whole receipts, a mighty sum, and was gratified with the round of applause by way of offset to the hisses. This event would have looked most horrible in anticipation,—a thing to make a man shoot himself, or run amuck, or hide himself in caverns where he might not see his own burning blush; but the reality was not so very hard to bear. It is a fact that I was more deeply grieved by an almost parallel misfortune which happened to my companion on the same evening. In my own behalf I was angry and excited, not depressed; my blood ran quick, my spirits rose buoyantly, and I had never felt such a confidence of future success and determination to achieve it as at that trying moment. I resolved to persevere, if it were only to wring the reluctant praise from my enemies.

Hitherto I had immensely underrated the difficulties of my idle trade; now I recognized that it demanded nothing short of my whole powers, cultivated to the utmost, and exerted with the same prodigality as if I were speaking for a great party or for the nation at large on the floor of the Capitol. No talent or attainment could come amiss; everything, indeed, was requisite—wide observation, varied knowledge, deep thoughts, and sparkling ones; pathos and levity, and a mixture of both, like sunshine in a raindrop; lofty imagination, veiling itself in the garb of common life; and the practised art which alone could render these gifts, and more than these, available. Not that I ever hoped to be thus qualified. But my despair was no ignoble one, for knowing the impossibility of satisfying myself, even should the world be satisfied, I did my best to overcome it; investigated the causes of every defect; and strove, with patient stubbornness, to remove them in the next attempt. It is one of my few sources of pride, that, ridiculous as the object was, I followed it up with the firmness and energy of a man.

I manufactured a great variety of plots and skeletons of tales, and kept them ready for use, leaving the filling up to the inspiration of the moment; though I cannot remember ever to have told a tale which did not vary considerably from my preconceived idea, and acquire a novelty of aspect as often as I repeated it. Oddly enough, my success was generally in proportion to the difference between the conception and accomplishment. I provided two or more commencements and catastrophes to many of the tales,—a happy expedient, suggested by the double sets of sleeves and trimmings which diversified the suits in Sir Piercy Shafton's wardrobe. But my best efforts had a unity, a wholeness, and a separate character that did not admit of this sort of mechanism.

THE VILLAGE THEATRE

About the first of September my fellow-traveller and myself arrived at a country town, where a small company of actors, on their return from a summer's campaign in the British provinces, were giving a series of dramatic exhibitions. A moderately sized hall of the tavern had been converted into a theatre. The performances that evening were, The Heir at Law, and No Song, no Supper, with the recitation of Alexander's Feast between the play and farce. The house was thin and dull. But the next day there appeared to be brighter prospects, the play-bills announcing at every corner, on the town pump, and—awful sacrilege!—on the very door of the meeting-house, an Unprecedented Attraction! After setting forth the ordinary entertainments of a theatre, the public were informed, in the hugest type that the printing-office could supply, that the manager had been fortunate enough to accomplish an engagement with the celebrated Story Teller. He would make his first appearance that evening, and recite his famous tale of Mr. Higginbotham's Catastrophe, which had been received with rapturous applause by audiences in all the principal cities. This outrageous flourish of trumpets, be it known, was wholly unauthorized by me, who had merely made an engagement for a single evening, without assuming any more celebrity than the little I possessed. As for the tale, it could hardly have been applauded by rapturous audiences, being as yet an unfilled plot; nor even when I stepped upon the stage was it decided whether Mr. Higginbotham should live or die.

In two or three places, underneath the flaming bills which announced the Story Teller, was pasted a small slip of paper, giving notice, in tremulous characters, of a religious meeting to be held at the school-house, where, with divine permission, Eliakim Abbott would address sinners on the welfare of their immortal souls.

In the evening, after the commencement of the tragedy of Douglas, I took a ramble through the town to quicken my ideas by active motion. My spirits were good, with a certain glow of mind which I had already learned to depend upon as the sure prognostic of success. Passing a small and solitary school-house, where a light was burning dimly and a few people were entering the door, I went in with them, and saw my friend Eliakim at the desk. He had collected about fifteen hearers, mostly females. Just as I entered he was beginning to pray in accents so low and interrupted that he seemed to doubt the reception of his efforts both with God and man. There was room for distrust in regard to the latter. At the conclusion of the prayer several of the little audience went out, leaving him to begin his discourse under such discouraging circumstances, added to his natural and agonizing diffidence. Knowing that my presence on these occasions increased his embarrassment, I had stationed myself in a dusky place near the door, and now stole softly out.

On my return to the tavern the tragedy was already concluded; and, being a feeble one in itself and indifferently performed, it left so much the better chance for the Story Teller. The bar was thronged with customers, the toddy stick keeping a continual tattoo; while in the hall there was a broad, deep, buzzing sound, with an occasional peal of impatient thunder,—all symptoms of an overflowing house and an eager audience. I drank a glass of wine and water, and stood at the side scene conversing with a young person of doubtful sex. If a gentleman, how could he have performed the singing girl the night before in No Song, no Supper? Or, if a lady, why did she enact Young Norval, and now wear a green coat and white pantaloons in the character of Little Pickle? In either case the dress was pretty and the wearer bewitching; so that, at the proper moment, I stepped forward with a gay heart and a bold one; while the orchestra played a tune that had resounded at many a country ball, and the curtain as it rose discovered something like a country bar-room. Such a scene was well enough adapted to such a tale.

The orchestra of our little theatre consisted of two fiddles and a clarinet; but, if the whole harmony of the Tremont had been there, it might have swelled in vain beneath the tumult of applause that greeted me. The good people of the town, knowing that the world contained innumerable persons of celebrity undreamed of by them, took it for granted that I was one, and that their roar of welcome was but a feeble echo of those which had thundered around me in lofty theatres. Such an enthusiastic uproar was never heard. Each person seemed a Briareus clapping a hundred hands, besides keeping his feet and several cudgels in play with stamping and thumping on the floor; while the ladies flourished their white cambric handkerchiefs, intermixed with yellow and red bandanna, like the flags of different nations. After such a salutation, the celebrated Story Teller felt almost ashamed to produce so humble an affair as Mr. Higginbotham's Catastrophe.

This story was originally more dramatic than as there presented, and afforded good scope for mimicry and buffoonery, neither of which, to my shame, did I spare. I never knew the "magic of a name" till I used that of Mr. Higginbotham. Often as I repeated it, there were louder bursts of merriment than those which responded to what, in my opinion, were more legitimate strokes of humor. The success of the piece was incalculably heightened by a stiff cue of horse hair, which Little Pickle, in the spirit of that mischief-loving character, had fastened to my collar, where, unknown to me, it kept making the queerest gestures of its own in correspondence with all mine. The audience, supposing that some enormous joke was appended to this long tail behind, were ineffably delighted, and gave way to such a tumult of approbation that, just as the story closed, the benches broke beneath them and left one whole row of my admirers on the floor. Even in that predicament they continued their applause. In after times, when I had grown a bitter moralizer, I took this scene for an example how much of fame is humbug; how much the meed of what our better nature blushes at; how much an accident; how much bestowed on mistaken principles; and how small and poor the remnant. From pit and boxes there was now a universal call for the Story Teller.

That celebrated personage came not when they did call to him. As I left the stage, the landlord, being also the postmaster, had given me a letter with the postmark of my native village, and directed to my assumed name in the stiff old handwriting of Parson Thumpcushion. Doubtless he had heard of the rising renown of the Story Teller, and conjectured at once that such a nondescript luminary could be no other than his lost ward. His epistle, though I never read it, affected me most painfully. I seemed to see the Puritanic figure of my guardian standing among the fripperies of the theatre and pointing to the players,—the fantastic and effeminate men, the painted women, the giddy girl in boy's clothes, merrier than modest,—pointing to these with solemn ridicule, and eying me with stern rebuke. His image was a type of the austere duty, and they of the vanities of life.

I hastened with the letter to my chamber and held it unopened in my hand while the applause of my buffoonery yet sounded through the theatre. Another train of thought came over me. The stern old man appeared again, but now with the gentleness of sorrow, softening his authority with love as a father might, and even bending his venerable head, as if to say that my errors had an apology in his own mistaken discipline. I strode twice across the chamber, then held the letter in the flame of the candle, and beheld it consume unread. It is fixed in my mind, and was so at the time, that he had addressed me in a style of paternal wisdom, and love, and reconciliation, which I could not have resisted had I but risked the trial. The thought still haunts me that then I made my irrevocable choice between good and evil fate.

Meanwhile, as this occurrence had disturbed my mind, and indisposed me to the present exercise of my profession, I left the town, in spite of a laudatory critique in the newspaper, and untempted by the liberal offers of the manager. As we walked onward, following the same road, on two such different errands, Eliakim groaned in spirit, and labored with tears to convince me of the guilt and madness of my life.

THE ARTIST OF THE BEAUTIFUL

An elderly man, with his pretty daughter on his arm, was passing along the street, and emerged from the gloom of the cloudy evening into the light that fell across the pavement from the window of a small shop. It was a projecting window; and on the inside were suspended a variety of watches, pinchbeck, silver, and one or two of gold, all with their faces turned from the streets, as if churlishly disinclined to inform the wayfarers what o'clock it was. Seated within the shop, sidelong to the window, with his pale face bent earnestly over some delicate piece of mechanism on which was thrown the concentrated lustre of a shade lamp, appeared a young man.

"What can Owen Warland be about?" muttered old Peter Hovenden, himself a retired watchmaker, and the former master of this same young man whose occupation he was now wondering at. "What can the fellow be about? These six months past I have never come by his shop without seeing him just as steadily at work as now. It would be a flight beyond his usual foolery to seek for the perpetual motion; and yet I know enough of my old business to be certain that what he is now so busy with is no part of the machinery of a watch."

"Perhaps, father," said Annie, without showing much interest in the question, "Owen is inventing a new kind of timekeeper. I am sure he has ingenuity enough."

"Poh, child! He has not the sort of ingenuity to invent anything better than a Dutch toy," answered her father, who had formerly been put to much vexation by Owen Warland's irregular genius. "A plague on such ingenuity! All the effect that ever I knew of it was to spoil the accuracy of some of the best watches in my shop. He would turn the sun out of its orbit and derange the whole course of time, if, as I said before, his ingenuity could grasp anything bigger than a child's toy!"

"Hush, father! He hears you!" whispered Annie, pressing the old man's arm. "His ears are as delicate as his feelings; and you know how easily disturbed they are. Do let us move on."

So Peter Hovenden and his daughter Annie plodded on without further conversation, until in a by-street of the town they found themselves passing the open door of a blacksmith's shop. Within was seen the forge, now blazing up and illuminating the high and dusky roof, and now confining its lustre to a narrow precinct of the coal-strewn floor, according as the breath of the bellows was puffed forth or again inhaled into its vast leathern lungs. In the intervals of brightness it was easy to distinguish objects in remote corners of the shop and the horseshoes that hung upon the wall; in the momentary gloom the fire seemed to be glimmering amidst the vagueness of unenclosed space. Moving about in this red glare and alternate dusk was the figure of the blacksmith, well worthy to be viewed in so picturesque an aspect of light and shade, where the bright blaze struggled with the black night, as if each would have snatched his comely strength from the other. Anon he drew a white-hot bar of iron from the coals, laid it on the anvil, uplifted his arm of might, and was soon enveloped in the myriads of sparks which the strokes of his hammer scattered into the surrounding gloom.

"Now, that is a pleasant sight," said the old watchmaker. "I know what it is to work in gold; but give me the worker in iron after all is said and done. He spends his labor upon a reality. What say you, daughter Annie?"

"Pray don't speak so loud, father," whispered Annie, "Robert Danforth will hear you."

"And what if he should hear me?" said Peter Hovenden. "I say again, it is a good and a wholesome thing to depend upon main strength and reality, and to earn one's bread with the bare and brawny arm of a blacksmith. A watchmaker gets his brain puzzled by his wheels within a wheel, or loses his health or the nicety of his eyesight, as was my case, and finds himself at middle age, or a little after, past labor at his own trade and fit for nothing else, yet too poor to live at his ease. So I say once again, give me main strength for my money. And then, how it takes the nonsense out of a man! Did you ever hear of a blacksmith being such a fool as Owen Warland yonder?"

"Well said, uncle Hovenden!" shouted Robert Danforth from the forge, in a full, deep, merry voice, that made the roof reëcho. "And what says Miss Annie to that doctrine? She, I suppose, will think it a genteeler business to tinker up a lady's watch than to forge a horseshoe or make a gridiron."

Annie drew her father onward without giving him time for reply.

But we must return to Owen Warland's shop, and spend more meditation upon his history and character than either Peter Hovenden, or probably his daughter Annie, or Owen's old school-fellow, Robert Danforth, would have thought due to so slight a subject. From the time that his little fingers could grasp a penknife, Owen had been remarkable for a delicate ingenuity, which sometimes produced pretty shapes in wood, principally figures of flowers and birds, and sometimes seemed to aim at the hidden mysteries of mechanism. But it was always for purposes of grace, and never with any mockery of the useful. He did not, like the crowd of school-boy artisans, construct little windmills on the angle of a barn or watermills across the neighboring brook. Those who discovered such peculiarity in the boy as to think it worth their while to observe him closely, sometimes saw reason to suppose that he was attempting to imitate the beautiful movements of Nature as exemplified in the flight of birds or the activity of little animals. It seemed, in fact, a new development of the love of the beautiful, such as might have made him a poet, a painter, or a sculptor, and which was as completely refined from all utilitarian coarseness as it could have been in either of the fine arts. He looked with singular distaste at the stiff and regular processes of ordinary machinery. Being once carried to see a steam-engine, in the expectation that his intuitive comprehension of mechanical principles would be gratified, he turned pale and grew sick, as if something monstrous and unnatural had been presented to him. This horror was partly owing to the size and terrible energy of the iron laborer; for the character of Owen's mind was microscopic, and tended naturally to the minute, in accordance with his diminutive frame and the marvellous smallness and delicate power of his fingers. Not that his sense of beauty was thereby diminished into a sense of prettiness. The beautiful idea has no relation to size, and may be as perfectly developed in a space too minute for any but microscopic investigation as within the ample verge that is measured by the arc of the rainbow. But, at all events, this characteristic minuteness in his objects and accomplishments made the world even more incapable than it might otherwise have been of appreciating Owen Warland's genius. The boy's relatives saw nothing better to be done—as perhaps there was not—than to bind him apprentice to a watchmaker, hoping that his strange ingenuity might thus be regulated and put to utilitarian purposes.

Peter Hovenden's opinion of his apprentice has already been expressed. He could make nothing of the lad. Owen's apprehension of the professional mysteries, it is true, was inconceivably quick; but he altogether forgot or despised the grand object of a watchmaker's business, and cared no more for the measurement of time than if it had been merged into eternity. So long, however, as he remained under his old master's care, Owen's lack of sturdiness made it possible, by strict injunctions and sharp oversight, to restrain his creative eccentricity within bounds; but when his apprenticeship was served out, and he had taken the little shop which Peter Hovenden's failing eyesight compelled him to relinquish, then did people recognize how unfit a person was Owen Warland to lead old blind Father Time along his daily course. One of his most rational projects was to connect a musical operation with the machinery of his watches, so that all the harsh dissonances of life might be rendered tuneful, and each flitting moment fall into the abyss of the past in golden drops of harmony. If a family clock was intrusted to him for repair,—one of those tall, ancient clocks that have grown nearly allied to human nature by measuring out the lifetime of many generations,—he would take upon himself to arrange a dance or funeral procession of figures across its venerable face, representing twelve mirthful or melancholy hours. Several freaks of this kind quite destroyed the young watchmaker's credit with that steady and matter-of-fact class of people who hold the opinion that time is not to be trifled with, whether considered as the medium of advancement and prosperity in this world or preparation for the next. His custom rapidly diminished—a misfortune, however, that was probably reckoned among his better accidents by Owen Warland, who was becoming more and more absorbed in a secret occupation which drew all his science and manual dexterity into itself, and likewise gave full employment to the characteristic tendencies of his genius. This pursuit had already consumed many months.

After the old watchmaker and his pretty daughter had gazed at him out of the obscurity of the street, Owen Warland was seized with a fluttering of the nerves, which made his hand tremble too violently to proceed with such delicate labor as he was now engaged upon.

"It was Annie herself!" murmured he. "I should have known it, by this throbbing of my heart, before I heard her father's voice. Ah, how it throbs! I shall scarcely be able to work again on this exquisite mechanism to-night. Annie! dearest Annie! thou shouldst give firmness to my heart and hand, and not shake them thus; for if I strive to put the very spirit of beauty into form and give it motion, it is for thy sake alone. O throbbing heart, be quiet! If my labor be thus thwarted, there will come vague and unsatisfied dreams which will leave me spiritless to-morrow."

As he was endeavoring to settle himself again to his task, the shop door opened and gave admittance to no other than the stalwart figure which Peter Hovenden had paused to admire, as seen amid the light and shadow of the blacksmith's shop. Robert Danforth had brought a little anvil of his own manufacture, and peculiarly constructed, which the young artist had recently bespoken. Owen examined the article and pronounced it fashioned according to his wish.

"Why, yes," said Robert Danforth, his strong voice filling the shop as with the sound of a bass viol, "I consider myself equal to anything in the way of my own trade; though I should have made but a poor figure at yours with such a fist as this," added he, laughing, as he laid his vast hand beside the delicate one of Owen. "But what then? I put more main strength into one blow of my sledge hammer than all that you have expended since you were a 'prentice. Is not that the truth?"

"Very probably," answered the low and slender voice of Owen. "Strength is an earthly monster. I make no pretensions to it. My force, whatever there may be of it, is altogether spiritual."

"Well, but, Owen, what are you about?" asked his old school-fellow, still in such a hearty volume of tone that it made the artist shrink, especially as the question related to a subject so sacred as the absorbing dream of his imagination. "Folks do say that you are trying to discover the perpetual motion."

"The perpetual motion? Nonsense!" replied Owen Warland, with a movement of disgust; for he was full of little petulances. "It can never be discovered. It is a dream that may delude men whose brains are mystified with matter, but not me. Besides, if such a discovery were possible, it would not be worth my while to make it only to have the secret turned to such purposes as are now effected by steam and water power. I am not ambitious to be honored with the paternity of a new kind of cotton machine."

"That would be droll enough!" cried the blacksmith, breaking out into such an uproar of laughter that Owen himself and the bell glasses on his work-board quivered in unison. "No, no, Owen! No child of yours will have iron joints and sinews. Well, I won't hinder you any more. Good night, Owen, and success, and if you need any assistance, so far as a downright blow of hammer upon anvil will answer the purpose, I'm your man."

And with another laugh the man of main strength left the shop.

"How strange it is," whispered Owen Warland to himself, leaning his head upon his hand, "that all my musings, my purposes, my passion for the beautiful, my consciousness of power to create it,—a finer, more ethereal power, of which this earthly giant can have no conception,—all, all, look so vain and idle whenever my path is crossed by Robert Danforth! He would drive me mad were I to meet him often. His hard, brute force darkens and confuses the spiritual element within me; but I, too, will be strong in my own way. I will not yield to him."

He took from beneath a glass a piece of minute machinery, which he set in the condensed light of his lamp, and, looking intently at it through a magnifying glass, proceeded to operate with a delicate instrument of steel. In an instant, however, he fell back in his chair and clasped his hands, with a look of horror on his face that made its small features as impressive as those of a giant would have been.

"Heaven! What have I done?" exclaimed he. "The vapor, the influence of that brute force,—it has bewildered me and obscured my perception. I have made the very stroke—the fatal stroke—that I have dreaded from the first. It is all over—the toil of months, the object of my life. I am ruined!"

And there he sat, in strange despair, until his lamp flickered in the socket and left the Artist of the Beautiful in darkness.

Thus it is that ideas, which grow up within the imagination and appear so lovely to it and of a value beyond whatever men call valuable, are exposed to be shattered and annihilated by contact with the practical. It is requisite for the ideal artist to possess a force of character that seems hardly compatible with its delicacy; he must keep his faith in himself while the incredulous world assails him with its utter disbelief; he must stand up against mankind and be his own sole disciple, both as respects his genius and the objects to which it is directed.

For a time Owen Warland succumbed to this severe but inevitable test. He spent a few sluggish weeks with his head so continually resting in his hands that the towns-people had scarcely an opportunity to see his countenance. When at last it was again uplifted to the light of day, a cold, dull, nameless change was perceptible upon it. In the opinion of Peter Hovenden, however, and that order of sagacious understandings who think that life should be regulated, like clockwork, with leaden weights, the alteration was entirely for the better. Owen now, indeed, applied himself to business with dogged industry. It was marvellous to witness the obtuse gravity with which he would inspect the wheels of a great old silver watch; thereby delighting the owner, in whose fob it had been worn till he deemed it a portion of his own life, and was accordingly jealous of its treatment. In consequence of the good report thus acquired, Owen Warland was invited by the proper authorities to regulate the clock in the church steeple. He succeeded so admirably in this matter of public interest that the merchants gruffly acknowledged his merits on 'Change; the nurse whispered his praises as she gave the potion in the sick-chamber; the lover blessed him at the hour of appointed interview; and the town in general thanked Owen for the punctuality of dinner time. In a word, the heavy weight upon his spirits kept everything in order, not merely within his own system, but wheresoever the iron accents of the church clock were audible. It was a circumstance, though minute, yet characteristic of his present state, that, when employed to engrave names or initials on silver spoons, he now wrote the requisite letters in the plainest possible style, omitting a variety of fanciful flourishes that had heretofore distinguished his work in this kind.

One day, during the era of this happy transformation, old Peter Hovenden came to visit his former apprentice.

"Well, Owen," said he, "I am glad to hear such good accounts of you from all quarters, and especially from the town clock yonder, which speaks in your commendation every hour of the twenty-four. Only get rid altogether of your nonsensical trash about the beautiful, which I nor nobody else, nor yourself to boot, could ever understand,—only free yourself of that, and your success in life is as sure as daylight. Why, if you go on in this way, I should even venture to let you doctor this precious old watch of mine; though, except my daughter Annie, I have nothing else so valuable in the world."

"I should hardly dare touch it, sir," replied Owen, in a depressed tone; for he was weighed down by his old master's presence.

"In time," said the latter,—"in time, you will be capable of it."

The old watchmaker, with the freedom naturally consequent on his former authority, went on inspecting the work which Owen had in hand at the moment, together with other matters that were in progress. The artist, meanwhile, could scarcely lift his head. There was nothing so antipodal to his nature as this man's cold, unimaginative sagacity, by contact with which everything was converted into a dream except the densest matter of the physical world. Owen groaned in spirit and prayed fervently to be delivered from him.

"But what is this?" cried Peter Hovenden abruptly, taking up a dusty bell glass, beneath which appeared a mechanical something, as delicate and minute as the system of a butterfly's anatomy. "What have we here? Owen! Owen! there is witchcraft in these little chains, and wheels, and paddles. See! with one pinch of my finger and thumb I am going to deliver you from all future peril."

"For Heaven's sake," screamed Owen Warland, springing up with wonderful energy, "as you would not drive me mad, do not touch it! The slightest pressure of your finger would ruin me forever."

"Aha, young man! And is it so?" said the old watchmaker, looking at him with just enough of penetration to torture Owen's soul with the bitterness of worldly criticism. "Well, take your own course; but I warn you again that in this small piece of mechanism lives your evil spirit. Shall I exorcise him?"

"You are my evil spirit," answered Owen, much excited,—"you and the hard, coarse world! The leaden thoughts and the despondency that you fling upon me are my clogs, else I should long ago have achieved the task that I was created for."

Peter Hovenden shook his head, with the mixture of contempt and indignation which mankind, of whom he was partly a representative, deem themselves entitled to feel towards all simpletons who seek other prizes than the dusty one along the highway. He then took his leave, with an uplifted finger and a sneer upon his face that haunted the artist's dreams for many a night afterwards. At the time of his old master's visit, Owen was probably on the point of taking up the relinquished task; but, by this sinister event, he was thrown back into the state whence he had been slowly emerging.

But the innate tendency of his soul had only been accumulating fresh vigor during its apparent sluggishness. As the summer advanced he almost totally relinquished his business, and permitted Father Time, so far as the old gentleman was represented by the clocks and watches under his control, to stray at random through human life, making infinite confusion among the train of bewildered hours. He wasted the sunshine, as people said, in wandering through the woods and fields and along the banks of streams. There, like a child, he found amusement in chasing butterflies or watching the motions of water insects. There was something truly mysterious in the intentness with which he contemplated these living playthings as they sported on the breeze or examined the structure of an imperial insect whom he had imprisoned. The chase of butterflies was an apt emblem of the ideal pursuit in which he had spent so many golden hours; but would the beautiful idea ever be yielded to his hand like the butterfly that symbolized it? Sweet, doubtless, were these days, and congenial to the artist's soul. They were full of bright conceptions, which gleamed through his intellectual world as the butterflies gleamed through the outward atmosphere, and were real to him, for the instant, without the toil, and perplexity, and many disappointments of attempting to make them visible to the sensual eye. Alas that the artist, whether in poetry, or whatever other material, may not content himself with the inward enjoyment of the beautiful, but must chase the flitting mystery beyond the verge of his ethereal domain, and crush its frail being in seizing it with a material grasp. Owen Warland felt the impulse to give external reality to his ideas as irresistibly as any of the poets or painters who have arrayed the world in a dimmer and fainter beauty, imperfectly copied from the richness of their visions.

The night was now his time for the slow progress of re-creating the one idea to which all his intellectual activity referred itself. Always at the approach of dusk he stole into the town, locked himself within his shop, and wrought with patient delicacy of touch for many hours. Sometimes he was startled by the rap of the watchman, who, when all the world should be asleep, had caught the gleam of lamplight through the crevices of Owen Warland's shutters. Daylight, to the morbid sensibility of his mind, seemed to have an intrusiveness that interfered with his pursuits. On cloudy and inclement days, therefore, he sat with his head upon his hands, muffling, as it were, his sensitive brain in a mist of indefinite musings; for it was a relief to escape from the sharp distinctness with which he was compelled to shape out his thoughts during his nightly toil.

From one of these fits of torpor he was aroused by the entrance of Annie Hovenden, who came into the shop with the freedom of a customer, and also with something of the familiarity of a childish friend. She had worn a hole through her silver thimble, and wanted Owen to repair it.

"But I don't know whether you will condescend to such a task," said she, laughing, "now that you are so taken up with the notion of putting spirit into machinery."

"Where did you get that idea, Annie?" said Owen, starting in surprise.

"Oh, out of my own head," answered she, "and from something that I heard you say, long ago, when you were but a boy and I a little child. But come; will you mend this poor thimble of mine?"

"Anything for your sake, Annie," said Owen Warland,—"anything, even were it to work at Robert Danforth's forge."

"And that would be a pretty sight!" retorted Annie, glancing with imperceptible slightness at the artist's small and slender frame. "Well; here is the thimble."

"But that is a strange idea of yours," said Owen, "about the spiritualization of matter."

And then the thought stole into his mind that this young girl possessed the gift to comprehend him better than all the world besides. And what a help and strength would it be to him in his lonely toil if he could gain the sympathy of the only being whom he loved! To persons whose pursuits are insulated from the common business of life—who are either in advance of mankind or apart from it—there often comes a sensation of moral cold that makes the spirit shiver as if it had reached the frozen solitudes around the pole. What the prophet, the poet, the reformer, the criminal, or any other man with human yearnings, but separated from the multitude by a peculiar lot, might feel, poor Owen felt.

"Annie," cried he, growing pale as death at the thought, "how gladly would I tell you the secret of my pursuit! You, methinks, would estimate it rightly. You, I know, would hear it with a reverence that I must not expect from the harsh, material world."

"Would I not? to be sure I would!" replied Annie Hovenden, lightly laughing. "Come; explain to me quickly what is the meaning of this little whirligig, so delicately wrought that it might be a plaything for Queen Mab. See! I will put it in motion."

"Hold!" exclaimed Owen, "hold!"

Annie had but given the slightest possible touch, with the point of a needle, to the same minute portion of complicated machinery which has been more than once mentioned, when the artist seized her by the wrist with a force that made her scream aloud. She was affrighted at the convulsion of intense rage and anguish that writhed across his features. The next instant he let his head sink upon his hands.

"Go, Annie," murmured he; "I have deceived myself, and must suffer for it. I yearned for sympathy, and thought, and fancied, and dreamed that you might give it me; but you lack the talisman, Annie, that should admit you into my secrets. That touch has undone the toil of months and the thought of a lifetime! It was not your fault, Annie; but you have ruined me!"

Poor Owen Warland! He had indeed erred, yet pardonably; for if any human spirit could have sufficiently reverenced the processes so sacred in his eyes, it must have been a woman's. Even Annie Hovenden, possibly, might not have disappointed him had she been enlightened by the deep intelligence of love.

The artist spent the ensuing winter in a way that satisfied any persons who had hitherto retained a hopeful opinion of him that he was, in truth, irrevocably doomed to inutility as regarded the world, and to an evil destiny on his own part. The decease of a relative had put him in possession of a small inheritance. Thus freed from the necessity of toil, and having lost the steadfast influence of a great purpose,—great, at least, to him,—he abandoned himself to habits from which it might have been supposed the mere delicacy of his organization would have availed to secure him. But when the ethereal portion of a man of genius is obscured, the earthly part assumes an influence the more uncontrollable, because the character is now thrown off the balance to which Providence had so nicely adjusted it, and which, in coarser natures, is adjusted by some other method. Owen Warland made proof of whatever show of bliss may be found in riot. He looked at the world through the golden medium of wine, and contemplated the visions that bubble up so gayly around the brim of the glass, and that people the air with shapes of pleasant madness, which so soon grow ghostly and forlorn. Even when this dismal and inevitable change had taken place, the young man might still have continued to quaff the cup of enchantments, though its vapor did but shroud life in gloom and fill the gloom with spectres that mocked at him. There was a certain irksomeness of spirit, which, being real, and the deepest sensation of which the artist was now conscious, was more intolerable than any fantastic miseries and horrors that the abuse of wine could summon up. In the latter case he could remember, even out of the midst of his trouble, that all was but a delusion; in the former, the heavy anguish was his actual life.

From this perilous state he was redeemed by an incident which more than one person witnessed, but of which the shrewdest could not explain or conjecture the operation on Owen Warland's mind. It was very simple. On a warm afternoon of spring, as the artist sat among his riotous companions with a glass of wine before him, a splendid butterfly flew in at the open window and fluttered about his head.

"Ah," exclaimed Owen, who had drank freely, "are you alive again, child of the sun and playmate of the summer breeze, after your dismal winter's nap? Then it is time for me to be at work!"

And, leaving his unemptied glass upon the table, he departed and was never known to sip another drop of wine.

And now, again, he resumed his wanderings in the woods and fields. It might be fancied that the bright butterfly, which had come so spirit-like into the window as Owen sat with the rude revellers, was indeed a spirit commissioned to recall him to the pure, ideal life that had so etherealized him among men. It might be fancied that he went forth to seek this spirit in its sunny haunts; for still, as in the summer time gone by, he was seen to steal gently up wherever a butterfly had alighted, and lose himself in contemplation of it. When it took flight his eyes followed the winged vision, as if its airy track would show the path to heaven. But what could be the purpose of the unseasonable toil, which was again resumed, as the watchman knew by the lines of lamplight through the crevices of Owen Warland's shutters? The towns-people had one comprehensive explanation of all these singularities. Owen Warland had gone mad! How universally efficacious—how satisfactory, too, and soothing to the injured sensibility of narrowness and dulness—is this easy method of accounting for whatever lies beyond the world's most ordinary scope! From St. Paul's days down to our poor little Artist of the Beautiful, the same talisman had been applied to the elucidation of all mysteries in the words or deeds of men who spoke or acted too wisely or too well. In Owen Warland's case the judgment of his towns-people may have been correct. Perhaps he was mad. The lack of sympathy—that contrast between himself and his neighbors which took away the restraint of example—was enough to make him so. Or possibly he had caught just so much of ethereal radiance as served to bewilder him, in an earthly sense, by its intermixture with the common daylight.

One evening, when the artist had returned from a customary ramble and had just thrown the lustre of his lamp on the delicate piece of work so often interrupted, but still taken up again, as if his fate were embodied in its mechanism, he was surprised by the entrance of old Peter Hovenden. Owen never met this man without a shrinking of the heart. Of all the world he was most terrible, by reason of a keen understanding which saw so distinctly what it did see, and disbelieved so uncompromisingly in what it could not see. On this occasion the old watchmaker had merely a gracious word or two to say.

"Owen, my lad," said he, "we must see you at my house to-morrow night."

The artist began to mutter some excuse.

"Oh, but it must be so," quoth Peter Hovenden, "for the sake of the days when you were one of the household. What, my boy! don't you know that my daughter Annie is engaged to Robert Danforth? We are making an entertainment, in our humble way, to celebrate the event."

"Ah!" said Owen.

That little monosyllable was all he uttered; its tone seemed cold and unconcerned to an ear like Peter Hovenden's; and yet there was in it the stifled outcry of the poor artist's heart, which he compressed within him like a man holding down an evil spirit. One slight outbreak, however, imperceptible to the old watchmaker, he allowed himself. Raising the instrument with which he was about to begin his work, he let it fall upon the little system of machinery that had, anew, cost him months of thought and toil. It was shattered by the stroke!

Owen Warland's story would have been no tolerable representation of the troubled life of those who strive to create the beautiful, if, amid all other thwarting influences, love had not interposed to steal the cunning from his hand. Outwardly he had been no ardent or enterprising lover; the career of his passion had confined its tumults and vicissitudes so entirely within the artist's imagination that Annie herself had scarcely more than a woman's intuitive perception of it; but, in Owen's view, it covered the whole field of his life. Forgetful of the time when she had shown herself incapable of any deep response, he had persisted in connecting all his dreams of artistical success with Annie's image; she was the visible shape in which the spiritual power that he worshipped, and on whose altar he hoped to lay a not unworthy offering, was made manifest to him. Of course he had deceived himself; there were no such attributes in Annie Hovenden as his imagination had endowed her with. She, in the aspect which she wore to his inward vision, was as much a creature of his own as the mysterious piece of mechanism would be were it ever realized. Had he become convinced of his mistake through the medium of successful love,—had he won Annie to his bosom, and there beheld her fade from angel into ordinary woman,—the disappointment might have driven him back, with concentrated energy, upon his sole remaining object. On the other hand, had he found Annie what he fancied, his lot would have been so rich in beauty that out of its mere redundancy he might have wrought the beautiful into many a worthier type than he had toiled for; but the guise in which his sorrow came to him, the sense that the angel of his life had been snatched away and given to a rude man of earth and iron, who could neither need nor appreciate her ministrations,—this was the very perversity of fate that makes human existence appear too absurd and contradictory to be the scene of one other hope or one other fear. There was nothing left for Owen Warland but to sit down like a man that had been stunned.

He went through a fit of illness. After his recovery his small and slender frame assumed an obtuser garniture of flesh than it had ever before worn. His thin cheeks became round; his delicate little hand, so spiritually fashioned to achieve fairy task-work, grew plumper than the hand of a thriving infant. His aspect had a childishness such as might have induced a stranger to pat him on the head—pausing, however, in the act, to wonder what manner of child was here. It was as if the spirit had gone out of him, leaving the body to flourish in a sort of vegetable existence. Not that Owen Warland was idiotic. He could talk, and not irrationally. Somewhat of a babbler, indeed, did people begin to think him; for he was apt to discourse at wearisome length of marvels of mechanism that he had read about in books, but which he had learned to consider as absolutely fabulous. Among them he enumerated the Man of Brass, constructed by Albertus Magnus, and the Brazen Head of Friar Bacon; and, coming down to later times, the automata of a little coach and horses, which it was pretended had been manufactured for the Dauphin of France; together with an insect that buzzed about the ear like a living fly, and yet was but a contrivance of minute steel springs. There was a story, too, of a duck that waddled, and quacked, and ate; though, had any honest citizen purchased it for dinner, he would have found himself cheated with the mere mechanical apparition of a duck.

"But all these accounts," said Owen Warland, "I am now satisfied are mere impositions."

Then, in a mysterious way, he would confess that he once thought differently. In his idle and dreamy days he had considered it possible, in a certain sense, to spiritualize machinery, and to combine with the new species of life and motion thus produced a beauty that should attain to the ideal which Nature has proposed to herself in all her creatures, but has never taken pains to realize. He seemed, however, to retain no very distinct perception either of the process of achieving this object or of the design itself.

"I have thrown it all aside now," he would say. "It was a dream such as young men are always mystifying themselves with. Now that I have acquired a little common sense, it makes me laugh to think of it."

Poor, poor and fallen Owen Warland! These were the symptoms that he had ceased to be an inhabitant of the better sphere that lies unseen around us. He had lost his faith in the invisible, and now prided himself, as such unfortunates invariably do, in the wisdom which rejected much that even his eye could see, and trusted confidently in nothing but what his hand could touch. This is the calamity of men whose spiritual part dies out of them and leaves the grosser understanding to assimilate them more and more to the things of which alone it can take cognizance; but in Owen Warland the spirit was not dead nor passed away; it only slept.

How it awoke again is not recorded. Perhaps the torpid slumber was broken by a convulsive pain. Perhaps, as in a former instance, the butterfly came and hovered about his head and reinspired him,—as indeed this creature of the sunshine had always a mysterious mission for the artist,—reinspired him with the former purpose of his life. Whether it were pain or happiness that thrilled through his veins, his first impulse was to thank Heaven for rendering him again the being of thought, imagination, and keenest sensibility that he had long ceased to be.

"Now for my task," said he. "Never did I feel such strength for it as now."

Yet, strong as he felt himself, he was incited to toil the more diligently by an anxiety lest death should surprise him in the midst of his labors. This anxiety, perhaps, is common to all men who set their hearts upon anything so high, in their own view of it, that life becomes of importance only as conditional to its accomplishment. So long as we love life for itself, we seldom dread the losing it. When we desire life for the attainment of an object, we recognize the frailty of its texture. But, side by side with this sense of insecurity, there is a vital faith in our invulnerability to the shaft of death while engaged in any task that seems assigned by Providence as our proper thing to do, and which the world would have cause to mourn for should we leave it unaccomplished. Can the philosopher, big with the inspiration of an idea that is to reform mankind, believe that he is to be beckoned from this sensible existence at the very instant when he is mustering his breath to speak the word of light? Should he perish so, the weary ages may pass away—the world's, whose life sand may fall, drop by drop—before another intellect is prepared to develop the truth that might have been uttered then. But history affords many an example where the most precious spirit, at any particular epoch manifested in human shape, has gone hence untimely, without space allowed him, so far as mortal judgment could discern, to perform his mission on the earth. The prophet dies, and the man of torpid heart and sluggish brain lives on. The poet leaves his song half sung, or finishes it, beyond the scope of mortal ears, in a celestial choir. The painter—as Allston did—leaves half his conception on the canvas to sadden us with its imperfect beauty, and goes to picture forth the whole, if it be no irreverence to say so, in the hues of heaven. But rather such incomplete designs of this life will be perfected nowhere. This so frequent abortion of man's dearest projects must be taken as a proof that the deeds of earth, however etherealized by piety or genius, are without value, except as exercises and manifestations of the spirit. In heaven, all ordinary thought is higher and more melodious than Milton's song. Then, would he add another verse to any strain that he had left unfinished here?

But to return to Owen Warland. It was his fortune, good or ill, to achieve the purpose of his life. Pass we over a long space of intense thought, yearning effort, minute toil, and wasting anxiety, succeeded by an instant of solitary triumph: let all this be imagined; and then behold the artist, on a winter evening, seeking admittance to Robert Danforth's fireside circle. There he found the man of iron, with his massive substance thoroughly warmed and attempered by domestic influences. And there was Annie, too, now transformed into a matron, with much of her husband's plain and sturdy nature, but imbued, as Owen Warland still believed, with a finer grace, that might enable her to be the interpreter between strength and beauty. It happened, likewise, that old Peter Hovenden was a guest this evening at his daughter's fireside; and it was his well-remembered expression of keen, cold criticism that first encountered the artist's glance.

"My old friend Owen!" cried Robert Danforth, starting up, and compressing the artist's delicate fingers within a hand that was accustomed to gripe bars of iron. "This is kind and neighborly to come to us at last. I was afraid your perpetual motion had bewitched you out of the remembrance of old times."

"We are glad to see you," said Annie, while a blush reddened her matronly cheek. "It was not like a friend to stay from us so long."

"Well, Owen," inquired the old watchmaker, as his first greeting, "how comes on the beautiful? Have you created it at last?"

The artist did not immediately reply, being startled by the apparition of a young child of strength that was tumbling about on the carpet,—a little personage who had come mysteriously out of the infinite, but with something so sturdy and real in his composition that he seemed moulded out of the densest substance which earth could supply. This hopeful infant crawled towards the new-comer, and setting himself on end, as Robert Danforth expressed the posture, stared at Owen with a look of such sagacious observation that the mother could not help exchanging a proud glance with her husband. But the artist was disturbed by the child's look, as imagining a resemblance between it and Peter Hovenden's habitual expression. He could have fancied that the old watchmaker was compressed into this baby shape, and looking out of those baby eyes, and repeating, as he now did, the malicious question:—

"The beautiful, Owen! How comes on the beautiful? Have you succeeded in creating the beautiful?"

"I have succeeded," replied the artist, with a momentary light of triumph in his eyes and a smile of sunshine, yet steeped in such depth of thought that it was almost sadness. "Yes, my friends, it is the truth. I have succeeded."

"Indeed!" cried Annie, a look of maiden mirthfulness peeping out of her face again. "And is it lawful, now, to inquire what the secret is?"

"Surely; it is to disclose it that I have come," answered Owen Warland. "You shall know, and see, and touch, and possess the secret! For, Annie,—if by that name I may still address the friend of my boyish years,—Annie, it is for your bridal gift that I have wrought this spiritualized mechanism, this harmony of motion, this mystery of beauty. It comes late, indeed; but it is as we go onward in life, when objects begin to lose their freshness of hue and our souls their delicacy of perception, that the spirit of beauty is most needed. If,—forgive me, Annie,—if you know how to value this gift, it can never come too late."

He produced, as he spoke, what seemed a jewel box. It was carved richly out of ebony by his own hand, and inlaid with a fanciful tracery of pearl, representing a boy in pursuit of a butterfly, which, elsewhere, had become a winged spirit, and was flying heavenward; while the boy, or youth, had found such efficacy in his strong desire that he ascended from earth to cloud, and from cloud to celestial atmosphere, to win the beautiful. This case of ebony the artist opened, and bade Annie place her finger on its edge. She did so, but almost screamed as a butterfly fluttered forth, and, alighting on her finger's tip, sat waving the ample magnificence of its purple and gold-speckled wings, as if in prelude to a flight. It is impossible to express by words the glory, the splendor, the delicate gorgeousness which were softened into the beauty of this object. Nature's ideal butterfly was here realized in all its perfection; not in the pattern of such faded insects as flit among earthly flowers, but of those which hover across the meads of paradise for child-angels and the spirits of departed infants to disport themselves with. The rich down was visible upon its wings; the lustre of its eyes seemed instinct with spirit. The firelight glimmered around this wonder—the candles gleamed upon it; but it glistened apparently by its own radiance, and illuminated the finger and outstretched hand on which it rested with a white gleam like that of precious stones. In its perfect beauty, the consideration of size was entirely lost. Had its wings overreached the firmament, the mind could not have been more filled or satisfied.

"Beautiful! beautiful!" exclaimed Annie. "Is it alive? Is it alive?"

"Alive? To be sure it is," answered her husband. "Do you suppose any mortal has skill enough to make a butterfly, or would put himself to the trouble of making one, when any child may catch a score of them in a summer's afternoon? Alive? Certainly! But this pretty box is undoubtedly of our friend Owen's manufacture; and really it does him credit."

At this moment the butterfly waved its wings anew, with a motion so absolutely lifelike that Annie was startled, and even awestricken; for, in spite of her husband's opinion, she could not satisfy herself whether it was indeed a living creature or a piece of wondrous mechanism.

"Is it alive?" she repeated, more earnestly than before.

"Judge for yourself," said Owen Warland, who stood gazing in her face with fixed attention.

The butterfly now flung itself upon the air, fluttered round Annie's head, and soared into a distant region of the parlor, still making itself perceptible to sight by the starry gleam in which the motion of its wings enveloped it. The infant on the floor followed its course with his sagacious little eyes. After flying about the room, it returned in a spiral curve and settled again on Annie's finger.

"But is it alive?" exclaimed she again; and the finger on which the gorgeous mystery had alighted was so tremulous that the butterfly was forced to balance himself with his wings. "Tell me if it be alive, or whether you created it."

"Wherefore ask who created it, so it be beautiful?" replied Owen Warland. "Alive? Yes, Annie; it may well be said to possess life, for it has absorbed my own being into itself; and in the secret of that butterfly, and in its beauty, —which is not merely outward, but deep as its whole system,—is represented the intellect, the imagination, the sensibility, the soul of an Artist of the Beautiful! Yes; I created it. But"—and here his countenance somewhat changed—"this butterfly is not now to me what it was when I beheld it afar off in the daydreams of my youth."

"Be it what it may, it is a pretty plaything," said the blacksmith, grinning with childlike delight. "I wonder whether it would condescend to alight on such a great clumsy finger as mine? Hold it hither, Annie."

By the artist's direction, Annie touched her finger's tip to that of her husband; and, after a momentary delay, the butterfly fluttered from one to the other. It preluded a second flight by a similar, yet not precisely the same, waving of wings as in the first experiment; then, ascending from the blacksmith's stalwart finger, it rose in a gradually enlarging curve to the ceiling, made one wide sweep around the room, and returned with an undulating movement to the point whence it had started.

"Well, that does beat all nature!" cried Robert Danforth, bestowing the heartiest praise that he could find expression for; and, indeed, had he paused there, a man of finer words and nicer perception could not easily have said more. "That goes beyond me, I confess. But what then? There is more real use in one downright blow of my sledge hammer than in the whole five years' labor that our friend Owen has wasted on this butterfly."

Here the child clapped his hands and made a great babble of indistinct utterance, apparently demanding that the butterfly should be given him for a plaything.

Owen Warland, meanwhile, glanced sidelong at Annie, to discover whether she sympathized in her husband's estimate of the comparative value of the beautiful and the practical. There was, amid all her kindness towards himself, amid all the wonder and admiration with which she contemplated the marvellous work of his hands and incarnation of his idea, a secret scorn—too secret, perhaps, for her own consciousness, and perceptible only to such intuitive discernment as that of the artist. But Owen, in the latter stages of his pursuit, had risen out of the region in which such a discovery might have been torture. He knew that the world, and Annie as the representative of the world, whatever praise might be bestowed, could never say the fitting word nor feel the fitting sentiment which should be the perfect recompense of an artist who, symbolizing a lofty moral by a material trifle,—converting what was earthly to spiritual gold,—had won the beautiful into his handiwork. Not at this latest moment was he to learn that the reward of all high performance must be sought within itself, or sought in vain. There was, however, a view of the matter which Annie and her husband, and even Peter Hovenden, might fully have understood, and which would have satisfied them that the toil of years had here been worthily bestowed. Owen Warland might have told them that this butterfly, this plaything, this bridal gift of a poor watchmaker to a blacksmith's wife, was, in truth, a gem of art that a monarch would have purchased with honors and abundant wealth, and have treasured it among the jewels of his kingdom as the most unique and wondrous of them all. But the artist smiled and kept the secret to himself.

"Father," said Annie, thinking that a word of praise from the old watchmaker might gratify his former apprentice, "do come and admire this pretty butterfly."

"Let us see," said Peter Hovenden, rising from his chair, with a sneer upon his face that always made people doubt, as he himself did, in everything but a material existence. "Here is my finger for it to alight upon. I shall understand it better when once I have touched it."

But, to the increased astonishment of Annie, when the tip of her father's finger was pressed against that of her husband, on which the butterfly still rested, the insect drooped its wings and seemed on the point of falling to the floor. Even the bright spots of gold upon its wings and body, unless her eyes deceived her, grew dim, and the glowing purple took a dusky hue, and the starry lustre that gleamed around the blacksmith's hand became faint and vanished.

"It is dying! it is dying!" cried Annie, in alarm.

"It has been delicately wrought," said the artist, calmly. "As I told you, it has imbibed a spiritual essence—call it magnetism, or what you will. In an atmosphere of doubt and mockery its exquisite susceptibility suffers torture, as does the soul of him who instilled his own life into it. It has already lost its beauty; in a few moments more its mechanism would be irreparably injured."

"Take away your hand, father!" entreated Annie, turning pale. "Here is my child; let it rest on his innocent hand. There, perhaps, its life will revive and its colors grow brighter than ever."

Her father, with an acrid smile, withdrew his finger. The butterfly then appeared to recover the power of voluntary motion, while its hues assumed much of their original lustre, and the gleam of starlight, which was its most ethereal attribute, again formed a halo round about it. At first, when transferred from Robert Danforth's hand to the small finger of the child, this radiance grew so powerful that it positively threw the little fellow's shadow back against the wall. He, meanwhile, extended his plump hand as he had seen his father and mother do, and watched the waving of the insect's wings with infantine delight. Nevertheless, there was a certain odd expression of sagacity that made Owen Warland feel as if here were old Peter Hovenden, partially, and but partially, redeemed from his hard scepticism into childish faith.

"How wise the little monkey looks!" whispered Robert Danforth to his wife.

"I never saw such a look on a child's face," answered Annie, admiring her own infant, and with good reason, far more than the artistic butterfly. "The darling knows more of the mystery than we do."

As if the butterfly, like the artist, were conscious of something not entirely congenial in the child's nature, it alternately sparkled and grew dim. At length it arose from the small hand of the infant with an airy motion that seemed to bear it upward without an effort, as if the ethereal instincts with which its master's spirit had endowed it impelled this fair vision involuntarily to a higher sphere. Had there been no obstruction, it might have soared into the sky and grown immortal. But its lustre gleamed upon the ceiling; the exquisite texture of its wings brushed against that earthly medium; and a sparkle or two, as of stardust, floated downward and lay glimmering on the carpet. Then the butterfly came fluttering down, and, instead of returning to the infant, was apparently attracted towards the artist's hand.

"Not so! not so!" murmured Owen Warland, as if his handiwork could have understood him. "Thou has gone forth out of thy master's heart. There is no return for thee."

With a wavering movement, and emitting a tremulous radiance, the butterfly struggled, as it were, towards the infant, and was about to alight upon his finger; but while it still hovered in the air, the little child of strength, with his grandsire's sharp and shrewd expression in his face, made a snatch at the marvellous insect and compressed it in his hand. Annie screamed. Old Peter Hovenden burst into a cold and scornful laugh. The blacksmith, by main force, unclosed the infant's hand, and found within the palm a small heap of glittering fragments, whence the mystery of beauty had fled forever. And as for Owen Warland, he looked placidly at what seemed the ruin of his life's labor, and which was yet no ruin. He had caught a far other butterfly than this. When the artist rose high enough to achieve the beautiful, the symbol by which he made it perceptible to mortal senses became of little value in his eyes while his spirit possessed itself in the enjoyment of the reality.

A VIRTUOSO'S COLLECTION

The other day, having a leisure hour at my disposal, I stepped into a new museum to which my notice was casually drawn by a small and unobtrusive sign: "To be seen here, a Virtuoso's Collection." Such was the simple, yet not altogether unpromising, announcement that turned my steps aside for a little while from the sunny sidewalk of our principal thoroughfare. Mounting a sombre staircase, I pushed open a door at its summit, and found myself in the presence of a person, who mentioned the moderate sum that would entitle me to admittance.

"Three shillings, Massachusetts tenor," said he. "No, I mean half a dollar, as you reckon in these days."

While searching my pocket for the coin I glanced at the doorkeeper, the marked character and individuality of whose aspect encouraged me to expect something not quite in the ordinary way. He wore an old-fashioned greatcoat, much faded, within which his meagre person was so completely enveloped that the rest of his attire was undistinguishable. But his visage was remarkably wind-flushed, sunburnt, and weather-worn, and had a most unquiet, nervous, and apprehensive expression. It seemed as if this man had some all-important object in view, some point of deepest interest to be decided, some momentous question to ask, might he but hope for a reply. As it was evident, however, that I could have nothing to do with his private affairs, I passed through an open doorway, which admitted me into the extensive hall of the museum.

Directly in front of the portal was the bronze statue of a youth with winged feet. He was represented in the act of flitting away from earth, yet wore such a look of earnest invitation that it impressed me like a summons to enter the hall.

"It is the original statue of Opportunity, by the ancient sculptor Lysippus," said a gentleman who now approached me. "I place it at the entrance of my museum, because it is not at all times that one can gain admittance to such a collection."

The speaker was a middle-aged person, of whom it was not easy to determine whether he had spent his life as a scholar or as a man of action; in truth, all outward and obvious peculiarities had been worn away by an extensive and promiscuous intercourse with the world. There was no mark about him of profession, individual habits, or scarcely of country; although his dark complexion and high features made me conjecture that he was a native of some southern clime of Europe. At all events, he was evidently the virtuoso in person.

"With your permission," said he, "as we have no descriptive catalogue, I will accompany you through the museum and point out whatever may be most worthy of attention. In the first place, here is a choice collection of stuffed animals."

Nearest the door stood the outward semblance of a wolf, exquisitely prepared, it is true, and showing a very wolfish fierceness in the large glass eyes which were inserted into its wild and crafty head. Still it was merely the skin of a wolf, with nothing to distinguish it from other individuals of that unlovely breed.

"How does this animal deserve a place in your collection?" inquired I.

"It is the wolf that devoured Little Red Riding-Hood," answered the virtuoso; "and by his side—with a milder and more matronly look, as you perceive—stands the she-wolf that suckled Romulus and Remus."

"Ah, indeed!" exclaimed I. "And what lovely lamb is this with the snow-white fleece, which seems to be of as delicate a texture as innocence itself?"

"Methinks you have but carelessly read Spenser," replied my guide, "or you would at once recognize the 'milk-white lamb' which Una led. But I set no great value upon the lamb. The next specimen is better worth our notice."

"What!" cried I, "this strange animal, with the black head of an ox upon the body of a white horse? Were it possible to suppose it, I should say that this was Alexander's steed Bucephalus."

"The same," said the virtuoso. "And can you likewise give a name to the famous charger that stands beside him?"

Next to the renowned Bucephalus stood the mere skeleton of a horse, with the white bones peeping through his ill-conditioned hide; but, if my heart had not warmed towards that pitiful anatomy, I might as well have quitted the museum at once. Its rarities had not been collected with pain and torn from the four quarters of the earth, and from the depths of the sea, and from the palaces and sepulchres of ages, for those who could mistake this illustrious steed.

"It is Rosinante!" exclaimed I, with enthusiasm.

And so it proved. My admiration for the noble and gallant horse caused me to glance with less interest at the other animals, although many of them might have deserved the notice of Cuvier himself. There was the donkey which Peter Bell cudgelled so soundly, and a brother of the same species who had suffered a similar infliction from the ancient prophet Balaam. Some doubts were entertained, however, as to the authenticity of the latter beast. My guide pointed out the venerable Argus, that faithful dog of Ulysses, and also another dog (for so the skin bespoke it), which, though imperfectly preserved, seemed once to have had three heads. It was Cerberus. I was considerably amused at detecting in an obscure corner the fox that became so famous by the loss of his tail. There were several stuffed cats, which, as a dear lover of that comfortable beast, attracted my affectionate regards. One was Dr. Johnson's cat Hodge; and in the same row stood the favorite cats of Mahomet, Gray, and Walter Scott, together with Puss in Boots, and a cat of very noble aspect who had once been a deity of ancient Egypt. Byron's tame bear came next. I must not forget to mention the Erymanthean boar, the skin of St. George's dragon, and that of the serpent Python; and another skin with beautifully variegated hues, supposed to have been the garment of the "spirited sly snake" which tempted Eve. Against the walls were suspended the horns of the stag that Shakespeare shot; and on the floor lay the ponderous shell of the tortoise which fell upon the head of Æschylus. In one row, as natural as life, stood the sacred bull Apis, the "cow with the crumpled horn," and a very wild-looking young heifer, which I guessed to be the cow that jumped over the moon. She was probably killed by the rapidity of her descent. As I turned away, my eyes fell upon an indescribable monster, which proved to be a griffin.

"I look in vain," observed I, "for the skin of an animal which might well deserve the closest study of a naturalist—the winged horse, Pegasus."

"He is not yet dead," replied the virtuoso; "but he is so hard ridden by many young gentlemen of the day that I hope soon to add his skin and skeleton to my collection."

We now passed to the next alcove of the hall, in which was a multitude of stuffed birds. They were very prettily arranged, some upon the branches of trees, others brooding upon nests, and others suspended by wires so artificially that they seemed in the very act of flight. Among them was a white dove, with a withered branch of olive leaves in her mouth.

"Can this be the very dove," inquired I, "that brought the message of peace and hope to the tempest-beaten passengers of the ark?"

"Even so," said my companion.

"And this raven, I suppose," continued I, "is the same that fed Elijah in the wilderness."

"The raven? No," said the virtuoso; "it is a bird of modern date. He belonged to one Barnaby Rudge; and many people fancied that the devil himself was disguised under his sable plumage. But poor Grip has drawn his last cork, and has been forced to 'say die' at last. This other raven, hardly less curious, is that in which the soul of King George I revisited his lady love, the Duchess of Kendall."

My guide next pointed out Minerva's owl and the vulture that preyed upon the liver of Prometheus. There was likewise the sacred ibis of Egypt, and one of the Stymphalides which Hercules shot in his sixth labor. Shelley's skylark, Bryant's water-fowl, and a pigeon from the belfry of the Old South Church, preserved by N. P. Willis, were placed on the same perch. I could not but shudder on beholding Coleridge's albatross, transfixed with the Ancient Mariner's cross-bow shaft. Beside this bird of awful poesy stood a gray goose of very ordinary aspect.

"Stuffed goose is no such rarity," observed I. "Why do you preserve such a specimen in your museum?"

"It is one of the flock whose cackling saved the Roman Capitol," answered the virtuoso. "Many geese have cackled and hissed both before and since; but none, like these, have clamored themselves into immortality."

There seemed to be little else that demanded notice in this department of the museum, unless we except Robinson Crusoe's parrot, a live phœnix, a footless bird of paradise, and a splendid peacock, supposed to be the same that once contained the soul of Pythagoras. I therefore passed to the next alcove, the shelves of which were covered with a miscellaneous collection of curiosities such as are usually found in similar establishments. One of the first things that took my eye was a strange-looking cap, woven of some substance that appeared to be neither woollen, cotton, nor linen.

"Is this a magician's cap?" I asked.

"No," replied the virtuoso; "it is merely Dr. Franklin's cap of asbestos. But here is one which, perhaps, may suit you better. It is the wishing cap of Fortunatus. Will you try it on?"

"By no means," answered I, putting it aside with my hand. "The day of wild wishes is past with me. I desire nothing that may not come in the ordinary course of Providence."

"Then probably," returned the virtuoso, "you will not be tempted to rub this lamp?"

While speaking, he took from the shelf an antique brass lamp, curiously wrought with embossed figures, but so covered with verdigris that the sculpture was almost eaten away.

"It is a thousand years," said he, "since the genius of this lamp constructed Aladdin's palace in a single night. But he still retains his power; and the man who rubs Aladdin's lamp has but to desire either a palace or a cottage."

"I might desire a cottage," replied I; "but I would have it founded on sure and stable truth, not on dreams and fantasies. I have learned to look for the real and the true."

My guide next showed me Prospero's magic wand, broken into three fragments by the hand of its mighty master. On the same shelf lay the gold ring of ancient Gyges, which enabled the wearer to walk invisible. On the other side of the alcove was a tall looking-glass in a frame of ebony, but veiled with a curtain of purple silk, through the rents of which the gleam of the mirror was perceptible.

"This is Cornelius Agrippa's magic glass," observed the virtuoso. "Draw aside the curtain, and picture any human form within your mind, and it will be reflected in the mirror."

"It is enough if I can picture it within my mind," answered I. "Why should I wish it to be repeated in the mirror? But, indeed, these works of magic have grown wearisome to me. There are so many greater wonders in the world, to those who keep their eyes open and their sight undimmed by custom, that all the delusions of the old sorcerers seem flat and stale. Unless you can show me something really curious, I care not to look farther into your museum."

"Ah, well, then," said the virtuoso, composedly, "perhaps you may deem some of my antiquarian rarities deserving of a glance."

He pointed out the iron mask, now corroded with rust; and my heart grew sick at the sight of this dreadful relic, which had shut out a human being from sympathy with his race. There was nothing half so terrible in the axe that beheaded King Charles, nor in the dagger that slew Henry of Navarre, nor in the arrow that pierced the heart of William Rufus—all of which were shown to me. Many of the articles derived their interest, such as it was, from having been formerly in the possession of royalty. For instance, here was Charlemagne's sheepskin cloak, the flowing wig of Louis Quatorze, the spinning-wheel of Sardanapalus, and King Stephen's famous breeches which cost him but a crown. The heart of the Bloody Mary, with the word "Calais" worn into its diseased substance, was preserved in a bottle of spirits; and near it lay the golden case in which the queen of Gustavus Adolphus treasured up that hero's heart. Among these relics and heirlooms of kings I must not forget the long, hairy ears of Midas, and a piece of bread which had been changed to gold by the touch of that unlucky monarch. And as Grecian Helen was a queen, it may here be mentioned that I was permitted to take into my hand a lock of her golden hair and the bowl which a sculptor modelled from the curve of her perfect breast. Here, likewise, was the robe that smothered Agamemnon, Nero's fiddle, the Czar Peter's brandy bottle, the crown of Semiramis, and Canute's sceptre which he extended over the sea. That my own land may not deem itself neglected, let me add that I was favored with a sight of the skull of King Philip, the famous Indian chief, whose head the Puritans smote off and exhibited upon a pole.

"Show me something else," said I to the virtuoso. "Kings are in such an artificial position that people in the ordinary walks of life cannot feel an interest in their relics. If you could show me the straw hat of sweet little Nell, I would far rather see it than a king's golden crown."

"There it is," said my guide, pointing carelessly with his staff to the straw hat in question. "But, indeed, you are hard to please. Here are the seven-league boots. Will you try them on?"

"Our modern railroads have superseded their use," answered I; "and as to these cowhide boots, I could show you quite as curious a pair at the Transcendental community in Roxbury."

We next examined a collection of swords and other weapons, belonging to different epochs, but thrown together without much attempt at arrangement. Here was Arthur's sword Excalibar, and that of the Cid Campeador, and the sword of Brutus rusted with Cæsar's blood and his own, and the sword of Joan of Arc, and that of Horatius, and that with which Virginius slew his daughter, and the one which Dionysius suspended over the head of Damocles. Here also was Arria's sword, which she plunged into her own breast, in order to taste of death before her husband. The crooked blade of Saladin's cimeter next attracted my notice. I know not by what chance, but so it happened, that the sword of one of our own militia generals was suspended between Don Quixote's lance and the brown blade of Hudibras. My heart throbbed high at the sight of the helmet of Miltiades and the spear that was broken in the breast of Epaminondas. I recognized the shield of Achilles by its resemblance to the admirable cast in the possession of Professor Felton. Nothing in this apartment interested me more than Major Pitcairn's pistol, the discharge of which, at Lexington, began the War of the Revolution, and was reverberated in thunder around the land for seven long years. The bow of Ulysses, though unstrung for ages, was placed against the wall, together with a sheaf of Robin Hood's arrows and the rifle of Daniel Boone.

"Enough of weapons," said I, at length; "although I would gladly have seen the sacred shield which fell from heaven in the time of Numa. And surely you should obtain the sword which Washington unsheathed at Cambridge. But the collection does you much credit. Let us pass on."

In the next alcove we saw the golden thigh of Pythagoras, which had so divine a meaning; and, by one of the queer analogies to which the virtuoso seemed to be addicted, this ancient emblem lay on the same shelf with Peter Stuyvesant's wooden leg, that was fabled to be of silver. Here was a remnant of the Golden Fleece, and a sprig of yellow leaves that resembled the foliage of a frost-bitten elm, but was duly authenticated as a portion of the golden branch by which Æneas gained admittance to the realm of Pluto. Atalanta's golden apple and one of the apples of discord were wrapped in the napkin of gold which Rampsinitus brought from Hades; and the whole were deposited in the golden vase of Bias, with its inscription: "TO THE WISEST."

"And how did you obtain this vase?" said I to the virtuoso.

"It was given me long ago," replied he, with a scornful expression in his eye, "because I had learned to despise all things."

It had not escaped me that, though the virtuoso was evidently a man of high cultivation, yet he seemed to lack sympathy with the spiritual, the sublime, and the tender. Apart from the whim that had led him to devote so much time, pains, and expense to the collection of this museum, he impressed me as one of the hardest and coldest men of the world whom I had ever met.

"To despise all things!" repeated I. "This, at best, is the wisdom of the understanding. It is the creed of a man whose soul, whose better and diviner part, has never been awakened, or has died out of him."

"I did not think that you were still so young," said the virtuoso. "Should you live to my years, you will acknowledge that the vase of Bias was not ill bestowed."

Without further discussion of the point, he directed my attention to other curiosities. I examined Cinderella's little glass slipper, and compared it with one of Diana's sandals, and with Fanny Elssler's shoe, which bore testimony to the muscular character of her illustrious foot. On the same shelf were Thomas the Rhymer's green velvet shoes, and the brazen shoe of Empedocles which was thrown out of Mount Ætna. Anacreon's drinking-cup was placed in apt juxtaposition with one of Tom Moore's wineglasses and Circe's magic bowl. These were symbols of luxury and riot; but near them stood the cup whence Socrates drank his hemlock, and that which Sir Philip Sidney put from his death-parched lips to bestow the draught upon a dying soldier. Next appeared a cluster of tobacco-pipes, consisting of Sir Walter Raleigh's, the earliest on record, Dr. Parr's, Charles Lamb's, and the first calumet of peace which was ever smoked between a European and an Indian. Among other musical instruments, I noticed the lyre of Orpheus and those of Homer and Sappho,

Dr. Franklin's famous whistle, the trumpet of Anthony Van Corlear, and the flute which Goldsmith played upon in his rambles through the French provinces. The staff of Peter the Hermit stood in a corner with that of good old Bishop Jewel, and one of ivory, which had belonged to Papirius, the Roman senator. The ponderous club of Hercules was close at hand. The virtuoso showed me the chisel of Phidias, Claude's palette, and the brush of Apelles, observing that he intended to bestow the former either on Greenough, Crawford, or Powers, and the two latter upon Washington Allston. There was a small vase of oracular gas from Delphos, which I trust will be submitted to the scientific analysis of Professor Silliman. I was deeply moved on beholding a vial of the tears into which Niobe was dissolved; nor less so on learning that a shapeless fragment of salt was a relic of that victim of despondency and sinful regrets—Lot's wife. My companion appeared to set great value upon some Egyptian darkness in a blacking jug. Several of the shelves were covered by a collection of coins, among which, however, I remember none but the Splendid Shilling, celebrated by Phillips, and a dollar's worth of the iron money of Lycurgus, weighing about fifty pounds.

Walking carelessly onward, I had nearly fallen over a huge bundle, like a pedlar's pack, done up in sackcloth and very securely strapped and corded.

"It is Christian's burden of sin," said the virtuoso.

"Oh, pray let us open it!" cried I. "For many a year I have longed to know its contents."

"Look into your own consciousness and memory," replied the virtuoso. "You will there find a list of whatever it contains."

As this was an undeniable truth, I threw a melancholy look at the burden and passed on. A collection of old garments, hanging on pegs, was worthy of some attention, especially the shirt of Nessus, Cæsar's mantle, Joseph's coat of many colors, the Vicar of Bray's cassock, Goldsmith's peach-bloom suit, a pair of President Jefferson's scarlet breeches, John Randolph's red baize hunting shirt, the drab smallclothes of the Stout Gentleman, and the rags of the "man all tattered and torn." George Fox's hat impressed me with deep reverence as a relic of perhaps the truest apostle that has appeared on earth for these eighteen hundred years. My eye was next attracted by an old pair of shears, which I should have taken for a memorial of some famous tailor, only that the virtuoso pledged his veracity that they were the identical scissors of Atropos. He also showed me a broken hour-glass which had been thrown aside by Father Time, together with the old gentleman's gray forelock, tastefully braided into a brooch. In the hour-glass was the handful of sand, the grains of which had numbered the years of the Cumæan sibyl. I think it was in this alcove that I saw the inkstand which Luther threw at the devil, and the ring which Essex, while under sentence of death, sent to Queen Elizabeth. And here was the blood-incrusted pen of steel with which Faust signed away his salvation.

The virtuoso now opened the door of a closet and showed me a lamp burning, while three others stood unlighted by its side. One of the three was the lamp of Diogenes, another that of Guy Fawkes, and the third that which Hero set forth to the midnight breeze in the high tower of Abydos.

"See!" said the virtuoso, blowing with all his force at the lighted lamp.

The flame quivered and shrank away from his breath, but clung to the wick, and resumed its brilliancy as soon as the blast was exhausted.

"It is an undying lamp from the tomb of Charlemagne," observed my guide. "That flame was kindled a thousand years ago."

"How ridiculous to kindle an unnatural light in tombs!" exclaimed I. "We should seek to behold the dead in the light of heaven. But what is the meaning of this chafing-dish of glowing coals?"

"That," answered the virtuoso, "is the original fire which Prometheus stole from heaven. Look steadfastly into it, and you will discern another curiosity."

I gazed into that fire,—which, symbolically, was the origin of all that was bright and glorious in the soul of man,—and in the midst of it, behold, a little reptile, sporting with evident enjoyment of the fervid heat! It was a salamander.

"What a sacrilege!" cried I, with inexpressible disgust. "Can you find no better use for this ethereal fire than to cherish a loathsome reptile in it? Yet there are men who abuse the sacred fire of their own souls to as foul and guilty a purpose."

The virtuoso made no answer except by a dry laugh and an assurance that the salamander was the very same which Benvenuto Cellini had seen in his father's household fire. He then proceeded to show me other rarities; for this closet appeared to be the receptacle of what he considered most valuable in his collection.

"There," said he, "is the Great Carbuncle of the White Mountains."

I gazed with no little interest at this mighty gem, which it had been one of the wild projects of my youth to discover. Possibly it might have looked brighter to me in those days than now; at all events, it had not such brilliancy as to detain me long from the other articles of the museum. The virtuoso pointed out to me a crystalline stone which hung by a gold chain against the wall.

"That is the philosopher's stone," said he.

"And have you the elixir vitæ which generally accompanies it?" inquired I.

"Even so; this urn is filled with it," he replied. "A draught would refresh you. Here is Hebe's cup; will you quaff a health from it?"

My heart thrilled within me at the idea of such a reviving draught; for methought I had great need of it after travelling so far on the dusty road of life. But I know not whether it were a peculiar glance in the virtuoso's eye, or the circumstance that this most precious liquid was contained in an antique sepulchral urn, that made me pause. Then came many a thought with which, in the calmer and better hours of life, I had strengthened myself to feel that Death is the very friend whom, in his due season, even the happiest mortal should be willing to embrace.

"No; I desire not an earthly immortality," said I. "Were man to live longer on the earth, the spiritual would die out of him. The spark of ethereal fire would be choked by the material, the sensual. There is a celestial something within us that requires, after a certain time, the atmosphere of heaven to preserve it from decay and ruin. I will have none of this liquid. You do well to keep it in a sepulchral urn; for it would produce death while bestowing the shadow of life."

"All this is unintelligible to me," responded my guide, with indifference. "Life—earthly life—is the only good. But you refuse the draught? Well, it is not likely to be offered twice within one man's experience. Probably you have griefs which you seek to forget in death. I can enable you to forget them in life. Will you take a draught of Lethe?"

As he spoke, the virtuoso took from the shelf a crystal vase containing a sable liquor, which caught no reflected image from the objects around.

"Not for the world!" exclaimed I, shrinking back. "I can spare none of my recollections, not even those of error or sorrow. They are all alike the food of my spirit. As well never to have lived as to lose them now."

Without further parley we passed to the next alcove, the shelves of which were burdened with ancient volumes and with those rolls of papyrus in which was treasured up the eldest wisdom of the earth. Perhaps the most valuable work in the collection, to a bibliomaniac, was the Book of Hermes. For my part, however, I would have given a higher price for those six of the Sibyl's books which Tarquin refused to purchase, and which, the virtuoso informed me, he had himself found in the cave of Trophonius. Doubtless these old volumes contain prophecies of the fate of Rome, both as respects the decline and fall of her temporal empire and the rise of her spiritual one. Not without value, likewise, was the work of Anaxagoras on Nature, hitherto supposed to be irrecoverably lost, and the missing treatises of Longinus, by which modern criticism might profit, and those books of Livy for which the classic student has so long sorrowed without hope. Among these precious tomes I observed the original manuscript of the Koran, and also that of the Mormon Bible in Joe Smith's authentic autograph. Alexander's copy of the Iliad was also there, enclosed in the jewelled casket of Darius, still fragrant of the perfumes which the Persian kept in it.

Opening an iron-clasped volume, bound in black leather, I discovered it to be Cornelius Agrippa's book of magic; and it was rendered still more interesting by the fact that many flowers, ancient and modern, were pressed between its leaves. Here was a rose from Eve's bridal bower, and all those red and white roses which were plucked in the garden of the Temple by the partisans of York and Lancaster. Here was Halleck's Wild Rose of Alloway. Cowper had contributed a Sensitive Plant, and Wordsworth an Eglantine, and Burns a Mountain Daisy, and Kirke White a Star of Bethlehem, and Longfellow a Sprig of Fennel, with its yellow flowers. James Russell Lowell had given a Pressed Flower, but fragrant still, which had been shadowed in the Rhine. There was also a sprig from Southey's Holly-Tree. One of the most beautiful specimens was a Fringed Gentian, which had been plucked and preserved for immortality by Bryant. From Jones Very, a poet whose voice is scarcely heard among us by reason of its depth, there was a Wind Flower and a Columbine.

As I closed Cornelius Agrippa's magic volume, an old, mildewed letter fell upon the floor. It proved to be an autograph from the Flying Dutchman to his wife. I could linger no longer among books; for the afternoon was waning, and there was yet much to see. The bare mention of a few more curiosities must suffice. The immense skull of Polyphemus was recognizable by the cavernous hollow in the centre of the forehead where once had blazed the giant's single eye. The tub of Diogenes, Medea's caldron, and Psyche's vase of beauty were placed one within another. Pandora's box, without the lid, stood next, containing nothing but the girdle of Venus, which had been carelessly flung into it. A bundle of birch rods which had been used by Shenstone's schoolmistress were tied up with the Countess of Salisbury's garter. I knew not which to value most, a roc's egg as big as an ordinary hogshead, or the shell of the egg which Columbus set upon its end. Perhaps the most delicate article in the whole museum was Queen Mab's chariot, which to guard it from the touch of meddlesome fingers, was placed under a glass tumbler.

Several of the shelves were occupied by specimens of entomology. Feeling but little interest in the science I noticed only Anacreon's grasshopper, and a humble bee which had been presented to the virtuoso by Ralph Waldo Emerson.

In the part of the hall which we had now reached I observed a curtain that descended from the ceiling to the floor in voluminous folds, of a depth, richness, and magnificence which I had never seen equalled. It was not to be doubted that this splendid though dark and solemn veil concealed a portion of the museum even richer in wonders than that through which I had already passed; but, on my attempting to grasp the edge of the curtain and draw it aside, it proved to be an illusive picture.

"You need not blush," remarked the virtuoso; "for that same curtain deceived Zeuxis. It is the celebrated painting of Parrhasius."

In a range with the curtain there were a number of other choice pictures by artists of ancient days. Here was the famous cluster of grapes by Zeuxis, so admirably depicted that it seemed as if the ripe juice were bursting forth. As to the picture of the old woman by the same illustrious painter, and which was so ludicrous that he himself died with laughing at it, I cannot say that it particularly moved my risibility. Ancient humor seems to have little power over modern muscles. Here, also, was the horse painted by Apelles which living horses neighed at; his first portrait of Alexander the Great, and his last unfinished picture of Venus asleep. Each of these works of art, together with others by Parrhasius, Timanthes, Polygnotus, Apollodorus, Pausias, and Pamphilus, required more time and study than I could bestow for the adequate perception of their merits. I shall therefore leave them undescribed and uncriticised, nor attempt to settle the question of superiority between ancient and modern art.

For the same reason I shall pass lightly over the specimens of antique sculpture which this indefatigable and fortunate virtuoso had dug out of the dust of fallen empires. Here was Ætion's cedar statue of Æsculapius, much decayed, and Alcon's iron statue of Hercules, lamentably rusted. Here was the statue of Victory, six feet high, which the Jupiter Olympus of Phidias had held in his hand. Here was a forefinger of the Colossus of Rhodes, seven feet in length. Here was the Venus Urania of Phidias, and other images of male and female beauty or grandeur, wrought by sculptors who appear never to have debased their souls by the sight of any meaner forms than those of gods or godlike mortals. But the deep simplicity of these great works was not to be comprehended by a mind excited and disturbed, as mine was, by the various objects that had recently been presented to it. I therefore turned away with merely a passing glance, resolving on some future occasion to brood over each individual statue and picture until my inmost spirit should feel their excellence. In this department, again, I noticed the tendency to whimsical combinations and ludicrous analogies which seemed to influence many of the arrangements of the museum. The wooden statue so well known as the Palladium of Troy was placed in close apposition with the wooden head of General Jackson which was stolen a few years since from the bows of the frigate Constitution.

We had now completed the circuit of the spacious hall, and found ourselves again near the door. Feeling somewhat wearied with the survey of so many novelties and antiquities, I sat down upon Cowper's sofa, while the virtuoso threw himself carelessly into Rabelais' easy chair. Casting my eyes upon the opposite wall, I was surprised to perceive the shadow of a man flickering unsteadily across the wainscot, and looking as if it were stirred by some breath of air that found its way through the door or windows. No substantial figure was visible from which this shadow might be thrown; nor, had there been such, was there any sunshine that would have caused it to darken upon the wall.

"It is Peter Schlemihl's shadow," observed the virtuoso, "and one of the most valuable articles in my collection."

"Methinks a shadow would have made a fitting door-keeper to such a museum," said I; "although, indeed, yonder figure has something strange and fantastic about him, which suits well enough with many of the impressions which I have received here. Pray, who is he?"

While speaking, I gazed more scrutinizingly than before at the antiquated presence of the person who had admitted me, and who still sat on his bench with the same restless aspect, and dim, confused questioning anxiety that I had noticed on my first entrance. At this moment he looked eagerly towards us, and, half starting from his seat, addressed me.

"I beseech you, kind sir," said he, in a cracked, melancholy tone, "have pity on the most unfortunate man in the world. For Heaven's sake, answer me a single question! Is this the town of Boston?"

"You have recognized him now," said the virtuoso. "It is Peter Rugg, the missing man. I chanced to meet him the other day still in search of Boston, and conducted him hither; and, as he could not succeed in finding his friends, I have taken him into my service as door-keeper. He is somewhat too apt to ramble, but otherwise a man of trust and integrity."

"And might I venture to ask," continued I, "to whom am I indebted for this afternoon's gratification?"

The virtuoso, before replying, laid his hand upon an antique dart, or javelin, the rusty steel head of which seemed to have been blunted, as if it had encountered the resistance of a tempered shield, or breastplate.

"My name has not been without its distinction in the world for a longer period than that of any other man alive," answered he. "Yet many doubt of my existence; perhaps you will do so to-morrow. This dart which I hold in my hand was once grim Death's own weapon. It served him well for the space of four thousand years; but it fell blunted, as you see, when he directed it against my breast."

These words were spoken with the calm and cold courtesy of manner that had characterized this singular personage throughout our interview. I fancied, it is true, that there was a bitterness indefinably mingled with his tone, as of one cut off from natural sympathies and blasted with a doom that had been inflicted on no other human being, and by the results of which he had ceased to be human. Yet, withal, it seemed one of the most terrible consequences of that doom that the victim no longer regarded it as a calamity, but had finally accepted it as the greatest good that could have befallen him.

"You are the Wandering Jew!" exclaimed I.

The virtuoso bowed without emotion of any kind; for, by centuries of custom, he had almost lost the sense of strangeness in his fate, and was but imperfectly conscious of the astonishment and awe with which it affected such as are capable of death.

"Your doom is indeed a fearful one!" said I, with irrepressible feeling and a frankness that afterwards startled me; "yet perhaps the ethereal spirit is not entirely extinct under all this corrupted or frozen mass of earthly life. Perhaps the immortal spark may yet be rekindled by a breath of Heaven. Perhaps you may yet be permitted to die before it is too late to live eternally. You have my prayers for such a consummation. Farewell."

"Your prayers will be in vain," replied he, with a smile of cold triumph. "My destiny is linked with the realities of earth. You are welcome to your visions and shadows of a future state; but give me what I can see, and touch, and understand, and I ask no more."

"It is indeed too late," thought I. "The soul is dead within him."

Struggling between pity and horror, I extended my hand, to which the virtuoso gave his own, still with the habitual courtesy of a man of the world, but without a single heart throb of human brotherhood. The touch seemed like ice, yet I know not whether morally or physically. As I departed, he bade me observe that the inner door of the hall was constructed with the ivory leaves of the gateway through which Æneas and the Sibyl had been dismissed from Hades.

FROM

The Snow-Image And Other Twice-Told Tales

THE SNOW IMAGE: A CHILDISH MIRACLE

One afternoon of a cold winter's day, when the sun shone forth with chilly brightness, after a long storm, two children asked leave of their mother to run out and play in the new-fallen snow. The elder child was a little girl, whom, because she was of a tender and modest disposition, and was thought to be very beautiful, her parents, and other people who were familiar with her, used to call Violet. But her brother was known by the style and title of Peony, on account of the ruddiness of his broad and round little phiz, which made everybody think of sunshine and great scarlet flowers. The father of these two children, a certain Mr. Lindsey, it is important to say, was an excellent but exceedingly matter-of-fact sort of man, a dealer in hardware, and was sturdily accustomed to take what is called the common-sense view of all matters that came under his consideration. With a heart about as tender as other people's, he had a head as hard and impenetrable, and therefore, perhaps, as empty, as one of the iron pots which it was a part of his business to sell. The mother's character, on the other hand, had a strain of poetry in it, a trait of unworldly beauty,—a delicate and dewy flower, as it were, that had survived out of her imaginative youth, and still kept itself alive amid the dusty realities of matrimony and motherhood.

So, Violet and Peony, as I began with saying, besought their mother to let them run out and play in the new snow; for, though it had looked so dreary and dismal, drifting downward out of the gray sky, it had a very cheerful aspect, now that the sun was shining on it. The children dwelt in a city, and had no wider play-place than a little garden before the house, divided by a white fence from the street, and with a pear-tree and two or three plum-trees overshadowing it, and some rose-bushes just in front of the parlor-windows. The trees and shrubs, however, were now leafless, and their twigs were enveloped in the light snow, which thus made a kind of wintry foliage, with here and there a pendent icicle for the fruit.

"Yes, Violet,—yes, my little Peony," said their kind mother, "you may go out and play in the new snow."

Accordingly, the good lady bundled up her darlings in woollen jackets and wadded sacks, and put comforters round their necks, and a pair of striped gaiters on each little pair of legs, and worsted mittens on their hands, and gave them a kiss apiece, by way of a spell to keep away Jack Frost. Forth sallied the two children, with a hop-skip-and-jump, that carried them at once into the very heart of a huge snow-drift, whence Violet emerged like a snow-bunting, while little Peony floundered out with his round face in full bloom. Then what a merry time had they! To look at them, frolicking in the wintry garden, you would have thought that the dark and pitiless storm had been sent for no other purpose but to provide a new plaything for Violet and Peony; and that they themselves had been created, as the snow-birds were, to take delight only in the tempest, and in the white mantle which it spread over the earth.

At last, when they had frosted one another all over with handfuls of snow, Violet, after laughing heartily at little Peony's figure, was struck with a new idea.

"You look exactly like a snow-image, Peony," said she, "if your cheeks were not so red. And that puts me in mind! Let us make an image out of snow,—an image of a little girl,—and it shall be our sister, and shall run about and play with us all winter long. Won't it be nice?"

"Oh yes!" cried Peony, as plainly as he could speak, for he was but a little boy. "That will be nice! And mamma shall see it!"

"Yes," answered Violet; "mamma shall see the new little girl. But she must not make her come into the warm parlor; for, you know, our little snow-sister will not love the warmth."

And forthwith the children began this great business of making a snow-image that should run about; while their mother, who was sitting at the window and overheard some of their talk, could not help smiling at the gravity with which they set about it. They really seemed to imagine that there would be no difficulty whatever in creating a live little girl out of the snow. And, to say the truth, if miracles are ever to be wrought, it will be by putting our hands to the work in precisely such a simple and undoubting frame of mind as that in which Violet and Peony now undertook to perform one, without so much as knowing that it was a miracle. So thought the mother; and thought, likewise, that the new snow, just fallen from heaven, would be excellent material to make new beings of, if it were not so very cold. She gazed at the children a moment longer, delighting to watch their little figures,—the girl, tall for her age, graceful and agile, and so delicately colored that she looked like a cheerful thought more than a physical reality; while Peony expanded in breadth rather than height, and rolled along on his short and sturdy legs as substantial as an elephant, though not quite so big. Then the mother resumed her work. What it was I forget; but she was either trimming a silken bonnet for Violet, or darning a pair of stockings for little Peony's short legs. Again, however, and again, and yet other agains, she could not help turning her head to the window to see how the children got on with their snow-image.

Indeed, it was an exceedingly pleasant sight, those bright little souls at their task! Moreover, it was really wonderful to observe how knowingly and skilfully they managed the matter. Violet assumed the chief direction, and told Peony what to do, while, with her own delicate fingers, she shaped out all the nicer parts of the snow-figure. It seemed, in fact, not so much to be made by the children, as to grow up under their hands, while they were playing and prattling about it. Their mother was quite surprised at this; and the longer she looked, the more and more surprised she grew.

"What remarkable children mine are!" thought she, smiling with a mother's pride; and, smiling at herself, too, for being so proud of them. "What other children could have made anything so like a little girl's figure out of snow at the first trial? Well; but now I must finish Peony's new frock, for his grandfather is coming to-morrow, and I want the little fellow to look handsome."

So she took up the frock, and was soon as busily at work again with her needle as the two children with their snow-image. But still, as the needle travelled hither and thither through the seams of the dress, the mother made her toil light and happy by listening to the airy voices of Violet and Peony.

They kept talking to one another all the time, their tongues being quite as active as their feet and hands. Except at intervals, she could not distinctly hear what was said, but had merely a sweet impression that they were in a most loving mood, and were enjoying themselves highly, and that the business of making the snow-image went prosperously on. Now and then, however, when Violet and Peony happened to raise their voices, the words were as audible as if they had been spoken in the very parlor where the mother sat. Oh how delightfully those words echoed in her heart, even though they meant nothing so very wise or wonderful, after all!

But you must know a mother listens with her heart much more than with her ears; and thus she is often delighted with the trills of celestial music, when other people can hear nothing of the kind.

"Peony, Peony!" cried Violet to her brother, who had gone to another part of the garden, "bring me some of that fresh snow, Peony, from the very farthest corner, where we have not been trampling. I want it to shape our little snow-sister's bosom with. You know that part must be quite pure, just as it came out of the sky!"

"Here it is, Violet!" answered Peony, in his bluff tone,—but a very sweet tone, too,—as he came floundering through the half-trodden drifts. "Here is the snow for her little bosom. O Violet, how beau-ti-ful she begins to look!"

"Yes," said Violet, thoughtfully and quietly; "our snow-sister does look very lovely. I did not quite know, Peony, that we could make such a sweet little girl as this."

The mother, as she listened, thought how fit and delightful an incident it would be, if fairies, or still better, if angel-children were to come from paradise, and play invisibly with her own darlings, and help them to make their snow-image, giving it the features of celestial babyhood! Violet and Peony would not be aware of their immortal playmates,—only they would see that the image grew very beautiful while they worked at it, and would think that they themselves had done it all.

"My little girl and boy deserve such playmates, if mortal children ever did!" said the mother to herself; and then she smiled again at her own motherly pride.

Nevertheless, the idea seized upon her imagination; and, ever and anon, she took a glimpse out of the window, half dreaming that she might see the golden-haired children of paradise sporting with her own golden-haired Violet and bright-cheeked Peony.

Now, for a few moments, there was a busy and earnest, but indistinct hum of the two children's voices, as Violet and Peony wrought together with one happy consent. Violet still seemed to be the guiding spirit, while Peony acted rather as a laborer, and brought her the snow from far and near. And yet the little urchin evidently had a proper understanding of the matter, too!

"Peony, Peony!" cried Violet; for her brother was again at the other side of the garden. "Bring me those light wreaths of snow that have rested on the lower branches of the pear-tree. You can clamber on the snow-drift, Peony, and reach them easily. I must have them to make some ringlets for our snow-sister's head!"

"Here they are, Violet!" answered the little boy. "Take care you do not break them. Well done! Well done! How pretty!"

"Does she not look sweetly?" said Violet, with a very satisfied tone; "and now we must have some little shining bits of ice, to make the brightness of her eyes. She is not finished yet. Mamma will see how very beautiful she is; but papa will say, 'Tush! nonsense!—come in out of the cold!' "

"Let us call mamma to look out," said Peony; and then he shouted lustily, "Mamma! mamma!! mamma!!! Look out, and see what a nice 'ittle girl we are making!"

The mother put down her work for an instant, and looked out of the window. But it so happened that the sun—for this was one of the shortest days of the whole year—had sunken so nearly to the edge of the world that his setting shine came obliquely into the lady's eyes. So she was dazzled, you must understand, and could not very distinctly observe what was in the garden. Still, however, through all that bright, blinding dazzle of the sun and the new snow, she beheld a small white figure in the garden, that seemed to have a wonderful deal of human likeness about it. And she saw Violet and Peony,—indeed, she looked more at them than at the image,—she saw the two children still at work; Peony bringing fresh snow, and Violet applying it to the figure as scientifically as a sculptor adds clay to his model. Indistinctly as she discerned the snow-child, the mother thought to herself that never before was there a snow-figure so cunningly made, nor ever such a dear little girl and boy to make it.

"They do everything better than other children," said she, very complacently. "No wonder they make better snow-images!"

She sat down again to her work, and made as much haste with it as possible; because twilight would soon come, and Peony's frock was not yet finished, and grandfather was expected, by railroad, pretty early in the morning. Faster and faster, therefore, went her flying fingers. The children, likewise, kept busily at work in the garden, and still the mother listened, whenever she could catch a word. She was amused to observe how their little imaginations had got mixed up with what they were doing, and carried away by it. They seemed positively to think that the snow-child would run about and play with them.

"What a nice playmate she will be for us, all winter long!" said Violet. "I hope papa will not be afraid of her giving us a cold! Sha'n't you love her dearly, Peony?"

"Oh yes!" cried Peony. "And I will hug her, and she shall sit down close by me, and drink some of my warm milk!"

"Oh no, Peony!" answered Violet, with grave wisdom. "That will not do at all. Warm milk will not be wholesome for our little snow-sister. Little snow-people, like her, eat nothing but icicles. No, no, Peony; we must not give her anything warm to drink!"

There was a minute or two of silence; for Peony, whose short legs were never weary, had gone on a pilgrimage again to the other side of the garden. All of a sudden, Violet cried out, loudly and joyfully,—

"Look here, Peony! Come quickly! A light has been shining on her cheek out of that rose-colored cloud! and the color does not go away! Is not that beautiful!"

"Yes; it is beau-ti-ful," answered Peony, prounouncing the three syllables with deliberate accuracy. "O Violet, only look at her hair! It is all like gold!"

"Oh certainly," said Violet, with tranquillity, as if it were very much a matter of course. "That color, you know, comes from the golden clouds, that we see up there in the sky. She is almost finished now. But her lips must be made very red,—redder than her cheeks. Perhaps, Peony, it will make them red if we both kiss them!"

Accordingly, the mother heard two smart little smacks, as if both her children were kissing the snow-image on its frozen mouth. But, as this did not seem to make the lips quite red enough, Violet next proposed that the snow-child should be invited to kiss Peony's scarlet cheek.

"Come, 'ittle snow-sister, kiss me!" cried Peony.

"There! she has kissed you," added Violet, "and now her lips are very red. And she blushed a little, too!"

"Oh, what a cold kiss!" cried Peony.

Just then, there came a breeze of the pure west-wind, sweeping through the garden and rattling the parlor-windows. It sounded so wintry cold, that the mother was about to tap on the window-pane with her thimbled finger, to summon the two children in, when they both cried out to her with one voice. The tone was not a tone of surprise, although they were evidently a good deal excited; it appeared rather as if they were very much rejoiced at some event that had now happened, but which they had been looking for, and had reckoned upon all along.

"Mamma! mamma! We have finished our little snow-sister, and she is running about the garden with us!"

"What imaginative little beings my children are!" thought the mother, putting the last few stitches into Peony's frock. "And it is strange, too, that they make me almost as much a child as they themselves are! I can hardly help believing, now, that the snow-image has really come to life!"

"Dear mamma!" cried Violet, "pray look out and see what a sweet playmate we have!"

The mother, being thus entreated, could no longer delay to look forth from the window. The sun was now gone out of the sky, leaving, however, a rich inheritance of his brightness among those purple and golden clouds which make the sunsets of winter so magnificent. But there was not the slightest gleam or dazzle, either on the window or on the snow; so that the good lady could look all over the garden, and see everything and everybody in it. And what do you think she saw there? Violet and Peony, of course, her own two darling children. Ah, but whom or what did she see besides? Why, if you will believe me, there was a small figure of a girl, dressed all in white, with rose-tinged cheeks and ringlets of golden hue, playing about the garden with the two children! A stranger though she was, the child seemed to be on as familiar terms with Violet and Peony, and they with her, as if all the three had been playmates during the whole of their little lives. The mother thought to herself that it must certainly be the daughter of one of the neighbors, and that, seeing Violet and Peony in the garden, the child had run across the street to play with them. So this kind lady went to the door, intending to invite the little runaway into her comfortable parlor; for, now that the sunshine was withdrawn, the atmosphere, out of doors, was already growing very cold.

But, after opening the house-door, she stood an instant on the threshold, hesitating whether she ought to ask the child to come in, or whether she should even speak to her. Indeed, she almost doubted whether it were a real child after all, or only a light wreath of the new-fallen snow, blown hither and thither about the garden by the intensely cold west-wind. There was certainly something very singular in the aspect of the little stranger. Among all the children of the neighborhood, the lady could remember no such face, with its pure white, and delicate rose-color, and the golden ringlets tossing about the forehead and cheeks. And as for her dress, which was entirely of white, and fluttering in the breeze, it was such as no reasonable woman would put upon a little girl, when sending her out to play, in the depth of winter. It made this kind and careful mother shiver only to look at those small feet, with nothing in the world on them, except a very thin pair of white slippers. Nevertheless, airily as she was clad, the child seemed to feel not the slightest inconvenience from the cold, but danced so lightly over the snow that the tips of her toes left hardly a print in its surface; while Violet could but just keep pace with her, and Peony's short legs compelled him to lag behind.

Once, in the course of their play, the strange child placed herself between Violet and Peony, and taking a hand of each, skipped merrily forward, and they along with her. Almost immediately, however, Peony pulled away his little fist, and began to rub it as if the fingers were tingling with cold; while Violet also released herself, though with less abruptness, gravely remarking that it was better not to take hold of hands. The white-robed damsel said not a word, but danced about, just as merrily as before. If Violet and Peony did not choose to play with her, she could make just as good a playmate of the brisk and cold west-wind, which kept blowing her all about the garden, and took such liberties with her, that they seemed to have been friends for a long time. All this while, the mother stood on the threshold, wondering how a little girl could look so much like a flying snow-drift, or how a snow-drift could look so very like a little girl.

She called Violet, and whispered to her.

"Violet my darling, what is this child's name?" asked she. "Does she live near us?"

"Why, dearest mamma," answered Violet, laughing to think that her mother did not comprehend so very plain an affair, "this is our little snow-sister whom we have just been making!"

"Yes, dear mamma," cried Peony, running to his mother, and looking up simply into her face. "This is our snow-image! Is it not a nice 'ittle child?"

At this instant a flock of snow-birds came flitting through the air. As was very natural, they avoided Violet and Peony. But—and this looked strange—they flew at once to the white-robed child, fluttered eagerly about her head, alighted on her shoulders, and seemed to claim her as an old acquaintance. She, on her part, was evidently as glad to see these little birds, old Winter's grandchildren, as they were to see her, and welcomed them by holding out both her hands. Hereupon, they each and all tried to alight on her two palms and ten small fingers and thumbs, crowding one another off, with an immense fluttering of their tiny wings. One dear little bird nestled tenderly in her bosom; another put its bill to her lips. They were as joyous, all the while, and seemed as much in their element, as you may have seen them when sporting with a snow-storm.

Violet and Peony stood laughing at this pretty sight; for they enjoyed the merry time which their new playmate was having with these small-winged visitants, almost as much as if they themselves took part in it.

"Violet," said her mother, greatly perplexed, "tell me the truth, without any jest. Who is this little girl?"

"My darling mamma," answered Violet, looking seriously into her mother's face, and apparently surprised that she should need any further explanation, "I have told you truly who she is. It is our little snow-image, which Peony and I have been making. Peony will tell you so, as well as I."

"Yes, mamma," asseverated Peony, with much gravity in his crimson little phiz; "this is 'ittle snow-child. Is not she a nice one? But, mamma, her hand is, oh, so very cold!"

While mamma still hesitated what to think and what to do, the street-gate was thrown open, and the father of Violet and Peony appeared, wrapped in a pilot-cloth sack, with a fur cap drawn down over his ears, and the thickest of gloves upon his hands. Mr. Lindsey was a middle-aged man, with a weary and yet a happy look in his wind-flushed and frost-pinched face, as if he had been busy all the day long, and was glad to get back to his quiet home. His eyes brightened at the sight of his wife and children, although he could not help uttering a word or two of surprise, at finding the whole family in the open air, on so bleak a day, and after sunset too. He soon perceived the little white stranger sporting to and fro in the garden, like a dancing snow-wreath, and the flock of snow-birds fluttering about her head.

"Pray, what little girl may that be?" inquired this very sensible man. "Surely her mother must be crazy to let her go out in such bitter weather as it has been to-day, with only that flimsy white gown and those thin slippers!"

"My dear husband," said his wife, "I know no more about the little thing than you do. Some neighbor's child, I suppose. Our Violet and Peony," she added, laughing at herself for repeating so absurd a story, "insist that she is nothing but a snow-image, which they have been busy about in the garden, almost all the afternoon."

As she said this, the mother glanced her eyes toward the spot where the children's snow-image had been made. What was her surprise, on perceiving that there was not the slightest trace of so much labor!—no image at all!—no piled up heap of snow!—nothing whatever, save the prints of little footsteps around a vacant space!

"This is very strange!" said she.

"What is strange, dear mother?" asked Violet. "Dear father, do not you see how it is? This is our snow-image, which Peony and I have made, because we wanted another playmate. Did not we, Peony?"

"Yes, papa," said crimson Peony. "This be our 'ittle snow-sister. Is she not beau-ti-ful? But she gave me such a cold kiss!"

"Poh, nonsense, children!" cried their good, honest father, who, as we have already intimated, had an exceedingly common-sensible way of looking at matters. "Do not tell me of making live figures out of snow. Come, wife; this little stranger must not stay out in the bleak air a moment longer. We will bring her into the parlor; and you shall give her a supper of warm bread and milk, and make her as comfortable as you can. Meanwhile, I will inquire among the neighbors; or, if necessary, send the city-crier about the streets, to give notice of a lost child."

So saying, this honest and very kind-hearted man was going toward the little white damsel, with the best intentions in the world. But Violet and Peony, each seizing their father by the hand, earnestly besought him not to make her come in.

"Dear father," cried Violet, putting herself before him, "it is true what I have been telling you! This is our little snow-girl, and she cannot live any longer than while she breathes the cold west-wind. Do not make her come into the hot room!"

"Yes, father," shouted Peony, stamping his little foot, so mightily was he in earnest, "this be nothing but our 'ittle snow-child! She will not love the hot fire!"

"Nonsense, children, nonsense, nonsense!" cried the father, half vexed, half laughing at what he considered their foolish obstinacy. "Run into the house, this moment! It is too late to play any longer, now. I must take care of this little girl immediately, or she will catch her death-a-cold!"

"Husband! dear husband!" said his wife, in a low voice,—for she had been looking narrowly at the snow-child, and was more perplexed than ever,—"there is something very singular in all this. You will think me foolish,—but—but—may it not be that some invisible angel has been attracted by the simplicity and good faith with which our children set about their undertaking? May he not have spent an hour of his immortality in playing with those dear little souls? and so the result is what we call a miracle. No, no! Do not laugh at me; I see what a foolish thought it is!"

"My dear wife," replied the husband, laughing heartily, "you are as much a child as Violet and Peony."

And in one sense so she was, for all through life she had kept her heart full of childlike simplicity and faith, which was as pure and clear as crystal; and, looking at all matters through this transparent medium, she sometimes saw truths so profound that other people laughed at them as nonsense and absurdity.

But now kind Mr. Lindsey had entered the garden, breaking away from his two children, who still sent their shrill voices after him, beseeching him to let the snow-child stay and enjoy herself in the cold west-wind. As he approached, the snow-birds took to flight. The little white damsel, also, fled backward, shaking her head, as if to say, "Pray, do not touch me!" and roguishly, as it appeared, leading him through the deepest of the snow. Once, the good man stumbled, and floundered down upon his face, so that, gathering himself up again, with the snow sticking to his rough pilot-cloth sack, he looked as white and wintry as a snow-image of the largest size. Some of the neighbors, meanwhile, seeing him from their windows, wondered what could possess poor Mr. Lindsey to be running about his garden in pursuit of a snow-drift, which the west-wind was driving hither and thither! At length, after a vast deal of trouble, he chased the little stranger into a corner, where she could not possibly escape him. His wife had been looking on, and, it being nearly twilight, was wonder-struck to observe how the snow-child gleamed and sparkled, and how she seemed to shed a glow all round about her; and when driven into the corner, she positively glistened like a star! It was a frosty kind of brightness, too, like that of an icicle in the moonlight. The wife thought it strange that good Mr. Lindsey should see nothing remarkable in the snow-child's appearance.

"Come, you odd little thing!" cried the honest man, seizing her by the hand, "I have caught you at last, and will make you comfortable in spite of yourself. We will put a nice warm pair of worsted stockings on your frozen little feet, and you shall have a good thick shawl to wrap yourself in. Your poor white nose, I am afraid, is actually frost-bitten. But we will make it all right. Come along in."

And so, with a most benevolent smile on his sagacious visage, all purple as it was with the cold, this very well-meaning gentleman took the snow-child by the hand and led her towards the house. She followed him, droopingly and reluctant; for all the glow and sparkle was gone out of her figure; and whereas just before she had resembled a bright, frosty, star-gemmed evening, with a crimson gleam on the cold horizon, she now looked as dull and languid as a thaw. As kind Mr. Lindsey led her up the steps of the door, Violet and Peony looked into his face,—their eyes full of tears, which froze before they could run down their cheeks,—and again entreated him not to bring their snow-image into the house.

"Not bring her in!" exclaimed the kind-hearted man. "Why, you are crazy, my little Violet!—quite crazy, my small Peony! She is so cold, already, that her hand has almost frozen mine, in spite of my thick gloves. Would you have her freeze to death?"

His wife, as he came up the steps, had been taking another long, earnest, almost awe-stricken gaze at the little white stranger. She hardly knew whether it was a dream or no; but she could not help fancying that she saw the delicate print of Violet's fingers on the child's neck. It looked just as if while Violet was shaping out the image, she had given it a gentle pat with her hand, and had neglected to smooth the impression quite away.

"After all, husband," said the mother, recurring to her idea that the angels would be as much delighted to play with Violet and Peony as she herself was,—"after all, she does look strangely like a snow-image! I do believe she is made of snow!"

A puff of the west-wind blew against the snow-child, and again she sparkled like a star.

"Snow!" repeated good Mr. Lindsey, drawing the reluctant guest over his hospitable threshold. "No wonder she looks like snow. She is half frozen, poor little thing! But a good fire will put everything to rights!"

Without further talk, and always with the same best intentions, this highly benevolent and common-sensible individual led the little white damsel—drooping, drooping, drooping, more and more—out of the frosty air, and into his comfortable parlor. A Heidenberg stove, filled to the brim with intensely burning anthracite, was sending a bright gleam through the isinglass of its iron door, and causing the vase of water on its top to fume and bubble with excitement. A warm, sultry smell was diffused throughout the room. A thermometer on the wall farthest from the stove stood at eighty degrees. The parlor was hung with red curtains, and covered with a red carpet, and looked just as warm as it felt. The difference betwixt the atmosphere here and the cold, wintry twilight out of doors, was like stepping at once from Nova Zembla to the hottest part of India, or from the North Pole into an oven. Oh, this was a fine place for the little white stranger!

The common-sensible man placed the snow-child on the hearth-rug, right in front of the hissing and fuming stove.

"Now she will be comfortable!" cried Mr. Lindsey, rubbing his hands and looking about him, with the pleasantest smile you ever saw. "Make yourself at home, my child."

Sad, sad and drooping, looked the little white maiden, as she stood on the hearth-rug, with the hot blast of the stove striking through her like a pestilence. Once, she threw a glance wistfully toward the windows, and caught a glimpse, through its red curtains, of the snow-covered roofs, and the stars glimmering frostily, and all the delicious intensity of the cold night. The bleak wind rattled the window-panes, as if it were summoning her to come forth. But there stood the snow-child, drooping, before the hot stove!

But the common-sensible man saw nothing amiss.

"Come wife," said he, "let her have a pair of thick stockings and a woollen shawl or blanket directly; and tell Dora to give her some warm supper as soon as the milk boils. You, Violet and Peony, amuse your little friend. She is out of spirits, you see, at finding herself in a strange place. For my part, I will go around among the neighbors, and find out where she belongs."

The mother, meanwhile, had gone in search of the shawl and stockings; for her own view of the matter, however subtle and delicate, had given way, as it always did, to the stubborn materialism of her husband. Without heeding the remonstrances of his two children, who still kept murmuring that their little snow-sister did not love the warmth, good Mr. Lindsey took his departure, shutting the parlor-door carefully behind him. Turning up the collar of his sack over his ears, he emerged from the house, and had barely reached the street-gate, when he was recalled by the screams of Violet and Peony, and the rapping of a thimbled finger against the parlor window.

"Husband! husband!" cried his wife, showing her horror-stricken face through the window-panes. "There is no need of going for the child's parents!"

"We told you so, father!" screamed Violet and Peony, as he re-entered the parlor. "You would bring her in; and now our poor—dear—beau-ti-ful little snow-sister is thawed!"

And their own sweet little faces were already dissolved in tears; so that their father, seeing what strange things occasionally happen in this every-day world, felt not a little anxious lest his children might be going to thaw too! In the utmost perplexity, he demanded an explanation of his wife. She could only reply, that, being summoned to the parlor by the cries of Violet and Peony, she found no trace of the little white maiden, unless it were the remains of a heap of snow, which, while she was gazing at it, melted quite away upon the hearth-rug.

"And there you see all that is left of it!" added she, pointing to a pool of water in front of the stove.

"Yes, father," said Violet looking reproachfully at him, through her tears, "there is all that is left of our dear little snow-sister!"

"Naughty father!" cried Peony, stamping his foot, and—I shudder to say—shaking his little fist at the common-sensible man. "We told you how it would be! What for did you bring her in?"

And the Heidenberg stove, through the isinglass of its door, seemed to glare at good Mr. Lindsey, like a red-eyed demon, triumphing in the mischief which it had done!

This, you will observe, was one of those rare cases, which yet will occasionally happen, where common-sense finds itself at fault. The remarkable story of the snow-image, though to that sagacious class of people to whom good Mr. Lindsey belongs it may seem but a childish affair, is, nevertheless, capable of being moralized in various methods, greatly for their edification. One of its lessons, for instance, might be, that it behooves men, and especially men of benevolence, to consider well what they are about, and, before acting on their philanthropic purposes, to be quite sure that they comprehend the nature and all the relations of the business in hand. What has been established as an element of good to one being may prove absolute mischief to another; even as the warmth of the parlor was proper enough for children of flesh and blood, like Violet and Peony,—though by no means very wholesome, even for them,—but involved nothing short of annihilation to the unfortunate snow-image.

But, after all, there is no teaching anything to wise men of good Mr. Lindsey's stamp. They know everything,—oh, to be sure!—everything that has been, and everything that is, and everything that, by any future possibility, can be. And, should some phenomenon of nature or providence transcend their system, they will not recognize it, even if it come to pass under their very noses.

"Wife," said Mr. Lindsey, after a fit of silence, "see what a quantity of snow the children have brought in on their feet! It has made quite a puddle here before the stove. Pray tell Dora to bring some towels and sop it up!"

THE GREAT STONE FACE

One afternoon, when the sun was going down, a mother and her little boy sat at the door of their cottage, talking about the Great Stone Face. They had but to lift their eyes, and there it was plainly to be seen, though miles away, with the sunshine brightening all its features.

And what was the Great Stone Face?

Embosomed amongst a family of lofty mountains, there was a valley so spacious that it contained many thousand inhabitants. Some of these good people dwelt in log-huts, with the black forest all around them, on the steep and difficult hill-sides. Others had their homes in comfortable farm-houses, and cultivated the rich soil on the gentle slopes or level surfaces of the valley. Others, again, were congregated into populous villages, where some wild, highland rivulet, tumbling down from its birthplace in the upper mountain region, had been caught and tamed by human cunning, and compelled to turn the machinery of cotton-factories. The inhabitants of this valley, in short, were numerous, and of many modes of life. But all of them, grown people and children, had a kind of familiarity with the Great Stone Face, although some possessed the gift of distinguishing this grand natural phenomenon more perfectly than many of their neighbors.

The Great Stone Face, then, was a work of Nature in her mood of majestic playfulness, formed on the perpendicular side of a mountain by some immense rocks, which had been thrown together in such a position as, when viewed at a proper distance, precisely to resemble the features of the human countenance. It seemed as if an enormous giant, or a Titan, had sculptured his own likeness on the precipice. There was the broad arch of the forehead, a hundred feet in height; the nose, with its long bridge; and the vast lips, which, if they could have spoken, would have rolled their thunder accents from one end of the valley to the other. True it is, that if the spectator approached too near, he lost the outline of the gigantic visage, and could discern only a heap of ponderous and gigantic rocks, piled in chaotic ruin one upon another. Retracing his steps, however, the wondrous features would again be seen; and the farther he withdrew from them, the more like a human face, with all its original divinity intact, did they appear; until, as it grew dim in the distance, with the clouds and glorified vapor of the mountains clustering about it, the Great Stone Face seemed positively to be alive.

It was a happy lot for children to grow up to manhood or womanhood with the Great Stone Face before their eyes, for all the features were noble, and the expression was at once grand and sweet, as if it were the glow of a vast, warm heart, that embraced all mankind in its affections, and had room for more. It was an education only to look at it. According to the belief of many people, the valley owed much of its fertility to this benign aspect that was continually beaming over it, illuminating the clouds, and infusing its tenderness into the sunshine.

As we began with saying, a mother and her little boy sat at their cottage-door, gazing at the Great Stone Face, and talking about it. The child's name was Ernest.

"Mother," said he, while the Titanic visage smiled on him, "I wish that it could speak, for it looks so very kindly that its voice must needs be pleasant. If I were to see a man with such a face, I should love him dearly."

"If an old prophecy should come to pass," answered his mother, "we may see a man, some time or other, with exactly such a face as that."

"What prophecy do you mean, dear mother?" eagerly inquired Ernest. "Pray tell me all about it!"

So his mother told him a story that her own mother had told to her, when she herself was younger than little Ernest; a story, not of things that were past, but of what was yet to come; a story, nevertheless, so very old, that even the Indians, who formerly inhabited this valley, had heard it from their forefathers, to whom, as they affirmed, it had been murmured by the mountain streams, and whispered by the wind among the tree-tops. The purport was, that, at some future day, a child should be born hereabouts, who was destined to become the greatest and noblest personage of his time, and whose countenance, in manhood, should bear an exact resemblance to the Great Stone Face. Not a few old-fashioned people, and young ones likewise, in the ardor of their hopes, still cherished an enduring faith in this old prophecy. But others, who had seen more of the world, had watched and waited till they were weary, and had beheld no man with such a face, nor any man that proved to be much greater or nobler than his neighbors, concluded it to be nothing but an idle tale. At all events, the great man of the prophecy had not yet appeared.

"O mother, dear mother!" cried Ernest, clapping his hands above his head, "I do hope that I shall live to see him!"

His mother was an affectionate and thoughtful woman, and felt that it was wisest not to discourage the generous hopes of her little boy. So she only said to him, "Perhaps you may."

And Ernest never forgot the story that his mother told him. It was always in his mind, whenever he looked upon the Great Stone Face. He spent his childhood in the log-cottage where he was born, and was dutiful to his mother, and helpful to her in many things, assisting her much with his little hands, and more with his loving heart. In this manner, from a happy yet often pensive child, he grew up to be a mild, quiet, unobtrusive boy, and sun-browned with labor in the fields, but with more intelligence brightening his aspect than is seen in many lads who have been taught at famous schools. Yet Ernest had had no teacher, save only that the Great Stone Face became one to him. When the toil of the day was over, he would gaze at it for hours, until he began to imagine that those vast features recognized him, and gave him a smile of kindness and encouragement, responsive to his own look of veneration. We must not take upon us to affirm that this was a mistake, although the Face may have looked no more kindly at Ernest than at all the world besides. But the secret was that the boy's tender and confiding simplicity discerned what other people could not see; and thus the love, which was meant for all, became his peculiar portion.

About this time there went a rumor throughout the valley, that the great man, foretold from ages long ago, who was to bear a resemblance to the Great Stone Face, had appeared at last. It seems that, many years before, a young man had migrated from the valley and settled at a distant seaport, where, after getting together a little money, he had set up as a shopkeeper. His name—but I could never learn whether it was his real one, or a nickname that had grown out of his habits and success in life—was Gathergold. Being shrewd and active, and endowed by Providence with that inscrutable faculty which develops itself in what the world calls luck, he became an exceedingly rich merchant, and owner of a whole fleet of bulky-bottomed ships. All the countries of the globe appeared to join hands for the mere purpose of adding heap after heap to the mountainous accumulation of this one man's wealth. The cold regions of the north, almost within the gloom and shadow of the Arctic Circle, sent him their tribute in the shape of furs; hot Africa sifted for him the golden sands of her rivers, and gathered up the ivory tusks of her great elephants out of the forests; the East came bringing him the rich shawls, and spices, and teas, and the effulgence of diamonds, and the gleaming purity of large pearls. The ocean, not to be behindhand with the earth, yielded up her mighty whales, that Mr. Gathergold might sell their oil, and make a profit on it. Be the original commodity what it might, it was gold within his grasp. It might be said of him, as of Midas in the fable, that whatever he touched with his finger immediately glistened, and grew yellow, and was changed at once into sterling metal, or, which suited him still better, into piles of coin. And, when Mr. Gathergold had become so very rich that it would have taken him a hundred years only to count his wealth, he bethought himself of his native valley, and resolved to go back thither, and end his days where he was born. With this purpose in view, he sent a skilful architect to build him such a palace as should be fit for a man of his vast wealth to live in.

As I have said above, it had already been rumored in the valley that Mr. Gathergold had turned out to be the prophetic personage so long and vainly looked for, and that his visage was the perfect and undeniable similitude of the Great Stone Face. People were the more ready to believe that this must needs be the fact, when they beheld the splendid edifice that rose, as if by enchantment, on the site of his father's old weather-beaten farm-house. The exterior was of marble, so dazzlingly white that it seemed as though the whole structure might melt away in the sunshine, like those humbler ones which Mr. Gathergold, in his young play-days, before his fingers were gifted with the touch of transmutation, had been accustomed to build of snow. It had a richly ornamented portico, supported by tall pillars, beneath which was a lofty door, studded with silver knobs, and made of a kind of variegated wood that had been brought from beyond the sea. The windows, from the floor to the ceiling of each stately apartment, were composed, respectively, of but one enormous pane of glass, so transparently pure that it was said to be a finer medium than even the vacant atmosphere. Hardly anybody had been permitted to see the interior of this palace; but it was reported, and with good semblance of truth, to be far more gorgeous than the outside, insomuch that whatever was iron or brass in other houses was silver or gold in this; and Mr. Gathergold's bedchamber, especially, made such a glittering appearance that no ordinary man would have been able to close his eyes there. But, on the other hand, Mr. Gathergold was now so inured to wealth, that perhaps he could not have closed his eyes unless where the gleam of it was certain to find its way beneath his eyelids.

In due time, the mansion was finished; next came the upholsterers, with magnificent furniture; then, a whole troop of black and white servants, the harbingers of Mr. Gathergold, who, in his own majestic person, was expected to arrive at sunset. Our friend Ernest, meanwhile, had been deeply stirred by the idea that the great man, the noble man, the man of prophecy, after so many ages of delay, was at length to be made manifest to his native valley. He knew, boy as he was, that there were a thousand ways in which Mr. Gathergold, with his vast wealth, might transform himself into an angel of beneficence, and assume a control over human affairs as wide and benignant as the smile of the Great Stone Face. Full of faith and hope, Ernest doubted not that what the people said was true, and that now he was to behold the living likeness of those wondrous features on the mountain-side. While the boy was still gazing up the valley, and fancying, as he always did, that the Great Stone Face returned his gaze and looked kindly at him, the rumbling of wheels was heard, approaching swiftly along the winding road.

"Here he comes!" cried a group of people who were assembled to witness the arrival. "Here comes the great Mr. Gathergold!"

A carriage, drawn by four horses, dashed round the turn of the road. Within it, thrust partly out of the window, appeared the physiognomy of the old man, with a skin as yellow as if his own Midas-hand had transmuted it. He had a low forehead, small, sharp eyes, puckered about with innumerable wrinkles, and very thin lips, which he made still thinner by pressing them forcibly together.

"The very image of the Great Stone Face!" shouted the people. "Sure enough, the old prophecy is true; and here we have the great man come, at last!"

And, what greatly perplexed Ernest, they seemed actually to believe that here was the likeness which they spoke of. By the roadside there chanced to be an old beggar-woman and two little beggar-children, stragglers from some far-off region, who, as the carriage rolled onward, held out their hands and lifted up their doleful voices, most piteously beseeching charity. A yellow claw—the very same that had clawed together so much wealth—poked itself out of the coach-window, and dropt some copper coins upon the ground; so that, though the great man's name seems to have been Gathergold, he might just as suitably have been nicknamed Scattercopper. Still, nevertheless, with an earnest shout, and evidently with as much good faith as ever, the people bellowed,—

"He is the very image of the Great Stone Face!"

But Ernest turned sadly from the wrinkled shrewdness of that sordid visage, and gazed up the valley, where, amid a gathering mist, gilded by the last sunbeams, he could still distinguish those glorious features which had impressed themselves into his soul. Their aspect cheered him. What did the benign lips seem to say?

"He will come! Fear not, Ernest; the man will come!"

The years went on, and Ernest ceased to be a boy. He had grown to be a young man now. He attracted little notice from the other inhabitants of the valley; for they saw nothing remarkable in his way of life, save that, when the labor of the day was over, he still loved to go apart and gaze and meditate upon the Great Stone Face. According to their idea of the matter, it was a folly, indeed, but pardonable, inasmuch as Ernest was industrious, kind, and neighborly, and neglected no duty for the sake of indulging this idle habit. They knew not that the Great Stone Face had become a teacher to him, and that the sentiment which was expressed in it would enlarge the young man's heart, and fill it with wider and deeper sympathies than other hearts. They knew not that thence would come a better wisdom than could be learned from books, and a better life than could be moulded on the defaced example of other human lives. Neither did Ernest know that the thoughts and affections which came to him so naturally, in the fields and at the fireside, and wherever he communed with himself, were of a higher tone than those which all men shared with him. A simple soul,—simple as when his mother first taught him the old prophecy,—he beheld the marvellous features beaming adown the valley, and still wondered that their human counterpart was so long in making his appearance.

By this time poor Mr. Gathergold was dead and buried; and the oddest part of the matter was, that his wealth, which was the body and spirit of his existence, had disappeared before his death, leaving nothing of him but a living skeleton, covered over with a wrinkled, yellow skin. Since the melting away of his gold, it had been very generally conceded that there was no such striking resemblance, after all, betwixt the ignoble features of the ruined merchant and that majestic face upon the mountain-side. So the people ceased to honor him during his lifetime, and quietly consigned him to forgetfulness after his decease. Once in a while, it is true, his memory was brought up in connection with the magnificent palace which he had built, and which had long ago been turned into a hotel for the accommodation of strangers, multitudes of whom came, every summer, to visit that famous natural curiosity, the Great Stone Face. Thus, Mr. Gathergold being discredited and thrown into the shade, the man of prophecy was yet to come.

It so happened that a native-born son of the valley, many years before, had enlisted as a soldier, and, after a great deal of hard fighting, had now become an illustrious commander. Whatever he may be called in history, he was known in camps and on the battle-field under the nickname of Old Blood-and-Thunder. This war-worn veteran, being now infirm with age and wounds, and weary of the turmoil of a military life, and of the roll of the drum and the clangor of the trumpet, that had so long been ringing in his ears, had lately signified a purpose of returning to his native valley, hoping to find repose where he remembered to have left it. The inhabitants, his old neighbors and their grown-up children, were resolved to welcome the renowned warrior with a salute of cannon and a public dinner; and all the more enthusiastically, it being affirmed that now, at last, the likeness of the Great Stone Face had actually appeared. An aid-de-camp of Old Blood-and-Thunder, travelling through the valley, was said to have been struck with the resemblance. Moreover the schoolmates and early acquaintances of the general were ready to testify, on oath, that, to the best of their recollection, the aforesaid general had been exceedingly like the majestic image, even when a boy, only that the idea had never occurred to them at that period. Great, therefore, was the excitement throughout the valley; and many people, who had never once thought of glancing at the Great Stone Face for years before, now spent their time in gazing at it, for the sake of knowing exactly how General Blood-and-Thunder looked.

On the day of the great festival, Ernest, with all the other people of the valley, left their work, and proceeded to the spot where the sylvan banquet was prepared. As he approached, the loud voice of the Rev. Dr. Battleblast was heard, beseeching a blessing on the good things set before them, and on the distinguished friend of peace in whose honor they were assembled. The tables were arranged in a cleared space of the woods, shut in by the surrounding trees, except where a vista opened eastward, and afforded a distant view of the Great Stone Face. Over the general's chair, which was a relic from the home of Washington, there was an arch of verdant boughs, with the laurel profusely intermixed, and surmounted by his country's banner, beneath which he had won his victories. Our friend Ernest raised himself on his tiptoes, in hopes to get a glimpse of the celebrated guest; but there was a mighty crowd about the tables anxious to hear the toasts and speeches, and to catch any word that might fall from the general in reply; and a volunteer company, doing duty as a guard, pricked ruthlessly with their bayonets at any particularly quiet person among the throng. So Ernest, being of an unobtrusive character, was thrust quite into the background, where he could see no more of Old Blood-and-Thunder's physiognomy than if it had been still blazing on the battle-field. To console himself, he turned towards the Great Stone Face, which, like a faithful and long-remembered friend, looked back and smiled upon him through the vista of the forest. Meantime, however, he could overhear the remarks of various individuals, who were comparing the features of the hero with the face on the distant mountain-side.

"'T is the same face, to a hair!" cried one man, cutting a caper for joy.

"Wonderfully like, that's a fact!" responded another.

"Like! why, I call it Old Blood-and-Thunder himself, in a monstrous looking-glass!" cried a third. "And why not? He's the greatest man of this or any other age, beyond a doubt."

And then all three of the speakers gave a great shout, which communicated electricity to the crowd, and called forth a roar from a thousand voices, that went reverberating for miles among the mountains, until you might have supposed that the Great Stone Face had poured its thunder-breath into the cry. All these comments, and this vast enthusiasm, served the more to interest our friend; nor did he think of questioning that now, at length, the mountain-visage had found its human counterpart. It is true, Ernest had imagined that this long-looked-for personage would appear in the character of a man of peace, uttering wisdom, and doing good, and making people happy. But, taking an habitual breadth of view, with all his simplicity, he contended that Providence should choose its own method of blessing mankind, and could conceive that this great end might be effected even by a warrior and a bloody sword, should inscrutable wisdom see fit to order matters so.

"The general! the general!" was now the cry. "Hush! silence! Old Blood-and-Thunder's going to make a speech."

Even so; for, the cloth being removed, the general's health had been drunk, amid shouts of applause, and he now stood upon his feet to thank the company. Ernest saw him. There he was, over the shoulders of the crowd, from the two glittering epaulets and embroidered collar upward, beneath the arch of green boughs with intertwined laurel, and the banner drooping as if to shade his brow! And there, too, visible in the same glance, through the vista of the forest, appeared the Great Stone Face! And was there, indeed, such a resemblance as the crowd had testified? Alas, Ernest could not recognize it! He beheld a war-worn and weather-beaten countenance, full of energy, and expressive of an iron will; but the gentle wisdom, the deep, broad, tender sympathies, were altogether wanting in Old Blood-and-Thunder's visage; and even if the Great Stone Face had assumed his look of stern command, the milder traits would still have tempered it.

"This is not the man of prophecy," sighed Ernest to himself, as he made his way out of the throng. "And must the world wait longer yet?"

The mists had congregated about the distant mountain-side, and there were seen the grand and awful features of the Great Stone Face, awful but benignant, as if a mighty angel were sitting among the hills, and enrobing himself in a cloud-vesture of gold and purple. As he looked, Ernest could hardly believe but that a smile beamed over the whole visage, with a radiance still brightening, although without motion of the lips. It was probably the effect of the western sunshine, melting through the thinly diffused vapors that had swept between him and the object that he gazed at. But—as it always did—the aspect of his marvellous friend made Ernest as hopeful as if he had never hoped in vain.

"Fear not, Ernest," said his heart, even as if the Great Face were whispering him,—"fear not, Ernest; he will come."

More years sped swiftly and tranquilly away. Ernest still dwelt in his native valley, and was now a man of middle age. By imperceptible degrees, he had become known among the people. Now, as heretofore, he labored for his bread, and was the same simple-hearted man that he had always been. But he had thought and felt so much, he had given so many of the best hours of his life to unworldly hopes for some great good to mankind, that it seemed as though he had been talking with the angels, and had imbibed a portion of their wisdom unawares. It was visible in the calm and well-considered beneficence of his daily life, the quiet stream of which had made a wide green margin all along its course. Not a day passed by, that the world was not the better because this man, humble as he was, had lived. He never stepped aside from his own path, yet would always reach a blessing to his neighbor. Almost involuntarily, too, he had become a preacher. The pure and high simplicity of his thought, which, as one of its manifestations, took shape in the good deeds that dropped silently from his hand, flowed also forth in speech. He uttered truths that wrought upon and moulded the lives of those who heard him. His auditors, it may be, never suspected that Ernest, their own neighbor and familiar friend, was more than an ordinary man; least of all did Ernest himself suspect it; but, inevitably as the murmur of a rivulet, came thoughts out of his mouth that no other human lips had spoken.

When the people's minds had had a little time to cool, they were ready enough to acknowledge their mistake in imagining a similarity between General Blood-and-Thunder's truculent physiognomy and the benign visage on the mountain-side. But now, again, there were reports and many paragraphs in the newspapers, affirming that the likeness of the Great Stone Face had appeared upon the broad shoulders of a certain eminent statesman. He, like Mr. Gathergold and Old Blood-and-Thunder, was a native of the valley, but had left it in his early days, and taken up the trades of law and politics. Instead of the rich man's wealth and the warrior's sword, he had but a tongue, and it was mightier than both together. So wonderfully eloquent was he, that whatever he might choose to say, his auditors had no choice but to believe him; wrong looked like right, and right like wrong; for when it pleased him, he could make a kind of illuminated fog with his mere breath, and obscure the natural daylight with it. His tongue, indeed, was a magic instrument: sometimes it rumbled like the thunder; sometimes it warbled like the sweetest music. It was the blast of war,—the song of peace; and it seemed to have a heart in it, when there was no such matter. In good truth, he was a wondrous man; and when his tongue had acquired him all other imaginable success,—when it had been heard in halls of state, and in the courts of princes and potentates,—after it had made him known all over the world, even as a voice crying from shore to shore,—it finally persuaded his countrymen to select him for the Presidency. Before this time,—indeed, as soon as he began to grow celebrated,—his admirers had found out the resemblance between him and the Great Stone Face; and so much were they struck by it, that throughout the country this distinguished gentleman was known by the name of Old Stony Phiz. The phrase was considered as giving a highly favorable aspect to his political prospects; for, as is likewise the case with the Popedom, nobody ever becomes President without taking a name other than his own.

While his friends were doing their best to make him President, Old Stony

Phiz, as he was called, set out on a visit to the valley where he was born. Of course, he had no other object than to shake hands with his fellow-citizens, and neither thought nor cared about any effect which his progress through the country might have upon the election. Magnificent preparations were made to receive the illustrious statesman; a cavalcade of horsemen set forth to meet him at the boundary line of the State, and all the people left their business and gathered along the wayside to see him pass. Among these was Ernest. Though more than once disappointed, as we have seen, he had such a hopeful and confiding nature, that he was always ready to believe in whatever seemed beautiful and good. He kept his heart continually open, and thus was sure to catch the blessing from on high when it should come. So now again, as buoyantly as ever, he went forth to behold the likeness of the Great Stone Face.

The cavalcade came prancing along the road, with a great clattering of hoofs and a mighty cloud of dust, which rose up so dense and high that the visage of the mountain-side was completely hidden from Ernest's eyes. All the great men of the neighborhood were there on horseback; militia officers, in uniform; the member of Congress; the sheriff of the county; the editors of newspapers; and many a farmer, too, had mounted his patient steed, with his Sunday coat upon his back. It really was a very brilliant spectacle, especially as there were numerous banners flaunting over the cavalcade, on some of which were gorgeous portraits of the illustrious statesman and the Great Stone Face, smiling familiarly at one another, like two brothers. If the pictures were to be trusted, the mutual resemblance, it must be confessed, was marvellous. We must not forget to mention that there was a band of music, which made the echoes of the mountains ring and reverberate with the loud triumph of its strains; so that airy and soul-thrilling melodies broke out among all the heights and hollows, as if every nook of his native valley had found a voice, to welcome the distinguished guest. But the grandest effect was when the far-off mountain precipice flung back the music; for then the Great Stone Face itself seemed to be swelling the triumphant chorus, in acknowledgment that, at length, the man of prophecy was come.

All this while the people were throwing up their hats and shouting, with enthusiasm so contagious that the heart of Ernest kindled up, and he likewise threw up his hat, and shouted, as loudly as the loudest, "Huzza for the great man! Huzza for Old Stony Phiz!" But as yet he had not seen him.

"Here he is, now!" cried those who stood near Ernest. "There! There! Look at Old Stony Phiz and then at the Old Man of the Mountain, and see if they are not as like as two twin-brothers!"

In the midst of all this gallant array came an open barouche, drawn by four white horses; and in the barouche, with his massive head uncovered, sat the illustrious statesman, Old Stony Phiz himself.

"Confess it," said one of Ernest's neighbors to him, "the Great Stone Face has met its match at last!"

Now, it must be owned that, at his first glimpse of the countenance which was bowing and smiling from the barouche, Ernest did fancy that there was a resemblance between it and the old familiar face upon the mountain-side. The brow, with its massive depth and loftiness, and all the other features, indeed, were boldly and strongly hewn, as if in emulation of a more than heroic, of a

Titanic model. But the sublimity and stateliness, the grand expression of a divine sympathy, that illuminated the mountain visage and etherealized its ponderous granite substance into spirit, might here be sought in vain. Something had been originally left out, or had departed. And therefore the marvellously gifted statesman had always a weary gloom in the deep caverns of his eyes, as of a child that has outgrown its playthings or a man of mighty faculties and little aims, whose life, with all its high performances, was vague and empty, because no high purpose had endowed it with reality.

Still, Ernest's neighbor was thrusting his elbow into his side, and pressing him for an answer.

"Confess! confess! Is not he the very picture of your Old Man of the Mountain?"

"No!" said Ernest, bluntly, "I see little or no likeness."

"Then so much the worse for the Great Stone Face!" answered his neighbor; and again he set up a shout for Old Stony Phiz.

But Ernest turned away, melancholy, and almost despondent: for this was the saddest of his disappointments, to behold a man who might have fulfilled the prophecy, and had not willed to do so. Meantime, the cavalcade, the banners, the music, and the barouches swept past him, with the vociferous crowd in the rear, leaving the dust to settle down, and the Great Stone Face to be revealed again, with the grandeur that it had worn for untold centuries.

"Lo, here I am, Ernest!" the benign lips seemed to say. "I have waited longer than thou, and am not yet weary. Fear not; the man will come."

The years hurried onward, treading in their haste on one another's heels. And now they began to bring white hairs, and scatter them over the head of Ernest; they made reverend wrinkles across his forehead, and furrows in his cheeks. He was an aged man. But not in vain had he grown old: more than the white hairs on his head were the sage thoughts in his mind; his wrinkles and furrows were inscriptions that Time had graved, and in which he had written legends of wisdom that had been tested by the tenor of a life. And Ernest had ceased to be obscure. Unsought for, undesired, had come the fame which so many seek, and made him known in the great world, beyond the limits of the valley in which he had dwelt so quietly. College professors, and even the active men of cities, came from far to see and converse with Ernest; for the report had gone abroad that this simple husbandman had ideas unlike those of other men, not gained from books, but of a higher tone,—a tranquil and familiar majesty, as if he had been talking with the angels as his daily friends. Whether it were sage, statesman, or philanthropist, Ernest received these visitors with the gentle sincerity that had characterized him from boyhood, and spoke freely with them of whatever came uppermost, or lay deepest in his heart or their own. While they talked together, his face would kindle, unawares, and shine upon them, as with a mild evening light. Pensive with the fulness of such discourse, his guests took leave and went their way; and passing up the valley, paused to look at the Great Stone Face, imagining that they had seen its likeness in a human countenance, but could not remember where.

While Ernest had been growing up and growing old, a bountiful Providence had granted a new poet to this earth. He, likewise, was a native of the valley, but had spent the greater part of his life at a distance from that romantic region, pouring out his sweet music amid the bustle and din of cities. Often, however, did the mountains which had been familiar to him in his childhood lift their snowy peaks into the clear atmosphere of his poetry. Neither was the Great Stone Face forgotten, for the poet had celebrated it in an ode, which was grand enough to have been uttered by its own majestic lips. This man of genius, we may say, had come down from heaven with wonderful endowments. If he sang of a mountain, the eyes of all mankind beheld a mightier grandeur reposing on its breast, or soaring to its summit, than had before been seen there. If his theme were a lovely lake, a celestial smile had now been thrown over it, to gleam forever on its surface. If it were the vast old sea, even the deep immensity of its dread bosom seemed to swell the higher, as if moved by the emotions of the song. Thus the world assumed another and a better aspect from the hour that the poet blessed it with his happy eyes. The Creator had bestowed him, as the last best touch to his own handiwork. Creation was not finished till the poet came to interpret, and so complete it.

The effect was no less high and beautiful, when his human brethren were the subject of his verse. The man or woman, sordid with the common dust of life, who crossed his daily path, and the little child who played in it, were glorified if he beheld them in his mood of poetic faith. He showed the golden links of the great chain that intertwined them with an angelic kindred; he brought out the hidden traits of a celestial birth that made them worthy of such kin. Some, indeed, there were, who thought to show the soundness of their judgment by affirming that all the beauty and dignity of the natural world existed only in the poet's fancy. Let such men speak for themselves, who undoubtedly appear to have been spawned forth by Nature with a contemptuous bitterness; she having plastered them up out of her refuse stuff, after all the swine were made. As respects all things else, the poet's ideal was the truest truth.

The songs of this poet found their way to Ernest. He read them after his customary toil, seated on the bench before his cottage-door, where for such a length of time he had filled his repose with thought, by gazing at the Great Stone Face. And now as he read stanzas that caused the soul to thrill within him, he lifted his eyes to the vast countenance beaming on him so benignantly.

"O majestic friend," he murmured, addressing the Great Stone Face, "is not this man worthy to resemble thee?"

The Face seemed to smile, but answered not a word.

Now it happened that the poet, though he dwelt so far away, had not only heard of Ernest, but had meditated much upon his character, until he deemed nothing so desirable as to meet this man, whose untaught wisdom walked hand in hand with the noble simplicity of his life. One summer morning, therefore, he took passage by the railroad, and, in the decline of the afternoon, alighted from the cars at no great distance from Ernest's cottage. The great hotel, which had formerly been the palace of Mr. Gathergold, was close at hand, but the poet, with his carpet-bag on his arm, inquired at once where Ernest dwelt, and was resolved to be accepted as his guest.

Approaching the door, he there found the good old man, holding a volume in his hand, which alternately he read, and then, with a finger between the leaves, looked lovingly at the Great Stone Face.

"Good evening," said the poet. "Can you give a traveller a night's lodging?"

"Willingly," answered Ernest; and then he added, smiling, "Methinks I never saw the Great Stone Face look so hospitably at a stranger."

The poet sat down on the bench beside him, and he and Ernest talked together. Often had the poet held intercourse with the wittiest and the wisest, but never before with a man like Ernest, whose thoughts and feelings gushed up with such a natural freedom, and who made great truths so familiar by his simple utterance of them. Angels, as had been so often said, seemed to have wrought with him at his labor in the fields; angels seemed to have sat with him by the fireside; and, dwelling with angels as friend with friends, he had imbibed the sublimity of their ideas, and imbued it with the sweet and lowly charm of household words. So thought the poet. And Ernest, on the other hand, was moved and agitated by the living images which the poet flung out of his mind, and which peopled all the air about the cottage-door with shapes of beauty, both gay and pensive. The sympathies of these two men instructed them with a profounder sense than either could have attained alone. Their minds accorded into one strain, and made delightful music which neither of them could have claimed as all his own, nor distinguished his own share from the other's. They led one another, as it were, into a high pavilion of their thoughts, so remote, and hitherto so dim, that they had never entered it before, and so beautiful that they desired to be there always.

As Ernest listened to the poet, he imagined that the Great Stone Face was bending forward to listen too. He gazed earnestly into the poet's glowing eyes.

"Who are you, my strangely gifted guest?" he said.

The poet laid his finger on the volume that Ernest had been reading.

"You have read these poems," said he. "You know me, then,—for I wrote them."

Again, and still more earnestly than before, Ernest examined the poet's features; then turned towards the Great Stone Face; then back, with an uncertain aspect, to his guest. But his countenance fell; he shook his head, and sighed.

"Wherefore are you sad?" inquired the poet.

"Because," replied Ernest, "all through life I have awaited the fulfilment of a prophecy; and, when I read these poems, I hoped that it might be fulfilled in you."

"You hoped," answered the poet, faintly smiling, "to find in me the likeness of the Great Stone Face. And you are disappointed, as formerly with Mr. Gathergold, and Old Blood-and-Thunder, and Old Stony Phiz. Yes Ernest, it is my doom. You must add my name to the illustrious three, and record another failure of your hopes. For—in shame and sadness do I speak it, Ernest—I am not worthy to be typified by yonder benign and majestic image."

"And why?" asked Ernest. He pointed to the volume. "Are not those thoughts divine?"

"They have a strain of the Divinity," replied the poet. "You can hear in them the far-off echo of a heavenly song. But my life, dear Ernest, has not corresponded with my thought. I have had grand dreams, but they have been only dreams, because I have lived—and that, too, by my own choice—among poor and mean realities. Sometimes even—shall I dare to say it?—I lack faith in the grandeur, the beauty, and the goodness, which my own works are said to have made more evident in nature and in human life. Why, then, pure seeker of the good and true, shouldst thou hope to find me, in yonder image of the divine?"

The poet spoke sadly, and his eyes were dim with tears. So, likewise, were those of Ernest.

At the hour of sunset, as had long been his frequent custom, Ernest was to discourse to an assemblage of the neighboring inhabitants in the open air. He and the poet, arm in arm, still talking together as they went along, proceeded to the spot. It was a small nook among the hills, with a gray precipice behind, the stern front of which was relieved by the pleasant foliage of many creeping plants that made a tapestry for the naked rock, by hanging their festoons from all its rugged angles. At a small elevation above the ground, set in a rich framework of verdure, there appeared a niche, spacious enough to admit a human figure, with freedom for such gestures as spontaneously accompany earnest thought and genuine emotion. Into this natural pulpit Ernest ascended, and threw a look of familiar kindness around upon his audience. They stood, or sat, or reclined upon the grass, as seemed good to each, with the departing sunshine falling obliquely over them, and mingling its subdued cheerfulness with the solemnity of a grove of ancient trees, beneath and amid the boughs of which the golden rays were constrained to pass. In another direction was seen the Great Stone Face, with the same cheer, combined with the same solemnity, in its benignant aspect.

Ernest began to speak, giving to the people of what was in his heart and mind. His words had power, because they accorded with his thoughts; and his thoughts had reality and depth, because they harmonized with the life which he had always lived. It was not mere breath that this preacher uttered; they were the words of life, because a life of good deeds and holy love was melted into them. Pearls, pure and rich, had been dissolved into this precious draught. The poet, as he listened, felt that the being and character of Ernest were a nobler strain of poetry than he had ever written. His eyes glistening with tears, he gazed reverentially at the venerable man, and said within himself that never was there an aspect so worthy of a prophet and a sage as that mild, sweet, thoughtful countenance, with the glory of white hair diffused about it. At a distance, but distinctly to be seen, high up in the golden light of the setting sun, appeared the Great Stone Face, with hoary mists around it, like the white hairs around the brow of Ernest. Its look of grand beneficence seemed to embrace the world.

At that moment, in sympathy with a thought which he was about to utter, the face of Ernest assumed a grandeur of expression, so imbued with benevolence, that the poet, by an irresistible impulse, threw his arms aloft, and shouted,—

"Behold! Behold! Ernest is himself the likeness of the Great Stone Face!"

Then all the people looked, and saw that what the deep-sighted poet said was true. The prophecy was fulfilled. But Ernest, having finished what he had to say, took the poet's arm, and walked slowly homeward, still hoping that some wiser and better man than himself would by and by appear, bearing a resemblance to the GREAT STONE FACE.

ETHAN BRAND

A CHAPTER FROM AN ABORTIVE ROMANCE

Bartram the lime-burner, a rough, heavy-looking man, begrimed with charcoal, sat watching his kiln at nightfall, while his little son played at building houses with the scattered fragments of marble, when, on the hill-side below them, they heard a roar of laughter, not mirthful, but slow, and even solemn, like a wind shaking the boughs of the forest.

"Father, what is that?" asked the little boy, leaving his play, and pressing betwixt his father's knees.

"Oh, some drunken man, I suppose," answered the lime-burner; "some merry fellow from the bar-room in the village, who dared not laugh loud enough within doors lest he should blow the roof of the house off. So here he is, shaking his jolly sides at the foot of Graylock."

"But, father," said the child, more sensitive than the obtuse, middle-aged clown, "he does not laugh like a man that is glad. So the noise frightens me!"

"Don't be a fool, child!" cried his father, gruffly. "You will never make a man, I do believe; there is too much of your mother in you. I have known the rustling of a leaf startle you. Hark! Here comes the merry fellow now. You shall see that there is no harm in him."

Bartram and his little son, while they were talking thus, sat watching the same lime-kiln that had been the scene of Ethan Brand's solitary and meditative life, before he began his search for the Unpardonable Sin. Many years, as we have seen, had now elapsed, since that portentous night when the IDEA was first developed. The kiln, however, on the mountain-side, stood unimpaired, and was in nothing changed since he had thrown his dark thoughts into the intense glow of its furnace, and melted them, as it were, into the one thought that took possession of his life. It was a rude, round, tower-like structure about twenty feet high, heavily built of rough stones, and with a hillock of earth heaped about the larger part of its circumference; so that the blocks and fragments of marble might be drawn by cart-loads, and thrown in at the top. There was an opening at the bottom of the tower, like an oven-mouth, but large enough to admit a man in a stooping posture, and provided with a massive iron door. With the smoke and jets of flame issuing from the chinks and crevices of this door, which seemed to give admittance into the hill-side, it resembled nothing so much as the private entrance to the infernal regions, which the shepherds of the Delectable Mountains were accustomed to show to pilgrims.

There are many such lime-kilns in that tract of country, for the purpose of burning the white marble which composes a large part of the substance of the hills. Some of them, built years ago, and long deserted, with weeds growing in the vacant round of the interior, which is open to the sky, and grass and wild-flowers rooting themselves into the chinks of the stones, look already like relics of antiquity, and may yet be overspread with the lichens of centuries to come. Others, where the lime-burner still feeds his daily and night-long fire, afford points of interest to the wanderer among the hills, who seats himself on a log of wood or a fragment of marble, to hold a chat with the solitary man. It is a lonesome, and, when the character is inclined to thought, may be an intensely thoughtful occupation; as it proved in the case of Ethan Brand, who had mused to such strange purpose, in days gone by, while the fire in this very kiln was burning.

The man who now watched the fire was of a different order, and troubled himself with no thoughts save the very few that were requisite to his business. At frequent intervals, he flung back the clashing weight of the iron door, and, turning his face from the insufferable glare, thrust in huge logs of oak, or stirred the immense brands with a long pole. Within the furnace were seen the curling and riotous flames, and the burning marble, almost molten with the intensity of heat; while without, the reflection of the fire quivered on the dark intricacy of the surrounding forest, and showed in the foreground a bright and ruddy little picture of the hut, the spring beside its door, the athletic and coal-begrimed figure of the lime-burner, and the half-frightened child, shrinking into the protection of his father's shadow. And when, again, the iron door was closed, then reappeared the tender light of the half-full moon, which vainly strove to trace out the indistinct shapes of the neighboring mountains; and, in the upper sky, there was a flitting congregation of clouds, still faintly tinged with the rosy sunset, though thus far down into the valley the sunshine had vanished long and long ago.

The little boy now crept still closer to his father, as footsteps were heard ascending the hill-side, and a human form thrust aside the bushes that clustered beneath the trees.

"Halloo! who is it?" cried the lime-burner, vexed at his son's timidity, yet half infected by it. "Come forward, and show yourself, like a man, or I'll fling this chunk of marble at your head!"

"You offer me a rough welcome," said a gloomy voice, as the unknown man drew nigh. "Yet I neither claim nor desire a kinder one, even at my own fireside."

To obtain a distincter view, Bartram threw open the iron door of the kiln, whence immediately issued a gush of fierce light, that smote full upon the stranger's face and figure. To a careless eye there appeared nothing very remarkable in his aspect, which was that of a man in a coarse, brown, country-made suit of clothes, tall and thin, with the staff and heavy shoes of a wayfarer. As he advanced, he fixed his eyes—which were very bright—intently upon the brightness of the furnace, as if he beheld, or expected to behold, some object worthy of note within it.

"Good evening, stranger," said the lime-burner; "whence come you, so late in the day?"

"I come from my search," answered the wayfarer; "for, at last, it is finished."

"Drunk!—or crazy!" muttered Bartram to himself. "I shall have trouble with the fellow. The sooner I drive him away, the better."

The little boy, all in a tremble, whispered to his father, and begged him to shut the door of the kiln, so that there might not be so much light; for that there was something in the man's face which he was afraid to look at, yet could not look away from. And, indeed, even the lime-burner's dull and torpid sense began to be impressed by an indescribable something in that thin, rugged, thoughtful visage, with the grizzled hair hanging wildly about it, and those deeply sunken eyes, which gleamed like fires within the entrance of a mysterious cavern. But, as he closed the door, the stranger turned towards him, and spoke in a quiet, familiar way, that made Bartram feel as if he were a sane and sensible man, after all.

"Your task draws to an end, I see," said he. "This marble has already been burning three days. A few hours more will convert the stone to lime."

"Why, who are you?" exclaimed the lime-burner. "You seem as well acquainted with my business as I am myself."

"And well I may be," said the stranger; "for I followed the same craft many a long year, and here, too, on this very spot. But you are a new-comer in these parts. Did you never hear of Ethan Brand?"

"The man that went in search of the Unpardonable Sin?" asked Bartram, with a laugh.

"The same," answered the stranger. "He has found what he sought, and therefore he comes back again."

"What! then you are Ethan Brand himself?" cried the lime-burner, in amazement. "I am a newcomer here, as you say, and they call it eighteen years since you left the foot of Graylock. But, I can tell you, the good folks still talk about Ethan Brand, in the village yonder, and what a strange errand took him away from his lime-kiln. Well, and so you have found the Unpardonable Sin?"

"Even so!" said the stranger, calmly.

"If the question is a fair one," proceeded Bartram, "where might it be?"

Ethan Brand laid his finger on his own heart.

"Here!" replied he.

And then, without mirth in his countenance, but as if moved by an involuntary recognition of the infinite absurdity of seeking throughout the world for what was the closest of all things to himself, and looking into every heart, save his own, for what was hidden in no other breast, he broke into a laugh of scorn. It was the same slow, heavy laugh, that had almost appalled the lime-burner when it heralded the wayfarer's approach.

The solitary mountain-side was made dismal by it. Laughter, when out of place, mistimed, or bursting forth from a disordered state of feeling, may be the most terrible modulation of the human voice. The laughter of one asleep, even if it be a little child,—the madman's laugh,—the wild, screaming laugh of a born idiot,—are sounds that we sometimes tremble to hear, and would always willingly forget. Poets have imagined no utterance of fiends or hobgoblins so fearfully appropriate as a laugh. And even the obtuse lime-burner felt his nerves shaken, as this strange man looked inward at his own heart, and burst into laughter that rolled away into the night, and was indistinctly reverberated among the hills.

"Joe," said he to his little son, "scamper down to the tavern in the village, and tell the jolly fellows there that Ethan Brand has come back, and that he has found the Unpardonable Sin!"

The boy darted away on his errand, to which Ethan Brand made no objection, nor seemed hardly to notice it. He sat on a log of wood, looking steadfastly at the iron door of the kiln. When the child was out of sight, and his swift and light footsteps ceased to be heard treading first on the fallen leaves and then on the rocky mountain-path, the lime-burner began to regret his departure. He felt that the little fellow's presence had been a barrier between his guest and himself, and that he must now deal, heart to heart, with a man who, on his own confession, had committed the one only crime for which Heaven could afford no mercy. That crime, in its indistinct blackness, seemed to overshadow him. The lime-burner's own sins rose up within him, and made his memory riotous with a throng of evil shapes that asserted their kindred with the Master Sin, whatever it might be, which it was within the scope of man's corrupted nature to conceive and cherish. They were all of one family; they went to and fro between his breast and Ethan Brand's, and carried dark greetings from one to the other.

Then Bartram remembered the stories which had grown traditionary in reference to this strange man, who had come upon him like a shadow of the night, and was making himself at home in his old place, after so long absence, that the dead people, dead and buried for years, would have had more right to be at home, in any familiar spot, than he. Ethan Brand, it was said, had conversed with Satan himself in the lurid blaze of this very kiln. The legend had been matter of mirth heretofore, but looked grisly now. According to this tale, before Ethan Brand departed on his search, he had been accustomed to evoke a fiend from the hot furnace of the lime-kiln, night after night, in order to confer with him about the Unpardonable Sin; the man and the fiend each laboring to frame the image of some mode of guilt which could neither be atoned for nor forgiven. And, with the first gleam of light upon the mountain-top, the fiend crept in at the iron door, there to abide the intensest element of fire until again summoned forth to share in the dreadful task of extending man's possible guilt beyond the scope of Heaven's else infinite mercy.

While the lime-burner was struggling with the horror of these thoughts, Ethan Brand rose from the log, and flung open the door of the kiln. The action was in such accordance with the idea in Bartram's mind, that he almost expected to see the Evil One issue forth, red-hot, from the raging furnace.

"Hold! hold!" cried he, with a tremulous attempt to laugh; for he was ashamed of his fears, although they overmastered him. "Don't, for mercy's sake, bring out your Devil now!"

"Man!" sternly replied Ethan Brand, "what need have I of the Devil? I have left him behind me, on my track. It is with such half-way sinners as you that he busies himself. Fear not, because I open the door. I do but act by old custom, and am going to trim your fire, like a lime-burner, as I was once."

He stirred the vast coals, thrust in more wood, and bent forward to gaze into the hollow prison-house of the fire, regardless of the fierce glow that reddened upon his face. The lime-burner sat watching him, and half suspected this strange guest of a purpose, if not to evoke a fiend, at least to plunge bodily into the flames, and thus vanish from the sight of man. Ethan Brand, however, drew quietly back, and closed the door of the kiln.

"I have looked," said he, "into many a human heart that was seven times hotter with sinful passions than yonder furnace is with fire. But I found not there what I sought. No, not the Unpardonable Sin!"

"What is the Unpardonable Sin?" asked the lime-burner; and then he shrank farther from his companion, trembling lest his question should be answered.

"It is a sin that grew within my own breast," replied Ethan Brand, standing erect, with a pride that distinguishes all enthusiasts of his stamp. "A sin that grew nowhere else! The sin of an intellect that triumphed over the sense of brotherhood with man and reverence for God, and sacrificed everything to its own mighty claims! The only sin that deserves a recompense of immortal agony! Freely, were it to do again, would I incur the guilt. Unshrinkingly I accept the retribution!"

"The man's head is turned," muttered the lime-burner to himself. "He may be a sinner like the rest of us,—nothing more likely,—but, I'll be sworn, he is a madman too."

Nevertheless, he felt uncomfortable at his situation, alone with Ethan Brand on the wild mountain-side, and was right glad to hear the rough murmur of tongues, and the footsteps of what seemed a pretty numerous party, stumbling over the stones and rustling through the underbrush. Soon appeared the whole lazy regiment that was wont to infest the village tavern, comprehending three or four individuals who had drunk flip beside the bar-room fire through all the winters, and smoked their pipes beneath the stoop through all the summers, since Ethan Brand's departure. Laughing boisterously, and mingling all their voices together in unceremonious talk, they now burst into the moonshine and narrow streaks of firelight that illuminated the open space before the lime-kiln. Bartram set the door ajar again, flooding the spot with light, that the whole company might get a fair view of Ethan Brand, and he of them.

There, among other old acquaintances, was a once ubiquitous man, now almost extinct, but whom we were formerly sure to encounter at the hotel of every thriving village throughout the country. It was the stage-agent. The present specimen of the genus was a wilted and smoke-dried man, wrinkled and red-nosed, in a smartly cut, brown, bobtailed coat, with brass buttons, who, for a length of time unknown, had kept his desk and corner in the bar-room, and was still puffing what seemed to be the same cigar that he had lighted twenty years before. He had great fame as a dry joker, though, perhaps, less on account of any intrinsic humor than from a certain flavor of brandy-toddy and tobacco-smoke, which impregnated all his ideas and expressions, as well as his person. Another well-remembered, though strangely altered, face was that of Lawyer Giles, as people still called him in courtesy; an elderly ragamuffin, in his soiled shirt-sleeves and tow-cloth trousers. This poor fellow had been an attorney, in what he called his better days, a sharp practitioner, and in great vogue among the village litigants; but flip, and sling, and toddy, and cocktails, imbibed at all hours, morning, noon, and night, had caused him to slide from intellectual to various kinds and degrees of bodily labor, till at last, to adopt his own phrase, he slid into a soap-vat. In other words, Giles was now a soap-boiler, in a small way. He had come to be but the fragment of a human being, a part of one foot having been chopped off by an axe, and an entire hand torn away by the devilish grip of a steam-engine. Yet, though the corporeal hand was gone, a spiritual member remained; for, stretching forth the stump, Giles steadfastly averred that he felt an invisible thumb and fingers with as vivid a sensation as before the real ones were amputated. A maimed and miserable wretch he was; but one, nevertheless, whom the world could not trample on, and had no right to scorn, either in this or any previous stage of his misfortunes, since he had still kept up the courage and spirit of a man, asked nothing in charity, and with his one hand—and that the left one—fought a stern battle against want and hostile circumstances.

Among the throng, too, came another personage, who, with certain points of similarity to Lawyer Giles, had many more of difference. It was the village doctor; a man of some fifty years, whom, at an earlier period of his life, we introduced as paying a professional visit to Ethan Brand during the latter's supposed insanity. He was now a purple-visaged, rude, and brutal, yet half-gentlemanly figure, with something wild, ruined, and desperate in his talk, and in all the details of his gesture and manners. Brandy possessed this man like an evil spirit, and made him as surly and savage as a wild beast, and as miserable as a lost soul; but there was supposed to be in him such wonderful skill, such native gifts of healing, beyond any which medical science could impart, that society caught hold of him, and would not let him sink out of its reach. So, swaying to and fro upon his horse, and grumbling thick accents at the bedside, he visited all the sick-chambers for miles about among the mountain towns, and sometimes raised a dying man, as it were, by miracle, or quite as often, no doubt, sent his patient to a grave that was dug many a year too soon. The doctor had an everlasting pipe in his mouth, and, as somebody said, in allusion to his habit of swearing, it was always alight with hell-fire.

These three worthies pressed forward, and greeted Ethan Brand each after his own fashion, earnestly inviting him to partake of the contents of a certain black bottle, in which, as they averred, he would find something far better worth seeking for than the Unpardonable Sin. No mind, which has wrought itself by intense and solitary meditation into a high state of enthusiasm, can endure the kind of contact with low and vulgar modes of thought and feeling to which Ethan Brand was now subjected. It made him doubt—and, strange to say, it was a painful doubt—whether he had indeed found the Unpardonable Sin, and found it within himself. The whole question on which he had exhausted life, and more than life, looked like a delusion.

"Leave me," he said bitterly, "ye brute beasts, that have made yourselves so, shrivelling up your souls with fiery liquors! I have done with you. Years and years ago, I groped into your hearts and found nothing there for my purpose. Get ye gone!"

"Why, you uncivil scoundrel," cried the fierce doctor, "is that the way you respond to the kindness of your best friends? Then let me tell you the truth. You have no more found the Unpardonable Sin than yonder boy Joe has. You are but a crazy fellow,—I told you so twenty years ago,—neither better nor worse than a crazy fellow, and the fit companion of old Humphrey, here!"

He pointed to an old man, shabbily dressed, with long white hair, thin visage, and unsteady eyes. For some years past this aged person had been wandering about among the hills, inquiring of all travellers whom he met for his daughter. The girl, it seemed, had gone off with a company of circus-performers, and occasionally tidings of her came to the village, and fine stories were told of her glittering appearance as she rode on horseback in the ring, or performed marvellous feats on the tight-rope.

The white-haired father now approached Ethan Brand, and gazed unsteadily into his face.

"They tell me you have been all over the earth," said he, wringing his hands with earnestness. "You must have seen my daughter, for she makes a grand figure in the world, and everybody goes to see her. Did she send any word to her old father, or say when she was coming back?"

Ethan Brand's eye quailed beneath the old man's. That daughter, from whom he so earnestly desired a word of greeting, was the Esther of our tale, the very girl whom, with such cold and remorseless purpose, Ethan Brand had made the subject of a psychological experiment, and wasted, absorbed, and perhaps annihilated her soul, in the process.

"Yes," murmured he, turning away from the hoary wanderer, "it is no delusion. There is an Unpardonable Sin!"

While these things were passing, a merry scene was going forward in the area of cheerful light, beside the spring and before the door of the hut. A number of the youth of the village, young men and girls, had hurried up the hill-side, impelled by curiosity to see Ethan Brand, the hero of so many a legend familiar to their childhood. Finding nothing, however, very remarkable in his aspect,—nothing but a sunburnt wayfarer, in plain garb and dusty shoes, who sat looking into the fire as if he fancied pictures among the coals,—these young people speedily grew tired of observing him. As it happened, there was other amusement at hand. An old German Jew travelling with a diorama on his back, was passing down the mountain-road towards the village just as the party turned aside from it, and, in hopes of eking out the profits of the day, the showman had kept them company to the lime-kiln.

"Come, old Dutchman," cried one of the young men, "let us see your pictures, if you can swear they are worth looking at!"

"Oh yes, Captain," answered the Jew,—whether as a matter of courtesy or craft, he styled everybody Captain,—"I shall show you, indeed, some very superb pictures!"

So, placing his box in a proper position, he invited the young men and girls to look through the glass orifices of the machine, and proceeded to exhibit a series of the most outrageous scratchings and daubings, as specimens of the fine arts, that ever an itinerant showman had the face to impose upon his circle of spectators. The pictures were worn out, moreover, tattered, full of cracks and wrinkles, dingy with tobacco-smoke, and otherwise in a most pitiable condition. Some purported to be cities, public edifices, and ruined castles in Europe; others represented Napoleon's battles and Nelson's sea-fights; and in the midst of these would be seen a gigantic, brown, hairy hand,—which might have been mistaken for the Hand of Destiny, though, in truth, it was only the showman's,—pointing its forefinger to various scenes of the conflict, while its owner gave historical illustrations. When, with much merriment at its abominable deficiency of merit, the exhibition was concluded, the German bade little Joe put his head into the box. Viewed through the magnifying-glasses, the boy's round, rosy visage assumed the strangest imaginable aspect of an immense Titanic child, the mouth grinning broadly, and the eyes and every other feature overflowing with fun at the joke. Suddenly, however, that merry face turned pale, and its expression changed to horror, for this easily impressed and excitable child had become sensible that the eye of Ethan Brand was fixed upon him through the glass.

"You make the little man to be afraid, Captain," said the German Jew, turning up the dark and strong outline of his visage from his stooping posture.

"But look again, and, by chance, I shall cause you to see somewhat that is very fine, upon my word!"

Ethan Brand gazed into the box for an instant, and then starting back, looked fixedly at the German. What had he seen? Nothing, apparently; for a curious youth, who had peeped in almost at the same moment, beheld only a vacant space of canvas.

"I remember you now," muttered Ethan Brand to the showman.

"Ah, Captain," whispered the Jew of Nuremburg, with a dark smile, "I find it to be a heavy matter in my show-box,—this Unpardonable Sin! By my faith, Captain, it has wearied my shoulders, this long day, to carry it over the mountain."

"Peace," answered Ethan Brand, sternly, "or get thee into the furnace yonder!"

The Jew's exhibition had scarcely concluded, when a great, elderly dog—who seemed to be his own master, as no person in the company laid claim to him—saw fit to render himself the object of public notice. Hitherto, he had shown himself a very quiet, well-disposed old dog, going round from one to another, and, by way of being sociable, offering his rough head to be patted by any kindly hand that would take so much trouble. But now, all of a sudden, this grave and venerable quadruped, of his own mere motion, and without the slightest suggestion from anybody else, began to run round after his tail, which, to heighten the absurdity of the proceeding, was a great deal shorter than it should have been. Never was seen such headlong eagerness in pursuit of an object that could not possibly be attained; never was heard such a tremendous outbreak of growling, snarling, barking, and snapping,—as if one end of the ridiculous brute's body were at deadly and most unforgivable enmity with the other. Faster and faster, round about went the cur; and faster and still faster fled the unapproachable brevity of his tail; and louder and fiercer grew his yells of rage and animosity; until, utterly exhausted, and as far from the goal as ever, the foolish old dog ceased his performance as suddenly as he had begun it. The next moment he was as mild, quiet, sensible, and respectable in his deportment, as when he first scraped acquaintance with the company.

As may be supposed, the exhibition was greeted with universal laughter, clapping of hands, and shouts of encore, to which the canine performer responded by wagging all that there was to wag of his tail, but appeared totally unable to repeat his very successful effort to amuse the spectators.

Meanwhile, Ethan Brand had resumed his seat upon the log, and moved, it might be, by a perception of some remote analogy between his own case and that of this self-pursuing cur, he broke into the awful laugh, which, more than any other token, expressed the condition of his inward being. From that moment, the merriment of the party was at an end; they stood aghast, dreading lest the inauspicious sound should be reverberated around the horizon, and that mountain would thunder it to mountain, and so the horror be prolonged upon their ears. Then, whispering one to another that it was late,—that the moon was almost down,—that the August night was growing chill,—they hurried homewards, leaving the lime-burner and little Joe to deal as they might with their unwelcome guest. Save for these three human beings, the open space on the hill-side was a solitude, set in a vast gloom of forest. Beyond that darksome verge, the firelight glimmered on the stately trunks and almost black foliage of pines, intermixed with the lighter verdure of sapling oaks, maples, and poplars, while here and there lay the gigantic corpses of dead trees, decaying on the leaf-strewn soil. And it seemed to little Joe—a timorous and imaginative child—that the silent forest was holding its breath until some fearful thing should happen.

Ethan Brand thrust more wood into the fire, and closed the door of the kiln; then looking over his shoulder at the lime-burner and his son, he bade, rather than advised, them to retire to rest.

"For myself, I cannot sleep," said he. "I have matters that it concerns me to meditate upon. I will watch the fire, as I used to do in the old time."

"And call the Devil out of the furnace to keep you company, I suppose," muttered Bartram, who had been making intimate acquaintance with the black bottle above mentioned. "But watch, if you like, and call as many devils as you like! For my part, I shall be all the better for a snooze. Come, Joe!"

As the boy followed his father into the hut, he looked back at the wayfarer, and the tears came into his eyes, for his tender spirit had an intuition of the bleak and terrible loneliness in which this man had enveloped himself.

When they had gone, Ethan Brand sat listening to the crackling of the kindled wood, and looking at the little spirts of fire that issued through the chinks of the door. These trifles, however, once so familiar, had but the slightest hold of his attention, while deep within his mind he was reviewing the gradual but marvellous change that had been wrought upon him by the search to which he had devoted himself. He remembered how the night dew had fallen upon him,—how the dark forest had whispered to him,—how the stars had gleamed upon him,—a simple and loving man, watching his fire in the years gone by, and ever musing as it burned. He remembered with what tenderness, with what love and sympathy for mankind, and what pity for human guilt and woe, he had first begun to contemplate those ideas which afterwards became the inspiration of his life; with what reverence he had then looked into the heart of man, viewing it as a temple originally divine, and, however desecrated, still to be held sacred by a brother; with what awful fear he had deprecated the success of his pursuit, and prayed that the Unpardonable Sin might never be revealed to him. Then ensued that vast intellectual development, which, in its progress, disturbed the counterpoise between his mind and heart. The Idea that possessed his life had operated as a means of education; it had gone on cultivating his powers to the highest point of which they were susceptible; it had raised him from the level of an unlettered laborer to stand on a star-lit eminence, whither the philosophers of the earth, laden with the lore of universities, might vainly strive to clamber after him. So much for the intellect! But where was the heart? That, indeed, had withered,—had contracted,—had hardened,—had perished! It had ceased to partake of the universal throb. He had lost his hold of the magnetic chain of humanity. He was no longer a brother-man, opening the chambers or the dungeons of our common nature by the key of holy sympathy, which gave him a right to share in all its secrets; he was now a cold observer, looking on mankind as the subject of his experiment, and, at length, converting man and woman to be his puppets, and pulling the wires that moved them to such degrees of crime as were demanded for his study.

Thus Ethan Brand became a fiend. He began to be so from the moment that his moral nature had ceased to keep the pace of improvement with his intellect. And now, as his highest effort and inevitable development,—as the bright and gorgeous flower, and rich, delicious fruit of his life's labor,—he had produced the Unpardonable Sin!

"What more have I to seek? what more to achieve?" said Ethan Brand to himself. "My task is done, and well done!"

Starting from the log with a certain alacrity in his gait and ascending the hillock of earth that was raised against the stone circumference of the lime-kiln, he thus reached the top of the structure. It was a space of perhaps ten feet across, from edge to edge, presenting a view of the upper surface of the immense mass of broken marble with which the kiln was heaped. All these innumerable blocks and fragments of marble were red-hot and vividly on fire, sending up great spouts of blue flame, which quivered aloft and danced madly, as within a magic circle, and sank and rose again, with continual and multitudinous activity. As the lonely man bent forward over this terrible body of fire, the blasting heat smote up against his person with a breath that, it might be supposed, would have scorched and shrivelled him up in a moment.

Ethan Brand stood erect, and raised his arms on high. The blue flames played upon his face, and imparted the wild and ghastly light which alone could have suited its expression; it was that of a fiend on the verge of plunging into his gulf of intensest torment.

"O Mother Earth," cried he, "who art no more my Mother, and into whose bosom this frame shall never be resolved! O mankind, whose brotherhood I have cast off, and trampled thy great heart beneath my feet! O stars of heaven, that shone on me of old, as if to light me onward and upward!—farewell all, and forever. Come, deadly element of Fire,—henceforth my familiar friend! Embrace me, as I do thee!"

That night the sound of a fearful peal of laughter rolled heavily through the sleep of the lime-burner and his little son; dim shapes of horror and anguish haunted their dreams, and seemed still present in the rude hovel, when they opened their eyes to the daylight.

"Up, boy, up!" cried the lime-burner, staring about him. "Thank Heaven, the night is gone, at last; and rather than pass such another, I would watch my lime-kiln, wide awake, for a twelvemonth. This Ethan Brand, with his humbug of an Unpardonable Sin, has done me no such mighty favor, in taking my place!"

He issued from the hut, followed by little Joe, who kept fast hold of his father's hand. The early sunshine was already pouring its gold upon the mountaintops, and though the valleys were still in shadow, they smiled cheerfully in the promise of the bright day that was hastening onward. The village, completely shut in by hills, which swelled away gently about it, looked as if it had rested peacefully in the hollow of the great hand of Providence. Every dwelling was distinctly visible; the little spires of the two churches pointed upwards, and caught a fore-glimmering of brightness from the sun-gilt skies upon their gilded weathercocks. The tavern was astir, and the figure of the old, smoke-dried stage-agent, cigar in mouth, was seen beneath the stoop. Old Graylock was glorified with a golden cloud upon his head. Scattered likewise over the breasts of the surrounding mountains, there were heaps of hoary mist, in fantastic shapes, some of them far down into the valley, others high up towards the summits, and still others, of the same family of mist or cloud, hovering in the gold radiance of the upper atmosphere. Stepping from one to another of the clouds that rested on the hills, and thence to the loftier brotherhood that sailed in air, it seemed almost as if a mortal man might thus ascend into the heavenly regions. Earth was so mingled with sky that it was a day-dream to look at it.

To supply that charm of the familiar and homely, which Nature so readily adopts into a scene like this, the stage-coach was rattling down the mountain-road, and the driver sounded his horn, while Echo caught up the notes, and intertwined them into a rich and varied and elaborate harmony, of which the original performer could lay claim to little share. The great hills played a concert among themselves, each contributing a strain of airy sweetness.

Little Joe's face brightened at once.

"Dear father," cried he, skipping cheerily to and fro, "that strange man is gone, and the sky and the mountains all seem glad of it!"

"Yes," growled the lime-burner, with an oath, "but he has let the fire go down, and no thanks to him if five hundred bushels of lime are not spoiled. If I catch the fellow hereabouts again, I shall feel like tossing him into the furnace!"

With his long pole in his hand, he ascended to the top of the kiln. After a moment's pause, he called to his son.

"Come up here, Joe!" said he.

So little Joe ran up the hillock, and stood by his father's side. The marble was all burnt into perfect, snow-white lime. But on its surface, in the midst of the circle,—snow-white too, and thoroughly converted into lime,—lay a human skeleton, in the attitude of a person who, after long toil, lies down to long repose. Within the ribs—strange to say—was the shape of a human heart.

"Was the fellow's heart made of marble?" cried Bartram, in some perplexity at this phenomenon. "At any rate, it is burnt into what looks like special good lime; and, taking all the bones together, my kiln is half a bushel the richer for him."

So saying, the rude lime-burner lifted his pole, and, letting it fall upon the skeleton, the relics of Ethan Brand were crumbled into fragments.

SYLPH ETHEREGE

On a bright summer evening, two persons stood among the shrubbery of a garden, stealthily watching a young girl who sat in the window-seat of a neighboring mansion. One of these unseen observers, a gentleman, was youthful, and had an air of high breeding and refinement, and a face marked with intellect, though otherwise of unprepossessing aspect. His features wore even an ominous, though somewhat mirthful expression, while he pointed his long forefinger at the girl, and seemed to regard her as a creature completely within the scope of his influence.

"The charm works!" said he, in a low, but emphatic whisper.

"Do you know, Edward Hamilton,—since so you choose to be named,—do you know," said the lady beside him, "that I have almost a mind to break the spell at once? What if the lesson should prove too severe! True, if my ward could be thus laughed out of her fantastic nonsense, she might be the better for it through life. But then, she is such a delicate creature! And, besides, are you not ruining your own chance by putting forward this shadow of a rival?"

"But will he not vanish into thin air, at my bidding?" rejoined Edward Hamilton. "Let the charm work!"

The girl's slender and sylph-like figure, tinged with radiance from the sunset clouds, and overhung with the rich drapery of the silken curtains, and set within the deep frame of the window, was a perfect picture; or, rather, it was like the original loveliness in a painter's fancy, from which the most finished picture is but an imperfect copy. Though her occupation excited so much interest in the two spectators, she was merely gazing at a miniature which she held in her hand, encased in white satin and red morocco; nor did there appear to be any other cause for the smile of mockery and malice with which Hamilton regarded her.

"The charm works!" muttered he, again. "Our pretty Sylvia's scorn will have a dear retribution!"

At this moment the girl raised her eyes, and, instead of a life-like semblance of the miniature, beheld the ill-omened shape of Edward Hamilton, who now stepped forth from his concealment in the shrubbery.

Sylvia Etherege was an orphan girl, who had spent her life, till within a few months past, under the guardianship, and in the secluded dwelling, of an old bachelor uncle. While yet in her cradle, she had been the destined bride of a cousin, who was no less passive in the betrothal than herself. Their future union had been projected, as the means of uniting two rich estates, and was rendered highly expedient, if not indispensable, by the testamentary dispositions of the parents on both sides. Edgar Vaughan, the promised bridegroom, had been bred from infancy in Europe, and had never seen the beautiful girl whose heart he was to claim as his inheritance. But already, for several years, a correspondence had been kept up between the cousins, and had produced an intellectual intimacy, though it could but imperfectly acquaint them with each other's character.

Sylvia was shy, sensitive, and fanciful; and her guardian's secluded habits had shut her out from even so much of the world as is generally open to maidens of her age. She had been left to seek associates and friends for herself in the haunts of imagination, and to converse with them, sometimes in the language of dead poets, oftener in the poetry of her own mind. The companion whom she chiefly summoned up was the cousin with whose idea her earliest thoughts had been connected. She made a vision of Edgar Vaughan, and tinted it with stronger hues than a mere fancy-picture, yet graced it with so many bright and delicate perfections, that her cousin could nowhere have encountered so dangerous a rival. To this shadow she cherished a romantic fidelity. With its airy presence sitting by her side, or gliding along her favorite paths, the loneliness of her young life was blissful; her heart was satisfied with love, while yet its virgin purity was untainted by the earthliness that the touch of a real lover would have left there. Edgar Vaughan seemed to be conscious of her character; for, in his letters, he gave her a name that was happily appropriate to the sensitiveness of her disposition, the delicate peculiarity of her manners, and the ethereal beauty both of her mind and person. Instead of Sylvia, he called her Sylph,—with the prerogative of a cousin and a lover,—his dear Sylph Etherege.

When Sylvia was seventeen, her guardian died, and she passed under the care of Mrs. Grosvenor, a lady of wealth and fashion, and Sylvia's nearest relative, though a distant one. While an inmate of Mrs. Grosvenor's family, she still preserved somewhat of her life-long habits of seclusion, and shrank from a too familiar intercourse with those around her. Still, too, she was faithful to her cousin, or to the shadow which bore his name.

The time now drew near when Edgar Vaughan, whose education had been completed by an extensive range of travel, was to revisit the soil of his nativity. Edward Hamilton, a young gentleman who had been Vaughan's companion, both in his studies and rambles, had already recrossed the Atlantic, bringing letters to Mrs. Grosvenor and Sylvia Etherege. These credentials insured him an earnest welcome, which, however, on Sylvia's part, was not followed by personal partiality, or even the regard that seemed due to her cousin's most intimate friend. As she herself could have assigned no cause for her repugnance, it might be termed instinctive. Hamilton's person, it is true, was the reverse of attractive, especially when beheld for the first time. Yet, in the eyes of the most fastidious judges, the defect of natural grace was compensated by the polish of his manners, and by the intellect which so often gleamed through his dark features. Mrs. Grosvenor, with whom he immediately became a prodigious favorite, exerted herself to overcome Sylvia's dislike. But, in this matter, her ward could neither be reasoned with nor persuaded. The presence of Edward Hamilton was sure to render her cold, shy, and distant, abstracting all the vivacity from her deportment, as if a cloud had come betwixt her and the sunshine.

The simplicity of Sylvia's demeanor rendered it easy for so keen an observer as Hamilton to detect her feelings. Whenever any slight circumstance made him sensible of them, a smile might be seen to flit over the young man's sallow visage. None, that had once beheld this smile, were in any danger of forgetting it; whenever they recalled to memory the features of Edward Hamilton, they were always duskily illuminated by this expression of mockery and malice.

In a few weeks after Hamilton's arrival, he presented to Sylvia Etherege a miniature of her cousin, which, as he informed her, would have been delivered sooner, but was detained with a portion of his baggage. This was the miniature in the contemplation of which we beheld Sylvia so absorbed, at the commencement of our story. Such, in truth, was too often the habit of the shy and musing girl. The beauty of the pictured countenance was almost too perfect to represent a human creature, that had been born of a fallen and world-worn race, and had lived to manhood amid ordinary troubles and enjoyments, and must become wrinkled with age and care. It seemed too bright for a thing formed of dust, and doomed to crumble into dust again. Sylvia feared that such a being would be too refined and delicate to love a simple girl like her. Yet, even while her spirit drooped with that apprehension, the picture was but the masculine counterpart of Sylph Etherege's sylph-like beauty. There was that resemblance between her own face and the miniature which is said often to exist between lovers whom Heaven had destined for each other, and which, in this instance, might be owing to the kindred blood of the two parties. Sylvia felt, indeed, that there was something familiar in the countenance, so like a friend did the eyes smile upon her, and seem to imply a knowledge of her thoughts. She could account for this impression only by supposing that, in some of her day-dreams, imagination had conjured up the true similitude of her distant and unseen lover.

But now could Sylvia give a brighter semblance of reality to those day-dreams. Clasping the miniature to her heart, she could summon forth, from that haunted cell of pure and blissful fantasies, the life-like shadow, to roam with her in the moonlight garden. Even at noontide it sat with her in the arbor, when the sunshine threw its broken flakes of gold into the clustering shade. The effect upon her mind was hardly less powerful than if she had actually listened to, and reciprocated, the vows of Edgar Vaughan; for, though the illusion never quite deceived her, yet the remembrance was as distinct as of a remembered interview. Those heavenly eyes gazed forever into her soul, which drank at them as at a fountain, and was disquieted if reality threw a momentary cloud between. She heard the melody of a voice breathing sentiments with which her own chimed in like music. O happy, yet hapless girl! Thus to create the being whom she loves, to endow him with all the attributes that were most fascinating to her heart, and then to flit with the airy creature into the realm of fantasy and moonlight where dwelt his dreamy kindred! For her lover wiled Sylvia away from earth, which seemed strange, and dull, and darksome, and lured her to a country where her spirit roamed in peaceful rapture, deeming that it had found its home. Many, in their youth, have visited that land of dreams, and wandered so long in its enchanted groves that, when banished thence, they feel like exiles everywhere.

The dark-browed Edward Hamilton, like the villain of a tale, would often glide through the romance wherein poor Sylvia walked. Sometimes, at the most blissful moment of her ecstasy, when the features of the miniature were pictured brightest in the air, they would suddenly change, and darken, and be transformed into his visage. And always, when such change occurred, the intrusive visage wore that peculiar smile with which Hamilton had glanced at Sylvia.

Before the close of summer, it was told Sylvia Etherege that Vaughan had arrived from France, and that she would meet him—would meet, for the first time, the loved of years—that very evening. We will not tell how often and how earnestly she gazed upon the miniature, thus endeavoring to prepare herself for the approaching interview, lest the throbbing of her timorous heart should stifle the words of welcome. While the twilight grew deeper and duskier, she sat with Mrs. Grosvenor in an inner apartment, lighted only by the softened gleam from an alabaster lamp, which was burning at a distance on the centre-table of the drawing-room. Never before had Sylph Etherege looked so sylph-like. She had communed with a creature of imagination, till her own loveliness seemed but the creation of a delicate and dreamy fancy. Every vibration of her spirit was visible in her frame, as she listened to the rattling of wheels and the tramp upon the pavement, and deemed that even the breeze bore the sound of her lover's footsteps, as if he trode upon the viewless air.

Mrs. Grosvenor, too, while she watched the tremulous flow of Sylvia's feelings, was deeply moved; she looked uneasily at the agitated girl, and was about to speak, when the opening of the street-door arrested the words upon her lips.

Footsteps ascended the staircase, with a confident and familiar tread, and some one entered the drawing-room. From the sofa where they sat, in the inner apartment, Mrs. Grosvenor and Sylvia could not discern the visitor.

"Sylph!" cried a voice. "Dearest Sylph! Where are you, sweet Sylph Etherege? Here is your Edgar Vaughan!"

But instead of answering, or rising to meet her lover,—who had greeted her by the sweet and fanciful name, which, appropriate as it was to her character, was known only to him,—Sylvia grasped Mrs. Grosvenor's arm, while her whole frame shook with the throbbing of her heart.

"Who is it?" gasped she. "Who calls me Sylph?"

Before Mrs. Grosvenor could reply, the stranger entered the room, bearing the lamp in his hand. Approaching the sofa, he displayed to Sylvia the features of Edward Hamilton, illuminated by that evil smile, from which his face derived so marked an individuality.

"Is not the miniature an admirable likeness?" inquired he.

Sylvia shuddered, but had not power to turn away her white face from his gaze. The miniature, which she had been holding in her hand, fell down upon the floor, where Hamilton, or Vaughan, set his foot upon it, and crushed the ivory counterfeit to fragments.

"There, my sweet Sylph," he exclaimed. "It was I that created your phantom-lover, and now I annihilate him! Your dream is rudely broken. Awake, Sylph Etherege, awake to truth! I am the only Edgar Vaughan!"

"We have gone too far, Edgar Vaughan," said Mrs. Grosvenor, catching Sylvia in her arms. The revengeful freak, which Vaughan's wounded vanity had suggested, had been countenanced by this lady, in the hope of curing Sylvia of her romantic notions, and reconciling her to the truths and realities of life. "Look at the poor child!" she continued. "I protest I tremble for the consequences!"

"Indeed, madam!" replied Vaughan, sneeringly, as he threw the light of the lamp on Sylvia's closed eyes and marble features. "Well, my conscience is clear. I did but look into this delicate creature's heart; and with the pure fantasies that I found there I made what seemed a man,—and the delusive shadow has wiled her away to Shadow-land, and vanished there! It is no new tale. Many a sweet maid has shared the lot of poor Sylph Etherege!"

"And now, Edgar Vaughan," said Mrs. Grosvenor, as Sylvia's heart began faintly to throb again, "now try, in good earnest, to win back her love from the phantom which you conjured up. If you succeed, she will be the better, her whole life long, for the lesson we have given her."

Whether the result of the lesson corresponded with Mrs. Grosvenor's hopes may be gathered from the closing scene of our story. It had been made known to the fashionable world that Edgar Vaughan had returned from France, and, under the assumed name of Edward Hamilton, had won the affections of the lovely girl to whom he had been affianced in his boyhood. The nuptials were to take place at an early date. One evening, before the day of anticipated bliss arrived, Edgar Vaughan entered Mrs. Grosvenor's drawing-room, where he found that lady and Sylph Etherege.

"Only that Sylvia makes no complaint," remarked Mrs. Grosvenor, "I should apprehend that the town air is ill-suited to her constitution. She was always, indeed, a delicate creature; but now she is a mere gossamer. Do but look at her! Did you ever imagine anything so fragile?"

Vaughan was already attentively observing his mistress, who sat in a shadowy and moonlighted recess of the room, with her dreamy eyes fixed steadfastly upon his own. The bough of a tree was waving before the window, and sometimes enveloped her in the gloom of its shadow, into which she seemed to vanish.

"Yes," he said, to Mrs. Grosvenor. "I can scarcely deem her 'of the earth, earthy.' No wonder that I call her Sylph! Methinks she will fade into the moonlight, which falls upon her through the window. Or, in the open air, she might flit away upon the breeze, like a wreath of mist!"

Sylvia's eyes grew yet brighter. She waved her hand to Edgar Vaughan, with a gesture of ethereal triumph.

"Farewell!" she said. "I will neither fade into the moonlight, nor flit away upon the breeze. Yet you cannot keep me here!"

There was something in Sylvia's look and tones that startled Mrs. Grosvenor with a terrible apprehension. But, as she was rushing towards the girl, Vaughan held her back.

"Stay!" cried he, with a strange smile of mockery and anguish. "Can our sweet Sylph be going to heaven, to seek the original of the miniature?"

THE CANTERBURY PILGRIMS

The summer moon, which shines in so many a tale, was beaming over a broad extent of uneven country. Some of its brightest rays were flung into a spring of water, where no traveller, toiling, as the writer has, up the hilly road beside which it gushes, ever failed to quench his thirst. The work of neat hands and considerate art was visible about this blessed fountain. An open cistern, hewn and hollowed out of solid stone, was placed above the waters, which filled it to the brim, but by some invisible outlet were conveyed away without dripping down its sides. Though the basin had not room for another drop, and the continual gush of water made a tremor on the surface, there was a secret charm that forbade it to overflow. I remember, that when I had slaked my summer thirst, and sat panting by the cistern, it was my fanciful theory that Nature could not afford to lavish so pure a liquid, as she does the waters of all meaner fountains.

While the moon was hanging almost perpendicularly over this spot, two figures appeared on the summit of the hill, and came with noiseless footsteps down towards the spring. They were then in the first freshness of youth; nor is there a wrinkle now on either of their brows, and yet they wore a strange, old-fashioned garb. One, a young man with ruddy cheeks, walked beneath the canopy of a broad-brimmed gray hat; he seemed to have inherited his great-grandsire's square-skirted coat, and a waistcoat that extended its immense flaps to his knees; his brown locks, also, hung down behind, in a mode unknown to our times. By his side was a sweet young damsel, her fair features sheltered by a prim little bonnet, within which appeared the vestal muslin of a cap; her close, long-waisted gown, and indeed her whole attire, might have been worn by some rustic beauty who had faded half a century before. But that there was something too warm and life-like in them, I would here have compared this couple to the ghosts of two young lovers who had died long since in the glow of passion, and now were straying out of their graves, to renew the old vows, and shadow forth the unforgotten kiss of their earthly lips, beside the moonlit spring.

"Thee and I will rest here a moment, Miriam," said the young man, as they drew near the stone cistern, "for there is no fear that the elders know what we have done; and this may be the last time we shall ever taste this water."

Thus speaking, with a little sadness in his face, which was also visible in that of his companion, he made her sit down on a stone, and was about to place himself very close to her side; she, however, repelled him, though not unkindly.

"Nay, Josiah," said she, giving him a timid push with her maiden hand, "thee must sit farther off, on that other stone, with the spring between us. What would the sisters say, if thee were to sit so close to me?"

"But we are of the world's people now, Miriam," answered Josiah.

The girl persisted in her prudery, nor did the youth, in fact, seem altogether free from a similar sort of shyness; so they sat apart from each other, gazing up the hill, where the moonlight discovered the tops of a group of buildings. While their attention was thus occupied, a party of travellers, who had come wearily up the long ascent, made a halt to refresh themselves at the spring. There were three men, a woman, and a little girl and boy. Their attire was mean, covered with the dust of the summer's day, and damp with the night-dew; they all looked woebegone, as if the cares and sorrows of the world had made their steps heavier as they climbed the hill; even the two little children appeared older in evil days than the young man and maiden who had first approached the spring.

"Good evening to you, young folks," was the salutation of the travellers; and "Good evening, friends," replied the youth and damsel.

"Is that white building the Shaker meeting-house?" asked one of the strangers. "And are those the red roofs of the Shaker village?"

"Friend, it is the Shaker village," answered Josiah, after some hesitation.

The travellers, who, from the first, had looked suspiciously at the garb of these young people, now taxed them with an intention which all the circumstances, indeed, rendered too obvious to be mistaken.

"It is true, friends," replied the young man, summoning up his courage. "Miriam and I have a gift to love each other, and we are going among the world's people, to live after their fashion. And ye know that we do not transgress the law of the land; and neither ye, nor the elders themselves, have a right to hinder us."

"Yet you think it expedient to depart without leave-taking," remarked one of the travellers.

"Yea, ye-a," said Josiah, reluctantly, "because father Job is a very awful man to speak with; and being aged himself, he has but little charity for what he calls the iniquities of the flesh."

"Well," said the stranger, "we will neither use force to bring you back to the village, nor will we betray you to the elders. But sit you here awhile, and when you have heard what we shall tell you of the world which we have left, and into which you are going, perhaps you will turn back with us of your own accord. What say you?" added he, turning to his companions. "We have travelled thus far without becoming known to each other. Shall we tell our stories, here by this pleasant spring, for our own pastime, and the benefit of these misguided young lovers?"

In accordance with this proposal, the whole party stationed themselves round the stone cistern; the two children, being very weary, fell asleep upon the damp earth, and the pretty Shaker girl, whose feelings were those of a nun or a Turkish lady, crept as close as possible to the female traveller, and as far as she well could from the unknown men. The same person who had hitherto been the chief spokesman now stood up, waving his hat in his hand, and suffered the moonlight to fall full upon his front.

"In me," said he, with a certain majesty of utterance,—"in me, you behold a poet."

Though a lithographic print of this gentleman is extant, it may be well to notice that he was now nearly forty, a thin and stooping figure, in a black coat, out at elbows; notwithstanding the ill condition of his attire, there were about him several tokens of a peculiar sort of foppery, unworthy of a mature man, particularly in the arrangement of his hair, which was so disposed as to give all possible loftiness and breadth to his forehead. However, he had an intelligent eye, and, on the whole, a marked countenance.

"A poet!" repeated the young Shaker, a little puzzled how to understand such a designation, seldom heard in the utilitarian community where he had spent his life. "Oh, ay, Miriam, he means a varse-maker, thee must know."

This remark jarred upon the susceptible nerves of the poet; nor could he help wondering what strange fatality had put into this young man's mouth an epithet, which ill-natured people had affirmed to be more proper to his merit than the one assumed by himself.

"True, I am a verse-maker," he resumed, "but my verse is no more than the material body into which I breathe the celestial soul of thought. Alas! how many a pang has it cost me, this same insensibility to the ethereal essence of poetry, with which you have here tortured me again, at the moment when I am to relinquish my profession forever! O Fate! why hast thou warred with Nature, turning all her higher and more perfect gifts to the ruin of me, their possessor? What is the voice of song, when the world lacks the ear of taste? How can I rejoice in my strength and delicacy of feeling, when they have but made great sorrows out of little ones? Have I dreaded scorn like death, and yearned for fame as others pant for vital air, only to find myself in a middle state between obscurity and infamy? But I have my revenge! I could have given existence to a thousand bright creations. I crush them into my heart, and there let them putrefy! I shake off the dust of my feet against my countrymen! But posterity, tracing my footsteps up this weary hill, will cry shame upon the unworthy age that drove one of the fathers of American song to end his days in a Shaker village!"

During this harangue, the speaker gesticulated with great energy, and, as poetry is the natural language of passion, there appeared reason to apprehend his final explosion into an ode extempore. The reader must understand that, for all these bitter words, he was a kind, gentle, harmless, poor fellow enough, whom Nature, tossing her ingredients together without looking at her recipe, had sent into the world with too much of one sort of brain, and hardly any of another.

"Friend," said the young Shaker, in some perplexity, "thee seemest to have met with great troubles; and, doubtless, I should pity them, if—if I could but understand what they were."

"Happy in your ignorance!" replied the poet, with an air of sublime superiority. "To your coarser mind, perhaps, I may seem to speak of more important griefs when I add, what I had wellnigh forgotten, that I am out at elbows, and almost starved to death. At any rate, you have the advice and example of one individual to warn you back; for I am come hither, a disappointed man, flinging aside the fragments of my hopes, and seeking shelter in the calm retreat which you are so anxious to leave."

"I thank thee, friend," rejoined the youth, "but I do not mean to be a poet, nor, Heaven be praised! do I think Miriam ever made a varse in her life. So we need not fear thy disappointments. But, Miriam," he added, with real concern, "thee knowest that the elders admit nobody that has not a gift to be useful. Now, what under the sun can they do with this poor varse-maker?"

"Nay, Josiah, do not thee discourage the poor man," said the girl, in all simplicity and kindness. "Our hymns are very rough, and perhaps they may trust him to smooth them."

Without noticing this hint of professional employment, the poet turned away, and gave himself up to a sort of vague reverie, which he called thought. Sometimes he watched the moon, pouring a silvery liquid on the clouds, through which it slowly melted till they became all bright; then he saw the same sweet radiance dancing on the leafy trees which rustled as if to shake it off, or sleeping on the high tops of hills, or hovering down in distant valleys, like the material of unshaped dreams; lastly, he looked into the spring, and there the light was mingling with the water. In its crystal bosom, too, beholding all heaven reflected there, he found an emblem of a pure and tranquil breast. He listened to that most ethereal of all sounds, the song of crickets, coming in full choir upon the wind, and fancied that, if moonlight could be heard, it would sound just like that. Finally, he took a draught at the Shaker spring, and, as if it were the true Castalia, was forthwith moved to compose a lyric, a Farewell to his Harp, which he swore should be its closing strain, the last verse that an ungrateful world should have from him. This effusion, with two or three other little pieces, subsequently written, he took the first opportunity to send, by one of the Shaker brethren, to Concord, where they were published in the New Hampshire Patriot.

Meantime, another of the Canterbury pilgrims, one so different from the poet that the delicate fancy of the latter could hardly have conceived of him, began to relate his sad experience. He was a small man, of quick and unquiet gestures, about fifty years old, with a narrow forehead, all wrinkled and drawn together. He held in his hand a pencil, and a card of some commission-merchant in foreign parts, on the back of which, for there was light enough to read or write by, he seemed ready to figure out a calculation.

"Young man," said he, abruptly, "what quantity of land do the Shakers own here, in Canterbury?"

"That is more than I can tell thee, friend," answered Josiah, "but it is a very rich establishment, and for a long way by the roadside thee may guess the land to be ours, by the neatness of the fences."

"And what may be the value of the whole," continued the stranger, "with all the buildings and improvements, pretty nearly, in round numbers?"

"Oh, a monstrous sum,—more than I can reckon," replied the young Shaker.

"Well, sir," said the pilgrim, "there was a day, and not very long ago, neither, when I stood at my counting-room window, and watched the signal flags of three of my own ships entering the harbor, from the East Indies, from Liverpool, and from up the Straits, and I would not have given the invoice of the least of them for the title-deeds of this whole Shaker settlement. You stare. Perhaps, now, you won't believe that I could have put more value on a little piece of paper, no bigger than the palm of your hand, than all these solid acres of grain, grass, and pasture-land would sell for?"

"I won't dispute it, friend," answered Josiah, "but I know I had rather have fifty acres of this good land than a whole sheet of thy paper."

"You may say so now," said the ruined merchant, bitterly, "for my name would not be worth the paper I should write it on. Of course, you must have heard of my failure?"

And the stranger mentioned his name, which, however mighty it might have been in the commercial world, the young Shaker had never heard of among the Canterbury hills.

"Not heard of my failure!" exclaimed the merchant, considerably piqued. "Why, it was spoken of on 'Change in London, and from Boston to New Orleans men trembled in their shoes. At all events, I did fail, and you see me here on my road to the Shaker village, where, doubtless (for the Shakers are a shrewd sect), they will have a due respect for my experience, and give me the management of the trading part of the concern, in which case I think I can pledge myself to double their capital in four or five years. Turn back with me, young man; for though you will never meet with my good luck, you can hardly escape my bad."

"I will not turn back for this," replied Josiah, calmly, "any more than for the advice of the varse-maker, between whom and thee, friend, I see a sort of likeness, though I can't justly say where it lies. But Miriam and I can earn our daily bread among the world's people as well as in the Shaker village. And do we want anything more, Miriam?"

"Nothing more, Josiah," said the girl, quietly.

"Yea, Miriam, and daily bread for some other little mouths, if God send them," observed the simple Shaker lad.

Miriam did not reply, but looked down into the spring, where she encountered the image of her own pretty face, blushing within the prim little bonnet. The third pilgrim now took up the conversation. He was a sunburnt countryman, of tall frame and bony strength, on whose rude and manly face there appeared a darker, more sullen and obstinate despondency, than on those of either the poet or the merchant.

"Well, now, youngster," he began, "these folks have had their say, so I'll take my turn. My story will cut but a poor figure by the side of theirs; for I never supposed that I could have a right to meat and drink, and great praise besides, only for tagging rhymes together, as it seems this man does; nor ever tried to get the substance of hundreds into my own hands, like the trader there. When I was about of your years, I married me a wife,—just such a neat and pretty young woman as Miriam, if that's her name,—and all I asked of Providence was an ordinary blessing on the sweat of my brow, so that we might be decent and comfortable, and have daily bread for ourselves, and for some other little mouths that we soon had to feed. We had no very great prospects before us; but I never wanted to be idle; and I thought it a matter of course that the Lord would help me, because I was willing to help myself."

"And didn't He help thee, friend?" demanded Josiah, with some eagerness.

"No," said the yeoman, sullenly; "for then you would not have seen me here. I have labored hard for years; and my means have been growing narrower, and my living poorer, and my heart colder and heavier, all the time; till at last I could bear it no longer. I set myself down to calculate whether I had best go on the Oregon expedition, or come here to the Shaker village; but I had not hope enough left in me to begin the world over again; and, to make my story short, here I am. And now, youngster, take my advice, and turn back; or else, some few years hence, you'll have to climb this hill, with as heavy a heart as mine."

This simple story had a strong effect on the young fugitives. The misfortunes of the poet and merchant had won little sympathy from their plain good sense and unworldly feelings, qualities which made them such unprejudiced and inflexible judges, that few men would have chosen to take the opinion of this youth and maiden as to the wisdom or folly of their pursuits. But here was one whose simple wishes had resembled their own, and who, after efforts which almost gave him a right to claim success from fate, had failed in accomplishing them.

"But thy wife, friend?" exclaimed the young man. "What became of the pretty girl, like Miriam? Oh, I am afraid she is dead!"

"Yea, poor man, she must be dead,—she and the children, too," sobbed Miriam.

The female pilgrim had been leaning over the spring, wherein latterly a tear or two might have been seen to fall, and form its little circle on the surface of the water. She now looked up, disclosing features still comely, but which had acquired an expression of fretfulness, in the same long course of evil fortune that had thrown a sullen gloom over the temper of the unprosperous yeoman.

"I am his wife," said she, a shade of irritability just perceptible in the sadness of her tone. "These poor little things, asleep on the ground, are two of our children. We had two more, but God has provided better for them than we could, by taking them to Himself."

"And what would thee advise Josiah and me to do?" asked Miriam, this being the first question which she had put to either of the strangers.

"'T is a thing almost against nature for a woman to try to part true lovers," answered the yeoman's wife, after a pause; "but I'll speak as truly to you as if these were my dying words. Though my husband told you some of our troubles, he didn't mention the greatest, and that which makes all the rest so hard to bear. If you and your sweetheart marry, you'll be kind and pleasant to each other for a year or two, and while that's the case, you never will repent; but, by and by, he'll grow gloomy, rough, and hard to please, and you'll be peevish, and full of little angry fits, and apt to be complaining by the fireside, when he comes to rest himself from his troubles out of doors; so your love will wear away by little and little, and leave you miserable at last. It has been so with us; and yet my husband and I were true lovers once, if ever two young folks were."

As she ceased, the yeoman and his wife exchanged a glance, in which there was more and warmer affection than they had supposed to have escaped the frost of a wintry fate, in either of their breasts. At that moment, when they stood on the utmost verge of married life, one word fitly spoken, or perhaps one peculiar look, had they had mutual confidence enough to reciprocate it, might have renewed all their old feelings, and sent them back, resolved to sustain each other amid the struggles of the world. But the crisis passed and never came again. Just then, also, the children, roused by their mother's voice, looked up, and added their wailing accents to the testimony borne by all the Canterbury pilgrims against the world from which they fled.

"We are tired and hungry!" cried they. "Is it far to the Shaker village?"

The Shaker youth and maiden looked mournfully into each other's eyes. They had but stepped across the threshold of their homes, when lo! the dark array of cares and sorrows that rose up to warn them back. The varied narratives of the strangers had arranged themselves into a parable; they seemed not merely instances of woful fate that had befallen others, but shadowy omens of disappointed hope and unavailing toil, domestic grief and estranged affection, that would cloud the onward path of these poor fugitives. But after one instant's hesitation, they opened their arms, and sealed their resolve with as pure and fond an embrace as ever youthful love had hallowed.

"We will not go back," said they. "The world never can be dark to us, for we will always love one another."

Then the Canterbury pilgrims went up the hill, while the poet chanted a drear and desperate stanza of the Farewell to his Harp, fitting music for that melancholy band. They sought a home where all former ties of nature or society would be sundered, and all old distinctions levelled, and a cold and passionless security be substituted for mortal hope and fear, as in that other refuge of the world's weary outcasts, the grave. The lovers drank at the Shaker spring, and then, with chastened hopes, but more confiding affections, went on to mingle in an untried life.

THE MAN OF ADAMANT

AN APOLOGUE

In the old times of religious gloom and intolerance lived Richard Digby, the gloomiest and most intolerant of a stern brotherhood. His plan of salvation was so narrow, that, like a plank in a tempestuous sea, it could avail no sinner but himself, who bestrode it triumphantly, and hurled anathemas against the wretches whom he saw struggling with the billows of eternal death. In his view of the matter, it was a most abominable crime—as, indeed, it is a great folly—for men to trust to their own strength, or even to grapple to any other fragment of the wreck, save this narrow plank, which, moreover, he took special care to keep out of their reach. In other words, as his creed was like no man's else, and being well pleased that Providence had intrusted him alone, of mortals, with the treasure of a true faith, Richard Digby determined to seclude himself to the sole and constant enjoyment of his happy fortune.

"And verily," thought he, "I deem it a chief condition of Heaven's mercy to myself, that I hold no communion with those abominable myriads which it hath cast off to perish. Peradventure, were I to tarry longer in the tents of Kedar, the gracious boon would be revoked, and I also be swallowed up in the deluge of wrath, or consumed in the storm of fire and brimstone, or involved in whatever new kind of ruin is ordained for the horrible perversity of this generation."

So Richard Digby took an axe, to hew space enough for a tabernacle in the wilderness, and some few other necessaries, especially a sword and gun, to smite and slay any intruder upon his hallowed seclusion, and plunged into the dreariest depths of the forest. On its verge, however, he paused a moment, to shake off the dust of his feet against the village where he had dwelt, and to invoke a curse on the meeting-house, which he regarded as a temple of heathen idolatry. He felt a curiosity, also, to see whether the fire and brimstone would not rush down from heaven at once, now that the one righteous man had provided for his own safety. But, as the sunshine continued to fall peacefully on the cottages and fields, and the husbandmen labored and children played, and as there were many tokens of present happiness, and nothing ominous of a speedy judgment, he turned away, somewhat disappointed. The farther he went, however, and the lonelier he felt himself, and the thicker the trees stood along his path, and the darker the shadow overhead, so much the more did Richard Digby exult. He talked to himself as he strode onward; he read his Bible to himself as he sat beneath the trees; and, as the gloom of the forest hid the blessed sky, I had almost added, that, at morning, noon, and eventide, he prayed to himself. So congenial was this mode of life to his disposition, that he often laughed to himself, but was displeased when an echo tossed him back the long loud roar.

In this manner he journeyed onward three days and two nights, and came, on the third evening, to the mouth of a cave, which, at first sight, reminded him of Elijah's cave at Horeb, though perhaps it more resembled Abraham's sepulchral cave at Machpelah. It entered into the heart of a rocky hill. There was so dense a veil of tangled foliage about it, that none but a sworn lover of gloomy recesses would have discovered the low arch of its entrance, or have dared to step within its vaulted chamber, where the burning eyes of a panther might encounter him. If Nature meant this remote and dismal cavern for the use of man, it could only be to bury in its gloom the victims of a pestilence, and then to block up its mouth with stones, and avoid the spot forever after. There was nothing bright nor cheerful near it, except a bubbling fountain, some twenty paces off, at which Richard Digby hardly threw away a glance. But he thrust his head into the cave, shivered, and congratulated himself.

"The finger of Providence hath pointed my way!" cried he, aloud, while the tomb-like den returned a strange echo, as if some one within were mocking him. "Here my soul will be at peace; for the wicked will not find me. Here I can read the Scriptures, and be no more provoked with lying interpretations. Here I can offer up acceptable prayers, because my voice will not be mingled with the sinful supplications of the multitude. Of a truth, the only way to heaven leadeth through the narrow entrance of this cave,—and I alone have found it!"

In regard to this cave it was observable that the roof, so far as the imperfect light permitted it to be seen, was hung with substances resembling opaque icicles; for the damps of unknown centuries, dripping down continually, had become as hard as adamant; and wherever that moisture fell, it seemed to possess the power of converting what it bathed to stone. The fallen leaves and sprigs of foliage, which the wind had swept into the cave, and the little feathery shrubs, rooted near the threshold, were not wet with a natural dew, but had been embalmed by this wondrous process. And here I am put in mind that Richard Digby, before he withdrew himself from the world, was supposed by skilful physicians to have contracted a disease for which no remedy was written in their medical books. It was a deposition of calculous particles within his heart, caused by an obstructed circulation of the blood; and, unless a miracle should be wrought for him, there was danger that the malady might act on the entire substance of the organ, and change his fleshy heart to stone. Many, indeed, affirmed that the process was already near its consummation. Richard Digby, however, could never be convinced that any such direful work was going on within him; nor when he saw the sprigs of marble foliage, did his heart even throb the quicker, at the similitude suggested by these once tender herbs. It may be that this same insensibility was a symptom of the disease.

Be that as it might, Richard Digby was well contented with his sepulchral cave. So dearly did he love this congenial spot, that, instead of going a few paces to the bubbling spring for water, he allayed his thirst with now and then a drop of moisture from the roof, which, had it fallen anywhere but on his tongue, would have been congealed into a pebble. For a man predisposed to stoniness of the heart, this surely was unwholesome liquor. But there he dwelt for three days more, eating herbs and roots, drinking his own destruction, sleeping, as it were, in a tomb, and awaking to the solitude of death, yet esteeming this horrible mode of life as hardly inferior to celestial bliss. Perhaps superior; for above the sky, there would be angels to disturb him. At the close of the third day, he sat in the portal of his mansion, reading the Bible aloud, because no other ear could profit by it, and reading it amiss, because the rays of the setting sun did not penetrate the dismal depth of shadow round about him, nor fall upon the sacred page. Suddenly, however, a faint gleam of light was thrown over the volume, and raising his eyes, Richard Digby saw that a young woman stood before the mouth of the cave, and that the sunbeams bathed her white garment, which thus seemed to possess a radiance of its own.

"Good evening, Richard," said the girl; "I have come from afar to find thee."

The slender grace and gentle loveliness of this young woman were at once recognized by Richard Digby. Her name was Mary Goffe. She had been a convert to his preaching of the word in England, before he yielded himself to that exclusive bigotry which now enfolded him with such an iron grasp that no other sentiment could reach his bosom. When he came a pilgrim to America, she had remained in her father's hall; but now, as it appeared, had crossed the ocean after him, impelled by the same faith that led other exiles hither, and perhaps by love almost as holy. What else but faith and love united could have sustained so delicate a creature, wandering thus far into the forest, with her golden hair dishevelled by the boughs, and her feet wounded by the thorns? Yet, weary and faint though she must have been, and affrighted at the dreariness of the cave, she looked on the lonely man with a mild and pitying expression, such as might beam from an angel's eyes, towards an afflicted mortal. But the recluse, frowning sternly upon her, and keeping his finger between the leaves of his half-closed Bible, motioned her away with his hand.

"Off!" cried he. "I am sanctified, and thou art sinful. Away!"

"O Richard," said she, earnestly, "I have come this weary way because I heard that a grievous distemper had seized upon thy heart; and a great Physician hath given me the skill to cure it. There is no other remedy than this which I have brought thee. Turn me not away, therefore, nor refuse my medicine; for then must this dismal cave be thy sepulchre."

"Away!" replied Richard Digby, still with a dark frown. "My heart is in better condition than thine own. Leave me, earthly one; for the sun is almost set; and when no light reaches the door of the cave, then is my prayer-time."

Now, great as was her need, Mary Goffe did not plead with this stony-hearted man for shelter and protection, nor ask anything whatever for her own sake. All her zeal was for his welfare.

"Come back with me!" she exclaimed, clasping her hands,—"come back to thy fellow-men; for they need thee, Richard, and thou hast tenfold need of them. Stay not in this evil den; for the air is chill, and the damps are fatal; nor will any that perish within it ever find the path to heaven. Hasten hence, I entreat thee, for thine own soul's sake; for either the roof will fall upon thy head, or some other speedy destruction is at hand."

"Perverse woman!" answered Richard Digby, laughing aloud,—for he was moved to bitter mirth by her foolish vehemence,—"I tell thee that the path to heaven leadeth straight through this narrow portal where I sit. And, moreover, the destruction thou speakest of is ordained, not for this blessed cave, but for all other habitations of mankind, throughout the earth. Get thee hence speedily, that thou mayst have thy share!"

So saying, he opened his Bible again, and fixed his eyes intently on the page, being resolved to withdraw his thoughts from this child of sin and wrath, and to waste no more of his holy breath upon her. The shadow had now grown so deep, where he was sitting, that he made continual mistakes in what he read, converting all that was gracious and merciful to denunciations of vengeance and unutterable woe on every created being but himself. Mary Goffe, meanwhile, was leaning against a tree, beside the sepulchral cave, very sad, yet with something heavenly and ethereal in her unselfish sorrow. The light from the setting sun still glorified her form, and was reflected a little way within the darksome den, discovering so terrible a gloom that the maiden shuddered for its self-doomed inhabitant. Espying the bright fountain near at hand, she hastened thither, and scooped up a portion of its water in a cup of birchen bark. A few tears mingled with the draught, and perhaps gave it all its efficacy. She then returned to the mouth of the cave, and knelt down at Richard Digby's feet.

"Richard," she said, with passionate fervor, yet a gentleness in all her passion, "I pray thee, by thy hope of heaven, and as thou wouldst not dwell in this tomb forever, drink of this hallowed water, be it but a single drop! Then, make room for me by thy side, and let us read together one page of that blessed volume; and, lastly, kneel down with me and pray! Do this, and thy stony heart shall become softer than a babe's and all be well."

But Richard Digby, in utter abhorrence of the proposal, cast the Bible at his feet, and eyed her with such a fixed and evil frown, that he looked less like a living man than a marble statue, wrought by some dark-imagined sculptor to express the most repulsive mood that human features could assume. And, as his look grew even devilish, so, with an equal change did Mary Goffe become more sad, more mild, more pitiful, more like a sorrowing angel. But, the more heavenly she was, the more hateful did she seem to Richard Digby, who at length raised his hand, and smote down the cup of hallowed water upon the threshold of the cave, thus rejecting the only medicine that could have cured his stony heart. A sweet perfume lingered in the air for a moment, and then was gone.

"Tempt me no more, accursed woman," exclaimed he, still with his marble frown, "lest I smite thee down also! What hast thou to do with my Bible?—what with my prayers?—what with my heaven?"

No sooner had he spoken these dreadful words, than Richard Digby's heart ceased to beat; while—so the legend says—the form of Mary Goffe melted into the last sunbeams, and returned from the sepulchral cave to heaven. For Mary Goffe had been buried in an English churchyard, months before; and either it was her ghost that haunted the wild forest, or else a dream-like spirit, typifying pure Religion.

Above a century afterwards, when the trackless forest of Richard Digby's day had long been interspersed with settlements, the children of a neighboring farmer were playing at the foot of a hill. The trees, on account of the rude and broken surface of this acclivity, had never been felled, and were crowded so densely together as to hide all but a few rocky prominences, wherever their roots could grapple with the soil. A little boy and girl, to conceal themselves from their playmates, had crept into the deepest shade, where not only the darksome pines, but a thick veil of creeping plants suspended from an overhanging rock, combined to make a twilight at noonday, and almost a midnight at all other seasons. There the children hid themselves, and shouted, repeating the cry at intervals, till the whole party of pursuers were drawn thither, and, pulling aside the matted foliage, let in a doubtful glimpse of daylight. But scarcely was this accomplished, when the little group uttered a simultaneous shriek, and tumbled headlong down the hill, making the best of their way homeward, without a second glance into the gloomy recess. Their father, unable to comprehend what had so startled them, took his axe, and, by felling one or two trees, and tearing away the creeping plants, laid the mystery open to the day. He had discovered the entrance of a cave, closely resembling the mouth of a sepulchre, within which sat the figure of a man, whose gesture and attitude warned the father and children to stand back, while his visage wore a most forbidding frown. This repulsive personage seemed to have been carved in the same gray stone that formed the walls and portal of the cave. On minuter inspection, indeed, such blemishes were observed as made it doubtful whether the figure were really a statue, chiselled by human art, and somewhat worn and defaced by the lapse of ages, or a freak of Nature, who might have chosen to imitate, in stone, her usual handiwork of flesh. Perhaps it was the least unreasonable idea, suggested by this strange spectacle, that the moisture of the cave possessed a petrifying quality, which had thus awfully embalmed a human corpse.

There was something so frightful in the aspect of this Man of Adamant, that the farmer, the moment that he recovered from the fascination of his first gaze, began to heap stones into the mouth of the cavern. His wife, who had followed him to the hill, assisted her husband's efforts. The children, also, approached as near as they durst, with their little hands full of pebbles, and cast them on the pile. Earth was then thrown into the crevices, and the whole fabric overlaid with sods. Thus all traces of the discovery were obliterated, leaving only a marvellous legend, which grew wilder from one generation to another, as the children told it to their grandchildren, and they to their posterity, till few believed that there had ever been a cavern or a statue, where now they saw but a grassy patch on the shadowy hill-side. Yet grown people avoid the spot, nor do children play there. Friendship, and Love, and Piety, all human and celestial sympathies, should keep aloof from that hidden cave; for there still sits, and, unless an earthquake crumble down the roof upon his head, shall sit forever, the shape of Richard Digby, in the attitude of repelling the whole race of mortals,—not from heaven,—but from the horrible loneliness of his dark, cold sepulchre!

THE DEVIL IN MANUSCRIPT

On a bitter evening of December, I arrived by mail in a large town, which was then the residence of an intimate friend, one of those gifted youths who cultivate poetry and the belles-lettres, and call themselves students at law. My first business, after supper, was to visit him at the office of his distinguished instructor. As I have said, it was a bitter night, clear starlight, but cold as Nova Zembla,—the shop-windows along the street being frosted, so as almost to hide the lights, while the wheels of coaches thundered equally loud over frozen earth and pavements of stone. There was no snow, either on the ground or the roofs of the houses. The wind blew so violently, that I had but to spread my cloak like a main-sail, and scud along the street at the rate of ten knots, greatly envied by other navigators, who were beating slowly up, with the gale right in their teeth. One of these I capsized, but was gone on the wings of the wind before he could even vociferate an oath.

After this picture of an inclement night, behold us seated by a great blazing fire, which looked so comfortable and delicious that I felt inclined to lie down and roll among the hot coals. The usual furniture of a lawyer's office was around us,—rows of volumes in sheepskin, and a multitude of writs, summonses, and other legal papers, scattered over the desks and tables. But there were certain objects which seemed to intimate that we had little dread of the intrusion of clients, or of the learned counsellor himself, who, indeed, was attending court in a distant town. A tall, decanter-shaped bottle stood on the table, between two tumblers, and beside a pile of blotted manuscripts, altogether dissimilar to any law documents recognized in our courts. My friend, whom I shall call Oberon,—it was a name of fancy and friendship between him and me,—my friend Oberon looked at these papers with a peculiar expression of disquietude.

"I do believe," said he, soberly, "or, at least, I could believe, if I chose, that there is a devil in this pile of blotted papers. You have read them, and know what I mean,—that conception in which I endeavored to embody the character of a fiend, as represented in our traditions and the written records of witchcraft. Oh, I have a horror of what was created in my own brain, and shudder at the manuscripts in which I gave that dark idea a sort of material existence! Would they were out of my sight!"

"And of mine, too," thought I.

"You remember," continued Oberon, "how the hellish thing used to suck away the happiness of those who, by a simple concession that seemed almost innocent, subjected themselves to his power. Just so my peace is gone, and all by these accursed manuscripts. Have you felt nothing of the same influence?"

"Nothing," replied I, "unless the spell be hid in a desire to turn novelist, after reading your delightful tales."

"Novelist!" exclaimed Oberon, half seriously. "Then, indeed, my devil has his claw on you! You are gone! You cannot even pray for deliverance! But we will be the last and only victims; for this night I mean to burn the manuscripts, and commit the fiend to his retribution in the flames."

"Burn your tales!" repeated I, startled at the desperation of the idea.

"Even so," said the author, despondingly. "You cannot conceive what an effect the composition of these tales has had on me. I have become ambitious of a bubble, and careless of solid reputation. I am surrounding myself with shadows, which bewilder me, by aping the realities of life. They have drawn me aside from the beaten path of the world, and led me into a strange sort of solitude,—a solitude in the midst of men,—where nobody wishes for what I do, nor thinks nor feels as I do. The tales have done all this. When they are ashes, perhaps I shall be as I was before they had existence. Moreover, the sacrifice is less than you may suppose, since nobody will publish them."

"That does make a difference, indeed," said I.

"They have been offered, by letter," continued Oberon, reddening with vexation, "to some seventeen booksellers. It would make you stare to read their answers; and read them you should, only that I burnt them as fast as they arrived. One man publishes nothing but school-books; another has five novels already under examination."

"What a voluminous mass the unpublished literature of America must be!" cried I.

"Oh, the Alexandrian manuscripts were nothing to it!" said my friend. "Well, another gentleman is just giving up business, on purpose, I verily believe, to escape publishing my book. Several, however, would not absolutely decline the agency, on my advancing half the cost of an edition, and giving bonds for the remainder, besides a high percentage to themselves, whether the book sells or not. Another advises a subscription."

"The villain!" exclaimed I.

"A fact!" said Oberon. "In short, of all the seventeen booksellers, only one has vouchsafed even to read my tales; and he—a literary dabbler himself, I should judge—has the impertinence to criticise them, proposing what he calls vast improvements, and concluding, after a general sentence of condemnation, with the definitive assurance that he will not be concerned on any terms."

"It might not be amiss to pull that fellow's nose," remarked I.

"If the whole 'trade' had one common nose, there would be some satisfaction in pulling it," answered the author. "But, there does seem to be one honest man among these seventeen unrighteous ones; and he tells me fairly, that no American publisher will meddle with an American work,—seldom if by a known writer, and never if by a new one,—unless at the writer's risk."

"The paltry rogues!" cried I. "Will they live by literature, and yet risk nothing for its sake? But, after all, you might publish on your own account."

"And so I might," replied Oberon. "But the devil of the business is this. These people have put me so out of conceit with the tales, that I loathe the very thought of them, and actually experience a physical sickness of the stomach, whenever I glance at them on the table. I tell you there is a demon in them! I anticipate a wild enjoyment in seeing them in the blaze; such as I should feel in taking vengeance on an enemy, or destroying something noxious."

I did not very strenuously oppose this determination, being privately of opinion, in spite of my partiality for the author, that his tales would make a more brilliant appearance in the fire than anywhere else. Before proceeding to execution, we broached the bottle of champagne, which Oberon had provided for keeping up his spirits in this doleful business. We swallowed each a tumblerful, in sparkling commotion; it went bubbling down our throats, and brightened my eyes at once, but left my friend sad and heavy as before. He drew the tales towards him, with a mixture of natural affection and natural disgust, like a father taking a deformed infant into his arms.

"Pooh! Pish! Pshaw!" exclaimed he, holding them at arm's-length. "It was Gray's idea of heaven, to lounge on a sofa and read new novels. Now, what more appropriate torture would Dante himself have contrived, for the sinner who perpetrates a bad book, than to be continually turning over the manuscript?"

"It would fail of effect," said I, "because a bad author is always his own great admirer."

"I lack that one characteristic of my tribe,—the only desirable one," observed Oberon. "But how many recollections throng upon me, as I turn over these leaves! This scene came into my fancy as I walked along a hilly road, on a starlight October evening; in the pure and bracing air, I became all soul, and felt as if I could climb the sky, and run a race along the Milky-Way. Here is another tale, in which I wrapt myself during a dark and dreary night-ride in the month of March, till the rattling of the wheels and the voices of my companions seemed like faint sounds of a dream, and my visions a bright reality. That scribbled page describes shadows which I summoned to my bedside at midnight: they would not depart when I bade them; the gray dawn came, and found me wide awake and feverish, the victim of my own enchantments!"

"There must have been a sort of happiness in all this," said I, smitten with a strange longing to make proof of it.

"There may be happiness in a fever fit," replied the author. "And then the various moods in which I wrote! Sometimes my ideas were like precious stones under the earth, requiring toil to dig them up, and care to polish and brighten them; but often a delicious stream of thought would gush out upon the page at once, like water sparkling up suddenly in the desert; and when it had passed, I gnawed my pen hopelessly, or blundered on with cold and miserable toil, as if there were a wall of ice between me and my subject."

"Do you now perceive a corresponding difference," inquired I, "between the passages which you wrote so coldly, and those fervid flashes of the mind?"

"No," said Oberon, tossing the manuscripts on the table. "I find no traces of the golden pen with which I wrote in characters of fire. My treasure of fairy coin is changed to worthless dross. My picture, painted in what seemed the loveliest hues, presents nothing but a faded and indistinguishable surface. I have been eloquent and poetical and humorous in a dream,—and behold! it is all nonsense, now that I am awake."

My friend now threw sticks of wood and dry chips upon the fire, and seeing it blaze like Nebuchadnezzar's furnace, seized the champagne-bottle, and drank two or three brimming bumpers, successively. The heady liquor combined with his agitation to throw him into a species of rage. He laid violent hands on the tales. In one instant more, their faults and beauties would alike have vanished in a glowing purgatory. But, all at once, I remembered passages of high imagination, deep pathos, original thoughts, and points of such varied excellence, that the vastness of the sacrifice struck me most forcibly. I caught his arm.

"Surely, you do not mean to burn them!" I exclaimed.

"Let me alone!" cried Oberon, his eyes flashing fire. "I will burn them! Not a scorched syllable shall escape! Would you have me a damned author?—To undergo sneers, taunts, abuse, and cold neglect, and faint praise, bestowed, for pity's sake, against the giver's conscience! A hissing and a laughing-stock to my own traitorous thoughts! An outlaw from the protection of the grave,—one whose ashes every careless foot might spurn, unhonored in life, and remembered scornfully in death! Am I to bear all this, when yonder fire will insure me from the whole? No! There go the tales! May my hand wither when it would write another!"

The deed was done. He had thrown the manuscripts into the hottest of the fire, which at first seemed to shrink away, but soon curled around them, and made them a part of its own fervent brightness. Oberon stood gazing at the conflagration, and shortly began to soliloquize, in the wildest strain, as if Fancy resisted and became riotous, at the moment when he would have compelled her to ascend that funeral pile. His words described objects which he appeared to discern in the fire, fed by his own precious thoughts; perhaps the thousand visions which the writer's magic had incorporated with these pages became visible to him in the dissolving heat, brightening forth ere they vanished forever; while the smoke, the vivid sheets of flame, the ruddy and whitening coals, caught the aspect of a varied scenery.

"They blaze," said he, "as if I had steeped them in the intensest spirit of genius. There I see my lovers clasped in each other's arms. How pure the flame that bursts from their glowing hearts! And yonder the features of a villain writhing in the fire that shall torment him to eternity. My holy men, my pious and angelic women, stand like martyrs amid the flames, their mild eyes lifted heavenward. Ring out the bells! A city is on fire. See!—destruction roars through my dark forests, while the lakes boil up in steaming billows, and the mountains are volcanoes, and the sky kindles with a lurid brightness! All elements are but one pervading flame! Ha! The fiend!"

I was somewhat startled by this latter exclamation. The tales were almost consumed, but just then threw forth a broad sheet of fire, which flickered as with laughter, making the whole room dance in its brightness, and then roared portentously up the chimney.

"You saw him? You must have seen him!" cried Oberon. "How he glared at me and laughed, in that last sheet of flame, with just the features that I imagined for him! Well! The tales are gone."

The papers were indeed reduced to a heap of black cinders, with a multitude of sparks hurrying confusedly among them, the traces of the pen being now represented by white lines, and the whole mass fluttering to and fro in the draughts of air. The destroyer knelt down to look at them.

"What is more potent than fire!" said he, in his gloomiest tone. "Even thought, invisible and incorporeal as it is, cannot escape it. In this little time, it has annihilated the creations of long nights and days, which I could no more reproduce, in their first glow and freshness, than cause ashes and whitened bones to rise up and live. There, too, I sacrificed the unborn children of my mind. All that I had accomplished—all that I planned for future years—has perished by one common ruin, and left only this heap of embers! The deed has been my fate. And what remains? A weary and aimless life,—a long repentance of this hour,—and at last an obscure grave, where they will bury and forget me!"

As the author concluded his dolorous moan, the extinguished embers arose and settled down and arose again, and finally flew up the chimney, like a demon with sable wings. Just as they disappeared, there was a loud and solitary cry in the street below us. "Fire!" Fire! Other voices caught up that terrible word, and it speedily became the shout of a multitude. Oberon started to his feet, in fresh excitement.

"A fire on such a night!" cried he. "The wind blows a gale, and wherever it whirls the flames, the roofs will flash up like gunpowder. Every pump is frozen up, and boiling water would turn to ice the moment it was flung from the engine. In an hour, this wooden town will be one great bonfire! What a glorious scene for my next—Pshaw!"

The street was now all alive with footsteps, and the air full of voices. We heard one engine thundering round a corner, and another rattling from a distance over the pavements. The bells of three steeples clanged out at once, spreading the alarm to many a neighboring town, and expressing hurry, confusion, and terror, so inimitably that I could almost distinguish in their peal the burden of the universal cry,—"Fire! Fire! Fire!"

"What is so eloquent as their iron tongues!" exclaimed Oberon. "My heart leaps and trembles, but not with fear. And that other sound, too,—deep and awful as a mighty organ,—the roar and thunder of the multitude on the pavement below! Come! We are losing time. I will cry out in the loudest of the uproar, and mingle my spirit with the wildest of the confusion, and be a bubble on the top of the ferment!"

From the first outcry, my forebodings had warned me of the true object and centre of alarm. There was nothing now but uproar, above, beneath, and around us; footsteps stumbling pell-mell up the public staircase, eager shouts and heavy thumps at the door, the whiz and dash of water from the engines, and the crash of furniture thrown upon the pavement. At once, the truth flashed upon my friend. His frenzy took the hue of joy, and, with a wild gesture of exultation, he leaped almost to the ceiling of the chamber.

"My tales!" cried Oberon. "The chimney! The roof! The Fiend has gone forth by night, and startled thousands in fear and wonder from their beds! Here I stand,—a triumphant author! Huzza! Huzza! My brain has set the town on fire! Huzza!"

JOHN INGLEFIELD'S THANKSGIVING

On the evening of Thanksgiving Day, John Inglefield, the blacksmith, sat in his elbow-chair, among those who had been keeping festival at his board. Being the central figure of the domestic circle, the fire threw its strongest light on his massive and sturdy frame, reddening his rough visage, so that it looked like the head of an iron statue, all aglow from his own forge, and with its features rudely fashioned on his own anvil. At John Inglefield's right hand was an empty chair. The other places round the hearth were filled by the members of the family, who all sat quietly, while, with a semblance of fantastic merriment, their shadows danced on the wall behind them. One of the group was John Inglefield's son, who had been bred at college, and was now a student of theology at Andover. There was also a daughter of sixteen, whom nobody could look at without thinking of a rose-bud almost blossomed. The only other person at the fireside was Robert Moore, formerly an apprentice of the blacksmith, but now his journeyman, and who seemed more like an own son of John Inglefield than did the pale and slender student.

Only these four had kept New England's festival beneath that roof. The vacant chair at John Inglefield's right hand was in memory of his wife, whom death had snatched from him since the previous Thanksgiving. With a feeling that few would have looked for in his rough nature, the bereaved husband had himself set the chair in its place next his own; and often did his eye glance thitherward, as if he deemed it possible that the cold grave might send back its tenant to the cheerful fireside, at least for that one evening. Thus did he cherish the grief that was dear to him. But there was another grief which he would fain have torn from his heart; or, since that could never be, have buried it too deep for others to behold, or for his own remembrance. Within the past year another member of his household had gone from him, but not to the grave. Yet they kept no vacant chair for her.

While John Inglefield and his family were sitting round the hearth with the shadows dancing behind them on the wall, the outer door was opened, and a light footstep came along the passage. The latch of the inner door was lifted by some familiar hand, and a young girl came in, wearing a cloak and hood, which she took off, and laid on the table beneath the looking-glass. Then, after gazing a moment at the fireside circle, she approached, and took the seat at John Inglefield's right hand, as if it had been reserved on purpose for her.

"Here I am, at last, father," said she. "You ate your Thanksgiving dinner without me, but I have come back to spend the evening with you."

Yes, it was Prudence Inglefield. She wore the same neat and maidenly attire which she had been accustomed to put on when the household work was over for the day, and her hair was parted from her brow, in the simple and modest fashion that became her best of all. If her cheek might otherwise have been pale, yet the glow of the fire suffused it with a healthful bloom. If she had spent the many months of her absence in guilt and infamy, yet they seemed to have left no traces on her gentle aspect. She could not have looked less altered, had she merely stepped away from her father's fireside for half an hour, and returned while the blaze was quivering upwards from the same brands that were burning at her departure. And to John Inglefield she was the very image of his buried wife, such as he remembered her on the first Thanksgiving which they had passed under their own roof. Therefore, though naturally a stern and rugged man, he could not speak unkindly to his sinful child, nor yet could he take her to his bosom.

"You are welcome home, Prudence," said he, glancing sideways at her, and his voice faltered. "Your mother would have rejoiced to see you, but she has been gone from us these four months."

"I know it, father, I know it," replied Prudence, quickly. "And yet, when I first came in, my eyes were so dazzled by the firelight, that she seemed to be sitting in this very chair!"

By this time the other members of the family had begun to recover from their surprise, and became sensible that it was no ghost from the grave, nor vision of their vivid recollections, but Prudence, her own self. Her brother was the next that greeted her. He advanced and held out his hand affectionately, as a brother should; yet not entirely like a brother, for, with all his kindness, he was still a clergyman, and speaking to a child of sin.

"Sister Prudence," said he, earnestly, "I rejoice that a merciful Providence hath turned your steps homeward, in time for me to bid you a last farewell. In a few weeks, sister, I am to sail as a missionary to the far islands of the Pacific. There is not one of these beloved faces that I shall ever hope to behold again on this earth. Oh, may I see all of them—yours and all—beyond the grave!"

A shadow flitted across the girl's countenance.

"The grave is very dark, brother," answered she, withdrawing her hand somewhat hastily from his grasp. "You must look your last at me by the light of this fire."

While this was passing, the twin-girl—the rose-bud that had grown on the same stem with the castaway—stood gazing at her sister, longing to fling herself upon her bosom, so that the tendrils of their hearts might intertwine again. At first she was restrained by mingled grief and shame, and by a dread that Prudence was too much changed to respond to her affection, or that her own purity would be felt as a reproach by the lost one. But, as she listened to the familiar voice, while the face grew more and more familiar, she forgot everything save that Prudence had come back. Springing forward, she would have clasped her in a close embrace. At that very instant, however, Prudence started from her chair, and held out both her hands, with a warning gesture.

"No, Mary,—no, my sister," cried she, "do not you touch me. Your bosom must not be pressed to mine!"

Mary shuddered and stood still, for she felt that something darker than the grave was between Prudence and herself, though they seemed so near each other in the light of their father's hearth, where they had grown up together. Meanwhile Prudence threw her eyes around the room, in search of one who had not yet bidden her welcome. He had withdrawn from his seat by the fireside, and was standing near the door, with his face averted, so that his features could be discerned only by the flickering shadow of the profile upon the wall. But Prudence called to him, in a cheerful and kindly tone:—

"Come, Robert," said she, "won't you shake hands with your old friend?"

Robert Moore held back for a moment, but affection struggled powerfully, and overcame his pride and resentment; he rushed towards Prudence, seized her hand, and pressed it to his bosom.

"There, there, Robert!" said she, smiling sadly, as she withdrew her hand, "you must not give me too warm a welcome."

And now, having exchanged greetings with each member of the family, Prudence again seated herself in the chair at John Inglefield's right hand. She was naturally a girl of quick and tender sensibilities, gladsome in her general mood, but with a bewitching pathos interfused among her merriest words and deeds. It was remarked of her, too, that she had a faculty, even from childhood, of throwing her own feelings, like a spell, over her companions. Such as she had been in her days of innocence, so did she appear this evening. Her friends, in the surprise and bewilderment of her return, almost forgot that she had ever left them, or that she had forfeited any of her claims to their affection. In the morning, perhaps, they might have looked at her with altered eyes, but by the Thanksgiving fireside they felt only that their own Prudence had come back to them, and were thankful. John Inglefield's rough visage brightened with the glow of his heart, as it grew warm and merry within him; once or twice, even, he laughed till the room rang again, yet seemed startled by the echo of his own mirth. The grave young minister became as frolicksome as a school-boy. Mary, too, the rose-bud, forgot that her twin-blossom had ever been torn from the stem, and trampled in the dust. And as for Robert Moore, he gazed at Prudence with the bashful earnestness of love new-born, while she, with sweet maiden coquetry, half smiled upon and half discouraged him.

In short, it was one of those intervals when sorrow vanishes in its own depth of shadow, and joy starts forth in transitory brightness. When the clock struck eight, Prudence poured out her father's customary draught of herb-tea, which had been steeping by the fireside ever since twilight.

"God bless you, child!" said John Inglefield, as he took the cup from her hand; "you have made your old father happy again. But we miss your mother sadly, Prudence, sadly. It seems as if she ought to be here now."

"Now, father, or never," replied Prudence.

It was now the hour for domestic worship. But while the family were making preparations for this duty, they suddenly perceived that Prudence had put on her cloak and hood, and was lifting the latch of the door.

"Prudence, Prudence! where are you going?" cried they all, with one voice.

As Prudence passed out of the door she turned towards them, and flung back her hand with a gesture of farewell. But her face was so changed that they hardly recognized it. Sin and evil passions glowed through its comeliness, and wrought a horrible deformity; a smile gleamed in her eyes, as of triumphant mockery, at their surprise and grief.

"Daughter," cried John Inglefield, between wrath and sorrow, "stay and be your father's blessing, or take his curse with you!"

For an instant Prudence lingered and looked back into the fire-lighted room, while her countenance wore almost the expression as if she were struggling with a fiend, who had power to seize his victim even within the hallowed precincts of her father's hearth. The fiend prevailed; and Prudence vanished into the outer darkness. When the family rushed to the door, they could see nothing, but heard the sound of wheels rattling over the frozen ground.

That same night, among the painted beauties at the theatre of a neighboring city, there was one whose dissolute mirth seemed inconsistent with any sympathy for pure affections, and for the joys and griefs which are hallowed by them. Yet this was Prudence Inglefield. Her visit to the Thanksgiving fireside was the realization of one of those waking dreams in which the guilty soul will sometimes stray back to its innocence. But Sin, alas! is careful of her bond-slaves; they hear her voice, perhaps, at the holiest moment, and are constrained to go whither she summons them. The same dark power that drew

Prudence Inglefield from her father's hearth—the same in its nature, though heightened then to a dread necessity—would snatch a guilty soul from the gate of heaven, and make its sin and its punishment alike eternal.

THE WIVES OF THE DEAD

The following story, the simple and domestic incidents of which may be deemed scarcely worth relating, after such a lapse of time, awakened some degree of interest, a hundred years ago, in a principal seaport of the Bay Province. The rainy twilight of an autumn day,—a parlor on the second floor of a small house, plainly furnished, as beseemed the middling circumstances of its inhabitants, yet decorated with little curiosities from beyond the sea, and a few delicate specimens of Indian manufacture,—these are the only particulars to be premised in regard to scene and season. Two young and comely women sat together by the fireside, nursing their mutual and peculiar sorrows. They were the recent brides of two brothers, a sailor and a landsman, and two successive days had brought tidings of the death of each, by the chances of Canadian warfare and the tempestuous Atlantic. The universal sympathy excited by this bereavement drew numerous condoling guests to the habitation of the widowed sisters. Several, among whom was the minister, had remained till the verge of evening, when, one by one, whispering many comfortable passages of Scripture that were answered by more abundant tears, they took their leave, and departed to their own happier homes. The mourners, though not insensible to the kindness of their friends, had yearned to be left alone. United, as they had been, by the relationship of the living, and now more closely so by that of the dead, each felt as if whatever consolation her grief admitted were to be found in the bosom of the other. They joined their hearts, and wept together silently. But after an hour of such indulgence, one of the sisters, all of whose emotions were influenced by her mild, quiet, yet not feeble character, began to recollect the precepts of resignation and endurance which piety had taught her when she did not think to need them. Her misfortune, besides, as earliest known, should earliest cease to interfere with her regular course of duties; accordingly, having placed the table before the fire, and arranged a frugal meal, she took the hand of her companion.

"Come, dearest sister; you have eaten not a morsel to-day," she said. "Arise, I pray you, and let us ask a blessing on that which is provided for us."

Her sister-in-law was of a lively and irritable temperament, and the first pangs of her sorrow had been expressed by shrieks and passionate lamentation. She now shrunk from Mary's words, like a wounded sufferer from a hand that revives the throb.

"There is no blessing left for me, neither will I ask it!" cried Margaret, with a fresh burst of tears. "Would it were His will that I might never taste food more!"

Yet she trembled at these rebellious expressions, almost as soon as they were uttered, and, by degrees, Mary succeeded in bringing her sister's mind nearer to the situation of her own. Time went on, and their usual hour of repose arrived. The brothers and their brides, entering the married state with no more than the slender means which then sanctioned such a step, had confederated themselves in one household, with equal rights to the parlor, and claiming exclusive privileges in two sleeping-rooms contiguous to it. Thither the widowed ones retired, after heaping ashes upon the dying embers of their fire, and placing a lighted lamp upon the hearth. The doors of both chambers were left open, so that a part of the interior of each, and the beds, with their unclosed curtains, were reciprocally visible. Sleep did not steal upon the sisters at one and the same time. Mary experienced the effect often consequent upon grief quietly borne, and soon sunk into temporary forgetfulness; while Margaret became more disturbed and feverish, in proportion as the night advanced with its deepest and stillest hours. She lay listening to the drops of rain that came down in monotonous succession, unswayed by a breath of wind; and a nervous impulse continually caused her to lift her head from the pillow, and gaze into Mary's chamber and the intermediate apartment. The cold light of the lamp threw the shadows of the furniture up against the wall, stamping them immovably there, except when they were shaken by a sudden flicker of the flame. Two vacant arm-chairs were in their old positions on opposite sides of the hearth, where the brothers had been wont to sit in young and laughing dignity, as heads of families; two humbler seats were near them, the true thrones of that little empire, where Mary and herself had exercised in love a power that love had won. The cheerful radiance of the fire had shone upon the happy circle, and the dead glimmer of the lamp might have befitted their reunion now. While Margaret groaned in bitterness, she heard a knock at the street-door.

"How would my heart have leapt at that sound but yesterday!" thought she, remembering the anxiety with which she had long awaited tidings from her husband. "I care not for it now; let them begone, for I will not arise."

But even while a sort of childish fretfulness made her thus resolve, she was breathing hurriedly, and straining her ears to catch a repetition of the summons. It is difficult to be convinced of the death of one whom we have deemed another self. The knocking was now renewed in slow and regular strokes, apparently given with the soft end of a doubled fist, and was accompanied by words, faintly heard through several thicknesses of wall. Margaret looked to her sister's chamber, and beheld her still lying in the depths of sleep. She arose, placed her foot upon the floor, and slightly arrayed herself, trembling between fear and eagerness as she did so.

"Heaven help me!" sighed she. "I have nothing left to fear, and methinks I am ten times more a coward than ever."

Seizing the lamp from the hearth, she hastened to the window that overlooked the street-door. It was a lattice, turning upon hinges; and having thrown it back, she stretched her head a little way into the moist atmosphere. A lantern was reddening the front of the house, and melting its light in the neighboring puddles, while a deluge of darkness overwhelmed every other object. As the window grated on its hinges, a man in a broad-brimmed hat and blanket-coat stepped from under the shelter of the projecting story, and looked upward to discover whom his application had aroused. Margaret knew him as a friendly innkeeper of the town.

"What would you have, Goodman Parker?" cried the widow.

"Lackaday, is it you, Mistress Margaret?" replied the innkeeper. "I was afraid it might be your sister Mary; for I hate to see a young woman in trouble, when I haven't a word of comfort to whisper her."

"For Heaven's sake, what news do you bring?" screamed Margaret.

"Why, there has been an express through the town within this half-hour," said Goodman Parker, "travelling from the eastern jurisdiction with letters from the governor and council. He tarried at my house to refresh himself with a drop and a morsel, and I asked him what tidings on the frontiers. He tells me we had the better in the skirmish you wot of, and that thirteen men reported slain are well and sound, and your husband among them. Besides, he is appointed of the escort to bring the captivated Frenchers and Indians home to the province jail. I judged you wouldn't mind being broke of your rest, and so I stepped over to tell you. Good night."

So saying, the honest man departed; and his lantern gleamed along the street, bringing to view indistinct shapes of things, and the fragments of a world, like order glimmering through chaos, or memory roaming over the past. But Margaret stayed not to watch these picturesque effects. Joy flashed into her heart, and lighted it up at once; and breathless, and with winged steps, she flew to the bedside of her sister. She paused, however, at the door of the chamber, while a thought of pain broke in upon her.

"Poor Mary!" said she to herself. "Shall I waken her, to feel her sorrow sharpened by my happiness? No; I will keep it within my own bosom till the morrow."

She approached the bed, to discover if Mary's sleep were peaceful. Her face was turned partly inward to the pillow, and had been hidden there to weep; but a look of motionless contentment was now visible upon it, as if her heart, like a deep lake, had grown calm because its dead had sunk down so far within. Happy is it, and strange, that the lighter sorrows are those from which dreams are chiefly fabricated. Margaret shrunk from disturbing her sister-in-law, and felt as if her own better fortune had rendered her involuntarily unfaithful, and as if altered and diminished affection must be the consequence of the disclosure she had to make. With a sudden step she turned away. But joy could not long be repressed, even by circumstances that would have excited heavy grief at another moment. Her mind was thronged with delightful thoughts, till sleep stole on, and transformed them to visions, more delightful and more wild, like the breath of winter (but what a cold comparison!) working fantastic tracery upon a window.

When the night was far advanced, Mary awoke with a sudden start. A vivid dream had latterly involved her in its unreal life, of which, however, she could only remember that it had been broken in upon at the most interesting point. For a little time, slumber hung about her like a morning mist, hindering her from perceiving the distinct outline of her situation. She listened with imperfect consciousness to two or three volleys of a rapid and eager knocking; and first she deemed the noise a matter of course, like the breath she drew; next, it appeared a thing in which she had no concern; and lastly, she became aware that it was a summons necessary to be obeyed. At the same moment, the pang of recollection darted into her mind; the pall of sleep was thrown back from the face of grief; the dim light of the chamber, and the objects therein revealed, had retained all her suspended ideas, and restored them as soon as she unclosed her eyes. Again there was a quick peal upon the street-door. Fearing that her sister would also be disturbed, Mary wrapped herself in a cloak and hood, took the lamp from the hearth, and hastened to the window. By some accident, it had been left unhasped, and yielded easily to her hand.

"Who's there?" asked Mary, trembling as she looked forth.

The storm was over, and the moon was up; it shone upon broken clouds above, and below upon houses black with moisture, and upon little lakes of the fallen rain, curling into silver beneath the quick enchantment of a breeze. A young man in a sailor's dress, wet as if he had come out of the depths of the sea, stood alone under the window. Mary recognized him as one whose livelihood was gained by short voyages along the coast; nor did she forget that, previous to her marrriage, he had been an unsuccessful wooer of her own.

"What do you seek here, Stephen?" said she.

"Cheer up, Mary, for I seek to comfort you," answered the rejected lover. "You must know I got home not ten minutes ago, and the first thing my good mother told me was the news about your husband. So, without saying a word to the old woman, I clapped on my hat, and ran out of the house. I couldn't have slept a wink before speaking to you, Mary, for the sake of old times."

"Stephen, I thought better of you!" exclaimed the widow, with gushing tears and preparing to close the lattice; for she was no whit inclined to imitate the first wife of Zadig.

"But stop, and hear my story out," cried the young sailor. "I tell you we spoke a brig yesterday afternoon, bound in from Old England. And whom do you think I saw standing on deck, well and hearty, only a bit thinner than he was five months ago?"

Mary leaned from the window, but could not speak.

"Why, it was your husband himself," continued the generous seaman. "He and three others saved themselves on a spar, when the Blessing turned bottom upwards. The brig will beat into the bay by daylight, with this wind, and you'll see him here to-morrow. There's the comfort I bring you, Mary, and so good night."

He hurried away, while Mary watched him with a doubt of waking reality, that seemed stronger or weaker as he alternately entered the shade of the houses, or emerged into the broad streaks of moonlight. Gradually, however, a blessed flood of conviction swelled into her heart, in strength enough to overwhelm her, had its increase been more abrupt. Her first impulse was to rouse her sister-in-law, and communicate the new-born-gladness. She opened the chamber-door, which had been closed in the course of the night, though not latched, advanced to the bedside, and was about to lay her hand upon the slumberer's shoulder. But then she remembered that Margaret would awake to thoughts of death and woe, rendered not the less bitter by their contrast with her own felicity. She suffered the rays of the lamp to fall upon the unconscious form of the bereaved one. Margaret lay in unquiet sleep, and the drapery was displaced around her; her young cheek was rosy-tinted, and her lips half opened in a vivid smile; an expression of joy, debarred its passage by her sealed eyelids, struggled forth like incense from the whole countenance.

"My poor sister! you will waken too soon from that happy dream," thought Mary.

Before retiring, she set down the lamp, and endeavored to arrange the bedclothes so that the chill air might not do harm to the feverish slumberer. But her hand trembled against Margaret's neck, a tear also fell upon her cheek, and she suddenly awoke.

LITTLE DAFFYDOWNDILLY

Daffydowndilly was so called because in his nature he resembled a flower, and loved to do only what was beautiful and agreeable, and took no delight in labor of any kind. But while Daffydowndilly was yet a little boy, his mother sent him away from his pleasant home, and put him under the care of a very strict schoolmaster, who went by the name of Mr. Toil. Those who knew him best affirmed that this Mr. Toil was a very worthy character; and that he had done more good, both to children and grown people, than anybody else in the world. Certainly he had lived long enough to do a great deal of good; for, if all stories be true, he had dwelt upon earth ever since Adam was driven from the garden of Eden.

Nevertheless, Mr. Toil had a severe and ugly countenance, especially for such little boys or big men as were inclined to be idle; his voice, too, was harsh; and all his ways and customs seemed very disagreeable to our friend Daffydowndilly. The whole day long, this terrible old schoolmaster sat at his desk overlooking the scholars, or stalked about the school-room with a certain awful birch rod in his hand. Now came a rap over the shoulders of a boy whom Mr. Toil had caught at play; now he punished a whole class who were behindhand with their lessons; and, in short, unless a lad chose to attend quietly and constantly to his book, he had no chance of enjoying a quiet moment in the school-room of Mr. Toil.

"This will never do for me," thought Daffydowndilly.

Now, the whole of Daffydowndilly's life had hitherto been passed with his dear mother, who had a much sweeter face than old Mr. Toil and who had always been very indulgent to her little boy. No wonder, therefore, that poor Daffydowndilly found it a woful change, to be sent away from the good lady's side, and put under the care of this ugly-visaged schoolmaster, who never gave him any apples or cakes, and seemed to think that little boys were created only to get lessons.

"I can't bear it any longer," said Daffydowndilly to himself, when he had been at school about a week. "I'll run away, and try to find my dear mother; and, at any rate, I shall never find anybody half so disagreeable as this old Mr. Toil!"

So, the very next morning, off started poor Daffydowndilly, and began his rambles about the world, with only some bread and cheese for his breakfast, and very little pocket-money to pay his expenses. But he had gone only a short distance when he overtook a man of grave and sedate appearance, who was trudging at a moderate pace along the road.

"Good morning, my fine lad," said the stranger; and his voice seemed hard and severe, but yet had a sort of kindness in it; "whence do you come so early, and whither are you going?"

Little Daffydowndilly was a boy of very ingenuous disposition, and had never been known to tell a lie in all his life. Nor did he tell one now. He hesitated a moment or two, but finally confessed that he had run away from school, on account of his great dislike to Mr. Toil; and that he was resolved to find some place in the world where he should never see or hear of the old schoolmaster again.

"Oh, very well, my little friend!" answered the stranger. "Then we will go together; for I, likewise, have had a good deal to do with Mr. Toil, and should be glad to find some place where he was never heard of."

Our friend Daffydowndilly would have been better pleased with a companion of his own age, with whom he might have gathered flowers along the roadside, or have chased butterflies, or have done many other things to make the journey pleasant. But he had wisdom enough to understand that he should get along through the world much easier by having a man of experience to show him the way. So he accepted the stranger's proposal, and they walked on very sociably together.

They had not gone far, when the road passed by a field where some haymakers were at work, mowing down the tall grass, and spreading it out in the sun to dry. Daffydowndilly was delighted with the sweet smell of the new-mown grass, and thought how much pleasanter it must be to make hay in the sunshine, under the blue sky, and with the birds singing sweetly in the neighboring trees and bushes, than to be shut up in a dismal school-room, learning lessons all day long, and continually scolded by old Mr. Toil. But, in the midst of these thoughts, while he was stopping to peep over the stone wall, he started back and caught hold of his companion's hand.

"Quick, quick!" cried he. "Let us run away, or he will catch us!"

"Who will catch us?" asked the stranger.

"Mr. Toil, the old schoolmaster!" answered Daffydowndilly. "Don't you see him amongst the haymakers?"

And Daffydowndilly pointed to an elderly man, who seemed to be the owner of the field, and the employer of the men at work there. He had stripped off his coat and waistcoat, and was busily at work in his shirt-sleeves. The drops of sweat stood upon his brow; but he gave himself not a moment's rest, and kept crying out to the haymakers to make hay while the sun shone. Now, strange to say, the figure and features of this old farmer were precisely the same as those of old Mr. Toil, who, at that very moment, must have been just entering his school-room.

"Don't be afraid," said the stranger. "This is not Mr. Toil the schoolmaster, but a brother of his, who was bred a farmer; and people say he is the most disagreeable man of the two. However, he won't trouble you, unless you become a laborer on the farm."

Little Daffydowndilly believed what his companion said, but was very glad, nevertheless, when they were out of sight of the old farmer, who bore such a singular resemblance to Mr. Toil. The two travellers had gone but little farther, when they came to a spot where some carpenters were erecting a house. Daffydowndilly begged his companion to stop a moment; for it was a very pretty sight to see how neatly the carpenters did their work, with their broad-axes, and saws, and planes, and hammers, shaping out the doors, and putting in the window-sashes, and nailing on the clapboards; and he could not help thinking that he should like to take a broad-axe, a saw, a plane, and a hammer, and build a little house for himself. And then, when he should have a house of his own, old Mr. Toil would never dare to molest him.

But, just while he was delighting himself with this idea, little Daffydowndilly beheld something that made him catch hold of his companion's hand, all in a fright.

"Make haste. Quick, quick!" cried he. "There he is again!"

"Who?" asked the stranger, very quietly.

"Old Mr. Toil," said Daffydowndilly, trembling. "There! he that is overseeing the carpenters. 'T is my old schoolmaster, as sure as I 'm alive!"

The stranger cast his eyes where Daffydowndilly pointed his finger; and he saw an elderly man, with a carpenter's rule and compasses in his hand. This person went to and fro about the unfinished house, measuring pieces of timber, and marking out the work that was to be done, and continually exhorting the other carpenters to be diligent. And wherever he turned his hard and wrinkled visage, the men seemed to feel that they had a task-master over them, and sawed, and hammered, and planed, as if for dear life.

"Oh no! this is not Mr. Toil, the schoolmaster," said the stranger. "It is another brother of his, who follows the trade of carpenter."

"I am very glad to hear it," quoth Daffydowndilly; "but if you please, sir, I should like to get out of his way as soon as possible."

Then they went on a little farther, and soon heard the sound of a drum and fife. Daffydowndilly pricked up his ears at this, and besought his companion to hurry forward, that they might not miss seeing the soldiers. Accordingly, they made what haste they could, and soon met a company of soldiers, gayly dressed, with beautiful feathers in their caps, and bright muskets on their shoulders. In front marched two drummers and two fifers, beating on their drums and playing on their fifes with might and main, and making such lively music that little Daffydowndilly would gladly have followed them to the end of the world. And if he was only a soldier, then, he said to himself, old Mr. Toil would never venture to look him in the face.

"Quick step! Forward march!" shouted a gruff voice.

Little Daffydowndilly started, in great dismay; for this voice which had spoken to the soldiers sounded precisely the same as that which he had heard every day in Mr. Toil's school-room, out of Mr. Toil's own mouth. And, turning his eyes to the captain of the company, what should he see but the very image of old Mr. Toil himself, with a smart cap and feather on his head, a pair of gold epaulets on his shoulders, a laced coat on his back, a purple sash round his waist, and a long sword, instead of a birch rod, in his hand. And though he held his head so high, and strutted like a turkey-cock, still he looked quite as ugly and disagreeable as when he was hearing lessons in the school-room.

"This is certainly old Mr. Toil," said Daffydowndilly, in a trembling voice. "Let us run away, for fear he should make us enlist in his company!"

"You are mistaken again, my little friend," replied the stranger, very composedly. "This is not Mr. Toil, the schoolmaster, but a brother of his, who has served in the army all his life. People say he's a terribly severe fellow; but you and I need not be afraid of him."

"Well, well," said little Daffydowndilly, "but, if you please, sir, I don't want to see the soldiers any more."

So the child and the stranger resumed their journey; and, by and by, they came to a house by the roadside, where a number of people were making merry. Young men and rosy-cheeked girls, with smiles on their faces, were dancing to the sound of a fiddle. It was the pleasantest sight that Daffydowndilly had yet met with, and it comforted him for all his disappointments.

"Oh, let us stop here," cried he to his companion; "for Mr. Toil will never dare to show his face where there is a fiddler, and where people are dancing and making merry. We shall be quite safe here!"

But these last words died away upon Daffydowndilly's tongue; for, happening to cast his eyes on the fiddler, whom should he behold again but the likeness of Mr. Toil, holding a fiddle-bow instead of a birch rod, and flourishing it with as much ease and dexterity as if he had been a fiddler all his life! He had somewhat the air of a Frenchman, but still looked exactly like the old schoolmaster; and Daffydowndilly even fancied that he nodded and winked at him, and made signs for him to join in the dance.

"Oh dear me!" whispered he, turning pale. "It seems as if there was nobody but Mr. Toil in the world. Who could have thought of his playing on a fiddle!"

"This is not your old schoolmaster," observed the stranger, "but another brother of his, who was bred in France, where he learned the profession of a fiddler. He is ashamed of his family, and generally calls himself Monsieur le Plaisir; but his real name is Toil, and those who have known him best think him still more disagreeable than his brothers."

"Pray let us go a little farther," said Daffydowndilly. "I don't like the looks of this fiddler at all."

Well, thus the stranger and little Daffydowndilly went wandering along the highway, and in shady lanes, and through pleasant villages; and whithersoever they went, behold! there was the image of old Mr. Toil. He stood like a scarecrow in the cornfields. If they entered a house, he sat in the parlor; if they peeped into the kitchen, he was there. He made himself at home in every cottage, and stole, under one disguise or another, into the most splendid mansions. Everywhere there was sure to be somebody wearing the likeness of Mr. Toil, and who, as the stranger affirmed, was one of the old schoolmaster's innumerable brethren.

Little Daffydowndilly was almost tired to death, when he perceived some people reclining lazily in a shady place, by the side of the road. The poor child entreated his companion that they might sit down there, and take some repose.

"Old Mr. Toil will never come here," said he; "for he hates to see people taking their ease."

But, even while he spoke, Daffydowndilly's eyes fell upon a person who seemed the laziest, and heaviest, and most torpid of all those lazy and heavy and torpid people who had lain down to sleep in the shade. Who should it be, again, but the very image of Mr. Toil!

"There is a large family of these Toils," remarked the stranger. "This is another of the old schoolmaster's brothers, who was bred in Italy, where he acquired very idle habits, and goes by the name of Signor Far Niente. He pretends to lead an easy life, but is really the most miserable fellow in the family."

"Oh take me back!—take me back!" cried poor little Daffydowndilly, bursting into tears. "If there is nothing but Toil all the world over, I may just as well go back to the school-house!"

"Yonder it is,—there is the school-house!" said the stranger; for though he and little Daffydowndilly had taken a great many steps, they had travelled in a circle instead of a straight line. "Come; we will go back to school together."

There was something in his companion's voice that little Daffydowndilly now remembered, and it is strange that he had not remembered it sooner. Looking up into his face, behold! there again was the likeness of old Mr. Toil; so that the poor child had been in company with Toil all day, even while he was doing his best to run away from him. Some people, to whom I have told little Daffydowndilly's story, are of opinion that old Mr. Toil was a magician, and possessed the power of multiplying himself into as many shapes as he saw fit.

Be this as it may, little Daffydowndilly had learned a good lesson, and from that time forward was diligent at his task, because he knew that diligence is not a whit more toilsome than sport or idleness. And when he became better acquainted with Mr. Toil, he began to think that his ways were not so very disagreeable, and that the old schoolmaster's smile of approbation made his face almost as pleasant as even that of Daffydowndilly's mother.

MY KINSMAN, MAJOR MOLINEUX

After the kings of Great Britain had assumed the right of appointing the colonial governors, the measures of the latter seldom met with the ready and general approbation which had been paid to those of their predecessors, under the original charters. The people looked with most jealous scrutiny to the exercise of power which did not emanate from themselves, and they usually rewarded their rulers with slender gratitude for the compliances by which, in softening their instructions from beyond the sea, they had incurred the reprehension of those who gave them. The annals of Massachusetts Bay will inform us, that of six governors in the space of about forty years from the surrender of the old charter, under James II., two were imprisoned by a popular insurrection; a third, as Hutchinson inclines to believe, was driven from the province by the whizzing of a musket-ball; a fourth, in the opinion of the same historian, was hastened to his grave by continual bickerings with the House of Representatives; and the remaining two, as well as their successors, till the Revolution, were favored with few and brief intervals of peaceful sway. The inferior members of the court party, in times of high political excitement, led scarcely a more desirable life. These remarks may serve as a preface to the following adventures, which chanced upon a summer night, not far from a hundred years ago. The reader, in order to avoid a long and dry detail of colonial affairs, is requested to dispense with an account of the train of circumstances that had caused much temporary inflammation of the popular mind.

It was near nine o'clock of a moonlight evening, when a boat crossed the ferry with a single passenger, who had obtained his conveyance at that unusual hour by the promise of an extra fare. While he stood on the landing-place, searching in either pocket for the means of fulfilling his agreement, the ferryman lifted a lantern, by the aid of which, and the newly risen moon, he took a very accurate survey of the stranger's figure. He was a youth of barely eighteen years, evidently country-bred, and now, as it should seem, upon his first visit to town. He was clad in a coarse gray coat, well worn, but in excellent repair; his under garments were durably constructed of leather, and fitted tight to a pair of serviceable and well-shaped limbs: his stockings of blue yarn were the incontrovertible work of a mother or a sister; and on his head was a three-cornered hat, which in its better days had perhaps sheltered the graver brow of the lad's father. Under his left arm was a heavy cudgel formed of an oak sapling, and retaining a part of the hardened root; and his equipment was completed by a wallet, not so abundantly stocked as to incommode the vigorous shoulders on which it hung. Brown, curly hair, well-shaped features, and bright, cheerful eyes were nature's gifts, and worth all that art could have done for his adornment.

The youth, one of whose names was Robin, finally drew from his pocket the half of a little province bill of five shillings, which, in the depreciation in that sort of currency, did but satisfy the ferryman's demand, with the surplus of a sexangular piece of parchment, valued at three pence. He then walked forward into the town, with as light a step as if his day's journey had not already exceeded thirty miles, and with as eager an eye as if he were entering London city, instead of the little metropolis of a New England colony. Before Robin had proceeded far, however, it occurred to him that he knew not whither to direct his steps; so he paused, and looked up and down the narrow street, scrutinizing the small and mean wooden buildings that were scattered on either side.

"This low hovel cannot be my kinsman's dwelling," thought he, "nor yonder old house, where the moonlight enters at the broken casement; and truly I see none hereabouts that might be worthy of him. It would have been wise to inquire my way of the ferryman, and doubtless he would have gone with me, and earned a shilling from the Major for his pains. But the next man I meet will do as well."

He resumed his walk, and was glad to perceive that the street now became wider, and the houses more respectable in their appearance. He soon discerned a figure moving on moderately in advance, and hastened his steps to overtake it. As Robin drew nigh, he saw that the passenger was a man in years, with a full periwig of gray hair, a wide-skirted coat of dark cloth, and silk stockings rolled above his knees. He carried a long and polished cane, which he struck down perpendicularly before him at every step; and at regular intervals he uttered two successive hems, of a peculiarly solemn and sepulchral intonation.

Having made these observations, Robin laid hold of the skirt of the old man's coat, just when the light from the open door and windows of a barber's shop fell upon both their figures.

"Good evening to you, honored sir," said he, making a low bow, and still retaining his hold of the skirt. "I pray you tell me whereabouts is the dwelling of my kinsman, Major Molineux."

The youth's question was uttered very loudly; and one of the barbers, whose razor was descending on a well-soaped chin, and another who was dressing a Ramillies wig, left their occupations, and came to the door. The citizen, in the meantime, turned a long-favored countenance upon Robin, and answered him in a tone of excessive anger and annoyance. His two sepulchral hems, however, broke into the very centre of his rebuke, with most singular effect, like a thought of the cold grave obtruding among wrathful passions.

"Let go my garment, fellow! I tell you, I know not the man you speak of. What! I have authority, I have—hem, hem—authority; and if this be the respect you show for your betters, your feet shall be brought acquainted with the stocks by daylight, to-morrow morning!"

Robin released the old man's skirt, and hastened away, pursued by an ill-mannered roar of laughter from the barber's shop. He was at first considerably surprised by the result of his question, but, being a shrewd youth, soon thought himself able to account for the mystery.

"This is some country representative," was his conclusion, "who has never seen the inside of my kinsman's door, and lacks the breeding to answer a stranger civilly. The man is old, or verily—I might be tempted to turn back and smite him on the nose. Ah, Robin, Robin! even the barber's boys laugh at you for choosing such a guide! You will be wiser in time, friend Robin."

He now became entangled in a succession of crooked and narrow streets, which crossed each other, and meandered at no great distance from the water-side. The smell of tar was obvious to his nostrils, the masts of vessels pierced the moonlight above the tops of the buildings, and the numerous signs, which Robin paused to read, informed him that he was near the centre of business. But the streets were empty, the shops were closed, and lights were visible only in the second stories of a few dwelling-houses. At length, on the corner of a narrow lane, through which he was passing, he beheld the broad countenance of a British hero swinging before the door of an inn, whence proceeded the voices of many guests. The casement of one of the lower windows was thrown back, and a very thin curtain permitted Robin to distinguish a party at supper, round a well-furnished table. The fragrance of the good cheer steamed forth into the outer air, and the youth could not fail to recollect that the last remnant of his travelling stock of provision had yielded to his morning appetite, and that noon had found and left him dinnerless.

"Oh, that a parchment three-penny might give me a right to sit down at yonder table!" said Robin, with a sigh. "But the Major will make me welcome to the best of his victuals; so I will even step boldly in, and inquire my way to his dwelling."

He entered the tavern, and was guided by the murmur of voices and the fumes of tobacco to the public-room. It was a long and low apartment, with oaken walls, grown dark in the continual smoke, and a floor which was thickly sanded, but of no immaculate purity. A number of persons—the larger part of whom appeared to be mariners, or in some way connected with the sea—occupied the wooden benches, or leather-bottomed chairs, conversing on various matters, and occasionally lending their attention to some topic of general interest. Three or four little groups were draining as many bowls of punch, which the West India trade had long since made a familiar drink in the colony. Others, who had the appearance of men who lived by regular and laborious handicraft, preferred the insulated bliss of an unshared potation, and became more taciturn under its influence. Nearly all, in short, evinced a predilection for the Good Creature in some of its various shapes, for this is a vice to which, as Fast Day sermons of a hundred years ago will testify, we have a long hereditary claim. The only guests to whom Robin's sympathies inclined him were two or three sheepish countrymen, who were using the inn somewhat after the fashion of a Turkish caravansary; they had gotten themselves into the darkest corner of the room, and heedless of the Nicotian atmosphere, were supping on the bread of their own ovens, and the bacon cured in their own chimney-smoke. But though Robin felt a sort of brotherhood with these strangers, his eyes were attracted from them to a person who stood near the door, holding whispered conversation with a group of ill-dressed associates. His features were separately striking almost to grotesqueness, and the whole face left a deep impression on the memory. The forehead bulged out into a double prominence, with a vale between; the nose came boldly forth in an irregular curve, and its bridge was of more than a finger's breadth; the eyebrows were deep and shaggy, and the eyes glowed beneath them like fire in a cave.

While Robin deliberated of whom to inquire respecting his kinsman's dwelling, he was accosted by the innkeeper, a little man in a stained white apron, who had come to pay his professional welcome to the stranger. Being in the second generation from a French Protestant, he seemed to have inherited the courtesy of his parent nation; but no variety of circumstances was ever known to change his voice from the one shrill note in which he now addressed Robin.

"From the country, I presume, sir?" said he, with a profound bow. "Beg leave to congratulate you on your arrival, and trust you intend a long stay with us. Fine town here, sir, beautiful buildings, and much that may interest a stranger. May I hope for the honor of your commands in respect to supper?"

"The man sees a family likeness! the rogue has guessed that I am related to the Major!" thought Robin, who had hitherto experienced little superfluous civility.

All eyes were now turned on the country lad, standing at the door, in his worn three-cornered hat, gray coat, leather breeches, and blue yarn stockings, leaning on an oaken cudgel, and bearing a wallet on his back.

Robin replied to the courteous innkeeper, with such an assumption of confidence as befitted the Major's relative. "My honest friend," he said, "I shall make it a point to patronize your house on some occasion, when"—here he could not help lowering his voice—"when I may have more than a parchment three-pence in my pocket. My present business," continued he, speaking with lofty confidence, "is merely to inquire my way to the dwelling of my kinsman, Major Molineux."

There was a sudden and general movement in the room, which Robin interpreted as expressing the eagerness of each individual to become his guide. But the innkeeper turned his eyes to a written paper on the wall, which he read, or seemed to read, with occasional recurrences to the young man's figure.

"What have we here?" said he, breaking his speech into little dry fragments. " 'Left the house of the subscriber, bounden servant, Hezekiah Mudge,—had on, when he went away, gray coat, leather breeches, master's third-best hat. One pound currency reward to whosoever shall lodge him in any jail of the province.' Better trudge, boy; better trudge!"

Robin had begun to draw his hand towards the lighter end of the oak cudgel, but a strange hostility in every countenance induced him to relinquish his purpose of breaking the courteous innkeeper's head. As he turned to leave the room, he encountered a sneering glance from the bold-featured personage whom he had before noticed; and no sooner was he beyond the door, than he heard a general laugh, in which the innkeeper's voice might be distinguished, like the dropping of small stones into a kettle.

"Now, is it not strange," thought Robin, with his usual shrewdness,—"is it not strange that the confession of an empty pocket should outweigh the name of my kinsman, Major Molineux? Oh, if I had one of those grinning rascals in the woods, where I and my oak sapling grew up together, I would teach him that my arm is heavy though my purse be light!"

On turning the corner of the narrow lane, Robin found himself in a spacious street, with an unbroken line of lofty houses on each side, and a steepled building at the upper end, whence the ringing of a bell announced the hour of nine. The light of the moon, and the lamps from the numerous shop-windows, discovered people promenading on the pavement, and amongst them Robin hoped to recognize his hitherto inscrutable relative. The result of his former inquiries made him unwilling to hazard another, in a scene of such publicity, and he determined to walk slowly and silently up the street, thrusting his face close to that of every elderly gentleman, in search of the Major's lineaments. In his progress, Robin encountered many gay and gallant figures. Embroidered garments of showy colors, enormous periwigs, gold-laced hats, and silver-hilted swords glided past him and dazzled his optics. Travelled youths, imitators of the European fine gentlemen of the period, trod jauntily along, half dancing to the fashionable tunes which they hummed, and making poor Robin ashamed of his quiet and natural gait. At length, after many pauses to examine the gorgeous display of goods in the shop-windows, and after suffering some rebukes for the impertinence of his scrutiny into people's faces, the Major's kinsman found himself near the steepled building, still unsuccessful in his search. As yet, however, he had seen only one side of the thronged street; so Robin crossed, and continued the same sort of inquisition down the opposite pavement, with stronger hopes than the philosopher seeking an honest man, but with no better fortune. He had arrived about midway towards the lower end, from which his course began, when he overheard the approach of some one who struck down a cane on the flag-stones at every step, uttering, at regular intervals, two sepulchral hems.

"Mercy on us!" quoth Robin, recognizing the sound.

Turning a corner, which chanced to be close at his right hand, he hastened to pursue his researches in some other part of the town. His patience now was wearing low, and he seemed to feel more fatigue from his rambles since he crossed the ferry, than from his journey of several days on the other side. Hunger also pleaded loudly within him, and Robin began to balance the propriety of demanding, violently, and with lifted cudgel, the necessary guidance from the first solitary passenger whom he should meet. While a resolution to this effect was gaining strength, he entered a street of mean appearance, on either side of which a row of ill-built houses was straggling towards the harbor. The moonlight fell upon no passenger along the whole extent, but in the third domicile which Robin passed there was a half-opened door, and his keen glance detected a woman's garment within.

"My luck may be better here," said he to himself.

Accordingly, he approached the door, and beheld it shut closer as he did so; yet an open space remained, sufficing for the fair occupant to observe the stranger, without a corresponding display on her part. All that Robin could discern was a strip of scarlet petticoat, and the occasional sparkle of an eye, as if the moonbeams were trembling on some bright thing.

"Pretty mistress," for I may call her so with a good conscience, thought the shrewd youth, since I know nothing to the contrary,—"my sweet pretty mistress, will you be kind enough to tell me whereabouts I must seek the dwelling of my kinsman, Major Molineux?"

Robin's voice was plaintive and winning, and the female, seeing nothing to be shunned in the handsome country youth, thrust open the door, and came forth into the moonlight. She was a dainty little figure, with a white neck, round arms, and a slender waist, at the extremity of which her scarlet petticoat jutted out over a hoop, as if she were standing in a balloon. Moreover, her face was oval and pretty, her hair dark beneath the little cap, and her bright eyes possessed a sly freedom, which triumphed over those of Robin.

"Major Molineux dwells here," said this fair woman.

Now, her voice was the sweetest Robin had heard that night, the airy counterpart of a stream of melted silver; yet he could not help doubting whether that sweet voice spoke Gospel truth. He looked up and down the mean street, and then surveyed the house before which they stood. It was a small, dark edifice of two stories, the second of which projected over the lower floor, and the front apartment had the aspect of a shop for petty commodities.

"Now, truly, I am in luck," replied Robin, cunningly, "and so indeed is my kinsman, the Major, in having so pretty a housekeeper. But I prithee trouble him to step to the door; I will deliver him a message from his friends in the country, and then go back to my lodgings at the inn."

"Nay, the Major has been abed this hour or more," said the lady of the scarlet petticoat; "and it would be to little purpose to disturb him to-night, seeing his evening draught was of the strongest. But he is a kind-hearted man, and it would be as much as my life's worth to let a kinsman of his turn away from the door. You are the good old gentleman's very picture, and I could swear that was his rainy-weather hat. Also he has garments very much resembling those leather small-clothes. But come in, I pray, for I bid you hearty welcome in his name."

So saying, the fair and hospitable dame took our hero by the hand; and the touch was light, and the force was gentleness, and though Robin read in her eyes what he did not hear in her words, yet the slender-waisted woman in the scarlet petticoat proved stronger than the athletic country youth. She had drawn his half-willing footsteps nearly to the threshold, when the opening of a door in the neighborhood startled the Major's housekeeper, and, leaving the Major's kinsman, she vanished speedily into her own domicile. A heavy yawn preceded the appearance of a man, who, like the Moonshine of Pyramus and Thisbe, carried a lantern, needlessly aiding his sister luminary in the heavens. As he walked sleepily up the street, he turned his broad, dull face on Robin, and displayed a long staff, spiked at the end.

"Home, vagabond, home!" said the watchman, in accents that seemed to fall asleep as soon as they were uttered. "Home, or we'll set you in the stocks by peep of day!"

"This is the second hint of the kind," thought Robin. "I wish they would end my difficulties, by setting me there to-night."

Nevertheless, the youth felt an instinctive antipathy towards the guardian of midnight order, which at first prevented him from asking his usual question. But just when the man was about to vanish behind the corner, Robin resolved not to lose the opportunity, and shouted lustily after him,—

"I say, friend! will you guide me to the house of my kinsman, Major Molineux?"

The watchman made no reply, but turned the corner and was gone; yet Robin seemed to hear the sound of drowsy laughter stealing along the solitary street. At that moment, also, a pleasant titter saluted him from the open window above his head; he looked up, and caught the sparkle of a saucy eye; a round arm beckoned to him, and next he heard light footsteps descending the staircase within. But Robin, being of the household of a New England clergyman, was a good youth, as well as a shrewd one; so he resisted temptation, and fled away.

He now roamed desperately, and at random, through the town, almost ready to believe that a spell was on him, like that by which a wizard of his country had once kept three pursuers wandering, a whole winter night, within twenty paces of the cottage which they sought. The streets lay before him, strange and desolate, and the lights were extinguished in almost every house. Twice, however, little parties of men, among whom Robin distinguished individuals in outlandish attire, came hurrying along; but, though on both occasions they paused to address him, such intercourse did not at all enlighten his perplexity. They did but utter a few words in some language of which Robin knew nothing, and perceiving his inability to answer, bestowed a curse upon him in plain English and hastened away. Finally, the lad determined to knock at the door of every mansion that might appear worthy to be occupied by his kinsman, trusting that perseverance would overcome the fatality that had hitherto thwarted him. Firm in this resolve, he was passing beneath the walls of a church, which formed the corner of two streets, when, as he turned into the shade of its steeple, he encountered a bulky stranger, muffled in a cloak. The man was proceeding with the speed of earnest business, but Robin planted himself full before him, holding the oak cudgel with both hands across his body as a bar to further passage.

"Halt, honest man, and answer me a question," said he, very resolutely. "Tell me, this instant, whereabouts is the dwelling of my kinsman, Major Molineux!"

"Keep your tongue between your teeth, fool, and let me pass!" said a deep, gruff voice, which Robin partly remembered. "Let me pass, I say, or I'll strike you to the earth!"

"No, no, neighbor!" cried Robin, flourishing his cudgel, and then thrusting its larger end close to the man's muffled face. "No, no, I'm not the fool you take me for, nor do you pass till I have an answer to my question. Whereabouts is the dwelling of my kinsman, Major Molineux?"

The stranger, instead of attempting to force his passage, stepped back into the moonlight, unmuffled his face, and stared full into that of Robin.

"Watch here an hour, and Major Molineux will pass by," said he.

Robin gazed with dismay and astonishment on the unprecedented physiognomy of the speaker. The forehead with its double prominence, the broad hooked nose, the shaggy eyebrows, and fiery eyes were those which he had noticed at the inn, but the man's complexion had undergone a singular, or, more properly, a twofold change. One side of the face blazed an intense red, while the other was black as midnight, the division line being in the broad bridge of the nose; and a mouth which seemed to extend from ear to ear was black or red, in contrast to the color of the cheek. The effect was as if two individual devils, a fiend of fire and a fiend of darkness, had united themselves to form this infernal visage. The stranger grinned in Robin's face, muffled his party-colored features, and was out of sight in a moment.

"Strange things we travellers see!" ejaculated Robin.

He seated himself, however, upon the steps of the church-door, resolving to wait the appointed time for his kinsman. A few moments were consumed in philosophical speculations upon the species of man who had just left him; but having settled this point shrewdly, rationally, and satisfactorily, he was compelled to look elsewhere for his amusement. And first he threw his eyes along the street. It was of more respectable appearance than most of those into which he had wandered; and the moon, creating, like the imaginative power, a beautiful strangeness in familiar objects, gave something of romance to a scene that might not have possessed it in the light of day. The irregular and often quaint architecture of the houses, some of whose roofs were broken into numerous little peaks, while others ascended, steep and narrow, into a single point, and others again were square; the pure snow-white of some of their complexions, the aged darkness of others, and the thousand sparklings, reflected from bright substances in the walls of many; these matters engaged Robin's attention for a while, and then began to grow wearisome. Next he endeavored to define the forms of distant objects, starting away, with almost ghostly indistinctness, just as his eye appeared to grasp them; and finally he took a minute survey of an edifice which stood on the opposite side of the street, directly in front of the church-door, where he was stationed. It was a large, square mansion, distinguished from its neighbors by a balcony, which rested on tall pillars, and by an elaborate Gothic window, communicating therewith.

"Perhaps this is the very house I have been seeking," thought Robin.

Then he strove to speed away the time, by listening to a murmur which swept continually along the street, yet was scarcely audible, except to an unaccustomed ear like his; it was a low, dull, dreamy sound, compounded of many noises, each of which was at too great a distance to be separately heard. Robin marvelled at this snore of a sleeping town, and marvelled more whenever its continuity was broken by now and than a distant shout, apparently loud where it originated. But altogether it was a sleep-inspiring sound, and, to shake off its drowsy influence, Robin arose, and climbed a window-frame, that he might view the interior of the church. There the moonbeams came trembling in, and fell down upon the deserted pews, and extended along the quiet aisles. A fainter yet more awful radiance was hovering around the pulpit, and one solitary ray had dared to rest upon the open page of the great Bible. Had nature, in that deep hour, become a worshipper in the house which man had builded? Or was that heavenly light the visible sanctity of the place,—visible because no earthly and impure feet were within the walls? The scene made Robin's heart shiver with a sensation of loneliness stronger than he had ever felt in the remotest depths of his native woods; so he turned away and sat down again before the door. There were graves around the church, and now an uneasy thought obtruded into Robin's breast. What if the object of his search, which had been so often and so strangely thwarted, were all the time mouldering in his shroud? What if his kinsman should glide through yonder gate, and nod and smile to him in dimly passing by?

"Oh that any breathing thing were here with me!" said Robin.

Recalling his thoughts from this uncomfortable track, he sent them over forest, hill, and stream, and attempted to imagine how that evening of ambiguity and weariness had been spent by his father's household. He pictured them assembled at the door, beneath the tree, the great old tree, which had been spared for its huge twisted trunk and venerable shade, when a thousand leafy brethren fell. There, at the going down of the summer sun, it was his father's custom to perform domestic worship, that the neighbors might come and join with him like brothers of the family, and that the wayfaring man might pause to drink at that fountain, and keep his heart pure by freshening the memory of home. Robin distinguished the seat of every individual of the little audience; he saw the good man in the midst, holding the Scriptures in the golden light that fell from the western clouds; he beheld him close the book and all rise up to pray. He heard the old thanksgivings for daily mercies, the old supplications for their continuance, to which he had so often listened in weariness, but which were now among his dear remembrances. He perceived the slight inequality of his father's voice when he came to speak of the absent one; he noted how his mother turned her face to the broad and knotted trunk; how his elder brother scorned, because the beard was rough upon his upper lip, to permit his features to be moved; how the younger sister drew down a low hanging branch before her eyes; and how the little one of all, whose sports had hitherto broken the decorum of the scene, understood the prayer for her playmate, and burst into clamorous grief. Then he saw them go in at the door; and when Robin would have entered also, the latch tinkled into its place, and he was excluded from his home.

"Am I here, or there?" cried Robin, starting; for all at once, when his thoughts had become visible and audible in a dream, the long, wide, solitary street shone out before him.

He aroused himself, and endeavored to fix his attention steadily upon the large edifice which he had surveyed before. But still his mind kept vibrating between fancy and reality; by turns, the pillars of the balcony lengthened into the tall, bare stems of pines, dwindled down to human figures, settled again into their true shape and size, and then commenced a new succession of changes. For a single moment, when he deemed himself awake, he could have sworn that a visage—one which he seemed to remember, yet could not absolutely name as his kinsman's—was looking towards him from the Gothic window. A deeper sleep wrestled with and nearly overcame him, but fled at the sound of footsteps along the opposite pavement. Robin rubbed his eyes, discerned a man passing at the foot of the balcony, and addressed him in a loud, peevish, and lamentable cry.

"Hallo, friend! must I wait here all night for my kinsman, Major Molineux?"

The sleeping echoes awoke, and answered the voice; and the passenger, barely able to discern a figure sitting in the oblique shade of the steeple, traversed the street to obtain a nearer view. He was himself a gentleman in his prime, of open, intelligent, cheerful, and altogether prepossessing countenance. Perceiving a country youth, apparently homeless and without friends, he accosted him in a tone of real kindness, which had become strange to Robin's ears.

"Well, my good lad, who are you sitting here?" inquired he. "Can I be of service to you in any way?"

"I am afraid not, sir," replied Robin, despondingly; "yet I shall take it kindly, if you'll answer me a single question. I've been searching, half the night, for one Major Molineux; now, sir, is there really such a person in these parts, or am I dreaming?"

"Major Molineux! The name is not altogether strange to me," said the gentleman, smiling. "Have you any objection to telling me the nature of your business with him?"

Then Robin briefly related that his father was a clergyman, settled on a small salary, at a long distance back in the country, and that he and Major Molineux were brothers' children. The Major, having inherited riches, and acquired civil and military rank, had visited his cousin, in great pomp, a year or two before; had manifested much interest in Robin and an elder brother, and, being childless himself, had thrown out hints respecting the future establishment of one of them in life. The elder brother was destined to succeed to the farm which his father cultivated in the interval of sacred duties; it was therefore determined that Robin should profit by his kinsman's generous intentions, especially as he seemed to be rather the favorite, and was thought to possess other necessary endowments.

"For I have the name of being a shrewd youth," observed Robin, in this part of his story.

"I doubt not you deserve it," replied his new friend, good-naturedly; "but pray proceed."

"Well, sir, being nearly eighteen years old, and well grown, as you see," continued Robin, drawing himself up to his full height, "I thought it high time to begin the world. So my mother and sister put me in handsome trim, and my father gave me half the remnant of his last year's salary, and five days ago I started for this place, to pay the Major a visit. But, would you believe it, sir! I crossed the ferry a little after dark, and have yet found nobody that would show me the way to his dwelling; only, an hour or two since, I was told to wait here, and Major Molineux would pass by."

"Can you describe the man who told you this?" inquired the gentleman.

"Oh, he was a very ill-favored fellow, sir," replied Robin, "with two great bumps on his forehead, a hook nose, fiery eyes; and, what struck me as the strangest, his face was of two different colors. Do you happen to know such a man, sir?"

"Not intimately," answered the stranger, "but I chanced to meet him a little time previous to your stopping me. I believe you may trust his word, and that the Major will very shortly pass through this street. In the meantime, as I have a singular curiosity to witness your meeting, I will sit down here upon the steps and bear you company."

He seated himself accordingly, and soon engaged his companion in animated discourse. It was but of brief continuance, however, for a noise of shouting, which had long been remotely audible, drew so much nearer that Robin inquired its cause.

"What may be the meaning of this uproar?" asked he. "Truly, if your town be always as noisy, I shall find little sleep while I am an inhabitant."

"Why, indeed, friend Robin, there do appear to be three or four riotous fellows abroad to-night," replied the gentleman. "You must not expect all the stillness of your native woods here in our streets. But the watch will shortly be at the heels of these lads and"—

"Ay, and set them in the stocks by peep of day," interrupted Robin, recollecting his own encounter with the drowsy lantern-bearer. "But, dear sir, if I may trust my ears, an army of watchmen would never make head against such a multitude of rioters. There were at least a thousand voices went up to make that one shout."

"May not a man have several voices, Robin, as well as two complexions?" said his friend.

"Perhaps a man may; but Heaven forbid that a woman should!" responded the shrewd youth, thinking of the seductive tones of the Major's housekeeper.

The sounds of a trumpet in some neighboring street now became so evident and continual, that Robin's curiosity was strongly excited. In addition to the shouts, he heard frequent bursts from many instruments of discord, and a wild and confused laughter filled up the intervals. Robin rose from the steps, and looked wistfully towards a point whither people seemed to be hastening.

"Surely some prodigious merry-making is going on," exclaimed he. "I have laughed very little since I left home, sir, and should be sorry to lose an opportunity. Shall we step round the corner by that darkish house, and take our share of the fun?"

"Sit down again, sit down, good Robin," replied the gentleman, laying his hand on the skirt of the gray coat. "You forget that we must wait here for your kinsman; and there is reason to believe that he will pass by, in the course of a very few moments."

The near approach of the uproar had now disturbed the neighborhood; windows flew open on all sides; and many heads, in the attire of the pillow, and confused by sleep suddenly broken, were protruded to the gaze of whoever had leisure to observe them. Eager voices hailed each other from house to house, all demanding the explanation, which not a soul could give. Half-dressed men hurried towards the unknown commotion, stumbling as they went over the stone steps that thrust themselves into the narrow foot-walk. The shouts, the laughter, and the tuneless bray, the antipodes of music, came onwards with increasing din, till scattered individuals, and then denser bodies, began to appear round a corner at the distance of a hundred yards.

"Will you recognize your kinsman, if he passes in this crowd?" inquired the gentleman.

"Indeed, I can't warrant it, sir; but I'll take my stand here, and keep a bright lookout," answered Robin, descending to the outer edge of the pavement.

A mighty stream of people now emptied into the street, and came rolling slowly towards the church. A single horseman wheeled the corner in the midst of them, and close behind him came a band of fearful wind-instruments, sending forth a fresher discord now that no intervening buildings kept it from the ear. Then a redder light disturbed the moonbeams, and a dense multitude of torches shone along the street, concealing, by their glare, whatever object they illuminated. The single horseman, clad in a military dress, and bearing a drawn sword, rode onward as the leader, and, by his fierce and variegated countenance, appeared like war personified; the red of one cheek was an emblem of fire and sword; the blackness of the other betokened the mourning that attends them. In his train were wild figures in the Indian dress, and many fantastic shapes without a model, giving the whole march a visionary air, as if a dream had broken forth from some feverish brain, and were sweeping visibly through the midnight streets. A mass of people, inactive, except as applauding spectators, hemmed the procession in; and several women ran along the sidewalk, piercing the confusion of heavier sounds with their shrill voices of mirth or terror.

"The double-faced fellow has his eye upon me," muttered Robin, with an indefinite but an uncomfortable idea that he was himself to bear a part in the pageantry.

The leader turned himself in the saddle, and fixed his glance full upon the country youth, as the steed went slowly by. When Robin had freed his eyes from those fiery ones, the musicians were passing before him, and the torches were close at hand; but the unsteady brightness of the latter formed a veil which he could not penetrate. The rattling of wheels over the stones sometimes found its way to his ear, and confused traces of a human form appeared at intervals, and then melted into the vivid light. A moment more, and the leader thundered a command to halt: the trumpets vomited a horrid breath, and then held their peace; the shouts and laughter of the people died away, and there remained only a universal hum, allied to silence. Right before Robin's eyes was an uncovered cart. There the torches blazed the brightest, there the moon shone out like day, and there, in tar-and-feathery dignity, sat his kinsman, Major Molineux!

He was an elderly man, of large and majestic person, and strong, square features, betokening a steady soul; but steady as it was, his enemies had found means to shake it. His face was pale as death, and far more ghastly; the broad forehead was contracted in his agony, so that his eyebrows formed one grizzled line; his eyes were red and wild, and the foam hung white upon his quivering lip. His whole frame was agitated by a quick and continual tremor, which his pride strove to quell, even in those circumstances of overwhelming humiliation. But perhaps the bitterest pang of all was when his eyes met those of Robin; for he evidently knew him on the instant, as the youth stood witnessing the foul disgrace of a head grown gray in honor. They stared at each other in silence, and Robin's knees shook, and his hair bristled, with a mixture of pity and terror. Soon, however, a bewildering excitement began to seize upon his mind; the preceding adventures of the night, the unexpected appearance of the crowd, the torches, the confused din and the hush that followed, the spectre of his kinsman reviled by that great multitude,—all this, and, more than all, a perception of tremendous ridicule in the whole scene, affected him with a sort of mental inebrity. At that moment a voice of sluggish merriment saluted Robin's ears; he turned instinctively, and just behind the corner of the church stood the lantern-bearer, rubbing his eyes, and drowsily enjoying the lad's amazement. Then he heard a peal of laughter like the ringing of silvery bells; a woman twitched his arm, a saucy eye met his, and he saw the lady of the scarlet petticoat. A sharp, dry cachinnation appealed to his memory, and, standing on tiptoe in the crowd, with his white apron over his head, he beheld the courteous little innkeeper. And lastly, there sailed over the heads of the multitude a great, broad laugh, broken in the midst by two sepulchral hems; thus, "Haw, haw, haw,—hem, hem,—haw, haw, haw, haw!"

The sound proceeded from the balcony of the opposite edifice, and thither Robin turned his eyes. In front of the Gothic window stood the old citizen, wrapped in a wide gown, his gray periwig exchanged for a nightcap, which was thrust back from his forehead, and his silk stockings hanging about his legs. He supported himself on his polished cane in a fit of convulsive merriment, which manifested itself on his solemn old features like a funny inscription on a tombstone. Then Robin seemed to hear the voices of the barbers, of the guests of the inn, and of all who had made sport of him that night. The contagion was spreading among the multitude, when all at once, it seized upon Robin, and he sent forth a shout of laughter that echoed through the street,—every man shook his sides, every man emptied his lungs, but Robin's shout was the loudest there. The cloud-spirits peeped from their silvery islands, as the congregated mirth went roaring up the sky! The Man in the Moon heard the far bellow. "Oho," quoth he, "the old earth is frolicsome to-night!"

When there was a momentary calm in that tempestuous sea of sound, the leader gave the sign, the procession resumed its march. On they went, like fiends that throng in mockery around some dead potentate, mighty no more, but majestic still in his agony. On they went, in counterfeited pomp, in senseless uproar, in frenzied merriment, trampling all on an old man's heart. On swept the tumult, and left a silent street behind.

"Well, Robin, are you dreaming?" inquired the gentleman, laying his hand on the youth's shoulder.

Robin started, and withdrew his arm from the stone post to which he had instinctively clung, as the living stream rolled by him. His cheek was somewhat pale, and his eye not quite as lively as in the earlier part of the evening.

"Will you be kind enough to show me the way to the ferry?" said he, after a moment's pause.

"You have, then, adopted a new subject of inquiry?" observed his companion, with a smile.

"Why, yes, sir," replied Robin, rather dryly. "Thanks to you, and to my other friends, I have at last met my kinsman, and he will scarce desire to see my face again. I begin to grow weary of a town life, sir. Will you show me the way to the ferry?"

"No, my good friend Robin,—not to-night, at least," said the gentleman. "Some few days hence, if you wish it, I will speed you on your journey. Or, if you prefer to remain with us, perhaps, as you are a shrewd youth, you may rise in the world without the help of your kinsman, Major Molineux."

Miscellaneous Tales

THE ANTIQUE RING

"Yes, indeed: the gem is as bright as a star, and curiously set," said Clara Pemberton, examining an antique ring, which her betrothed lover had just presented to her, with a very pretty speech. "It needs only one thing to make it perfect."

"And what is that?" asked Mr. Edward Caryl, secretly anxious for the credit of his gift. "A modern setting, perhaps?"

"Oh, no! That would destroy the charm at once," replied Clara. "It needs nothing but a story. I long to know how many times it has been the pledge of faith between two lovers, and whether the vows, of which it was the symbol, were always kept or often broken. Not that I should be too scrupulous about facts. If you happen to be unacquainted with its authentic history, so much the better. May it not have sparkled upon a queen's finger? Or who knows but it is the very ring which Posthumus received from Imogen? In short, you must kindle your imagination at the lustre of this diamond, and make a legend for it."

Now such a task—and doubtless Clara knew it—was the most acceptable that could have been imposed on Edward Caryl. He was one of that multitude of young gentlemen—limbs, or rather twigs, of the law—whose names appear in gilt letters on the front of Tudor's Buildings, and other places in the vicinity of the Court House, which seem to be the haunt of the gentler as well as the severer Muses. Edward, in the dearth of clients, was accustomed to employ his much leisure in assisting the growth of American Literature, to which good cause he had contributed not a few quires of the finest letter-paper, containing some thought, some fancy, some depth of feeling, together with a young writer's abundance of conceits. Sonnets, stanzas of Tennysonian sweetness, tales imbued with German mysticism, versions from Jean Paul, criticisms of the old English poets, and essays smacking of Dialistic philosophy, were among his multifarious productions. The editors of the fashionable periodicals were familiar with his autography, and inscribed his name in those brilliant bead-rolls of ink-stained celebrity which illustrate the first page of their covers. Nor did fame withhold her laurel. Hillard had included him among the lights of the New England metropolis, in his "Boston Book;" Bryant had found room for some of his stanzas, in the "Selections from American Poetry;" and Mr. Griswold, in his recent assemblage of the sons and daughters of song, had introduced Edward Caryl into the inner court of the temple, among his four-score choicest bards. There was a prospect, indeed, of his assuming a still higher and more independent position. Interviews had been held with Ticknor, and a correspondence with the Harpers, respecting a proposed volume, chiefly to consist of Mr. Caryl's fugitive pieces in the Magazines, but to be accompanied with a poem of some length, never before published. Not improbably, the public may yet be gratified with this collection.

Meanwhile, we sum up our sketch of Edward Caryl, by pronouncing him, though somewhat of a carpet knight in literature, yet no unfavorable specimen of a generation of rising writers, whose spirit is such that we may reasonably expect creditable attempts from all, and good and beautiful results from some. And, it will be observed, Edward was the very man to write pretty legends, at a lady's instance, for an old-fashioned diamond ring. He took the jewel in his hand, and turned it so as to catch its scintillating radiance, as if hoping, in accordance with Clara's suggestion, to light up his fancy with that star-like gleam.

"Shall it be a ballad?—a tale in verse?" he inquired. "Enchanted rings often glisten in old English poetry; I think something may be done with the subject; but it is fitter for rhyme than prose."

"No, no," said Miss Pemberton, "we will have no more rhyme than just enough for a posy to the ring. You must tell the legend in simple prose; and when it is finished, I will make a little party to hear it read."

The young gentleman promised obedience; and going to his pillow, with his head full of the familiar spirits that used to be worn in rings, watches, and sword-hilts, he had the good fortune to possess himself of an available idea in a dream. Connecting this with what he himself chanced to know of the ring's real history, his task was done. Clara Pemberton invited a select few of her friends, all holding the stanchest faith in Edward's genius, and therefore the most genial auditors, if not altogether the fairest critics, that a writer could possibly desire. Blessed be woman for her faculty of admiration, and especially for her tendency to admire with her heart, when man, at most, grants merely a cold approval with his mind!

Drawing his chair beneath the blaze of a solar lamp, Edward Caryl untied a roll of glossy paper, and began as follows:—

THE LEGEND

After the death-warrant had been read to the Earl of Essex, and on the evening before his appointed execution, the Countess of Shrewsbury paid his lordship a visit, and found him, as it appeared, toying childishly with a ring. The diamond, that enriched it, glittered like a little star, but with a singular tinge of red. The gloomy prison-chamber in the Tower, with its deep and narrow windows piercing the walls of stone, was now all that the earl possessed of worldly prospect; so that there was the less wonder that he should look steadfastly into the gem, and moralize upon earth's deceitful splendor, as men in darkness and ruin seldom fail to do. But the shrewd observations of the countess,—an artful and unprincipled woman,—the pretended friend of Essex, but who had come to glut her revenge for a deed of scorn which he himself had forgotten,—her keen eye detected a deeper interest attached to this jewel. Even while expressing his gratitude for her remembrance of a ruined favorite, and condemned criminal, the earl's glance reverted to the ring, as if all that remained of time and its affairs were collected within that small golden circlet.

"My dear lord," observed the countess, "there is surely some matter of great moment wherewith this ring is connected, since it so absorbs your mind. A token, it may be, of some fair lady's love,—alas, poor lady, once richest in possessing such a heart! Would you that the jewel be returned to her?"

"The queen! the queen! It was her Majesty's own gift," replied the earl, still gazing into the depths of the gem. "She took it from her finger, and told me, with a smile, that it was an heirloom from her Tudor ancestors, and had once been the property of Merlin, the British wizard, who gave it to the lady of his love. His art had made this diamond the abiding-place of a spirit, which, though of fiendish nature, was bound to work only good, so long as the ring was an unviolated pledge of love and faith, both with the giver and receiver. But should love prove false, and faith be broken, then the evil spirit would work his own devilish will, until the ring were purified by becoming the medium of some good and holy act, and again the pledge of faithful love. The gem soon lost its virtue; for the wizard was murdered by the very lady to whom he gave it."

"An idle legend!" said the countess.

"It is so," answered Essex, with a melancholy smile. "Yet the queen's favor, of which this ring was the symbol, has proved my ruin. When death is nigh, men converse with dreams and shadows. I have been gazing into the diamond, and fancying—but you will laugh at me—that I might catch a glimpse of the evil spirit there. Do you observe this red glow,—dusky, too, amid all the brightness? It is the token of his presence; and even now, methinks, it grows redder and duskier, like an angry sunset."

Nevertheless, the earl's manner testified how slight was his credence in the enchanted properties of the ring. But there is a kind of playfulness that comes in moments of despair, when the reality of misfortune, if entirely felt, would crush the soul at once. He now, for a brief space, was lost in thought, while the countess contemplated him with malignant satisfaction.

"This ring," he resumed, in another tone, "alone remains, of all that my royal mistress's favor lavished upon her servant. My fortune once shone as brightly as the gem. And now, such a darkness has fallen around me, methinks it would be no marvel if its gleam—the sole light of my prison-house—were to be forthwith extinguished; inasmuch as my last earthly hope depends upon it."

"How say you, my lord?" asked the Countess of Shrewsbury. "The stone is bright; but there should be strange magic in it, if it can keep your hopes alive, at this sad hour. Alas! these iron bars and ramparts of the Tower are unlike to yield to such a spell."

Essex raised his head involuntarily; for there was something in the countess's tone that disturbed him, although he could not suspect that an enemy had intruded upon the sacred privacy of a prisoner's dungeon, to exult over so dark a ruin of such once brilliant fortunes. He looked her in the face, but saw nothing to awaken his distrust. It would have required a keener eye than even Cecil's to read the secret of a countenance, which had been worn so long in the false light of a court, that it was now little better than a mask, telling any story save the true one. The condemned nobleman again bent over the ring, and proceeded:—

"It once had power in it,—this bright gem,—the magic that appertains to the talisman of a great queen's favor. She bade me, if hereafter I should fall into her disgrace,—how deep soever, and whatever might be the crime,—to convey this jewel to her sight, and it should plead for me. Doubtless, with her piercing judgment, she had even then detected the rashness of my nature, and foreboded some such deed as has now brought destruction upon my head. And knowing, too, her own hereditary rigor, she designed, it may be, that the memory of gentler and kindlier hours should soften her heart in my behalf, when my need should be the greatest. I have doubted,—I have distrusted,—yet who can tell, even now, what happy influence this ring might have?"

"You have delayed full long to show the ring, and plead her Majesty's gracious promise," remarked the countess,—"your state being what it is."

"True," replied the earl: "but for my honor's sake, I was loath to entreat the queen's mercy, while I might hope for life, at least, from the justice of the laws. If, on a trial by my peers, I had been acquitted of meditating violence against her sacred life, then would I have fallen at her feet, and, presenting the jewel, have prayed no other favor than that my love and zeal should be put to the severest test. But now—it were confessing too much—it were cringing too low—to beg the miserable gift of life, on no other score than the tenderness which her Majesty deems me to have forfeited!"

"Yet it is your only hope," said the countess.

"And besides," continued Essex, pursuing his own reflections, "of what avail will be this token of womanly feeling, when, on the other hand, are arrayed the all-prevailing motives of state policy, and the artifices and intrigues of courtiers, to consummate my downfall? Will Cecil or Raleigh suffer her heart to act for itself, even if the spirit of her father were not in her? It is in vain to hope it."

But still Essex gazed at the ring with an absorbed attention, that proved how much hope his sanguine temperament had concentrated here, when there was none else for him in the wide world, save what lay in the compass of that hoop of gold. The spark of brightness within the diamond, which gleamed like an intenser than earthly fire, was the memorial of his dazzling career. It had not paled with the waning sunshine of his mistress's favor; on the contrary, in spite of its remarkable tinge of dusky red, he fancied that it never shone so brightly. The glow of festal torches,—the blaze of perfumed lamps,—bonfires that had been kindled for him, when he was the darling of the people,—the splendor of the royal court, where he had been the peculiar star,—all seemed to have collected their moral or material glory into the gem, and to burn with a radiance caught from the future, as well as gathered from the past. That radiance might break forth again. Bursting from the diamond, into which it was now narrowed, it might beam first upon the gloomy walls of the Tower,—then wider, wider, wider,—till all England, and the seas around her cliffs, should be gladdened with the light. It was such an ecstasy as often ensues after long depression, and has been supposed to precede the circumstances of darkest fate that may befall mortal man. The earl pressed the ring to his heart as if it were indeed a talisman, the habitation of a spirit, as the queen had playfully assured him,—but a spirit of happier influences than her legend spake of.

"Oh, could I but make my way to her footstool!" cried he, waving his hand aloft, while he paced the stone pavement of his prison-chamber with an impetuous step. "I might kneel down, indeed, a ruined man, condemned to the block, but how should I rise again? Once more the favorite of Elizabeth!—England's proudest noble!—with such prospects as ambition never aimed at!

Why have I tarried so long in this weary dungeon? The ring has power to set me free! The palace wants me! Ho, jailer, unbar the door!"

But then occurred the recollection of the impossibility of obtaining an interview with his fatally estranged mistress, and testing the influence over her affections, which he still flattered himself with possessing. Could he step beyond the limits of his prison, the world would be all sunshine; but here was only gloom and death.

"Alas!" said he, slowly and sadly, letting his head fall upon his hands. "I die for the lack of one blessed word."

The Countess of Shrewsbury, herself forgotten amid the earl's gorgeous visions, had watched him with an aspect that could have betrayed nothing to the most suspicious observer; unless that it was too calm for humanity, while witnessing the flutterings, as it were, of a generous heart in the death-agony. She now approached him.

"My good lord," she said, "what mean you to do?"

"Nothing,—my deeds are done!" replied he, despondingly; "yet, had a fallen favorite any friends, I would entreat one of them to lay this ring at her Majesty's feet; albeit with little hope, save that, hereafter, it might remind her that poor Essex, once far too highly favored, was at last too severely dealt with."

"I will be that friend," said the countess. "There is no time to be lost. Trust this precious ring with me. This very night the queen's eye shall rest upon it; nor shall the efficacy of my poor words be wanting, to strengthen the impression which it will doubtless make."

The earl's first impulse was to hold out the ring. But looking at the countess, as she bent forward to receive it, he fancied that the red glow of the gem tinged all her face, and gave it an ominous expression. Many passages of past times recurred to his memory. A preternatural insight, perchance caught from approaching death, threw its momentary gleam, as from a meteor, all round his position.

"Countess," he said, "I know not wherefore I hesitate, being in a plight so desperate, and having so little choice of friends. But have you looked into your own heart? Can you perform this office with the truth—the earnestness—the zeal, even to tears, and agony of spirit—wherewith the holy gift of human life should be pleaded for? Woe be unto you, should you undertake this task, and deal towards me otherwise than with utmost faith! For your own soul's sake, and as you would have peace at your death-hour, consider well in what spirit you receive this ring!"

The countess did not shrink.

"My lord!—my good lord!" she exclaimed, "wrong not a woman's heart by these suspicions. You might choose another messenger; but who, save a lady of her bedchamber, can obtain access to the queen at this untimely hour? It is for your life,—for your life,—else I would not renew my offer."

"Take the ring," said the earl.

"Believe that it shall be in the queen's hands before the lapse of another hour," replied the countess, as she received this sacred trust of life and death. "To-morrow morning look for the result of my intercession."

She departed. Again the earl's hopes rose high. Dreams visited his slumber, not of the sable-decked scaffold in the Tower-yard, but of canopies of state, obsequious courtiers, pomp, splendor, the smile of the once more gracious queen, and a light beaming from the magic gem, which illuminated his whole future.

History records how foully the Countess of Shrewsbury betrayed the trust, which Essex, in his utmost need, confided to her. She kept the ring, and stood in the presence of Elizabeth, that night, without one attempt to soften her stern hereditary temper in behalf of the former favorite. The next day the earl's noble head rolled upon the scaffold. On her death-bed, tortured, at last, with a sense of the dreadful guilt which she had taken upon her soul, the wicked countess sent for Elizabeth, revealed the story of the ring, and besought forgiveness for her treachery. But the queen, still obdurate, even while remorse for past obduracy was tugging at her heart-strings, shook the dying woman in her bed, as if struggling with death for the privilege of wreaking her revenge and spite. The spirit of the countess passed away, to undergo the justice, or receive the mercy, of a higher tribunal; and tradition says, that the fatal ring was found upon her breast, where it had imprinted a dark red circle, resembling the effect of the intensest heat. The attendants, who prepared the body for burial, shuddered, whispering one to another, that the ring must have derived its heat from the glow of infernal fire. They left it on her breast, in the coffin, and it went with that guilty woman to the tomb.

Many years afterward, when the church, that contained the monuments of the Shrewsbury family, was desecrated by Cromwell's soldiers, they broke open the ancestral vaults, and stole whatever was valuable from the noble personages who reposed there. Merlin's antique ring passed into the possession of a stout sergeant of the Ironsides, who thus became subject to the influences of the evil spirit that still kept his abode within the gem's enchanted depths. The sergeant was soon slain in battle, thus transmitting the ring, though without any legal form of testament, to a gay cavalier, who forthwith pawned it, and expended the money in liquor, which speedily brought him to the grave. We next catch the sparkle of the magic diamond at various epochs of the merry reign of Charles the Second. But its sinister fortune still attended it. From whatever hand this ring of portent came, and whatever finger it encircled, ever it was the pledge of deceit between man and man, or man and woman, of faithless vows, and unhallowed passion; and whether to lords and ladies, or to village-maids,—for sometimes it found its way so low,—still it brought nothing but sorrow and disgrace. No purifying deed was done, to drive the fiend from his bright home in this little star. Again, we hear of it at a later period, when Sir Robert Walpole bestowed the ring, among far richer jewels, on the lady of a British legislator, whose political honor he wished to undermine. Many a dismal and unhappy tale might be wrought out of its other adventures. All this while, its ominous tinge of dusky red had been deepening and darkening, until, if laid upon white paper, it cast the mingled hue of night and blood, strangely illuminated with scintillating light, in a circle round about. But this peculiarity only made it the more valuable.

Alas, the fatal ring! When shall its dark secret be discovered, and the doom of ill, inherited from one possessor to another, be finally revoked?

The legend now crosses the Atlantic, and comes down to our own immediate time. In a certain church of our city, not many evenings ago, there was a contribution for a charitable object. A fervid preacher had poured out his whole soul in a rich and tender discourse, which had at least excited the tears, and perhaps the more effectual sympathy, of a numerous audience. While the choristers sang sweetly, and the organ poured forth its melodious thunder, the deacons passed up and down the aisles, and along the galleries, presenting their mahogany boxes, in which each person deposited whatever sum he deemed it safe to lend to the Lord, in aid of human wretchedness. Charity became audible,—chink, chink, chink,—as it fell drop by drop, into the common receptacle. There was a hum,—a stir,—the subdued bustle of people putting their hands into their pockets; while, ever and anon, a vagrant coin fell upon the floor, and rolled away, with long reverberation, into some inscrutable corner.

At length, all having been favored with an opportunity to be generous, the two deacons placed their boxes on the communion-table, and thence, at the conclusion of the services, removed them into the vestry. Here these good old gentlemen sat down together, to reckon the accumulated treasure.

"Fie, fie, Brother Tilton," said Deacon Trott, peeping into Deacon Tilton's box, "what a heap of copper you have picked up! Really, for an old man, you must have had a heavy job to lug it along. Copper! copper! copper! Do people expect to get admittance into heaven at the price of a few coppers?"

"Don't wrong them, brother," answered Deacon Tilton, a simple and kindly old man. "Copper may do more for one person, than gold will for another. In the galleries, where I present my box, we must not expect such a harvest as you gather among the gentry in the broad aisle, and all over the floor of the church. My people are chiefly poor mechanics and laborers, sailors, seamstresses, and servant-maids, with a most uncomfortable intermixture of roguish schoolboys."

"Well, well," said Deacon Trott; "but there is a great deal, Brother Tilton, in the method of presenting a contribution-box. It is a knack that comes by nature, or not at all."

They now proceeded to sum up the avails of the evening, beginning with the receipts of Deacon Trott. In good sooth, that worthy personage had reaped an abundant harvest, in which he prided himself no less, apparently, than if every dollar had been contributed from his own individual pocket. Had the good deacon been meditating a jaunt to Texas, the treasures of the mahogany box might have sent him on his way rejoicing. There were bank-notes, mostly, it is true, of the smallest denomination in the giver's pocketbook, yet making a goodly average upon the whole. The most splendid contribution was a check for a hundred dollars, bearing the name of a distinguished merchant, whose liberality was duly celebrated in the newspapers of the next day. No less than seven half-eagles, together with an English sovereign, glittered amidst an indiscriminate heap of silver; the box being polluted with nothing of the copper kind, except a single bright new cent, wherewith a little boy had performed his first charitable act.

"Very well! very well indeed!" said Deacon Trott, self-approvingly. "A handsome evening's work! And now, Brother Tilton, let's see whether you can match it." Here was a sad contrast! They poured forth Deacon Tilton's treasure upon the table, and it really seemed as if the whole copper coinage of the country, together with an amazing quantity of shop-keeper's tokens, and English and Irish half-pence, mostly of base metal, had been congregated into the box.

There was a very substantial pencil-case, and the semblance of a shilling; but the latter proved to be made of tin, and the former of German-silver. A gilded brass button was doing duty as a gold coin, and a folded shop-bill had assumed the character of a bank-note. But Deacon Tilton's feelings were much revived by the aspect of another bank-note, new and crisp, adorned with beautiful engravings, and stamped with the indubitable word, TWENTY, in large black letters. Alas! it was a counterfeit. In short, the poor old Deacon was no less unfortunate than those who trade with fairies, and whose gains are sure to be transformed into dried leaves, pebbles, and other valuables of that kind.

"I believe the Evil One is in the box," said he, with some vexation.

"Well done, Deacon Tilton!" cried his Brother Trott, with a hearty laugh. "You ought to have a statue in copper."

"Never mind, brother," replied the good Deacon, recovering his temper. "I'll bestow ten dollars from my own pocket, and may Heaven's blessing go along with it. But look! what do you call this?"

Under the copper mountain, which it had cost them so much toil to remove, lay an antique ring! It was enriched with a diamond, which, so soon as it caught the light, began to twinkle and glimmer, emitting the whitest and purest lustre that could possibly be conceived. It was as brilliant as if some magician had condensed the brightest star in heaven into a compass fit to be set in a ring, for a lady's delicate finger.

"How is this?" said Deacon Trott, examining it carefully, in the expectation of finding it as worthless as the rest of his colleague's treasure. "Why, upon my word, this seems to be a real diamond, and of the purest water. Whence could it have come?"

"Really, I cannot tell," quoth Deacon Tilton, "for my spectacles were so misty that all faces looked alike. But now I remember, there was a flash of light came from the box, at one moment; but it seemed a dusky red, instead of a pure white, like the sparkle of this gem. Well; the ring will make up for the copper; but I wish the giver had thrown its history into the box along with it."

It has been our good luck to recover a portion of that history. After transmitting misfortune from one possessor to another, ever since the days of British Merlin, the identical ring which Queen Elizabeth gave to the Earl of Essex was finally thrown into the contribution-box of a New England church. The two deacons deposited it in the glass case of a fashionable jeweller, of whom it was purchased by the humble rehearser of this legend, in the hope that it may be allowed to sparkle on a fair lady's finger. Purified from the foul fiend, so long its inhabitant, by a deed of unostentatious charity, and now made the symbol of faithful and devoted love, the gentle bosom of its new possessor need fear no sorrow from its influence.

"Very pretty!—Beautiful!—How original!—How sweetly written!—What nature!—What imagination!—What power!—What pathos!—What exquisite humor!"—were the exclamations of Edward Caryl's kind and generous auditors, at the conclusion of the legend.

"It is a pretty tale," said Miss Pemberton, who, conscious that her praise was to that of all others as a diamond to a pebble, was therefore the less liberal in awarding it. "It is really a pretty tale, and very proper for any of the

Annuals. But, Edward, your moral does not satisfy me. What thought did you embody in the ring?"

"O Clara, this is too bad!" replied Edward, with a half-reproachful smile. "You know that I can never separate the idea from the symbol in which it manifests itself. However, we may suppose the Gem to be the human heart, and the Evil Spirit to be Falsehood, which, in one guise or another, is the fiend that causes all the sorrow and trouble in the world. I beseech you to let this suffice."

"It shall," said Clara, kindly. "And, believe me, whatever the world may say of the story, I prize it far above the diamond which enkindled your imagination."

GRAVES AND GOBLINS

Now talk we of graves and goblins! Fit themes,—start not! gentle reader,—fit for a ghost like me. Yes; though an earth-clogged fancy is laboring with these conceptions, and an earthly hand will write them down, for mortal eyes to read, still their essence flows from as airy a ghost as ever basked in the pale starlight, at twelve o'clock. Judge them not by the gross and heavy form in which they now appear. They may be gross, indeed, with the earthly pollution contracted from the brain, through which they pass; and heavy with the burden of mortal language, that crushes all the finer intelligences of the soul. This is no fault of mine. But should aught of ethereal spirit be perceptible, yet scarcely so, glimmering along the dull train of words,—should a faint perfume breathe from the mass of clay,—then, gentle reader, thank the ghost, who thus embodies himself for your sake! Will you believe me, if I say that all true and noble thoughts, and elevated imaginations, are but partly the offspring of the intellect which seems to produce them? Sprites, that were poets once, and are now all poetry, hover round the dreaming bard, and become his inspiration; buried statesmen lend their wisdom, gathered on earth and mellowed in the grave, to the historian; and when the preacher rises nearest to the level of his mighty subject, it is because the prophets of old days have communed with him. Who has not been conscious of mysteries within his mind, mysteries of truth and reality, which will not wear the chains of language? Mortal, then the dead were with you! And thus shall the earth-dulled soul, whom I inspire, be conscious of a misty brightness among his thoughts, and strive to make it gleam upon the page,—but all in vain. Poor author! How will he despise what he can grasp, for the sake of the dim glory that eludes him!

So talk we of graves and goblins. But, what have ghosts to do with graves? Mortal man, wearing the dust which shall require a sepulchre, might deem it more a home and resting-place than a spirit can, whose earthly clod has returned to earth. Thus philosophers have reasoned. Yet wiser they who adhere to the ancient sentiment, that a phantom haunts and hallows the marble tomb or grassy hillock where its material form was laid. Till purified from each stain of clay; till the passions of the living world are all forgotten; till it have less brotherhood with the wayfarers of earth than with spirits that never wore mortality,—the ghost must linger round the grave. Oh, it is a long and dreary watch to some of us!

Even in early childhood, I had selected a sweet spot, of shade and glimmering sunshine, for my grave. It was no burial-ground, but a secluded nook of virgin earth, where I used to sit, whole summer afternoons, dreaming about life and death. My fancy ripened prematurely, and taught me secrets which I could not otherwise have known. I pictured the coming years,—they never came to me, indeed; but I pictured them like life, and made this spot the scene of all that should be brightest, in youth, manhood, and old age. There, in a little while, it would be time for me to breathe the bashful and burning vows of first-love; thither, after gathering fame abroad, I would return to enjoy the loud plaudit of the world, a vast but unobtrusive sound, like the booming of a distant sea; and thither, at the far-off close of life, an aged man would come, to dream, as the boy was dreaming, and be as happy in the past as he was in futurity. Finally, when all should be finished, in that spot so hallowed, in that soil so impregnated with the most precious of my bliss, there was to be my grave. Methought it would be the sweetest grave that ever a mortal frame reposed in, or an ethereal spirit haunted. There, too, in future times, drawn thither by the spell which I had breathed around the place, boyhood would sport and dream, and youth would love, and manhood would enjoy, and age would dream again, and my ghost would watch but never frighten them. Alas, the vanity of mortal projects, even when they centre in the grave! I died in my first youth, before I had been a lover; at a distance, also, from the grave which fancy had dug for me; and they buried me in the thronged cemetery of a town, where my marble slab stands unnoticed amid a hundred others. And there are coffins on each side of mine!

"Alas, poor ghost!" will the reader say. Yet I am a happy ghost enough, and disposed to be contented with my grave, if the sexton will but let it be my own, and bring no other dead man to dispute my title. Earth has left few stains upon me, and it will be but a short time that I need haunt the place. It is good to die in early youth. Had I lived out three-score years and ten, or half of them, my spirit would have been so earth-incrusted, that centuries might not have purified it for a better home than the dark precincts of the grave. Meantime, there is good choice of company amongst us. From twilight till near sunrise, we are gliding to and fro, some in the graveyard, others miles away; and, would we speak with any friend, we do but knock against his tombstone, and pronounce the name engraved on it: in an instant, there the shadow stands!

Some are ghosts of considerable antiquity. There is an old man, hereabout; he never had a tombstone, and is often puzzled to distinguish his own grave; but hereabouts he haunts, and long is doomed to haunt. He was a miser in his lifetime, and buried a strong box of ill-gotten gold, almost fresh from the mint, in the coinage of William and Mary. Scarcely was it safe, when the sexton buried the old man, and his secret with him. I could point out the place where the treasure lies; it was at the bottom of the miser's garden; but a paved thoroughfare now passes beside the spot, and the corner-stone of a market-house presses right down upon it. Had the workmen dug six inches deeper, they would have found the hoard. Now thither must this poor old miser go, whether in starlight, moonshine, or pitch darkness, and brood above his worthless treasure, recalling all the petty crimes by which he gained it. Not a coin must he fail to reckon in his memory, nor forget a pennyworth of the sin that made up the sum, though his agony is such as if the pieces of gold, red-hot, were stamped into his naked soul. Often, while he is in torment there, he hears the steps of living men, who love the dross of earth as well as he did. May they never groan over their miserable wealth like him! Night after night, for above a hundred years, hath he done this penance, and still must he do it, till the iron box he brought to light, and each separate coin be cleansed by grateful tears of a widow or an orphan. My spirit sighs for his long vigil at the corner of the market-house!

There are ghosts whom I tremble to meet, and cannot think of without a shudder. One has the guilt of blood upon him. The soul which he thrust untimely forth has long since been summoned from our gloomy graveyard, and dwells among the stars of heaven, too far and too high for even the recollection of mortal anguish to ascend thither. Not so the murderer's ghost! It is his doom to spend all the hours of darkness in the spot which he stained with innocent blood, and to feel the hot stream—hot as when it first gushed upon his hand—incorporating itself with his spiritual substance. Thus his horrible crime is ever fresh within him. Two other wretches are condemned to walk arm in arm. They were guilty lovers in their lives, and still, in death, must wear the guise of love, though hatred and loathing have become their very nature and existence. The pollution of their mutual sin remains with them, and makes their souls sick continually. Oh, that I might forget all the dark shadows which haunt about these graves! This passing thought of them has left a stain, and will weigh me down among dust and sorrow, beyond the time that my own transgressions would have kept me here.

There is one shade among us, whose high nature it is good to meditate upon. He lived a patriot, and is a patriot still. Posterity has forgotten him. The simple slab, of red freestone, that bore his name, was broken long ago, and is now covered by the gradual accumulation of the soil. A tuft of thistles is his only monument. This upright spirit came to his grave, after a lengthened life, with so little stain of earth, that he might, almost immediately, have trodden the pathway of the sky. But his strong love of country chained him down, to share its vicissitudes of weal or woe. With such deep yearning in his soul, he was unfit for heaven. That noblest virtue has the effect of sin, and keeps his pure and lofty spirit in a penance, which may not terminate till America be again a wilderness. Not that there is no joy for the dead patriot. Can he fail to experience it, while he contemplates the mighty and increasing power of the land, which he protected in its infancy? No; there is much to gladden him. But sometimes I dread to meet him, as he returns from the bedchambers of rulers and politicians, after diving into their secret motives, and searching out their aims. He looks round him with a stern and awful sadness, and vanishes into his neglected grave. Let nothing sordid or selfish defile your deeds or thoughts, ye great men of the day, lest ye grieve the noble dead.

Few ghosts take such an endearing interest as this, even in their own private affairs. It made me rather sad, at first, to find how soon the flame of love expires amid the chill damps of the tomb; so much the sooner, the more fiercely it may have burned. Forget your dead mistress, youth! She has already forgotten you. Maiden, cease to weep for your buried lover! He will know nothing of your tears, nor value them if he did. Yet it were blasphemy to say that true love is other than immortal. It is an earthly passion, of which I speak, mingled with little that is spiritual, and must therefore perish with the perishing clay. When souls have loved, there is no falsehood or forgetfulness. Maternal affection, too, is strong as adamant. There are mothers here, among us, who might have been in heaven fifty years ago, if they could forbear to cherish earthly joy and sorrow, reflected from the bosoms of their children. Husbands and wives have a comfortable gift of oblivion, especially when secure of the faith of their living halves. Jealousy, it is true, will play the devil with a ghost, driving him to the bedside of secondary wedlock, there to scowl, unseen, and gibber inaudible remonstrances. Dead wives, however jealous in their lifetime, seldom feel this posthumous torment so acutely.

Many, many things, that appear most important while we walk the busy street, lose all their interest the moment we are borne into the quiet graveyard which borders it. For my own part, my spirit had not become so mixed up with earthly existence, as to be now held in an unnatural combination, or tortured much with retrospective cares. I still love my parents and a younger sister, who remain among the living, and often grieve me by their patient sorrow for the dead. Each separate tear of theirs is an added weight upon my soul, and lengthens my stay among the graves. As to other matters, it exceedingly rejoices me that my summons came before I had time to write a projected poem, which was highly imaginative in conception, and could not have failed to give me a triumphant rank in the choir of our native bards. Nothing is so much to be deprecated as posthumous renown. It keeps the immortal spirit from the proper bliss of his celestial state, and causes him to feed upon the impure breath of mortal man, till sometimes he forgets that there are starry realms above him. Few poets—infatuated that they are!—soar upward while the least whisper of their name is heard on earth. On Sabbath evenings, my sisters sit by the fireside, between our father and mother, and repeat some hymns of mine, which they have often heard from my own lips, ere the tremulous voice left them forever. Little do they think, those dear ones, that the dead stands listening in the glimmer of the firelight, and is almost gifted with a visible shape by the fond intensity of their remembrance.

Now shall the reader know a grief of the poor ghost that speaks to him; a grief, but not a helpless one. Since I have dwelt among the graves, they bore the corpse of a young maiden hither, and laid her in the old ancestral vault, which is hollowed in the side of a grassy bank. It has a door of stone, with rusty iron hinges, and above it, a rude sculpture of the family arms, and inscriptions of all their names who have been buried there, including sire and son, mother and daughter, of an ancient colonial race. All of her lineage had gone before, and when the young maiden followed, the portal was closed forever. The night after her burial, when the other ghosts were flitting about their graves, forth came the pale virgin's shadow, with the rest, but knew not whither to go, nor whom to haunt, so lonesome had she been on earth. She stood by the ancient sepulchre, looking upward to the bright stars, as if she would, even then, begin her flight. Her sadness made me sad. That night and the next, I stood near her, in the moonshine, but dared not speak, because she seemed purer than all the ghosts, and fitter to converse with angels than with men. But the third bright eve, still gazing upward to the glory of the heavens, she sighed, and said, "When will my mother come for me?" Her low, sweet voice emboldened me to speak, and she was kind and gentle, though so pure, and answered me again. From that time, always at the ghostly hour, I sought the old tomb of her fathers, and either found her standing by the door, or knocked, and she appeared. Blessed creature, that she was; her chaste spirit hallowed mine, and imparted such a celestial buoyancy, that I longed to grasp her hand, and fly,—upward, aloft, aloft! I thought, too, that she only lingered here, till my earthlier soul should be purified for heaven. One night, when the stars threw down the light that shadows love, I stole forth to the accustomed spot, and knocked, with my airy fingers, at her door. She answered not. Again I knocked, and breathed her name. Where was she? At once, the truth fell on my miserable spirit and crushed it to the earth, among dead men's bones and mouldering dust, groaning in cold and desolate agony. Her penance was over! She had taken her trackless flight, and had found a home in the purest radiance of the upper stars, leaving me to knock at the stone portal of the darksome sepulchre. But I know—I know, that angels hurried her away, or surely she would have whispered ere she fled!

She is gone! How could the grave imprison that unspotted one! But her pure, ethereal spirit will not quite forget me, nor soar too high in bliss, till I ascend to join her. Soon, soon be that hour! I am weary of the earth-damps; they burden me; they choke me! Already, I can float in the moonshine; the faint starlight will almost bear up my footsteps; the perfume of flowers, which grosser spirits love, is now too earthly a luxury for me. Grave! Grave! thou art not my home. I must flit a little longer in thy night gloom, and then be gone,—far from the dust of the living and the dead,—far from the corruption that is around me, but no more within!

A few times I have visited the chamber of one who walks, obscure and lonely, on his mortal pilgrimage. He will leave not many living friends, when he goes to join the dead, where his thoughts often stray, and he might better be. I steal into his sleep, and play my part among the figures of his dreams. I glide through the moonlight of his waking fancy, and whisper conceptions, which, with a strange thrill of fear, he writes down as his own. I stand beside him now, at midnight, telling these dreamy truths with a voice so dream-like, that he mistakes them for fictions of a brain too prone to such. Yet he glances behind him and shivers, while the lamp burns pale. Farewell, dreamer,—waking or sleeping! Your brightest dreams are fled; your mind grows too hard and cold for a spiritual guest to enter; you are earthly, too, and have all the sins of earth. The ghost will visit you no more.

But where is the maiden, holy and pure, though wearing a form of clay, that would have me bend over her pillow at midnight, and leave a blessing there? With a silent invocation, let her summon me. Shrink not, maiden, when I come! In life, I was a high-souled youth, meditative, yet seldom sad, full of chaste fancies, and stainless from all grosser sin. And now, in death, I bring no loathsome smell of the grave, nor ghostly terrors,—but gentle, and soothing, and sweetly pensive influences. Perhaps, just fluttering for the skies, my visit may hallow the wellsprings of thy thought, and make thee heavenly here on earth. Then shall pure dreams and holy meditations bless thy life; nor thy sainted spirit linger round the grave, but seek the upper stars, and meet me there!

DR. BULLIVANT

This person was not eminent enough, either by nature or circumstance, to deserve a public memorial simply for his own sake, after the lapse of a century and a half from the era in which he flourished. His character, in the view which we propose to take of it, may give a species of distinctness and point to some remarks on the tone and composition of New England society, modified as it became by new ingredients from the eastern world, and by the attrition of sixty or seventy years over the rugged peculiarities of the original settlers. We are perhaps accustomed to employ too sombre a pencil in picturing the earlier times among the Puritans, because, at our cold distance, we form our ideas almost wholly from their severest features. It is like gazing on some scenes in the land which we inherit from them; we see the mountains, rising sternly and with frozen summits up to heaven, and the forests, waving in massy depths where sunshine seems a profanation, and we see the gray mist, like the duskiness of years, shedding a chill obscurity over the whole; but the green and pleasant spots in the hollow of the hills, the warm places in the heart of what looks desolate, are hidden from our eyes. Still, however, a prevailing characteristic of the age was gloom, or something which cannot be more accurately expressed than by that term, and its long shadow, falling over all the intervening years, is visible, though not too distinctly, upon ourselves. Without material detriment to a deep and solid happiness, the frolic of the mind was so habitually chastened, that persons have gained a nook in history by the mere possession of animal spirits, too exuberant to be confined within the established bounds. Every vain jest and unprofitable word was deemed an item in the account of criminality, and whatever wit, or semblance thereof, came into existence, its birthplace was generally the pulpit, and its parent some sour old Genevan divine. The specimens of humor and satire, preserved in the sermons and controversial tracts of those days, are occasionally the apt expressions of pungent thoughts; but oftener they are cruel torturings and twistings of trite ideas, disgusting by the wearisome ingenuity which constitutes their only merit. Among a people where so few possessed, or were allowed to exercise, the art of extracting the mirth which lies hidden like latent caloric in almost everything, a gay apothecary, such as Dr. Bullivant, must have been a phenomenon.

We will suppose ourselves standing in Cornhill, on a pleasant morning of the year 1670, about the hour when the shutters are unclosed, and the dust swept from the doorsteps, and when Business rubs its eyes, and begins to plod sleepily through the town. The street, instead of running between lofty and continuous piles of brick, is but partially lined with wooden buildings of various heights and architecture, in each of which the mercantile department is connected with the domicile, like the gingerbread and candy shops of an after-date. The signs have a singular appearance to a stranger's eye. These are not a barren record of names and occupations, yellow letters on black boards, but images and hieroglyphics, sometimes typifying the principal commodity offered for sale, though generally intended to give an arbitrary designation to the establishment. Overlooking the bearded Saracens, the Indian Queens, and the wooden Bibles, let us direct our attention to the white post newly erected at the corner of the street, and surmounted by a gilded countenance which flashes in the early sunbeams like veritable gold. It is a bust of Æsculapius, evidently of the latest London manufacture; and from the door behind it steams forth a mingled smell of musk and assafœtida, and other drugs of potent perfume, as if an appropriate sacrifice were just laid upon the altar of the medical deity. Five or six idle people are already collected, peeping curiously in at the glittering array of gallipots and phials, and deciphering the labels which tell their contents in the mysterious and imposing nomenclature of ancient physic. They are next attracted by the printed advertisement of a Panacea, promising life but one day short of eternity, and youth and health commensurate. An old man, his head as white as snow, totters in with a hasty clattering of his staff, and becomes the earliest purchaser, hoping that his wrinkles will disappear more swiftly than they gathered. The Doctor (so styled by courtesy) shows the upper half of his person behind the counter, and appears to be a slender and rather tall man; his features are difficult to describe, possessing nothing peculiar, except a flexibility to assume all characters in turn, while his eye, shrewd, quick, and saucy, remains the same throughout. Whenever a customer enters the shop, if he desire a box of pills, he receives with them an equal number of hard, round, dry jokes,—or if a dose of salts, it is mingled with a portion of the salt of Attica,—or if some hot, Oriental drug, it is accompanied by a racy word or two that tingle on the mental palate,—all without the least additional cost. Then there are twistings of mouths which never lost their gravity before. As each purchaser retires, the spectators see a resemblance of his visage pass over that of the apothecary, in which all the ludicrous points are made most prominent, as if a magic looking-glass had caught the reflection, and were making sport with it. Unwonted titterings arise and strengthen into bashful laughter, but are suddenly hushed as some minister, heavy-eyed from his last night's vigil, or magistrate, armed with the terror of the whipping-post and pillory, or perhaps the governor himself, goes by like a dark cloud intercepting the sunshine.

About this period, many causes began to produce an important change on and beneath the surface of colonial society. The early settlers were able to keep within the narrowest limits of their rigid principles, because they had adopted them in mature life, and from their own deep conviction, and were strengthened in them by that species of enthusiasm, which is as sober and as enduring as reason itself. But if their immediate successors followed the same line of conduct, they were confined to it, in a great degree, by habits forced upon them, and by the severe rule under which they were educated, and, in short, more by restraint than by the free exercise of the imagination and understanding.

When therefore the old original stock, the men who looked heavenward without a wandering glance to earth, had lost a part of their domestic and public influence, yielding to infirmity or death, a relaxation naturally ensued in their theory and practice of morals and religion, and became more evident with the daily decay of its most strenuous opponents. This gradual but sure operation was assisted by the increasing commercial importance of the colonies, whither a new set of emigrants followed unworthily in the track of the pure-hearted Pilgrims. Gain being now the allurement, and almost the only one, since dissenters no longer dreaded persecution at home, the people of New England could not remain entirely uncontaminated by an extensive intermixture with worldly men. The trade carried on by the colonists (in the face of several inefficient acts of Parliament) with the whole maritime world, must have had a similar tendency; nor are the desperate and dissolute visitants of the country to be forgotten among the agents of a moral revolution. Freebooters from the West Indies and the Spanish Main,—state criminals, implicated in the numerous plots and conspiracies of the period,—felons, loaded with private guilt,—numbers of these took refuge in the provinces, where the authority of the English king was obstructed by a zealous spirit of independence, and where a boundless wilderness enabled them to defy pursuit. Thus the new population, temporary and permanent, was exceedingly unlike the old, and far more apt to disseminate their own principles than to imbibe those of the Puritans. All circumstances unfavorable to virtue acquired double strength by the licentious reign of Charles II.; though perhaps the example of the monarch and nobility was less likely to recommend vice to the people of New England than to those of any other part of the British Empire.

The clergy and the elder magistrates manifested a quick sensibility to the decline of godliness, their apprehensions being sharpened in this particular no less by a holy zeal than because their credit and influence were intimately connected with the primitive character of the country. A Synod, convened in the year 1679, gave its opinion that the iniquity of the times had drawn down judgments from Heaven, and proposed methods to assuage the Divine wrath by a renewal of former sanctity. But neither the increased numbers, nor the altered spirit of the people, nor the just sense of a freedom to do wrong, within certain limits, would now have permitted the exercise of that inquisitorial strictness, which had been wont to penetrate to men's firesides and watch their domestic life, recognizing no distinction between private ill conduct and crimes that endanger the community. Accordingly, the tide of worldly principles encroached more and more upon the ancient landmarks, hitherto esteemed the outer boundaries of virtue. Society arranged itself into two classes, marked by strong shades of difference, though separated by an uncertain line: in one were included the small and feeble remnant of the first settlers, many of their immediate descendants, the whole body of the clergy, and all whom a gloomy temperament, or tenderness of conscience, or timidity of thought, kept up to the strictness of their fathers; the other comprehended the new emigrants, the gay and thoughtless natives, the favorers of Episcopacy, and a various mixture of liberal and enlightened men with most of the evil-doers and unprincipled adventurers in the country. A vivid and rather a pleasant idea of New England manners, when this change had become decided, is given in the journal of John Dunton, a cockney bookseller, who visited Boston and other towns of Massachusetts with a cargo of pious publications, suited to the Puritan market. Making due allowance for the flippancy of the writer, which may have given a livelier tone to his descriptions than truth precisely warrants, and also for his character, which led him chiefly among the gayer inhabitants, there still seems to have been many who loved the winecup and the song, and all sorts of delightful naughtiness. But the degeneracy of the times had made far less progress in the interior of the country than in the seaports, and until the people lost the elective privilege, they continued the government in the hands of those upright old men who had so long possessed their confidence. Uncontrollable events, alone, gave a temporary ascendency to persons of another stamp. James II., during the four years of his despotic reign revoked the charters of the American colonies, arrogated the appointment of their magistrates, and annulled all those legal and prescriptive rights which had hitherto constituted them nearly independent states. Among the foremost advocates of the royal usurpations was Dr. Bullivant. Gifted with a smart and ready intellect, busy and bold, he acquired great influence in the new government, and assisted Sir Edmund Andros, Edward Randolph, and five or six others, to browbeat the council, and misrule the Northern provinces according to their pleasure. The strength of the popular hatred against this administration, the actual tyranny that was exercised, and the innumerable fears and jealousies, well grounded and fantastic, which harassed the country, may be best learned from a work of Increase Mather, the "Remarkable Providences of the Earlier Days of American Colonization." The good divine (though writing when a lapse of nearly forty years should have tamed the fierceness of party animosity) speaks with the most bitter and angry scorn of "'Pothecary Bullivant," who probably indulged his satirical propensities, from the seat of power, in a manner which rendered him an especial object of public dislike. But the people were about to play off a piece of practical fun on the Doctor and the whole of his coadjutors, and have the laugh all to themselves. By the first faint rumor of the attempt of the Prince of Orange on the throne, the power of James was annihilated in the colonies, and long before the abdication of the latter became known, Sir Edmund Andros, Governor-General of New England and New York, and fifty of the most obnoxious leaders of the court party, were tenants of a prison. We will visit our old acquaintance in his adversity.

The scene now represents a room of ten feet square, the floor of which is sunk a yard or two below the level of the ground; the walls are covered with a dirty and crumbling plaster, on which appear a crowd of ill-favored and lugubrious faces done in charcoal, and the autographs and poetical attempts of a long succession of debtors and petty criminals. Other features of the apartment are a deep fireplace (superfluous in the sultriness of the summer's day), a door of hard-hearted oak, and a narrow window high in the wall, where the glass has long been broken, while the iron bars retain all their original strength. Through this opening come the sound of passing footsteps in the public street, and the voices of children at play. The furniture consists of a bed, or rather an old sack of barley straw, thrown down in the corner farthest from the door, and a chair and table, both aged and infirm, and leaning against the side of the room, besides lending a friendly support to each other. The atmosphere is stifled and of an ill smell, as if it had been kept close prisoner for half a century, and had lost all its pure and elastic nature by feeding the tainted breath of the vicious and the sighs of the unfortunate. Such is the present abode of the man of medicine and politics, and his own appearance forms no contrast to the accompaniments. His wig is unpowdered, out of curl, and put on awry; the dust of many weeks has worked its way into the web of his coat and smallclothes, and his knees and elbows peep forth to ask why they are so ill clad; his stockings are ungartered, his shoes down at the heel, his waistcoat is without a button, and discloses a shirt as dingy as the remnant of snow in a showery April day. His shoulders have become rounder, and his whole person is more bent and drawn together, since we last saw him, and his face has exchanged the glory of wit and humor for a sheepish dulness. At intervals, the Doctor walks the room, with an irregular and shuffling pace; anon he throws himself flat on the sack of barley straw, muttering very reprehensible expressions between his teeth; then again he starts to his feet, and journeying from corner to corner, finally sinks into the chair, forgetful of its three-legged infirmity till it lets him down upon the floor. The grated window, his only medium of intercourse with the world, serves but to admit additional vexations. Every few moments the steps of the passengers are heard to pause, and some well-known face appears in the free sunshine behind the iron bars, brimful of mirth and drollery, the owner whereof stands on tiptoe to tickle poor Dr. Bullivant with a stinging sarcasm. Then laugh the little boys around the prison door, and the wag goes chuckling away. The apothecary would fain retaliate, but all his quips and repartees, and sharp and facetious fancies, once so abundant, seem to have been transferred from himself to the sluggish brains of his enemies. While endeavoring to condense his whole intellect into one venomous point, in readiness for the next assailant, he is interrupted by the entrance of the turnkey with the prison fare of Indian bread and water. With these dainties we leave him.

When the turmoil of the Revolution had subsided, and the authority of William and Mary was fixed on a quiet basis throughout the colonies, the deposed governor and some of his partisans were sent home to the new court, and the others released from imprisonment. The New-Englanders, as a people, are not apt to retain a revengeful sense of injury, and nowhere, perhaps, could a politician, however odious in his power, live more peacefully in his nakedness and disgrace. Dr. Bullivant returned to his former occupation, and spent rather a desirable old age. Though he sometimes hit hard with a jest, yet few thought of taking offence; for whenever a man habitually indulges his tongue at the expense of all his associates, they provide against the common annoyance by tacitly agreeing to consider his sarcasms as null and void. Thus for many years, a gray old man with a stoop in his gait, he continued to sweep out his shop at eight o'clock in summer mornings, and nine in the winter, and to waste whole hours in idle talk and irreverent merriment, making it his glory to raise the laughter of silly people, and his delight to sneer at them in his sleeve. At length, one pleasant day, the door and shutters of his establishment kept closed from sunrise till sunset, and his cronies marvelled a moment, and passed on; a week after, the rector of King's Chapel said the death-rite over Dr. Bullivant; and within the month a new apothecary, and a new stock of drugs and medicines, made their appearance at the gilded Head of Æsculapius.

AN OLD WOMAN'S TALE

In the house where I was born, there used to be an old woman crouching all day long over the kitchen fire, with her elbows on her knees and her feet in the ashes. Once in a while she took a turn at the spit, and she never lacked a coarse gray stocking in her lap, the foot about half finished; it tapered away with her own waning life, and she knit the toe-stitch on the day of her death. She made it her serious business and sole amusement to tell me stories at any time from morning till night, in a mumbling, toothless voice, as I sat on a log of wood, grasping her check-apron in both my hands. Her personal memory included the better part of a hundred years, and she had strangely jumbled her own experience and observation with those of many old people who died in her young days; so that she might have been taken for a contemporary of Queen Elizabeth, or of John Rogers in the Primer. There are a thousand of her traditions lurking in the corners and by-places of my mind, some more marvellous than what is to follow, some less so, and a few not marvellous in the least, all of which I should like to repeat, if I were as happy as she in having a listener. But I am humble enough to own, that I do not deserve a listener half so well as that old toothless woman, whose narratives possessed an excellence attributable neither to herself, nor to any single individual. Her groundplots, seldom within the widest scope of probability, were filled up with homely and natural incidents, the gradual accretions of a long course of years, and fiction hid its grotesque extravagance in this garb of truth, like the Devil (an appropriate simile, for the old woman supplies it) disguising himself, cloven-foot and all, in mortal attire. These tales generally referred to her birthplace, a village in the valley of the Connecticut, the aspect of which she impressed with great vividness on my fancy. The houses in that tract of country, long a wild and dangerous frontier, were rendered defensible by a strength of architecture that has preserved many of them till our own times, and I cannot describe the sort of pleasure with which, two summers since, I rode through the little town in question, while one object after another rose familiarly to my eye, like successive portions of a dream becoming realized. Among other things equally probable, she was wont to assert that all the inhabitants of this village (at certain intervals, but whether of twenty-five or fifty years, or a whole century, remained a disputable point) were subject to a simultaneous slumber, continuing one hour's space. When that mysterious time arrived, the parson snored over his half-written sermon, though it were Saturday night and no provision made for the morrow,—the mother's eyelids closed as she bent over her infant, and no childish cry awakened,—the watcher at the bed of mortal sickness slumbered upon the death-pillow,—and the dying man anticipated his sleep of ages by one as deep and dreamless. To speak emphatically, there was a soporific influence throughout the village, stronger than if every mother's son and daughter were reading a dull story; notwithstanding which the old woman professed to hold the substance of the ensuing account from one of those principally concerned in it.

One moonlight summer evening, a young man and a girl sat down together in the open air. They were distant relatives, sprung from a stock once wealthy, but of late years so poverty-stricken, that David had not a penny to pay the marriage fee, if Esther should consent to wed. The seat they had chosen was in an open grove of elm and walnut-trees, at a right angle of the road; a spring of diamond water just bubbled into the moonlight beside them, and then whimpered away through the bushes and long grass, in search of a neighboring mill-stream. The nearest house (situate within twenty yards of them, and the residence of their great-grandfather in his lifetime) was a venerable old edifice, crowned with many high and narrow peaks, all overrun by innumerable creeping plants, which hung curling about the roof like a nice young wig on an elderly gentleman's head. Opposite to this establishment was a tavern, with a well and horse-trough before it, and a low green bank running along the left side of the door. Thence, the road went onward, curving scarce perceptibly, through the village, divided in the midst by a narrow lane of verdure, and bounded on each side by a grassy strip of twice its own breadth. The houses had generally an odd look. Here, the moonlight tried to get a glimpse of one, a rough old heap of ponderous timber, which, ashamed of its dilapidated aspect, was hiding behind a great thick tree; the lower story of the next had sunk almost under ground, as if the poor little house were a-weary of the world, and retiring into the seclusion of its own cellar; farther on stood one of the few recent structures, thrusting its painted face conspicuously into the street, with an evident idea that it was the fairest thing there. About midway in the village was a grist-mill, partly concealed by the descent of the ground towards the stream which turned its wheel. At the southern extremity, just so far distant that the window-panes dazzled into each other, rose the meeting-house, a dingy old barnlike building, with an enormously disproportioned steeple sticking up straight into heaven, as high as the Tower of Babel, and the cause of nearly as much confusion in its day. This steeple, it must be understood, was an afterthought, and its addition to the main edifice, when the latter had already begun to decay, had excited a vehement quarrel, and almost a schism in the church, some fifty years before. Here the road wound down a hill, and was seen no more, the remotest object in view being the graveyard gate, beyond the meeting-house. The youthful pair sat hand in hand beneath the trees, and for several moments they had not spoken, because the breeze was hushed, the brook scarce tinkled, the leaves had ceased their rustling, and everything lay motionless and silent as if Nature were composing herself to slumber.

"What a beautiful night it is, Esther!" remarked David, somewhat drowsily.

"Very beautiful," answered the girl, in the same tone.

"But how still!" continued David.

"Ah, too still!" said Esther, with a faint shudder, like a modest leaf when the wind kisses it.

Perhaps they fell asleep together, and, united as their spirits were by close and tender sympathies, the same strange dream might have wrapped them in its shadowy arms. But they conceived, at the time, that they still remained wakeful by the spring of bubbling water, looking down through the village, and all along the moon-lighted road, and at the queer old houses, and at the trees, which thrust their great twisted branches almost into the windows.

There was only a sort of mistiness over their minds like the smoky air of an early autumn night. At length, without any vivid astonishment, they became conscious that a great many people were either entering the village or already in the street, but whether they came from the meeting-house, or from a little beyond it, or where the devil they came from, was more than could be determined. Certainly a crowd of people seemed to be there, men, women, and children, all of whom were yawning and rubbing their eyes, stretching their limbs, and staggering from side to side of the road, as if but partially awakened from a sound slumber. Sometimes they stood stock-still, with their hands over their brows to shade their sight from the moonbeams. As they drew near, most of their countenances appeared familiar to Esther and David, possessing the peculiar features of families in the village, and that general air and aspect by which a person would recognize his own townsmen in the remotest ends of the earth. But though the whole multitude might have been taken, in the mass, for neighbors and acquaintances, there was not a single individual whose exact likeness they had ever before seen. It was a noticeable circumstance, also, that the newest fashioned garment on the backs of these people might have been worn by the great-grandparents of the existing generation. There was one figure behind all the rest, and not yet near enough to be perfectly distinguished.

"Where on earth, David, do all these odd people come from?" said Esther, with a lazy inclination to laugh.

"Nowhere on earth, Esther," replied David, unknowing why he said so.

As they spoke, the strangers showed some symptoms of disquietude, and looked towards the fountain for an instant, but immediately appeared to assume their own trains of thought and previous purposes. They now separated to different parts of the village, with a readiness that implied intimate local knowledge, and it may be worthy of remark, that, though they were evidently loquacious among themselves, neither their footsteps nor their voices reached the ears of the beholders. Wherever there was a venerable old house, of fifty years' standing and upwards, surrounded by its elm or walnut-trees, with its dark and weather-beaten barn, its well, its orchard and stone-walls, all ancient and all in good repair around it, there a little group of these people assembled. Such parties were mostly composed of an aged man and woman, with the younger members of a family; their faces were full of joy, so deep that it assumed the shade of melancholy; they pointed to each other the minutest objects about the homesteads, things in their hearts, and were now comparing them with the originals. But where hollow places by the wayside, grass-grown, and uneven, with unsightly chimneys rising ruinous in the midst, gave indications of a fallen dwelling and of hearths long cold, there did a few of the strangers sit them down on the mouldering beams, and on the yellow moss that had overspread the door-stone. The men folded their arms, sad and speechless; the women wrung their hands with a more vivid expression of grief; and the little children tottered to their knees, shrinking away from the open grave of domestic love. And wherever a recent edifice reared its white and flashy front on the foundation of an old one, there a gray-haired man might be seen to shake his staff in anger at it, while his aged dame and their offspring appeared to join in their maledictions, forming a fearful picture in the ghostly moonlight. While these scenes were passing, the one figure in the rear of all the rest was descending the hollow towards the mill, and the eyes of David and Esther were drawn thence to a pair with whom they could fully sympathize. It was a youth in a sailor's dress and a pale slender maiden, who met each other with a sweet embrace in the middle of the street.

"How long it must be since they parted," observed David.

"Fifty years at least," said Esther.

They continued to gaze with wondering calmness and quiet interest, as the dream (if such it were) unrolled its quaint and motley semblance before them, and their notice was now attracted by several little knots of people apparently engaged in conversation. Of these one of the earliest collected and most characteristic was near the tavern, the persons who composed it being seated on the low green bank along the left side of the door. A conspicuous figure here was a fine corpulent old fellow in his shirt-sleeves and flame-colored breeches, and with a stained white apron over his paunch, beneath which he held his hands, and wherewith at times he wiped his ruddy face. The stately decrepitude of one of his companions, the scar of an Indian tomahawk on his crown, and especially his worn buff-coat, were appropriate marks of a veteran belonging to an old Provincial garrison, now deaf to the roll-call. Another showed his rough face under a tarry hat and wore a pair of wide trousers, like an ancient mariner who had tossed away his youth upon the sea, and was returned, hoary and weather-beaten, to his inland home. There was also a thin young man, carelessly dressed, who ever and anon cast a sad look towards the pale maiden above mentioned. With these there sat a hunter, and one or two others, and they were soon joined by a miller, who came upward from the dusty mill, his coat as white as if besprinkled with powdered starlight. All these (by the aid of jests, which might indeed be old, but had not been recently repeated) waxed very merry, and it was rather strange, that just as their sides shook with the heartiest laughter, they appeared greatly like a group of shadows flickering in the moonshine. Four personages, very different from these, stood in front of the large house with its periwig of creeping plants. One was a little elderly figure, distinguished by the gold on his three-cornered hat and sky-blue coat, and by the seal of arms annexed to his great gold watch-chain; his air and aspect befitted a Justice of Peace and County Major, and all earth's pride and pomposity were squeezed into this small gentleman of five feet high. The next in importance was a grave person of sixty or seventy years, whose black suit and band sufficiently indicated his character, and the polished baldness of whose head was worthy of a famous preacher in the village, half a century before, who had made wigs a subject of pulpit denunciation. The two other figures, both clad in dark gray, showed the sobriety of Deacons; one was ridiculously tall and thin, like a man of ordinary bulk infinitely produced, as the mathematicians say; while the brevity and thickness of his colleague seemed a compression of the same man. These four talked with great earnestness, and their gestures intimated that they had revived the ancient dispute about the meeting-house steeple. The grave person in black spoke with composed solemnity, as if he were addressing a Synod; the short deacon grunted out occasional sentences, as brief as himself; his tall brother drew the long thread of his argument through the whole discussion, and (reasoning from analogy) his voice must indubitably have been small and squeaking. But the little old man in gold-lace was evidently scorched by his own red-hot eloquence; he bounced from one to another, shook his cane at the steeple, at the two deacons, and almost in the parson's face, stamping with his foot fiercely enough to break a hole through the very earth; though, indeed, it could not exactly be said that the green grass bent beneath him. The figure, noticed as coming behind all the rest, had now surmounted the ascent from the mill, and proved to be an elderly lady with something in her hand.

"Why does she walk so slow?" asked David.

"Don't you see she is lame?" said Esther.

This gentlewoman, whose infirmity had kept her so far in the rear of the crowd, now came hobbling on, glided unobserved by the polemic group, and paused on the left brink of the fountain, within a few feet of the two spectators. She was a magnificent old dame, as ever mortal eye beheld. Her spangled shoes and gold-clocked stockings shone gloriously within the spacious circle of a red hoop-petticoat, which swelled to the very point of explosion, and was bedecked all over with embroidery a little tarnished. Above the petticoat, and parting in front so as to display it to the best advantage, was a figured blue damask gown. A wide and stiff ruff encircled her neck, a cap of the finest muslin, though rather dingy, covered her head, and her nose was bestridden by a pair of gold-bowed spectacles with enormous glasses. But the old lady's face was pinched, sharp, and sallow, wearing a niggardly and avaricious expression, and forming an odd contrast to the splendor of her attire, as did likewise the implement which she held in her hand. It was a sort of iron shovel (by housewives termed a "slice"), such as is used in clearing the oven, and with this, selecting a spot between a walnut-tree and the fountain, the good dame made an earnest attempt to dig. The tender sods, however, possessed a strange impenetrability. They resisted her efforts like a quarry of living granite, and, losing her breath, she cast down the shovel and seemed to bemoan herself most piteously, gnashing her teeth (what few she had) and wringing her thin yellow hands. Then, apparently with new hope, she resumed her toil, which still had the same result,—a circumstance the less surprising to David and Esther, because at times they would catch the moonlight shining through the old woman, and dancing in the fountain beyond. The little man in gold-lace now happened to see her, and made his approach on tiptoe.

"How hard this elderly lady works!" remarked David.

"Go and help her, David," said Esther, compassionately.

As their drowsy voices spoke, both the old woman and the pompous little figure behind her lifted their eyes, and for a moment they regarded the youth and damsel with something like kindness and affection; which, however, were dim and uncertain, and passed away almost immediately. The old woman again betook herself to the shovel, but was startled by a hand suddenly laid upon her shoulder; she turned round in great trepidation, and beheld the dignitary in the blue coat; then followed an embrace of such closeness as would indicate no remoter connection than matrimony between these two decorous persons. The gentleman next pointed to the shovel, appearing to inquire the purpose of this lady's occupation; while she as evidently parried his interrogatories, maintaining a demure and sanctified visage as every good woman ought, in similar cases. Howbeit, she could not forbear looking askew, behind her spectacles, towards the spot of stubborn turf. All the while, their figures had a strangeness in them, and it seemed as if some cunning jeweller had made their golden ornaments of the yellowest of the setting sunbeams, and that the blue of their garments was brought from the dark sky near the moon, and that the gentleman's silk waistcoat was the bright side of a fiery cloud, and the lady's scarlet petticoat a remnant of the blush of morning,—and that they both were two unrealities of colored air. But now there was a sudden movement throughout the multitude. The Squire drew forth a watch as large as the dial on the famous steeple, looked at the warning hands and got him gone, nor could his lady tarry; the party at the tavern door took to their heels, headed by the fat man in the flaming breeches; the tall deacon stalked away immediately, and the short deacon waddled after, making four steps to the yard; the mothers called their children about them and set forth, with a gentle and sad glance behind. Like cloudy fantasies that hurry by a viewless impulse from the sky, they all were fled, and the wind rose up and followed them with a strange moaning down the lonely street. Now whither these people went is more than may be told; only David and Esther seemed to see the shadowy splendor of the ancient dame, as she lingered in the moonshine at the graveyard gate, gazing backward to the fountain.

"O Esther! I have had such a dream!" cried David, starting up, and rubbing his eyes.

"And I such another!" answered Esther, gaping till her pretty red lips formed a circle.

"About an old woman with gold-bowed spectacles," continued David.

"And a scarlet hoop-petticoat," added Esther. They now stared in each other's eyes, with great astonishment and some little fear. After a thoughtful moment or two, David drew a long breath and stood upright.

"If I live till to-morrow morning," said he, "I'll see what may be buried between that tree and the spring of water."

"And why not to-night, David?" asked Esther; for she was a sensible little girl, and bethought herself that the matter might as well be done in secrecy.

David felt the propriety of the remark, and looked round for the means of following her advice. The moon shone brightly on something that rested against the side of the old house, and, on a nearer view, it proved to be an iron shovel, bearing a singular resemblance to that which they had seen in their dreams. He used it with better success than the old woman, the soil giving way so freely to his efforts, that he had soon scooped a hole as large as the basin of the spring. Suddenly, he poked his head down to the very bottom of this cavity. "Oho!—what have we here?" cried David.

ALICE DOANE'S APPEAL

On a pleasant afternoon of June, it was my good fortune to be the companion of two young ladies in a walk. The direction of our course being left to me, I led them neither to Legge's Hill, nor to the Cold Spring, nor to the rude shores and old batteries of the Neck, nor yet to Paradise; though if the latter place were rightly named, my fair friends would have been at home there.

We reached the outskirts of the town, and turning aside from a street of tanners and curriers, began to ascend a hill, which at a distance, by its dark slope and the even line of its summit, resembled a green rampart along the road. It was less steep than its aspect threatened. The eminence formed part of an extensive tract of pasture land, and was traversed by cow paths in various directions; but, strange to tell, though the whole slope and summit were of a peculiarly deep green, scarce a blade of grass was visible from the base upward. This deceitful verdure was occasioned by a plentiful crop of "wood-wax," which wears the same dark and glossy green throughout the summer, except at one short period, when it puts forth a profusion of yellow blossoms. At that season, to a distant spectator, the hill appears absolutely overlaid with gold, or covered with a glory of sunshine, even beneath a clouded sky. But the curious wanderer on the hill will perceive that all the grass, and everything that should nourish man or beast, has been destroyed by this vile and ineradicable weed: its tufted roots make the soil their own, and permit nothing else to vegetate among them; so that a physical curse may be said to have blasted the spot, where guilt and frenzy consummated the most execrable scene that our history blushes to record. For this was the field where superstition won her darkest triumph; the high place where our fathers set up their shame, to the mournful gaze of generations far remote. The dust of martyrs was beneath our feet. We stood on Gallows Hill.

For my own part, I have often courted the historic influence of the spot. But it is singular how few come on pilgrimage to this famous hill; how many spend their lives almost at its base, and never once obey the summons of the shadowy past, as it beckons them to the summit. Till a year or two since, this portion of our history had been very imperfectly written, and, as we are not a people of legend or tradition, it was not every citizen of our ancient town that could tell, within half a century, so much as the date of the witchcraft delusion. Recently, indeed, an historian has treated the subject in a manner that will keep his name alive, in the only desirable connection with the errors of our ancestry, by converting the hill of their disgrace into an honorable monument of his own antiquarian lore, and of that better wisdom, which draws the moral while it tells the tale. But we are a people of the present, and have no heartfelt interest in the olden time. Every fifth of November, in commemoration of they know not what, or rather without an idea beyond the momentary blaze, the young men scare the town with bonfires on this haunted height, but never dream of paying funeral honors to those who died so wrongfully, and, without a coffin or a prayer, were buried here.

Though with feminine susceptibility, my companions caught all the melancholy associations of the scene, yet these could but imperfectly overcome the gayety of girlish spirits. Their emotions came and went with quick vicissitude, and sometimes combined to form a peculiar and delicious excitement, the mirth brightening the gloom into a sunny shower of feeling, and a rainbow in the mind. My own more sombre mood was tinged by theirs. With now a merry word and next a sad one, we trod among the tangled weeds, and almost hoped that our feet would sink into the hollow of a witch's grave. Such vestiges were to be found within the memory of man, but have vanished now, and with them, I believe, all traces of the precise spot of the executions. On the long and broad ridge of the eminence, there is no very decided elevation of any one point, nor other prominent marks, except the decayed stumps of two trees, standing near each other, and here and there the rocky substance of the hill, peeping just above the wood-wax.

There are few such prospects of town and village, woodland and cultivated field, steeples and country seats, as we beheld from this unhappy spot. No blight had fallen on old Essex; all was prosperity and riches, healthfully distributed. Before us lay our native town, extending from the foot of the hill to the harbor, level as a chess board embraced by two arms of the sea, and filling the whole peninsula with a close assemblage of wooden roofs, overtopped by many a spire, and intermixed with frequent heaps of verdure, where trees threw up their shade from unseen trunks. Beyond was the bay and its islands, almost the only objects, in a country unmarked by strong natural features, on which time and human toil had produced no change. Retaining these portions of the scene, and also the peaceful glory and tender gloom of the declining sun, we threw, in imagination, a veil of deep forest over the land, and pictured a few scattered villages, and this old town itself a village, as when the prince of hell bore sway there. The idea thus gained of its former aspect, its quaint edifices standing far apart, with peaked roofs and projecting stories, and its single meeting-house pointing up a tall spire in the midst; the vision, in short, of the town in 1692, served to introduce a wondrous tale of those old times.

I had brought the manuscript in my pocket. It was one of a series written years ago, when my pen, now sluggish and perhaps feeble, because I have not much to hope or fear, was driven by stronger external motives, and a more passionate impulse within, than I am fated to feel again. Three or four of these tales had appeared in the "Token," after a long time and various adventures, but had encumbered me with no troublesome notoriety, even in my birthplace. One great heap had met a brighter destiny: they had fed the flames; thoughts meant to delight the world and endure for ages had perished in a moment, and stirred not a single heart but mine. The story now to be introduced, and another, chanced to be in kinder custody at the time, and thus, by no conspicuous merits of their own, escaped destruction.

The ladies, in consideration that I had never before intruded my performances on them, by any but the legitimate medium, through the press, consented to hear me read. I made them sit down on a moss-grown rock, close by the spot where we chose to believe that the death tree had stood. After a little hesitation on my part, caused by a dread of renewing my acquaintance with fantasies that had lost their charm in the ceaseless flux of mind, I began the tale, which opened darkly with the discovery of a murder.

A hundred years, and nearly half that time, have elapsed since the body of a murdered man was found, at about the distance of three miles, on the old road to Boston. He lay in a solitary spot, on the bank of a small lake, which the severe frost of December had covered with a sheet of ice. Beneath this, it seemed to have been the intention of the murderer to conceal his victim in a chill and watery grave, the ice being deeply hacked, perhaps with the weapon that had slain him, though its solidity was too stubborn for the patience of a man with blood upon his hand. The corpse therefore reclined on the earth, but was separated from the road by a thick growth of dwarf pines. There had been a slight fall of snow during the night, and as if nature were shocked at the deed, and strove to hide it with her frozen tears, a little drifted heap had partly buried the body, and lay deepest over the pale dead face. An early traveller, whose dog had led him to the spot, ventured to uncover the features, but was affrighted by their expression. A look of evil and scornful triumph had hardened on them, and made death so life-like and so terrible, that the beholder at once took flight, as swiftly as if the stiffened corpse would rise up and follow.

I read on, and identified the body as that of a young man, a stranger in the country, but resident during several preceding months in the town which lay at our feet. The story described, at some length, the excitement caused by the murder, the unavailing quest after the perpetrator, the funeral ceremonies, and other commonplace matters, in the course of which, I brought forward the personages who were to move among the succeeding events. They were but three. A young man and his sister; the former characterized by a diseased imagination and morbid feelings; the latter, beautiful and virtuous, and instilling something of her own excellence into the wild heart of her brother, but not enough to cure the deep taint of his nature. The third person was a wizard; a small, gray, withered man, with fiendish ingenuity in devising evil, and superhuman power to execute it, but senseless as an idiot and feebler than a child to all better purposes. The central scene of the story was an interview between this wretch and Leonard Doane, in the wizard's hut, situated beneath a range of rocks at some distance from the town. They sat beside a mouldering fire, while a tempest of wintry rain was beating on the roof. The young man spoke of the closeness of the tie which united him and Alice, the consecrated fervor of their affection from childhood upwards, their sense of lonely sufficiency to each other, because they only of their race had escaped death, in a night attack by the Indians. He related his discovery or suspicion of a secret sympathy between his sister and Walter Brome, and told how a distempered jealousy had maddened him. In the following passage, I threw a glimmering light on the mystery of the tale.

"Searching," continued Leonard, "into the breast of Walter Brome, I at length found a cause why Alice must inevitably love him. For he was my very counterpart! I compared his mind by each individual portion, and as a whole, with mine. There was a resemblance from which I shrunk with sickness, and loathing, and horror, as if my own features had come and stared upon me in a solitary place, or had met me in struggling through a crowd. Nay! the very same thoughts would often express themselves in the same words from our lips, proving a hateful sympathy in our secret souls. His education, indeed, in the cities of the old world, and mine in this rude wilderness, had wrought a superficial difference. The evil of his character, also, had been strengthened and rendered prominent by a reckless and ungoverned life, while mine had been softened and purified by the gentle and holy nature of Alice. But my soul had been conscious of the germ of all the fierce and deep passions, and of all the many varieties of wickedness, which accident had brought to their full maturity in him. Nor will I deny that, in the accursed one, I could see the withered blossom of every virtue, which, by a happier culture, had been made to bring forth fruit in me. Now, here was a man whom Alice might love with all the strength of sisterly affection, added to that impure passion which alone engrosses all the heart. The stranger would have more than the love which had been gathered to me from the many graves of our household—and I be desolate!"

Leonard Doane went on to describe the insane hatred that had kindled his heart into a volume of hellish flame. It appeared, indeed, that his jealousy had grounds, so far as that Walter Brome had actually sought the love of Alice, who also had betrayed an undefinable, but powerful interest in the unknown youth. The latter, in spite of his passion for Alice, seemed to return the loathful antipathy of her brother; the similarity of their dispositions made them like joint possessors of an individual nature, which could not become wholly the property of one, unless by the extinction of the other. At last, with the same devil in each bosom, they chanced to meet, they two on a lonely road. While Leonard spoke, the wizard had sat listening to what he already knew, yet with tokens of pleasurable interest, manifested by flashes of expression across his vacant features, by grisly smiles and by a word here and there, mysteriously filling up some void in the narrative. But when the young man told how Walter Brome had taunted him with indubitable proofs of the shame of Alice, and, before the triumphant sneer could vanish from his face, had died by her brother's hand, the wizard laughed aloud. Leonard started, but just then a gust of wind came down the chimney, forming itself into a close resemblance of the slow, unvaried laughter, by which he had been interrrupted. "I was deceived," thought he; and thus pursued his fearful story.

"I trod out his accursed soul, and knew that he was dead; for my spirit bounded as if a chain had fallen from it and left me free. But the burst of exulting certainty soon fled, and was succeeded by a torpor over my brain and a dimness before my eyes, with the sensation of one who struggles through a a dream. So I bent down over the body of Walter Brome, gazing into his face, and striving to make my soul glad with the thought, that he, in very truth, lay dead before me. I know not what space of time I had thus stood, nor how the vision came. But it seemed to me that the irrevocable years since childhood had rolled back, and a scene, that had long been confused and broken in my memory, arrayed itself with all its first distinctness. Methought I stood a weeping infant by my father's hearth; by the cold and blood-stained hearth where he lay dead. I heard the childish wail of Alice, and my own cry arose with hers, as we beheld the features of our parent, fierce with the strife and distorted with the pain, in which his spirit had passed away. As I gazed, a cold wind whistled by, and waved my father's hair. Immediately I stood again in the lonesome road, no more a sinless child, but a man of blood, whose tears were falling fast over the face of his dead enemy. But the delusion was not wholly gone; that face still wore a likeness of my father; and because my soul shrank from the fixed glare of the eyes, I bore the body to the lake, and would have buried it there. But before his icy sepulchre was hewn, I heard the voices of two travellers and fled."

Such was the dreadful confession of Leonard Doane. And now tortured by the idea of his sister's guilt, yet sometimes yielding to a conviction of her purity; stung with remorse for the death of Walter Brome, and shuddering with a deeper sense of some unutterable crime, perpetrated, as he imagined, in madness or a dream; moved also by dark impulses, as if a fiend were whispering him to meditate violence against the life of Alice; he had sought this interview with the wizard, who, on certain conditions, had no power to withhold his aid in unravelling the mystery. The tale drew near its close.

The moon was bright on high; the blue firmament appeared to glow with an inherent brightness; the greater stars were burning in their spheres; the northern lights threw their mysterious glare far over the horizon; the few small clouds aloft were burdened with radiance; but the sky, with all its variety of light, was scarcely so brilliant as the earth. The rain of the preceding night had frozen as it fell, and, by that simple magic, had wrought wonders. The trees were hung with diamonds and many-colored gems; the houses were overlaid with silver, and the streets paved with slippery brightness; a frigid glory was flung over all familiar things, from the cottage chimney to the steeple of the meeting-house, that gleamed upward to the sky. This living world, where we sit by our firesides, or go forth to meet beings like ourselves, seemed rather the creation of wizard power, with so much of the resemblance to known objects that a man might shudder at the ghostly shape of his old beloved dwelling, and the shadow of a ghostly tree before his door. One looked to behold inhabitants suited to such a town, glittering in icy garments, with the motionless features, cold, sparkling eyes, and just sensation enough in their frozen hearts to shiver at each other's presence.

By this fantastic piece of description, and more in the same style, I intended to throw a ghostly glimmer round the reader, so that his imagination might view the town through a medium that should take off its every-day aspect, and make it a proper theatre for so wild a scene as the final one. Amid this unearthly show, the wretched brother and sister were represented as setting forth, at midnight, through the gleaming streets, and directing their steps to a graveyard, where all the dead had been laid, from the first corpse in that ancient town, to the murdered man who was buried three days before. As they went, they seemed to see the wizard gliding by their sides, or walking dimly on the path before them. But here I paused, and gazed into the faces of my two fair auditors, to judge whether, even on the hill where so many had been brought to death by wilder tales than this, I might venture to proceed. Their bright eyes were fixed on me; their lips apart. I took courage, and led the fated pair to a new made grave, where for a few moments, in the bright and silent midnight, they stood alone. But suddenly there was a multitude of people among the graves.

Each family tomb had given up its inhabitants, who, one by one, through distant years, had been borne to its dark chamber, but now came forth and stood in a pale group together. There was the gray ancestor, the aged mother, and all their descendants, some withered and full of years, like themselves, and others in their prime; there, too, were the children who went prattling to the tomb, and there the maiden who yielded her early beauty to death's embrace, before passion had polluted it. Husbands and wives arose, who had lain many years side by side, and young mothers who had forgotten to kiss their first babes, though pillowed so long on their bosoms. Many had been buried in the habiliments of life, and still wore their ancient garb; some were old defenders of the infant colony, and gleamed forth in their steel-caps and bright breast-plates, as if starting up at an Indian war-cry; other venerable shapes had been pastors of the church, famous among the New England clergy, and now leaned with hands clasped over their gravestones, ready to call the congregation to prayer. There stood the early settlers, those old illustrious ones, the heroes of tradition and fireside legends, the men of history whose features had been so long beneath the sod that few alive could have remembered them. There, too, were faces of former towns-people, dimly recollected from childhood, and others, whom Leonard and Alice had wept in later years, but who now were most terrible of all, by their ghastly smile of recognition. All, in short, were there; the dead of other generations, whose moss-grown names could scarce be read upon their tombstones, and their successors, whose graves were not yet green; all whom black funerals had followed slowly thither now reappeared where the mourners left them. Yet none but souls accursed were there, and fiends counterfeiting the likeness of departed saints.

The countenances of those venerable men, whose very features had been hallowed by lives of piety, were contorted now by intolerable pain or hellish passion, and now by an unearthly and derisive merriment. Had the pastors prayed, all saintlike as they seemed, it had been blasphemy. The chaste matrons, too, and the maidens with untasted lips, who had slept in their virgin graves apart from all other dust, now wore a look from which the two trembling mortals shrank, as if the unimaginable sin of twenty worlds were collected there. The faces of fond lovers, even of such as had pined into the tomb, because there their treasure was, were bent on one another with glances of hatred and smiles of bitter scorn, passions that are to devils what love is to the blest. At times, the features of those who had passed from a holy life to heaven would vary to and fro, between their assumed aspect and the fiendish lineaments whence they had been transformed. The whole miserable multitude, both sinful souls and false spectres of good men, groaned horribly and gnashed their teeth, as they looked upward to the calm loveliness of the midnight sky, and beheld those homes of bliss where they must never dwell. Such was the apparition, though too shadowy for language to portray; for here would be the moonbeams on the ice, glittering through a warrior's breastplate, and there the letters of a tombstone, on the form that stood before it; and whenever a breeze went by, it swept the old men's hoary heads, the women's fearful beauty, and all the unreal throng, into one indistinguishable cloud together.

I dare not give the remainder of the scene, except in a very brief epitome. This company of devils and condemned souls had come on a holiday, to revel in the discovery of a complicated crime; as foul a one as ever was imagined in their dreadful abode. In the course of the tale, the reader had been permitted to discover that all the incidents were results of the machinations of the wizard, who had cunningly devised that Walter Brome should tempt his unknown sister to guilt and shame, and himself perish by the hand of his twin-brother. I described the glee of the fiends at this hideous conception, and their eagerness to know if it were consummated. The story concluded with the Appeal of Alice to the spectre of Walter Brome; his reply, absolving her from every stain; and the trembling awe with which ghost and devil fled, as from the sinless presence of an angel.

The sun had gone down. While I held my page of wonders in the fading light, and read how Alice and her brother were left alone among the graves, my voice mingled with the sigh of a summer wind, which passed over the hilltop, with the broad and hollow sound as of the flight of unseen spirits. Not a word was spoken till I added that the wizard's grave was close beside us, and that the wood-wax had sprouted originally from his unhallowed bones. The ladies started; perhaps their cheeks might have grown pale had not the crimson west been blushing on them; but after a moment they began to laugh, while the breeze took a livelier motion, as if responsive to their mirth. I kept an awful solemnity of visage, being, indeed, a little piqued that a narrative which had good authority in our ancient superstitions, and would have brought even a church deacon to Gallows Hill, in old witch times, should now be considered too grotesque and extravagant for timid maids to tremble at. Though it was past supper time, I detained them a while longer on the hill, and made a trial whether truth were more powerful than fiction.

We looked again towards the town, no longer arrayed in that icy splendor of earth, tree, and edifice, beneath the glow of a wintry midnight, which shining afar through the gloom of a century had made it appear the very home of visions in visionary streets. An indistinctness had begun to creep over the mass of buildings and blend them with the intermingled tree-tops, except where the roof of a statelier mansion, and the steeples and brick towers of churches, caught the brightness of some cloud that yet floated in the sunshine. Twilight over the landscape was congenial to the obscurity of time. With such eloquence as my share of feeling and fancy could supply, I called back hoar antiquity, and bade my companions imagine an ancient multitude of people, congregated on the hillside, spreading far below, clustering on the steep old roofs, and climbing the adjacent heights, wherever a glimpse of this spot might be obtained. I strove to realize and faintly communicate the deep, unutterable loathing and horror, the indignation, the affrighted wonder, that wrinkled on every brow, and filled the universal heart. See! the whole crowd turns pale and shrinks within itself, as the virtuous emerge from yonder street. Keeping pace with that devoted company, I described them one by one; here tottered a woman in her dotage, knowing neither the crime imputed her, nor its punishment; there another, distracted by the universal madness, till feverish dreams were remembered as realities, and she almost believed her guilt. One, a proud man once, was so broken down by the intolerable hatred heaped upon him, that he seemed to hasten his steps, eager to hide himself in the grave hastily dug at the foot of the gallows. As they went slowly on, a mother looked behind, and beheld her peaceful dwelling; she cast her eyes elsewhere, and groaned inwardly yet with bitterest anguish, for there was her little son among the accusers. I watched the face of an ordained pastor, who walked onward to the same death; his lips moved in prayer; no narrow petition for himself alone, but embracing all his fellow-sufferers and the frenzied multitude; he looked to Heaven and trod lightly up the hill.

Behind their victims came the afflicted, a guilty and miserable band; villains who had thus avenged themselves on their enemies, and viler wretches, whose cowardice had destroyed their friends; lunatics, whose ravings had chimed in with the madness of the land; and children, who had played a game that the imps of darkness might have envied them, since it disgraced an age, and dipped a people's hands in blood. In the rear of the procession rode a figure on horseback, so darkly conspicuous, so sternly triumphant, that my hearers mistook him for the visible presence of the fiend himself; but it was only his good friend, Cotton Mather, proud of his well-won dignity, as the representative of all the hateful features of his time; the one blood-thirsty man, in whom were concentrated those vices of spirit and errors of opinion that sufficed to madden the whole surrounding multitude. And thus I marshalled them onward, the innocent who were to die, and the guilty who were to grow old in long remorse—tracing their every step, by rock, and shrub, and broken track, till their shadowy visages had circled round the hill-top, where we stood. I plunged into my imagination for a blacker horror, and a deeper woe, and pictured the scaffold——

But here my companions seized an arm on each side; their nerves were trembling; and, sweeter victory still, I had reached the seldom trodden places of their hearts, and found the well-spring of their tears. And now the past had done all it could. We slowly descended, watching the lights as they twinkled gradually through the town, and listening to the distant mirth of boys at play, and to the voice of a young girl warbling somewhere in the dusk, a pleasant sound to wanderers from old witch times. Yet, ere we left the hill, we could not but regret that there is nothing on its barren summit, no relic of old, nor lettered stone of later days, to assist the imagination in appealing to the heart. We build the memorial column on the height which our fathers made sacred with their blood, poured out in a holy cause. And here, in dark, funereal stone, should rise another monument, sadly commemorative of the errors of an earlier race, and not to be cast down, while the human heart has one infirmity that may result in crime.

THE GHOST OF DOCTOR HARRIS

I am afraid this ghost story will bear a very faded aspect when transferred to paper. Whatever effect it had on you, or whatever charm it retains in your memory, is perhaps to be attributed to the favorable circumstances under which it was originally told.

We were sitting, I remember, late in the evening, in your drawing-room, where the lights of the chandelier were so muffled as to produce a delicious obscurity through which the fire diffused a dim red glow. In this rich twilight the feelings of the party had been properly attuned by some tales of English superstition, and the lady of Smithills Hall had just been describing that Bloody Footstep which marks the threshold of her old mansion, when your Yankee guest (zealous for the honor of his country, and desirous of proving that his dead compatriots have the same ghostly privileges as other dead people, if they think it worth while to use them) began a story of something wonderful that long ago happened to himself. Possibly in the verbal narrative he may have assumed a little more license than would be allowable in a written record. For the sake of the artistic effect, he may then have thrown in, here and there, a few slight circumstances which he will not think it proper to retain in what he now puts forth as the sober statement of a veritable fact.

A good many years ago (it must be as many as fifteen, perhaps more, and while I was still a bachelor) I resided at Boston, in the United States. In that city there is a large and long-established library, styled the Athenæum, connected with which is a reading-room, well supplied with foreign and American periodicals and newspapers. A splendid edifice has since been erected by the proprietors of the institution; but, at the period I speak of, it was contained within a large, old mansion, formerly the town residence of an eminent citizen of Boston. The reading-room (a spacious hall, with the group of the Laocoon at one end, and the Belvidere Apollo at the other) was frequented by not a few elderly merchants, retired from business, by clergymen and lawyers, and by such literary men as we had amongst us. These good people were mostly old, leisurely, and somnolent, and used to nod and doze for hours together, with the newspapers before them—ever and anon recovering themselves so far as to read a word or two of the politics of the day—sitting, as it were, on the boundary of the Land of Dreams, and having little to do with this world, except through the newspapers which they so tenaciously grasped.

One of these worthies, whom I occasionally saw there, was the Reverend Doctor Harris, a Unitarian clergyman of considerable repute and eminence. He was very far advanced in life, not less than eighty years old, and probably more; and he resided, I think, at Dorchester, a suburban village in the immediate vicinity of Boston. I had never been personally acquainted with this good old clergyman, but had heard of him all my life as a noteworthy man; so that when he was first pointed out to me I looked at him with a certain specialty of attention, and always subsequently eyed him with a degree of interest whenever I happened to see him at the Athenæum or elsewhere. He was a small, withered, infirm, but brisk old gentleman, with snow-white hair, a somewhat stooping figure, but yet a remarkable alacrity of movement. I remember it was in the street that I first noticed him. The Doctor was plodding along with a staff, but turned smartly about on being addressed by the gentleman who was with me, and responded with a good deal of vivacity.

"Who is he?" I inquired, as soon as he had passed. "The Reverend Doctor Harris, of Dorchester," replied my companion; and from that time I often saw him, and never forgot his aspect. His especial haunt was the Athenæum. There I used to see him daily, and almost always with a newspaper—the Boston Post, which was the leading journal of the Democratic party in the Northern States. As old Doctor Harris had been a noted Democrat during his more active life, it was a very natural thing that he should still like to read the Boston Post. There his reverend figure was accustomed to sit day after day, in the self-same chair by the fireside; and, by degrees, seeing him there so constantly, I began to look towards him as I entered the reading-room, and felt that a kind of acquaintance, at least on my part, was established. Not that I had any reason (as long as this venerable person remained in the body) to suppose that he ever noticed me; but by some subtle connection, this small, white-haired, infirm, yet vivacious figure of an old clergyman became associated with my idea and recollection of the place. One day especially (about noon, as was generally his hour) I am perfectly certain that I had seen this figure of old Doctor Harris, and taken my customary note of him, although I remember nothing in his appearance at all different from what I had seen on many previous occasions.

But, that very evening, a friend said to me, "Did you hear that old Doctor Harris is dead?" "No," said I very quietly, "and it cannot be true; for I saw him at the Athenæum to-day." "You must be mistaken," rejoined my friend. "He is certainly dead!" and confirmed the fact with such special circumstances that I could no longer doubt it. My friend has often since assured me that I seemed much startled at the intelligence; but, as well as I can recollect, I believe that I was very little disturbed, if at all, but set down the apparition as a mistake of my own, or, perhaps, the interposition of a familiar idea into the place and amid the circumstances with which I had been accustomed to associate it.

The next day, as I ascended the steps of the Athenæum, I remember thinking within myself, "Well, I never shall see old Doctor Harris again!" With this thought in my mind, as I opened the door of the reading-room, I glanced towards the spot and chair where Doctor Harris usually sat, and there, to my astonishment, sat the gray, infirm figure of the deceased Doctor, reading the newspaper as was his wont! His own death must have been recorded, that very morning, in that very newspaper! I have no recollection of being greatly discomposed at the moment, nor indeed that I felt any extraordinary emotion whatever. Probably, if ghosts were in the habit of coming among us, they would coincide with the ordinary train of affairs, and melt into them so familiarly that we should not be shocked at their presence. At all events, so it was in this instance. I looked through the newspapers as usual, and turned over the periodicals, taking about as much interest in their contents as at other times. Once or twice, no doubt, I may have lifted my eyes from the page to look again at the venerable Doctor, who ought then to have been lying in his coffin dressed out for the grave, but who felt such interest in the Boston Post as to come back from the other world to read it the morning after his death. One might have supposed that he would have cared more about the novelties of the sphere to which he had just been introduced than about the politics he had left behind him!

The apparition took no notice of me, nor behaved otherwise in any respect than on any previous day. Nobody but myself seemed to notice him; and yet the old gentlemen round about the fire, beside his chair, were his lifelong acquaintances, who were perhaps thinking of his death, and who in a day or two would deem it a proper courtesy to attend his funeral.

I have forgotten how the ghost of Doctor Harris took its departure from the Athenæum on this occasion, or, in fact, whether the ghost or I went first. This equanimity, and almost indifference, on my part—the careless way in which I glanced at so singular a mystery and left it aside—is what now surprises me as much as anything else in the affair.

From that time, for a long while thereafter—for weeks at least, and I know not but for months—I used to see the figure of Doctor Harris quite as frequently as before his death. It grew to be so common that at length I regarded the venerable defunct no more than any other of the old fogies who basked before the fire and dozed over the newspapers.

It was but a ghost—nothing but thin air—not tangible nor appreciable, nor demanding any attention from a man of flesh and blood! I cannot recollect any cold shudderings, any awe, any repugnance, any emotion whatever, such as would be suitable and decorous on beholding a visitant from the spiritual world. It is very strange, but such is the truth. It appears excessively odd to me now that I did not adopt such means as I readily might to ascertain whether the appearance had solid substance, or was merely gaseous and vapory. I might have brushed against him, have jostled his chair, or have trodden accidentally on his poor old toes. I might have snatched the Boston Post—unless that were an apparition too—out of his shadowy hands. I might have tested him in a hundred ways; but I did nothing of the kind.

Perhaps I was loath to destroy the illusion, and to rob myself of so good a ghost story, which might probably have been explained in some very commonplace way. Perhaps, after all, I had a secret dread of the old phenomenon, and therefore kept within my limits, with an instinctive caution which I mistook for indifference. Be this as it may, here is the fact. I saw the figure, day after day, for a considerable space of time, and took no pains to ascertain whether it was a ghost or no. I never, to my knowledge, saw him come into the reading-room or depart from it. There sat Doctor Harris in his customary chair, and I can say little else about him.

After a certain period—I really know not how long—I began to notice, or to fancy, a peculiar regard in the old gentleman's aspect towards myself. I sometimes found him gazing at me, and, unless I deceived myself, there was a sort of expectancy in his face. His spectacles, I think, were shoved up, so that his bleared eyes might meet my own. Had he been a living man I should have flattered myself that good Doctor Harris was, for some reason or other, interested in me and desirous of a personal acquaintance. Being a ghost, and amenable to ghostly laws, it was natural to conclude that he was waiting to be spoken to before delivering whatever message he wished to impart. But, if so, the ghost had shown the bad judgment common among the spiritual brotherhood, both as regarded the place of interview and the person whom he had selected as the recipient of his communications. In the reading-room of the Athenæum conversation is strictly forbidden, and I could not have addressed the apparition without drawing the instant notice and indignant frowns of the slumbrous old gentlemen around me. I myself, too, at that time, was as shy as any ghost, and followed the ghosts' rule never to speak first. And what an absurd figure should I have made, solemnly and awfully addressing what must have appeared, in the eyes of all the rest of the company, an empty chair! Besides, I had never been introduced to Doctor Harris, dead or alive, and I am not aware that social regulations are to be abrogated by the accidental fact of one of the parties having crossed the imperceptible line which separates the other party from the spiritual world. If ghosts throw off all conventionalism among themselves, it does not therefore follow that it can safely be dispensed with by those who are still hampered with flesh and blood.

For such reasons as these—and reflecting, moreover, that the deceased Doctor might burden me with some disagreeable task, with which I had no business nor wish to be concerned—I stubbornly resolved to have nothing to say to him. To this determination I adhered; and not a syllable ever passed between the ghost of Doctor Harris and myself.

To the best of my recollection, I never observed the old gentleman either enter the reading-room or depart from it, or move from his chair, or lay down the newspaper, or exchange a look with any person in the company, unless it were myself. He was not by any means invariably in his place. In the evening, for instance, though often at the reading-room myself, I never saw him. It was at the brightest noontide that I used to behold him, sitting within the most comfortable focus of the glowing fire, as real and lifelike an object (except that he was so very old, and of an ashen complexion) as any other in the room. After a long while of this strange intercourse, if such it can be called, I remember—once, at least, and I know not but oftener—a sad, wistful, disappointed gaze, which the ghost fixed upon me from beneath his spectacles; a melancholy look of helplessness, which, if my heart had not been as hard as a paving-stone, I could hardly have withstood. But I did withstand it; and I think I saw him no more after this last appealing look, which still dwells in my memory as perfectly as while my own eyes were encountering the dim and bleared eyes of the ghost. And whenever I recall this strange passage of my life, I see the small, old, withered figure of Doctor Harris, sitting in his accustomed chair, the Boston Post in his hand, his spectacles shoved upwards—and gazing at me as I close the door of the reading-room, with that wistful, appealing, hopeless, helpless look. It is too late now; his grave has been grass-grown this many and many a year; and I hope he has found rest in it without any aid from me.

I have only to add that it was not until long after I had ceased to encounter the ghost that I became aware how very odd and strange the whole affair had been; and even now I am made sensible of its strangeness chiefly by the wonder and incredulity of those to whom I tell the story.

THE YOUNG PROVINCIAL

"Now, father, tell us all about the old gun," were the words of one of a number of children, who were seated around the hearth of a New England cottage. The old man sat in an arm-chair at one side of the fireplace, and his wife was installed in one of smaller dimensions on the other. The boys, that they might not disturb the old man's meditations, seemed to keep as much silence as was possible for individuals of their age; the fire burned high, with a sound like that of a trumpet, and its blaze occasionally shone on an old rifle which was suspended horizontally above the mantel.

"Willingly, my boys," said the old man, apparently animated by his returning recollections. "It may help to give you an idea of old times, when boys could not stay in their quiet homes like you, but were forced, or rather glad, to do what little they could for their country. My father lived in Tewksbury, a small town in Middlesex county. We were not generally much interested in the news of the day, but the spirit of resistance had then spread to every cottage in the country. The younger men of our village, following the example of others, had formed themselves into military bands, who were obliged by the terms of their association to be ready to march at a moment's warning, and were, therefore, called Minute Men. Perhaps if you accent the last syllable of that word minute, it would better describe a considerable portion of our number, of whom I was one. I armed myself with that rifle which you see over the mantel, though it was a weary labor to me to bear it on a march, and this, with a leathern bag for bullets, and a powder-horn, completed my equipment. We relied more upon the justice of our cause, not to mention our skill in sharp-shooting, than upon military discipline, and thence derived courage which was not a little needed; for the name of Roger was a very formidable one to every American ear.

"Having completed our preparations, such as they were, we waited for an opportunity, which the British were expected soon to afford us. It was understood that their purpose was to possess themselves of certain military stores at Concord, and a secret arrangement was made with the friends of liberty in Boston, that when they marched out for that purpose, lights should be displayed in certain spires, to alarm the country. One night in April, after a day of unusually hard labor, we were suddenly startled with a heavy sound which shook all the windows of the house. Another followed it, and we said in deep and half breathless tones to each other, 'It is the signal gun!' I must confess that my heart beat hard at the sound, and my cheek was cold with dismay; but my father, who was lame with a wound received in the old French War, encouraged us by his animation. 'Now,' said he, 'the time is come. Go, my boys, and do your best.' We had no time for sad reflections, so we ran hastily to the meeting-house, where the rest of our number were already collected by the light of lanterns. With your ideas of military show, you might, in a calmer moment, have smiled at our display. The younger men were gathered in groups round certain veterans who rejoiced in that opportunity of fighting their battles over again; but the arrival of the colonel broke up their conference. He came, not in state with his staff around him, but with that sign of authority in his hand. He was a man whose equanimity nothing ever disturbed, and I am free to confess that I heartily envied him, when I heard his quiet tones calling to his men to mind their business; and when they had sufficiently arranged their ranks, saying, 'Come, we'd as good's go along.' Along he went, as quietly as he had followed his plough that day, but there were hearts among his followers that were sorely oppressed by the excitement of the scene.

"We moved in darkness and silence on the road to Lexington. As we came near the town, we thought we heard the sound of some unusual motion, and, as the day began to dawn, were on the watch to discover the cause, when suddenly, as we turned the base of a hill, the martial music burst upon the ear, and the bright colors and the long red files of the British army came full in view. As if by one consent we all stood still for a time; and I declare to you, that helpless as we were in comparison to such a force, and young as I was for such encounters, the moment I saw what the danger was, I felt at once relieved, and, nothing doubting that an engagement must take place, I longed for it to begin.

"In a few moments we heard the sound of irregular firing, and saw our countrymen dispersing in every direction. Then our senior officer gave orders—not after a military sort, but still the best that could be given on such an occasion—for each man to go into the fields and fight 'upon his own hook.' This was done at once, and with surprising execution. A close fire was poured in on the regulars from all quarters, though not an American was to be seen. They fired passionately and at random, but every moment they saw their best men falling, and found themselves obliged to retreat without revenge. Closely did we follow them throughout that day. Unused as we were to blood, we felt a triumph when each one of our enemies fell. I received two balls in my clothes, and one passed through my hat, but so engaged was I in firing, that I hardly noticed them at the time.

"When my powder was gone, I went out on the track of the retreating army, with a high heart and burning cheek, I assure you. The first of the fallen that I saw before me was a young officer, not older than myself, who had received a wound in the breast, and was lying by the wayside. There was a calm repose in the expression of his features, which I have often seen in those who died of gunshot wounds; his lips were gently parted, and he seemed like one neither dead nor sleeping, but profoundly wrapped in meditations on distant scenes and friends. I went up to him with the same proud feeling which I had maintained throughout the battle; but when I saw him lying there in his beauty, and thought of all the hopes that were crushed by that blow, of those who were dreaming of him as one free from danger, and waiting the happy moment that was to restore him to their arms; and, more than all, when I thought that I might have been the cause of all this destruction, my heart relented within me, and I confess to you that I sat down by that poor youth and wept like a child. I left the spot with the heavy steps of one who feels the weight of blood upon his head, and returned to my father's house resolved to expiate my crime. The image of that youth, pale and bleeding, was before my eyes by day, and at my bedside by night, for weeks after, and in every wind I thought I heard the voice of the avenger of blood."

"And did you fight no more, father?"

"O yes, my boy. As soon as Boston was invested, we heard that our services were called for, and nothing more was wanted to fill the ranks of the army. I arrived at the camp the evening before the battle of Bunker Hill. Though weary with the march of the day, I went to the hill upon which our men were throwing up the breastwork in silence, and happened to reach the spot just as the morning was breaking in the sky. It was clear and calm; the sky was like pearl, the mist rolled lightly from the still water, and the large vessels of the enemy lay quiet as the islands. Never shall I forget the earthquake-voice with which that silence was broken. A smoke like that of a conflagration burst from the sides of the ships, and the first thunders of the revolutionary storm rolled over our heads. The bells of the city spread the alarm, the lights flashed in a thousand windows, the drums and trumpets mustered their several bands, and the sounds, in their confusion, seemed like an articulate voice foretelling the strife of that day.

"We took our places mechanically, side by side, behind the breastwork, and waited for the struggle to begin. We waited long and in silence. There was no noise but of the men at the breastwork strengthening their rude fortifications. We saw the boats put off from the city, and land the forces on the shore beneath our station. Still there was silence, except when the tall figure of our commander moved along our line, directing us not to fire until the word was given. For my part, as I saw those gallant forces march up the hill in well ordered ranks, with the easy confidence of those who had been used to victory, I was motionless with astonishment and delight. I thought only on their danger, and the steady courage with which they advanced to meet it, the older officers moving with mechanical indifference, the younger with impatient daring. Then a fire blazed along their ranks, but the shot struck in the redoubt or passed harmlessly over our heads. Not a solitary musket answered, and if you had seen the redoubt, you would have said that some mighty charm had turned all its inmates to stone. But when they stood so near us that every shot would tell, a single gun from the right was the signal for us to begin, and we poured upon them a fire, under which a single glance, before the smoke covered all, showed us their columns reeling like some mighty wall which the elements are striving to overthrow. As the vapor passed away, their line appeared as if a scythe of destruction had cut it down, for one long line of dead and dying marked the spot where their ranks had stood. Again they returned to the charge; again they were cut down; and then the heavy masses of smoke from the burning town added magnificence to the scene. By this time my powder-horn was empty, and most of those around me had but a single charge remaining. It was evident that our post must be abandoned, but I resolved to resist them once again. They came upon us with double fury. An officer happened to be near me; raising my musket, and putting all my strength into the blow, I laid him dead at my feet. But, meantime, the British line passed me in pursuit of the flying Americans, and thus cut off my retreat; one of their soldiers fired, and the ball entered my side. I fell, and was beaten with muskets on the head until they left me for dead upon the field. When I recovered, the soldiers were employed in burying their dead. An officer inquired if I could walk; but finding me unable, he directed his men to drag me by the feet to their boats, where I was thrown in, fainting with agony, and carried with the rest of the prisoners to Boston. One of my comrades, who saw me fallen, returned with the news to my parents. They heard nothing more concerning me, but had no doubt that I was slain. They mourned for me as lost, and a rude stone was erected near the graves of my family, in the burying-ground, to record the fate of the one who was not permitted to sleep with his fathers. I doubt not that the mourning was sincere, nor do I doubt that there was in all their sorrow a feeling of exultation, that one of their number was counted worthy to suffer death in the service of his country. The old schoolmaster, who was a learned man, said it was like the monument to the slain at Marathon, a great field of ancient times, and often pointed it out to his scholars from his school window, to encourage that spirit of freedom which was the passion of that day.

"I was carried to the hospital in Boston, and never shall I forget the scene presented in that abode of woe. The rooms were small and crowded; the regular and provincial were thrown in together, to be visited, that is, looked upon, if perchance they could catch his eye, once a day, by an indifferent physician, who neither understood nor cared for his duty. It was dire and dreadful to hear the curses poured out by some dying wretch upon the rebels who had given him his death wound; but my heart sank still more at hearing the last words of some of my countrymen, who entreated the surviving to tell their friends that in death they remembered them, and gave up their lives calmly and religiously, as brave men should. One youth of my age do I especially remember; his bed was next to mine. One night his gasping informed me that his death was drawing nigh. I rose upon my elbow and looked upon him, as a pale lamp shone upon his features. There was a tear in his eye, and his thoughts were far away, evidently returning to that home which never was to behold him again. Long time he lay thus, and I remained gazing on him, expecting myself soon to pass through the same change. At last the expression of his countenance altered; he raised his hands and clasped them as if in supplication, his eyes were turned upwards, and in that prayer, when sleep had happily sealed the eyes of the blasphemers around him, he gave up his soul unto God.

"When the British were obliged to retire from Boston, I was taken to Halifax, with the rest of the prisoners, in the fleet. I was first placed in a prison-ship, but soon removed to a prison in the town. The confinement grew intolerable, as my limbs recovered strength, and the prison door was hardly closed before I resolved, with my companions, that we would not rest till we had made one great endeavor. Every day we were insulted by the wretches employed to guard us; our food was hardly sufficient to sustain us; we were not permitted to know anything of the success of our countrymen, and as often as any favor was requested, it was denied with bitter scorn. Our apartment, in which six were confined, resembled a dungeon; but this, while it added to the gloom of our condition, aided our attempts at escape. I was fortunate enough to find an old bayonet upon the floor, with which I loosened the masonry of the prison wall. Long and wearily did we labor, relieving each other at the task, and thus keeping constantly employed day and night, except when the grating of rusty hinges informed us that the turnkey was coming near our room. We had hung up our clothing on the wall where we labored as soon as we entered the jail, so that it was not suspected to be a screen for our labors. In the course of four long weeks we succeeded in penetrating through the wall, and never did my heart bound with such delight, as when I saw the first gleam of a star through the opening.

"We waited for a night suitable to our purpose, and it seemed as if the elements had conspired against us; for seven days passed, and each night it was as clear and calm as possible. At last the night set in dark and stormy. The wind, as it howled from the ocean, and sent the rain rattling against our little window, was music to our ears. We heard the toll of midnight from the bells of the town, and then began our operations. We took the stones of the wall and placed them within the dungeon, removing them silently and one by one. When the passage was opened, we saw that it was not very high above the ground. We doubted not that the sentry would conceal himself in his box from the storm, but lest he should discover us, each armed himself with a stone. He was sheltered, as we supposed, but hearing the sound we made in letting ourselves down from the breach, he came toward us. Before he could give his challenge we threw our stones at the unfortunate man, and heard him sink heavily to the earth, his musket ringing as he fell.

"Four of our number were strong, but one, with myself, was infirm from the effect of wounds. They, therefore, at our request, left us behind, though with much apparent reluctance. It was an evil hour for them when they did so, for they were afterwards retaken, and committed to prison again, where ill treatment and depression put an end to their lives before the close of the war. I went with my companion into a swamp about a mile from the town, and we had hardly secured our retreat, and laid ourselves down to rest, when the roar of a gun came floating upon the wind, a signal that our retreat was discovered. It was followed by the martial shout of the bugle; but, near as it was, we could go no farther, and could only quietly employ ourselves in gathering boughs of pine to form a kind of couch and covering. Thus we lay sheltered till the day dawned, listening in no pleasing suspense to the sounds of alarm that reached us from the town. In a few hours the sounds grew near us; we could even see our pursuers as they passed by. A small party employed a stratagem to draw us from the swamp, in which they thought it possible we had taken shelter. Suddenly crying out, 'Here they are,' they fired into the shrubbery; but though the balls fell all around us, we saw their motions, and were not frightened from our hiding place. We rose at night, and went on our way, subsisting upon roots and berries, together with a little miserable bread, which we had saved for this expedition; but we were tortured with hunger, and on passing a barn my companion secured a fowl, which we ate, raw as it was, with delight.

"Thus we travelled for seven days, almost without food, and entirely without shelter; but our strength began to give way. I deliberated with my companion, who was resolute, though still more feeble than I, and we determined to throw ourselves on the mercy of some passing traveller. We had no other possible chance of relief, and though this was hazardous, and almost hopeless, we resolved if we met but one person, we would make ourselves known, and ask his protection. Soon after we had decided on this adventure, we heard the lingering tramp of a horse, and saw a venerable-looking person, who reminded us of one of our New England farmers, going to market with well-filled saddlebags, from which the claws of poultry made their appearance in the attitude of supplication. He was to all appearance just the man we wanted to see, and our first impressions were not disappointed. I came out from the hedge, and requested him to hear me; but he looked at me with his eyes and mouth wide open, and saying, 'Can't stop,' endeavored, with much clamor, to urge his beast into a quicker step. But the steed was my friend on this occasion, and absolutely refused to hasten his movements without some better reason than he saw at the time. I took advantage of his delay to state my condition to the old man, whose countenance changed at once on hearing my story. 'Conscience!' said he, 'I thought ye no better than a picaroon; but ye look 'most starved.' So saying, he got off his horse, and, opening his saddle-bags, he gave me the bread and cheese which he had provided for his own journey. This I shared with my companion, who came forward and joined me. 'I was going to ask you to ride double,' said the farmer, 'but the creature can't carry three, though ye are both of ye rather meagre. However, wait here till I come back at night, then I will lend a hand to help you. I don't know as it's quite right, but I took a notion for the Americans myself, when I heard you were angry about the price of tea. It's dear enough here, that's certain. But whether or no, I can't see how I should help King George by carrying you back to Halifax, to be hanged, maybe, though I would do anything for the old gentleman in reason.' With many cautions and encouragements he left us.

"We concealed ourselves through the day, and many suspicions came over us, that our friend might be induced by the reward to give us up to our pursuers. But we did him injustice. At night he came back, and seemed glad to see us when we made our appearance. 'I might have come back before,' said he, 'but I thought we could work better in the dark.' He then dismounted, and without delay directed us to mount the horse, while he would walk by its side. For a long time we refused to suffer him, aged as he was, to encounter such fatigue, but we were really worn out, and at last consented. We went on all that night, the old man keeping up our spirits by his conversation. It was daybreak before he showed any intention of making a permanent halt; but as the morning grew red in the sky, he urged us forward till we stopped under the windows of a solitary farmhouse, with its large buildings round it, not neat as they are seen in New England, but still indicating thrift and industry in its possessor. 'Thank Heaven, here we are,' said the farmer, 'for I do not know how it is, I am not the man for a walk I once was;' and truly the weight of eighty years might have exempted him from such labors. He went to what appeared to be a bedroom window, where he knocked with some caution. Forthwith a nightcapped head made its appearance, and at once declared its native land by the exclamation, 'Law for me! what brings you home at this time o' night!' But the question was only answered by a request that the individual, who was no less than the old man's helpmate, would rise and open the door. She rose with cheerful alacrity, and immediately began to make preparations for the morning's meal, without troubling herself much about the character of her husband's guests; though it should not be forgotten, that he condescended to make some little explanations. When the breakfast was over, which, however, was a work of time, we were invited to spend all that day in rest after our long and painful labor.

"In the evening we met again in the huge kitchen, which was the gathering place of the family, who were amused with some feigned account of our character, and the object of our visit. When the miscellaneous collection had retired, leaving us with the old man and his wife, we gave him a full account of our adventures, finding from his unconcern as to politics that we were in a place of security. He told us there was much confusion in the town on account of our escape, and that a reward was offered for our detection, while at the same time detachments of soldiers were sent in pursuit. He himself was strictly examined, and he said that he did not feel quite easy in his mind, when he thought of the lies of all sorts and sizes which he had felt obliged to tell. 'However,' said he, 'I did not do evil that good might come. I did the good first and then the evil followed, which was no lookout of mine.'

"We proposed to leave him that night, but he would by no means consent to this, and insisted on our remaining with him for some time, as he said, 'to pick up our crumbs.' On the third night we took leave of our Samaritan with the deepest emotion of gratitude for his kindness. I always looked on the bright side of human nature; but I never received an impression in its favor so decided and reviving as from the conduct of this humble man. I never saw nor heard of him again.

"Our friend had given us directions to a place where we could take passage for Falmouth, now Portland. We succeeded in reaching it without difficulty, and, though we had no money, his recommendation gained us a place in the vessel. I felt relieved when once more upon the waters, and standing gallantly out to sea. With what different feelings had I traversed the same ocean-roads before! Then my heart died within me, as I stood on the battlements of the floating castle that bore me through the waves; every moment increased the distance that separated me from my home and country, which grew dearer to me in the hour of its own distress and mine; now, as our little whaleboat bounded over the waves, I felt bold, joyous, and triumphant. I thought then that there were moments in a life of changes, which atone for the heaviness of many of its hours. I have since learned that the only real happiness is that which I then unconsciously felt, arising from the reflection that I had done my duty.

"From Falmouth we went home on foot. Before I reached my native village, my companion left me. His society had become endeared to me by our partnership in misfortune, and I parted from him with sorrow. He has ceased from the number of the living long ago, but I hope to meet him again. I entered my native place on a clear summer afternoon; the air was calm, the sky was clear, and there was stillness like that of the Sabbath through the whole extent of the place. I remembered hearing the distant bell, and knew that they were assembled for the lecture which preceded the Communion service, according to the custom of our fathers. I went to my father's door, and entered it softly. My mother was sitting in her usual place by the fireside, though there were green boughs instead of fagots in the chimney before her. When she saw me, she gave a wild look, grew deadly pale, and making an ineffectual effort to speak to me, fainted away. With much difficulty I restored her, but it was long before I could make her understand that the supposed apparition was in truth her son whom she had so long mourned for as dead. My little brother had also caught a glimpse of me, and with that superstition which was in that day so much more common than it is in this, he was sadly alarmed. In his fright he ran to the meeting-house to give the alarm; when he reached that place, the service had ended, and the congregation were just coming from its doors. Breathless with fear, he gave them his tidings, losing even his dread, in that moment, for the venerable minister and the snowy wigs of the deacons. Having told them what he had seen, they turned, with the whole assembly after them, towards my father's house; and such was their impatience to arrive at the spot, that minister, deacons, old men and matrons, young men and maidens, quickened their steps to a run.

"Never was there such a confusion in our village. The young were eloquent in their amazement, and the old put on their spectacles to see the strange being who had thus returned as from the dead. I told my story over and over again. As often as I concluded it, new detachments arrived, who insisted on hearing all the particulars in their turn. The house was crowded with visitors till far into the night, when the minister dismissed them, by calling on my father and mother to join him in an offering of praise, 'for this son which was dead and is alive again, which was lost and is found.'"

THE HAUNTED QUACK

A TALE OF A CANAL BOAT

In the summer of 18—, I made an excursion to Niagara. At Schenectady, finding the roads nearly impassable, I took passage in a canal boat for Utica. The weather was dull and lowering. There were but few passengers on board; and of those few, none were sufficiently inviting in appearance to induce me to make any overtures to a travelling acquaintance. A stupid answer, or a surly monosyllable, were all that I got in return for the few simple questions I hazarded. An occasional drizzling rain, and the wet and slippery condition of the tow-path, along which the lazy beasts that dragged the vessel travelled, rendered it impossible to vary the monotony of the scene by walking. I had neglected to provide myself with books, and as we crept along at the dull rate of four miles per hour, I soon felt the foul fiend *Ennui* coming upon me with all her horrors.

"Time and the hour," however, "run through the roughest day," and night at length approached. By degrees the passengers, seemingly tired of each other's company, began to creep slowly away to their berths; most of them fortifying themselves with a potation, before resigning themselves to the embrace of Morpheus. One called for a glass of hot whiskey punch, because he felt cold; another took some brandy toddy to prevent his taking cold; some took mint juleps; some gin-slings, and some rum and water. One took his dram because he felt sick; another to make him sleep well; and a third because he had nothing else to do. The last who retired from the cabin, was an old gentleman who had been deeply engaged in a well-thumbed volume all day, and whose mental abstraction I had more than once envied. He now laid down his book, and, pulling out a red nightcap, called for a pint of beer, to take the vapors out of his head.

As soon as he had left the cabin, I took up the volume, and found it to be Glanville's marvellous book, entitled the History of Witches, or the Wonders of the Invisible World Displayed. I began to peruse it, and soon got so deeply interested in some of his wonderful narrations, that the hours slipped unconsciously away, and midnight found me poring half asleep over the pages. From this dreamy state I was suddenly aroused by a muttering, as of a suppressed voice, broken by groans and sounds of distress. Upon looking round, I saw that they proceeded from the figure of a man enveloped in a cloak who was lying asleep upon one of the benches of the cabin whom I had not previously noticed. I recognized him to be a young man, with whose singular appearance and behavior during the day, I had been struck. He was tall and thin in person, rather shabbily dressed, with long, lank, black hair, and large gray eyes, which gave a visionary character to one of the most pallid and cadaverous countenances I had ever beheld. Since he had come on board, he had appeared restless and unquiet, keeping away from the table at meal times, and seeming averse from entering into conversation with the passengers. Once or twice, on catching my eye, he had slunk away as if, conscience-smitten by the remembrance of some crime, he dreaded to meet the gaze of a fellow mortal. From this behavior I suspected that he was either a fugitive from justice, or else a little disordered in mind; and had resolved to keep my eye on him and observe what course he should take when we reached Utica.

Supposing that the poor fellow was now under the influence of nightmare, I got up with the intention of giving him a shake to rouse him, when the words, "murder," "poison," and others of extraordinary import, dropping unconnectedly from his lips, induced me to stay my hand. "Go away, go away," exclaimed he, as if conscious of my approach, but mistaking me for another. "Why do you continue to torment me? If I did poison you, I did n't mean to do it, and they can't make that out more than manslaughter. Besides, what's the use of haunting me now? Ain't I going to give myself up, and tell all? Begone! I say, you bloody old hag, begone!" Here the bands of slumber were broken by the intensity of his feelings, and with a wild expression of countenance and a frame shaking with emotion, he started from the bench, and stood trembling before me.

Though convinced that he was a criminal, I could not help pitying him from the forlorn appearance he now exhibited. As soon as he had collected his wandering ideas, it seemed as if he read in my countenance, the mingled sentiments of pity and abhorrence, with which I regarded him. Looking anxiously around, and seeing that we were alone, he drew the corner of the bench towards me, and sitting down, with an apparent effort to command his feelings, thus addressed me. His tone of voice was calm and distinct; and his countenance, though deadly pale, was composed.

"I see, Sir, that from what I am conscious of having uttered in my disturbed sleep, you suspect me of some horrid crime. You are right. My conscience convicts me, and an awful nightly visitation, worse than the waking pangs of remorse, compels me to confess it. Yes, I am a murderer. I have been the unhappy cause of blotting out the life of a fellow being from the page of human existence. In these pallid features, you may read enstamped, in the same characters which the first murderer bore upon his brow, Guilt—guilt—guilt!"

Here the poor young man paused, evidently agitated by strong internal emotion. Collecting himself, however, in a few moments, he thus continued.

"Yet still, when you have heard my sad story, I think you will bestow upon me your pity. I feel that there is no peace for me, until I have disburthened my mind. Your countenance promises sympathy. Will you listen to my unhappy narrative?"

My curiosity being strongly excited by this strange exordium, I told him I was ready to hear whatever he had to communicate. Upon this, he proceeded as follows:—

"My name is Hippocrates Jenkins. I was born in Nantucket, but my father emigrated to these parts when I was young. I grew up in one of the most flourishing villages on the borders of the canal. My father and mother both dying of the lake fever, I was bound apprentice to an eminent operative in the boot and shoe making line, who had lately come from New York. Would that I had remained content with this simple and useful profession. Would that I had stuck to my waxed ends and awl, and never undertaken to cobble up people's bodies. But my legs grew tired of being trussed beneath my haunches; my elbows wearied with their monotonous motion; my eyes became dim with gazing forever upon the dull brick wall which faced our shop window; and my whole heart was sick of my sedentary, and, as I foolishly deemed it, particularly mean occupation. My time was nearly expired, and I had long resolved, should any opportunity offer of getting into any other employment, I would speedily embrace it.

"I had always entertained a predilection for the study of medicine. What had given my mind this bias, I know not. Perhaps it was the perusal of an old volume of Doctor Buchan, over whose pages it was the delight of my youthful fancy to pore. Perhaps it was the oddness of my Christian cognomen, which surely was given me by my parents in a prophetic hour. Be this as it may, the summit of my earthly happiness was to be a doctor. Conceive then my delight and surprise, one Saturday evening, after having carried home a pair of new white-topped boots for Doctor Ephraim Ramshorne, who made the care of bodies his care, in the village, to hear him ask me, how I should like to be a doctor. He then very generously offered to take me as a student. From my earliest recollections, the person and character of Doctor Ramshorne had been regarded by me with the most profound and awful admiration. Time out of mind the successful practitioner for many miles around, I had looked upon him as the *beau idéal* of a doctor—a very Apollo in the healing art. When I speak of him, however, as the *successful* practitioner, I mean it not to be inferred that death was less busy in his doings, or funerals scarcer during his dynasty; but only that he had, by some means or other, contrived to force all those who had ventured to contest the palm with him, to quit the field. He was large and robust in person, and his ruby visage showed that if he grew fat upon drugs, it was not by swallowing them himself. It was never exactly ascertained from what college the Doctor had received his diploma; nor was he very forward to exhibit his credentials. When hard pressed, however, he would produce a musty old roll of parchment, with a red seal as broad as the palm of his hand, which looked as if it might have been the identical diploma of the great Boerhaave himself, and some cramped manuscript of a dozen pages, in an unknown tongue, said by the Doctor to be his Greek thesis. These documents were enough to satisfy the doubts of the most sceptical. By the simple country people, far and near, the Doctor was regarded, in point of occult knowledge and skill, as a second Faustus. It is true, the village lawyer, a rival in popularity, used to whisper, that the Doctor's Greek thesis was nothing but a bundle of prescriptions for the bots, wind-galls, spavins, and other veterinary complaints, written in high Dutch by a Hessian horse doctor; that the diploma was all a sham, and that Ephraim was no more a doctor than his jackass. But these assertions were all put down to the score of envy on the part of the lawyer. Be this as it may, on the strength of one or two remarkable cures, which he was said to have performed, and by dint of wheedling some and bullying others, it was certain that Ramshorne had worked himself into very good practice. The Doctor united in his own person, the attributes of apothecary and physician; and as he vended, as well as prescribed his own drugs, it was not his interest to stint his patients in their enormous boluses, or nauseous draughts. His former medical student had been worried into a consumption over the mortar and pestle; in consequence of which he had pitched upon me for his successor.

"By the kindness of a few friends I was fitted out with the necessary requisitions for my metamorphosis. The Doctor required no fee, and, in consideration of certain little services to be rendered him, such as taking care of his horse, cleaning his boots, running errands, and doing little jobs about the house, had promised to board and lodge me, besides giving me my professional education. So with a rusty suit of black, and an old plaid cloak, behold equipped the disciple of Æsculapius.

"I cannot describe my elation of mind, when I found myself fairly installed in the Doctor's office. Golden visions floated before my eyes. I fancied my fortune already made, and blessed my happy star, that had fallen under the benign influence of so munificent a patron.

"The Doctor's office, as it was called *par excellence*, was a little nook of a room, communicating with a larger apartment denominated the shop. The paraphernalia of this latter place had gotten somewhat into disorder since the last student had gone away, and I soon learnt that it was to be my task to arrange the heterogeneous mass of bottles, boxes, and gallipots, that were strewed about in promiscuous confusion. In the office, there was a greater appearance of order. A small regiment of musty looking books, were drawn up in line upon a couple of shelves, where, to judge from the superincumbent strata of dust, they appeared to have peacefully reposed for many years. A rickety wooden clock, which the Doctor had taken in part payment from a peddler, and the vital functions of which, to use his own expression, had long since ceased to act, stood in one corner. A mouldy plaster bust of some unknown worthy, a few bottles of pickled, and one or two dried specimens of morbid anatomy, a small chest of drawers, a table, and a couple of chairs, completed the furniture of this *sanctum*. The single window commanded a view of the churchyard, in which, it was said, many of the Doctor's former patients were quietly slumbering. With a feeling of reverence I ventured to dislodge one of the dusty tomes, and began to try to puzzle out the hard words with which it abounded; when suddenly, as if he had been conjured back, like the evil one by Cornelius Agrippa's book, the Doctor made his appearance. With a gruff air, he snatched the volume from my hands, and telling me not to meddle with what I could not understand, bade me go and take care of his horse, and make haste back, as he wanted me to spread a pitch plaster, and carry the same, with a bottle of his patent catholicon, to farmer Van Pelt, who had the rheumatism. On my return, I was ordered by Mrs. Ramshorne to split some wood, and kindle a fire in the parlor, as she expected company; after which Miss Euphemia Ramshorne, a sentimental young lady, who was as crooked in person and crabbed in temper as her own name, despatched me to the village circulating library, in quest of the Mysteries of Udolpho. I soon found out that my place was no sinecure. The greater part of my time was occupied in compounding certain quack medicines, of Ramshorne's own invention, from which he derived great celebrity, and no inconsiderable profit. Besides his patent catholicon, and universal panacea, there was his anti-pertusso-balsamico drops, his patent calorific refrigerating anodyne, and his golden restorative of nature. Into the business of compounding these, and other articles with similar high-sounding titles, I was gradually initiated, and soon acquired so much skill in their manipulation, that my services became indispensable to my master; so much so, that he was obliged to hire a little negro to take care of his horse, and clean his boots. What chiefly reconciled me to the drudgery of the shop, was the seeing how well the Doctor got paid for his villainous compounds. A mixture of a little brick dust, rosin, and treacle, dignified with the title of the anthelminthic amalgam, he sold for half a dollar; and a bottle of vinegar and alum, with a little rose water to give it a flavor, yclept the anti-scrofulous abstergent lotion, brought twice that sum. I longed for the day when I should dispense my own medicines, and in my hours of castle-building, looked forward to fortunes far beyond those of the renowned Dr. Solomon. Alas! my fond hopes have been blighted in their bud. I have drunk deeply of the nauseous draught of adversity, and been forced to swallow many bitter pills of disappointment. But I find I am beginning to smell of the shop. I must return to my sad tale. The same accident, which not unfrequently before had put a sudden stop to the Doctor's patients' taking any more of his nostrums, at length prevented him from reaping any longer their golden harvest. One afternoon, after having dined with his friend, Squire Gobbledown, he came home, and complained of not feeling very well. By his directions, I prepared for him some of his elixir sanitatis, composed of brandy and bitters, of which he took an inordinate dose. Shortly after, he was seized with a fit of apoplexy, and before bedtime, in spite of all the drugs in the shop, which I poured down with unsparing hand, he had breathed his last. In three days, Ramshorne was quietly deposited in the churchyard, in the midst of those he had sent there before him.

"Having resided with the Doctor for several years, I had become pretty well known throughout the neighborhood, particularly among the old ladies, whose good graces I had always sedulously cultivated. I accordingly resolved to commence quacking—I mean practising—on my own account. Having obtained my late master's stock of drugs from his widow at an easy rate, and displaying my own name in golden letters as his successor, to work I went, with the internal resolve that where Ramshorne had given one dose, I would give six.

"For a time, Fortune seemed to smile upon me, and everything went on well. All the old women were loud in sounding my praises, far and near. The medicaments of my master, continued to be in demand, and treacle, brick dust, and alum came to a good market. Some drawbacks, however, I occasionally met with. Having purchased the patent right of one of Thompson's steam baths, in my first experiment I came near flaying alive a rheumatic tanner, who had submitted himself to the operation. By an unfortunate mistake in regulating the steam he was nearly parboiled; and it was supposed that the thickness of his hide alone preserved his vitals uninjured. I was myself threatened with the fate of Marsyas, by the enraged sufferer; which he was happily prevented from attempting to inflict, by a return of his malady, which has never since left him. I however after this gave up steaming, and confined myself to regular practice. At length, either the charm of novelty wearing off, or people beginning to discover the inefficacy of the old nostrums, I was obliged to exert my wits to invent new ones. These I generally took the precaution to try upon cats or dogs, before using them upon the human system. They were, however, mostly of an innocent nature, and I satisfied my conscience with the reflection, that if they did no good, they could at least do no harm. Happy would it have been for me, could I always have done thus. Meeting with success in my first efforts, I by degrees ventured upon more active ingredients. At length in an evil hour, I invented a curious mixture composed of forty-nine different articles. This I dubbed in high-flowing terms 'The Antidote to Death, or the Eternal Elixir of Longevity;' knowing full well that though

'A rose might smell as sweet by any other name,'

yet would not my drugs find as good a sale under a more humble title. This cursed compound proved the antidote to all my hopes of success. Besides forcing me to quit the village in a confounded hurry, it has embittered my life ever since, and reduced me to the ragged and miserable plight in which you see me.

"I dare say you have met with that species of old women, so frequent in all country towns, who, seeming to have outlived the common enjoyments of life, and outworn the ordinary sources of excitement, seek fresh stimulus in scenes of distress, and appear to take a morbid pleasure in beholding the varieties of human suffering and misery. One of the most noted characters in the village was an old beldame of this description. Granny Gordon, so she was familiarly denominated, was the rib of the village Vulcan, and the din of her eternal tongue was only equalled by the ringing of her husband's anvil. Thin and withered away in person and redolent with snuff, she bore no small resemblance to a newly-exhumed mummy, and to all appearance promised to last as long as one of those ancient dames of Egypt. Not a death, a burial, a fit of sickness, a casualty, nor any of the common calamities of life ever occurred in the vicinity, but Granny Gordon made it her especial business to be present. Wrapped in an old scarlet cloak,—that hideous cloak! the thought of it makes me shudder—she might be seen hovering about the dwelling of the sick. Watching her opportunity, she would make her way into the patient's chamber, and disturb his repose with long dismal stories and ill-boding predictions; and if turned from the house, which was not unfrequently the case, she would depart, muttering threats and abuse.

"As the Indians propitiate the favor of the devil, so had I, in my eagerness to acquire popularity, made a firm friend and ally, though rather a troublesome one, of this old woman. She was one of my best customers, and, provided it was something new, and had a high-sounding name to recommend it, would take my most nauseous compounds with the greatest relish. Indeed the more disgusting was the dose, the greater in her opinion was its virtue.

"I had just corked the last bottle of my antidote, when a message came to tell me that Granny Gordon had one of her old fits, and wanted some new doctor-stuff, as the old physic did n't do her any more good. Not having yet given my new pharmaceutic preparation a trial, I felt a little doubtful about its effects, but trusting to the toughness of the old woman's system, I ventured to send a potion, with directions to take it cautiously. Not many minutes had elapsed, before the messenger returned, in breathless haste, to say that Mrs. Gordon was much worse, and that though she had taken all the stuff, they believed she was dying. With a vague foreboding of evil, I seized my hat, and hastened to the blacksmith's. On entering the chamber my eyes were greeted with a sad spectacle. Granny Gordon, bolstered up in the bed, holding in her hand the bottle I had sent her, drained of its contents, sat gasping for breath, and occasionally agitated by strong convulsions. A cold sweat rested on her forehead, her eyes seemed dim and glazed, her nose, which was usually of a ruby hue, was purple and peaked, and her whole appearance evidently betokened approaching dissolution.

"Around the bed were collected some half dozen withered beldames who scowled upon me, as I entered, with ill-omened visages. Her husband, a drunken brute, who used to beat his better half six times a week, immediately began to load me with abuse, accusing me of having poisoned his dear, dear wife, and threatening to be the death of me, if she died.

"My conscience smote me. I felt stupefied and bewildered, and knew not which way to turn. At this moment, the patient perceiving me, with a hideous contortion of countenance, the expression of which I shall carry to my dying hour, and a voice between a scream and a groan, held up the empty bottle, and exclaimed, 'This is your doing, you villainous quack you' (here she was seized with hiccup);—'you have poisoned me, you have' (here fearful spasms shook her whole frame);—'but I'll be revenged; day and night my ghost shall haunt'—here her voice became inarticulate, and shaking her withered arm at me, she fell back, and to my extreme horror, gave up the ghost. This was too much for my nerves. I rushed from the house, and ran home with the dying curse ringing in my ears, fancying that I saw her hideous physiognomy, grinning from every bush and tree that I passed. Knowing that as soon as the noise of this affair should get abroad, the village would be too hot to hold me, I resolved to decamp as silently as possible. First throwing all my recently manufactured anodyne into the canal, that it should not rise in judgment against me, I made up a little bundle of clothes, and taking my seat in the mail stage, which was passing at the time and fortunately empty, in a couple of days I found myself in the great city of New York. Having a little money with me, I hired a mean apartment in an obscure part of the city, in the hope that I might remain concealed till all search after me should be over, when I might find some opportunity of getting employment, or of resuming my old profession, under happier auspices. By degrees the few dollars I brought with me were expended, and after pawning my watch and some of my clothes, I found myself reduced to the last shilling. But not the fear of impending starvation, nor the dread of a jail, are to be compared to the horrors I nightly suffer. Granny Gordon has been as good as her word. Every night, at the solemn hour of twelve" (here he looked fearfully around)—"her ghost appears to me, wrapped in a red cloak, with her gray hairs streaming from beneath an old nightcap of the same color, brandishing the vial, and accusing me of having poisoned her. These visitations have at length become so insupportable, that I have resolved to return and give myself up to justice; for I feel that hanging itself is better than this state of torment."

Here the young man ceased. I plainly saw that he was a little disordered in his intellect. To comfort him, however, I told him that if he had killed fifty old women, they could do nothing to him, if he had done it professionally. And as for the ghost, we would take means to have that put at rest, when we reached Utica.

About the gray of the morning, we arrived at the place of our destination.

My *protégé* having unburthened his mind, seemed more at his ease, and taking a mint julep, prepared to accompany me on shore. As we were leaving the boat, several persons in a wagon drove down to the wharf. As soon as my companion observed them, he exclaimed with a start of surprise, "Hang me, if there is n't old Graham the sheriff, and lawyer Dickson, and Bill Gordon come to take me." As he spoke, his foot slipping, he lost his balance, and fell backwards into the canal. We drew him from the water, and as soon as the persons in the wagon perceived him, they one and all sprang out, and ran up with the greatest expressions of joyful surprise. "Why, Hippy, my lad," exclaimed the sheriff, "where have you been? All our town has been in a snarl about you. We all supposed you had been forcibly abducted. Judge Bates offered a reward of twenty dollars for your corpse. We have dragged the canal for more than a mile, and found a mass of bottles, which made us think you had been spirited away. Betsey Wilkins made her affidavit that she heard Bill Gordon swear that he would take your life, and here you see we have brought him down to have his trial. But come, come, jump in the wagon, we'll take you up to the tavern, to get your duds dried, and tell you all about it."

Here a brawny fellow with a smutty face, who I found was Gordon the blacksmith, came up, and shaking Hippocrates by the hand, said, "By goles, Doctor, I am glad to see you. If you hadn't come back I believe it would have gone hard with me. Come, man, you must forgive the hard words I gave you. My old woman soon got well of her fit, after you went away, and says she thinks the stuff did her a mortal sight o' good."

It is impossible to describe the singular expression the countenance of the young man now exhibited. For some time he stood in mute amazement, shaking with cold, and gazing alternately at each of his friends as they addressed him; and it required their reiterated assurance to convince him, that Granny Gordon was still in the land of the living, and that he had not been haunted by a veritable ghost.

Wishing to obtain a further explanation of this strange scene, I accompanied them to the tavern. A plain-looking man in a farmer's dress, who was of the party, confirmed what the blacksmith had said, as to the supposed death of his wife and her subsequent recovery. "She was only in a swoond," said he, "but came to, soon after the Doctor had left her." He added that it was his private opinion that she would now last forever. He spoke of Hippocrates as a " 'nation smart doctor, who had a power of larning, but gave severe doses."

After discussing a good breakfast, my young friend thanked me for the sympathy and interest I had taken in his behalf. He told me he intended returning to the practice of his profession. I admonished him to be more careful in the exhibition of his patent medicines, telling him that all old women had not nine lives. He shook hands with me, and, gayly jumping into the wagon, rode off with his friends.

THE NEW ENGLAND VILLAGE

Some years ago it was my destiny to reside in a New England village. Nothing can be pleasanter than its situation. All that nature ever did for a place, she has done for this. It is sheltered on the north by high hills, and fringed on the south with forests of oaks and elms; it has waterfalls and cascades, and, what is more surprising, they are suffered to flow on through meadow and valley, without being condemned to the treadmill. In this country everything is compelled to do duty. Our forests are cut down for firewood; our rocks hewn into state prisons, and some of our modern speculators mean to make old Niagara, that has roared and bellowed so many hundred years for its own amusement, actually work for its living, and support cotton and woollen manufactures.

But to return to my village. It is not called a flourishing one, for there is no distillery, and no jail in it. But they have straw bonnet manufactories, working societies, and reading societies, and the females actually raised ten dollars fifty-two cents for the emancipation of the Greeks.

While I resided there, I became intimately acquainted with the clergyman, and it was my constant habit to call on him every evening for a stroll. He was just such a man as the ladies call a marrying man, yet, strange to tell, he was still a bachelor. There was a village legend that he had been crossed in love; but disappointments of the heart generate suspicion and misanthropy, and no one could be more confiding and guileless than he was. His sensibilities seemed to be in their first spring. His fair smooth forehead, his broad chest and Boanerges voice, gave no evidence that he had wasted his health in scientific or theological pursuits; yet he was well read in Scripture, and could quote chapter and verse on every contested point. For many years he had made no use of a Concordance, for he was a living one himself. The practical part of his profession formed its beauty in him. He might well teach temperance, for necessary articles of food were all he coveted; he could talk of charity with the "tongue of an angel," for it was not with him tinkling brass or empty sound; from his five hundred dollars salary there was always an overplus, that brought upon him "the blessing of those that were ready to perish." Perhaps there was a little too much minuteness about worldly affairs, and yet it was an excellent example for others. There was also a bit too much of the parish register in his cast of mind; he could tell how many he had married, how many he had christened, and how many he had buried; how many prayers he had made, and how many sermons he had written. All this was very well; but when he undertook to know people's ages better than they did themselves, it would have been intolerably provoking, if he had not always been able to prove he was right by parish records. He had a love for agriculture that contributed to his health, and agreeably diversified his employments. The piece of land that was set off to the parsonage was always in excellent order, and the invalids of his parish might count upon the first mess of peas and the first plate of strawberries from his garden.

Our walk often led by a farm that had once been the summer residence of an opulent family. The grounds were laid out originally with much taste; but it had passed into the hands of various owners. They had cut down the trees that they might not obstruct the view of the road, and suffered the buildings to go to decay, because it cost money to repair them. There was an air of desolate grandeur about the house, that inspired sensations wholly unlike the trim, square houses of the village. It was too far from the road, and too large to be tenanted. Besides, the farm was run out. In short, it was unpopular, and nobody would live on it. It was said that it might be "bought for a song," but it was so out of repair and so comfortless, that nobody appeared to purchase it. It had gone through the "pitiless pelting" of a severe winter uninhabited, and nothing could be more dreary than it looked, half buried in snow. But when the spring came on, and the grass grew green, and the wild roses blossomed, and the creepers hung clustering about the doors and windows, it was a place that might have tempted any lover of solitude and nature.

In a small country village, however, there are few who come under this class. All have a practical love of nature, but not many a sentimental one; and it was with a degree of contempt that it was discovered, in the month of June, that the house was actually inhabited. Much speculation was excited, and the place that stood in desolate neglect became an object of curiosity and interest.

I had had some thoughts of purchasing the place, and tried to persuade myself that it would be a good way of investing a small sum, when I learnt that a Mr. Forester had been beforehand with me, and had taken possession of the house. I felt a degree of disappointment that the previously irresolute state of my mind by no means authorized. Soon after this occurrence, I quitted the village, and removed to a different part of the country.

Ten years passed away, and I made no effort to renew my intercourse with my old friend the clergyman. In consequence of indisposition I found it actually necessary last year to journey. My recollections immediately turned to the village where I had before found health, and I once more directed my course towards it.

It was on Sunday morning that I entered the town of H——, about ten miles from the village. I knew too well the primitive habits of my friend the clergyman, to break in upon his Sabbath morning, and I determined to remain where I was till the next day.

It is a church-going place. When I saw couple after couple pass the window of the tavern at which I had stationed myself in mere idleness, I began to feel an inclination to go to church too.

I entered the nearest one, and when the minister arose, found to my surprise that it was my old friend. He did not appear to have altered since I last saw him; his voice was equally powerful, his person rather fuller. I recognized in his prayers and sermon, the same expressions he had used ten years ago—and why not? They were drawn from his book of knowledge. There was still the same simplicity and the same fervor that had first interested me, and when the services were over, and I shook hands with him, it seemed even to me, who am not given to illusion, that we had parted but yesterday. I tried to make out by his appearance whether he had married, but I was baffled—

the outer man had undergone no change. He told me that he should return home after the evening service, and invited me to take a seat in his chaise with him. I readily accepted the invitation. When he called for me, he said, "Don't forget your portmanteau, for I must keep you at my house for a few days."

As we jogged along, for his horse never departed from his Sunday pace even on week days, I asked him what had become of the Foresters. "Do they still retain the farm that ought to have been mine?" said I. A color like the mellow tint of a russetine apple that had been perfectly preserved through the winter, rose in his cheek as he replied: "Part of the family are there; if you like I will give you an account of them." I assented; but when I found he was settling himself as if for a long story, my heart died within me. I knew his minuteness on every subject, and that to have added or diminished an iota would have been to him palpable fraud and injustice. By degrees, however, I became interested in his narrative.

"Soon after you left me, I became intimate with Mr. Forester. He was a sensible, intelligent man, and his wife was a very worthy woman. They had two children, who were full of health and gayety. Mr. Forester entered upon farming with great zeal, and the place soon wore a different aspect. The venerable trees that had been cut down could not be restored, but repairs were made, the stone walls rebuilt, and all indicated that the new tenant was a man of order and good habits. He had not been accustomed to farming, but he was assiduous in finding out the best and most approved methods of ploughing, planting, and managing his land. Nothing could be more successful than his industry. The third year his crops were abundant, and his wife began to talk of her dairy, and exhibit her butter and cheese in the country style. The inhabitants of the village found they managed their affairs so well, that they were content to let them go on without interfering. Mrs. Forester accommodated herself to the habits and customs of those around her with wonderful facility, and was a general favorite.

"Instead of passing the house as you and I used to in our walk, I now every evening turned up the avenue, and spent half an hour with them. The children called me uncle, and ran to meet me; their mother, too, would follow them with a step almost as light. She played upon the guitar, and though I was not acquainted with the instrument, and thought it feeble compared to the bass viol, yet I loved to hear it chiming with her sweet voice.

"When I looked at this happy family, I felt new sympathies springing up in my heart, and began to be almost dissatisfied with my solitary home. I sometimes thought Mr. Forester was not as tranquil and contented as his wife; but he had lived in the world, and it was natural that he should feel the want of that society to which he had been accustomed.

"It was on the third year of their residence in the village, that I was invited to visit them with more form than usual. Mrs. Forester said, that she and the children were going to celebrate the fifth anniversary of her marriage. She had many of the fanciful contrivances of her sex to give interest to the daily routine of life. She had placed her table under an arbor, covered with honeysuckles and sweetbrier, and loaded it with fruit and the abundance of her good housewifery. The grass that had been newly mown was distributed around us in heaps. At a little distance from the arbor, and behind it, stood the large barn, with the huge folding doors open at each end. Through this we had a view of the house, and beyond it the country round, with its fields waving with grain, its peaceful streams, its green valleys, its distant hills, and, what in my opinion added greatly to the beauty of the prospect, the spire of my own church rising from a grove of trees. I must not forget to mention the Merrimack that was in front of us, moving on in the majesty of its deep, blue waters, and bearing on its bosom the various craft of inland navigation. It was a glorious scene, and we all felt it such. 'Here at least,' said I, 'we may worship God in the temple of his own beauty!' I looked at Mrs. Forester. Women have quick sensibilities. I saw the tears were coursing each other down her cheeks; but they were like the raindrops of summer, and her smiles returned more gayly. The children had taken many a trip from the house to the arbor, with their baskets and aprons loaded with cakes and fruits. We all gathered round the table. Mrs. Forester was as gay as her children. She played upon her guitar, and sang modern songs, which I am sorry to say had more music than sense in them. In the midst of one of these we heard footsteps. A man stood at the entrance of the arbor, and laid his hand on Mr. Forester's shoulder. He started, and turned round; then, taking the man by the arm, walked away. 'I wish,' said Mrs. Forester impatiently, 'he had not interrupted us just as we were so happy.'

" 'Do you know him?' said I. 'No,' she replied, 'I can't say I do, and yet I remember seeing him soon after we were married. I believe,' added she, coloring and laughing, 'I never told you that ours was a runaway match. It has turned out so well, and our troubles have terminated so happily, that I am not afraid to confess my imprudence to you. I was an orphan, and lived with my grandmother, who was as different from me in her habits and opinions as old people usually are from young ones. She thought singing was bad for the lungs, that dancing would throw me into a fever, and the night air into a consumption. I differed from her in all these opinions, and yet was obliged to conform. After I became acquainted with Mr. Forester, we differed still more. She said he was a stranger that nobody knew; I said I knew him perfectly. In short, she told me if I intended to marry him, she would forbid the banns. I thought it best to save her the trouble, and so I tied up a little bundle, and walked off with my husband that is now.

" 'The good old lady lived to see him well established in business as a lawyer, and became quite reconciled. I loved her sincerely, and now that I was independent, willingly accommodated myself to her habits. She died soon after birth of my first child, Ellen, who was named for her. She left me five thousand dollars, which is now invested in this farm, and I trust will be the inheritance of my children.'

" 'May I ask,' said I, 'why you left your native place?' 'I hardly know,' said she; 'my husband thought the air did not agree with him. He grew melancholy and abstracted, and then I began to dislike it too, and was quite ready to quit it. We removed to B——. My husband carried his reputation and talents with him, and was again successful in the practice of law. In the course of a few months his complaints returned, and he then thought it was country air he wanted, and an entire change of life. The event has proved so. We quitted the lanquid and enervating climate of the South, and travelled North. We gave up all our former associations, and to make the change more complete, my husband took the name of an uncle who brought him up, and relinquished his own. It is now three years since we have resided here, and I don't know that he has had any return of ill health or nervous affections since.'

"At that moment Mr. Forester returned, accompanied by the stranger. He approached his wife, and said, 'Here is an old acquaintance, Mary; you must make him welcome.' There was an expression in the countenance of the guest that appalled us. It seemed to communicate its baleful influence to the whole circle. Mr. Forester looked pale and anxious; the gayety was gone; nobody sung or laughed; we scarcely spoke. All was changed. The stranger seemed to have had a blighting effect on the master of the house; for from this time his health and spirits gradually forsook him. Signs of poverty appeared, and he announced to his wife that he must move elsewhere. She was thunderstruck. The legacy of her aunt had been invested in the purchase of the farm. To give up that was relinquishing the inheritance of her children. She remonstrated, but without effect; he declined all explanation. With deep regret I saw them quit the village.

"Mrs. Forester had promised to write me when they were again fixed in any permanent situation. It was nearly two years before I received a letter. That letter I have now in my pocket-book. It has remained there since I first received it. Here it is!"

I knew too well his exact habits to be surprised at the perfect state of preservation in which I saw it. It was as follows:—

"I rejoice that I can give you cheerful accounts, my much respected friend, of my husband and myself. After we left you, we removed to a remote town in the West, and here we are. We have given up farming, and my husband has opened an office. As he is the only lawyer in the place, he has made his way extremely well. I wish I could say I am as happy as you once saw me; but this mode of life is not to my taste, nor do I think it agrees with my husband. I have never seen him so tranquil as the three short years we passed at N——. There is something in the life of a farmer peculiarly soothing. The sun never rose so bright to me as at that period. I do not think Eve was as happy in her paradise as I was in mine; for her fruits grew spontaneously, but mine were produced by the united efforts of head and hands, and gave exercise to all my powers. My children are well. My husband's health is not very good; this plodding life does not agree with him; he is subject to low spirits. I sometimes have sad forebodings of the future; if I could only get back to N——, I think all would go well."

This was the purport of the letter. I returned it to my friend, and he resumed his narrative.

"About a year from the time I received the letter, I took a journey to Montreal to visit a sister who was settled there. In passing one of the streets I recognized Mr. Forester; but he was so altered in his appearance that I doubted if it could be he. He held out his hand, and I found, upon inquiring, that they had made another remove to Montreal. He was emaciated in his person, and there was a nervous agitation in his manner that alarmed me. I begged him to conduct me to his wife. 'With all my heart,' said he, 'but you will be surprised at our *ménage*.' I accompanied him to a low, dilapidated building, in which everything bespoke poverty. Mrs. Forester gave me a mournful welcome. She, too, was greatly changed; but her children were still blooming and healthy, and appeared unconscious of the cloud that hung over their parents.

"My visit was short; I perceived it was an embarrassing one; but in taking leave, I said, 'If you have any commands to your old friends at N——, here is my address.' I had not been home long, before William Forester brought me a note from his mother, requesting to see me. I immediately returned with him, and found her alone. She was free and undisguised in her communication; said there was some dreadful mystery hung over them, and that whatever it was, it was hurrying her husband to the grave. 'I should not have spoken,' added she, 'had not this conviction made all scruples weigh light in the balance. I think it possible he may reveal to you what he will not to me. At least, see him before you quit Montreal. If we could once more return to N——, we might yet be happy.'

"I again called to see him. Never was there a human being more changed. He was dull, abstracted, and silent; and I began to think his mind was impaired. I used every argument in my power to persuade him to return to N——, and tried to convince him it was a duty he owed to his wife and children. He only replied that it would do no good; neither they nor he would be happier; that there was nothing I could say to him with regard to himself that his own mind had not suggested. He acknowledged that he had a secret source of calamity, but said it was beyond human power to mitigate it, that the kindest part would be to let him alone; that he had never intruded his sorrows on others, and he asked no participation; that happily there was a termination to all things here, and his sufferings could not last forever. I told him, that if he was alone in the world, he might reason justly; but he must feel that there was one human being at least, that was doomed to participate in his good or bad fortune, and who was made wretched by his mysterious conduct.

" 'Has she spoken to you?' said he fiercely.

" 'There needs no other language,' replied I, 'than her pale cheek and wasted form. You, who see her daily, cannot realize the change that has taken place; but I, who saw her last at N——, blooming, and happy, full of health and gayety, alive to all that was beautiful in creation—can I agree with you that you alone are the sufferer?' I found I had touched the chord to which his heart vibrated; I pursued the subject, and finally obtained the victory. He promised me solemnly to return in the course of a few weeks.

"It was with heartfelt pleasure I set about preparing for them. I had the old shattered mansion put into comfortable repair, and took a half a year's salary in pork, grain, and live stock, much to the satisfaction of my parishioners, who had rather pay in produce than money, and it was all cheerfully transferred to the desolate building. It was the last day of November when they arrived, and the snow lay three feet deep on the ground. The old trees that remained with their dry, straggling branches, stood on each side of the avenue like a procession of mourners. In winter there is but little for a farmer to do, except foddering his cattle and preparing for the coming spring. Mr. Forester had no stock or materials, and his life was an idle one. I could not but think Providence had wonderfully marked its bounty to the other sex, when I saw how cheerfully and constantly Mrs. Forester found employment. Her color and spirit returned, and again I heard her singing songs that seemed only made for summer.

"I have hitherto said but little of myself. I had dwindled into a kind of insignificance in my own mind, and was thought to be a confirmed old bachelor. Even my neighbor, Miss Keziah Spinney, no longer attempted to pour in the oil and the wine, but passed on to the other side. I confess, however, that I sometimes looked back with lingering regret on the years I had loitered away. I could count up to fifty-two. After twenty-five they were all dull, cheerless blanks except in the way of duty, and every faithful minister knows how many omissions must press upon his recollection. March had arrived, and we had reasonable expectations that the severity of the winter was over; but it did not prove so. There came a violent driving snowstorm, and I did not visit the Foresters for several days. At length I received a message from them requesting to see me. Mrs. Forester met me at the door. 'My husband,' said she, 'is very ill. Do you remember our visitor on the fifth anniversary of our marriage? Twice since he has come. God knows what malignant power he has over us; but it is terrible in its effects. Yesterday he came suddenly upon us; his visit was short, but immediately after his departure, my husband complained of great oppression upon the lungs, and this morning he has been seized with a hemorrhage. O my dear friend,' continued she, wringing my hand, 'go to him, tell him there is nothing he can reveal so dreadful as this suspense. I can endure it no longer; my reason will be the sacrifice.'

"I hastened to his apartment. He was in bed; his countenance was pale, but calm. 'I am glad you have come,' said he; 'I have a confession to make.' At that moment his wife entered. He called her to his bedside, and, as she knelt down, he looked earnestly at her, and his courage appeared to fail. But in a few moments he resumed. 'I had hoped that I might die with my secret unrevealed; but now that I believe myself on my death-bed, the judgment of my fellow-creatures loses its importance. And yet,' said he, turning to his wife, 'to voluntarily relinquish your esteem, to be remembered by you only with horror! O, if suffering could expiate guilt, these pangs would atone!'

"Never shall I forget the expression of her countenance, the noble, the sublime expression, as she leaned over him. 'My friend, my husband,' said she, 'fear nothing from me. Whatever may be the circumstances to which you allude, they cannot now influence my affection. The years we have passed together are all that identify you with me. Speak without hesitation.'

"'I will be brief,' said he, 'for my strength is failing. My early life was one of dissipation and profligacy. My father gave me all the opportunities of a good education, and a lucrative profession. He died, and left my mother destitute. I persuaded myself it was a duty to run all risks to place her in an independent situation. Frequently I returned from the gambling table, and poured money into her lap. The poor, deceived parent blessed and applauded me. I went through all the changes of a gamester, and at length found myself deeply in debt. A horrible chance presented—it was one of fraud and treachery. I purloined a sum entrusted to me—was detected!'—he seemed unable to proceed. 'I was sentenced to two years' imprisonment,' continued he, in a low voice. 'Though sunk and degraded, I was not lost. I loathed the vices that had undone me. I turned with horror from the profligacy by which I was surrounded. My conduct was such that the term of my imprisonment was shortened. I received a pardon. My poor mother had died broken-hearted. I quitted Havana; for this was the scene of my guilt and disgrace. At Richmond

I by degrees gained access to good society. I was persevering and industrious. You know, my dear Mary, how I became acquainted with you, and now you may perceive that when I married you, I added a new crime, that of deception, to my catalogue of sins. I truly loved you, and I could not resist temptation. My business was lucrative, everything around me prosperous, and if vice had left no sting, I might have been the happiest of mortals. But not all the rivers of Damascus, nor the waters of Jordan, can wash out the stains of the soul. I was haunted by remembrance of the past. There was something so unlike retributive justice in my prosperity, that I felt as if even this success portended some dreadful reverse. Fool that I was, not to perceive that the terror and anxiety that consumed my hours, was retributive justice! When I pressed her whom I loved best to my bosom, I thought what would become of her if she knew she was the wife of a felon!

" 'Such was the state of my mind while everybody congratulated me on my happiness. I was nominated for an office of trust. A few days after the election had taken place, I received a note requesting me to come to a particular place if I would avoid public disgrace. I went to the spot with a beating heart, and found, to my horror, a fellow convict! When I quitted the prison, I had left him there. He had stayed out his term, and accident brought him to Richmond. His object was to extort money. I gave him what he asked, as the bribe of secrecy. Again and again he came. My anxiety grew insupportable. Horrible thoughts crossed my mind. I sometimes felt that either he or I must be sacrificed. I gave up all but my wife and children, and left Richmond in hopes of concealment from my persecutor. The rest you know. As soon as I began to acquire credit and property, my tormentor appeared, and nearly stripped me. For three years, I lived on this spot unmolested; and I began to think he was dead. You know how, in the midst of apparent security and happiness, he came upon us. Twice he has visited me since. Yesterday he arrived. But Heaven is merciful. The disorder that for months has been undermining my life is brought to a crisis. With the near prospect of death, I have gained fortitude. I might say something in extenuation of my guilt. But why should I?—There is a Judge, and he is merciful.'

"Such was the unhappy man's story. He was mistaken in believing his end so near. He lingered on for months. His confession had rendered the scourge of his persecutor powerless. His decay was gradual, and he lived till June. His wife and myself were his constant attendants. He saw that her affection was undiminished; that it was the labor of love, and not of compassion, that bound her to his side. He died, trusting in divine mercy, and commending to my care his wife and children."

"And you have performed this dying injunction most faithfully, I doubt not," said I to the good man.

Again the color rose to his cheek. "I have," said he, "to the best of my power. At the end of two years, Mrs. Forester kindly consented to marry me. Her children are as dear to me as if they were my own." We had now entered the little village of N——. It was still flourishing in its native beauty. The green banks, with their footpaths, still bordered the carriage road, and clusters of dandelions, purple thistles, and mallows were scattered by the wayside with their former profusion. The low schoolhouse with its tall chimney stood where I left it. The paths that led through the pastures still remained the same. We were now near the parsonage house. I asked no questions, for I was willing to wait the development of circumstances. I was not much surprised when we turned up the avenue that led to the old-fashioned house.

"This is my residence," said the clergyman, "and I let out the parsonage." We stopped. The lady came to the door to meet us. She seemed to have gone along with all things else. Her hair, when I last saw her, was glossy and brown; it was now covered with a white muslin cap, and was parted upon her forehead in a matron-like manner.

I passed a few days with them, and took leave with the novel conclusion, that if there was any happiness in this world, it was to be found in a country village, where there were no "improvements," and at the house of a country minister.

MY WIFE'S NOVEL

I was descending the Ohio, in a steamboat, in the month of May, 1830, when the waters were rather low for the season. Just before reaching Island Number Thirty-Eight, better known as Blennerhassett's Island, our boat struck a snag, which broke a hole in her bow, and threatened her total destruction. The newspapers have made us so familiar with incidents of this kind, that I shall not take up the time of the reader in describing the scene. The boat's company and crew were of course thrown into considerable disorder, but we were near both to the bank of the river, and to the island, and no great alarm was felt after the first shock. Some of the passengers went in the boat to the Ohio side. I preferred being landed on the island, and exploring a spot, which the eloquence of Wirt and the residence of Blennerhassett have rendered classical. His tasteful mansion had been, some years before, wantonly destroyed by lawless vagrants, from pure love of mischief; and his grounds had relapsed into the wilderness, out of which he created them. After having gratified my curiosity in exploring these vestiges, I pursued my walk, without any definite occupation; but indulging, as I strolled along, the delightful consciousness of remoteness from the world and solitude. At length I perceived a plain, substantial house, such as is usually constructed by emigrants, bringing with them a little capital. Everything about it was plain, orderly, and comfortable in its appearance, and formed an agreeable contrast with the scene of cultivation returning to chaos, which I had just surveyed. I drew nearer the house, and perceived the master of it sitting under the portico, and beneath the shade of a noble oak tree. He rose at my approach and courteously bade me welcome. An arrival was too unusual an occurrence, in this retreat, not to excite immediate attention; and pretty soon the other members of the family were collected round us. They consisted of the wife of my host, and three or four good-looking children. In the lady's countenance I soon traced a deeper expression than is often met with in the faces of those whom we encounter in the common walks of life. It was the *emigrant's look*; not the beaming, energetic look of the emigrant in the morning of life, who goes forth, like the young Hercules, to subdue the hardships of the wilderness; but the look of one who has sought and found in a new country a refuge from the cares and vicissitudes, which have harassed existence in the old settlements. It was the look of anxiety relieved, and sorrow comforted. The curious student of human nature may see a great deal more, in that mingled expression, than in the aspect of any of the simpler moods of feeling, whether cheerful or sad.

The usual interchange of courtesies passed. Having spoken of my situation, and the probability that the boat would require a day or two to be repaired, I was kindly urged to be at home, with my new friends. This invitation I was well pleased to accept, for I had, from the first moment, felt rather an undefined interest in the family, in which I had accidentally become a visitor. After dinner my kind host, whose name was Azureton, proposed a walk upon the island, through the woods, which he had partly cleared up. Our familiarity increased as we strolled along, conversing together. Acquaintance runs hastily through many degrees in a situation like ours, and it was not long before I thought I could venture to ask Mr. Azureton to communicate to me those incidents in his history which had brought him to the retirement in which I found him. After a moment's pause, and looking round as if to be assured that we were not overheard, he said, in reply to my request, that he did not know but he might venture.

"Your appearance and conversation, Sir," said he, "are those of a gentleman. You will perceive, when I relate my history to you, that I throw myself, in some measure, into your hands; but there is something in your aspect tells me I may do so with safety."

Having assured him that he might rely implicitly on my discretion, we seated ourselves on the trunk of a tree recently felled, in a position where we enjoyed a delightful view of the Ohio, winding away among its verdant hills. Rafts of timber from Olean, hundreds of miles up the Allegheny, were floating down to New Orleans; even there to be broken up, and distributed along the Mexican shore. Keel-boats, flats, arks, and steamboats were following each other down the stream; and a tide of life seemed pouring forward, toward the western wilds, strong enough to animate their stillest recesses. Oh, the plans, the hopes, the recollections, the expectations; the affections vibrating between what was left behind, and what was looked forward to! But this is aside from our subject. Mr. Azureton collected himself a moment, and then began:—

"I was established in good business, in the profession of the law, not far from Boston. The destiny of man is contained in the short sentence of Scripture, 'It is not good for man to be alone.' I felt the truth of this doctrine; and in due time I looked round for a partner. I was fortunate enough to meet with a young lady, whose appearance, connections, character, and age were everything I could wish. She had received the education, usually obtained at the respectable boarding schools, in the part of the country where she was born. Her natural capacity was good. In early life, she had learned what is usually taught, at home by intelligent parents, and at the town schools; and at a later period, had completed her education at Mr. Plainstyle's Academy, in Enfield. There was nothing ambitious or eccentric in her character. She had witnessed, in her mother, the display of those solid qualities, which mark the frugal and exemplary housewife in New England. She was early taught that it was the province of the mistress of a family to look well to the ways of her household. My friends, on my engagement, congratulated me on the treasure I had found; and prophesied that I should be more than commonly happy in the married state.

"The temper and manners of my wife were everything I could wish. She was judicious, kind, and firm in her deportment toward the domestics (I wish that excellent word, 'help,' which contains a whole volume of social philosophy, had not been blighted by the ridicule of English travellers, sneering at a state of society of which they have not the faintest comprehension); attentive to the neighbors, affable to her inferiors, assiduous in the care of my friends who visited the house; in short, good-humored and cheerful. Alas, that I had been content with what Providence and a virtuous, unpretending education had made her! but, I thank Heaven, we have outlived the sufferings, which my own false view of things brought upon us. Man is an imperfect being; we never know when to be content with our lot; we never are content. Fool that I was, I took it into my wise head, that my wife was too exclusively domestic in her character. I thought that it would improve her to read the new publications, the leading periodicals, and even the newspapers, in which she rarely went beyond the marriages and deaths. I wanted her to take a little interest in the question of the comparative merits of Locke and Reid, of Stewart and Brown. I heard, one evening, a very animated discussion of the subject of the classic and romantic schools of poetry, between a gentleman, just returned from Europe, and an accomplished lady; in which I thought the lady had the advantage. I could not, on my return home, help expressing to my spouse the wish that she would make herself acquainted with the question between the classic and romantic schools.

"In order that she might not neglect nor delay the cultivation of her mind, for want of the requisite means of pursuing it, I supplied myself, to the extent of my ability, with books. I subscribed for the Edinburgh, Quarterly, Westminster, and the North American reviews (the American Quarterly, and the Southern, were not then published), besides taking the principal magazines of both hemispheres. Whenever I came to town, I entered my name at the Athenæum, for the new books from England, and took home with me as many of the novelties which I found on the counters of the booksellers as I could afford. In writing, as I did occasionally myself, for the literary journals, I used to read my articles to my wife; and I must do her the credit to say that she listened to them with invariable interest, and frequently expressed the opinion that what I had read to her was one of the cleverest things she ever heard. This showed me that her judgment was naturally sound. I cultivated the acquaintance of the literary men. I never failed to bring home to dinner any of the distinguished literary characters of the day, who visited our village; although, to tell the truth, they were not always the liveliest company. I was very active in getting up a lyceum; and by way of setting a good example, and promoting the great end which I had secretly in view, I delivered the introductory lecture myself, and chose for the subject The Cultivation of Female Intellect.

"It will easily be supposed that I did not fail to give to the education of my children such a turn as would contribute to forward my purpose. The first plaything the little creatures had put into their hands was a book; and I did not scruple to furnish them with some of the less valuable volumes on my shelves, to build their baby-houses with. For this purpose I let them freely have—but the specification would be invidious, and, after all, but a feeble attempt to imitate the inimitable scene in Don Quixote. As soon as my children were old enough to read, a new storybook was the reward for every act of obedience; and when, on Wednesday and Saturday afternoons, the little things, oppressed with the burden of a vacant hour, would hang imploringly about me, and ask, 'what *should* they do?' the answer commonly was, 'Had you not better take a book, my child?' I made a pretty strong push to have our fourth daughter named Corinna, in honor of the greatest female authoress of the age; but her mother's aunt Jerusha expressed a wish that her own name might be selected; and of course I yielded. My oldest girl having brought me home a very pretty exercise in composition, in the form of a tale, I gave her on the spot a quarter of a dollar, as a reward; and took down Lempriere's biographical dictionary, and read her the notice of the illustrious Maria Schurmann, 'who not only excelled in music, painting, sculpture, and engraving, but in the knowledge of the Greek, Hebrew, Syriac, and Arabic, as well as the modern tongues.'

"I was pleased to observe the success of my efforts. My wife gradually assumed the literary tone of the house. Breathing, as it were, a bookish atmosphere, she became fonder and fonder of reading. She did not neglect her household; but she insensibly sewed less and read more. She listened evidently with greater satisfaction to the conversation of the literary men whom I took every opportunity of bringing to the house. She frequently herself threw in a remark on the last new publication. Sometimes she adventured a verbal criticism on my own compositions, which I showed her in manuscript. To encourage her I generally adopted her suggestions,—though, to tell the truth, I commonly thought it stood as well as it was. It was not very long before she produced herself an article for one of the annuals. I own it took me by surprise, and I was at some loss whether to advise its being sent for publication. It did not seem to me of a merit sufficiently decided to command brilliant success; nor had I as yet, in all my zeal to give my wife a literary taste, positively made up my mind that I wished her to become a writer. I could not, however, well discourage her *coup d'essai;* and I accordingly approved its publication. It was entitled The Characteristics of Female Mind; and, after all, made a very respectable appearance in print. Several of the newspapers awarded it the palm in the Anodyne for 1824, the annual in which it appeared. After this auspicious beginning, my wife made several similar attempts, more or less elaborate, in the following years, and, upon the whole, with very considerable success. Her style gradually formed itself, and she attained no small proficiency in the art which forms so important a part in the mystery of fine writing,—that of expanding a leading thought through several pages, in order that the reader may fully comprehend it.

"All at once, 'a change came o'er the spirit of my wife,'—a change which baffled my penetration. She showed the same love of literature, the same fondness for books; and, though she continued the same excellent housewife she had ever been, she was more than ever economical of the odd intervals of time. She never wasted a moment; proposed no parties of pleasure; sat up late, and rose betimes. There was an expression of thought in her countenance, beyond its wonted serenity,—an expression not only of intellectual action, but of moral purpose. All this seemed the stranger to me, because the season passed by, and my wife said nothing of a contribution to any of the annuals, which was hitherto about the only thing she had attempted, in the way of writing for the press.

" 'What will Mr. Poppystalk say, my dear,' I observed to her one day, 'if you send him nothing for this year's Anodyne?'

" 'Do you think he will be greatly disappointed, my love?' was her answer. 'Well, if *he* is disappointed, *you* shall not be,' she continued, with an air of mingled archness and conscious purpose, which I could not fathom.

"It is said that Dr. Burney, the father of Madame d'Arblay, to prevent that lady, while still quite young, from reading novels, for which he thought she showed an undue fondness, locked her up in her chamber. At the end of three months his dutiful daughter presented him with a copy of Evelina, which she had herself written, and procured to be printed, during her confinement. It was with something of the good doctor's surprise on that occasion that I received from my wife, at the end of about six months after the change in her manner which I have noticed, a clever-sized manuscript, which she handed me one morning, triumphantly, as a novel that she had been writing! It was entitled the Pleasures of Sentiment. The original misgiving with which my wife's first effort at composition affected me returned on me with renewed force. I felt the magnitude of the undertaking, the uncertainty of success. I remembered Madame de Staël's remark, in the preface to Delphine, on the small number of writers who had succeeded in the novel; which, when executed as it ought to be, I consider above a tragedy, and next to an epic poem. Common politeness, however, dictated to me to suppress these feelings as much as possible. I took the manuscript from my wife's hand, with a look in which I threw as much pleasure as I could; and which I own was a little checked by her saying, with a flush of eager resolution:—

" 'This very evening, dear husband, I shall begin The Forlorn Wanderer; or, The Mysterious Orphan. I have already sketched the plan.'

" 'Shall we not rather, my dear,' said I, 'devote the evening to reading this manuscript? You know I have never seen it before.' And to this Lucinda—for that was her name—readily assented.

"On reading the Pleasures of Sentiment, I can with truth say that I thought my wife had acquitted herself very tolerably. It was as good as I should have expected. The story was pretty ingeniously contrived, and well told; the language correct; the style a very decent imitation of my own; the moral unexceptionable. The great defect in the book, no doubt, was its want of interest. Candor obliges me to admit that it was rather dull. I am not sure whether I should have read it, had it been written by any person but my wife. What the particular difficulty about it was I could not exactly make out. It seemed to be all *first chapter*. There was no getting interested in it. The reader went on, page after page, expecting to find something that would pique his curiosity; but there was nothing that had that effect. It was a kind of mental treadmill, always stepping up, and even getting on in the story, but never rising into interest. You felt the disappointment which you do in going downstairs in the dark; when, at the bottom of the staircase, you make a motion for another step, where there is no other. Still there seemed nothing in the world to object to the novel; and I saw, by numerous indications, that my wife had determined to have it printed. Her views were not confined even to the applause she expected to receive for it. She asked me significantly, one day, whether I knew how many thousand pounds Sir Walter Scott received for one of the Waverley Novels.

"Three thousand, I replied, had been stated to be the amount.

" 'Three thousand pounds it was, my dear,' she pursued; 'fifteen thousand dollars, I believe, in our money. If the Pleasures of Sentiment is only one tenth as successful,—and that, I think,' said she, 'is not a very extravagant calculation,—we may promise ourselves fifteen hundred dollars from your wife's novel. No bad thing that, dear husband, is it?'

"A negotiation was soon entered into with Messrs. Frisket & Narrowform, respectable publishers at Boston, to print my wife's novel. The terms of the contract were such as we could not complain of, as they were designed to secure to us the entire profits of the work. Messrs. Frisket & Narrowform were to do the printing at the usual prices; sell the books at a fair commission; and all the profits were to be ours. Nothing was said of making up any deficiency, should the sales not cover the expense; for, to tell the truth, that certainly never crossed my wife's imagination, nor, I must own, mine. We neither of us were very conversant with the business of book-making, and our thoughts ran rather too much on Sir Walter's three thousand pounds.

"It would take too long to describe the state of my wife's mind, and, I may as well confess it, of her husband's too, during the progress of the publication. The proof sheets were sent us by Frisket & Narrowform, for I was determined the work should be correct. I ordered it done on a seven-dollar paper, and an English type, leaded, in order to make a fair, legible page, and such as could be read without pain by aged people. In this way the work was swelled to two sizable volumes. We hesitated as to the number which should be struck off. My wife named five thousand copies, understanding that ten thousand copies of Ivanhoe had been sold the first day. But as Messrs. Frisket & Narrowform stipulated for an advance, to pay for the seven-dollar paper, and the sum required for this purpose was not small, we concluded to limit the first edition to twelve hundred. I reconciled my wife to this arrangement, by reminding her that we could make the second edition as large as we pleased, as there would be the profits of the first to go on with.

"At length, on the first of November, 1825, my wife's novel appeared. The newspapers of the day announced the publication of the 'Pleasures of Sentiment, a novel, in two volumes, by Mrs. Lucinda Azureton.' A couple of dozen copies were ordered home, handsomely bound, as presents, one of which was given to each member of the family, old and young; for my wife was resolved to make a holiday of it, and thought it hard if each of her children could not have a copy of her first novel. My mind, I own, was not fully at ease about this expression, *first*. I knew The Mysterious Orphan was in progress; and Frisket & Narrowform had written me rather an obscure letter, speaking of the slowness with which sales of all books were effected, and dropping a hint that they should expect my note for the expenses of printing the Pleasures of Sentiment, a sum but little short of fifteen hundred dollars.

"After the bustle produced in the family by this occurrence was a little over, we began to bestow some attention on the reception the novel met with in the world. I took the Wachusett Universal Intelligencer, which was the newspaper nearest our residence, but saw nothing in its columns relative to my wife's novel. 'These country papers,' my wife exclaimed, 'really know nothing of what is going on in the world! Do, my dear, subscribe for the Boston Repository of Politics, Commerce, Literature, and the Fine Arts, that we may emerge a little into the light.' I accordingly remitted eight dollars by mail for the Repository, for my wife was not content with anything less than the daily paper. 'Now,' said she, 'we shall know what they say in town of the Pleasures of Sentiment.' Day after day the Repository came, but no notice of the novel. 'It is provoking,' cried my wife, at the end of the week, 'to see how these Boston editors are engrossed with politics, railroads, foreign news, and advertisments! Thank Heaven, the Reviews are devoted to literature.'

"This consideration reconciled us to wait till the end of the quarter. Meantime a copy of the novel was sent to the editors of each of the Reviews. The first of January came, and my wife sent a man in the sleigh to town, to get the North American. The man froze his face in a northeast storm, and nearly perished in a snowdrift; but we got the book a fortnight before it would have reached us. My wife went out into the kitchen, and took it herself from Thomas, and ran over the table of contents. There was no review of the Pleasures of Sentiment. There was an undisguised air of discontent in the tone with which she hummed over the list of articles,—Hebrew Poetry, Origin of the French Language, American System, Hieroglyphics. 'I must say, husband,' she exclaimed, 'I think the North American is rather falling off. However,' added she, 'there is the American Quarterly just started, quite able to take its place; do, husband, subscribe for the Quarterly.' I accordingly wrote on and ordered the Quarterly. In about six weeks the newspapers contained a notice, by anticipation, of the contents of the forthcoming number of the American Quarterly, and there was nothing on the Pleasures of Sentiment in the catalogue. 'Husband,' said my wife to me, as she threw the paper down, 'you did not subscribe for the Quarterly the other day, did you? It is hardly worth while, I think. These reviewers really seem to think the world cares for nothing but voyages and travels, political economy and finance.'

"In a word, for some cause or other, not the least notice was taken of my wife's novel in any of the leading periodicals of the day, and we became at last weary of looking forward with expectation. At the end of four months Messrs. Frisket & Narrowform wrote to me, informing me that they had sold but three copies of the work, and that they could not wait any longer for the large sum they had expended in the publication, which, agreeably to the contract, they required me to reimburse them. I had to sell three shares in the Grand Crash Manufacturing Company to meet this demand. The shares were seven hundred dollars at par. I had bought in at a moment of great activity in manufactures, and had got my shares of a friend, as a great favor, at a thousand dollars apiece. The stock happened to be down when I was obliged to sell, and I was glad to get five hundred dollars apiece for what had cost me a thousand. The publication of my wife's novel, accordingly, stood me in about three thousand dollars.

"It is a curious thing how much our opinion even of ourselves depends on the opinions of others of us. I suppose, when my wife first finished her novel, she felt herself but little, if anything, inferior to Scott or Cooper, Edgeworth or Sedgwick. But when she noticed the steady silence of the newspapers, the magazines, and the reviews, her opinion of the merits of her book was shaken. The tidings that but three copies had been sold in four months confirmed the growing doubt of its merit; and when she learned that instead of the fifteen hundred dollars which we had promised ourselves, it bid fair to cause us a loss of twice that magnitude, and that I had been obliged to sell my shares in the Grand Crash Manufacturing Company to meet the publishers' demand, her doubts changed to conviction, and her feelings for her own novel, from those of the fondest partiality, turned into a mingled sentiment of contempt and hatred. She could not bear to hear it named.

"A short time after I had paid the bill of Frisket & Narrowform, and while my wife's mind was thus embittered toward her first intellectual offspring, she took up the newspaper, and was casting her eye over the advertisement of one of the book auctions; and there, amidst a mass of the most melancholy trash ever swept from the shelves of a bookseller retiring from trade, was a copy of the Pleasures of Sentiment; one of the three, no doubt, which had been bought of the booksellers, and was already sent to auction. This incident affected her very unpleasantly.

"Determined, however, not to yield too readily to what might, after all, be a caprice of the public taste, I wrote to Frisket & Narrowform, without the knowledge of my wife, directing them to send the books, on commission, to the booksellers in New England, in quantities proportioned to the size of the towns where they were established. In this way they were scattered throughout the country, and I flattered myself that public attention would thereby be awakened to them. A week or two after this manœuvre, I received the account of Frisket & Narrowform for the expense of forwarding the various boxes and parcels containing the work; the booksellers in the interior having required that it should be transmitted to them free of expense. This bill amounted to eighty-three dollars. It accidentally fell under my wife's eye; she required an explanation of it, and I was obliged to give her one. I told her what I had done.

"This incident quite overturned the little equanimity with which my wife regarded her novel. She had made up her own mind that it was worthless; that it did not merit notice; that it deserved the obscurity to which it had sunk. In this view the silence of the papers and reviews was rather grateful to her. It was less grating than their faint praise or severe censure. She had not asked herself what was to become of the copies of the work on hand; and, in fact, had studiously averted her thoughts from all consideration of the subject. When she found, then, that by my well-meant officiousness it had been scattered through the country; that Mrs. Azureton's Pleasures of Sentiment was advertising in all the newspapers of New England, from the Ousatonic Emporium to the Passamaquoddy Central Enquirer, the cup of her affliction was full to overflowing, and she burst into tears. Her annoyance was not a little increased by reflecting that I had paid eighty-three dollars, in addition to my three thousand, for this judicious operation.

"At the time of ordering the distribution of the work in the manner mentioned, Frisket & Narrowform wrote me that one of the country traders had offered to purchase twenty-five copies outright, at a reduced price; and that they themselves could also dispose of fifty copies in town, if I could let them go quite cheap. I asked no questions about the price, but ordered them sold for the most they would bring. The country bookseller, as I afterwards learned, allowed four cents a volume for his twenty-five sets, and the fifty copies sold in town brought three dollars for the lot. These two sales, yielding but five dollars in the whole, were a source of great mischief to us. I had reason to rue the day when I gave my consent to them.

"The country trader intended, it seems, to send them round the villages in Massachusetts by a peddler. Late in a warm afternoon of July, we saw a wayworn chapman, with a large box held by straps over his shoulders, staggering towards our door. He was evidently oppressed with the heat of the day and the burden he was carrying. He asked permission to deposit his load on the doorstep, which was freely granted him, and a cup of beer was added, unasked, for his refreshment. The heart of the peddler warmed at this kind treatment; and as my wife approached him, herself, with the foaming glass in her hand, he told her that though he could not reward her with silver or gold, he would give her a nice new book from his box. My wife replied that 'he was welcome to the beer; and that she could not think of robbing him of his book, but perhaps she would buy one.'

" 'Nay, no robbery,' rejoined the peddler; 'but take it in welcome, and thank you to boot, for lightening my burden. It costs but a shilling, and if Mr. Scatterstuff, who employs me, is not satisfied, I will pay him for it myself, if it is only to say that I have sold one copy. Here I have been dragging the box about, nine whole days in July, up and down the Connecticut River, and not one copy have I been able to get rid of. Here, my lady,' said he, 'take a copy, and much good may it do you.'

"The family had by this time collected around the peddler and his chest; we were all straining forward to behold its contents. He raised the cover: the chest was filled with the Pleasures of Sentiment! That moment, I must confess, was one of the most awkward in my life. But the mortifications to which this unfortunate book was destined to reduce us were not yet at an end.

"My oldest boy had reached the age of eleven years. I am myself in favor of domestic education, and would prefer that every night my little flock should be safely folded beneath the paternal roof. There are, however, unquestionable advantages incident to a removal from home; and the disposition of Gustavus (that was his name) seemed to me such as would derive benefit from the rough and tumble of an academy, among boys of his own age. It was accordingly decided in family council that he should be sent to the academy at Templeton to prepare for college. Neighbor Edgebone, the butcher, was commissioned to purchase a trunk in the city, for his clothes and books, and all preparations were made for his departure. My wife, as her parting injunction, cautioned him against reading novels, a miserable, unprofitable sort of books. At length the eve of his departure arrived, and Mrs. Azureton engaged herself in the final preparations for his journey. For this purpose she left the parlor to pack his trunk, in season for the morning stage. As his stock of clothes and books was small, this was a task soon to be performed; but my wife did not come back to the parlor. After waiting much longer than was necessary for the performance of this duty, my anxiety was awakened, and I could not avoid going to inquire into the cause of her prolonged absence. I hastened to the chamber where I supposed her to be engaged in packing the trunk, and beheld her, to my great alarm and astonishment, stretched senseless on the floor in front of the open trunk. I flew to her relief, equally shocked at the situation in which I found her, and at a loss to conceive the cause. I stooped to raise her, and in so doing cast my eyes accidentally upon the inside of the open trunk. The mystery was explained; the cause of my wife's fainting was solved. The trunk-maker had lined the trunk with the sheets of the Pleasures of Sentiment; and was, in fact, the purchaser of the fifty copies which had been sold in a lot,—sold to a trunk-maker for the lining of his trunks!

"It was several days before my wife recovered her senses. She passed the time in a state intermediate between lethargy and delirium. She wandered in mind, and talked incoherently. She spoke of the trunk in which the Italian bride had accidentally shut herself on her bridal night, and was not found till years after her mysterious disappearance. The trunk in The Mysteries of Udolpho seemed to be in her mind. She was pursued with the idea of trunks and linings; and at times would repeat, 'The Pleasures—ah no! the Pains of Sentiment!' At length she recovered the exercise of her understanding, and talked calmly and rationally of the causes of her distress. She made no effort to palliate the cause nor the degree of her mortification. She traced it to its true and only source, the failure of the book, and declared that if every copy of it could be annihilated she could live in resignation and die in peace. But if her nerves were much longer to be exposed to these shocks, she felt an undoubted persuasion that her days were numbered. Nor did the thought alarm her, for she had rather die at once than live at the mercy of the peddlers and trunk-makers.

"I loved my wife tenderly; and on this occasion I felt the greater sympathy in her sufferings, for I regarded myself as, in no small degree, their unintentional cause. I had perseveringly formed her to the taste, in the gratification of which she was placed in her present distressing situation. I determined, accordingly, to leave no stone unturned for her relief. She had expressed her earnest conviction that nothing but the utter suppression of her work would give her peace; and, thinking no sacrifice too great to effect this object, I determined to set about it. I felt the rather encouraged in this purpose, as the little demand there appeared to be for my wife's novel led me to suppose the copies could all be bought up for a moderate sum.

"I accordingly went to work in good earnest. I determined to take a journey myself through the principal towns in New England; and where it was not convenient to go in person, I wrote to such friends as I could trust, to aid me in an operation of this delicate character. It will easily be understood that, as well from tenderness to my wife's feelings as my own, I proceeded about the business with the greatest caution and prudence. My object was to buy up all the copies of the Pleasures of Sentiment and destroy them; but I wished, on every ground, that it should not be known that I was thus occupied. I commenced my operations with a bookseller who had but three copies on hand. With the keen eye of the trade, he perceived that I had some particular motive and was very desirous of possessing the book. I inquired the price. It was a dollar per volume. 'Was not that dear?' I asked.

" 'Dear!' he exclaimed. 'Why, sir, look at the type; the paper seven dollars a ream, I have not a doubt. Besides, sir, it is a production of Mrs. Azureton, a lady of the highest literary eminence. It is her first work, but it is reported that she has another in preparation. You will find it for your convenience to take them as they come out.'

"I was ready to execrate the man's fluency; but I was too well able to bear witness to the truth of his statement relative to the cost of the work, and I own I was flattered by his respectful allusion to my wife's name. I took the three copies, on his abating two and a half per cent for cash payment.

"In this way I proceeded through the towns, while my friends and agents in all quarters, with the greatest secrecy and caution, were doing the same. We bought up the books wherever we found them. We were compelled, from the first, almost always to pay the full retail price; but I comforted myself that the edition was small, and that there would before long be an end of it. I had a few more shares in the Grand Crash Manufacturing Company, and was quite willing to devote them to effecting an object on which my wife's peace of mind and even life seemed to depend. I was a little vexed, I must own, at what, however, was a natural consequence of the mode in which I conducted the operation. The booksellers, finding themselves, and hearing from all quarters, that there was a sudden but general and steady demand for the Pleasures of Sentiment, raised the price, as by universal consent, to a dollar and a half, and at length two dollars a volume. This, of course, materially increased the expense of the suppression, and obliged me besides to sell my shares in the Plum Island and Squam Navigation Company. This was a stock which, however promising, was difficult to turn into cash at par. In fact, I sold it at eighty-seven per cent discount, realizing but about thirteen dollars on a hundred of my stock. As, however, it had never given a dividend, and as assessments were pretty frequently called for, I did not much regret to part with it.

"At length I succeeded in purchasing up the edition. With the exception of a few straggling copies I got them all into my possession. As it was my wife's wish that they should be destroyed, I would gladly have turned them to some economical account, and used them as fuel in the family; thus imitating the example of Omar, who heated the baths of his Saracen host for six months with the parchments of the Alexandrian Library. I was desirous, however, of avoiding the publicity of any such proceeding, which could not but be known to my children, domestics, and neighbors, besides harassing my wife's feelings. I accordingly had them stowed away in the loft of a ruinous outhouse, which stood isolated on my farm, resolving to watch the opportunity, when the wind blew in a direction opposite from the dwelling house, and privately set fire to it myself. But it was in the book of fate that these precautions should be unavailing.

"Scarcely had I begun to rest from the labor of collecting the books, when I learned, to my consternation, that two booksellers, at first without knowing each other's project, but afterwards in rivalry, were actually employed in striking off two new editions of the Pleasures of Sentiment. They had witnessed a sudden and rapid demand for the work. It had been in request everywhere. The town and country seemed equally eager of it. Their own copies had been sold; the neighboring booksellers had witnessed the like surprising demand; not a copy was to be had; the price had risen; the edition was exhausted. The measures which I had taken to prevent my agency in the suppression from being traced misled the booksellers as to the cause of the rapid demand. They ascribed it to the popularity of the work, which went off more rapidly than anything since the last Waverley Novel. I had neglected to take out a copyright. I was not conversant with publishing books myself, and Frisket & Narrowform, doubtless foreseeing the reception the book was likely to meet, did not think it worth while to advise this precaution against a reprint. It was therefore out of my power to interfere and stop the booksellers, who were preparing again to inundate New England with my wife's ill-starred novel. What were my feelings on reading on one and the same day, in the Naushaun General Advertiser and the Baker's Island Hemisphere, that new and revised editions were preparing of 'that admired and popular novel, the Pleasures of Sentiment, by Mrs. Azureton.' It was stated by one of these merciless creatures, that a large impression of the first edition had been taken off with unprecedented rapidity; and by the other, that it was understood to be the first of a series of productions, with which the fair and accomplished authoress intended to favor the American public.

"The conjuncture was full of embarrassment and difficulty. The idea of allowing the editions to proceed was a very painful one. I well knew that it would have no other effect than to send my wife's novel into every auction room, peddler's cart, trunk-maker's shop, and pastry cook's kitchen in New England. It would become dangerous for us to buy a pound of tea, for fear it should come home wrapped up in the sheets of this unlucky work; and the sight of a boy's kite would carry terror to us, when we thought of the materials out of which it would in great likelihood be constructed. In the bitterness of my spirit I began a lecture, for the next Lyceum, in which I intended to investigate the truth of the tradition that Dr. Faustus was helped to the invention of the art of printing by the devil. Something, however, was to be done; and I finally concluded that there was no possibility of averting the impending calamity except by going to the booksellers and frankly stating to them the manner in which the first edition had been taken up. I took with me an affidavit of Frisket & Narrowform, attesting the fact that three copies only had been sold in the regular course of trade, and seventy-five others disposed of as above mentioned. Fortified with this document, I called upon the booksellers, frankly made known to them the facts of the case, and urged the consequent inexpediency of their proceeding with their rival editions of a novel of which it was not possible that a single copy would sell. They were at first struck with the reasonableness of my representation; but, so merciless a thing is self-interest, it pretty soon occurred to these cruel men that the same motives which had prompted me to suppress one edition would lead me to buy up another; in short, that they had me in their power. They immediately began to hesitate, demur, to talk of their outlay. One had purchased a new font of type; another, seeing the beauty of the paper on which the first edition was printed (confound it), had ordered from Mr. Flimsyrag a seven-dollar paper expressly for the work; and, in short, their names had gone before the world pledged to the publication, and they scarce knew how to recede. At the same time, however, they said they were willing to do everything that was right and proper.

"I felt my case to be really a hard one. I was struggling more zealously to prevent my wife's book from being printed than ever the most self-satisfied author did to get a production before the public, and the more I exerted myself, the farther I seemed from the point. The emergency, however, was not to be trifled with. I knew well the publication of another edition of her novel would be the death of my wife. I had three shares left in the Grand Crash Manufacturing Company, and I asked the hard-hearted wretches what they would take not to go on. After humming and hawing a reasonable time, they finally agreed to take five hundred dollars each, and give up the enterprise. I knew it was more money than the dogs ever made in any year of their business; but I was glad to get out of their clutches, and closed the bargain. Grand Crash stock was rather lower than before; and my three shares brought me altogether just a thousand dollars. I divided it between them, and went off; not without being obliged to promise them (and I am not clear that they were not quizzing me, as they exacted my word to that effect), that if my wife published another novel, they should have the job. To make sure of their abandoning the undertaking, I obliged them to issue a joint notice in the newspapers, that 'they had relinquished the project of their new editions of the Pleasures of Sentiment.'

"This very notice, by which I thought to clinch the nail on their bargain, was but the occasion of driving me into new and unexpected trouble. I returned home, and having, as I thought, destroyed the hydra, I communicated the transaction, in all its stages, to my wife. She was gratified at my attention and zeal, but listened with a sort of incredulous melancholy, looking as if she feared that the malice of Fortune was not yet appeased. Nor did the event disappoint her forebodings. A few weeks after my return, on opening the newspaper, I was struck with horror at the following advertisement, inserted in the most conspicuous manner, and ordered for *epis 1 year:*—

NEW AND UNIFORM EDITION OF THE AMERICAN FEMALE NOVELISTS

Messrs. Silvertype, Vellumpage, Flauntwell, Fairtrash & Brown have the honor to announce to the friends of American literature in general, and more particularly to the admirers of female excellence, that they have made arrangements for the publication of a new uniform edition, in a continuous series, of the productions of the American Female Novelists. The work will be printed on a first-rate paper, with a new type cast expressly for this publication. It will be illustrated with engravings made for the purpose, by our most eminent artists. The series will commence with that highly popular work, the Pleasures of Sentiment, by Mrs. Lucinda Azureton. The rapidity with which the first edition of this favorite production has been exhausted, and the simultaneous annunciation of rival editions by two distinguished booksellers, who, from the difficulty of reconciling their conflicting claims, appear to have relinquished the enterprise, have decided Messrs. Silvertype, Vellumpage, Flauntwell, Fairtrash & Brown to select this work for the first of their series. Not doubting its popularity, they have resolved to print a very large edition, and shall consequently have it in their power to put it at a price which will enable every lover of female intellect to possess himself of this invaluable work. Messrs. S., V., F., F. & B. solicit the early orders of their friends and the trade.

Note. The Pleasures of Sentiment will be preceded by a biographical account of the fair authoress, accompanied with a critical essay on her genius and style. This portion of the enterprise will be conducted by Dr. Worrywell, who will immediately proceed to the residence of Mrs. Azureton, to ascertain from authentic sources the leading incidents of her life, and the circumstances connected with the origin and progress of her literary career. Messrs. Silvertype, Vellumpage, Flauntwell, Fairtrash & Brown feel assured that the result of his inquiries will present those encouragements and cheering examples to the ingenious fair of our country, which will prompt them in numbers to enter the noble career which has conducted the fair authoress of the Pleasures of Sentiment to the enviable reputation which she now enjoys.

"Such was this terrific advertisement; and scarcely had I finished reading it when the mail stagecoach stopped at the door. A considerable bustle immediately arose. A short, corpulent gentleman, dressed in black, jumped out of the stage, and began, with great volubility, to give his orders about the baggage. Two large travelling trunks, a box apparently containing a portable desk, a cloak bag, ivory-headed cane, umbrella, hat case, a large shaggy dog, and a fiddle case were successively unladen from the vehicle, which immediately drove off, leaving this fearful deposit at my door. The bustling man in black approached, holding his card in his hand, which he thrust, with a self-satisfied air, into mine, and which announced him to be Dr. Allbore Worrywell.

" 'The papers, I fancy, sir,' said he, with a brazen self-complacency, 'will have prepared you for this visit and made known to you my errand. You see, from my baggage, that I have come resolved to take ample time to do full justice to the noble theme which has been confided to me by Messrs. Silvertype, Vellumpage, Flauntwell, Fairtrash & Brown. Sir, your situation here is delightful,—fine prospect, sir, in the distance; woods in the background; spacious lawn; salubrious air; really, Mr. Azureton, I should not be sorry to make a season's job of it. But, sure enough,' continued the wretch, spying my man Arthur at a distance, 'sure enough, John,' said he to Arthur, 'you are coming to take in my little baggage. I had forgot my things were, all this time, in the road. Mr. Azureton, tell John what room to take my trunk to.'

"The volubility, the attic impertinence, the unexampled audacity of the creature really petrified me. My faculties were for a moment suspended; and, when Reason resumed her seat, the first thought that struck me was the effect which the Visigoth's presence, or his avowed errand, would have on Mrs. Azureton's nerves. I was casting about in my mind how I could get him off, or get my wife and myself out of his reach, when a shriek from the room where I had left her recalled me to myself. The newspaper, the fatal advertisement which it contained! My wife, while I was at the door, had taken it up; her eye had caught the withering proposals, and, uttering one piercing shriek, she swooned. I hastened into the house; the proper restoratives were applied, but she returned to herself only to fall into paroxysms of agitation and terror. For several days she continued in this state, the only alleviation of which was that, by confining her to her chamber, it enabled me to keep Dr. Worrywell away from her. I dropped several hints to him that, in the present state of Mrs. Azureton's health, it was inconvenient to entertain a visitor. The remorseless pedant affected to think I spoke only out of reluctance to detain him at my house at the sacrifice of his time; and he asseverated that, 'rather than endanger Mrs. Azureton's health by calling upon her prematurely for the mental effort, which he hoped eventually she would condescend to make, for the purpose of aiding him in his pleasing task, he would rather make an entire vacation of it at my charming retreat; or, even,' added he, 'commence the execution of another literary project which I have in hand,—the secret history of the Celestial Empire, comprehending personal anecdotes of the sovereigns of China, from the Emperor Fo-hi to the present moment, a period of ten thousand years, in forty-five volumes, folio.'

"Seeing that there was no hope of getting rid of my tormentor, and well aware that the first flash upon my wife's mind of his name and errand would be her instant death; persuaded, too, that even could I shake off this incubus, some other disaster connected with our standing trial would befall us, I made up my mind to emigrate to the Western Country. My wife, sunk into a state of stupor and inaction, was seldom in a condition to converse upon business. I acquainted her privately with my purpose. I spoke of her health as the motive, with a view to change of air, and alluded to the opening afforded the rising generation in the Western Country as an inducement to take our children to that region. She languidly assented. I do not know whether she penetrated the real reasons that influenced me. I succeeded in disposing of my house, furniture, and land (at a great sacrifice, I confess), to a friend, who agreed to take them off my hands. I observed the profoundest secrecy, for I feared that if Dr. Worrywell got wind of my project he would fasten himself on me for the journey. I gradually packed up, and sent off to Providence the few articles which I proposed to take with me. When I had made all my preparations, I took my wife and children with me to town, without giving the Doctor any reason to suspect that we proposed anything more than a day's visit. I left him delving into the scandalous chronicle of the ninety-ninth dynasty of the Ante-Tartarian Emperors of China. I had already made arrangements for disposing of my carriage in Boston, and had nothing to do but to take the stage to Providence, and thence, by the usual route, to the banks of the Ohio. Our journey was uncommonly prosperous: the steamboat, in which we took passage in the Sound, was run afoul of and sunk, but we escaped with our lives and baggage; and I had the good fortune to get two of my children down from the roof of a canal boat near Lockport, just as we grazed under a bridge, leaving an unlucky Frenchman, who did not understand the cry, behind us in the canal. On our way from Buffalo to Cleveland, on an alarm of fire, a few persons jumped into the lake, on hearing the cry of *Gunpowder aboard!* but before I could get up the cabin stairs, I was assured by the captain that the casks contained nothing but cut nails. This prevented my jumping overboard, but on reaching Cleveland I found they were filled with gunpowder nevertheless. However, the fire was extinguished in season, which I may truly call fortunate.

"On landing at Cleveland, one of the first persons I saw was the editor of the Cuyahoga Ararat; or, Indiscriminate Investigator. He was an emigrant from the North, an old neighbor and acquaintance of mine. He had come down to the landing to collect news from the steamboat. Never shall I forget the terror with which the sight of him at a distance inspired me. I saw already, in my mind's eye, in the next number of the Ararat, the annunciation of my poor wife's arrival, as the authoress of the Pleasures of Sentiment. Happily, however, Lowercase (that was his name) did not recognize me. I saw by this indication that time and care must have dealt roughly upon me. I was in truth sadly changed. Lowercase, as he passed me, looked hardly at me; but I put on a most *unknowing* air, and finally escaped him.

"After this I began to breathe the free air of the West. I crossed the State of Ohio, without further molestation from editors, publishers, biographers, and advertisements. My wife gradually recovered her health and spirits. I confess that I felt no little satisfaction in hearing, by letter, from the friend who had purchased my house, of the astonishment and vexation of Dr. Worrywell, on finding that I did not return. I had taken my measures so well, that my entire establishment was broken up and brought to a close the day on which I left the house. Like a faithful captain of a shipwrecked vessel, I was the last to leave it; and yet Dr. Worrywell did not suspect what was going on. The poor man was bewildered enough, when the hour of the evening repast came (the eating hours were all pretty closely watched by the Doctor), and no family nor preparation for supper appeared. A charitable cup of tea at a neighbor's carried him through the evening; and early the next morning my friend who had purchased the house arrived and took possession. Dr. Worrywell, as soon as he learned from this gentleman the present state of things, inquired whether he or his lady had appeared before the world as an author, and volunteered his services for a biography of one or both of them. But there was a shade of significance in the manner with which my friend flourished his horsewhip, and the Doctor thought it prudent to send word to the tavern for the stage to call and take him up. The report which he carried back to Messrs. Silvertype, Vellumpage, Flauntwell, Fairtrash & Brown probably induced those gentlemen to make such farther inquiries into the popularity of the Pleasures of Sentiment as led them, as far as that work was concerned, to abandon their project.

"Having reached the banks of *the beautiful river,* I took my passage on board a boat which was descending, resolved to be guided by my eye and my taste in selecting a secluded spot upon its shores, or on one of its islands, for the place of my retreat. Accident led me to this quiet residence, where we have passed a couple of years in retirement, tranquillity, and peace. My wife is fast recovering her cheerfulness, and divides with me the care of educating our children. The literary taste, which I took injudicious pains to strengthen in her, chastened of that extravagance to which I urged it, now performs its appropriate office, and furnishes resources for the amusement of herself and family. Books now entertain and instruct, without absorbing and engrossing us. Literature is the sauce, and not the food, of our mental system. The great active duties of life are our first care; and we read for relaxation, in the intervals of their performance. Thus occupied, contentment presides in our little circle; and so kindly has Time discharged his office as the great consoler, that we are able now to allude, without embarrassment or pain, to My Wife's Novel."

THE BALD EAGLE

"I'll have you chronicled, and chronicled, and cut and chronicled, and sung in all-to-be-praised sonnets, and grav'd in new brave ballads, that all tongues shall troule you in Sæcula Sæculorum."—OLD COMEDY.

In one of the little villages sprinkled along the delicious valley of the Connecticut, there stood, not many years ago, a little tavern called the Bald Eagle. It was an old-fashioned building with a small antique portico in front, where, of a lazy summer afternoon, the wise men of the village assembled to read newspapers, talk politics, and drink beer. Before the door stood a tall yellow signpost, from which hung a white sign emblazoned with a fierce bald-headed eagle, holding an olive branch in one claw, and a flash of forked lightning in the other. Underneath was written in large black letters, "The Bald Eagle: Good Entertainment for Man and Beast: by Jonathan Dewlap, Esq."

One calm, sultry summer evening, the knot of village politicians had assembled, according to custom, at the tavern door. At the entrance sat the landlord, Justice of the Peace and Quorum, lolling in a rocking-chair, and dozing over the columns of an electioneering handbill. Along the benches of the portico were seated the village attorney, the schoolmaster, the tailor, and other personages of less note, but not less idle, nor less devoted to the affairs of the nation.

To this worthy assembly of patriotic citizens the schoolmaster was drowsily doling forth the contents of the latest Gazette. It was at that memorable epoch of our national history when Lafayette returned to visit, in the evening of his days, the land that owed so much to his youthful enthusiasm; and to see, in the soft decline of life, the consummation of his singular glory, in the bosom of that country where it first began. His approach was everywhere hailed with heart-stirring joy. There was but one voice throughout the land, and every village through which he passed hailed him with rural festivities, addresses, odes, and a dinner at the tavern.

Every step of his journey was regularly and minutely recorded in those voluminous chronicles of our country, the newspapers; and column after column was filled with long notices of the dinners he had eaten, and of the toasts drank, and of the songs sung on the occasion.

As the schoolmaster detailed to the group around him an account of these busy festivals, which were so rapidly succeeding each other all over the country, the little soul he possessed kindled up within him. With true oratorical emphasis he repeated a long list of toasts, drank on a recent celebration of the kind,—"The American Eagle," "The Day we celebrate," "The New England Fair," "The Heroes who fought, bled, and died at Bunker Hill, of which I am one!"—and a thousand others equally patriotic. He was interrupted by the merry notes of the stage horn, twanging in long-drawn blasts over the blue hills that skirted the village; and shortly after a cloud of dust came rolling its light volume along the road, and the stagecoach wheeled up to the door.

It was driven by a stout, thick-set young fellow, with a glowing red face, that peeped out from under the wide brim of a white hat, like the setting sun from beneath a summer cloud. He was dressed in a wren-tailed gingham coat, with pocket holes outside, and a pair of gray linen pantaloons, buttoned down each leg with a row of yellow bell buttons. His vest was striped with red and blue, and around his neck he wore a colored silk handkerchief, tied in a loose knot before, and tucked in at the waistband. Beside him on his coach box sat two dusty travellers in riding-caps, and the group within presented an uncomfortable picture of the miseries of travelling in a stagecoach in the month of June.

In an instant all was noise and confusion in the bar-room of the inn. Travellers that had just arrived, and those about to set off in the evening coach, came crowding in with their baggage,—some eager to secure places, and others lodgings. A noisy group was gathered at the bar, within which the landlady was bouncing to and fro in a huff, and jingling a great bunch of keys, like some wild animal at a raree-show, stalking about its cage, whisking its tail, and jingling its iron chain.

The fireplace was filled with pine boughs and asparagus tops; and over it the wall was covered with advertisements of new-invented machines, patent medicines, tollgate and turnpike companies, and coarse prints of steamboats, stagecoaches, opposition lines, and Fortune's home forever. In one corner stood an old-fashioned oaken settee, with high back and crooked elbows, which served as a seat by day, and a bed by night; in another was a pile of trunks and different articles of a traveller's equipage; travelling-coats hung here and there about the room; and the atmosphere was thick with the smoke of tobacco and the fumes of brandy.

At length the sound of wheels was heard at the door. "Stage ready!" shouted the coachman, putting his head in at the door: there was a hurry and bustle about the room; the travellers crowded out; a short pause succeeded; the carriage door was slammed to in haste; and the coach wheeled away, and disappeared in the dusk of evening.

The sound of its wheels had hardly ceased to be heard, when the tailor entered the bar-room with a newspaper in his hand, and strutted up to the squire and the schoolmaster, who sat talking together upon the settee, with a step that would have done honor to the tragedy hero of a strolling theatre. He had just received the tidings that Lafayette was on his way north. The stage driver had brought the news; the passengers confirmed it; it was in the newspapers; and of course there could be no doubt upon the subject. It now became a general topic of conversation in the bar-room. The villagers came in one by one: all were on tiptoe; all talked together,—Lafayette, the Marquis, the Gin'ral! He would pass through the village in two days from then. What was to be done? The town authorities were at their wits' end, and were quite as anxious to know how they should receive their venerable guest as they were to receive him.

In the meantime the news took wing. There was a crowd at the door of the Post Office, talking with becoming zeal upon the subject: the boys in the street gave three cheers, and shouted "Lafayette forever!" and in less than ten minutes the approaching jubilee was known and talked of in every nook and corner of the village. The town authorities assembled in the little back parlor of the inn, to discuss the subject more at leisure over a mug of cider, and conclude upon the necessary arrangements for the occasion. Here they continued with closed doors until a late hour; and, after much debate, finally resolved to decorate the tavern hall, prepare a great dinner, order out the militia, and take the General by surprise. The lawyer was appointed to write an oration, and the schoolmaster an ode, for the occasion.

As night advanced, the crowd gradually dispersed from the street. Silence succeeded to the hum of rejoicing, and nothing was heard throughout the village but the occasional bark of a dog, the creaking of the tavern sign, and the no less musical accents of the one-keyed flute of the schoolmaster, who, perched at his chamber window in nightgown and slippers, serenaded the neighborhood with Fire on the Mountains and half of Washington's March; whilst the grocer, who lived next door, roused from sweet dreams of treacle and brown sugar, lay tossing in his bed, and wishing the deuce would take the schoolmaster, with his Latin and his one-keyed flute.

As day began to peep, next morning, the tailor was seen to issue out of the inn yard in the landlord's yellow wagon, with the negro hostler Cæsar mounted behind, thumping about in the tail of the vehicle, and grinning with huge delight. As the gray of morning mellowed, life began its course again in the little village. The cock hailed the daylight cheerly; the sheep bleated from the hills; the sky grew softer and clearer; the blue mountains caught the rising sun; and the mass of white vapor, that filled the valley, began to toss and roll itself away, like ebb of a feathery sea. Then the bustle of advancing day began: doors and windows were thrown open; the gate creaked on its hinge; carts rattled by; villagers were moving in the streets; and the little world began to go, like some ponderous machine, that, wheel after wheel, is gradually put in motion.

In a short time the tailor was seen slowly returning along the road, with a wagonload of pine boughs and evergreens. The wagon was unloaded at the tavern door, and its precious cargo carried up into the hall, where the tailor, in his shirt sleeves, danced and capered about the room, with a hatchet in one hand and a long knife in the other, like an Indian warrior before going to battle. In a moment the walls were stripped of the faded emblems of former holidays; garlands of withered roses were trampled underfoot; old stars, that had lost their lustre, were seen to fall; and the white pine chandelier was robbed of its yellow coat, and dangled from the ceiling, quite woe-begone and emaciated. But erelong the whole room was again filled with arches, and garlands, and festoons, and stars, and all kinds of singular devices in green leaves and asparagus tops. Over the chimney-piece were suspended two American flags, with a portrait of General Washington beneath them; and the names of Trenton, Yorktown, Bunker Hill, etc., peeped out from between the evergreens, cut in red morocco, and fastened to the wall with a profusion of brass nails. Every part of the room was liberally decorated with paper eagles; and in a corner hung a little black ship, rigged with twine, and armed with a whole broadside of umbrella tips.

It were in vain to attempt a description of all the wonders that started up beneath the tailor's hand, as from the touch of a magician's wand. In a word, before night everything was in readiness. Travellers, that arrived in the evening, brought information that the General would pass through the village at noon the next day, but without the slightest expectation of the jubilee that awaited him. The tailor was beside himself with joy, at the news, and pictured to himself with good-natured self-complacency the surprise and delight of the venerable patriot, when he should receive the public honors prepared for him, and the new blue coat, with bright buttons and velvet collar, which was then making at his shop.

In the meantime the landlady had been busy in making preparations for a sumptuous dinner; the lawyer had been locked up all day, hard at work upon his oration; and the pedagogue was hard ridden by the phantom of a poetic eulogy, that bestrode his imagination like the nightmare. Nothing was heard in the village but the bustle of preparation, and the martial music of drums and fifes. For a while the ponderous wheel of labor seemed to stand still. The clatter of the cooper's mallet was silent; the painter left his brush, the cobbler his awl; and the blacksmith's bellows lay sound asleep, with its nose buried in the ashes.

The next morning at daybreak the whole military force of the town was marshalled forth in front of the tavern, "armed and equipped as the law directs." Conspicuous among this multitude stood the tailor, arrayed in a coat of his own making, all lace and buttons, and a pair of buff pantaloons, drawn up so tight that he could hardly touch his feet to the ground. He wore a military hat, shaped like a clam shell, with little white goose feathers stuck all round the edge. By his side stood the gigantic figure of the blacksmith, in rusty regimentals. At length the roll of the drum announced the order for forming the ranks, and the valiant host displayed itself in a long wavering line. Here stood a tall lantern-jawed fellow, all legs, furbished up with a red waistcoat and shining green coat, a little round wool hat perched on the back of his head, and downward tapering off in a pair of yellow nankeens, twisted and wrinkled about the knees, as if his legs had been screwed into them. Beside him stood a long-waisted being, with a head like a hurra's nest, set off with a willow hat, and a face that looked as if it were made of sole leather, and a gash cut in the middle of it for a mouth. Next came a little man with fierce black whiskers and sugar-loaf hat, equipped with a long fowling piece, a powder horn, and a white canvas knapsack with a red star on the back of it; then a country bumpkin standing bolt upright, his head elevated, his toes turned out, holding fast to his gun with one hand, and keeping the other spread out upon his right thigh. Then figured the descendant of some Revolutionary veteran, arrayed in the uniform and bearing the arms and accoutrements of his ancestor, a cocked hat on his head, a heavy musket on his shoulder, and on his back a large knapsack marked U.S. Here was a man in straw hat and gingham jacket; and there a pale, nervous fellow, buttoned up to the chin in a drab greatcoat, to guard him against the morning air, and keep out the fever and ague.

"Attention the whole! Front face! Eyes right! Eyes left! Steady! Attention to the roll call!" shouted the blacksmith, in a voice like a volcano.

"Peleg Popgun!"

"Here."

"Tribulation Sheepshanks!"

"He-e-e-re."

"Return Jonathan Babcock!"

"Here."

And so on through a whole catalogue of long, hard names.

"Attention! Shoulder—arms! Very well. Fall back there on the extreme left! No talking in the ranks! Present—arms! Squire Wiggins, you're not in the line; if you please, a little farther in, a little farther out; there, I guess that will do! Carry—arms! Very well done. Quick time, upon your post—march!"

The little red-coated drummer flourished his drumsticks, the bandy-legged fifer struck up Yankee Doodle, Cæsar showed his flat face over the horizon of a great bass drum, like the moon in an eclipse, the tailor brandished his sword, and the whole company, wheeling with some confusion round the tavern signpost, streamed down the road, covered with dust, and followed by a troop of draggle-tailed boys.

As soon as this company had disappeared, and the dub of its drum ceased to be heard, the too-too of a shrill trumpet sounded across the plains, and a troop of horse came riding up. The leader was a jolly, round-faced butcher, with a red foxtail nodding over his head, and came spurring on, with his elbows flapping up and down like a pair of wings. As he approached the tavern, he ordered the troop to wheel, and form a line in front,—a manœuvre which, though somewhat arduous, was nevertheless executed with wonderful skill and precision.

This body of light horse was the pride of the whole country round, and was mounted and caparisoned in a style of splendor that dazzled the eyes of all the village. Each horseman wore a cap of bearskin crested with a foxtail, a short blue jacket faced with yellow and profusely ornamented with red morocco and quality binding. The pantaloons were of the same color as the jacket, and were trimmed with yellow cord. Some rode with long stirrups, some with short stirrups, and some with no stirrups at all; some sat perpendicular upon their saddles, some at an obtuse angle, and others at an angle of forty-five. One was mounted on a tall one-eyed bone setter, with his tail and ears cropped; another on a little red nag, with shaggy mane and long switch tail, and as vicious as if the very devil were in him. Here was a great fellow, with long curly whiskers, looking as fierce as Mars himself; there, a little hook-nosed creature, with red crest, short spurs, elbows stuck out, and jacket cocked up behind, looking like a barn door *"rooster,"* with his tail clipped, just preparing to crow.

When this formidable troop was formed to the satisfaction of their leader, the word of command was given, and they went through the sword exercise, hewing and cutting the air in all directions with the most cool and deliberate courage. The order was then given to draw pistols. Ready! Aim! Fire! Pop-pop-poo, went the pistols. Too-too-too, went the trumpet. The horses took fright at the sound: some plunged; others reared and kicked; and others started out of the line, and capered up and down *"like mad."* The captain being satisfied with this display of the military discipline of his troop, they wheeled off in sections, and rode gallantly into the tavern yard, to recruit from the fatigues of the morning.

Crowds of country people now came driving in from all directions, to see the fun and the General. The honest farmer, in broad-brimmed hat and broad-skirted coat, jogged slowly on, with his wife and half a dozen blooming daughters, in a square top chaise; and country beaux, in all their Sunday finery, came racing along in wagons, or parading round on horseback to win a sidelong look from some fair country lass in gypsy hat and blue ribbons.

In the meantime the schoolmaster was far from being idle. His scholars had been assembled at an early hour, and after a deal of drilling and good advice were arranged in a line in front of the schoolhouse, to bask in the sun and wait for the General. The little girls had wreaths of roses upon their heads, and baskets of flowers in their hands; and the boys carried Bibles, and wore papers on their hats inscribed "Welcome, Lafayette." The schoolmaster walked up and down before them, with a rattan in his hand, repeating to himself his poetic eulogy; stopping now and then to rap some unlucky little rogue over the knuckles for misdemeanor; shaking one to make him turn out his toes, and pulling another's ear to make him hold up his head and look like a man.

In this manner the morning wore away, and the hour at which it had been rumored that the General was to arrive drew near. The whole military force, both foot and horse, was then summoned together in front of the tavern, and formed into a hollow square, and the colonel, a swarthy knight of the forge, by the aid of a scrawl, written by the squire and placed in the crown of his hat, made a most eloquent and patriotic harangue, in which he called the soldiers his "brothers in arms, the hope of their country, the terror of their enemies, the bulwark of liberty, and the safeguard of the fair sex." They were then wheeled back again into a line, and dismissed for ten minutes.

An hour or two previous, an honest old black, named Boaz, had been stationed upon the highroad, not far from the entrance of the village, equipped with a loaded gun, which he was ordered to discharge by way of signal, as soon as the General should appear. Full of the importance and dignity of his office, Boaz marched to and fro across the dusty road, with his musket ready cocked and his finger on the trigger. This manœuvring in the sun, however, diminished the temperature of his enthusiasm in proportion as it increased that of his body, till at length he sat down on a stump in the shade, and, leaning his musket against the trunk of a tree, took a short-stemmed pipe out of his pocket, and began to smoke. As noon drew near, he grew hungry and homesick; his heart sunk into his stomach. His African philosophy dwindled apace into a mere theory. Overpowered by the heat of the weather he grew drowsy; his pipe fell from his mouth; his head lost its equipoise, and dropped, like a poppy, upon his breast; and sliding gently from his seat, he fell asleep at the root of the tree. He was aroused from his slumber by the noise of an empty wagon, that came rattling along a crossroad near him. Thus suddenly awakened, the thought of the General's approach, the idea of being caught sleeping at his post, and the shame of having given the signal too late flashed together across his bewildered mind, and springing upon his feet, he caught his musket, shut both eyes, and fired, to the utter consternation of the wagoner, whose horses took fright at the sound, and became unmanageable. Poor Boaz, when he saw the mistake he had made and the mischief he had done, did not wait long to deliberate, but, throwing his musket over his shoulder, bounded into the woods, and was out of sight in the twinkling of an eye.

The sharp report of the gun rang far and wide through the hush of noontide, awakening many a drowsy echo that grumbled in the distance, like a man aroused untimely from his rest. At the sound of the long-expected signal gun, the whole village was put in motion. The drum beat to order, the ranks were formed in haste, and the whole military force moved off to escort the General in, amid the waving of banners, the roll of drums, the scream of fifes, and the twang of the horse trumpet.

All was now anxious expectation at the village. The moments passed like hours. The lawyer appeared at the tavern door, with his speech in his hand; the schoolmaster and his scholars stood broiling in the sun, and many a searching look was cast along the dusty highway to descry some indication of their guest's approach. Sometimes a little cloud of dust, rolling along the distant road, would cheat them with a vain illusion. Then the report of musketry and the roll of drums, rattling among the hills and dying on the breeze, would inspire the fugitive hope that he had at length arrived, and a murmur of eager expectation would run from mouth to mouth. "There he comes!—That's he!" and the people would crowd into the street, to be again disappointed.

One o'clock arrived; two, three, but no General! The dinner was overdone, —the landlady in great tribulation, the cook in a great passion. The gloom of disappointment began to settle on many a countenance. The people looked doubtingly at each other, and guessed. The sky, too, began to lower. Volumes of black clouds piled themselves up in the west, and threatened a storm. The ducks were unusually noisy and quarrelsome around the green pool in the stable yard, and a flock of ill-boding crows were holding ominous consultation round the top of a tall pine. Everything gave indication of an approaching thunder gust. A distant irregular peal rattled along the sky, like a volley of musketry. They thought it was a salute to the General. Soon after the air grew damp and misty, it began to drizzle, a few scattered drops pattered on the roofs, and it set in to rain.

A scene of confusion ensued. The pedagogue and his disciples took shelter in the schoolhouse; the crowd dispersed in all directions, with handkerchiefs thrown over their heads and their gowns tucked up; and everything looked dismal and disheartening. The bar-room was full of disconsolate faces. Some tried to keep their spirits up by drinking; others wished to laugh the matter off; and others stood with their hands in their pockets, looking out of the window to see it rain, and making wry faces.

Night drew on apace, and the rain continued. Still nothing was to be heard of the General. Some were for despatching a messenger to ascertain the cause of this delay, but who would go out in such a storm! At length the monotonous too-too of the horse trumpet was heard, there was a great clattering and splashing of hoofs at the door, and the troop reined up, spattered with mud, drenched through and through, and completely crestfallen. Not long after, the foot company came straggling in, dripping wet, and diminished to one half its number by desertions. The tailor entered the bar-room, reeking and disconsolate, a complete epitome of the miseries of human life written in his face. The feathers were torn out of his clam-shell hat, his coat was thoroughly sponged, his boots full of water, and his buff pantaloons clung tighter than ever to his little legs. He trembled like a leaf: one might have taken him for Fever and Ague personified. The blacksmith, on the contrary, seemed to dread the water as little as if it were his element. The rain did not penetrate him, and he rolled into the bar-room like a great sea calf, that, after sporting about in the waves, tumbles himself out upon the sand to dry.

A thousand questions were asked at once about the General, but there was nobody to answer them. They had seen nothing of him, they had heard nothing of him, they knew nothing of him! Their spirit and patience were completely soaked out of them; no patriotism was proof against such torrents of rain.

Every heart seemed now to sink in despair. Every hope had given way, when the twang of the stage horn was heard, sending forth its long-drawn cadences, and enlivening the gloom of a rainy twilight. The coach dashed up to the door. It was empty, not a solitary passenger. The coachman came in without a dry thread about him. A little stream of water trickled down his back from the rim of his hat. There was something dismally ominous in his look; he seemed to be a messenger of bad news.

"The Gin'ral! the Gin'ral! where's the Gin'ral?"

"He's gone on by another road. So much for the opposition line and the new turnpike!" said the coachman, as he tossed off a glass of New England.

"He has lost a speech!" said the lawyer.

"He has lost a coat!" said the tailor.

"He has lost a dinner!" said the landlord.

It was a gloomy night at the Bald Eagle. A few boon companions sat late over their bottle, drank hard, and tried to be merry; but it would not do. Good humor flagged, the jokes were bad, the laughter forced, and one after another slunk away to bed, full of bad liquor, and reeling with the fumes of brandy and beer.